HOMECOMING
Harmony

HOMECOMING
Harmony

THE MEMORY OF EARTH
THE CALL OF EARTH
THE SHIPS OF EARTH

Orson Scott Card

Published by arrangement with Tor Books.
Tom Doherty Associates, Inc.
175 Fifth Avenue
New York, N.Y. 10010

ISBN 1-56865-089-2

PRINTED IN THE UNITED STATES OF AMERICA

Contents

Major
Streets
of Basilica

High
Mountain
Road

Cold
House

Low
Gate
Street

Seggidugu
Road

N

Districts of Basilica

Back Gate

The Wells

The Cisterns

Wall Town

Gaballufix's House

New Schools

Girls' Schools

The Fountains

Scholars

Rasa's House

Holy Road

Long Street

Old Town

Holy

Funnel Gate

Edgetown

Dogtown

The Funnel

Old Dance

West Shelf

North High Road

Scholar Street

The

Boys Town

The Temple

High Gate

High Market

The Pier

High Town

Black Fields

Inner Market

The Pens

South High Road

Gate Town

Outer Market

Low Market

Low Gate

Low

Twisting Trail

Gaballufix's
Household

Twisting Trail

Caravan
Road

High
Gate
Road

Ridge Road

Wetchik's
Household

Sidescraper
Trail

Plains Road

N

Seggidugu
Road

Environs of Basilica

Notes on Parentage

Because of the marriage customs in the city of Basilica, family relationships can be somewhat complex. Perhaps these parentage charts can help keep things straight. Women's names are in italics.

WETCHIK'S FAMILY

Volemak, the Wetchik

(by *Hosni*) (by *Kilvishevex*) (by *Rasa*)

Elemak Mebbekew Issib Nafai

RASA'S FAMILY

Rasa

(by Wetchik)	(by Gaballufix)	(by Wetchik 2nd contract)
Issib	Sevet Kokor	Nafai

RASA'S NIECES

(her prize students, "adopted" into a permanent relationship of sponsorship)

Shedemei   *Dol*   *Eiadh*   *Hushidh* and *Luet* (sisters)

HOSNI'S FAMILY

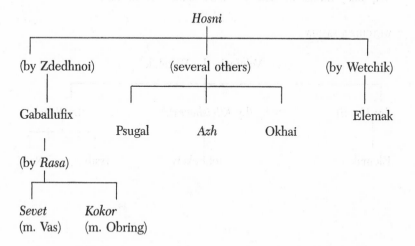

Hosni

(by Zdedhnoi)	(several others)	(by Wetchik)
Gaballufix	Psugal *Azh* Okhai	Elemak
(by *Rasa*)		
Sevet *Kokor*		
(m. Vas) (m. Obring)		

Nicknames

Most names have diminutive or familiar forms. Thus Gaballufix's near kin, close friends, current mate, and former mates could call him Gabya. Other nicknames are listed here. (Again, because these names are so unfamiliar, names of female characters are set off in italics.)

Basilikya—Syelsika—Skiya

Chveya—Veya

Dabrota—Dabya

Dhelembuvex—Dhel

Dol—Dolya

Drotik—Dorya

Dza—Dazya

Eiadh—Edhya

Elemak—Elya

Hosni—Hosya

Hushidh—Shuya

Issib—Issya

Izuchaya—Zuya

Kokor—Koya

Krasata—Krassya

Luet—Lutya

Mebbekew—Meb

Motiga—Motya

Nadezhny—Nadya

Nafai—Nyef

Obring—Briya

Oykib—Okya

Padarok—Rokya

Panimanya—Panya-Manya

Protchnu—Proya

Rasa—(no diminutive)

Rashgallivak—Rash

Roptat—Rop

Serp—Sepya

Sevet—Sevya

Shedemei—Shedya

Smelost—Smelya

Spel—Spelya

Truzhnisha—Truzhya

Umene—Umya   Yasai—Yaya
Vas—Vasya   *Zalatoya—Toya*
Vasnaminanya—Vasnya   Zaxodh—Xodhya
Volemak—Volya   Zdorab—Zodya
Wetchik—(no diminutive;   Zhatva—Zhyat
   Volemak's family title)   *Zhavaronok—Nokya*

Notes on Names

For the purpose of reading this story, it hardly matters whether the reader pronounces the names of the characters correctly. But for those who might be interested, here is some information concerning the pronunciation of names.

The rules of vowel formation in the language of Basilica require that in most words, at least one vowel be pronounced with a leading *y* sound. With names, it can be almost any vowel, and it can legitimately be changed at the speaker's preference. Thus the name Gaballufix could be pronounced G*yah*-BAH-loo-fix or Gah-BAH-l*yoo*-fix; it happens that Gaballufix himself preferred to pronounce it Gah-B*YAH*-loo-fix, and of course most people followed that usage.

Basilikya [byah-see-lee-KEE-ya]

Chveya [shvey-YA]

Dabrota [dah-BROH-tyah]

Dhelembuvex [thel-EM-byoo-vex]

Dol [DYOHL]

Drotik [DROHT-yik]

Dza [dzee-YAH]

Eiadh [A-yahth]

Elemak [EL-yeh-mahk]

Hosni [HYOZ-nee]

Hushidh [HYOO-sheeth]

Issib [IS-yib]

Izuchaya [yee-zoo-CHA-yah]

Kokor [KYOH-kor]

Krasata [krah-SSYAH-tah]

Luet [LYOO-et]

Mebbekew [MEB-bek-kyoo]

Motiga [myoh-TEE-gah]

Nadezhny [nah-DYEZH-nee]

Nafai [NYAH-fie]

Obring [OB-rying]

Oykib [OY-kyib]

Padarok [PYAH-dah-rohk]

Panimanya

Protchnu [PRYO-tchnu]

Rasa [RAHZ-yah]

Rashgallivak [rahsh-GYAH-lih-vahk]

Roptat [ROPE-taht]

Serp [SYAIRP]

Sevet [SEV-yet]

Shedemei [SHYED-eh-may]

Smelost [SMYE-lost]

Spel [SPYEHL]

Truzhnisha [troozh-NYEE-shah]

Umene [ooh-MYEH-neh]

Vas [VYAHSS]

Vasnaminanya [vahss-nah-mee-NAH-nyah]

Volemak [VOHL-yeh-mak]

Wetchik [WET-chyick]

Yasai [YAH-sai]

Zalatoya [zah-lyah-TOH-yah]

Zaxodh [ZYAH-chothe]

Zdorab [ZDOR-yab]

Zhatva [ZHYAT-vah]

Zhavaronok [zhah-VYA-roh-nohk]

THE MEMORY
OF EARTH

To a good reader, a good friend,
and, most important, a good man,
Jeff Alton

Acknowledgments

I owe many debts in the creation of this work, some more obvious than others.

My wife, Kristine, as always was my reader of first resort; with this book, however, she was joined in this labor by our oldest son, Geoffrey, who proved himself to be a reader of great insight and an editor with a good eye for detail. The world has too few good editors. I'm proud to have found another one.

I must also thank the many friends working with me on other projects, who waited patiently until this book was finished, so that I could return to other labors too long delayed. And thanks, again and always, to my agent, Barbara Bova, who proves that it *is* possible to do good business with a good friend.

Contents

Contents

Prologue

The master computer of the planet Harmony was afraid. Not in a way that any human would recognize—no clammy palms, no dry mouth, no sick dread in the pit of the stomach. It was only a machine without moving parts, drawing power from the sun and data from its satellites, its memory, and the minds of half a billion human beings. Yet it could feel a kind of fear, a sense that things were slipping out of its control, that it no longer had the power to influence the world as it had before.

What it felt was, in short, the fear of death. Not its own death, for the master computer had no ego and cared not at all whether it continued to exist or not. Instead it had a mission, programmed into it millions of years before, to be the guardian of humanity on this world. If the computer became so feeble that it could no longer fulfil its mission, then it knew without doubt—every projection it was capable of making confirmed it—that within a few thousand years humanity would once again be faced with the one enemy that could destroy it: humanity itself, armed with such weapons that a whole planet could be killed.

Now is the time, the master computer decided. I must act now, while I still have some influence in the world, or a world will die again.

Yet the master computer had no idea *how* to act. One of the symptoms of its decline was the very confusion that kept it from being able to make a decision. It couldn't trust its own conclusions, even if it could reach one. It needed guidance. It needed to be clarified, reprogrammed, or perhaps even replaced with a machine more sophisticated, better able to deal with the new challenges evolving among the human race.

The trouble was, there was only one source it could trust to give valid advice, and that source was so far away that the Oversoul would have to go there to get it. Once the Oversoul had been capable of movement, but that was forty million years ago, and even inside a stasis field there had been decay. The Oversoul could not undertake its quest alone. It needed human help.

For two weeks the master computer searched its vast database, evaluating the potential usefulness of every human being currently alive. Most were too stupid or unreceptive; of those who could still receive direct communications from the master computer, only a few were in a position where they could do what was needed.

Thus it was that the master computer turned its attention to a handful of human beings in the ancient city Basilica. In the dark of night, as one of the master computer's most reliable satellites passed overhead, it began its work, sending a steady stream of information and instructions in a tightbeam transmission to those who might be useful in the effort to save a world named Harmony.

1
Father's House

Nafai woke before dawn on his mat in his father's house. He wasn't allowed to sleep in his mother's house anymore, being fourteen years old. No self-respecting woman of Basilica would put her daughter in Rasa's household if a fourteen-year-old boy were in residence—especially since Nafai had started a growth spurt at the age of twelve that showed no signs of stopping even though he was already near two meters in height.

Only yesterday he had overheard his mother talking with her friend Dhelembuvex. "People are beginning to speculate on when you're going to find an auntie for him," said Dhel.

"He's still just a boy," said Mother.

Dhel hooted with laughter. "Rasa, my dear, are you *so* afraid of growing old that you can't admit your little baby is a man?"

"It's not fear of age," said Mother. "There's time enough for aunties and mates and all that business when he starts thinking about it himself."

"Oh, he's *thinking* about it already," said Dhel. "He's just not talking to *you* about it."

It was true enough; it had made Nafai blush when he heard her say it, and it made him blush again when he remembered it. How did Dhel know, just to look at him for a moment that day, that his thoughts were so often on "that business"? But no, Dhel didn't know it because of anything she had seen in Nafai. She knew it because she knew men. I'm just going through an age, thought Nafai. All boys start thinking these thoughts at about this age. Anyone can point at a male who's near two meters in height but still beardless and say, "That boy is thinking about sex right now," and most of the time they'll be right.

But I'm *not* like all the others, thought Nafai. I hear Mebbekew and his friends talking, and it makes me sick. I don't like thinking of women that crudely, sizing them up like mares to see what they're likely to be useful for. A pack animal or can I ride her? Is she a walker or can we gallop? Do I keep her in the stable or bring her out to show my friends?

That wasn't the way Nafai thought about women at all. Maybe because he was still in school, still talking to women every day about intellectual subjects. I'm not in love with Eiadh because she's the most beautiful young woman in Basilica and therefore quite probably in the entire world. I'm in love with her because we can talk together, because of the way she thinks, the sound of her voice, the way she cocks her head to listen to an idea she doesn't agree with, the way she rests her hand on mine when she's trying to persuade me.

Nafai suddenly realized that the sky was starting to grow light outside his window, and here he was lying in bed dreaming of Eiadh, when if he had any brains at all he'd get up and get into the city and *see* her in person.

No sooner thought of than done. He sat up, knelt beside his mat, slapped his bare thighs and chest and offered the pain to the Oversoul, then rolled up his bed and put it in his box in the corner. I don't really need a bed, thought Nafai. If I were a real man I could sleep on the floor and not mind it. That's how I'll become as hard and lean as Father. As Elemak. I won't use the bed tonight.

He walked out into the courtyard to the water tank. He dipped his hands into the small sink, moistened the soap, and rubbed it all over. The air was cool and the water was cooler, but he pretended not to notice until he was lathered up. He knew that this chill was nothing compared to what would happen in a moment. He stood under the shower and reached up for the cord—and then hesitated, bracing himself for the misery to come.

"Oh, just pull it," said Issib.

Nafai looked over toward Issib's room. He was floating in the air just in front of the doorway. "Easy for *you* to say," Nafai answered him.

Issib, being a cripple, couldn't use the shower; his floats weren't supposed to get wet. So one of the servants took his floats off and bathed him every night. "You're such a baby about cold water," said Issib.

"Remind me to put ice down your neck at supper."

"As long as you woke me up with all your shivering and chattering out here—"

"I didn't make a sound," said Nafai.

"I decided to go with you into the city today."

"Fine, fine. Fine as wine," said Nafai.

"Are you planning to let the soap dry? It gives your skin a charming sort of whiteness, but after a few hours it might begin to itch."

Nafai pulled the cord.

Immediately ice-cold water cascaded out of the tank over his head. He gasped—it always hit with a shock—and then bent and turned and twisted and splashed water into every nook and crevice of his body to rinse the soap off. He had only thirty seconds to get clean before the shower stopped, and if he didn't finish in that time he either had to live with the unrinsed soap for the rest of the day—and it *did* itch, like a thousand fleabites—or wait a couple of minutes, freezing his butt off, for the little shower tank to refill from the big water tank. Neither consequence was any fun, so he had long since learned the routine so well that he was always clean before the water stopped.

"I love watching that little dance you do," said Issib.

"Dance?"

"Bend to the left, rinse the armpit, bend the other way, rinse the left armpit, bend over and spread your cheeks to rinse your butt, bend over backward—"

"All right, I get it," said Nafai.

"I'm serious, I think it's a wonderful little routine. You ought to show it to the manager of the Open Theatre. Or even the Orchestra. You could be a star."

"A fourteen-year-old dancing naked under a stream of water," said Nafai. "I think they'd show that in a different kind of theatre."

"But still in Dolltown! You'd still be a hit in Dolltown!"

By now Nafai had toweled himself dry—except his hair, which was still freezing cold. He wanted to run for his room the way he used to do when he was little, jabbering nonsense words—"ooga-booga looga-booga" had been a favorite—while he pulled on his clothes and rubbed himself to get warm. But he was a man now, and it was only autumn, not winter yet, so he forced himself to walk casually toward his room. Which is why he was still in the courtyard, stark naked and cold as ice, when Elemak strode through the gate.

"A hundred and twenty-eight days," he bellowed.

"Elemak!" cried Issib. "You're back!"

"No thanks to the hill robbers," said Elemak. He walked straight to the shower, pulling off his clothes as he went. "They hit us only two days ago, way too close to Basilica. I think we killed one this time."

"Don't you know whether you did or not?" asked Nafai.

"I used the pulse, of course."

Of course? thought Nafai. To use a hunting weapon against a *person?*

"I saw him drop, but I wasn't about to go back and check, so maybe he just tripped and fell down at the exact moment that I fired."

Elemak pulled the shower cord *before* he soaped. The moment the water hit him he yowled, and then did his own little splash dance, shaking his head and flipping water all over the courtyard while jabbering "ooga-booga looga-booga" just like a little kid.

It was all right for Elemak to act that way. He was twenty-four now, he had just got his caravan safely back from purchasing exotic plants in the jungle city of Tishchetno, the first time anyone from Basilica had gone *there* in years, and he might actually have killed a robber on the way. No one could think of Elemak as anything but a man. Nafai knew the rules: When a man acts like a child, he's boyish, and everyone's delighted; when a boy acts the same way, he's childish, and everyone tells him to be a man.

Elemak was soaping up now. Nafai—freezing still, even with his arms folded across his chest—was about to go into his room and snag his clothes, when Elemak started talking again.

"You've grown since I left, Nyef."

"I've been doing that lately."

"Looks good on you. Muscling up pretty well. You take after the old man in all the right ways. Got your mother's face, though."

Nafai liked the tone of approval in Elemak's voice, but it was also vaguely demeaning to stand there naked as a jaybird while his brother sized him up.

Issib, of course, only made it worse. "Got Father's most important feature, fortunately," he said.

"Well, we *all* got that," said Elemak. "All of the old man's babies have been boys—or at least all his babies that we *know* about." He laughed.

Nafai hated it when Elemak talked about Father that way. Everyone knew that Father was a chaste man who only had sex with his lawful mate. And for the past fifteen years that mate had been Rasa, Nafai's and Issib's mother, the contract renewed every year. He was so faithful that women had given up coming to visit and hint around about availability when his contract lapsed. Of course, Mother was just as faithful and there were still plenty of men plying *her* with gifts and innuendoes —but that's how some men were, they found faithfulness even more enticing than wantonness, as if Rasa were staying so faithful to Wetchik only to goad them on in their pursuit of her. Also, mating with Rasa meant sharing what some thought was the finest house and what all agreed was the finest *view* in Basilica. I'd never mate with a woman just for her house, thought Nafai.

"Are you crazy or what?" asked Elemak.

"What?" asked Nafai.

"It's cold as a witch's tit out here and you're standing there sopping wet and buck naked."

"Yeah," said Nafai. But he didn't run for his room—that would be admitting that the cold was bothering him. So he grinned at Elemak first. "Welcome home," he said.

"Don't be such a show-off, Nyef," said Elemak. "I know you're dying of the cold—your dangling parts are shriveling up."

Nafai sauntered to his room and pulled on his pants and shirt. It really bothered him that Elemak always seemed to know what was going on in Nafai's head. Elemak could never imagine that maybe Nafai was so hardened and manly that the cold simply didn't bother him. No, Elemak always assumed that if Nafai did something manly it was nothing but an act. Of course, it *was* an act, so Elemak was right, but that only made it more annoying. How do men become manly, if not by putting it on as an act until it becomes habit and then, finally, their character? Besides, it wasn't *completely* an act. For a minute there, seeing Elemak home again, hearing him talk about maybe killing a man on his trip, Nafai had forgotten that he was cold, had forgotten everything.

There was a shadow in the doorway. It was Issib. "You shouldn't let him get to you like that, Nafai."

"What do you mean?"

"Make you so angry. When he teases you."

Nafai was genuinely puzzled. "What do you mean, angry? I wasn't angry."

"When he made that joke about how cold you were," said Issib. "I thought you were going to go over and knock his head off."

"But I wasn't mad."

"Then you're a genuine mental case, my boy," said Issib. "*I* thought you were mad. *He* thought you were mad. The *Oversoul* thought you were mad."

"The Oversoul knows that I wasn't angry at all."

"Then learn to control your face, Nyef, because apparently it's showing emotions that you don't even feel. As soon as you turned your back he jammed his finger at you, that's how mad he thought you were."

Issib floated away. Nafai pulled on his sandals and criss-crossed the laces up around his pantlegs. The style among young men around Basilica was to wear long laces up the thighs and tie them together just under the crotch, but Nafai cut the laces short and wore them knee-high, like a serious workingman. Having a thick leather knot between their legs caused young men to swagger, rolling side to side when they walked, trying to keep their thighs from rubbing together and chafing from the knot. Nafai didn't swagger and loathed the whole idea of a fashion that made clothing *less* comfortable.

Of course, rejecting fashion meant that he didn't fit in as easily with boys his age, but Nafai hardly minded that. It was women whose company he enjoyed most, and the women whose good opinion he valued were the ones who were not swayed by trivial fashions. Eiadh, for one, had often joined him in ridiculing the high-laced sandals. "Imagine wearing those *riding a horse,*" she had said once.

"Enough to make a bull into a steer," Nafai had quipped in reply, and Eiadh had laughed and then repeated his joke several times later in the day. If a woman like that existed in the world, why should a man bother with silly fashions?

When Nafai got to the kitchen, Elemak was just sliding a frozen rice pudding into the oven. The pudding looked large enough to feed them all, but Nafai knew from experience that Elemak intended the whole thing for himself. He'd been traveling for months, eating mostly cold food, moving almost entirely at night—Elemak would eat the entire pudding in about six swallows and then go collapse on his bed and sleep till dawn tomorrow.

"Where's Father?" asked Elemak.

"A short trip," said Issib, who was breaking raw eggs over his toast, preparing them for the oven. He did it quite deftly, considering that simply grasping an egg in one hand took all his strength. He would hold the egg a few inches over the table, then clench just the right muscle to release the float that was holding up his arm, causing it to drop, egg and all, onto the table surface. The egg would split exactly right—every time—and then he'd clench another muscle, the float would swing his arm up over the plate, and then he'd open the egg with his other hand and it would pour out onto the toast. There wasn't much Issib couldn't do for himself, with the floats taking care of gravity for him. But it meant Issib could never go traveling the way Father and Elemak and, sometimes, Mebbekew did. Once he was away from the magnetics of the city, Issib had to ride in his chair, a clumsy machine that he could only ride from place to place. It wouldn't help him *do* anything. Away from the city, confined to his chair, Issib was *really* crippled.

"Where's Mebbekew?" asked Elemak. The pudding was done— overdone, actually, but that's the way Elemak always ate breakfast, cooked until it was so soft you didn't need teeth to eat it. Nafai figured it was because he could swallow it faster that way.

"Spent the night in the city," said Issib.

Elemak laughed. "That's what he'll say when he gets back. But I think Meb is all plow and no planting."

There was only one way for a man of Mebbekew's age to spend a night inside the walls of Basilica, and that was if some woman had him in her home. Elemak might tease that Mebbekew claimed to have more women than he got, but Nafai had seen the way Meb acted with *some* women, at least. Mebbekew didn't have to pretend to spend a night in the city; he probably accepted fewer invitations than he got.

Elemak took a huge bite of pudding. Then he cried out, opened his mouth, and poured in wine straight from the table jug. "Hot," he said, when he could talk again.

"Isn't it always?" asked Nafai.

He had meant it as a joke, a little jest between brothers. But for some reason Elemak took it completely wrong, as if Nafai had been calling him stupid for taking the bite. "Listen, little boy," said Elemak, "when you've been out on the road eating cold food and sleeping in dust and mud for two-and-a-half months, maybe you forget just how hot a pudding can be."

"Sorry," said Nafai. "I didn't mean anything bad."

"Just be careful who you make fun of," said Elemak. "You're only my *half*-brother, after all."

"That's all right," said Issib cheerfully. "He has the same effect on full brothers, too." Issib was obviously trying to smooth things over and keep a quarrel from developing.

Elemak seemed willing enough to go along. "I imagine it's harder on *you*," he said. "Good thing you're a cripple or Nafai here probably wouldn't have lived to be eighteen."

If the remark about being a cripple stung Issib, he didn't show it. It infuriated Nafai, however. Here Issib was trying to keep the peace, and Elemak casually insulted him for it. So, while Nafai hadn't had the slightest intention of picking a fight before, he was ready for one *now*. Elemak's having counted his age in planting years instead of temple years was a good enough pretext. "I'm fourteen," said Nafai. "Not eighteen."

"Temple years, planting years," said Elemak. "If you were a horse you'd be eighteen."

Nafai walked over and stood about a pace from Elemak's chair. "But I'm *not* a horse," said Nafai.

"You're not a man yet, either," said Elemak. "And I'm too tired to want to beat you senseless right now. So fix your breakfast and let me eat mine." He turned to Issib. "Did Father take Rashgallivak with him?"

Nafai was surprised at the question. How could Father take the estate manager with him, when Elemak was also gone? Truzhnisha would keep the household running, of course; but without Rashgallivak, who would manage the greenhouses, the stables, the gossips, the booths? Certainly not Mebbekew—he had no interest in the day-to-day duties of Father's business. And the men would hardly take orders from Issib—they regarded him with tenderness or pity, not respect.

"No, Father left Rash in charge," Issib said. "Rash was probably sleeping out at the coldhouse tonight. But you know Father never leaves without seeing that everything's in order."

Elemak cast a quick, sidelong glance at Nafai. "Just wondered why certain people were getting so cocky."

Then it dawned on Nafai: Elemak's question was really a back-handed compliment—he had wondered whether Father had put Nafai in charge of things in his absence. And plainly Elemak didn't like the idea of Nafai running any part of the Wetchik family's rare-plant business.

"I'm not interested in taking over the weed trade," said Nafai, "if that's what you're worried about."

"I'm not *worried* about anything at all," said Elemak. "Isn't it time for you to go to Mama's school? She'll be afraid her little boy got robbed and beaten on the road."

Nafai knew he should let Elemak's taunt go unanswered, shouldn't provoke him anymore. The last thing he wanted was to have Elemak as an enemy. But the very fact that he looked up to Elemak so much, wanted so much to be like him, made it impossible for Nafai to leave the gibe unanswered. As he headed for the courtyard door, he turned back to say, "I have much higher aims in life than skulking around shooting at robbers and sleeping with camels and carrying tundra plants to the tropics and tropical plants to the glaciers. I'll leave that game to you."

Suddenly Elemak's chair flew across the room as he jumped to his feet and in two strides had Nafai's face pressed against the doorframe. It hurt, but Nafai hardly noticed the pain, or even the fear that Elemak might hurt him even worse. Instead there was a strange feeling of triumph. I made Elemak lose his temper. He doesn't get to keep pretending that he thinks I'm not worth noticing.

"That *game*, as you call it, pays for everything you have and everything you are," said Elemak. "If it wasn't for the money that Father and Rash and I bring in, do you think anybody'd pay attention to you in Basilica? Do you think your *mother* has so much honor that it would actually transfer to her *sons*? If you think that, then you don't know how the world works. Your mother might be able to make her daughters into hot stuff, but the only thing a woman can do for a *son* is make a scholar out of him." He practically spat the word *scholar*. "And believe me, boy, that's all you're ever going to be. I don't know why the Oversoul even bothered putting a boy's parts on you, little girl, because all you're going to have in this world when you grow up is what a *woman* gets."

Again, Nafai knew that he should keep his silence and let Elemak
have the last word. But the retort no sooner came to his mind than it
came out of his mouth. "Is calling me a woman your subtle way of
telling me you've got some heat for me? I think you've been out on the
road too long if *I'm* starting to look irresistible."

At once Elemak let go of him. Nafai turned around, half-expecting to
see Elemak laughing, shaking his head about how their playing sometimes got out of hand. Instead his brother was standing there red-
faced, breathing heavily, like an animal poised to lunge. "Get out of
this house," said Elemak, "and don't come back while I'm here."

"It's not your house," Nafai pointed out.

"The next time I see you here I'll kill you."

"Come on, Elya, you know I was only joking."

Issib floated blithely between them and cast an arm clumsily across
Nafai's shoulders. "We're late getting into the city, Nyef. Mother *will*
be worried about us."

This time Nafai had sense enough to shut his mouth and let things
go. He *did* know how to hold his tongue—he just never remembered
to do it soon enough. Now Elemak was furious at him. Might be angry
for days. Where will I sleep if I can't go home? Nafai wondered. Immediately there flashed in his mind an image of Eiadh whispering to
him, "Why not stay tonight in *my* room? After all, we're surely going to
be mates one day. A woman trains her favorite nieces to be mates for
her sons, doesn't she? I've known that since I first knew you, Nafai.
Why should we wait any longer? After all, you're only about the
stupidest human being in all of Basilica."

Nafai came out of his reverie to realize that it was Issib speaking to
him, not Eiadh. "Why do you keep goading him like that," Issib was
saying, "when you know it's all Elemak can do to keep from killing you
sometimes?"

"I think of things and sometimes I say them when I shouldn't," said
Nafai.

"You think of *stupid* things and you're so stupid that you *say* them
every time."

"Not *every* time."

"Oh, you mean there are even *stupider* things that you *don't* say?
What a mind you've got! A treasure!" Issib was floating ahead of him.
He always did that going up the ridge road, forgetting that for people

who had to deal with gravity, a slower pace might be more comfortable.

"I like Elemak," said Nafai miserably. "I don't understand why he doesn't like me."

"I'll get him to make you a list sometime," said Issib. "I'll paste it onto the end of my own."

2

Mother's House

It was a long but familiar road from the Wetchik house to Basilica. Until the age of eight, Nafai had always made the round trip in the other direction, when Mother took him and Issib to Father's house for holidays. In those days it was magical to be in a household of men. Father, with his mane of white hair, was almost a god—indeed, until he was five Nafai had thought that Father *was* the Oversoul. Mebbekew, only six years older than Nafai, had always been a vicious, merciless tease, but in those early years Elemak was kind and playful. Ten years older than Nafai, Elya was already mansize in Nafai's first memories of Wetchik's house; but instead of Father's ethereal look, he had the dark rugged appearance of a fighter, a man who was kind only because he wanted to be, not because he was incapable of harshness when it was needed. In those days Nafai had pleaded to be released from Mother's household and allowed to live with Wetchik—and Elemak. Having Mebbekew around all the time would simply be the unavoidable price for living in the place of the gods.

Mother and Father met with him together to explain why they wouldn't release him from his schooling. "Boys who are sent to their fathers at this age are the ones without promise," said Father. "The ones who are too violent to get along well in a household of study, too disrespectful to abide in a household of women."

"And the stupid ones go to their fathers at age eight," said Mother. "Beyond rudimentary reading and arithmetic, what use does a stupid man have for learning?"

Even now, remembering, Nafai felt a little stab of pleasure at that— for Mebbekew had often bragged that, unlike Nyef and Issya, and Elya in his day, *Meb* had gone home to Father at the age of eight. Nafai was sure that Meb had met every criterion for early entry into the household of men.

So they managed to persuade Nafai that it was a good thing for him to stay with his mother. There were other reasons, too—to keep Issib company, the prestige of his mother's household, the association with his sisters—but it was Nafai's ambition that made him content to stay. I'm one of the boys with real promise. I will have value to the land of Basilica, perhaps to the whole world. Perhaps one day my writings will be sent into the sky for the Oversoul to share them with the people of other cities and other languages. Perhaps I will even be one of the great ones whose ideas are encoded into glass and saved in an archive, to be read during all the rest of human history as one of the giants of Harmony.

Still, because he had pleaded so earnestly to be allowed to live with Father, from the age of eight until he was thirteen, he and Issib had spent almost every weekend at the Wetchik house, becoming as familiar with it as with Rasa's house in the city. Father had insisted that they work hard, experiencing what a man does to earn his living, so their weekends were not holidays. "You study for six days, working with your mind while your body takes a holiday. Here you'll work in the stables and the greenhouses, working with your body while your mind learns the peace that comes from honest labor."

That was the way Father talked, a sort of continuous oratory; Mother said he took that tone because he wasn't sure how to talk naturally with children. But Nafai had overheard enough adult conversations to know that Father talked that way with everybody except Rasa herself. It showed that Father was never at ease, never truly himself with anyone; but over the years Nafai had also learned that no matter how elevated and hortatory Father's conversation might be, he was never a fool; his words were never empty or stupid or ignorant. This is how a man speaks, Nafai had thought when he was young, and so he practiced an

elegant style and made a point of learning classical Emeznetyi as well
as the colloquial Basyat that was the language of most art and com-
merce in Basilica these days. More recently Nafai had realized that to
communicate effectively with real people he had to speak the common
language—but the rhythms, the melodies of Emeznetyi could still be
felt in his writing and heard in his speech. Even in his stupid jokes that
earned Elemak's wrath.

"I've just realized something," said Nafai.

Issib didn't answer—he was far enough ahead that Nafai wasn't sure
he could even hear. But Nafai went ahead and said it anyway, speaking
even more softly, because he was probably saying it only to himself. "I
think that I say those things that make people so angry, not because I
really *mean* them, but because I simply thought of a clever *way* to say
them. It's a kind of art, to think of the perfect way to say an idea, and
when you think of it then you have to say it, because words don't exist
until you say them."

"A pretty feeble kind of art, Nyef, and I say you should give it up
before it gets you killed."

So Issib *was* listening, after all.

"For a big strong guy you sure take a long time getting up Ridge
Road to Market Street," said Issib.

"I was thinking," said Nafai.

"You really ought to learn how to think and walk at the same time."

Nafai reached the top of the road, where Issib was waiting. I really
was dawdling, he thought. I'm not even out of breath.

But because Issib had paused there, Nafai also waited, turning as
Issib had turned, to look back down the road they had just traveled.
Ridge Road was named exactly right, since it ran along a ridge that
sloped down toward the great well-watered coastal plain. It was a clear
morning, and from the crest they could see all the way to the ocean,
with a patchwork quilt of farms and orchards, stitched with roads and
knotted with towns and villages, spread out like a bedcover between
the mountains and the sea. Looking down Ridge Road they could see
the long line of farmers coming up for market, leading strings of pack
animals. If Nafai and Issib had delayed even ten minutes more they
would have had to make this trip in the noise and stink of horses,
donkeys, mules, and kurelomi, the swearing of the men and the gossip
of the women. Once that had been a pleasure, but Nafai had traveled

with them often enough to know that the gossip and the swearing were always the same. Not everything that comes from a garden is a rose.

Issib turned to the west, and so did Nafai, to see a landscape as opposite as any could possibly be: the jumbled rocky plateau of the Besporyadok, the near-waterless waste that went on and on toward the west. A thousand poets at least had made the same observation, that the sun rose from the sea, surrounded by jewels of light dancing on the water, and then settled down in red fire in the west, lost in the dust that was always blowing across the desert. But Nafai always thought that, at least where weather was concerned, the sun ought to go the other way. It didn't bring water from the ocean to the land—it brought dry fire from the desert toward the sea.

The vanguard of the market crowd was close enough now that they could hear the drivers and the donkeys. So they turned and started walking toward Basilica, sections of the redrock wall shining in the first rays of sunlight. Basilica, where the forested mountains of the north met the desert of the west and the garden seacoast of the east. How the poets had sung of this place: Basilica, the City of Women, the Harbor of Mists, Red-walled Garden of the Oversoul, the haven where all the waters of the world come together to conceive new clouds, to pour out fresh water again over the earth.

Or, as Mebbekew put it, the best town in the world for getting laid.

The path between the Market Gate of Basilica and the Wetchik house on Ridge Road had never changed in all these years—Nafai knew when as much as a stone of it had been changed. But when Nafai turned thirteen, he had reached a turning point that changed the meaning of that road. At thirteen, even the most promising boys went to live with their fathers, leaving their schooling behind forever. The only ones who remained behind were the ones who meant to reject a man's trade and become scholars. When Nafai was eight he had pleaded to live with his father, at thirteen he argued the other way. No, I haven't decided to be a scholar, he said, but I also haven't decided *not* to be. Why should I decide now? Let me live with you, Father, if I must—but let me also stay at Mother's school until things become clearer. You don't need me in your work, the way you need Elemak. And I don't want to be another Mebbekew.

So, though the path between Father's house and the city was unchanged, Nafai now walked it in the other direction. The round trip now wasn't from Rasa's city house out into the country and back again;

now it was a trek from Wetchik's country house into the city. Even though he actually owned more possessions in the city—all his books, papers, tools, and toys—and often slept three or four of the eight nights of the week there, home was Father's house now.

Which was inevitable. No man could call anything in Basilica truly his own; everything came as a gift from a woman. And even a man who, like Father, had every reason to feel secure with a mate of many years —even he could never truly be at home in Basilica, because of the lake. The deep rift valley in the heart of the city—the reason why the city existed at all—took half the space within Basilica's walls, and no man could ever go there, no man could even walk into the surrounding forest far enough to catch a glimpse of the shining water. If it *did* shine. For all Nafai knew, the rift valley was so deep that sunlight never touched the waters of the lake of Basilica.

No place can ever be home if there is a place within it where you are forbidden to go. No man is ever *truly* a citizen of Basilica. And I am becoming a stranger in my mother's house.

Elemak had spoken often, in years past, about cities where men owned everything, places where men had many wives and the wives had no choice about renewing their marriage contracts, and even one city where there was no marriage at all, but any man could take any woman and she was forbidden to refuse him unless she was already pregnant. Nafai wondered, though, if any of those stories was true. For why would women ever submit themselves to such treatment? Could it be that the women of Basilica were so much stronger than the women of any other place? Or were the men of this place weaker or more timid than the men of other cities?

Suddenly it became a question of great urgency. "Have you ever slept with a woman, Issya?"

Issib didn't answer.

"I just wondered," said Nafai.

Issib said nothing.

"I'm trying to figure out what's so wonderful about the women of Basilica that a man like Elya keeps coming back here when he could live in one of those places where men have their way all the time."

Only now did Issib answer. "In the first place, Nafai, there *is* no place where men have their way all the time. There *are* places where men pretend to have their way and women pretend to let them, just as women here pretend to have their way and *men* pretend to let them."

That was an interesting thought. It had never occurred to Nafai that perhaps things weren't as one-sided and simple as they seemed. But Issib hadn't finished, and Nafai wanted to hear the rest. "And in the second place?"

"In the second place, Nyef, Mother and Father *did* find an auntie for me several years ago and to be frank, it isn't all it's cracked up to be."

That wasn't what Nafai wanted to hear. "Meb seems to think it is."

"Meb has no brain," said Issib, "he simply goes wherever his most protuberant part leads him. Sometimes that means that he follows his nose, but usually not."

"What was it like?"

"It was nice. She was very sweet. But I didn't love her." Issib seemed a bit sad about it. "I felt like it was something being done to me, instead of something we were doing together."

"Was that because of . . ."

"Because I'm a cripple? Partly, I suppose, though she did teach me how to give pleasure in return and said I did surprisingly well. You'll probably enjoy it just like Meb."

"I hope not."

"Mother said that the best men don't enjoy their auntie all that much, because the best men don't want to receive their pleasure as a lesson, they want to be given it freely, out of love. But then she said that the worst men also don't like their auntie, because they can't stand having anyone but themselves be in control of things."

"I don't even want an auntie," said Nafai.

"Well, that's brilliant. How will you learn anything, then?"

"I want to learn it together with my mate."

"You're a romantic idiot," said Issib.

"Nobody has to teach birds or lizards."

"Nafai ab Wetchik mag Rasa, the famous lizard lover."

"I once watched a pair of lizards go at it for a whole hour."

"Learn any good techniques?"

"Sure. But you can only use them if you're proportioned like a lizard."

"Oh?"

"It's about half as long as their whole body."

Issib laughed. "Imagine buying pants."

"Imagine lacing your sandals!"

"You'd have to wrap it around your waist."

"Or loop it over your shoulder."

This conversation carried them through the market, where people were just starting to open their booths, expecting the immediate arrival of the farmers from the plain. Father maintained a couple of booths in the outer market, though none of the plains farmers had the money or the sophistication to want to buy a plant that took so much trouble to keep alive, and yet produced no worthwhile crop. The only sales in the outer market were to shoppers from Basilica itself, or, more rarely, to rich foreigners who browsed through the outer market on their way into or out of the city. With Father on a journey, it would be Rashgallivak supervising the set-up, and sure enough, there he was setting up a cold-plant display inside a chilled display table. They waved at him, though he only looked at them, not even nodding in recognition. That was Rash's way—he would be there if they needed him in some crisis. At the moment, his job was setting out plants, and so that had all of his attention. There was no rush, though. The best sales would come in the late afternoon, when Basilicans were looking for impressive gifts to bring their mate or lover, or to help win the heart of someone they were courting.

Meb once joked that people never bought exotic plants for themselves, since they were nothing but trouble to keep alive—and they only bought them as gifts because they were so expensive. "They make the perfect gift because the plant is beautiful and impressive for exactly as long as the love affair lasts—usually about a week. Then the plant dies, unless the recipients keep paying *us* to come take care of it. Either way their feelings toward the plant always match their feelings toward the lover who gave it to them. Either constant annoyance because he's still around, or distaste at the ugly dried-up memory. If a love is actually going to be *permanent* the lovers should buy a tree instead." It was when Meb started talking this way with customers that Father had banned him from the booths. No doubt that was exactly what Meb had been hoping for.

Nafai understood the desire to avoid helping in the business. There was nothing fun in the slugwork of selling a bunch of temperamental plants.

If I end my studies, thought Nafai, I'll have to work every day at one of these miserable jobs. And it'll lead nowhere. When Father dies Elemak will become the Wetchik, and he would never let me lead a caravan of my own, which is the only interesting part of the work. I don't want to spend my life in the hothouse or the dryhouse or the coldhouse, grafting and nurturing and propagating plants that will die almost as soon as they're sold. There's no greatness in that.

The outer market ended at the first gate, the vast doors standing open as they always did—Nafai wondered if they could even close anymore. It hardly mattered—this was always the most carefully guarded gate because it was the busiest. Everybody's retinas were scanned and checked against the roster of citizens and rightholders. Issib and Nafai, as sons of citizens, were technically citizens themselves, even though they weren't allowed to own property within the city, and when they came of age they'd be able to vote. So the guards treated them respectfully as they passed them through.

Between the outer gate and the inner gate, between the high red walls and protected by guards on every side, the city of Basilica conducted its most profitable business: the gold market. Actually, gold wasn't even the majority of what was bought and sold here, though moneylenders were thick as ever. What was traded in the gold market was any form of wealth that was easily portable and therefore easily stolen. Jewels, gold, silver, platinum, databases, libraries, deeds of property, deeds of trust, certificates of stock ownership, and warrants of uncollectible debt: All were traded here, and every booth had its computer to report transactions to the city recorder—the city's master computer. In fact, the constantly shifting holographic displays over all the computers caused a strange twinkling effect, so that no matter where you looked you always seemed to see motion out of the corner of your eye. Meb said that was why the lenders and vendors of the gold market were so sure someone was always spying on them.

No doubt most of the computers here had noticed Nafai and Issib as soon as their retinas were scanned at the gate, flashing their names, their status, and their financial standing into the computer display. Someday that would mean something, Nafai knew, but at the moment it meant nothing at all. Ever since Meb ran up huge debts last year when he turned eighteen, there was a tight restriction on all credit to the Wetchik family, and since credit was the only way Nafai was likely to get his hands on serious money, no one here would be interested in him. Father could probably have got all those restrictions removed, but since Father did all his business in cash, never borrowing, the restrictions did nothing to hurt him—and they kept Meb from borrowing any more. Nafai had listened to the whining and shouting and pouting and weeping that seemed to go on for months until Meb finally realized that Father was *never* going to relent and allow him financial independence. In recent months Meb had been fairly quiet about it. Now when he showed up in new clothes he always claimed they were borrowed from pitying friends, but Nafai was skeptical. Meb still spent money as if he had some, and since Nafai couldn't imagine Meb actually working at anything, he could only conclude that Meb had found someone to borrow from against his anticipated share in the Wetchik estate.

That would be just like Meb—to borrow against Father's anticipated death. But Father was still a vigorous and healthy man, only fifty years old. At some point Meb's creditors would get tired of waiting, and Meb would have to come to Father again, begging for help to free him from debt.

There was another retina check at the inner gate. Because they were citizens and the computers showed they not only hadn't bought anything, but hadn't even stopped at a booth, they didn't have to have their bodies scanned for what was euphemistically called "unauthorized borrowing." So in moments they passed through the gate into the city itself.

More specifically, they entered the inner market. It was almost as large as the outer market, but there the resemblance ended, for instead of selling meat and food, bolts of cloth and reaches of lumber, the inner market sold finished things: pastries and ices, spices and herbs; furniture and bedding, draperies and tapestries; fine-sewn shirts and trousers, sandals for the feet, gloves for the hands, and rings for toes and ears and fingers; and exotic trinkets and animals and plants, brought at great expense and risk from every corner of the world. Here was where Father offered his most precious plants, keeping his booths open day and night.

But none of these held any particular charm for Nafai—it was all the same to him, after passing through the market with little money for so many years. To him all that mattered were the many booths selling myachiks, the little glass balls that carried recordings of music, dance, sculpture, paintings; tragedies, comedies, and realities, recited as poems, acted out in plays, or sung in operas; and the works of historians, scientists, philosophers, orators, prophets, and satirists; lessons and demonstrations of every art or process ever thought of; and, of course, the great love songs for which Basilica was known throughout the world, combining music with wordless erotic plays that went on and on, repeating endlessly and randomly, like self-creating sculptures in the bedrooms and private gardens of every household in the city.

Of course, Nafai was too young to buy any love songs himself, but he had seen more than one when visiting in the homes of friends whose mothers or teachers were not as discreet as Rasa. They fascinated him, as much for the music and the implied story as for the eroticism. But he spent his time in the market searching for new works by Basilican poets, musicians, artists, and performers, or old ones that were just being revived, or strange works from other lands, either in translation or in the original. Father might have left his sons with little money, but Mother gave all her children—sons and nieces no more or less than mere pupils—a decent allowance for the purchase of myachiks.

Nafai found himself wandering toward a booth where a young man was singing in an exquisitely high and sweet tenor voice; the melody sounded like it might be a new one by the composer who called herself Sunrise—or at least one of her better imitators.

"No," said Issib. "You can come back this afternoon."

"You can go ahead," said Nafai.

"We're already late," said Issib.

"So I might as well be later."

"Grow up, Nafai," said Issib. "Every lesson you miss is one that either you or the teacher will have to make up later."

"I'll never learn everything anyway," said Nafai. "I want to hear the song."

"Then listen while you're walking. Or can't you walk and listen at the same time?"

Nafai let himself be led out of the market. The song faded quickly, lost in music from other booths, and the chatter and conversation of the market. Unlike the outer market, the inner market didn't wait for farmers from the plain, and so it never closed; half the people here, Nafai was sure, had not slept the night before, and were buying pastries and tea as their morning supper before going home to bed. Meb might well be one of them. And for a moment, Nafai envied him the freedom of his life. If I am ever a great historian or scientist, will I have freedom like that? To rise in the mid-afternoon, do my writing until dusk, and then venture out into the Basilican night to see the dances and plays, to hear the concerts, or perhaps to recite passages of the work I did myself that day before a discerning audience that will leave my recita-

tion abuzz with discussion and argument and praise and criticism of
my work—how could Elemak's dirty, wearying journeys ever compare
with such a life as that? And then to return at dawn to Eiadh's house,
and make love to her as we whisper and laugh about the night's adven-
tures and triumphs.

Only a few things were lacking to make the dream reality. For one
thing, Eiadh didn't have a house yet, and though she was gaining some
small reputation as a singer and reciter, it was clear that her career
would not be one of the dazzlingly brilliant ones; she was no prodigy,
and so her house would no doubt be a modest one for many years. No
matter, I will help her buy a finer one than she could afford on her
own, even though when a man helps a woman buy property in Basilica
the money can only be given as a gift. Eiadh is too loyal a woman ever
to lapse my contract and close me out of the house I helped her buy.

The only other thing lacking in the dream was that Nafai had never
actually written anything that was particularly good. Of course, that
was only because he had not yet chosen his field, and therefore he was
still testing himself, still dabbling a little in all of them. He'd settle on
one very soon, there'd be one in which he would show himself to have
a flair, and then there'd be myachiks of *his* works in the booths of the
inner market.

The Holy Road was having some kind of procession down into the
Rift Valley, and so—as men—they had to go all the way around it; even
so, they were soon enough at Mother's house. Issib immediately left
him, floating his way around to the outside stairway leading up into the
computer room, where he was spending all his time these days. The
next younger class was already in session out on the south curve of the
pillared porch, catching the sunlight slanting in. They were doing devotions, the boys slapping themselves sharply now and then, the girls
humming softly to themselves. His own class would be doing the same
thing inside somewhere, and Nafai was in no hurry to join them, since
it was considered vaguely impious to make a disturbance during a
devotion.

So he walked slowly, skirting the younger class on the porch, paus-
ing to lean on a pillar out of sight as he listened to the comfortable
music of small girlish voices humming randomly, yet finding momen-
tary chords that were lost in the moment they were discovered; and the
staccato, broken rhythms of boys slapping their trousered legs, their
shirted arms and chests, their bare cheeks.

As he stood there, a girl from the class suddenly appeared beside him. He knew her from gymnasium, of course. It was the witchling named Luet, who was rumored to have such remarkable visions that some of the ladies of the Shelf were already calling her a seer. Nafai didn't put much stock in such magical stories—the Oversoul couldn't know the future any more than a human being could, and as far as visions were concerned, people only remembered the ones that by sheer luck happened to match reality at some point.

"You're the one who's covered with fire," she said.

What was she talking about? How was he supposed to answer this kind of thing?

"No, I'm Nafai," he said.

"Not really fire. Little diamond sparks that turn to lightning when you're angry."

"I've got to go in."

She touched his sleeve; it held him as surely as if she had gripped his arm. "She'll never mate with you, you know."

"Who?"

"Eiadh. She'll offer, but you'll refuse her."

This was humiliating. How did this girl, probably only twelve, and from her size and shape *definitely* not a young woman yet, know anything about his feelings toward Eiadh? Was his love that obvious to everyone? Well, fine, so be it—he had nothing to hide. There was only honor in being known to love such a woman. And as for this girl being a seer, it wasn't too likely, not if she said that Eiadh would actually *offer* herself to him and he would turn her down! I'm more likely to bite my own finger off than to refuse to take the most perfect woman in Basilica as my mate.

"Excuse me," Nafai said, pulling his arm away. He didn't like this girl touching him anyway. They said that her mother was a wilder, one of those filthy naked solitary women who came into Basilica from the desert; supposedly they were holy women, but Nafai well knew that they also would sleep with any man who asked, right on the streets of the city, and it was permissible for any man to take one, even when he was in a contract with a mate. Decent and highborn men didn't do it, of course—even Meb had never bragged about "desert worship" or going on a "dust party," as couplings with wilders were crudely called. Nafai saw nothing holy in the whole business, and as far as he was concerned, this Luet was a bastard, conceived by a madwoman and a

bestial man in a coupling that was closer to rape than love. There was
no chance that the Oversoul really had anything to do with *that.*
"You're the bastard," said the girl. Then she walked away. The others
had finished their devotions—or perhaps had stopped them in order to
listen to what Luet was saying to him. Which meant that the story
would be spread all over the house by dinnertime and all over Basilica
before supper and no doubt Issib would tease him about it all the way
home and then Elemak and Mebbekew would *never* let him forget it
and he wished that the women of Basilica would keep crazy people like
Luet under lock and key instead of taking their stupid nonsense seriously all the time.

3

Fire

When he got inside he headed for the fountain room, where his class would be meeting all through the autumn. From the kitchen he could smell the preparations for dinner, and with a pang he remembered that, what with his argument with Elemak, he had completely forgotten to eat. Until this moment he hadn't felt even the tiniest bit hungry; but now that he realized it, he was completely famished. In fact, he felt just a little lightheaded. He should sit down. The fountain room was only a few steps away; surely they would understand why he was late if he arrived not feeling well. No one could be angry at him. No one could think he was a lazy slackwit if he was *sick*. They didn't have to know that he was sick with hunger.

He shuffled miserably into the room, playing his faintness to the hilt, leaning against a wall for a moment as he passed. He could feel their eyes on him, but he didn't look; he had a vague idea that genuinely sick people didn't easily meet other people's gaze. He half-expected the teacher of the day to speak up. What's wrong, Nafai? Aren't you well?

Instead there was silence until he had slid down the wall, folding himself into a sitting position on the wooden floor.

"We'll send out for a burial party, Nafai, in case you suddenly die."

Oh, no! It wasn't a teacher at all, one of the easily fooled young women who were so very impressed that Nafai was Rasa's own son. It was Mother here today. He looked up and met her gaze. She was smiling wickedly at him, not fooled a bit by his sick act.

"I was waiting for you. Issib is already on my portico. He didn't mention that you were dying, but I'm sure it was an oversight."

There was nothing left but to take it with good humor. Nafai sighed and got to his feet. "You know, Mother, that your unwillingness to suspend your disbelief will set back my acting career by several years."

"That's all right, Nafai, dear. Your acting career would set back Basilican theatre by centuries."

The other students laughed. Nafai grinned—but he also scanned the group to see who was enjoying it most. There was Eiadh, sitting near the fountain, where a few tiny drops of water had caught in her hair and were now reflecting light like jewels. *She* wasn't laughing at him. Instead she smiled beautifully, and winked. He grinned back—like a foolish clown, he was sure—and nearly tripped on the step leading up to the doorway to the back corridor. There was more laughter, of course, and so Nafai turned and took a deep bow. Then he walked away with dignity, deliberately running into the doorframe to earn another laugh before he finally made it out of the room.

"What's this about?" he asked Mother, hurrying to catch up with her.

"Family business," she said.

Then they passed through the doorway leading to Mother's private portico. They would stay, as always, in the screened-off area near the door, beyond the screen, out near the balustrade, the portico offered a beautiful view of the Rift Valley, so it was completely forbidden for men to go there. Such proscriptions in private houses were often ignored—Nafai knew several boys who talked about the Rift Valley, asserting that it was nothing special, just a steep craggy slope covered with trees and vines with a bunch of mist or clouds or fog blocking any view of the middle where, presumably, the sacred lake was located. But in Mother's house, decent respect was always shown, and Nafai was sure that even Father had never passed beyond the screen.

Once he was through with blinking, coming out into bright sunlight, Nafai was able to see who else was on the portico. Issib, of course; but to Nafai's surprise, Father himself was there, home from his journey. Why had he come to Rasa's house in the city, instead of going home first?

Father stood to greet him with an embrace.

"Elemak's at home, Father."

"So Issya informed me."

Father seemed very serious, very distant. He had something on his mind. It couldn't be anything good.

"Now that Nafai is finally here," said Mother, "we can perhaps make some sense out of all this."

Only now, as he seated himself in the best shade that wasn't already taken, did Nafai realize that there were two girls with them. At first glance, in the dazzling sunlight, he had assumed they were his sisters, Rasa's daughters Sevet and Kokor—in that context, an assembly of Rasa and her children, Father's presence was surprising, since he was father only to Issib and Nafai, not to the girls. But instead of Sevet and Kokor, it was two girls from the school—Hushidh, another of mother's nieces, the same age as Eiadh; and that witchling girl from the front porch, Luet. He looked at her in consternation—how had she got here so quickly? Not that he'd been hurrying. Mother must have sent for her even before she knew that Nafai had arrived.

What were Luet and Hushidh doing in a conference about family business?

"My dear mate Wetchik has something to tell us. We're hoping that you can—well, at least that Luet or Hushidh might—"

"Why don't I simply begin?" said Father.

Mother smiled and raised her hands in a graceful, elegant shrug.

"I saw something disturbing this morning," Father began. "Just before morning, actually. I was on my way home on the Desert Road—I was out on the desert, yesterday, to ponder and consult with myself and the Oversoul—when suddenly there came upon me a strong desire —a need, really—to leave the trail, even though that's a foolish thing to do in that dark time between moonset and sunrise. I didn't go far. I only had to move around a large rock, and it became quite clear to me why I had been led to that spot. For there in front of me I saw Basilica. But not the Basilica I would have expected, dotted with the lights of celebration in Dolltown or the inner market. What I saw was Basilica ablaze."

"On *fire?*" asked Issib.

"A vision, of course. I didn't know that at first, mind you—I lunged forward; I was intending to rush to the city—to rush here and see if you were all right, my dear—"

"As I would certainly expect you to do," said Mother.

"When the city disappeared as suddenly as it had appeared. Only the fire remained, rising up to form a pillar on the rock in front of me. It stood there for the longest time, a column of flame. And it was hot— as hot as if it had been real. I felt it singeing me, though of course there's not a mark on my clothing. And then the pillar of flame rose up into the sky, slowly at first, then faster and faster until it became a star moving across the sky, and then disappeared entirely."

"You were tired, Father," said Issib.

"I've been tired many times," said Father, "but I have never seen pillars of flame before. Or burning cities."

Mother spoke up again. "Your father came to me, Issya, because he hoped that I might help him understand the meaning of this. If it came from the Oversoul, or if it was just a mad sort of waking dream."

"I vote for the dream," said Issib.

"Even madness can come from the Oversoul," said Hushidh.

Everyone looked at her. She was a rather plainish girl, always quiet in class. Now that Nafai saw her and Luet side by side, he realized that they resembled each other closely. Were they sisters? More to the point, what was Hushidh doing here, and by what right did she speak out about family matters?

"It *can* come from the Oversoul," said Father. "But did it? And if it did, what does it mean?"

Nafai could see that Father was directing those questions, not at Rasa or even at Hushidh, but at Luet! He couldn't possibly believe what the women said about her, could he? Did a single vision turn a rational man of business into a superstitious pilgrim trying to find meanings in everything he saw?

"I can't tell you what your dream means," said Luet.

"Oh," said Father. "Not that I actually thought—"

"If the Oversoul sent the dream, and if she meant you to understand it, then she also sent the interpretation."

"There *was* no interpretation."

"Wasn't there?" asked Luet. "This is the first time you've had a dream like this, isn't it?"

"Definitely. This isn't a habit of mine, to see visions as I'm walking along the road at night."

"So you aren't used to recognizing the meanings that come along with a vision."

"I suppose not."

"Yet you *were* receiving messages."

"Was I?"

"Before you saw the flame, you knew that you were supposed to turn away from the road."

"Yes, well, *that.*"

"What do you think the voice of the Oversoul sounds like? Do you think she speaks Basyat or puts up signposts?"

Luet sounded vaguely scornful—an outrageous tone of voice for her to adopt with a man of Wetchik's status in the city. Yet he seemed to take no offense, accepting her rebuke as if she had a right to chastise him.

"The Oversoul puts the knowledge pure into our minds, unmixed with any human language," she said. "We are always given more than we can possibly comprehend, and we can comprehend far more than we're able to put into words."

Luet had a voice of such simple power. Not like the chanting sound that the witches and prophets of the inner market used when they were trying to attract business. She spoke as if she knew, as if there was no possibility of doubt.

"Let me ask you, then, sir. When you saw the city on fire, how did you know it was Basilica?"

"I've seen it a thousand times, from just that angle, coming in from the desert."

"But did you see the shape of the city and recognize it from that, or did you know first that it was Basilica on fire, and then your mind called forth the picture of the city that was already in your memory?"

"I don't know—how can I know that?"

"Think back. Was the knowledge there before the vision, or was the vision first?"

Instead of telling the girl to go away, Father closed his eyes and tried to remember.

"When you put it that way, I think—I knew it before I actually looked in that direction. I don't think I actually saw it until I was lunging toward it. I saw the *flame,* but not the burning city inside it. And now that you ask, I also knew that Rasa and my children were in terrible danger. I knew that first of all, as I was rounding the rock— that was part of the sense of urgency. I knew that if I left the trail and came to that exact spot, I'd be able to save them from the danger. It was only then that it came to mind what the danger was, and then last of all that I saw the flame and the city inside it."

"This is a true vision," said Luet.

Just from that? She knew just from the order of things? She probably would have said the same thing no matter *what* Father remembered. And maybe Father was only remembering it that way because Luet had suggested it that way. This was making Nafai furious, for Father to be nodding in acceptance when this twelve-year-old girl condescendingly treated him like an apprentice in a profession in which she was a widely respected master.

"But it wasn't true," said Father. "When I got here, there *was* no danger."

"No, I didn't think so," said Luet. "Back when you first felt that your mate and your children were in danger, what did you expect to *do* about it?"

"I was going to save them, of course."

"Specifically *how?*"

Again he closed his eyes. "Not to pull them from a burning building. That never occurred to me until later, as I was walking the rest of the way into the city. At the moment I wanted to shout out that the city was burning, that we had to—"

"What?"

"I was going to say, we had to get out of the city. But that wasn't what I wanted to say at first. When it started, I felt like I had to come to the city and tell everybody that there was a fire coming."

"And they had to get out?"

"I guess," said Father. "Of course, what else?"

Luet said nothing, but her gaze never left his face.

"No," Father said. "No, that *wasn't* it." Father sounded surprised. "I wasn't going to warn them to get out."

Luet leaned forward, looking somehow more intense, not so—analytical. "Sir, just a moment ago, when you were saying that you had wanted to warn them to get out of the city—"

"But that *wasn't* what I was going to do."

"But when you thought for a moment that—when you *assumed* that you were going to tell them to get out of the city—what did that feel like? When you told us that, why did you know that it was wrong?"

"I don't know. It just felt . . . *wrong.*"

"This is very important," said Luet. "How does feeling wrong *feel?*"

Again he closed his eyes. "I'm not used to thinking about how I think. And now I'm trying to remember how it felt when I thought I remembered something that I didn't actually remember—"

"Don't talk," said Luet.

He fell silent.

Nafai wanted to yell at somebody. What were they doing, listening to this ugly stupid little girl, letting her tell Father—the Wetchik himself, in case nobody remembered—to keep his mouth shut!

But everybody else was so intense that Nafai kept his own mouth shut. Issib would be so proud of him for actually refraining from saying something that he had thought of.

"What I felt," said Father, "was *nothing.*" He nodded slowly. "Right after you asked the question and I answered it—. Of course, what else —then you sat there looking at me and I had nothing in my head at all."

"Stupid," she said.

He raised an eyebrow. To Nafai's relief, he was finally noticing how disrespectfully Luet was speaking to him.

"You felt stupid," she said. "And so you knew that what you'd just said was wrong."

He nodded. "Yes, I guess that's it."

"What's all this about?" said Issib. "Analyzing your analysis of analyses of a completely subjective hallucination?"

Good work, Issya, said Nafai silently. You took the words right out of my mouth.

"I mean, you can play these games all morning, but you're just laying meanings on top of a meaningless experience. Dreams are nothing more than random firings of memories, which your brain then interprets so as to invent casual connections, which makes stories out of *nothing.*"

Father looked at Issib for a long moment, then shook his head. "You're right, of course," he said. "Even though I was wide awake and I've never had a hallucination before, it was nothing more than a random firing of synapses in my brain."

Nafai knew, as Issib and Mother certainly knew, that Father was being ironic, that he was telling Issib that his vision of the fire on the rock was *more* than a meaningless night dream. But Luet didn't know Father, so *she* thought he was backing away from mysticism and retreating into reality.

"You're wrong," she said. "It was a true vision, because it came to you the right way. The understanding came *before* the vision—that's why I was asking those questions. The meaning is there and then your brain supplies the pictures that let you understand it. That's the way the Oversoul talks to us."

"Talks to crazy people, you mean," Nafai said.

He regretted it immediately, but by then it was too late.

"Crazy people like *me?*" said Father.

"And I assure you that Luet is at least as sane as you are," Mother added.

Issib couldn't pass up the chance to cast a verbal dart. "As sane as Nyef? Then she's in deep trouble."

Father shut down Issib's teasing immediately. "You were saying the same thing yourself only a minute ago."

"I wasn't calling people crazy," said Issib.

"No, you didn't have Nafai's—what shall we call it?—*pointed eloquence.*"

Nafai knew he could save himself now by shutting up and letting Issib deflect the heat. But he was committed to skepticism, and self-control wasn't his strong suit. "This girl," said Nafai. "Don't you see how she was leading you on, Father? She asks you a question, but she doesn't tell you beforehand what the answer will mean—so no matter what you answer, she can say, That's it, it's a true vision, definitely the Oversoul talking."

Father didn't have an immediate answer. Nafai glanced at Luet, feeling triumphant, wanting to see her squirm. But she wasn't squirming. She was looking at him very calmly. The intensity had drained out of her and now she was simply—calm. It bothered him, the steadiness of her gaze. "What are you looking at?" he demanded.

"A fool," she answered.

Nafai jumped to his feet. "I don't have to listen to you calling me a—"

"Sit down!" roared Father.

Nafai sat, seething.

"She just listened to *you* calling *her* a fraud," said Father. "I appreciate how both of my sons are doing exactly what I wanted you here to do—providing a skeptical audience for my story. You analyzed the process very cleverly and your version of things accounts for everything you know about it, just as neatly as Luet's version does."

Nafai was ready to help him draw the correct conclusion. "Then the rule of simplicity requires you to—"

"The rule of your father requires you to hold your tongue, Nafai. What you're both forgetting is that there's a fundamental difference between you and me."

Father leaned toward Nafai.

"*I* saw the fire."

He leaned back again.

"Luet didn't tell me what to think or feel at the time. And her questions helped me remember—helped *me* remember—the way it really happened. Instead of the way I was already changing it to fit my preconceptions. She *knew* that it would be strange—in exactly the ways that it was strange. Of course, I can't convince you."

"No," said Nafai. "You can only convince yourself."

"In the end, Nafai, oneself is the only person anyone can convince."

The battle was lost if Father was already making up aphorisms. Nafai sat back to wait for it all to end. He took consolation from the fact that it had been, after all, merely a dream. It's not as if it was going to change his life or anything.

Father wasn't done yet. "Do you know what I actually wanted to do, when I felt such urgency to get to the city? I wanted to warn people— to follow the old ways, to go back to the laws of the Oversoul, or this place would burn."

"What place?" asked Luet, her intensity back again.

"This place. Basilica. The city. That's what I saw burning."

Again Father fell silent, looking into her burning eyes.

"Not the city," he said at last. "The city was only the picture that my mind supplied, wasn't it? Not the city. The whole world. All of Harmony, burning."

Rasa gasped. "Earth," she whispered.

"Oh, please," Nafai said. So Mother was going to connect Father's vision with that old story about the home planet that was burned by the Oversoul to punish humanity for whatever nastiness the current story-teller wanted to preach against. The all-purpose coercive myth: If you don't do what I say—I mean, what the *Oversoul* says—then the *whole world* will *burn*.

"*I* haven't seen the fire itself," said Luet, ignoring Nafai. "Maybe I'm not even seeing the same thing."

"What *have* you seen?" asked Father. Nafai cringed at how respectful he was being toward this girl.

"I saw the Deep Lake of Basilica, crusted over with blood and
ashes."

Nafai waited for her to finish. But she just sat there.

"That's it? That's all?" Nafai stood up, preparing to walk out. "This is
great, hearing the two of you compare visions. *I* saw a city on fire. Well,
I saw a scum-covered lake."

Luet stood up and faced him. No, faced him down—which was
ridiculous, since he was almost half a meter taller than her.

"You're only arguing against me," she said hotly, "because you don't
want to believe what I told you about Eiadh."

"That's ridiculous," said Nafai.

"You had a vision about Eiadh?" asked Rasa.

"What does Eiadh have to do with *Nyef?*" asked Issib.

Nafai hated her for mentioning it again, in front of his family. "You
can make up whatever you want about other people, but you'd better
leave *me* out of it."

"Enough," said Father. "We're done."

Rasa looked at him in surprise. "Are you dismissing me in my own
house?"

"I'm dismissing my sons."

"You have authority over *your* sons, of course." Mother was smiling,
but Nafai knew from her soft speech that she was seriously annoyed.
"However, I see no one here in *my* house but *my* students."

Father nodded, accepting the rebuke, then stood to leave. "Then I'm
dismissing myself—I may do *that*, I hope."

"You may always leave, my adored mate, as long as you promise to
come back to me."

His answer was to kiss her cheek.

"What are you going to do?" she asked.

"What the Oversoul told me to do."

"And what is *that?*"

"Warn people to return to the laws of the Oversoul or the world will
burn."

Issib was appalled. "That's crazy, Father!"

"I'm tired of hearing that word from the lips of my sons."

"But—prophets of the Oversoul don't say things like that. They're like poets, except all their metaphors have some moral lesson or they celebrate the Oversoul or—"

"Issya," said Wetchik, "all my life I've listened to these so-called prophecies—and the psalms and the histories and the temple priests— and I've always thought, if *this* is all the Oversoul has to say, why should I bother to listen? Why should the Oversoul even bother *speaking,* if this is all that's on his mind?"

"Then why did you teach *us* to speak to the Oversoul?" asked Issib.

"Because I believed in the ancient laws. And I *did* speak to the Oversoul myself, though more as a way of clarifying my own thoughts than because I actually thought that he was *listening.* Then last night— this morning—I had an experience that I never conceived of. I never wished for it. I didn't even know what it *was* until now, these last few minutes, talking to Luet. Now I know—what it feels like to have the Oversoul's voice inside you. Nothing like these poets and dreamers and deceivers, who write down whatever pops into their heads and then sell it as prophecy. What was in me was not myself, and Luet has shown me that she's had the same voice inside *her.* It means that the Oversoul is real and alive."

"So maybe it's real," said Issib. "That doesn't tell us what it *is.*"

"It's the guardian of the world," said Wetchik. "He asked me to help. *Told* me to help. And I will."

"That's all temple stuff," said Issib. "You don't know anything about it. You grow exotic plants."

Father dismissed Issib's objections with a gesture. "Anything the Oversoul needs me to know, he'll tell me." Then he headed for the door into the house.

Nafai followed him, only a few steps. "Father," he said.

Father waited.

The trouble was, Nafai didn't know what he was going to say. Only that he had to say it. That there was a very important question whose answer he had to have before Father left. He just didn't know what the question was.

"Father," he said again.

"Yes?"

And because Nafai couldn't think of the real question, the deep one, the important one, he asked the only question that came to mind. "What am *I* supposed to do?"

"Keep the old ways of the Oversoul," said Father.

"What does that *mean?*"

"Or the world will burn." And Father was gone.

Nafai looked at the empty door for a while. It didn't do anything, so he turned back to the others. They were all looking at him, as if they expected *him* to do something.

"*What!*" he demanded.

"Nothing," said Mother. She arose from her seat in the shade of the kaplya tree. "We'll all return to our work."

"That's all?" said Issib. "Our father—your mate—has just told us that the Oversoul is speaking to him, and we're supposed to go back to our studies?"

"You really don't understand, do you?" said Mother. "You've lived all these years as my sons, as my *students,* and you are still nothing more than the ordinary boys wandering the streets of Basilica hoping to find a willing woman and a bed for the night."

"What don't we understand here?" asked Nafai. "Just because you women all take this witchgirl so seriously doesn't mean that—"

"I have been down into the water myself," said Mother, her voice like metal. "You men can pretend to yourselves that the Oversoul is distracted or sleeping, or just a machine that collects our transmissions and sends them to libraries in distant cities. Whatever theory you happen to believe, it makes no difference to the *truth.* For *I* know, as most of the women in this city know, that the Oversoul is very much alive. At least as the keeper of the memories of this world, she is alive. We all receive those memories when we go into the water. Sometimes they seem random, sometimes we are given exactly the memory we needed. The Oversoul keeps the history of the world, as it was seen through other people's eyes. Only a few of us—like Luet and Hushidh—are given wisdom away from the water, and even fewer are given visions of real things that haven't happened yet. Since the great Izumina died, Luet is the only seer I know of in Basilica—so yes, we take her very, very seriously."

Women go down into the water and receive visions? This was the first time Nafai had ever heard a woman describe any part of the worship at the lake. He had always assumed that the women's worship was like the men's—physical, ascetic, painful, a dispassionate way of discharging emotion. Instead they were all mystics. What seemed like legends or madness to men was at the center of a woman's life. Nafai felt as though he had discovered that women were of another species after all. The question was, which of them, men or women, were the humans? The rational but brutal men? Or the irrational but gentle women?

"There's only one thing rarer than a girl like Luet," Mother was saying, "and that's a *man* who hears the voice of the Oversoul. We know now that your father does hear—Luet confirmed that for me. I don't know what the Oversoul wants, or why she spoke to your father, but I *am* wise enough to know that it matters."

As she passed Nafai, she reached up and caught his ear firmly, though not painfully, between her fingers. "As for the mythical burning of Earth, my dear boy, I've seen it myself. It happened. I can only guess how long ago—we estimate there's been at least thirty million years of human history on this world we named Harmony. But I saw the missiles fly, the bombs explode, and the world erupt in flame. The smoke filled the sky and blocked the sun, and underneath that blanket of darkness the oceans froze and the world was covered in ice and only a few human beings survived, to rise up out of the blackness as the world died, carrying their hopes and their regrets and their genes to other planets, hoping to start again. They did. We're here. Now the Oversoul has warned your father that our new start can lead to the same ending as before."

Nafai had seen Mother's public face—playful, brilliant, analytical, gracious—and he had seen her family face—frank of speech yet always kind, quick to anger yet quicker to forgive. Always he had assumed that the way she was with the family was her true self, with nothing held back. Instead, behind the faces that he thought he knew, she had kept this secret all the time, her bitter vision of the end of Earth. "You never told us about this," whispered Nafai.

"I most certainly told you about it," said Rasa. "It's not *my* fault that when you heard it, you thought I was telling you a myth." She let go of his ear and returned to the house.

Issib floated past him, mumbling something about waking up one morning to find that you've been living in a madhouse all your life. Hushidh went past him also, not meeting his gaze; he could imagine the gossip that she would spread in his class all the rest of the day.

He was alone with Luet.

"I shouldn't have spoken to you before," she said.

"And you shouldn't speak to me again, either," suggested Nafai.

"Some people hear a lie when they're told the truth. You're so proud of your status as the son of Rasa and Wetchik, but obviously whatever genes you got from your parents, they weren't the right ones."

"While I'm sure *you* got the finest your parents had to offer." She looked at him with obvious contempt, and then she was gone.

"What a wonderful day this is going to be," he said—to no one, since he was alone. "My entire family hates me." He thought for a moment. "I'm not even sure that I *want* them to like me."

For one dangerous moment, alone on the portico, he toyed with the idea of slipping past the screens and going to the edge, leaning out, and looking at the forbidden sight of the Valley of the Holy Women, casually referred to as the Rift Valley, and more crudely known as the Canyon of the Crones. I'll see it and I bet I don't even get struck blind.

But he didn't do it, even though he stood there thinking about it for a long time. It seemed that every time he was about to take a step toward the edge, his mind suddenly wandered and he hesitated, confused, forgetting for a moment what it was he wanted to do. Finally he lost interest and went back inside the house.

He should have gone back to class—it's what he *expected* to do when he went inside. But he couldn't bring himself to do it. Instead he wandered to the front door and out onto the porch, into the streets of Basilica. Mother would probably be furious at him but that was too bad.

He must have been seeing where he was going, since he didn't bump into anything, but he had no memory of what he saw or where he had been. He ended up in the Fountains district, not far from the neighborhood of Rasa's house; and in his mind, he had circled through the same thoughts over and over again, finally ending up not very far from where he started.

One thing he knew, though: He couldn't dismiss this all as madness. Father was *not* crazy, however new and strange he might seem; and as for Mother, if *her* vision of the burning of Earth was madness, then she had been mad since before he was born. So there *was* something that put ideas and desires and visions into his parents' minds—and into Luet's, too, couldn't forget *her*. People called this something the Oversoul, but that was just a name, a label. What *was* it? What did it want? What could it actually *do?* If it could talk to some people, why didn't it just talk to everybody?

Nafai stopped across a fairly wide street from what might be the largest house in Basilica. He knew it well enough, since the head of the

Palwashantu clan was mated with the woman who lived there. Nafai couldn't remember *her* name—she was nobody, everyone knew she had bought this ancient house with her mate's money, and if she didn't renew his contract then even *with* the house she'd be nobody—but *he* was Gaballufix. There was a family connection—his mother was Hosni, who later on became Wetchik's auntie and the mother of Elemak. Between that blood connection and the fact that Father was perhaps the second most prestigious Palwashantu clansman in Basilica, they had visited this house at least once, usually two or three times a year since as long ago as Nafai could remember.

As he stood there, stupidly watching the front of that landmark building, he suddenly came alert, for without meaning to he had recognized someone moving along the street. Elemak should have been home sleeping—he had traveled all night, hadn't he? Yet here he was, in mid-afternoon. For a panicked moment Nafai wondered if Elya was looking for *him*—was it possible that Mother had missed him and worried and now the whole family, perhaps even Father's employees as well, were combing the city looking for him?

But no. Elemak wasn't looking for anybody. He was moving too casually, too easily. Looking in no particular direction at all.

And then he was gone.

No, he had turned down into the gap between Gaballufix's house and the building next door. So he *did* have a destination.

Nafai had to know what Elemak was doing. He trotted along the street to where he had a clear view down the narrow road. He got there in time to see Elemak ducking into a low alley doorway into Gaballufix's house.

Nafai couldn't imagine what business Elya might have with Gaballufix—especially something so urgent that he had to go to his house the same day he got back from a long trip. True, Gaballufix was technically Elya's half-brother, but there were sixteen years between them and Gaballufix had never openly recognized Elya as his brother. That didn't mean, though, that they couldn't start behaving more like close kinsmen now. Still, it bothered Nafai that Elemak had never mentioned it and seemed to be concealing it now.

Whether the question bothered him or not, Nafai knew that it would be a very bad idea to ask Elemak about it directly. When Elya wanted anybody to know what he was doing with Gaballufix, he'd tell them. In the meantime, the secret would be safe inside Elya's head.

A secret inside somebody's head.

Luet had known that Nafai was in love with Eiadh. Well, it wasn't all *that* secret—Luet might have guessed it from the way that he looked at her. But there on the front porch of Mother's house, Luet had said, "*You're* the bastard," as if she were answering him for calling *her* a bastard. Only he hadn't *said* anything. He had only *thought* of her as a bastard. It wasn't an opinion he had expressed before. He had only thought of it at that moment, because he was annoyed with Luet. Yet she had known.

Was that the Oversoul, too? Not just putting ideas into people's heads, but also taking them out and telling them to other people? The Oversoul wasn't just a provider of strange dreams—it was a spy and a gossip as well.

It made Nafai afraid, to think that not only was the Oversoul real, but also that it had the power to read his most secret, transitory thoughts and tell them to someone else. And to someone as repulsive as the little bastard witchgirl, no less.

It frightened him like the first time he went out into the sea by himself. Father had taken them all on a holiday, down to the beach. The first afternoon there, they had all gone out into the sea together, and surrounded by his father and brothers—except Issib, of course, who watched them from his chair on the beach—he had felt the sea play with him, the waves shoving him toward shore, then trying to draw him out again. It was fun, exhilarating. He even dared to swim out to where his feet couldn't quite touch the bottom, all the while playing with Meb and Elya and Father. A good day, a great day, when his older brothers still liked him. But the next morning he got up early, left the tent and went out to the water alone. He could swim like a fish; he was in no danger. And yet as he walked out into the water he felt an inexplicable unease. The water tugging at him, pushing him; he was only a few meters from shore, and yet with no one else in the water, all by himself, he felt as if he had lost his place, as if he had already been washed out to sea, as if he were caught in the grasp of something so huge that any part of it could swallow him up. He panicked then. He ran to shore, struggling against the water, convinced that it would never let him go, dragging at him, sucking him down. And then he was on the sand, on the dry sand above the tide line, and he fell to his knees and wept because he was safe.

But for those few moments out in the water he had felt the terror of knowing how small and helpless he was, how much power there was in the world, and how easily it could do to him whatever it wanted and there was nothing he could do to resist it.

That was the fear he felt now. Not so strong, not so specific as it had been that day on the beach—but then, he wasn't a five-year-old anymore, either, and he was better at dealing with fear. The Oversoul wasn't an old legend, it was alive, and it could force visions into his own parents' minds and it could search out secrets inside Nafai's head and tell them to other people, to people that Nafai didn't like and who didn't like him.

The worst thing was knowing that the reason why Luet didn't like him was probably *because* of what the Oversoul had told her about his thoughts. His most private thoughts exposed to this unsympathetic little monster. What next? Would Father's next vision be Nafai's fantasies about Eiadh? Worse yet, would *Mother* be shown?

On the beach, he had been able to run for shore. Where did you run to get away from the Oversoul?

You didn't. You couldn't hide, either—how could you disguise your own thoughts so even you didn't know what you were thinking?

The only choice he had was to try to find out what the Oversoul was, to try to understand what it wanted, what it was trying to do to his family, to *him*. He had to understand the Oversoul and, if possible, get it to leave him alone.

4

Masks

There would be no point in going back to Mother's house so late in the school day. Explaining himself would probably take up what little time was left. Making excuses could wait until tomorrow.

Or maybe Nafai would never go back. There was a thought. After all, Mebbekew didn't go to school. In fact he didn't do *anything*, didn't even come home if he decided not to.

When had that started? Was Meb already doing that sort of thing at fourteen? Well, whether he was or not, Nafai could start now and who was going to stop him? He was as tall as any man, and he was old enough for a man's trade. Not Father's trade, though—never the plant business. If you followed *that* trade long enough, you started seeing visions in the dark beside desert roads.

But there were other trades. Maybe Nafai could apprentice himself to some artist. A poet, or a singer—Nafai's voice was young, but he could follow a tune, and with training maybe he could actually become good. Or maybe he was really a dancer, or an actor, in spite of Mother's joke this morning. Those arts had nothing to do with going to school— if he was supposed to pursue one, then staying on with Mother was a waste of time.

That notion possessed him through the afternoon, carrying him

south at first, toward the inner market, where there would be songs
and poems to hear, perhaps some fine new myachik to buy and listen to
at home. Of course, if he stopped attending school, Mother would no
doubt cut off his myachik allowance. But as an apprentice there'd probably be some spending money, and if not, so what? He'd be doing a
real art himself, in the flesh. Soon he would no longer even *want*
recordings of art on little glass balls.

By the time he reached the inner market, he had talked himself into
having no interest in recordings, now that he was going to be making a
career out of creating the real thing. He headed east, through the
neighborhoods called Pens and Gardens and Olive Grove, a few narrow streets of houses between the city wall and the rim of the valley
where men could not go. At last he came to the place that was narrow-
est of all, a single street with a high white wall behind the houses, so
that a man standing on the red wall of the city couldn't see over the
houses and down into the valley. He had only come this way a few
times in his life, and never alone.

Never alone, because Dolltown was a place for company and fellowship, a place for sitting in a crowded audience and watching dances
and plays, or listening to recitations and concerts. Now, though, Nafai
was coming to Dolltown as an artist, not to be part of the audience. It
wasn't fellowship he was looking for, but vocation.

The sun was still up, so the streets of Dolltown weren't crowded.
Dusk would bring out the frolicking apprentices and schoolboys, and
full dark would call forth the lovers and the connoisseurs and the
revelers. But even now, in late afternoon, some of the theatres were
open, and the galleries were doing good business in the daylight.

Nafai stopped into several galleries, more because they were open
than because he seriously thought he might apprentice himself to a
painter or a sculptor. Nafai's skill at drawing was never good, and when
he tried sculpture as a child his projects always had to have titles so
people could tell what they were supposed to be. Browsing through
the galleries, Nafai tried to look thoughtful and studious, but the art-
sellers were never fooled—Nafai might be tall as a man, but he was
still far too young to be a serious customer. So they never came up and
talked to him, the way they did when adults came into the shops. He
had to glean his information from what he overheard. The prices astonished him. Of course the cost of the originals was completely out of
reach, but even the high-resolution holographic copies were too expen-

sive for him to dream of buying one. Worst of all was the fact that the paintings and sculptures he liked the best were invariably the most expensive. Maybe that meant that he had excellent taste. Or maybe it meant that the artists who knew how to impress the ignorant were able to make the most money.

Bored at last with the galleries, and determined to see which art should be the channel for his future, Nafai wandered down to the open theatre, a series of tiny stages dotting the broad lawns near the wall. A few plays were in rehearsal. Since there was no real audience yet, the sound bubbles hadn't been turned on, and as Nafai walked from stage to stage, the sounds of more distant plays kept intruding into every pause in the one close at hand. After a while, though, Nafai discovered that if he stood and watched a rehearsal long enough to get interested, he stopped noticing any other noises.

What intrigued him most was a troupe of satirists. He had always thought satire must be the most exciting kind of play, because the scripts were always as new as today's gossip. And, just as he had imagined, there sat the satirist at the rehearsal, scribbling his verse on paper —on *paper*—and handing the scraps to a script boy who ran them up to the stage and handed them to the player that the lines were intended for. The players who weren't onstage at the moment were either pacing back and forth or hunched over on the lawn, saying their lines over and over again, to memorize them for tonight's performance. This was why satires were always sloppy and ill-timed, with sudden silences and absurd non sequiturs abounding. But no one expected a satire to be *good*—it only had to be funny and nasty and new.

This one seemed to be about an old man who sold love potions. The masker playing the old man seemed quite young, no more than twenty, and he wasn't very good at faking an older voice. But that was part of the fun of it—maskers were almost always apprentice actors who hadn't yet managed to get a part with a serious company of players. They *claimed* that the reason they wore masks instead of makeup was to protect them from reprisals from angry victims of satire—but, watching them, Nafai suspected that the mask was as much to protect the young actor from the ridicule of his peers.

The afternoon had turned hot, and some of the actors had taken off their shirts; those with pale skin seemed oblivious to the fact that they were burning to the color of tomatoes. Nafai laughed silently at the thought that maskers were probably the only people in Basilica who could get a sunburn everywhere *but* their faces.

The script boy handed a verse to a player who had been sitting hunched over in the grass. The young man looked at it, then got up and walked to the satirist.

"I can't say this," he said.

The satirist's back was to Nafai, so he couldn't hear the answer.

"What, is my part so unimportant that *my* lines don't have to rhyme?"

Now the satirist's answer was loud enough that Nafai caught a few phrases, ending with the clincher, "Write the thing yourself!"

The young man angrily pulled his mask off his face and shouted, "I couldn't do worse than *this!*"

The satirist burst into laughter. "Probably not," he said. "Go ahead, give it a try, I don't have time to be brilliant with *every* scene."

Mollified, the young man put his mask back on. But Nafai had seen enough. For the young masker who wanted his lines to rhyme was none other than Nafai's brother Mebbekew.

So this was the source of his income. Not borrowing at all. The idea that had seemed so clever and fresh to Nafai—apprenticing himself in an art to earn his independence—had long since occurred to Mebbekew, and he was *doing* it. In a way it was encouraging—if Mebbekew can do it, why can't I?—but it was also discouraging to think that of all people, Nafai had happened to choose Mebbekew to emulate. Meb, the brother who had hated him all his life instead of coming to hate him more recently, like Elya. Is this what I was born for? To become a second Mebbekew?

Then came the nastiest thought of all. Wouldn't it be funny if I entered the acting profession, years after Meb, and got a job with a serious company right away? It would be deliciously humiliating; Meb would be suicidal.

Well, maybe not. Meb was far more likely to turn murderous.

Nafai was drawn out of his spiteful little daydream by the scene on the stage. The old potion-seller was trying to persuade a reluctant young woman to buy an herb from him.

> Put the leaves in his tea
> Put the flower in your bed
> And by half past three

> He'll be dead—I beg your pardon,
> Just a slip of the tongue.

The plot was finally making sense. The old man wanted to poison the girl's lover by persuading her that the fatal herb was a love potion. She apparently didn't catch on—all characters in satire were amazingly stupid—but for other reasons she was still resisting the sale.

> I'd sooner be hung
> Than use a flower from your garden.
> I want nothing from you.
> I want his love to be true.

Suddenly the old man burst into an operatic song. His voice was actually not bad, even with exaggeration for comic effect.

> The dream of love is so enchanting!

At that moment Mebbekew, his mask back in place, bounded onto the stage and directly addressed the audience.

> Listen to the old man ranting!

They proceeded to perform a strange duet, the old potion-seller singing a line and Mebbekew's young character answering with a spoken comment to the audience.

> But love can come in many ways!
> (I've followed him for several days.)
> One lover might be very willing!
> (I know he plots her lover's killing.)
> The other endlessly delays!
> (Listen how the donkey brays!)
> Oh, do not make the wrong decision!
> (I think I'll give this ass a vision.)
> When I can take you to your goal!
> (He'll think it's from the Oversoul.)
> No limits bind the lover's game.
> (A vision needs a little flame . . .)
> No matter how you win it,
> Because your heart is in it,
> You'll love your lover's loving still the same.

A vision from the Oversoul. Flame. Nafai didn't like the turn this was taking. He didn't like the fact that the old potion-seller's mask had a wild mane of white hair and a full white beard. Was it possible that word had already spread so far and fast? Some satirists were famous for getting the gossip before anyone else—as often as not, people attended the satires just to find out what was happening—and many people left the satires asking each other, What was that *really* about?

Mebbekew was fiddling with a box on the stage. The satirist called out to him, "Never mind the fire effect. We'll pretend it's working."

"We have to try it sometime," Mebbekew answered.

"Not now."

"When?"

The satirist got to his feet, strode to the foot of the stage directly in front of Meb, cupped his hands around his mouth, and bellowed: "We . . . will . . . do . . . the . . . effect . . . later!"

"Fine," said Meb.

As the satirist returned to his place on the hill, he said, "And *you* wouldn't be setting off the fire effect anyway."

"Sorry," said Meb. He returned to his place behind the box that presumably would be spouting a column of flame tonight. The other maskers returned to their positions.

"End of song," said Meb. "Fire effect."

Immediately the potion-seller and the girl flung up their hands in a mockery of surprise.

"A pillar of fire!" cried the potion-seller.

"How could fire suddenly appear on a bare rock in the desert?" cried the girl. "It's a *miracle!*"

The potion-seller whirled on her. "You don't know what you're talking about, bitch! *I'm* the only one who can see this! It's a vision!"

"No!" shouted Mebbekew, in his deepest voice. "It's a special stage effect!"

"A stage effect!" cried the potion-seller. "Then you must be—"

"You got it!"

"That old humbug the Oversoul!"

"I'm proud of you, old trickster! Stupid girl—you almost fixed her."

"Oh, it's nothing much to take *her*—*you're* the master faker!"

"*No!*" bellowed the satirist. "Not 'take *her*,' you idiot! It's '*take* her,' emphasis on *take*, or it doesn't rhyme with *faker!*"

"Sorry," said the young masker playing the potion-seller. "It doesn't make *sense* your way, of course, but at least it'll *rhyme.*"

"It doesn't have to make sense, you uppity young rooster, it only has to make money!"

Everybody laughed—though it was clear that the actors still didn't really like the satirist much. They got back into the scene and a few moments later Meb and the potion-seller launched into a song-and-dance routine about how clever they were at hoodwinking people, and how unbelievably gullible most people were—especially women. It seemed that every couplet of the song was designed to mortally offend some portion of the audience, and the song went on until every conceivable group in Basilica had been darted. While they sang and danced, the girl pretended to roast some kind of meat in the flames.

Meb forgot his lyrics less than the other masker, and in spite of the fact that Nafai knew the whole sequence was aimed at humiliating Father, he couldn't help but notice that Meb was actually pretty good, especially at singing so every word was clear. I could do that, too, thought Nafai.

The song kept coming back to the same refrain:

I'm standing by a fire
With my favorite liar
No one stands a chance
When he starts his fancy dancing

When the song ended, the Oversoul—Meb—had persuaded the potion-seller that the best way to get the women of Basilica to do whatever he wanted was to persuade them that he was getting visions from the Oversoul. "They're so ready for deceiving," said Meb, "We'll have all these girls believing."

The scene closed with the potion-seller leading the girl off-stage, telling her how he had seen a vision of the city of Basilica burning up. The satirist had switched to alliterative verse, which Nafai thought sounded a little more natural than rhyming, but it wasn't as fun. "Do you want to waste the last weeks of the world clinging to some callow young cad? Wouldn't you be better off boffing your brains out with an ugly old man who has an understanding with the Oversoul?"

"Fine," said the satirist. "That'll work. Let's have the street scene now."

Another group of maskers came up on the stage. Nafai immediately headed across the lawn to where Mebbekew, his mask still in place, was already scribbling new dialogue on a scrap of paper.

"Meb," said Nafai.

Meb looked up, startled, trying to see better through the small eye-holes in the mask. "What did you call me?" Then he saw it was Nafai. Immediately he jumped to his feet and started walking away. "Get away from me, you little rat-eater."

"Meb, I've got to talk to you."

Mebbekew kept walking.

"Before you go on in this play tonight!" said Nafai.

Meb whirled on him. "It's not a play, it's a satire. I'm not an actor, I'm a masker. And you're not my brother, you're an ass."

Meb's fury astonished him. "What have I done to you?" asked Nafai.

"I know you, Nyef. No matter what I do or say to you, you're going to end up telling Father."

As if Father wouldn't eventually find out that his son was playing in a satire that was designed to dart him in front of the whole city. "What makes me sick," said Nafai, "is that all you care about is whether *you* get in trouble. You've got no family loyalty at all."

"This doesn't hurt my family. Masking is a perfectly legitimate way to get started as an actor, and it pays me a living and wins me just a little tiny scrap of respect and pleasure now and then, which is a lot more than working for Father ever did!"

What was Meb talking about? "I don't care that you're a masker. In fact, I think it's great. I was hanging around here today because I was thinking maybe I might try it myself."

Meb pulled his mask off and looked Nafai up and down. "You've got a body that might look all right on stage. But you still sound like a kid."

"Mebbekew, it doesn't matter right now. You a masker, me a masker —the point is that you can't do this to Father!"

"I'm not doing anything to Father! I'm doing this for myself."

It was always like this, talking to Mebbekew. He never seemed to grasp the thread of an argument. "Be a masker, fine," said Nafai. "But darting your own Father is too low even for you!"

Meb looked at him blankly. "Darting my father?"

"You can't tell me you don't know."

"What is there in this satire that darts *him*?"

"The scene you just finished, Meb."

"Father's not the *only* person in Basilica who believes in the Over-soul. In fact, I sometimes think *he* doesn't believe all that seriously."

"The vision, Meb! The fire in the desert, the prophecy about the end of the world! Who do you *think* it's about?"

"I don't know. Old Drotik doesn't tell us what these things are about. If we haven't heard the gossip then so what? We still say the lines anyway." Then Meb got a strange, quizzical expression on his face. "What does all this Oversoul stuff have to do with Father?"

"He had a vision," said Nafai. "On the Desert Road, this morning before dawn, returning from his journey. He saw a pillar of fire on a rock, and Basilica burning, and he thinks it means the destruction of the world, like Earth in the old legend. Mother believes him and he must already be talking to people about it or how else would your satirist know to include this bit in his satire?"

"This is the craziest thing I ever heard of," said Mebbekew.

"I'm not making it up," said Nafai. "I sat there this morning on Mother's portico and—"

"The portico scene! That's . . . He wrote how the apothecary—that's supposed to be *Father?*"

"What do you think I've been telling you?"

"Bastard," whispered Meb. "That bastard. And he put me on stage as the *Oversoul.*"

Meb turned and rushed toward the masker who played the apothe-cary. He stood in front of him for a few moments, looking at the mask and the costume. "It's so *obvious,* I must have the brains of a gnat—but a vision!"

"What are you talking about?" asked the masker.

"Give me that mask," said Mebbekew. "Give it to me!"

"Right, sure, here."

Meb tore it out of the other man's hands and ran up the hill toward the satirist. Nafai ran after him. Meb was waving the mask in front of the satirist's face. "How dare you, Drotik, you pus-hearted old fart!"

"Oh, don't pretend you didn't know, my boy."

"How would I know? I was asleep till rehearsal started. You put me on stage darting my *father* and it's just coincidence that you didn't happen to mention the fact, yes, I'm sure I believe *that.*"

"Hey, it brings an audience."

"What were you going to do, tell people who I am, after all your promises about keeping me anonymous? What are these masks supposed to *mean* anyway." Meb turned to the others, who were clearly baffled by the whole thing. "Listen, people, do you know what this old pimple was going to do? He was going to dart my father and then tell people that it was *me* playing the Oversoul. He was going to unmask me!"

The satirist was obviously worried by this turn of events. Though most of the maskers' faces were still hidden, they must be angry at the idea of a satirist exposing his maskers' identities. So the satirist had to get things back under control. "Don't waste a thought on this nonsense," he said to the others. "I just fired the boy because he had the audacity to rewrite my lines, and now he wants to wreck the entire show."

The maskers visibly relaxed.

Meb must have realized that he had lost the argument—the maskers *wanted* to believe the satirist because if they didn't, they'd lose a paying job. "My father isn't the liar," said Meb, "*you* are."

"Satire is wonderful, isn't it," said Drotik, "until the dart strikes at home."

Meb raised the white-maned apothecary mask over his head, as if he was going to strike the satirist with it. Drotik flung up an arm and shied away. But Meb never meant to hit him. Instead he brought the mask down over his knee, breaking it in half. Then he tossed both pieces into the satirist's lap.

The satirist lowered his arm and met Mebbekew's gaze again. "It'll take ten minutes for my maskmaker to put the beard onto another mask. Or were you trying to make a metaphorical threat?"

"I don't know," said Meb. "Were you trying to get me to metaphorically murder my father?"

The satirist shook his head in disbelief. "It's a *dart*, boy. Just words. A few laughs."

"A few extra tickets."

"It paid your wages."

"It made you rich." Meb turned his back and walked away. Nafai followed him. Behind them he could hear Drotik sending the script boy to the wall to ask for maskers who thought they could learn a part in three hours.

Mebbekew wouldn't let Nafai catch up with him. He walked faster and faster, until finally they were running full tilt along the streets, up and down the hills. But Mebbekew hadn't the endurance to outlast

Nafai, and finally he fetched up against the corner of a house, bowed over, panting, gasping for breath.

Nafai didn't know what to say. He hadn't meant to chase Meb down, only to tell him what he thought—that he'd been terrific, the way he put the satirist in his place, the way he called him a liar to his face and blasted every argument Drotik raised in his own defense. When you broke the mask in half, I wanted to cheer—that's what Nafai meant to tell him.

But when he got close enough to speak, he realized that Meb wasn't just panting for breath. He was crying, not in grief, but in rage, and when Nafai got there Meb started beating a fist against the wall. "How could he *do* it!" Meb was saying, over and over. "The selfish stupid old son-of-a-bitch!"

"Don't worry about it," said Nafai, meaning to comfort him. "Drotik isn't worth it."

"Not Drotik, you idiot," Meb answered. "Drotik's exactly what I always thought he was except that now I've lost my job and I'll *never* get another one, Drotik will spread the word on me that I walked out on a show three hours before lights."

"Then who are you mad at?"

"Father! Who do you think? A vision—I can't believe it, I thought Drotik would tell me that it wasn't Father he was darting, it was somebody else, and whatever gave me the idea it was Wetchik, what kind of cheese-brained fool would come up with the idea that the honorable *Wetchik* was off getting visions from the amazing unbelievable *Oversoul!*"

"Mother believes him," said Nafai.

"Mother has renewed his contract every year since the year you were conceived, *obviously* she's got a lot of judgment where he's concerned! Do *you* believe him? Does anybody who hasn't slept with him?"

"I don't know. I don't even know who knows about it."

"Let me tell you something. Six hours from now the entire city of Basilica will know about it, that's who knows about it. I want to *kill* him, the flatulent old pincushion!"

"Calm down, you don't mean that—"

"Don't I? Do you think I wouldn't love to push this fist right through his face?" Meb turned around and screamed his next sentence at the passersby on the street. "I'll show you some visions, you pebble-headed weed-hauler!"

People were stopped on the street, staring.

"Right," said Nafai, "Father's embarrassing *you*."

"I didn't ask you to follow me. *You're* the one who chased after me, so if you don't like being with me you can choke to death on your own snot, that's perfectly all right."

"Let's go home," said Nafai, mostly because he couldn't think of anything else to say.

5

Wheels

Home certainly wasn't where Nafai wanted to be, not tonight. He had been hoping Father would be somewhere else, so Meb would have a chance to calm down before they talked. But no, of course not, Father *wanted* to talk to Meb. He had already spent an hour talking with Elemak—Nafai wasn't too broken up about missing *that* scene—and now he seemed to have the fantasy that he might possibly persuade Meb to believe in his vision.

The yelling started as soon as Mebbekew located Father in the study. Nafai had seen what these arguments were like, and so he quickly retreated to his room. On his way through the courtyard, he caught a glimpse of Issib peering out of his doorway. Another refugee, thought Nafai.

For the first hour or so, all that could be heard was the low murmur of Father's voice, presumably trying to explain about his vision, interrupted every few minutes by Mebbekew's clear, piercing shout making comments that ranged from accusation to derision. Then it finally came out, amid all of Mebbekew's complaints about how Father was humiliating the family, that Meb had been doing a fair job of bringing the family into disrepute by working as a masker. Then it was Father's turn to shout and Mebbekew's to try to explain, which was good for another hour of quarreling before Meb left the house in a rage and Father went out to the stables to tend to the animals until he calmed down.

Only then did Nafai venture to the kitchen, absolutely starving by now, for his first serious meal of the day. To his surprise, Elemak was there, sitting with Issib at the table.

"Elya, I didn't know you were here," said Nafai.

Elemak looked up at him, blankly, and then remembered. "Forget it," he said. "I was angry this morning but it's nothing, forget it."

Nafai *had* forgotten, with all that had happened since, that Elemak had warned him not to come home. "I guess I already did," he said.

Elemak gave him a disgusted look and then went back to his food. "What did I say?"

"Never mind," said Issib. "We're trying to think what we should do."

Nafai headed for the freezer and started scanning the food that Truzhnisha had stocked there for occasions like this. He was dying of hunger and yet nothing looked good. "Is this all that's left?"

"No, I have the rest hidden in my pants," said Issib.

Nafai picked something that he remembered liking before, even though it didn't sound particularly good tonight. While it was heating he turned around and faced the others. "So, what have we decided?"

Elemak didn't look up.

"*We* haven't decided anything," said Issib.

"Oh, what, am I suddenly the only child in the house, while the *men* are making all the decisions?"

"Pretty much, yes," said Issib.

"And what decisions do *you* have to make? Who has any decisions to make at *all*, besides Father? It's his house, his business, his money, and his name that's getting laughed at all through Basilica."

Elemak shook his head. "Not *all* through Basilica."

"You mean somebody hasn't heard about this yet?"

"I mean," said Elemak, "that not everybody is laughing."

"They will if that satire runs long. I saw a rehearsal. Meb was really pretty good. Of course he quit since it was about Father, but I think he really has talent. Did you know he sings?"

Elemak looked at him with contempt. "Are you really this shallow, Nyef?"

"Yes," said Nafai. "I'm so shallow that I actually think our embarrassment isn't all that important, if Father really saw a vision."

"We know Father *saw* it," said Elemak. "The problem is what he's doing about it."

"What, he gets a vision from the Oversoul warning about the destruction of the world, and he should keep it a secret?"

"Just eat your food," said Elemak.

"He's going around telling people that the Oversoul wants us to go back to the old laws," said Issib.

"Which ones?"

"All of them."

"I mean which ones aren't we already following?"

Elemak apparently decided to go straight to the heart of things. "He went to the clan council and spoke against our decision to cooperate with Potokgavan in their war with the Wetheads."

"Who?"

"The Gorayni. The Wetheads."

They had got the nickname because of their habit of wearing their hair long, in ringlets, dripping with a perfumed oil. They were also known as vicious warriors with a habit of slaughtering prisoners who hadn't proved their valor by sustaining a serious wound before surrendering. "But they're hundreds of kilometers north of here," said Nafai, "and the Potoku are way to the southeast, and what do they have to fight about?"

"What do they teach you in your little school?" said Elemak. "The Potoku have extended their protection over all the coastal plain up to the Mochai River."

"Sure, right. Protection from what?"

"From the Gorayni, Nafai. We're between them. It's called geography."

"I know geography," said Nafai. "I just don't see why there should ever be a war between the Gorayni and the Potoku, and if there was, how they'd go about fighting it. I mean, Potokgavan has a fleet—all their *houses* are boats, for heaven's sake—but since Goraynivat has no seacoast—"

"*Had* no seacoast. They've conquered Usluvat."

"I guess I knew that."

"Oh, I'm sure you did," said Elemak. "They have horsewagons. Have you heard of those?"

"Wheels," said Nafai. "Horses pulling men in boxes into battle."

"And carrying supplies to feed an army on a long march. A *very* long

march. Horsewagons are changing everything." Suddenly Elemak
sounded enthusiastic. It had been a lot of years since Nafai had seen
Elya excited about anything. "I can envision a day when we'll widen
the Ridge Road and the Plains Road and Market Street so that the
farmers can haul their produce up here in horsewagons. The same
number of horses can haul ten times as much. One man, two horses,
and a wagon can bring what it takes a dozen men and twenty horses to
haul up here now. The price of food drops. The cost of transporting *our*
products downhill drops even lower—there's money there. I can envision roads going hundreds of kilometers, right across the desert—fewer
animals in our caravans, less feed to haul and no need to find as much
water on the journey. The world is getting smaller, and Father's trying
to block it."

"All this has something to do with his vision?"

"The old laws of the Oversoul. Wheels for anything other than gears
or toys are forbidden. Sacrilege. Abomination. Do you realize that
horsewagons have been known about for thousands and thousands of
years and *nobody* has ever built any?"

"Till now," said Issib.

"Maybe there was a good reason," said Nafai.

"The reason was superstition, that was the reason," said Elemak,
"but now we have a chance to build two hundred horsewagons with
Potokgavan paying for it and providing us with the designs, and the
price Gaballufix has negotiated is high enough that we can build two
hundred more for ourselves."

"Why don't the Potoku build their own wagons?"

"They're coming here on boats," said Elemak. "Instead of building
the wagons in Potokgavan and then floating them all the way, they'll
simply send their soldiers and have the wagons waiting for them here."

"Why *here?*"

"Because here is where they're going to draw the line. The Gorayni
go no farther, or they face the wrath of the Potoku. Don't try to understand it, Nafai, it's men's business."

"It sounds to me like Father would be right to try to block this just
on general principles," said Nafai. "I mean, if they find out we're building horsewagons for the Potoku, won't that just make the Gorayni send
an army here to stop us?"

"They won't know until it's too late."

"Why won't they know? Is Basilica so good at keeping secrets?"

"Even if they know, Nyef, the Potoku will be here to stop them from trying to punish us."

"But if the Potoku weren't coming, and therefore we weren't making wagons for them, there'd be nothing for the Gorayni to punish us *for*."

Elemak lowered his head to the table, making a show of his despair at trying to explain anything to Nafai.

"The world is changing," said Issib. "We're used to wars being local quarrels. But the Gorayni have changed it. They're conquering other countries that never did them any harm."

Elemak picked up the explanation. "Someday they'd reach us, with or without the Potoku here to protect us. Personally, I prefer letting the Potoku do the fighting."

"I can't believe all this has been going on and nobody's even talking about it in the city," said Nafai. "I really *don't* have my ears plugged with mud, and I haven't heard anything about us building wagons for Potokgavan."

Elemak shook his head. "It's a secret. Or it *was*, till Father brought it up before the entire clan council."

"You mean somebody was doing this and the clan council didn't even know?"

"It was a *secret*," said Elemak. "How many times do I have to say it?"

"So somebody was going to do this thing in the name of Basilica and the Palwashantu clan, and nobody in the clan council or the city council was going to be consulted about it?"

Issib laughed ruefully. "When you put it that way, it sounds pretty strange, doesn't it."

"It doesn't sound strange at all," said Elemak. "I can see that you're already with Roptat's party."

"Who's Roptat?"

Issib answered, "He's a Palwashantu, Elya's age is all, who's been using this war talk to build up his reputation as a prophet. Not like Father, he doesn't have visions from the Oversoul, he just writes prophecies that read like a shark tearing your leg off. And he keeps saying the same things that you just said."

"You mean this secret plan is so well known that there's already a party led by this Roptat trying to block it?"

"It wasn't *that* secret," said Elemak. "There's no plot. There's no conspiracy. There's just some good people trying to do something that's in Basilica's vital interest, and some traitors doing everything they can to stop it."

Clearly Elemak had a one-sided view of things. Nafai had to offer another point of view. "Or maybe it's some greedy profiteers putting our city in a terribly dangerous situation so they can get rich, and some good people are trying to save the city by stopping them. I'm just suggesting this as a possibility."

Elemak was furious. "The people working on this project are already so rich that they hardly need any more money," he said. "And what I don't get is how a fourteen-year-old *scholar* who's never had to do a *man's* work in his life suddenly has opinions about political issues that he didn't even know *existed* until ten minutes ago."

"I was just asking a question," said Nafai. "I wasn't accusing you of anything."

"Well of course you weren't accusing *me*," said Elemak. "I'm not part of the project anyway."

"Of course not," said Nafai. "It's a *secret* project."

"I should have beaten the teeth out of your mouth this morning," said Elemak.

Why did it always come down to threats? "Do you beat the teeth out of the mouth of everybody who asks you questions you don't have any good answers for?"

"Never before," said Elemak, getting up. "But now I'm going to make up for all those missed opportunities."

"Stop it!" shouted Issib. "Don't we have enough problems?"

Elemak hesitated, then sat back down. "I shouldn't let him get to me."

Nafai breathed again. He hadn't noticed that he wasn't breathing.

"He's a child, what does he know?" said Elemak. "Father's the one who should know better. He's making a lot of people very angry. Some very dangerous people."

"You mean they're threatening him?" asked Nafai.

"Nobody *threatens*," said Elemak. "That would be crude. They're just . . . concerned about Father."

"But if everybody's laughing at Father, why should they care what he says? It sounds like it's this Roptat they ought to be worried about."

"It's the vision thing," said Elemak. "The Oversoul. Most men don't take it all that seriously, but the women . . . the city council . . . your Mother isn't helping things."

"Or she *is* helping things, depending on which side you're on."

"Right," said Elemak. He got up from the table, but this time he wasn't threatening. "I can see which side *you're* on, Nyef, and I can only warn you that if Father has his way, we'll end up in Gorayni chains."

"Why are you so sure?" asked Nafai. "The Oversoul give you a vision or something?"

"I'm sure, my little *half*-friend, because I understand things. When you grow up, you might actually come to know what that means. But I doubt it." Elemak walked out of the kitchen.

Issib sighed. "Does anybody actually *like* anybody else in this family?"

Nafai's food was overcooked, but he didn't care. He was trembling so violently that he could hardly carry his tray to the table.

"Why are you shaking?"

"I don't know," said Nafai. "Maybe I'm afraid."

"Of Elemak?"

"Why should I be afraid of him?" said Nafai. "Just because he could break my neck with his elbow."

"Then why do you keep provoking him?"

"Maybe I'm also afraid *for* him."

"Why?"

"Don't you think it's funny, Issib? Elya can sit here and talk about Father being in danger from powerful people—and yet his solution for it isn't to denounce those dangerous people, it's to try to get Father to stop talking."

"Nobody's being rational."

"I actually *do* understand politics," said Nafai. "I study history all the time. I left my class behind years ago. I *know* something about how wars start and who wins them. And this is the stupidest plan I've ever heard. Potokgavan has no chance of holding this area and no compelling reason to try. All that will happen is they'll send an army, provoke the Gorayni into attacking, and then they'll realize they can't win and go home to their floodplain where the Wetheads can't touch them, leaving *us* to bear the brunt of the Gorayni wrath. Building war wagons for them is so *obviously* going to lead to disaster that only a person completely blinded by greed could possibly support it. And if the Oversoul is telling Father to oppose the building of wagons, then the Oversoul is right."

"I'm sure the Oversoul is relieved to have your approval."

"Anything I can do to help."

"Nafai, you're fourteen."

"So?"

"Elemak doesn't want to hear that kind of thing from you."

"Neither do you, right?"

"I'm really tired. It's been a long day." Issib floated out of the kitchen.

Nafai finally started to eat. To his disgust he had no appetite, even though he knew he was still hungry. Must eat, can't eat. Forget it. He flushed the food down the drain and put the plate in the cleaning rack.

He walked out into the courtyard, heading for his room. The night air was chilly already—they were close enough to the desert to get sharp falls in temperature when the sun was down. He was still trembling. He didn't know why. It wasn't because of Father's vision of the destruction of the world, and it wasn't because of the war that would probably come to Basilica if they went ahead with the idiotic alliance with Potokgavan. Those were dangers, yes, but distant ones. And it wasn't because of Elemak's threats of violence, he'd lived with those all his life.

It wasn't until he was lying on his mat, still shaking even though his room was *not* cold, that he finally realized what was bothering him. Elemak had mentioned that Gaballufix was involved in negotiating the price with the Potoku. Obviously this whole plan had Gaballufix's support—who else but the clan chief would think he could commit the Palwashantu to such a dangerous course of action without even consulting the council? And so it was reasonable to suppose that when Elya warned about the dangerous enemies Father was making, it was Gaballufix he was referring to.

Gaballufix, whose house Elemak secretly visited today.

Where was Elemak's loyalty? With Father? Or with his half-brother Gaballufix? Clearly Elya was involved with this war wagon plan. What else was he involved with? The dangerous people weren't making *threats*, he had said. So what *were* they making—plans? Was Elya in on a plan to do something ugly to Father, and his hints were an attempt to warn Father away?

Just today, Mebbekew had spoken of metaphorical patricide.

No, thought Nafai. No, I'm simply upset because all of this has happened so suddenly, in one day. Father has a vision, and suddenly

he's caught up in city politics in a way he never was before, almost as if
the Oversoul sent him this vision specifically *because* of this stupid
provocative project of Gaballufix's, because action needed to be taken
now.

Why? What did the fate of Basilica matter to the Oversoul? Countless cities and nations had risen and fallen—dozens every century,
thousands and thousands in all of human history. Maybe millions. The
Oversoul hadn't lifted a finger. It wasn't war that the Oversoul cared
about; it certainly wasn't preventing human suffering. So why was the
Oversoul getting involved now? What was the *urgency?* Was it worth
tearing their family apart? And even if maybe it was, who decided
anyway? Nobody had asked the Oversoul for this, so if they really were
getting bounced around as part of some master plan, it might be nice if
the Oversoul let them in on what it had in mind.

Nafai lay on his mat, trembling.

Then he remembered. I wasn't going to sleep on a mat tonight. I was
going to try to be a real man.

He almost laughed aloud. Sleeping on the bare floor—*that* would
make me a man? What an idiot I am. What an ass.

Laughing at himself, now he could sleep.

6
Enemies

"*Where* did you spend all day yesterday?"

Nafai didn't want this conversation, but there was no avoiding it. Mother was not one to let one of her students disappear for a day without an accounting.

"I walked around."

As he had expected, this was not going to be enough for Mother. "I didn't think that you *flew*," she said. "Though I'm surprised you didn't curl up somewhere and sleep. Where did you go?"

"To some very educational places," said Nafai. He had in mind Gaballufix's house and the Open Theatre, but of course Mother would interpret his words as she wished.

"Dolltown?" she asked.

"There's nothing much going on there in the daytime, Mother."

"And you shouldn't be going there at all," she said. "Or do you think you already know everything about everything, so that you have no further need of schooling?"

"There are some subjects you just don't teach here, Mother." Again, the truth—but not the truth.

"Ah," she said. "Dhelembuvex was right about you."

Oh, yes, wonderful. Time to get an Auntie for your little boy.

"I should have seen it coming. Your body is growing so fast—too fast, I fear, outstripping your maturity in every other area."

This was too much to bear. He had planned to listen calmly to everything she said, let her jump to her own conclusions, and then get back to class and have done with the whole thing. But to have her thinking that his gonads were running his life when, if anything, his mind was more mature than his body—

"Is that as smart as you know how to be, Mother?"

She raised an eyebrow.

He knew he was already overstepping himself, but he had begun, and the words were there in his mind, and so he said them. "You see something inexplicable going on, and if it's a boy doing it, you're sure it has to do with his sexual desires."

She half-smiled. "I do have some knowledge of men, Nafai, and the idea that the behavior of a fourteen-year-old might have some link to sexual desire is based on much evidence."

"But I'm your *son*, and still you don't know me from a pile of bricks."

"So you *didn't* go to Dolltown?"

"Not for any reason *you'd* imagine."

"Ah," she said. "I can imagine *many* reasons. But not one of the possible reasons for you to go to Dolltown suggests that you have very good judgment."

"Oh, and you're the expert on good judgment, I imagine."

His sarcasm was not playing well. "You forget, I think, that I am your mother and your schoolmistress."

"It was you, Mother, and not I who invited those two girls to that *family* meeting yesterday."

"And this showed poor judgment on my part?"

"Extremely poor. By the time I got to the Open Theatre it was still several hours before dark, and already the word was out about Father's vision."

"That's not surprising," said Mother. "Father went directly to the clan council. It would hardly be a secret after that."

"Not just his *vision*, Mother. There was already a satire in rehearsal —one of Drotik's, too, no less—that included a fascinating little portico scene. Since the only people present who were *not* family were those two witchgirls—"

"Hold your tongue!"

He immediately fell silent, but with an undeniable sense of victory.

Yes, Mother was furious—but he had also scored a point with her, to get her this angry.

"Your referring to them by that demeaning *manword* is offensive in the extreme," said Mother. Her voice was quiet now; she was *really* angry. "Luet is a seer and Hushidh is a raveler. Furthermore, both have been completely discreet, mentioning nothing to anyone."

"Oh, have you watched them every second since—"

"I said to hold your tongue." Her voice was like ice. "For your information, my bright, wise, *mature* little boy, the reason there was a portico scene in Drotik's satire—which, by the way, I *saw,* and it was very badly done, so it hardly worries me—the reason there was a portico scene was because while your father was going to the clan council, I was at the city council, and when *I* told the story I included the events on this portico. Why, asks my brilliant son with a deliciously stupid look on his face? Because the only thing that made the council take your father's vision seriously was the fact that Luet believed him and found his vision consonant with her own."

Mother had told. *Mother* had brought down ridicule and ruin upon the family. Unbelievable. "Ah," said Nafai.

"I thought you'd see things a little differently."

"I see that there was nothing wrong with having Luet and Hushidh at the family meeting," said Nafai. "It was *you* who should have been excluded."

Her hand lashed out across his face. If she had been aiming for his cheek, she missed, perhaps because he reflexively drew his head back. Instead her fingernail caught him on the chin, tearing the skin. It stung and drew blood.

"You forget yourself, sir," she said.

"Not as badly as you have forgotten yourself, Madam," he answered. Or rather, that was how he *meant* to answer. He even *began* to answer that way, but in the middle of the sentence the enormity of her having struck him that way, the shock and hurt of it, the sheer humiliation of his mother hitting him reduced him to tears. "I'm sorry," he said. Though what he really wanted to say was How dare you, I'm too old for that, I hate you. It was impossible to say such harsh things, however, when he was crying like a baby. Nafai hated it, how tears had always come so easily to him, and it wasn't getting any better as he got older.

"Maybe next time you'll remember to speak to me with proper respect," she said. But she, too, was unable to maintain her sharp tone, for even as she spoke he felt her arm around him as she sat beside him, comforted him.

She could not possibly understand that the way she nestled his head to her shoulder only added to the humiliation and confirmed him in his decision to regard her as an enemy. If she had the power to make him cry because of his love for her, then there was only possible solution for him: to cease loving her. This was the last time she would ever be able to do this to him.

"You're bleeding," she said.

"It's nothing," he said.

"Let me stanch it—here, with a clean handkerchief, not that horrible rag you carry in your pocket, you absurd little boy."

That's all I'll ever be in this house, isn't it? An absurd little boy. He pulled away from her, refused to let the handkerchief touch his chin. But she persisted, and dabbed at the wound, and the white cloth came away surprisingly bloody—so he took it from her hand and pressed it against the wound. "Deep, I guess," he said.

"If you hadn't moved your head back, my nails wouldn't have caught your chin like that."

If you hadn't slapped me, your nails would have been in your *lap*. But he held his tongue.

"I can see that you're taking our family's situation very much to heart, Nafai, but your values are a little twisted. What does the ridicule of the satirists matter? Everyone knows that every great figure in the history of Basilica was darted at one time or another, and usually for the very thing that made her—or him—great. We can bear that. What matters is that Father's vision was a very clear warning from the Oversoul, with immediate implications for our city's course of action over the next few days and weeks and months. The embarrassment will pass. And among the women in this city who really count, Father is viewed as quite a remarkable man—their respect for him is growing. So try to control your embarrassment at your Father's having come to the center of attention. All children in their early teens are excruciatingly sensitive to embarrassment, but in time you will learn that criticism and ridicule are not always bad. To earn the enmity of evil people can speak very well of you."

He could hardly believe she thought so little of him as to think he needed such a lecture as this one. Did she really believe that it was *embarrassment* he feared? If she had listened instead of lecturing, he might have told her about Elemak's warning about danger to Father, about his secret visit to Gaballufix's house. But it was clear that in her eyes he was still nothing but a child. She wouldn't take his warning seriously. Indeed, she'd probably give him another lecture about not letting fears and worries take possession of your mind, but instead to concentrate on his studies and let adults worry about the *real* problems in the world.

In her mind, I'm still six years old and I always will be. "I'm sorry, Mother. I'll not speak to you that way again." In fact, I doubt that I'll ever say anything serious or important to you again as long as you live.

"I accept your apology, Nafai, as I hope you'll accept mine for having struck you in my anger."

"Of course, Mother." I'll accept your apology—*when* you offer it and *when* I believe that you mean it. However, as a matter of fact, dear beloved breadbasket out of whom I sprang, you did not actually apologize to me at any point in our conversation. You only expressed the hope that I would accept an apology which in fact was never offered.

"I hope, Nafai, you will resume your studies and not allow these events in the city to disturb the normal routines of your life any further. You have a very keen mind, and there is no particular reason for you to let these things distract you from the honing of that mind."

Thank you for the dollop of praise, Mother. You've told me that I'm childish, that I'm a slave of lust, and that my views are to be silenced, not listened to. You'll pay serious attention to every word drooled from the mouth of that *witch*girl, but you start from the assumption that anything *I* say is worthless.

"Yes, Mother," said Nafai. "But I'd rather not go back to class right now, if you don't mind."

"Of course not," she said. "I understand completely."

Dear Oversoul, keep me from laughing.

"I can't have you out wandering the streets again, Nafai, I'm sure you can understand that. Father's vision has attracted enough attention that someone *will* say something that will make you angry, and I don't want you fighting."

So you're worried about *me* fighting, Mother? Kindly remember who struck whom here on your portico today.

"Why not spend the day in the library, with Issib? He'll be a good influence on you, I think—he's always so calm."

Issib, always calm? Poor Mother—she knows nothing at all about her own sons. Women never *do* understand men. Of course, men don't understand women any better—but at least we don't suffer from the delusion that we *do.*

"Yes, Mother. The library's fine."

She arose. "Then you must go there now. Keep the handkerchief, of course."

She left the portico, not waiting to see if he obeyed.

He immediately got to his feet and walked around the screen, straight to the balustrade, and looked out over the Rift Valley.

There was no sign of the lake. A thick cloud filled the lower reaches of the valley, and since the valley walls seemed to grow steeper just before the fog began, for all he knew the lake might be invisible from this spot even without the fog.

All he could see from here was the white cloud and the deep, lush greens of the forest that lined the valley. Here and there he could see smoke rising from a chimney, for there were women who lived on the valley slopes. Father's housekeeper, Truzhnisha, was one of them. She kept a house in the district called West Shelf, one of the twelve districts of Basilica where only women were allowed to live or even enter. The Women's Districts were far less populated than any of the twenty-four districts where men were allowed to live (though not own property, of course), yet on the City Council they wielded enormous power, since their representatives always voted as a bloc. Conservative, religious—no doubt those were the councilors who were most impressed by the fact that Luet had confirmed Father's vision. If *they* agreed with Father on the war wagon issue, then it would take the votes of only six other councilors to create stalemate, and of seven councilors to take positive action against Gaballufix's plans.

It was these same councilors from the Women's Districts who, for thousands of years, had refused to allow any subdivision of the thickly populated Open Districts, or to give a council vote to any of the districts outside the walls, or to allow men to own property within the wall, or anything else that might tend to dilute or weaken the absolute rule of women in Basilica. Now, looking out over the secret valley, filled with rage against his mother, Nafai could hardly see how beautiful this place was, how rich with mystery and life; all he could see was how unbelievably few the houses were.

How do they divide this into a dozen districts? There must be some districts where the three women who live there take turns being the councilor.

And outside the city, in the tiny but expensive cubicles where unmated men without households were forced to live, there was no legal recourse to demand fairer treatment, to insist on laws protecting bachelors from their landlords, or from women whose promises disappeared when they lost interest in a man, or even from each other's violence. For a moment, standing there looking out over the untamed greenery of the Rift, Nafai understood how a man like Gaballufix might easily gather men around him, struggling to gain some power in this city where men were unmanned by women every day and every hour of their lives.

Then, as the wind gusted a little over the valley, the cloud moved, and there was a shimmer of reflected light. The surface of a lake, not at the center of the deepest part of the rift, but higher, farther away. Without thinking, Nafai reflexively looked away. It was one thing to come to the balustrade in defiance of his Mother, it was another thing to look on the holy lake where women went for their worship. If there was one thing becoming clear in all this business, it was that the Oversoul might very well be real. There was no point in earning its wrath over something as stupid as looking at some lake over the edge of Mother's portico.

Nafai turned away from the view and hurried back around the screen, feeling foolish all the while. What if I'm caught? Well, so what if I am? No, no, the defiance wasn't worth the risk. He had more practical work to do. If Mother wasn't going to listen to his fears about the danger to Father, then Nafai would have to do something himself. But first he had to know more—about Gaballufix, about the Oversoul, about everything.

For a moment he toyed with the idea of going to Luet and asking her questions. *She* knew about the Oversoul, didn't she? She saw visions all the time, not just once, like Father. Surely she could explain.

But she was a woman, and at this moment Nafai knew that he'd get no help of any kind from women. On the contrary—women in Basilica were taught from childhood on how to oppress men and make them feel worthless. Luet would laugh at him and go straight to Mother to tell her about his questions.

If he could trust anyone in this, it would be other men—and precious few of them, since the danger to Father was coming from Gabal-

Iufix's party. Perhaps he could enlist the help of this Roptat that Elya had talked about. Or find out something about what the Oversoul was doing in the first place.

Issib wasn't thrilled to see him. "I'm busy and I don't need interruptions."

"This is the household library," said Nafai. "This is where we always come to do research."

"See? You're interrupting already."

"Look, I didn't say *anything*, I just came in here, and *you* started picking at me the second I walked in the door."

"I was hoping you'd walk back out."

"I can't. Mother sent me here." Nafai walked over behind Issib, who was floating comfortably in the air in front of his computer display. It was layered about thirty pages deep, but each page had only a few words on it, so he could see almost everything at once. Like a game of solitaire, in which Issib was simply moving fragments from place to place.

The fragments were all words in weird languages. The ones Nafai recognized were very old.

"What language is *that?*" Nafai asked, pointing to one.

Issib sighed. "I'm so glad you're not interrupting me."

"What is it, some ancient form of Vijati?"

"Very good. It's Slucajan, which came from Obilazati, the original form of Vijati. It's dead now."

"I read Vijati, you know."

"*I* don't."

"Oh, so you're specializing in ancient, obscure languages that nobody speaks anymore, including you?"

"I'm not *learning* these languages, I'm researching lost words."

"If the whole language is dead, then *all* the words are lost."

"Words that used to have meanings, but that died out or survived only in idiomatic expressions. Like 'dancing bear.' What's a *bear*, do you know?"

"I don't know. I always thought it was some kind of graceful bird."

"Wrong. It's an ancient mammal. Known only on Earth, I think, and not brought here. Or it died out soon. It was bigger than a man, very powerful. A predator."

"And it *danced?*"

"The expression used to mean something absurdly clumsy. Like a dog walking on its hind legs."

"And now it means the opposite. That's weird. How could it change?"

"Because there aren't any bears. The meaning used to be obvious, because everybody knew what a bear was and how clumsy it would look, dancing. But when the bears were gone, the meaning could go anywhere. Now we use it for a person who's extremely deft in getting out of an embarrassing social situation. It's the only case where we use the word *bear* anymore. And you see a lot of people misspelling it, too."

"Great stuff. You doing a linguistics project?"

"No."

"What's this for, then?"

"Me."

"Just collecting old idioms."

"Lost words."

"Like *bear?* The *word* isn't lost, Issya. It's the *bears* that are gone."

"Very good, Nyef. You get full credit for the assignment. Go away now."

"You're not researching lost words. You're researching words that have lost their meanings because the thing they refer to doesn't exist anymore."

Issya slowly turned his head to look at Nafai. "You mean that you've actually developed a brain?"

Nafai pointed at the screen. *"Kolesnisha.* That's a word in Kunic. You've got the meaning right there—war wagon. Kunic hasn't been spoken in ten million years. It's just a written language now. And yet they had a word for war wagon. Which was only just invented. Which means that there used to be war wagons a long time ago."

Issib laughed. A low chuckle, but it went on and on.

"What, am I wrong?"

"It just kills me, that's all. How *obvious* it is. Even *you* can just walk up to a computer display and see the whole thing at once. So why hasn't anybody noticed this before? Why hasn't anybody noticed the fact that we had the word *wagon* already, and we all knew what it meant, and yet as far as we know there have never been any wagons anywhere in the world *ever?*"

"That's really weird, isn't it?"

"It isn't weird, it's scary. Look at what the Wetheads are doing with their war wagons—their *kolesnishety*. It gives them a vital advantage in war. They're building a real empire, not just a system of alliances, but actual *control* over nations that are six days' travel away from their city. Now, if war wagons can do *that*, and people used to have them millions of years ago, *how did we ever forget what they were?*"

Nafai thought about that for a while. "You'd have to be really stupid," he said. "I mean, people don't forget things like that. Even if you had peace for a thousand years, you'd still have pictures in the library."

"No pictures of war wagons," said Issib.

"I mean, that's *stupid,*" said Nafai.

"And this word," said Issib.

"*Zrakoplov*," said Nafai. "That's definitely an Obilazati word."

"Right."

"What does it mean? 'Air' something."

"Broken down and loosely translated, yes, it means 'air swimmer.' "

Nafai thought about this for a while. He conjured up a picture in his mind—a fish moving through the air. "A flying fish?"

"It's a machine," said Issib.

"A really fast ship?"

"Listen to yourself, Nafai. It should be obvious to you. And yet you keep resisting the plain meaning of it."

"An underwater boat?"

"How would that be an *air* swimmer, Nyef?"

"I don't know." Nafai felt silly. "I forgot about the air part."

"You forgot about it—and yet you recognized the 'air part' right off, by yourself. You *knew* that *Zraky* was the Obilazati root for *air,* and yet you forgot the 'air part.' "

"So I'm really, *really* dumb."

"But you're *not,* Nyef. You're really really *smart,* and yet you're still standing here looking at the word and I'm telling you all this and you *still* can't think of what the word means."

"Well, what's *this* word," said Nafai, pointing at *puscani prah.* "I don't recognize the language."

Issib shook his head. "If I didn't see it happening to you, I wouldn't believe it."

"What?"

"Aren't you even curious to know what a *zrakoplov* is?"

"You told me. Air swimmer."

"A *machine* whose name is *air* swimmer."

"Sure. Right. So what's a *puscani prah?*"

Issib slowly turned around and faced Nafai. "Sit down, my dear beloved brilliant stupid brother, thou true servant of the Oversoul. I've got something to tell you about machines that swim through the air."

"I guess I'm interrupting you," said Nafai.

"I want to talk to you," said Issib. "It's not an interruption. I just want to explain the idea of flying—"

"I'd better go."

"Why? Why are you so eager to leave?"

"I don't know." Nafai walked to the door. "I need some air. I'm running out of air." He walked out of the room. Immediately he felt better. Not lightheaded anymore. What was all that about, anyway? The library was too stuffy. Too crowded. Too many people in there.

"Why did you leave?" asked Issib.

Nafai whirled. Issib was silently floating out of the library after him. Nafai immediately felt the same kind of claustrophobia that had driven him out into the hall. "Too crowded in there," said Nafai. "I need to be alone."

"I was the only person in there," said Issib.

"Really?" Nafai tried to remember. "I want to get outside. Just let me go."

"Think," said Issib. "Remember when Luet and Father were talking yesterday?"

Immediately Nafai relaxed. He didn't feel claustrophobic anymore. "Sure."

"And Luet was testing Father—about his memories. When his memory of the vision he saw was wrong, he felt kind of stupid, right?"

"He said."

"Stupid. Disconnected. He just stared into space."

"I guess."

"Like you," said Issib. "When I pushed you about the meaning of *zrakoplov.*"

Suddenly Nafai felt as if there were no air in his lungs. "I've got to get outside!"

"You are *really* sensitive to this," said Issib. "Even worse than Father and Mother when I tried to tell *them.*"

"Stop following me!" Nafai cried. But Issib continued to float down the hall after him, down the stairs, out into the street. There, in the open, Issib easily passed Nafai, floating here and there in front of him. As if he were herding Nafai back toward the house.

"Stop it!" cried Nafai. But he couldn't get away. He had never felt such panic before. Turning, he stumbled, fell to his knees.

"It's all right," said Issib softly. "Relax. It's nothing. Relax."

Nafai breathed more easily. Issib's voice sounded safe now. The panic subsided. Nafai lifted his head and looked around. "What are we doing out here on the street? Mother's going to kill me."

"You ran out here, Nafai."

"I did?"

"It's the Oversoul, Nafai."

"*What's* the Oversoul?"

"The force that sent you outside rather than listen to me talk about— about the thing that the Oversoul doesn't want people to know about."

"That's silly," said Nafai. "The Oversoul *spreads* information, it doesn't conceal it. We submit our writings, our music, everything, and the Oversoul transmits it from city to city, from library to library all over the world."

"Your reaction was much stronger than Father's," said Issib. "Of course, I pushed you harder, too."

"What do you mean?"

"The Oversoul is inside your head, Nafai. Inside all of our heads. But some have it more than others. It's there, watching what we think. I know it's hard to believe."

But Nafai remembered how Luet had known what was in his mind. "No, Issya, I already knew that."

"Really?" said Issib. "Well then. As soon as the Oversoul knew that you were getting close to a forbidden subject, it started making you stupid."

"*What* forbidden subject?"

"If I remind you, it'll just set you off again," said Issib.

"When did I get stupid?"

"Trust me. You got *very* stupid. Trying to change the subject without even realizing it. Normally you're extremely insightful, Nafai. Very bright. You *get* things. But this time up in the library you just stood there like an idiot, with the truth staring you in the face, and you didn't recognize it. When I reminded you, when I *pushed*, you got claustrophobic, right? Hard to breathe, had to get out of the room. I followed you, I pushed again, and here we are."

Nafai tried to think back over what had happened. Issib was right about the order of events. Only Nafai hadn't connected his need to get out of the house with anything Issib said. In fact, he couldn't for the life of him remember what it was that Issib had been talking about. "You pushed?"

"I know," said Issib. "I felt it, too, when I first started getting on the track of this a couple of years ago. I was playing around with lost words, just like that dancing bear thing. Making lists. I had a *long* list of terms like that, with definitions and explanations after each one, along with my best guess about what each lost word meant. And then one day I was looking at a list that I thought was complete and I realized that there were a couple of dozen words that had no meanings at all. That's stupid, I thought. That's ruining my list. So I deleted all those words."

"Deleted them?" Nafai was appalled. "Instead of researching them?"

"See how stupid it can make you?" said Issib. "And the moment I finished deleting them, it came to me—what am I doing! So reached for the undelete command, but instead of pushing those keys, I reflexively gave the kill command, completely wiping out the delete buffer, and then I saved the file right over the old one."

"That's too complicated to be clumsiness," said Nafai.

"Exactly. I knew that deleting them was a mistake, and yet instead of undoing that mistake and bringing the words back, I killed them, wiped them out of the system."

"And you think the Oversoul did that to you?"

"Nafai, haven't you ever wondered what the Oversoul is? What it does?"

"Sure."

"Me too. And now I know."

"Because of those words?"

"I haven't got them all back, but I retraced as much of my research as I could and I got a list of eight words. You have no idea how hard it was, because now I was sensitized to them. Before, I must have simply overlooked them, gotten stupid when I saw them—the way Father did when he was getting wrong ideas about the Oversoul's vision. That's how they got on my first list, but without definitions—I just got stupid whenever I thought of them. But now when I saw them I'd get that claustrophobic feeling. I needed air. I had to get out of the library. But I forced myself to go inside. It's the hardest thing I've ever done. I forced myself to stay and think about the unthinkable. To hold concepts in my mind that the Oversoul doesn't want us to remember. Concepts that once were so common that every language in the world has words for them. Ancient words. Lost words."

"The Oversoul is *hiding* things from us?"

"Yes."

"Like what?"

"If I tell you, Nafai, you'll take off again."

"No I won't."

"You *will*," said Issib. "Do you think I don't know? Do you think I haven't had my own struggle this past year? So you can imagine my surprise when last night Elemak sits there in the kitchen and explains to us about one of the forbidden things. War wagons."

"Forbidden? How could it be forbidden, it isn't even ancient."

"See? You've forgotten already. The word *kolesnisha*."

"Oh, yes. That's right. No, I remember that."

"But you *didn't* till I said it."

That's right, thought Nafai. A memory lapse.

"Last night you and Elemak were sitting there talking about war wagons, even though it took me *months* to be able to study the word *kolesnisha* without gasping the whole time."

"But we didn't *say* kolesnisha."

"What I'm telling you, Nafai, is that the Oversoul is breaking down."

"That's an old theory."

"But it's a true one," said Issib. "The Oversoul has certain concepts that it is protecting, that it refuses to let human beings think about. Only in the past few years the Wetheads have suddenly become able to think about one of them. And so have the Potoku. And so have *we*. And last night, hearing Elemak talk about it, I felt not one twinge of the panic."

"But it still made me forget the word. *Kolesnisha.*"

"A lingering residual effect. You remembered it *this* time, right? Nafai, the Oversoul has given up on keeping us away from the war wagon concept. After millions of years, it isn't trying anymore."

"What else?" asked Nafai. "What are the other concepts?"

"It hasn't given up on those yet. And you seem to be *really* sensitive to the Oversoul, Nyef. I don't know if I can tell you, or if you'd be able to remember for five minutes even if I did."

"You mean I can know that the Oversoul is keeping us from knowing things, only I can't know *which* things because the Oversoul is still keeping me from knowing them."

"Right."

"Then why doesn't the Oversoul stop people from thinking about *murder?* Why doesn't the Oversoul stop people from thinking about war, and rape, and stealing? If it can do this to *me*, why doesn't it do something useful?"

Issib shook his head. "It doesn't seem right. But I've been thinking about it—I've had a year, remember—and here's the best thing I've come up with. The Oversoul doesn't want to stop us from being human. Including all the rotten things we do to each other. It's just trying to hold down the *scale* of our rottenness. All the things that are forbidden—how can I tell you this without setting you off?—if we still had the machines that the forbidden words refer to, it would make it so that anything we did would reach farther, and each weapon would cause more damage, and everything would happen *faster.*"

"Time would speed up?"

"No," said Issib. He was obviously choosing his words carefully. "What if . . . what if the Gorayni could bring an army of five thousand men from Yabrev to Basilica in one day."

"Don't make me laugh."

"But if they *could?*"

"We'd be helpless, of course."

"Why?"

"Well, we'd have no time to get an army together."

"So if we knew other nations could do that, we'd have to keep an army all the time, wouldn't we, just in *case* somebody suddenly attacked."

"I guess."

"So then, knowing that, suppose the Gorayni found a way to get, not five thousand, but *fifty* thousand soldiers here, and not in a day, but in six hours."

"Impossible."

"What if I tell you that it's been done?"

"Whoever could do that would rule the whole world."

"Exactly, Nyef, unless everybody else could do it, too. But what kind of world would that be? It would be as if the world had turned small, and everybody was right next door to everybody else. A cruel, bullying, domineering nation like the Gorayni could put their armies on *any-*

body's doorstep. So all other nations of the world would have to band together to stop them. And instead of a few thousand people dying, a million, ten million people might die in a war."

"So that's why the Oversoul keeps us from thinking about . . . quick ways . . . to get lots of soldiers from one place to another."

"That was hard to say, wasn't it?"

"I kept . . . my mind kept wandering."

"It's a hard concept to keep in your mind, and you aren't even thinking about anything specific."

"I hate this," said Nafai. "You can't even tell me how anybody could do a trick like that. I can hardly even hold the concept in my mind as it is. I *hate* this."

"I don't think the Oversoul is used to having anybody notice. I think that the very fact that you're able to think about the concept of unthinkable concepts means that the Oversoul is losing control."

"Issya, I've never felt so helpless and stupid in my life."

"And it isn't just wars and armies," said Issib. "Remember the stories of Klati?"

"The slaughter man?"

"Climbing in through women's windows in the night and gutting them like cattle in the butcher's shop."

"Why couldn't the Oversoul have made *him* get stupid when he thought of doing that?"

"Because the Oversoul's job isn't to make us perfect," said Issib. "But imagine if Klati had been able to get on a—been able to travel very quickly and get to another city in six hours."

"They would have known he was a stranger and watched him so closely that he couldn't have done a thing."

"But you don't understand—thousands, millions of people every day are doing the same thing—"

"Butchering women?"

"Flying from one place to another."

"This is too crazy to think about!" shouted Nafai. He bounded to his feet and moved toward the house.

"Come back," cried Issib. "You don't really think that, you're being *made* to think it!"

Nafai leaned against one of the pillars of the front porch. Issib was right. He had been fine, and then suddenly Issib said whatever it was that he said and suddenly Nafai had to *leave*, had to get away and now here he was, panting, leaning up against the pillar, his heart pounding so hard that somebody else could probably hear it from a meter away. Could this really be the Oversoul, making him so stupid and fearful? If it was, then the Oversoul was his enemy. And Nafai refused to surrender. He *could* think about things whether the Oversoul liked it or not. He *could* think about the thing that Issib had said, and he could do it without running away.

In his mind Nafai retraced the last few moments of his conversation with Issib. About Klati. Going from city to city in a few hours. Other cities would notice him, of course—but then Issib said what if thousands of people . . . were . . . flying.

The picture that came into Nafai's mind was ludicrous. To imagine people in the air, like birds, soaring, swooping. He should laugh—but instead, thinking of it made his throat feel tight. His head felt tight, constrained. A sharp pain grew out of his neck and up into the back of his head. But he could think of it. People flying. And from there he could finish Issib's thought. People flying from city to city, thousands of them, so that the authorities in each city had no way of keeping track of one person.

"Klati could have killed once in each city and no one would ever have found him," said Nafai.

Issib was beside him again, his arm resting oh-so-lightly across Nafai's shoulder as he leaned against the pillar. "Yes," said Issib.

"But what would it mean to be a citizen of a place?" asked Nafai. "If a thousand people . . . *flew* here . . . to Basilica . . . today."

"It's all right," said Issib. "You don't have to say it."

"Yes I do," said Nafai. "I can think *anything*. It can't stop me."

"I was just trying to explain—that the Oversoul doesn't stop the evil in the world—it just stops it from getting out of hand. It keeps the damage local. But the good things—think about it, Nafai—we give our art and music and stories to the Oversoul, and it offers them to every other nation. The good things *do* spread. So it *does* make the world a better place."

"No," said Nafai. "In some ways better, yes, but how can it help but be a good thing to live in a world where people . . . where we could . . . *fly*."

The word almost choked him, but he said it, and even though he could hardly bear to stay in the same place, the air felt so close and unbreathable, nevertheless he *stayed*.

"You're good," said Issib. "I'm impressed."

But Nafai didn't feel impressive. He felt sick and angry and betrayed. "How does the Oversoul have the *right*," he said. "To take this all away from us."

"What, armies appearing at our gates without warning? I'm glad enough not to have that."

Nafai shook his head. "It's deciding what I can *think.*"

"Nyef, I know the feeling, I went through all this months ago, and I *know*, it makes you so angry and frightened. But I also know that you can overcome it. And yesterday, when Mother talked about her vision. Of a planet burning. There's a word for—well, you couldn't hear it now, I know that—but the Oversoul has been keeping us from *that*. For thirty or forty million years—don't you realize that this is a *long* time? More history than we can imagine. It's all stored away somewhere, but the most we can hold onto, the most that we can get into our minds is the most skeletal sort of plan of what's happened in the world for the last ten million years or so—and it takes years and years of study to comprehend even that much. There are kingdoms and languages we've never heard of even in the last million years, and yet nothing is really lost. When I went searching in the library, I was able to find references to works in other libraries and trace my way back until I read a crude translation from a book written thirty-two million years ago and do you know what it said? Even then the writer was saying that history was now too long, too full for the human mind to comprehend it. That if all of human history were compressed into a single thousand-page volume, the whole story of humankind on Earth would be only a single page. And that was thirty-two million years ago."

"So we've been here a long time."

"If I take that writer's arithmetic literally, that would mean that human history on Earth lasted only eight thousand years before the planet . . . burned."

Nafai understood. The Oversoul had kept human beings from expanding the scale of their destructiveness, and so humanity had lasted five thousand times longer on the planet Harmony than it did on Earth.

"So why didn't the Oversoul keep Earth from being destroyed?"

"I don't know," said Issib. "I have a guess."

"And what's that?"

"I don't know if you'll be allowed to think about it."

"Give me a try."

"The Oversoul wasn't made until people got to Harmony. It has the same meaning in every language, you know—the name of the planet. Sklad. Endrakt. Soglassye. Maybe when they got here, with Earth in ashes behind them, they decided never to let it happen again. Maybe that's when the Oversoul was put in place—to stop us from ever having such terrible power."

"Then the Oversoul would be—an artifact."

"Yes," said Issib. "This isn't hard for you to think about?"

"No," said Nafai. "Easy. It's not that uncommon a thought. People have talked about the Oversoul as a machine before."

"It was hard for *me*," said Issib. "But maybe because I came to the idea another way. Through a couple of unthinkable paths. Genetic alteration of the human brain so it could receive and transmit thoughts from communications satellites orbiting the planet."

Nafai heard the words, but they meant nothing to him.

"You didn't understand that, did you," said Issib.

"No," said Nafai.

"I didn't think you would."

"Issya, what is the Oversoul doing to us now?"

"That's what I've been working on. Trying to look through the forbidden words, find the pattern, find out what it means to be giving Father this vision of a world on fire. And Mother. And the dream of blood and ashes that Luet was given."

"It means that we're puppets."

"No, Nafai. Don't talk yourself into hating the Oversoul about this. That does no good at all—I *know* that now. We have to understand it. What it's doing. Because the world really *is* in danger, if the Oversoul's control is breaking down. And it is. It's given up on war wagons—what will it give up on next? What empire will be the next to get out of hand? Which one will discover—that word you asked about—puscani prah. It's a powder that when you put flame to it, it blows up. Pops like a balloon, only with thousands of times more force. Enough to make a wall fall down. Enough to kill people."

"Please stop," whispered Nafai. It was more than he could bear, fighting off the panic he felt as he heard these words.

"The Oversoul is not our enemy. In fact, I think—I think it called on Father because it needs help."

"Why haven't you said any of this before?"

"I have—to Father. To Mother. To some teachers. Other students. Other scholars. I even wrote it up in an article, but if nobody ever remembers receiving it, they can never find it. Even when I sent it to the same person four times. I gave up."

"But you told *me*."

"You came into the library," said Issib. "I thought—why not?"

"*Zrakoplov*," said Nafai.

"I can't believe you remembered the word," said Issib.

"A machine. The people don't just . . . fly. They use a machine."

"Don't push it," said Issib. "You'll just make yourself sick. You have a headache already, right?"

"But I'm right, yes?"

"My best guess is that it was hollow, like a house, and people got inside it to fly. Like a ship, only through the air. With wings. But we had them here, I think. You know the district of Black Fields?"

"Of course, just west of the market."

"The old name of it was Skyport. The name lasted until twenty million years ago, more or less. Skyport. When they changed it, nobody remembered what it even meant."

"I can't think about this anymore," said Nafai.

"Do you want to remember it, though?" asked Issib.

"How can I forget it?"

"You will, you know. If I don't remind you. Every day. Do you want me to? It'll feel like this every time. It'll make you sick. Do you want to just forget this, or do you want me to keep reminding you?"

"Who reminded *you*?"

"I left myself notes," said Issib. "In the library computers. Reminders. Why do you think it took me a year to get this far?"

"I want to remember," said Nafai.

"You'll get angry at me."

"Remind me not to."

"It'll make you sick."

"So I'll faint a lot." Nafai slid down the pillar and sat on the porch, looking out toward the street. "Why hasn't anybody noticed us out here? We haven't exactly been whispering."

Issib laughed. "Oh, they noticed. Mother came out once, and a couple of the teachers. They heard us talking for a couple of moments and then they just sort of forgot why they came out."

"This is great. If we want them to leave us alone, all we have to do is talk about the *zrakoplovs.*"

"Well," said Issib, "that only works with people who are still closely tied with the Oversoul."

"Who isn't?"

"Whoever thought of the war wagons, for instance."

"You said the Oversoul had given up on them."

"Sure, *recently,*" said Issib. "But there were people in Basilica planning to build war wagons, people dealing with the Potoku about them for a long time. More than a year. *They* had no trouble with the Oversoul. It's like they're deaf to it now. But most people aren't—which is why Gaballufix and his men were able to keep it secret for so long. Most people who heard anything about war wagons would simply have forgotten they even heard it. In fact," added Issib, "the Oversoul may have deliberately stopped forbidding that idea in the last little while precisely *because* there had to be open discussion of the war wagon thing in order to stop it."

"So the people who are deaf to the Oversoul—in order to stop them, the Oversoul has to stop controlling the rest of us, too."

"It's a double bind," said Issib. "In order to win, the Oversoul has to give up. I'd say that the Oversoul is in serious trouble."

It was making sense to Nafai, except for one thing. "But why did it start talking to *Father?*"

"That's what we need to figure out. That, and what it's going to tell Father to do next."

"Oh, hey, let's let the Oversoul keep a *few* surprises up its sleeve." Nafai laughed, but he didn't really think it was funny.

Neither did Issib. "Even if we believe in the Oversoul's cause, Nafai, somewhere along in here we may find out that the Oversoul is causing more harm than good. What do we do *then?*"

"Hey, Issya, it may be doing a bad job these days, but that doesn't mean that we'd do better without it."

"I guess we'll never know, will we?"

7

Prayer

For a week Nafai worked with Issib every day. They slept at Mother's house every night—they didn't ask, but then, Mother didn't send them away, either. It was a grueling time, not because the work was so hard but because the interference from the Oversoul was so painful. Issib was right, however. It *could* be overcome; and even though Nafai's aversive response was stronger than Issib's had been, he was able to get over it more quickly—mostly because Issib was there to help him, to assure him that it was worth doing, to remind him what it was about.

They began to work out a pretty clear picture of what it was that humans had once had, and that the Oversoul had long kept them from reinventing.

A communications system in which a person could talk instantly and directly to a person in any other city in the world.

Machines that could receive artwork and plays and stories transmitted through the air, not just from library to library, but right into people's homes.

Machines that moved swiftly over the ground, without horses.

Machines that flew, not just through the air, but out into space. "Of course there must be space traveling machines, or how did we get to

Harmony from Earth?" But until he had punched his way through the aversion, Nafai had never been able to conceive of such a thing.

And the weapons of war: Explosives. Projectile weapons. Some so small that they could be held in the hand. Others so terrible that they could devastate whole cities, and burn up a planet if hundreds were used at once. Self-mutating diseases. Poisonous gases. Seismic disruptors. Missiles. Orbital launch platforms. Gene-wrecking viruses. The picture that emerged was beautiful and terrible at once.

"I can see why the Oversoul does this to us," said Nafai. "To save us from these weapons. But the cost, Issya. The freedom we gave up."

Issib only nodded. "At least the Oversoul left us something. The ability to get power from the sun. Computers. Libraries. Refrigeration. All the machines of the kitchen, the greenhouses. The magnetics that allow my floats to work. And we *do* have some pretty sophisticated handweapons. Charged-wire blades. And pulses. So that large strong people don't have any particular advantage over smaller, weaker ones. The Oversoul could have stripped us. Stone and metal tools. Nothing with moving parts. Burning trees for all our heat."

"We wouldn't even be *human* then."

"Human is human," said Issib. "But civilized—that's the gift of the Oversoul. Civilization without self-destruction."

They tried explaining it to Mother once, but it went nowhere. She stupidly failed to understand anything they were talking about, and left them with a cheerful little jest about how nice it was that they could be friends and play these games together despite the age difference between them. There was no chance to talk to Father.

But there *was* someone who took an interest in them.

"Why don't you come to class anymore?" asked Hushidh.

She sat down on the porch steps beside Nafai and bit into her bread and cheese. A large mouthful, not the delicate bites that Eiadh took. Never mind that Mother was the one who taught all her girl students to use their *mouths* when they ate, and not to take the mincing little bites that were in fashion among the young women of Basilica these days. Nafai didn't have to find Hushidh's obedience to Mother *attractive.*

"I'm working on a project with Issib."

"The other students say that you're hiding," said Hushidh.

Hiding. Because Father was so notorious and controversial. "I'm not ashamed of my father."

"Of course not," said Hushidh. "*They* say you're hiding. Not me."

"And what do *you* think I'm doing? Or has the Oversoul told you?"

"I'm a raveler," she said, "not a seer."

"Right. I forgot." As if he should keep track of what kind of witch she was.

"The Oversoul doesn't have to tell me how you're weaving yourself into the world."

"Because you can see it."

She nodded. "And you're very brave."

He looked at her in consternation. "I sit in the library with Issya."

"You're weaving yourself into the weakest of the quarreling parties in Basilica, and yet it's the best of them. The one that *should* win, though no one can imagine how."

"I'm not party of *any* party."

She nodded. "I'll stop talking if you don't want to hear the truth."

As if she were going to be the fount of irresistible wisdom.

"I'll listen to a pig fart as long as it's the *truth,*" said Nafai.

Immediately she got to her feet and moved away.

That was really stupid, Nafai rebuked himself. She's just trying to help, and you make a stupid joke out of it. He got up and followed her. "I'm sorry," he said.

She shrugged away from him.

"I'm used to making stupid jokes like that," said Nafai. "It's a bad habit, but I didn't mean it. It's not as if I don't know for myself now that the Oversoul is real."

"I know that you *know,*" she said coldly. "But it's obvious that knowing the Oversoul exists doesn't mean you automatically get brains or kindness or even decency."

"I deserve it, and the next three nasty things you think of." Nafai stepped around her, to face her. This time she didn't turn away.

"I see patterns," she said. "I see the way things fit together. I see where *you* are starting to fit. You and Issib."

"I haven't been following things in the city," said Nafai. "Busy with the project we're working on. I don't really know what's going on."

"It's been wearing you out," she said.

"Yes," said Nafai. "I guess so."

"Gaballufix is the center of one party," she said. "It's the strongest, for more reasons than one. It isn't just about the war wagons anymore, or even about the alliance with Potokgavan. It's about men. Especially men from outside the city. So he's strong in numbers, and he's also strong because his men are asserting themselves with violence."

Nafai thought back to conversations he had overheard at mealtimes. About the tolchocks, men who were knocking down women in the street for no reason. "*His* men are the tolchocks?"

"He denies it. In fact, he claims that he's sending his soldiers out into the streets of Basilica in order to protect women from the tolchocks."

"Soldiers?"

"Officially they're the militia of the Palwashantu clan. But they all answer to Gaballufix, and the clan council hasn't been able to meet to discuss the way the militia are being used. You're Palwashantu, aren't you?"

"I'm too young for the militia yet."

"They're not really militia anymore," she said. "They're hired. Men from outside the walls, the hopeless kind of men, and very few of them really Palwashantu. Gaballufix is paying them. And he paid the tolchocks, too."

"How do you *know* this?"

"I was pushed. I've seen the soldiers. I know how they fit together."

More of the witchery. But how could he doubt it? Hadn't he felt the influence of the Oversoul whenever he thought about forbidden words? It made him sweat just to think of what he'd been through during the past week. So why *couldn't* Hushidh just look at a soldier and a tolchock and know things about them? Why couldn't camels fly? Anything was possible now.

Except that the Oversoul's influence was weakening. Hadn't he and Issib overcome its power, in order to think about forbidden things?

"And you know that I'm not one of them."

"But your brothers are."

"Tolchocks?"

"They're with Gaballufix. Not *Issib*, of course. But Elemak and Mebbekew."

"How do you know *them*? They never come here—they're not Mother's sons."

"Elemak has come here several times this week," said Hushidh. "Didn't you know?"

"Why would he come here?" But Nafai knew at once. Without being able to think the thought himself, he knew exactly why Elemak would come to Rasa's household. Mother's reputation in the city was of the highest; her nieces were courted by many, and Elemak was of an age—well into the age, in fact—for a serious mating, intended to produce an heir.

Nafai looked around the courtyard, where many girls and a few boys were eating their supper. All the students from outside were gone, and the younger children ate earlier. So most of the girls here were eligible for mating, including her nieces, if Rasa released them. Which of them would Elemak be courting?

"Eiadh," he whispered.

"One can assume," said Hushidh. "I know it isn't me."

Nafai looked at her in surprise. Of course it wasn't her. Then he was embarrassed; what if she realized how ridiculous it had seemed to him, that his brother might desire *her*.

But Hushidh continued as if she didn't even notice his silent insult. Certainly she was oblivious to how the idea of Elya courting Eiadh might hurt Nafai. "When your brother came, I knew at once that he was very close to Gaballufix. I'm sure that it's causing Aunt Rasa a great deal of sorrow, because she knows that Eiadh will say yes to him. Your brother has a great deal of prestige."

"Even with Father's visions causing such a scandal?"

"He's with Gaballufix," said Hushidh. "Within the Party of Men—those who favor Gaballufix—the worse your father looks, the better they like Elemak. Because if something happened to your father, then Elemak would be a very rich and powerful man."

Her words reawakened Nafai's worst fears about his brother. But it was a monstrous, unbearable thought. "Gaballufix wants Elya to influence Father, that's all."

Hushidh nodded. But was she nodding in agreement, or just silencing him so she could get on with what she had to say? "The other strong party is Roptat's people. They're being called the Party of Women now, though they are also led by a man. They want to ally with the Gorayni. And also they want to remove the vote from all men except those currently mated with a citizen, and require all non-mated men to leave the city every night by sundown, and not return until dawn. That's *their* solution to the tolchock problem—and to Gaballufix, as well. They have a wide following—among mated men and women."

"Is that the group that Father's with?"

"Everyone in the Party of Men thinks so, but Roptat's people know better."

"So what's the third group?"

"They call themselves the City Party, but what they truly are is the Party of the Oversoul. They refuse to ally with any warring nation. They want to return to the old ways, for the protection of the Lake. To make this a city above politics and conflict. To give away the great wealth of the city and live simply, so no other nation will desire to possess us."

"Nobody will agree to that."

"You're wrong," she said. "Many do agree. Your father and Aunt Rasa have won over almost all the women of the Lake Districts."

"But that's hardly anybody. Only a handful of people live in the Rift Valley."

"They have a third of the council votes."

Nafai thought about that. "I think that's very dangerous for them," he said.

"Why do you think so?"

"Because they don't have anything but tradition to back them up. The more Gaballufix pushes against tradition, the more he frightens people with tolchocks and soldiers, the more people will demand that something be done. All that Father and Mother are doing is making it impossible for anyone to get a majority on the council. They're blocking Roptat from stopping Gaballufix."

Hushidh smiled. "You're really very good at this."

"Politics is what I study most."

"You've seen the danger. But what you haven't told me is how we'll get out of it."

"We?"

"Basilica."

"No," said Nafai. "You said that you knew what party I was in."

"You're with the Oversoul, of course," she said.

"You don't know that. I don't even know that. I'm not sure I like the way the Oversoul manipulates us."

Hushidh shook her head. "You may not make the decision in your mind for many days yet, but the decision in your heart is already made. You reject Gaballufix. And you are drawn to the Oversoul."

"You're wrong," said Nafai. "I mean, yes, I'm drawn to the Oversoul, Issib came to that decision long ago and his reasons are good. Despite all its secret manipulation of people's minds, it's even more dangerous to reject the Oversoul. But that doesn't mean I'm ready to turn the future of Basilica over to the tiny minority of crazy religious fanatics who live in the Rift Valley and have visions all the time."

"We're the ones who are close to the Oversoul."

"The whole *world* has the Oversoul inside their brains," said Nafai. "You can't get closer than that."

"We're the ones who *choose* the Oversoul," she insisted. "And the whole world *doesn't* have her inside their brains, or they would never have started carrying war to faraway nations."

For a moment Nafai wondered if she, too, had somehow discovered how the Oversoul had blocked the discovery of war wagons until recently. Then he realized that of course *she* was thinking of the seventh codicil: "You have no dispute with your neighbor's neighbor's neighbor; when she quarrels, stay home and close your window." This had long been interpreted to be a prohibition of entangling alliances or quarrels with countries so far away that the outcome made no difference to you. Nafai and Issib knew the purpose and origin of such a law, and the way that the Oversoul had enforced it within people's minds. To Hushidh, though, it was the law itself that had fended off wars of imperial aggression for all these millennia. Never mind that many nations had *tried* to create empires, and only the lack of efficient means of travel and communication had hindered them.

"I'm not with you," said Nafai. "You can't turn back the clock."

"If you can't," she said, "then we're as good as destroyed already."

"Maybe so," said Nafai. "If Roptat wins, then when the Potoku fleet arrives, they come up the mountain and destroy us before the Wetheads can get here. And if Gaballufix wins, then when the Wetheads finally come they destroy the Potoku first and then *they* come up the mountains and destroy us in retaliation."

"So," said Hushidh. "You see that you *are* with us."

"No," said Nafai. "Because if the City Party keeps up this stalemate, either Gaballufix or Roptat will get impatient and people will start to die. Then we won't *need* outsiders to destroy us. We'll do it ourselves. How long do you think women will continue to rule in this city, if it comes to civil war between two powerful men?"

Hushidh looked off into space. "Do you think so?" she said.

"I may not be a *raveler*," said Nafai, "but I've read history."

"So many centuries we've kept this a city of women, a place of peace."

"You never should have given men the vote."

"They've had the vote for a million years."

Nafai nodded. "I know. What's happening now—it's the Oversoul."

He could see now that Hushidh was looking off into nothingness because her eyes were so full of tears. "She's dying, isn't she?"

It hadn't occurred to him that someone could take this so personally. As if the Oversoul were a dear relative. But to someone like Hushidh, perhaps it was so. Besides, she was the daughter of a wilder, a so-called holy woman. Even though everyone knew that wilders' children were usually the result of rape or casual coupling in the streets of the city, they were still called "children of the Oversoul." Maybe Hushidh really thought of the Oversoul as her father. But no—the women called the Oversoul *she*. And Hushidh *knew* that her mother was a wilder.

Still, Hushidh was barely containing her tears.

"What do you want from me?" asked Nafai. "I don't know what the Oversoul is doing. Your sister—like you said, *she's* the seer."

"The Oversoul hasn't spoken to her all week. Or to anyone."

Nafai was surprised. "You mean not even at the lake?"

"I knew that you and Issib were very, very closely tied to the Oversoul all this week. She was wearing you out, the way she does with Lutya and . . . and me, sometimes. The women have been going into the water, more and more of them, and yet they come out with nothing, or with silly sleep-dreams. It's making them afraid. But I told them, I said: Nafai and Issib, *they're* being touched by the Oversoul. So she's not dead. And they asked me . . . to find out from you."

"Find out what?"

The tears finally spilled out and slid down her cheeks. "I don't know," she said miserably. "What to do. What the Oversoul expects of us."

He touched her shoulder, to comfort her—Nafai didn't know what else to do. "I don't know," he said. "But you're right about one thing—the Oversoul is wearing down. Wearing *itself* out. Still, I'm surprised that it would stop giving visions. Maybe it's distracted. Maybe it's . . ."

"What?"

He shook his head. "Let me talk to Issib, will you?"

She nodded, ducking her head at the end to wipe away tears. "Please, yes," she said. *"I couldn't—talk to him."*

Why in the world *not?* But he didn't ask. He was too confused by all that she'd told him. All this time that he and Issib thought their research was secret, and here was Hushidh telling all the women of Basilica that the two of them were being worn out by the Oversoul! And yet, for all that they knew, the women were also hopelessly ignorant—how could he and Issib know anything about the reason why their visions had stopped?

Nafai went straight to the library and repeated to Issib all he could remember of his conversation with Hushidh. "So what I'm thinking is this. What if the Oversoul isn't all that powerful? What if the reason the visions have stopped is that the Oversoul can't deal with *us* and give visions all at the same time?"

Issib laughed. "Come on, Nyef, as if we're the center of the world or something."

"I'm serious. How much capacity would the Oversoul have to have, really? Most people are ignorant or stupid or weak enough that even if they thought of one of these forbidden subjects, they couldn't do anything about it, so why watch them? That means the Oversoul has to monitor relatively few people. And with them, if it checks in on them every now and then, it has plenty of time to turn them away from dangerous projects. But now, with the Oversoul weakening, you were able to desensitize yourself. That was a contest between you and the Oversoul, and you *won,* Issib. What if during all those struggles, the Oversoul was completely focused on you, giving no visions to anyone else, monitoring no one else. But you were going slowly enough that it still had time left over."

"But the two of us, working together," said Issib. "It had to concentrate on us, constantly. And it's losing, too—weakening even more."

"So I'm thinking, Issib—we're not helping here, we're *hurting.*"

Issib laughed again. "It can't *be,*" he said. "This is the Oversoul we're talking about, not a teacher with a couple of unruly students."

"The Oversoul has failed before. Or there wouldn't be any war wagons."

"So what should we do?"

"Stop," said Nafai. "For a day. Stay away from the forbidden subjects. See if people start getting visions again."

"You seriously think that we, the two of us, have taken up so much of

the Oversoul's time that it can't give visions to people? What about
during the time we sleep and eat? There are plenty of breaks."

"Maybe we've got it confused. Maybe it's panicking about us because it doesn't know what to do."

"Right," said Issib. "So let's not just *quit*. Let's give the Oversoul
some advice, why not!"

"Why not?" said Nafai. "It was made by human beings, wasn't it?"

"We *think*. Maybe."

"So we tell it to stop worrying about trying to block us. That's a
pointless assignment and it should stop wasting time on it *right now*,
because even if we easily think of every forbidden subject in the world,
we're not going to tell anybody else and we're not going to try to build
any ourselves. Are we?"

"We're not."

"So take an oath to that, Issib. I'll take it too. I swear it right now—
you listening, Oversoul?—we're not your enemies, so you don't need
to waste another second worrying about us. Go back and give visions to
the women again. And spend your time blocking the dangerous guys.
The Wetheads, for instance. Gaballufix. Roptat probably, too. And if
you can't block them, then at least let *us* know what to do so *we* can
block them."

"Who are you talking to?"

"The Oversoul."

"This feels really stupid," said Issib.

"It's been telling *us* what to think our whole lives," said Nafai.
"What's so stupid about giving *it* a suggestion now and then? Take the
oath, Issya."

"Yes, I promise, I take the most solemn oath. You listening, Oversoul?"

"It's listening," said Nafai. "That much we *know*."

"So," said Issib. "You think it's going to do what we say?"

"I don't know," said Nafai. "But I know *this*—we're not going to
learn anything more by hanging around the library for the rest of the
day. Let's get out of here. Spend the night at Father's house. Maybe
we'll have a really good idea. Or maybe Father will have a vision. Or
something."

It was only that afternoon, as he was leaving Mother's house, that
Nafai remembered that Elemak was courting Eiadh. Not that Nafai
had a right to hate him for it. Nafai had never said anything to anyone

about his feelings toward her, had he? And at fourteen he was far too young to be taken seriously as a possible legal mate. Of course Eiadh would look at Elemak and desire him. It explained everything—why she was so nice to Nafai and yet never seemed to get close to him. She wanted to keep his favor in case he had some influence over Elemak. But it would never have crossed her mind that she might give a contract to *Nafai*. After all, he was a *child*.

Then he remembered how Hushidh had spoken of Issib. I couldn't talk to *him*. Because he was a cripple? Not likely. No, Hushidh was shy with Issib because she was looking at him as a possible mate. Even *I* know enough about women to guess that, thought Nafai.

Hushidh is my age, and *she's* looking at my older brother when she thinks of mating. While *I* might as well be a tree or a brick for all the sexual interest a girl my age would have in *me*. And Eiadh is older than me—one of the oldest in my class, while I'm one of the youngest. How could I have ever thought . . .

He felt the hot blush of embarrassment on his cheeks, even though no one knew of his humiliation except himself.

Moving through the streets of Basilica, Nafai realized that except for an occasional walk in Rain Street he had not been out of Mother's house since he began his research with Issib. Perhaps because of what Hushidh had told him, he was aware of a change in the city. Were there fewer people on the streets? Perhaps—but the real difference was more in the *way* they walked. People in Basilica often moved with purpose, but usually they did not let that purpose close them to what was going on around them. Even people in a hurry could pause for a moment, or at least smile, when they passed a street musician or a juggler or a comic reciting his doggerel. And many people sauntered, taking things in with real pleasure, conversing with their companions, of course, but also freely speaking with strangers on the street, as if all the people of Basilica were neighbors, or even relatives.

This evening was different. As the sun silhouetted the western rooftops and cast angled slabs of blackness across the streets, the people seemed to dodge the sunlight as if it might burn their skin. They were closed off to each other. The street musicians were ignored, and even their music seemed more timid, as if they were ready to break off their song at the first sign of displeasure in a passerby. The streets were quieter because almost no one was talking.

Soon enough the reason became obvious. A troop of eight men

jogged up the street, pulses in their hands and charged-wire blades at their waists. Soldiers, thought Nafai. Gaballufix's men. No—officially, they were the militia of the Palwashantu, but Nafai felt no kinship with them.

They didn't seem to look to left or right, as if their errand were set. But Nafai and Issib noticed at once that the streets seemed to empty as the soldiers passed. Where had the people gone? They weren't actually hiding, but still it took several minutes after the soldiers had passed before people began emerging again. They had ducked into shops, pretending to have business. Some had simply taken alternate routes down side streets. And others had never left the street at all, but like Nafai and Issib they had stopped, had frozen in place, so that for a few minutes they were part of the architecture, not part of the life of the place.

It did not seem at all as though people thought the soldiers were making the city safer. Instead the soldiers had made them afraid.

"Basilica's in trouble," said Nafai.

"Basilica is *dead*," said Issib. "There are still people here, but the city isn't Basilica anymore."

Fortunately, it wasn't as bad when they got farther along Wing Street —the soldiers had passed where Wing crossed Wheat Street, only a few blocks from Gaballufix's house. When they got into Old Town there was more life in the streets. But changes were still visible.

For instance, Spring Street had been cleared. Spring was one of the major thoroughfares of Basilica, running in the most direct route from Funnel Gate through Old Town and right on to the edge of the Rift Valley. But as often happened in Basilica, some enterprising builder had decided that it was a shame to let all that empty space in the middle of the street go to waste, when people could be living there. On a long block between Wing and Temple, the builder had put up six buildings.

Now, when a Basilican builder started putting up a structure that blocked a street, several things could happen. If the street wasn't very busy, only a few people would object. They might scream and curse and even throw things at the builders, but since the workers were all such burly men, there would be little serious resistance. The building would go up, and people would find new routes. The people who owned houses or shops that used to front on the now-blocked road were the ones who suffered most. They had to bargain with neighbors to gain hallway rights that would give them street access—or *take* those rights, if the neighbor was weak. Sometimes they simply had to abandon their property. Either way, the new hallways or the abandoned property soon became thoroughfares in their own right. Eventually some enterprising soul would buy a couple of abandoned or decaying houses whose hallways were being used for traffic, tear out an open streetway, and thus a new road was born. The city council did nothing to interfere with this process—it was how the city evolved and changed over time, and it seemed pointless in a city tens of millions of years old to try to hold back the tide of time and history.

It was quite another thing when someone started building on a much-used thoroughfare like Spring Street. There, the passersby gained courage from their numbers—and from their outrage at the thought of losing a road they often used. So they would deliberately sabotage the construction as they passed, knocking down masonry, carrying away stones. If the builder was powerful and determined, with many strong workers, a brawl could easily start—but then it might easily come to a court trial, where the builder was *always* found to be at fault, since building in a street was regarded as ample provocation for legal assault.

The builder in Spring Street had been clever, though. She had designed her six buildings to stand on arches, so that the road was never actually blocked. The houses instead began on the first floor, above the street—and so, while passersby were annoyed, they weren't so provoked that they got serious about their sabotage. So the buildings had been finished early that summer, and some very wealthy people had taken up residence.

Inevitably, however, the archways became crowded with streetsellers and enterprising restaurateurs—which the builder surely knew would happen. Traffic slowed to a crawl, and other builders began to put up permanent shops and stalls, until only a few weeks ago it became physically impossible to get from Temple to Wing on Spring Street—the little buildings now completed blocked the way. Another street in Basilica had been killed, only this time it was a major thoroughfare and caused serious inconvenience to a lot of people. Only the original builder and the enterprising little shopkeepers truly profited; the people who bought the inner buildings now found it harder and harder to get to the stairways leading up to their houses, and people were already preparing to abandon old structures that no longer faced on a street.

Now, as Nafai and Issib passed Spring Street, they saw that someone had gone through the blocked section and torn down all the small structures. The new buildings were still there, arching over the street, but the passageway remained open underneath them. More significantly, a couple of soldiers stood at each end of the street. The message was clear: No new building would be tolerated.

"Gaballufix isn't a fool," said Issib.

Nafai knew what he meant. People might not like seeing soldiers trot by in the streets, with the threat of violence and the loss of freedom that they implied. But seeing Spring Street open would go a long way toward making the soldiers seem like a mixed evil, one perhaps worth tolerating.

Wing Street eventually fed into Temple Street, and Nafai and Issib followed it until it came to the great circle around the Temple itself. This was the one outpost of the men's religion in this city of women, the one place where the Oversoul was known to be male, and where blood rather than water was the holy fluid. On impulse, though he hadn't been inside since he was eight and his foreskin was drowned in his own blood, Nafai stopped at the north doors. "Let's go in," he said.

Issib shuddered. "I deeply hate this place," he said.

"If they used anesthetic, worship would be more popular with kids," said Nafai.

Issib grinned. "Painless worship. Now there's a thought. Maybe dry worship would catch on among the women, too."

They went through the door into the musty, dark, windowless outer chamber.

Though the temple was perfectly round, the inner chambers were designed to recall the chambers of the heart: the Indrawing Auricle, the Airward Ventricle, the Airdrawing Auricle, and the Outflowing Ventricle. The winding halls and tiny rooms between them were named for various veins and arteries. Before their circumcision boys had to learn all the names of all the rooms, but they did it by memorizing a song that remained meaningless to most who learned it. So there was nothing particularly familiar about the names written on each door lintel or keystone, and Issib and Nafai were immediately lost.

It didn't matter. Eventually, all halls and corridors funneled worshippers into the central courtyard, the only bright space in the temple,

open to the sky. Since it was so close to sunset, there was no direct
sunlight on the stone floor of the courtyard, but after so much darkness
even reflected sunlight was painfully dazzling.

At the gateway, a priest stopped them. "Prayer or meditation?" he
asked.

Issib shuddered—a convulsive movement, for him, since the floats
exaggerated every twitch his muscles made. "I think I'll wait in the
Airdrawing Auricle."

"Don't be a poddletease," said Nafai. "Just meditate for a minute, it
won't kill you."

"You mean *you're* going to *pray?*" said Issib.

"I guess so," said Nafai.

Truth to tell, Nafai wasn't sure why, or for what. He only knew that
his relationship with the Oversoul was getting more complicated every
day; he understood the Oversoul better than before, and the Oversoul
was meddling in his life now, so it had become important to try to
communicate clearly and directly, instead of all this slantwise guess-
work. It wasn't enough to slack off their research into forbidden words
and hope that the Oversoul got the hint. There had to be something
more.

He watched as the priests jabbed Issib's finger and wiped the tiny
wound over the bloodstone. Issib took it well enough—he really *wasn't*
a poddle, and he'd had enough pain in his life that a little fingerjab was
nothing. He just had little use for the rituals of the men's worship. He
called it "blood sports" and compared it to sharkfights, which always
started out by getting every shark in the pool to bleed. As soon as his
little red smear was on the rough stone, he drifted over toward the high
bench against the sunny wall, where there was still about a half-hour of
sunlight. The bench was full, of course, but Issib could always float just
beside it. "Hurry up," he murmured as he passed Nafai.

Since Nafai was here to pray, the priest didn't jab him. Instead he let
him reach into the golden bowl of prayer rings. The bowl was filled
with a powerful disinfectant, which had the double effect of keeping
the barbed prayer rings from spreading disease and also making it so
that every jab stung bitterly for several long seconds. Nafai usually took
only two rings, one for the middle finger of each hand, but this time he
felt that he needed more. That even though he had no idea what he
was praying *about,* he wanted to make sure that the Oversoul under-

stood that he was serious. So he found prayer rings for all four fingers of each hand, and thumb rings as well.

"It can't be that bad," said the priest.

"I'm not praying for forgiveness," said Nafai.

"I don't want you fainting on me, we're short-staffed today."

"I won't faint." Nafai walked to the center of the courtyard, near the fountain. The water of the fountain wasn't the normal pinkish color—it was almost dark red. Nafai well remembered the powerful frisson the first time he realized how the water got its color. Father said that when Basilica was in great need—during a drought, for instance, or when an enemy threatened—the fountain flowed with almost pure blood, there was so much blood. It was a strange and powerful feeling, to pull off his sandals and strip off his clothes, then kneel in the pool and know that the tepid liquid swirling around him, almost up to his waist if he sat back on his heels, was thick with the passionate bloody prayers of other men.

He held his barbed hands open in front of him for a long time, composing himself, readying himself for the conversation with the Oversoul. Then he slapped his hands vigorously against his upper arms, just as he did in his morning prayers; this time, though, the barbed rings cut into his flesh and the sting was deep and harsh. It was a good, vigorous opening, and he heard several of the meditators sigh or murmur. He knew that they had heard the sharp sound of his slap and seen his self-discipline as he restrained himself from so much as gasping in pain, and they respected this prayer for its strength and virtue.

Oversoul, he said silently. You started all this. Weak as you are, you decided to start intruding in my family's life. You'd better have a plan in mind. And if you do, isn't it about time you let us know what it is?

He slapped himself again, this time on the more sensitive skin of his chest. When the sting faded he could feel blood tickling through the invisible new hairs growing there. I offer this sacrifice to you, Oversoul, I offer my pain if you need it, I'll do whatever you want me to do but I expect a promise from you in return. I expect you to protect my father. I expect you to have a real purpose in mind, and to tell Father what it is. I expect you to keep my brothers from getting mixed up in some terrible crime against the city and particularly from getting involved in a crime against my father. If you protect Father and let us know what's going on, then I'll do everything I can to help your plan work, because I know that the purpose that was programmed into you from the beginning is to keep humanity from destroying itself, and I'll do all I can to serve that purpose. I am yours, as long as you treat us fairly.

He slapped his belly, the sharpest pain yet, and now he heard several of the meditators commenting out loud, and the priest came up behind him. Don't interrupt me, thought Nafai. Either the Oversoul is hearing this or it isn't, and if it *is* hearing me, then I want it to know that I'm serious about it. Serious enough to cut myself to ribbons if need be. Not because I think this bloodletting has anything to do with holiness, but because it shows my willingness to do what I'm told, even when it has a harsh personal cost. I'll do what you want, Oversoul, but you must keep faith.

"Young man," whispered the priest.

"Get lost," whispered Nafai in return.

The sandals shuffled away over the stone.

Nafai reached over his shoulders and scraped his hands up along his back. This was tearing now, not jabbing, and the wounds would not be trivial. Do you see this, Oversoul? You're inside my head, you know what I'm thinking and what I'm feeling. Issib and I are letting you alone so you can give people visions again. Now get to work and get this situation under control. And whatever you want me to do, I'll do. I will. If I can bear this pain, you know I can bear whatever you set me to suffer. And, knowing exactly how it hurts, I can do it again.

He scraped again. The pain this time, as new wounds crossed old ones, brought tears to his eyes—but not a sound to his lips.

Enough. Either the Oversoul heard him or it didn't.

He let himself fall forward into the bloody water, his eyes still closed. It closed over his head, and for a moment he was completely immersed. Then the water buoyed him up, and he felt the cool evening air on his back and buttocks as they floated on the surface.

A moment more. Hold your breath a moment more. Longer. Just a little longer. Wait for the voice of the Oversoul. Listen in the silence of the water.

But no answer came to him. Only the growing pain of the wounds in his upper back and shoulders.

He arose to his feet, dripping wet, and turned toward the edge of the fountain, opening his eyes for the first time since entering the pool. Someone was handing him a towel. Hands reached for him to help him over the lip of the pool. When his eyes were dry, he could see that almost all the meditators had come away from the wall, and were now gathered around, offering him towels, his clothes. "A mighty prayer," they were whispering. "May the Oversoul hear you." They would not let him towel himself, or even dress. "Such virtue in one so young." Instead it was other hands gently dabbing at his wounded back, vigorously toweling at his thighs. "Basilica is blessed to have such a prayer in this temple." It was other hands that pulled his shirt over his head and drew his trousers up his legs. "A Father's pride is a young son bowed with piety yet lifted up with courage." They laced his sandals up his legs, and when they found that the thongs ended below his knee, they nodded, they murmured. "No foolish styles in this one." "A working man's sandals."

And as Nafai followed Issib away from the fountain, he could hear the murmurs continuing behind him. "The Oversoul was here with us today."

At the doorway leading to the Outflowing Ventricle, Nafai was momentarily blocked by someone coming in through that door. Since his head was bowed, he saw only the man's feet. As one whose shirt was stained with the blood of prayer, he expected the man blocking him to make way for him, but it seemed he would not go.

"Meb," said Issib.

Nafai lifted his gaze from the man's shoes. It *was* Mebbekew. In a moment of piercing clarity, it seemed as though he saw his brother whole. He was no longer dressed in the flamboyant costume that had long been his style. Meb was now dressed as a man of business, in clothing that must have cost considerable money. It was not his clothing that Nafai cared about, nor the mystery of where he got the money to buy it—for *that* was no mystery at all. Looking at Mebbekew's face, Nafai knew—*knew*, without words, without reason—that Mebbekew was Gaballufix's man now. Maybe it was the expression on his face: Where once Meb had always had a jaunty sort of half-smile, a spark of malicious fun in his eyes, now he looked serious and important and just a little bit afraid of—of what? Of himself. Of the man he was becoming.

Of the man who owned him. There was nothing in his expression or his clothing to mark him as belonging to Gaballufix, and yet Nafai knew. This must be how it comes in Hushidh, he thought, to see the connections between people. To have no reason, and yet also to have no doubt.

"What were you praying for?" asked Mebbekew.

"For you," answered Nafai.

Inexplicable tears came to Mebbekew's eyes, but his face and voice refused to admit whatever feelings called them forth. "Pray for yourself," said Mebbekew, "and for this city."

"And for Father," said Nafai.

Mebbekew's eyes widened, just a bit, the tiniest bit, but Nafai knew that he had struck home.

"Step aside," said a quiet but angry voice behind him. One of the meditators, perhaps. A stranger, anyway. "Make way for the young man of mighty prayer."

Mebbekew stepped back into the dark shadow of the temple's interior. Nafai moved past him and rejoined Issib, who was waiting in the corridor just beyond Meb.

"Why would *Meb* be here?" asked Issib, once they were out of earshot.

"Maybe there are some things you can't do without speaking to the Oversoul first," said Nafai.

"Or maybe he's decided it's useful to be publicly seen to be a pious man." Issib laughed a little. "He *is* an actor, you know, and it looks like somebody's given him a new costume. I wonder what role he's going to play?"

8

Warning

When Nafai and Issib got home, Truzhnisha was still there. She had spent the day cooking, replenishing the meals in the freezer. But there was nothing hot and fresh for tonight's meal. Father was not one to let his housekeeper indulge his sons.

Truzhnisha saw at once, of course, how disappointed Nafai was. "How should I have known you were coming home for supper tonight?"

"We *do* sometimes."

"So I take your father's money and buy food and prepare it to be eaten hot and fresh on the table, and then nobody comes home at all. It happens as often as not, and then the meal is wasted because I prepare it *differently* for freezing."

"Yes, you overcook everything," said Issib.

"So it will be nice and soft for your feeble jaws," she said.

Issib growled at her—in the back of his throat, like a dog. It was the way they played with each other. Only Truzhya could play with him by exaggerating his weakness; only with Truzhya did Issib ever grunt or growl, in mockery of a manly strength that would always be out of his reach.

"Your frozen stuff is all right, anyway," said Nafai.

"*Thank* you," she said. Her exaggerated tone told him that she was offended at what he had said. But he had meant it sincerely, as a compliment. Why did everybody always think he was being sarcastic or insulting when he was just trying to be nice? Somewhere along the way he really had to learn what the signals were that other people were forever detecting in his speech, so that they were always so sure that he was trying to be offensive.

"Your father is out in the stables, but he wants to talk to the both of you."

"Separately?" asked Issib.

"Now, should I know this? Should I form you into a line outside his door?"

"Yes, you should," said Issib. Then he snapped his jaws at her, like a dog biting. "If you weren't such a worthless old goat."

"Mind who you're calling worthless, now," she said, laughing.

Nafai watched in awe. Issib could say genuinely insulting things, and she took it as play. Nafai complimented her cooking, and she took it as an insult. I should go out in the desert and become a wilder, thought Nafai. Except, of course, that only *women* could be wilders, protected from injury by both custom and law. In fact, on the desert a wilder woman was treated better than in the city—desert folk wouldn't lay a hand on the holy women, and they left them water and food when they noticed them. But a *man* living alone out on the desert was likely to be robbed and killed within a day. Besides, thought Nafai, I haven't the faintest idea of how to live in the desert. Father and Elemak do, but even then they only do it by carrying a lot of supplies with them. Out on the desert without supplies, they'd die as fast as I would. The difference is, they'd be *surprised* that they were dying, because they *think* they know how to survive there.

"Are you awake, Nafai?" asked Issib.

"Mm? Yes, of course."

"So you plan to keep that food sitting in front of you as a pet?"

Nafai looked down and saw that Truzhya had slid a loaded plate in front of him. "Thanks," he said.

"Giving food to you is like leaving it on the graves of your ancestors," said Truzhya.

"They don't say thanks," said Nafai.

"*Oh*, he said *thanks*," she grumbled.

"Well what am I *supposed* to say?" asked Nafai.

"Just eat your supper," said Issib.

"I want to know what was wrong with my saying thanks!"

"She was joking with you," said Issib. "She was *playing.* You've got no sense of humor, Nyef."

Nafai took a bite and chewed it angrily. So she was joking. How was he supposed to know that?

The gate swung open. A scuff of sandals, and then a door opening and closing immediately. It was Father, then, since he was the only one in the family who could reach his room without coming in view of the kitchen door. Nafai started to get up, to go see him.

"Finish your supper first," said Issib.

"He didn't say it was an emergency," added Truzhnisha.

"He didn't say it *wasn't,*" answer Nafai. He continued on out of the room.

Behind him, Issib called out. "Tell him I'll be there in a second."

Nafai stepped out into the courtyard, crossed in front of the gate, and entered the door into Father's public room. He wasn't there. Instead he was back in the library, with a book in the computer display that Nafai instantly recognized as the Testament of the Oversoul, perhaps the oldest of the holy writings, from a time so ancient that, according to the stories, the men's and women's religions were the same.

"She comes to you in the shadows of sleep," Nafai said aloud, reading from the first line on the screen.

"She whispers to you in the fears of your heart," Father answered.

"In the bright awareness of your eyes and in the dark stupor of your ignorance, there is her wisdom," Nafai continued.

"Only in her silence are you alone. Only in her silence are you wrong. Only in her silence should you despair." Father sighed. "It's all here, isn't it, Nafai?"

"The Oversoul isn't a man or a woman," said Nafai.

"Right, yes, of course, *you* know all about what the Oversoul is."

Father's tone was so weary that Nafai decided it wasn't worth arguing theology with him tonight. "You wanted to see me."

"You *and* Issib."

"He'll be here in a second."

As if on cue, Issib drifted through the door, still eating some cheesebread.

"Thank you for bringing crumbs into my library," said Father.

"Sorry," said Issib; he reversed direction and started floating out the door.

"Come back," said Father. "I don't care about the crumbs."

Issib came back.

"There's talk all over Basilica about the two of you."

Nafai traded glances with Issib. "We've just been doing some library research."

"The women are saying that the Oversoul is speaking to no one but you."

"We aren't exactly getting clear messages from it," said Nafai.

"Mostly we've just been monopolizing it by stimulating its aversive reflexes," said Issib.

"Mmm," said Father.

"But we've stopped," said Issib. "That's why we came home."

"We didn't want to interfere," said Nafai.

"Nafai prayed, though, on the way home," said Issib. "It was pretty impressive stuff."

Father sighed. "Oh, Nafai, if you've learned anything from me, couldn't you have learned that jabbing yourself and bleeding all over the place has nothing to do with prayer to the Oversoul?"

"Right," said Nafai. "This from the man who suddenly comes home with a vision of fire on a rock. I thought all bets were off."

"I got my vision without bleeding," said Father. "But never mind. I was hoping that the two of you might have received something from the Oversoul that would help me."

Nafai shook his head.

"No," said Issib. "Mostly what we got from the Oversoul was that stupor of thought. It was trying to keep us from thinking forbidden thoughts."

"Well, that's it, then," said Father. "I'm on my own."

"On your own with what?" asked Issib.

"Gaballufix sent word to me through Elemak today. It seems that Gaballufix is as unhappy as I am about the situation in Basilica today. If he had known that this war wagon business would cause such controversy he would never have begun it. He said that he wanted me to set up a meeting between him and Roptat. All Gaballufix really wants now is to find a way to back down without losing face—he says that all he needs is for Roptat also to back down, so that we don't make an alliance with anybody."

"So have you set up a meeting with Roptat?"

"Yes," said Father. "At dawn, at the coolhouse east of Market Gate."

"It sounds to me," said Nafai, "like Gaballufix has come around to the City Party's way of thinking."

"That's how it *sounds*," said Father.

"But you don't believe him," said Issib.

"I don't know," said Father. "His position is the only reasonable, intelligent one. But when has Gaballufix ever been reasonable or intelligent? All the years I've known him, even when he was a young man, before he maneuvered himself into the clan leadership, he's never done anything that wasn't designed to advance him relative to other people. There are always two ways of doing that—by building yourself up and by tearing your rivals down. In all these years, I've seen that Gaballufix has a definite preference for the latter."

"So you think he's using you," said Nafai. "To get at Roptat."

"Somehow he will betray Roptat and destroy him," said Father. "And in the end, I'll look back and see how he used me to help him accomplish that. I've seen it before."

"So why are you helping him?" asked Issib.

"Because there's a chance, isn't there? A chance that he means what he's saying. If I refuse to mediate between them, then it'll be *my* fault if things get worse in Basilica than they always are. So I have to take him at face value, don't I?"

"All you can do is your best," said Nafai, echoing Father's own pat phrase from many previous conversations.

"Keep your eyes open," said Issib, echoing another of Father's epigrams.

"Yes," said Father. "I'll do that."

Issib nodded wisely.

"Father," said Nafai. "May I go with you in the morning?"

Father shook his head.

"I want to. And maybe I can see something that you miss. Like while you're talking or something, I can be looking at other people and seeing their reactions. I could really help."

"No," said Father. "I won't be a credible mediator if I have others with me."

But Nafai knew that wasn't true. "I think you're afraid that something ugly will happen and you don't want me there."

Father shrugged. "I have my fears. I *am* a father."

"But I'm *not* afraid, Father."

"Then apparently you're stupider than I feared," said Father. "Go to bed now, both of you."

"It's way too early for that," said Issib.

"Then *don't* go to bed."

Father turned away from them and faced the computer display again. It was a clear signal of dismissal, but Nafai couldn't keep himself from questioning him. "If the Oversoul isn't speaking to you directly, Father, why do you hope to find anything helpful in its ancient, dead words?"

Father sighed and said nothing.

"Nafai," said Issib, "let Father contemplate in peace."

Nafai followed Issib out of the library. "Why won't anybody ever answer my questions?"

"Because you never stop asking them," said Issib, "and especially because you keep asking them even when it's clear that nobody knows the answers."

"Well how do I know that they don't know the answer unless I ask?"

"Go to your room and think dirty thoughts or something," said Issib. "Why can't you just act like a normal fourteen-year-old?"

"Right," said Nafai. "Like *I'm* supposed to be the one normal person in the family."

"Somebody's got to do it."

"Why do you think Meb was at the temple?"

"To pray for you to get a hemorrhoid every time you ask a question."

"No, that's why *you* were at the temple. Can you imagine Meb praying?"

"And marking up his beautiful body?" Issib laughed.

They were in the courtyard, in front of Issib's room. They heard a footstep and turned to see Mebbekew standing in the kitchen door. The kitchen had been dark; they had assumed that Truzhnisha had gone and that no one was in there. Meb must have overheard all their conversation.

Nafai couldn't think of anything to say. Of course, that didn't mean he held his tongue. "I guess you didn't stay long in the temple, did you, Meb?"

"No," said Meb. "But I *did* pray, if it's any of your business."

Nafai was ashamed. "I'm sorry."

Issib wasn't. "Oh, come on," he said. "Show me a scab, then."

"I have a question for you first, Issya," said Meb.

"Sure," said Issib.

"Do you have a float attached to your private lever to hold it up when you pee? Or do you just let it dribble down like a girl?"

It was too dark for Nafai to see whether Issib was blushing or not. All he was sure of was that Issib said nothing, just glided from the courtyard into his room.

"Bravely done," said Nafai. "Taunting a cripple."

"He called me a lair," said Meb. "Was I supposed to kiss him?"

"He was joking."

"It wasn't funny." Mebbekew went back into the kitchen.

Nafai went into his room, but he didn't feel like going to bed. He felt sweaty, even though the night was fairly chilly. His skin itched. It had to be the residue of blood and disinfectant from the temple fountain. Nafai didn't relish the idea of using soap on his wounds, but the slimy itchiness would be unbearable, too. So he stripped and went to the shower. This time he rinsed first, shockingly cold despite the day's warming of the water. And it stung bitterly to soap himself—perhaps worse now than when the wounds were first inflicted, though he knew that this was probably subjective. The pain of the moment is always the worst, Father had often said.

As he was soaping in miserable dark silence, he saw Elemak come in. He went directly into Father's rooms, and emerged not long after to lock the gate. And not just the outer gate; the inner one, too. That wasn't the usual thing; indeed, Nafai couldn't remember when he had last seen the inner gate locked. Maybe there was a storm once. Or a time when they were training a dog and kept it between the gates at night. But there was neither storm nor dog now.

Elemak went into his room. Nafai pulled the cord and plunged himself again in icy water, rubbing at his wounds to get the soap out before the water stopped flowing. Curse Father for his absurd insistence on toughening his sons and making men of them! Only the poor had to bathe in a sudden flow of cold water like this!

It took two rinsings this time, with a long wet wait in the chilly breeze for the shower tank to refill. When he finally got back to his room, Nafai was chattering and shaking with the cold, and even when he was dry and dressed again, he couldn't seem to get warm. He almost closed the door to his room, which would have triggered the heating system—but he and his brothers always competed to see who could be last to start closing the door of his room in the wintertime, and he wasn't about to surrender that battle tonight, confessing that a little prayer had weakened him so much. Instead he pulled all his clothes out of his chest and piled them on top of himself where he lay on his mat.

There was no comfortable position for sleeping, of course, but lying on his side was least painful. Anger and pain and worry kept him from sleeping easily; he felt as though he hadn't slept at all, listening to the small sounds of the others getting ready for sleep, and then the endless silence of the courtyard at night. Now and then a birdcall, or a wild dog in the hills, or a soft restless sound from the horses in the stable or the pack animals in the barns.

And then he must have slept, or how else could he have woken up so suddenly, startled. Was it a sound that woke him? Or a dream? What was he dreaming, anyway? Something dark and fearful. He was trembling, but it wasn't cold—in fact, he was sweating heavily under his pile of clothing.

He got up and tossed the clothes back into his chest. He tried to be quiet about opening and closing the box—he didn't want to waken anyone else. Every movement caused him pain. He must be fevered, he realized—he had the stiffness in his muscles, and the hotness under his covers. And yet his thinking seemed remarkably clear, and all his senses. If this was a fever, it was a strange one, for he had never felt so vivid and alive. In spite of the pain—or because of it—he felt as though he would hear it if a mouse ran across a beam in the stable.

He walked out into the courtyard and stood there in silence. The moon wasn't up yet, but the stars were many and bright on this clear night. The gate was still locked. But why had he wondered? What was he afraid of? What *had* he seen in his dream?

Meb's and Elya's doors were closed. What a laugh—here I am, wounded and sore, and I keep my door open, while these two go ahead and close their doors like little children.

Or maybe it's only little children who care about such meaningless contests of manliness.

It was colder than ever outside, and now he had cooled off the feverishness that had made him get up. But still he didn't return to his room, though he meant to. In fact, it finally dawned on him that he had already decided several times to return to his room, and each time his mind had wandered and he hadn't taken a step.

The Oversoul, he thought. The Oversoul wants me to be up. Perhaps wants me to be doing something. But what?

At this point in the month, the fact that the moon had not yet risen meant that it was a good three hours before dawn. Two hours, then, before Father was supposed to arise and go to his rendezvous at the cool house, where the plants from the icy north were nurtured and propagated.

Why was the meeting being held *there?*

Nafai felt an inexplicable desire to go outside and look northeast across the Tsivet Valley toward the high hills on the other side, where the Music Gate marked the southeast limit of Basilica. It was silly, and the noise of opening the gates might waken someone. But by now Nafai knew that the Oversoul was involved with him tonight, trying to keep him from going back to bed; couldn't this impulse to go outside also come from the Oversoul? Hadn't Nafai prayed today—couldn't this be an answer? Wasn't it possible that this desire to go outside was like the impulse Father had felt, that took him from the Desert Road to the place where he saw the vision of fire?

Wasn't it possible that Nafai, too, was about to receive a vision from the Oversoul?

He walked smoothly, quietly to the gate lifted the heavy bar. No noises; his senses and reflexes were so alert and alive that he could move with perfect silence. The gate creaked slightly as he opened it— but he didn't have to open it widely in order to slip through.

The outer gate was more often used, and so it worked more easily, and quietly, having been better maintained. Nafai stepped outside just as the moon first showed an arc over the top of the Seggidugu Mountains to the east. He headed out to walk around the house to where he could see the cool house, but before he had taken a few steps he realized that he could hear a sound coming from the traveler's room.

As was the custom in all the households in this part of the world, every house had a room whose door opened to the outside and was never locked—a decent place where a traveler could come and take refuge from storm or cold or weariness. Father took the obligation of hospitality to strangers more seriously than most, providing not just a room, but also a bed and clean linen, and a cupboard provisioned with traveling food. Nafai wasn't sure which servant had responsibility for the room, but he knew it was often used and just as often replenished.

So he should not be surprised at the idea that someone might be inside.

And yet he knew that he must stop at the door and peer inside.

Scant light fell into the traveler's room from the crack in the door. He opened it wider, and the light spilled onto the bed, where he found himself looking into the wide eyes of—Luet.

"You," he whispered.

"You," she answered. She sounded relieved.

"What are you doing here?" he asked. "Who's with you?"

"I'm alone," she said. "I wasn't sure who I was coming to. Whose house. I've never been outside of the city walls before."

"When did you get here?"

"Just now. The Oversoul led me."

Of course. "To what purpose?"

"I don't know," she said. "To tell my dream, I think. It woke me."

Nafai thought of his own dream, which he couldn't remember.

"I was so—glad," she said. "That the Oversoul had spoken again. But the dream was terrible."

"What was it?"

"Is it you I'm supposed to tell?" she asked.

"I should know?" he answered. "But I'm here."

"Did the Oversoul bring you out here?"

With the question put so directly, he couldn't evade it. "Yes," he said. "I think so."

She nodded. "Then I'll tell you. It makes sense, actually, that it be your family. Because there are so many people who hate your father because of his vision and his courage in proclaiming it."

"Yes," he said. And then, to prompt her: "The dream."

"I saw a man alone on foot, walking in the straight. He was walking through snow. Only I knew that it was tonight, even though there's not a speck of snow on the ground. Do you understand how I can know something, even though it's different from what the dream actually shows me?"

Remembering the conversation on the portico a week ago, Nafai nodded.

"So there was snow, and yet it was tonight. The moon was up. I knew it was almost dawn. And as the man walked along, two men wearing hoods sprang out into the road in front of him, holding blades. He seemed to know them, in spite of the hoods. And he said, 'Here's my throat. I carry no weapon. You could have killed me at any time, even when I knew you were my enemy. Why did you need to deceive me into trusting you first? Were you afraid that death wouldn't bother me enough, unless I felt betrayed?"

Nafai had already made the connection between her dream and Father's meeting, only a few hours away. "Gaballufix," said Nafai.

Luet nodded. "Now I understand that—but I didn't until I realized this was your father's house."

"No—Gaballufix arranged a meeting for Father and Roptat and him this morning, at the coolhouse."

"The snow," she said.

"Yes," he said. "It's always got frost in the corners."

"And Roptat," she whispered. "That explains—the next part of the dream."

"Tell me."

"One hooded man reached out and uncovered the face of his companion. For a moment I thought I saw a grin on his face, but then my vision clarified and I realized it wasn't his face that had the smile. It was his throat, slit clear back to the spine. As I watched him, his head lolled back and the wound in his throat opened completely, as if it were a mouth, trying to scream. And the man—the one that was me in the dream—"

"I understand," said Nafai. "Father."

"Yes. Only I didn't know that."

"Right," said Nafai. Impatiently, urging her to get on with it.

"Your father, if it was your father, said, 'I suppose it will be said that I killed him.' And the hooded man says, 'And you did, in very truth, my dear kinsman.'"

"He would say that," said Nafai. "So Roptat is supposed to die, too."

"I'm not done," said Luet. "Or rather, the dream wasn't finished. Because the man—your father—said, 'And who will they say killed me?' And the hooded one said, 'Not me. I'd never lift a hand against you, for I love you dearly. I will merely find your body here, and your bloody-handed murderers standing over it.' Then he laughed and disappeared back into the shadows."

"So he doesn't kill Father."

"No. Your father turned around then and saw two other hooded men standing behind him. And even though they didn't speak or lift their hoods, he knew them. I felt this terrible sadness. 'You couldn't wait,' he said to the one. 'You couldn't forgive me,' he said to the other. And then they reached out with their blades and killed him."

"No, by the Oversoul," said Nafai. "They wouldn't do it."

"Who? Do you know?"

"Tell no one of this last part of the dream," said Nafai. "Swear it to me with your most awful oath."

"I'll do no such thing," she said.

"My brothers are all home tonight," said Nafai. "Not lying in wait for Father."

"Is that who the hooded men are, then? Your brothers?"

"No!" he said. "Never."

She nodded. "I'll give you no oath. Only my promise. If your father is saved from death by my having come here, then I'll tell no one else of this part of the dream."

"Not even Hushidh," he said.

"But I make you another promise," she said. "If your father dies, I'll know that you didn't warn him. And that the hooded ones in the dream included *you*—because to know of the plot and fail to warn him is exactly the same as holding the charged-wire blade in your own hands."

"Do you think I don't know that?" said Nafai. He was angry for a moment, that she would think *he* needed to be taught the ethics of this situation. But then his thoughts moved on, as Luet's warning clarified other things that had happened that day. "That's why Meb went to pray," said Nafai, "and why Elya locked the inner gate. They knew—or maybe they just suspected something—and yet they were afraid to tell. That's what the dream meant—not that they would ever lift a hand against Father, but rather that they knew and were afraid to warn him."

She nodded. "It often works that way in dreams," she said. "That would be a true meaning, and it doesn't empty my head when I think that thought."

"Maybe the Oversoul itself doesn't know."

She reached out and patted his hand. It made him feel like a child, even though she was younger and much smaller than he. He resented her for it.

"The Oversoul knows," she said.

"Not everything," he said.

"Everything that *can* be known," she said. She walked to the door of the traveler's room. "Tell no one that I came," she said.

"Except Father," he said.

"Can't you say that it was *your* dream?"

"Why?" asked Nafai. "*Your* dream he would believe. Mine would be —nothing to him."

"You underestimate your father. And the Oversoul, too, I think. And yourself." She stepped out into the moonlit yard in front of the house. She started to turn right, heading for Ridge Road.

"No," he whispered, catching her arm—small and frail indeed, she was a girl so young and little-boned. "Don't pass in front of the gate."

She gave him a questioning look, eyes wide, reflecting the moon, which was half-risen now over his shoulder.

"Perhaps I woke someone when I opened it," he explained.

She nodded. "I'll go around the house on the other side."

"Luet," he said.

"Yes?"

"Will you be safe, going home now?"

"The moon is up," she said. "And the guard at the Funnel Gate will give me no trouble. The Oversoul made him sleep when I passed before."

"Luet," he said, calling her back again.

Again she stopped, waited for his words.

"Thank you," he said. The words were nothing compared to what he felt in his heart. She had saved his Father's life—and it was a brave thing for a girl who had never left the city to come all this way in the starlight, guided only by a dream.

She shrugged. "The Oversoul sent me. Thank *her*." Then she was gone.

Nafai returned to the gate, and this time deliberately made some noise coming in and latching it. If one of his brothers was listening or watching, he didn't want his return to surprise him. Let him hear and go back to his room before I come through the inner gate.

As he had hoped, the courtyard was empty when he returned. He went straight to Father's room, through the public room and the library to the private place where he slept alone. There he lay on the bare floor, without a mat of any kind, his white beard spilling onto the stone. Nafai stood there a moment, imagining the throat cut open and the beard stained brownish red with the gush of blood.

Then he noticed that Father's eyes were shining. He was awake.

"Are you the one?" whispered Father.

"What do you mean?" asked Nafai.

Father sat up, slowly, wearily. "I had a dream. It was nothing—just my fear."

"Someone else had a dream tonight," said Nafai. "I talked to her just now in the traveler's room. But it's better if you tell no one that she was here."

"Who?"

"Luet," he said. "And her dream was to warn you of the meeting tonight. There's murder waiting for you if you go."

Father sprang to his feet and turned on the light. Nafai blinked in the brightness of it. "Then it wasn't just a dream I had."

"I'm beginning to think there *are* no meaningless dreams," said Nafai. "I also dreamed, and it woke me, and the Oversoul brought me outside to talk to her."

"Murder waiting for me. I can guess the rest. He'll murder Roptat also, and make it look like one of us killed the other, and then someone else killed the murderer, and only then will Gaballufix arrive, probably with several believable witnesses who can swear that the murders took place before Gabya arrived. They'll tell of how shocked he was by the bloody scene. Why didn't I see it myself? How else could he get me and Roptat to the same place at the same time, with no followers or witnesses about?"

"So you won't go," said Nafai.

"Yes," said Father. "I'll go, yes."

"No!"

"But not to the coolhouse," said Father. "Because *my* dream showed me something else."

"What?"

"Tents," he said. "My tents, spread wide in the desert sun. If we stay, Gaballufix will only try again, in some other way. And—there are other reasons for leaving. For getting my sons out of this city before it destroys them."

Nafai knew that Father's dream must have been terrible indeed. Did it show him that one of his sons would kill him? That would explain Father's first words—Are you the one?

"So we're going into the desert?"

"Yes," said Father.

"When?"

"Now, of course."

"Now? Today?"

"Now, *tonight*. Before dawn. So we're over the ridge before his men can see us."

"But won't we pass right by Gaballufix's household, where Twisting Trail crosses Desert Road?"

"There's a back way," said Father. "Not the best for camels, but we'll have to do it. It puts us on Desert Road well past Gabya's place. Now come, help me waken your brothers."

"No," said Nafai.

Father turned to him, puzzlement making him hesitate to express his anger at being disobeyed.

"Luet asked—that no one be told it was her. And she was right. They shouldn't know about me, either. It should be *your* dream."

"Why?" asked Father. "To have three be touched tonight by the Oversoul—"

"Because if it's your dream, then they'll wonder what you know, what you saw. But if there are others, then to them it will seem that we're fooling and manipulating you. They'll argue. They'll resist you. And you have to bring them with you, Father."

Father nodded. "You're very wise," he said. "For a boy of fourteen."

But Nafai knew he was not wise. He simply had the benefit of knowing the rest of Luet's dream. If Meb and Elya stayed behind, they would be wholly swallowed up in Gaballufix's machinations. They would lose what decency remained in them. And there *must* be goodness in them. Perhaps they even planned to warn Father. Maybe that's why Elya closed the inner gate, so that he'd be wakened by the noise Father made as he left—then he could come out and warn Father not to go!

Or perhaps he meant only to follow Father, so he could be right behind him when he came upon Roptat's murdered body in the ice house.

No! cried Nafai inside himself. Not Elemak. It's monstrous of me even to think that he could do that. My brothers are not murderers, not one of them.

"Go to your room," said Father. "Or better still, to the toilet. And then come out and set an example of silent obedience. Not to me—to Elya. He knows how to pack for this kind of trip."

"Yes, Father," said Nafai.

At once he moved briskly from Father's room, through the library

and public room, and out into the courtyard. Elemak's and Mebbekew's doors were still closed. Nafai headed for the latrine, with its
two walls leaving it open to the courtyard. He was only just there when
he heard Father knocking on Mebbekew's door. "Wake up, but quietly," said Father. Then again, on Elemak's. "Come out into the courtyard."

He heard them all come out—Issib, too, though no one called him
directly.

"Where's Nyef?" asked Issib.

"Using the latrine," said Father.

"Now *that's* an idea," said Meb.

"You can wait a moment," said Father.

Nafai came out of the stall, letting the toilet wash itself automatically
behind him. At least Father hadn't made them live in a *completely*
primitive way.

"Sorry," said Nafai. "Didn't mean to keep you waiting." Meb
glowered at him, but too sleepily for Nafai to take it as a threat of a
fight to come.

"We're leaving," Father said. "Out into the desert."

"All of us?" asked Issib.

"I'm sorry, yes," said Father. "You'll be in your chair. It's not the
same as your floats, I know, but it's something."

"Why?" asked Elemak.

"I was warned by the Oversoul in a dream," said Father.

Meb made a contemptuous noise and started back for his room.

"You will stand and listen," said Father, "because if you stay, it will
not be as my son."

Meb stood and listened, though his back was still toward Father.

"There's a plot to kill me," said Father. "This morning. I was to go to
a meeting with Gaballufix and Roptat, and there I was going to die."

"Gabya gave me his word," said Elemak. "No harm to anyone."

So Elemak called Gaballufix by his boy-name now, did he?

"The Oversoul knows his heart better than his own mouth does,"
said Father. "If I go, I'll die. And even if I don't, it will be only a matter
of time. Now that Gaballufix has determined to kill me, my life is
worthless here. I would stay in the city if I thought some purpose
would be served by my dying here—I'm not afraid of it. But the Oversoul has told me to leave."

"In a dream," said Elemak.

"I don't need a dream to tell me that Gaballufix is dangerous when he's crossed," said Father, "and neither do you. When I don't show up at the coolhouse this morning, there's no telling what Gaballufix will do. I must already be out on the desert when he discovers it. We'll take Redstone Path."

"The camels can't do it," said Elemak.

"They can because they must," said Father. "We'll take enough to live for a year."

"This is monstrous," said Mebbekew. "I won't do it."

"What do we do after a year?" asked Elemak.

"The Oversoul will show me something by then," said Father.

"Maybe things will have calmed down in Basilica enough to return," suggested Issib.

"If we go now," said Elemak, "Gabya will think you betrayed him, Father."

"Will he?" said Father. "And if I stay, he'll betray *me.*"

"Said a dream."

"Said *my* dream," said Father. "I need you. Stay if you want, but not as my son."

"I did fine not as your son," said Mebbekew.

"No," said Elemak. "You did fine *pretending* not to be his son. But everyone knew."

"I lived from my talent."

"You lived from theatre people's hope of getting your Father to invest in their shows—or you, in the future, out of your inheritance."

Mebbekew looked like he had been slapped. "You too, is that it, Elya?"

"I'll talk to you later," said Elemak. "If Father says we're going then we're going—and we have no time to lose." He turned to Father. "Not because you threatened to disinherit me, old man. But because you're my father, and I won't have you going out into the desert with nothing but *these* to help you stay alive."

"I taught you everything you know, Elya," said Father.

"When you were younger," said Elemak. "And we always had servants. I assume we're leaving them all behind."

"Dismissing the household servants," said Father. "While you ready the animals and the supplies, Elya, I'll leave instructions for Rashgallivak."

For the next hour Nafai worked with more hurry than he had ever thought possible. Everyone, even Issib, had tasks to perform, and Nafai admired Elemak all over again for his great skill at this sort of thing. He always knew exactly what needed to be done, and who should do it, and how long it should take; he also knew how to make Nafai feel like an idiot for not learning his tasks more quickly, even though he was sure that he was doing at least as well as anyone could expect, considering that it was his first time.

At last they were ready—a true desert caravan, with nothing but camels, though they were the most temperamental of the pack animals, and the least comfortable to ride. Issib's chair was strapped to one side of a camel, bundles of powdered water on the other. The water would be for emergencies later; on the first part of their journey Father and Elemak knew all the watering places, and besides, an autumn occasional rain fell on the desert, and there would be ample water. Next summer, though, it would be drier, and then it would be too late to come back to Basilica for the precious powder. And what if they were followed, chased into untracked sections of the desert? Then they might need to pour some of the powder into a pan, light it, and watch it burn itself into water, taking oxygen from the air to accomplish it. Nafai had tasted it once—foul stuff, tinny and nasty with the chemicals used to bind the hydrogen into powdered form. But they'd be glad of it if they ever needed it.

It was Issib's chair that would bring the least gladness. Nafai knew that this journey would be hardest on Issya, deprived of his floats, and bound into the chair. The floats made him feel as though his own body were light and strong; in the chair, he felt gravity pressing him down, and it took all his strength to operate the controls. At the end of a day in the chair Issya was always wan and exhausted. How would it be for day after day, week after week, month after month? Maybe he would grow stronger. Maybe he would grow weaker. Maybe he would die. Maybe the Oversoul would sustain him.

Maybe angels would come and carry them to the moon.

It was still a good hour before dawn when they set out. They had been quiet enough that none of the servants had been wakened—or perhaps they *had*, but since nobody asked them to help and they weren't interested in volunteering for whatever mad task was going on at this hour of the night, they discreetly rolled over and went back to sleep.

Redstone Path was murderously treacherous, but the moonlight and

Elemak's instructions made it possible. Nafai was again filled with admiration for his eldest brother. Was there nothing Elya couldn't do?
Was there any hope of Nafai ever becoming so strong and competent?
At last they crossed Twisting Path, right at the crest of the highest
ridge; below them stretched the desert. The first light of dawn was
already strong in the east, but they had made good enough time. It was
downhill now, still difficult, but not long until they reached the great
plateau of the western desert. No one would follow them easily here—
no one from the city, anyway. Elemak passed out pulses to all of them
and made them practice aiming the tightbeam light at rocks he pointed
out. Issib was pretty useless—he couldn't hold the pulse steady enough
—but Nafai was proud of the fact that he held his aim better than
Father.

Whether he could actually kill a robber with it was another matter.
Surely he wouldn't have to. They were on the Oversoul's errand here
in the desert, weren't they? The Oversoul would steer the robbers
away from them. Just as the Oversoul would lead them to water and
food, when they ran out of their traveling supplies.

Then Nafai remembered that this whole business began because the
Oversoul wasn't as competent as it used to be. How did he know the
Oversoul could do *any* of those things? Or that it even had a plan? Yes,
it had sent Luet to warn them, and had wakened Nafai to go hear the
warning, and had sent Father his own dream. But that didn't mean that
the Oversoul actually had any intention of protecting them or even of
leading them anywhere except away from the city. Who knew what the
Oversoul's plans were? Maybe all it needed was to get rid of Wetchik
and his family.

With that grim thought, Nafai sat high above the desert, his leg
hooked around the pommel of his saddle, as he searched in all directions for robbers, for pursuers from the city, for any strange thing on
the road, for signs from the Oversoul. The only music was Mebbekew's
complaints and Elemak's orders and the occasional splatting as the
camels voided their bowels. Nafai's beast, oblivious to any worries
except where to put its feet, continued its rolling gait onward into the
heat of day.

9

Lies and Disguises

With the moon up, it was much easier for Luet to find her way back into the city than it had been for her to get to Wetchik's house. Besides, now she *knew* her destination; it's always easier to return home than to find a strange place.

Oddly, though, she didn't feel a sense of danger until she got back into the city itself. The guard at the Funnel Gate was away from his post—perhaps he had been caught sleeping, or perhaps the Oversoul made him think of some sudden errand. Luet had to smile to herself at the thought of the Oversoul troubling herself to make a man feel an urgent need to void his bladder, just for Luet's safe passage.

Within the city, though, the moon was less help. In fact, since it hadn't yet risen very high, it cast deep shadows, and the north-south streets were still in utter blackness at street level. Anyone might be abroad at this hour. Tolchocks were known to be abroad much earlier in the night, when there were still many women abroad in the streets. Now, though, in the loneliest hours before dawn, there might be much worse than Tolchocks about.

"Isn't she the pretty one?"

The voice startled her. It was a woman, though, a husky-voiced woman. It took a moment for Luet to find her in the shadows. "I'm not pretty," she said. "In the darkness your eyes deceived you."

It had to be a holy woman, to be on the street at this hour. As she stepped from the dark corner where she had taken shelter from the night breeze, the woman's dirty skin showed a bit paler than the surrounding shadow. She was naked from face to foot. Seeing her, Luet felt the cold of the autumn night. As long as Luet had been moving, she had kept warm from the exercise. Now, though, she wondered how this woman could live like this, with no barrier between her skin and the chilling air except for the dirt on her body.

Mother was a wilder, thought Luet. I was born to such a one as this. She slept in the desert when I was in her womb, and carried me, as naked as she was, into the city to leave me with Aunt Rasa. Not this one, though. My mother, wherever she is, is not a holy woman anymore. Only a year after I was born she left the Oversoul to follow a man, a farmer, to a hardscrabble life in the rocky soil of the Chalvasankhra Valley. Or so Aunt Rasa said.

"Beautiful are the eyes of the holy child," intoned the woman, "who sees in the darkness and burns with bright fire in the frozen night."

Luet permitted the woman to touch her face, but when the cold hands started to pull at her clothing, Luet covered them with her own. "Please," she said. "I am not holy, and the Oversoul doesn't shield me from the cold."

"Or from the prying eyes," said the holy woman. "The Oversoul sees you deep, and you *are* holy, yes you are."

Whose were the prying eyes? The Oversoul's? The eyes of men who sized up women as if they were horses? Gossips' eyes? Or this woman's? And as for being holy—Luet knew better. The Oversoul had chosen her, yes, but not for any virtue in herself. If anything, it was a punishment, always to be surrounded by people who saw her as an oracle instead of a girl. Hushidh, her own sister, had once said to her, "I wish I had your gift; everything is so clear to you." Nothing is clear to me, Luet wanted to say. The Oversoul doesn't confide in me, she merely uses me to transmit messages that I don't understand myself. Just as I don't understand what this holy woman wants with me, or why—if the Oversoul sent her—she was sent to me.

"Don't be afraid to take him beside the water," said the holy woman.

"Who?" asked Luet.

"The Oversoul wants you to save him alive, no matter what the danger. There is no sacrilege in obeying the Oversoul."

"Who?" asked Luet again. This confusion, this dread that she must decode the puzzle of these words or suffer some terrible loss—was this how others felt when she told them of her visions?

"You think all the visions should come to *you,*" said the holy woman. "But some things are too clear for you to see yourself. Eh?"

I think nothing of the kind, holy woman. I never asked for visions, and I often wish they had come to other people. But if you're going to insist on giving me some message, then have the decency to make it as intelligible as you can. It's what *I* try to do.

Luet tried to keep her resentment out of her voice, but she could not resist insisting on a clarifying answer. "Who is this *him* that you keep talking about?"

The woman slapped her sharply across the face. It brought tears to Luet's eyes—tears as much of shame as of pain. "What have I done?"

"I have punished you now for the defiling you will do," said the holy woman. "It's done, and no one can demand that you pay more."

Luet didn't dare ask questions again; the answer was not to her liking. Instead she studied at the woman, trying to see if there was understanding in her eyes. Was this madness after all? Did it have to be the true voice of the Oversoul? So much easier if it was madness.

The old woman reached her hand toward Luet's cheek again. Luet recoiled a little, but the woman's touch was gentle this time, and she brushed a tear from the hollow just under Luet's eye. "Don't be afraid of the blood on his hands. Like the water of vision, the Oversoul will receive it as a prayer."

Then the holy woman's face went slack and weary, and the light went out of her eyes. "It's cold," she said.

"Yes."

"I'm too old," she said.

Her hair wasn't even gray, but yes, thought Luet, you are very, very old.

"Nothing will hold," said the holy woman. "Silver and gold. Stolen or sold."

She was a rhymer. Luet knew that many people thought that when a holy woman went a-rhyming, it meant that the Oversoul was speaking through her. But it wasn't so—the rhyming was a sort of music, the voice of the trance that kept some of the holy women detached from their bleak and terrible life. It was when they *stopped* rhyming that there was a chance they might speak sense.

The holy woman wandered away, as if she had forgotten Luet was there. Since she seemed to have forgotten where her sheltered corner was, Luet took her by the hand and led her back there, encouraged her to sit down and curl up against the wall that blocked the wind. "Out of the wind," whispered the holy woman. "How they have sinned."

Luet left her there and went on into the night. The moon was higher now, but the better light did little to cheer her. Though the holy woman was harmless in herself, she had reminded Luet of how many people there might be, hiding in the shadows. And how vulnerable *she* was. There were stories of men who treated citizens the way that the law allowed them to deal with the holy women. But even that was not the worst fear.

There is murder in the city, thought Luet. Murder in this place, not holiness, and it is Gaballufix who first thought of it. If not for the vision and warning I carried for the Oversoul, good men would have died. She shuddered again at the memory of the slit throat in her vision.

At last she came to the place where the Holy Road widened out as it descended into the valley, becoming, not a road, but a canyon, with ancient stairs carved into the rock, leading directly down to the place where the lake steamed hot with a tinge of sulphur. Those who worshiped there always kept that smell about them for days. It might be holy, but Luet found it exceedingly unpleasant and never worshiped there herself. She preferred the place where the hot and cold waters mixed and the deepest fog arose, where currents swirled their varying temperatures all around her as she floated on the water. It was there that her body danced on the water with no volition of her own, where she could surrender herself utterly to the Oversoul.

Who was the holy woman speaking about? The "him" with blood on his hands, the "he" that she could take by the waters—presumably the waters of the lake.

No, it was nothing. The holy woman was one of the mad ones, making no sense.

The only man she could think of who had blood on his hands was Gaballufix. How could the Oversoul want such a man as that to come near the holy lake? Would the time come when she would have to save Gaballufix's life? How could such a thing possibly fit in with the purposes of the Oversoul?

She turned left onto Tower Street, then turned right onto Rain Street, which curved around until she stood before Rasa's house. Home, unharmed. Of course. The Oversoul had protected her. The message she had delivered was *not* the whole purpose the Oversoul had for her; Luet would live to do other work. It was a great relief to her. For hadn't her own mother told Aunt Rasa, on the day she put Luet as an infant into Rasa's arms, "This one will live only as long as she serves the Mother of Mothers?" The Mother of Mothers had preserved her for another night.

Luet had expected to get back into Aunt Rasa's house without waking anyone, but she hadn't taken into account how the new climate of fear in the city had changed even the household of the leading housemistress of Basilica. The front door was locked on the inside. Still hoping to enter unobserved, she looked for a window she might climb through. Only now did she realize that all the windows facing the street were solely for the passage of light and air—many vertical slits in the wall, carved or sculpted with delicate designs, but with no gap wide enough to let even the head and shoulders of a child pass through.

This is not the first time there has been fear in Basilica, she thought. This house is designed to keep someone from entering surreptitiously in the night. Protection from burglars, of course; but perhaps such windows were designed primarily to keep rejected suitors and lapsed mates from forcing their way back into a house that they had come to think of as their own.

The provisions that kept a man from entering also barred Luet, slight as she was. She knew, of course, that there was no way to get around the sides of the house, since the neighboring structures leaned against the massive stone walls of Rasa's house.

Why didn't she guess that getting back inside would be so much harder than getting out? She had left after dark, of course, but well before the house quieted down for the evening; Hushidh knew something of her errand and would keep anyone from discovering her absence. It simply hadn't occurred to either of them to arrange how Luet would get back in. Aunt Rasa had never locked the front door before. And later, after the Oversoul had made the guard doze on the way out and had kept him away from the gate entirely on her return, Luet had assumed that the Oversoul was smoothing the way for her.

Luet thought of staying out on the porch all night. But it was cold now. As long as she had been walking, it was all right, she had stayed warm enough. Sleep, though, would be dangerous. City women, at least those of good breeding, did not own the right clothing for sleeping out of doors. What the holy women did would make her ill.

There might be another way, however. Wasn't Aunt Rasa's portico on the valley-side of the house completely open? There might be a way to climb up from the valley. Of course, the area just east of Rasa's portico was the wildest, emptiest part of the Shelf—it wasn't even part of a district, and though Sour Street ran out into it, there was no road there; women never went that way to get to the lake.

Yet she knew that this was the way she must go, if she was to return to Aunt Rasa's house.

The Oversoul again, leading her. Leading her, but telling her nothing.

Why not? asked Luet for the thousandth time. Why can't you tell me your purpose? If you had told me I was going to Wetchik's house, I wouldn't have been so fearful all the way. How did my fear and ignorance serve your purpose? And now you send me around to the wild country east of Aunt Rasa's house—for what purpose? Do you take pleasure in toying with me? Or am I too stupid to understand your purpose? I'm your homing dove, able to carry your messages but never worth explaining them to.

And yet, despite her resentment, a few minutes she stepped from the last cobbles of Sour Street onto the grass and then plunged into the pathless woods of the Shelf.

The ground was rugged, and all the gaps and breaks in the underbrush seemed to lead downward, away from Rasa's portico and toward the cliffs looming over the canyon of the Holy Road. No wonder that even the Shelf women built no houses here. But Luet refused to be led astray by the easy paths—she knew they would disappear the moment she started following them. Instead she forced her way through the underbrush. The zarosel thorns snagged at her, and she knew they would leave tiny welts that would sting for days even under a layer of Aunt Rasa's balm. Worse, she was bone-weary, cold, and sleepy, so that at times she caught herself waking up, even though she had not been asleep. Still—she had set herself on this course, and she would finish.

She came into a small clearing where bright moonlight filtered through the canopy of leaves overhead. In a month all the leaves would be gone and these thickets would not be half so forbidding. Now, though, a patch of light came like a miracle, and she blinked.

In that eyeblink, the clearing changed. There was a woman standing there.

"Aunt Rasa," whispered Luet. How did she know to come looking for me here? Has the Oversoul spoken again to someone else?

But it was not Aunt Rasa, after all. It was Hushidh. How could she have made such a mistake?

No. Not a mistake. For now Hushidh had changed again. It was Eiadh now, that beautiful girl from Hushidh's class, the one that poor Nafai was so uselessly in love with. And again the woman was transformed, into the actress Dol, who had been so very famous as a young girl; she was one of Aunt Rasa's nieces, and in recent years had returned to the house to teach. Once it was said that Dolltown was named after her (though it had been named such for ten thousand years at least), she was so beautiful and broke so many hearts; but she was in her twenties now, and the features that, when she was a girl, made women want to mother her and ravished the eyes of men were not so astonishing in a woman. Still, Luet would give half her life if during the other half she could be as delicately, sweetly beautiful as Dol.

Why is the Oversoul showing me these women?

From Dol the apparition changed to Shedemei, another of Aunt Rasa's nieces. If anything, though, Shedya was the opposite of Dol and Eiadh. At twenty-six she was still in Aunt Rasa's house, helping to teach science to the older students as her own reputation as a geneticist grew. Most nights she actually slept in her laboratory, many streets away, instead of her room in Rasa's house, but still she was a strong, quiet presence there. Shedemei was unbeautiful; not so ugly as to startle the onlooker, but deeply plain, so that the longer one studied her face the less attractive it became. Yet her mind was like a magnet, drawn to truth: as soon as it came near enough, she would leap to it and cling. Of all Aunt Rasa's nieces, she was the one that Luet most admired; but Luet knew that no more had she the wit to emulate Shedemei than she had the beauty to follow Dol's career. The Oversoul had chosen to send her visions to one who had no other use to the world.

The woman was gone. Luet was alone in the clearing, and she felt again as if she had just awakened.

Was this only a dream, the kind that comes when you don't even know that you're asleep?

Behind where the apparitions had stood, she saw a single light burning in the dark of earliest morning. It had to be on Aunt Rasa's portico —in that direction there could be no other source of light. Maybe the vision had been right thus far. Aunt Rasa was awake, and waiting for her.

She pushed forward into the brush. Low twigs swiped at her, thorns snagged at her clothing and her skin, and the irregular ground deceived her, causing her to trip and stumble. Always, though, that light was her beacon, drawing her on until at last it went out of sight as she drew under the lip of Rasa's portico.

It rose in a single sheet of weathered stone, sheer from base to balustrade, with no handholds. And it was at least four meters from the ground to the top. Even if Aunt Rasa was there waiting for her, there'd be no way to climb up, not without calling for servants. And if she was going to have to disturb the house anyway, she might as well have pulled the bellcord at the front door!

It happened that after having been forced this way and that by the rough ground of the forest, Luet had finally approached Rasa's house almost from the south. Most of the face of the portico was hidden from her. It was possible that the house had been built with some access from the portico to the wood. Surely the builders had planned for more than a mere *view* of the Rift Valley. And even if there was no deliberate access, there had to be a spot where she would have some hope of climbing up.

Making her way around the curved stone surface, Luet at last found what she had hoped for—a place where the broken ground rose higher in relation to the portico. Now the top of the balustrade was only an arm's length out of her reach. And, as she reached up to try to find a handhold in the gaps of the balustrade, she saw Aunt Rasa's face, as welcome as sunrise, and her arms reaching down for her.

If Luet had been any larger, Aunt Rasa probably could not have lifted her weight; but then, had she been larger she might have climbed up without help.

When at last she sat on the bench with Aunt Rasa half-cradling her, on the verge of weeping with relief and exhaustion, Aunt Rasa asked the obvious question. "What under the moon were you doing out there instead of coming to the front door like any other student coming back

home after hours? Were you so afraid of a reprimand that you thought
it would be better to risk your neck in the woods at night?"

Luet shook her head. "In the wood I saw a vision," she said. "But I
might have seen it anyway, so coming around that way was probably
my own foolishness."

Then there was nothing for Luet to do but tell Aunt Rasa about all
that had happened—the vision she had told to Nafai, warning of the
plot to murder Wetchik; the words of the holy woman in the dark
street; and finally the vision of Rasa and a few of her nieces.

"I can't think what such a vision might mean," said Rasa. "If the
Oversoul didn't tell *you*, how can *I* guess?"

"I don't want to guess anything anyway," said Luet. "I don't want
any more visions or talk of visions or anything except I hurt all over and
I want to go to bed."

"Of course you do, of course," said Aunt Rasa. "You can sleep, and
leave it to Wetchik and me to think what course of action to take now.
Unless he was stupid enough to decide that honor required him to
keep that treacherous rendezvous at the coolhouse."

A terrible thought occurred to Luet. "What if Nafai didn't tell him?"

Aunt Rasa looked at her sharply. "Nafai, not warn his father about a
plot against his life? You're speaking of my son."

What could that mean to Luet, who had never known her mother
and whose father could be any man in the city, with the most brutish
men the likeliest candidates? Mother and son—it was a connection that
held no particular authority for her. In a world of faithless promises,
anything was possible.

No, it was her weariness telling her to trust no one. She was doubting Aunt Rasa's judgment here, not just Nafai's faithfulness. Obviously
her mind was not functioning clearly. She allowed Aunt Rasa to half-
lead, half-carry her up the stairs to Rasa's own room, and place Luet on
the great soft bed of the mistress of the house, where she slept almost
before realizing where she was.

"Out all night," said Hushidh.

Luet opened one eye. The light coming through the window was
very bright, but the air had a chill in it. Full day, and Luet was only
waking now.

"And then not even the brains to come in the front door."

"I don't always rely on my brains," said Luet quietly.

"That much I knew," said Hushidh. "You should have taken me with you."

"Two people are always less obvious than one."

"To Wetchik's house! Didn't it occur to you that I might actually know the way there and back?"

"I didn't know that was where I was going."

"Alone at night. Anything could have happened. And you binding me with that foolish oath to tell no one. Aunt Rasa almost skinned me alive and hung me out to dry on the front porch when she realized that I must have known you were gone and didn't tell her."

"Don't be cross with me, Hushidh."

"Whole city's in turmoil, you know."

A sudden fear stabbed through her. "No, Hushidh—don't tell me there was murder after all!"

"Murder? Not likely. Wetchik's gone, though, him and his sons all, and Gaballufix is claiming that it was because he uncovered Wetchik's plot to murder him and Roptat at a secret meeting that Wetchik arranged at his coolhouse near Music Gate."

"That's not true," said Luet.

"Well, I didn't think it was," said Hushidh. "I only told you what Gaballufix's people are saying. His soldiers are thick in the streets."

"I'm so tired, Hushidh, and there's nothing I can do about any of this."

"Aunt Rasa thinks you can do something," said Hushidh. "That's why she sent me to wake you."

"Did she?"

"Well, you know her. She sent me up twice to 'see if poor Luet is still getting some of that rest she needs so much.' The third time I finally caught on that she was waiting for you to wake up but didn't have the heart to give instructions for me to do it."

"How thoughtful of you to read between the lines, my darling jewel of a big sister."

"You can nap again later, my sweet yagda-berry of a little sister."

It took only moments to wash and dress, for Luet was young enough that Aunt Rasa did not insist on her learning how to make hair and clothing graceful and dignified before appearing in public. As a child, she could be her scrawny, gawky self, which certainly took less effort. When Luet got downstairs, Aunt Rasa was in her salon with a man, a stranger, but Rasa introduced him at once.

"This is Rashgallivak, dear Luet. He is perhaps the most loyal and trustworthy man alive, or so my beloved mate has always said."

"I have served the Wetchik estate all my life," said Rashgallivak, "and will do so until I die. I may not be of the great houses, but I am still a true Palwashantu."

Aunt Rasa nodded. Luet wondered whether she was supposed to hear this man with belief or with irony; Rasa seemed to be trusting him, however, and so Luet gave her tentative trust as well.

"I understand that it was you who brought warning," said Rashgallivak.

Luet looked at Aunt Rasa in surprise. "He'll tell no one else," said Aunt Rasa. "I have his oath. We don't want to involve you in the politics of murder, my dear. But Rash had to know it, so that he didn't think my Wetchik had lost his mind. Wetchik left him detailed instructions, you see, to do something quite mad."

"Close everything down," said Rashgallivak. "Dismiss all but the fewest possible employees, sell off all the pack animals, and liquidate the stock. I'm to hold only the land, the buildings, and the liquid assets, in untouchable accounts. Very suspicious, if my master is innocent. Or so some would say. *Do* say."

"Wetchik's absence wasn't known for half an hour before Gaballufix was at Wetchik's house, demanding as the head of the Palwashantu clan that all the property of the Wetchik family be turned over to him. He had the audacity to refer to my mate by his birth name, Volemak, as if he had forfeited his right to the family title."

"If my master has really left Basilica permanently," said Rashgallivak, "then Gaballufix would be within his rights. The property can never be sold or given away from the Palwashantu."

"And I'm trying to persuade Rashgallivak that it was *your* warning of immediate danger that caused Wetchik to flee, not some plot to leave the city and take the family fortune with him."

Luet understood her duty now, in this conversation. "I did speak with Nafai," Luet told Rashgallivak. "I warned him that Gaballufix meant to murder Wetchik and Roptat—or at least my dream certainly seemed to suggest that."

Rashgallivak nodded slowly. "This will not be enough to bring charges against Gaballufix, of course. In Basilica, even *men* are not tried for acts they plotted but never performed. But it's enough to persuade me to resist Gaballufix's efforts to obtain the property."

"I was mated with him once, you know," said Rasa. "I know Gabya very well. I suggest you take extraordinary measures to protect the fortune—liquid assets particularly."

"No one will have them but the head of the house of Wetchik," said Rashgallivak. "Madam, I thank you. And you, little wise one."

He said not another word, but left immediately. Not at all like the more stylish men—artists, scientists, men of government and finance—whom Luet had met in Aunt Rasa's salon before. That sort of man always lingered, until Aunt Rasa had to force their departure by feigning weariness or pretending that she had pressing duties in the school —as if her teaching staff were not competent to handle things without her direct supervision. But then, Rashgallivak was of a social class that could not reasonably contemplate mating with one like Aunt Rasa, or any of her nieces.

"I'm sorry you didn't get more sleep," said Aunt Rasa, "but glad that you happened to wake up at such a fortunate time."

Luet nodded. "So much of last night I felt as if I were walking in my sleep, perhaps I only needed half as much this morning."

"I would send you back to bed at once," said Aunt Rasa, "but I must ask you a question first."

"Unless it's something we've studied recently in class, I won't know the answer, my lady."

"Don't pretend you don't know what I'm talking about."

"Don't imagine that I actually understand anything about the Oversoul."

Luet knew at once that she had spoken too flippantly. Aunt Rasa's eyebrows rose, and her nostrils flared—but she contained her anger, and spoke without sharpness. "Sometimes, my dear, you forget yourself. You pretend to take no special honor to yourself because the Oversoul has made a seer of you, and yet you speak to me with impertinence that no other woman in this city, young or old, would dare to use. Which should I believe, your modest words or your proud manner?"

Luet bowed her head. "My words, Mistress. My manner is the natural rudeness of a child."

Laughing, Aunt Rasa answered, "*Those* words are the hardest to believe of all. I'll spare you my questions after all. Go back to bed now —but this time in your own bed—no one will disturb you there, I promise."

Luet was at the door of the salon when it opened and a young woman burst in, forcing her back inside the room.

"Mother, this is abominable!" cried the visitor.

"Sevet, I'm so delighted to see you after all these months—and without a word of notice that you were coming, or even the courtesy of waiting until I invited you into my salon."

Sevet—Aunt Rasa's oldest daughter. Luet had seen her only once before. As was the custom, Rasa did not teach her own daughters, but rather had given them to her dear friend Dhelembuvex to raise. This one, her oldest, was mated with a young scholar of some note—Vas?— but it hadn't hampered her career as a singer with a growing reputation for having a way with pichalny songs, the low melancholy songs of death and loss that were an ancient tradition in Basilica. There was nothing of pichalny about her now, though—she was sharp and angry, and her mother no less so. Luet decided to leave the room at once, before she overheard another word.

But Aunt Rasa wouldn't allow it. "Stay, Luet. I think it will be educational for you to see how little this daughter of mine takes after either her mother *or* her Aunt Dhel."

Sevet glared sharply at Luet. "What's *this*—are you taking charity cases now?"

"Her mother was a holy woman, Sevya. I think you may even have heard the name of Luet."

Sevet blushed at once. "I beg your pardon," she said.

Luet had no idea how to answer, since of course Luet *was* a charity case and therefore mustn't show that she had been offended by Sevet's slur.

Aunt Rasa saved her from having to think of a proper response. "I will consider that pardon has been begged and granted all around, and now we may begin our conversation with perhaps a more civil tone."

"Of course," said Sevet. "You must realize that I came here straight from Father."

"From your rude and offensive manner, I assumed you had spent at least an hour with him."

"Raging, the poor man. And how could he do otherwise, with his own mate spreading terrible lies about him!"

"Poor man indeed," said Aunt Rasa. "I'm surprised that little waif of a mate of his would have the courage to speak out against him—or the wit to make up a lie, for that matter. What has she been saying?"

"I meant *you*, of course, Mother, not his *present* mate, nobody thinks of *her*."

"But since I lapsed dear Gabya's contract fifteen years ago, he can hardly regard *me* as having a duty to refrain from telling the truth about him."

"Mother, don't be impossible."

"I'm never impossible. The most I ever allow myself is to be somewhat unlikely."

"You're the mother of Father's two daughters, both of us more than slightly famous—the *most* famous of your offspring, and all for honorable things, though of course little Koya's career has only at its beginning, with not a myachik of her own yet—"

"Spare me your rivalry with your sister, please."

"It's only a rivalry from *her* point of view, Mother—*I* don't even pay attention to the fact that her singing career seems a bit sluggish at the outset. It's always harder for a lyric soprano to be noticed—there are so *many* of them, one can hardly tell them apart, unless one is the soprano's own loving, loyal sister."

"Yes, I use you as an example of loyalty for all my girls."

For a moment Sevet's face brightened; then she realized her mother was teasing her, and scowled. "You really are too nasty with me."

"If your father sent you to get me to retract my remarks about this morning's events, you can tell him that I know what he was planning from an undoubtable source, and if he doesn't stop telling people that Wetchik was plotting murder, I'll bring my evidence before the council and have him banned."

"I can't—I can't tell Father that!" said Sevet.

"Then don't," said Aunt Rasa. "Let him find out when I do it."

"*Ban* him? Ban *Father*?"

"If you had studied more history—though come to think of it, I doubt that Dhelya taught you all that much anyway—you'd know that the more powerful and famous a man is, the more likely he is to be banned from Basilica. It's been done before, and it will be done again. After all, it's Gabya, not Wetchik or Roptat, whose soldiers roam the streets, pretending to protect us from thugs that Gabya probably hired in the first place. People will be glad to see him go—and that means they'll find it *useful* to believe every bit of evidence I bring."

Sevet's face grew grave. "Father may be a bit prone to rage and a little sneaky in business, Mother, but he's no murderer."

"Of course he's not a murderer. Wetchik left Basilica and Gabya would never dare to kill Roptat without Wetchik there to blame it on. Though I think that if Gabya had known at the time that Wetchik had fled, he would certainly have killed Roptat the moment he showed up and then used Wetchik's hasty departure as proof that my dear mate was the murderer."

"You make Father sound like a monster. Why did you take him as a mate, then?"

"Because I wanted to have a daughter with an extraordinary singing voice and no moral judgment whatsoever. It worked so well that I renewed with him for a second year and had another. And then I was done."

Sevet laughed. "You're such a silly thing, Mother. I *do* have moral judgment, you know. And every other kind. It was Vasya I married, not some second-rate actor."

"Stop sniping at your sister's choice of mate," said Aunt Rasa. "Kokor's Obring is a dear, even if he has no talent whatsoever and not the breath of a chance that Koya will actually bear him a child, let alone renew him."

"A *dear*," said Sevet. "I'll have to remember what that word *really* means, now that you've told me."

Sevet got up to leave. Luet opened the door for her. But Aunt Rasa stopped her daughter before she left.

"Sevya, dear," she said. "The time may come when you have to choose between your father and me."

"The two of you have made me do that at least once a month since I was very small. I've managed to sidestep you both so far, and I intend to continue."

Rasa clapped her hands together—loudly, a sharp report like one stone striking another. "Listen to me, child. I know the dance that you've done, and I've both admired you for the way you did it and pitied you for the fact that it was necessary. What I'm saying to you is that soon—very soon—it may no longer be possible to do that dance. So it's time for you to look at both your parents and decide which one deserves your loyalty. I do not say *love*, because I know you love us both. I say loyalty."

"You shouldn't speak to me this way, Mother," said Sevet. "I'm not your student. And even if you succeeded in banning Father, that still wouldn't mean I'd have to choose between you."

"What if your father sent soldiers to silence me? Or tolchocks—
which is more likely. What if it was a knife he paid for that slit your
mother's throat?"

Sevet regarded her mother in silence. "Then I'd have a pichalny
song to sing indeed, wouldn't I?"

"I believe that your father is the enemy of the Oversoul, and the
enemy of Basilica as well. Think about this seriously, my sad-voiced
Sevet, think deep and long, because when the day of choosing comes
there'll be no time to think."

"I have always honored you, Mother, for the fact that you never tried
to turn me against my father, despite all the vile things he said about
you. I'm sorry you have changed." With great dignity, Sevet swept
herself from the room. Luet, still a bit stunned by the brutal nature of
the conversation under the veneer of elegant speech, was slow to follow her out the door.

"Luet," whispered Aunt Rasa.

Luet turned to face the great woman, and trembled inside to see the
tears on her cheeks.

"Luet, you must tell me. What is the Oversoul doing to us? What
does the Oversoul plan?"

"I don't know," said Luet. "I wish I did."

"*If* you did, would you tell me?"

"Of course."

"Even if the Oversoul told you not to?"

Luet hadn't thought of such a possibility.

Aunt Rasa took her hesitation for an answer. "So," she said. "I
wouldn't have expected otherwise—the Oversoul does not choose
weak servants, or disloyal ones. But tell me this, if you can: Is it possible, is it *possible*, that there was no plot to kill Wetchik at all? That the
Oversoul merely sent that warning to get him to leave Basilica? You
must realize—I was thinking that—Lutya, what if the only thing the
Oversoul was doing was getting rid of Issib and Nafai? It makes sense,
doesn't it—they were interfering with the Oversoul, keeping her so
busy that she couldn't speak to anyone but them. Might she not have
sent your vision to make sure they left the city, because *they* were
threatening to *her?*"

Luet's first impulse was to shout her denial, to rebuke her for daring
to speak so sacrilegiously of the Oversoul—as if it would act for its own
private benefit.

But then, on sober reflection, she remembered with what wonderment Hushidh had told her of her realization that Issib and Nafai might well be the reason for the Oversoul's silence. And if the Oversoul thought that her ability to guide and protect her daughters was being hampered by these two boys, couldn't she act to remove them?

"No," said Luet. "I don't think so."

"Are you sure?"

"I'm never sure, except of the vision itself," said Luet. "But I've never known the Oversoul to deceive me. All my visions have been true."

"But this one would still be a true instrument of the Oversoul's will."

"No," said Luet again. "No, it couldn't be. Because Nafai and Issib had already stopped. Nafai even went and prayed—"

"So I heard, but then, so did Mebbekew, Wetchik's son by that miserable little whoreling Kilvishevex—"

"And the Oversoul spoke to Nafai and woke him up, and brought him outside to meet me in the traveler's room. If the Oversoul wanted Nafai to be still, she would have told him, and he would have obeyed. No, Aunt Rasa, I'm sure the message was real."

Aunt Rasa nodded. "I know. I knew it was. It would just be . . ."

"Simpler."

"Yes." She smiled ruefully. "Simpler if Gaballufix were as innocent as he pretends. But not true to character. You know why I lapsed him?"

"No," said Luet. Nor did she want to know—by long custom a woman never told her reasons for lapsing a man, and it was a hideous breach of etiquette to ask or even speculate on the subject.

"I shouldn't tell, but I will—because you're one who must know the truth in order to understand all things."

I'm also a child, thought Luet. You'd never tell any of your *other* thirteen-year-olds about such things. You'd never even tell your daughter. But I, *I* am a seer, and so everything is opened up before me and I am forbidden to remain innocent of anything except joy.

"I lapsed him because I learned that he . . ."

Luet braced herself for some sordid revelation, but it did not come.

"No, child, no. Just because the Oversoul speaks to you doesn't mean that I should burden you with my secrets. Go, sleep. Forget my questions, if you can. I know my Wetchik. And I know Gaballufix, too. Both of them, down to the deepest shadow of their souls. It was for my daughters' sake that I wished to find some impossible thing, like

Gabya's innocence." She chuckled. "I'm like a child, forever wishing for impossible things. Like your vision in the woods, before I drew you up to the portico. You saw all my most brilliant nieces, like a roll call of judgment."

Brilliant? Shedemei and Hushidh, yes, but Dol and Eiadh, those women of paint and tinsel?

"I was so happy to know that the Oversoul knew them, and linked them with me and you in the vision she sent. But where were my daughters, Lutya? I wish that you had seen my Sevya and my Koya. I do wish that—is that silly of me?"

Yes. "No."

"You should practice lying more," said Aunt Rasa, "so you'd be better at it. Go to bed, my sweet seer."

Luet obeyed, but slept little.

In the days that followed, the turmoil in the city increased, to the point where it was almost impossible for classes to continue in Aunt Rasa's house. It wasn't just the constant worry, either. It was the disappearance of so many faces, especially from the younger classes. Only a few children were withdrawn because their parents disapproved of Rasa's political stance. Children were being taken out of every teaching household, great or common, and restored to their families; many families had even closed up their houses and gone on unnamed holidays to unknown places, presumably waiting for whatever terrible day was coming to be over.

How Luet envied Nafai and Issib, safe as they were in some distant land, not having to live in constant fear in this city that had so long been known by the poets as the Mountain of Peace.

As the petition for the banning of Gaballufix gained support in the council, Gaballufix himself became bolder in the way he used his soldiers in the streets. There were more of them, for one thing, and there was no more pretense of protecting the citizenry from tolchocks. The soldiers accosted whomever they wanted, sending women and children home in tears, and beating men who spoke up to them.

"Is he a fool?" Hushidh asked Luet one day. "Doesn't he know that everything his soldiers do gives his enemies one more reason to ban him?"

"He must know," said Luet, "and so he must want to be banned."

"Then hasten the day," said Hushidh, "and good riddance to him."

Luet waited for a vision from the Oversoul, some message of warning she should take to the council. Instead the only vision that came was a word of comfort to an old woman in the district of Olive Grove, assuring her that her long-lost son was still alive, and homebound on a ship that would reach port before too long. Luet didn't know whether to be comforted that the Oversoul still took the time to answer the heartfelt prayers of broken-hearted women, or infuriated that the Oversoul was spending time on such matters instead of healing the city before it tore itself apart.

Then at last the most feared moment came. The doorbell clanged, and strong fists beat on the door, and when the door was thrown open, there stood a dozen soldiers. The servant who opened the door screamed, and not just because they were armed men in perilous times. Luet was among the first to come to the aid of the terrified servant, and saw what had so unnerved her. All the soldiers were in identical uniforms, with identical armor and helmets and charged-wire blades, as might be expected—but inside those helmets, each one also had an identical face.

It was Rasa's oldest niece, Shedemei, the geneticist, who spoke to the soldiers. "You have no legitimate business here," she said. "No one wants you. Go away."

"I'll see the mistress of this household or I'll never go," said the soldier who stood in front of the others.

"She has no business with you, I said."

But then Aunt Rasa was there, and her voice rang clear. "Close the door in the face of these hired criminals," she said.

At once the lead soldier laughed, and reached his hand to his waist. In an instant he was transformed before their eyes, from a youngish, dead-faced soldier to a middle-aged man with a grizzled beard and fiercely bright eyes, stout but not soft-bellied, clothed not in armor but in quietly elegant clothing. A man of style and power, who thought the whole situation was enormously amusing.

"Gabya," said Aunt Rasa.

"How do you like my new toys?" asked Gaballufix, striding into the house. Women and girls and young boys parted to make way for him. "Old theatrical equipment, out of style for centuries, but they were in a stasis bubble in the museum and the maker machines still remembered how to copy them. Holocostumes, they're called. All my soldiers have them now. It makes them somewhat hard to tell apart, I admit, but then, I have the master switch that can turn them all off when I want."

"Leave my house," said Rasa.

"But I don't want to," said Gaballufix. "I want to talk to you."

"Without *them*, you can speak to me any time. You know that, Gabya."

"I knew that *once*," said Gaballufix. "Truth to tell, O noblest of my mates, my unforgotten bed-bundle, I knew that my soldiers would never impress you—I just wanted to show you the latest fashion. Soon all the best people will be wearing them."

"Only in their coffins," said Aunt Rasa.

"Do you want to hold this conversation in front of the children, or shall we retire to your sacred portico?"

"Your soldiers wait outside the door. The *locked* door."

"Whatever you say, O mother of my duet of sweet songbirds. Though your door, with all its locks, would be no barrier if I wanted them inside."

"People who are sure of their power don't have to brag," said Aunt Rasa. She led the way down the corridor as Shedemei closed and barred the front door in the soldiers' faces.

Luet could still hear the conversation between Aunt Rasa and Gaballufix even after they turned a corner and were out of sight.

"I don't *have* to brag," Gaballufix was saying. "I do it for the sheer joy of it."

Instead of answering, though, Aunt Rasa called loudly down the corridor.

"Luet! Hushidh! Come with me. I want witnesses."

At once Luet strode forward, with Hushidh beside her at once. Because Aunt Rasa had brought them up, they didn't run, but their walk was brisk enough that they had turned the corner and could hear Gaballufix's last few whispered words before they caught up. ". . . not afraid of your witchlets," he was saying.

Luet gave no sign that she had heard, of course. She knew that Hushidh's face would be even less expressive.

Out on the portico, Gaballufix made no pretense of respecting the boundary of Aunt Rasa's screens. He strode directly to the balustrade, looking out at the view that was forbidden to the eyes of men. Aunt Rasa did not follow him, so Luet and Hushidh also remained behind the screens. At last Gaballufix returned to where they waited.

"Always a beautiful sight," he said.

"For that act alone you could be banned," said Aunt Rasa.

Gaballufix laughed. "Your sacred lake. How long do you think it will go unmuddied by the boots of men, if the Wetheads come? Have you thought of that—have Roptat and your beloved Volemak thought of it? The Wetheads have no reverence for women's religion."

"Even less than you?"

Gaballufix rolled his eyes to show his disdain for her accusation. "If Roptat and Volemak have their way, the Wetheads would own this city, and to them, the view from this portico would not be a view of holy land—it would all be city property, undeveloped land, potential building sites and hunting parks, and an extraordinary lake, with both hot and cold water for bathing in any weather."

Luet was astonished that so much of the nature of the lake had been explained to him. What woman had so forgotten herself as to speak of the sacred place?

Yet Aunt Rasa said nothing of the impropriety of his words. "Bringing the Wetheads is Roptat's plan. Wetchik and I have spoken for nothing but the ancient neutrality."

"Neutrality! Fools and children believe in that. There *is* no neutrality when great powers collide!"

"In the power of the Oversoul there is neutrality and peace," said Aunt Rasa, calm in the face of his storm. "She has the power to turn aside our enemies so they see us not at all."

"Power? Maybe he has power, all right, this Oversoul—but I've seen no evidence that he saves poor innocent cities from destruction. How did it happen that I alone am the champion of Basilica, the only one who can see that safety lies only in alliance with Potokgavan?"

"Save the patriotic speeches for the council, Gabya. In front of me, there's no point in hiding behind them. The wagons offered some easy profit. And as for war—you know so little about it that you think you want it to come. You think that you'll stand beside the mighty soldiers of Potokgavan and drive off the Wetheads, and your name will be remembered forever. But *I* tell you that when you stand against your enemy, you'll stand alone. No Potoku will be there beside you. And when you fall your name will be forgotten as quickly as last week's weather."

"*This* storm, my dear lapsatory mate, has a name, and will be remembered."

"Only for the damage that you caused, Gabya. When Basilica burns, every tongue of flame will be branded Gaballufix, and the dying curse of every citizen who falls will have your name in it."

"Now who fancies herself a prophet?" said Gaballufix. "Save your poetics for those who tremble at the thought of the Oversoul. And as for your banning—succeed or fail, it makes no difference."

"You mean that you don't intend to obey?"

"*Me?* Disobey the *council?* Unthinkable. No one will find me in the city after I am banned, you can be sure of that."

But with those words he reached down and switched on his holocostume. At once he was armored in illusion, his face an undetectable mask of a vaguely menacing soldier, like any of the hundreds of others he had so equipped. Luet knew then that he had no intention of obeying a banning. He would simply wear this most perfect of disguises, so that no one could identify him. He would stay within the city, doing whatever he wanted, flouting the council's edicts with impunity. Then the only hope of freeing the city from his rule would not be political. It would be civil war, and the streets would flow with blood.

Luet knew from her eyes that Aunt Rasa understood this. She looked steadily at the empty eyes that stared back at her from Gaballufix's holocostume. She said nothing when he turned and left; said nothing at all, in fact, until at last Luet took Hushidh's hand and they walked away to the edge of the portico, to look out over the Valley of Women.

"There's nothing between them anymore," said Hushidh. "I could see it fall, the last tie of love or even of concern. If he died tonight, she would be content."

To Luet this seemed the most terrible of tragedies. Once these two had been joined together in love, or something like love; they had made two babies, and yet, only fifteen years later, the last tie between them was broken now. All lost, all gone. Nothing lasted, nothing. Even this forty-million-year world that the Oversoul had preserved as if in ice, even it would melt before the fire. Permanence was always an illusion, and love was just the disguise that lovers wore to hide the death of their union from each other for a while.

10

Tents

Wetchik had pitched his tents away from any road, in a narrow river valley near the shores of the Rumen Sea. They had reached it at sunset, just as a troop of baboons moved away from their feeding area near the river's mouth, toward their sleeping niches in the steepest, craggiest cliff in the valley wall. It was the baboons' calls and hoots that guided them during the last of their journey; Elemak was careful to lead them well upstream of the baboons. "So we don't disturb them?" Issib asked.

"So they don't foul our water and steal our food," said Elemak.

Before Father allowed them to unburden the camels and water them, before they ate or drank anything themselves, Father sat atop his camel and gestured toward the stream. "Look—the end of the dry season, and yet it still has water in it. The name of this place is Elemak from now on. I name it for you, my eldest son. Be like the river, so that the purpose of your life is to flow forever toward the great ocean of the Oversoul."

Nafai glanced at Elemak and saw that he was taking the peroration with dignity. It was a sacred moment, the naming of a place, and even if Father laced the occasion with a sermon, Elemak knew that it was an honor, a sign that Father acknowledged him.

"And as for this green valley," said Father, "I name it Mebbekew, for my second son. Be like this valley, Mebbekew, a firm channel through which the waters of life can flow, and where life can take root and thrive."

Mebbekew nodded graciously.

There was nothing named for Issib and Nafai. Only a silence, and then Father's groan as his camel knelt for him to dismount. It was well after dark before they finally had the tents pitched, the scorpions swept outside, and the repellents set in place. Three tents—Father's, of course, the largest though he was only one man. The next largest for Elya and Meb. And the smallest for Issib and Nafai, even though Issib's chair took up an exorbitant amount of room inside.

Nafai couldn't help but brood about the inequities, and when, in the darkness of the tent, Issib asked him what he was thinking, Nafai went ahead and voiced his resentment. "He names the river and the valley for *them*, when Elemak's the one who was working with Gaballufix, and Mebbekew's the one who said all those terrible things to him and left home and everything."

"So?" said Issib, ever sympathetic.

"So here we are in the smallest tent. We've got two extras, still packed up, both of them larger than this one." Having undressed himself, Nafai now helped Issib undress—it was too hard for him, without his floats.

"Father's making a statement," said Issib.

"Yes, and I'm hearing it, and I don't like it. He's saying, Issib and Nafai, you're *nothing*."

"What was he going to do, name a *cloud* after us?" Issib fell silent for a moment as Nafai pulled the shirt off over Issib's head. "Or did you want him to name a bush for you?"

"I don't care about the naming, I care about justice."

"Get some perspective, Nafai. Father isn't going to sort out his children according to who's the most obedient or cooperative or polite from hour to hour. There's a clear ranking involved in the assignment of tent space here." Nafai laid his brother on his mat, farthest from the door. "The fact that Elya doesn't have a tent to himself, but shares with Meb," said Issib, "that's putting him in his place, reminding him that he's *not* the Wetchik, he's just the Wetchik's boy. But then putting us in such a tiny tent tells Elya and Meb that he *does* value them and honor them as his oldest sons. He's at once rebuking and encouraging them. I think he's been rather deft."

Nafai lay down on his own mat, near the door, in the traditional servant's position. "What about us?"

"What *about* us? Are you going to rebel against the Oversoul because your papa gave you a tiny tent?"

"No."

"Father trusts us to be loyal while he works on Elya and Meb. Father's trust is the greatest honor of all. I'm proud to be in this tent."

"When you put it that way," said Nafai, "so am I."

"Go to sleep."

"Wake me if you need anything."

"What can I need," said Issib, "when I have my chair beside me?"

Actually, the chair was down near his feet, and it was almost completely useless when Issib wasn't sitting in it. Nafai was puzzled for a moment, until he realized that Issib was giving him a small rebuke: Why are *you* complaining, Nafai, when being away from the magnetics of the city means that I can't use my floats, and have to be tended to like an infant? It must be humiliating for Issib to have me undress him, thought Nafai. And yet he bears it uncomplaining, for Father's sake.

Deep in the night, Nafai awoke, instantly alert. He lay there listening. Was it Issib who had called him? No—his brother was still taking the heavy, rhythmic breaths of sleep. Did he wake, then, because he was uncomfortable? No, for the sand under his mat made the floor more, not less, comfortable than his room at home. Nor was it the cold, nor the distant howling of a wild dog, and it could not have been the baboons, because they always slept the night in perfect silence.

The last time Nafai had awakened like this, he had found Luet outside in the traveler's room, and the Oversoul had spoken in the night to Father.

Was I dreaming, then? Did the Oversoul teach me in my sleep? But Nafai could remember no dreams. Just the sudden wakefulness.

He got up from his mat—quietly, so as not to disturb Issya—and slid under the netted fabric draped across the door. It was cooler outside the tent than inside, of course, but they had traveled far enough south that autumn hadn't yet arrived in this place, and the waters of the Rumen Sea were much warmer and more placid than the ocean that swept along the coastline east of Basilica.

The camels were peacefully asleep in their small temporary corral. The wards at the corners kept away even the smallest of animals not yet inured to the sound frequencies and pheromones the wards gave off. The stream splashed a syncopated music over the rocks. The leaves in the trees rustled now and then in the night breeze. If there is any place in all of Harmony where a man could sleep in peace, it's here, thought Nafai. And yet I couldn't sleep.

Nafai walked upstream and sat on a stone beside the water. The breeze was cool enough to chill him a little; for a moment he wished he had dressed before leaving the tent. But he hadn't intended to get up for the day. Soon enough he'd go back inside.

He looked around him, at the low hills not that far off. Unless a person stood on one of those hills, there was no sign of a watered valley here. Still, it was a wonder that no one lived here but the tribe of baboons downstream of them, that there wasn't even a sign of human habitation. Perhaps it had not been settled because it was so far from any trade route. The land here was barely enough to support a few dozen people, if it were all cultivated. It would be too lonely or unprofitable to settle here. Robbers might use it as a refuge, but it was too far from the caravan routes to be convenient for them. It was exactly what Father's family needed, during this time of exile from Basilica. As if it had been prepared for them.

For a moment Nafai wondered if perhaps this valley had not even existed until they needed it. Did the Oversoul have such power that it could transform landforms at will?

Impossible. The Oversoul might have such powers in myth and legend, but in the real world, the Oversoul's powers seemed to be entirely confined to communication—the sharing of works of art throughout the world, and mental influence over those who received visions or, more commonly, the stupor of thought that the Oversoul used to turn people away from forbidden ideas.

That's why this place was empty till we came, thought Nafai. It would be a simple thing for the Oversoul to make desert travelers get stupid whenever they thought of turning toward the Rumen Sea near here. The Oversoul prepared it for us, not by creating it out of the rock, not by causing some hidden pool of water to burst forth into a spring, a stream for us, but rather by keeping other people away from here, so that it was empty and ready for us when we came.

The Oversoul has some great purpose here, plans within plans. We listen for its voice, we heed the visions it puts into our minds, but we're still puppets, uncertain why our strings are being pulled, or what our dance will lead to in the end. It isn't right, thought Nafai. It isn't even good, for if the followers of the Oversoul are kept blind, if they can't judge the Oversoul's purpose for themselves, then they aren't freely choosing between good and evil, or between wise and foolish, but are only choosing to subsume themselves in the purposes of the Oversoul. How can the Oversoul's plans be well-served, if all its followers are the kind of weak-souled people who are willing to obey the Oversoul without understanding?

I will serve you, Oversoul, with my whole heart I'll serve you, if I understand what you're trying to do, what it *means*. And if your purpose is a good one.

Who am I to judge what's good and what isn't?

The thought came into Nafai's mind, and he laughed silently at his own arrogance. Who am I, to set myself up as the judge of the Oversoul?

Then he shuddered. What put such a thought into my mind? Couldn't it have been the Oversoul itself, trying to tame me? I will *not* be tamed, only persuaded. I will not be coerced or led blindly or tricked or bullied—I am willing only to be convinced. If you don't trust your own basic goodness enough to tell me what you're trying to do, Oversoul, then you're confessing your own moral weakness and I'll never serve you.

The moonlight sparkling on the shifting surface of the stream suddenly became sunlight reflected from metal satellites orbiting perpetually around the planet Harmony. In his mind's eye, Nafai saw how, one by one, the satellites stumbled in their orbit and fell, burning themselves into dust as they entered the atmosphere. The first human settlers of this world had built tools that would last ten or twenty million years. To them that had seemed like forever—it was longer than the existence of the human species, many times over. But now it had been forty million years, and the Oversoul had to do its work with only a quarter as many satellites as it had had in the beginning, barely half as many as it had had for the first thirty million years. No wonder the Oversoul had weakened.

But its plans were no less important. Its purpose still needed to be served. Issib and Nafai were right—the Oversoul had been set in place by the first human settlers in this place, for one purpose only: to make Harmony a world where humanity would never have the power to destroy itself.

Wouldn't it have been better, thought Nafai, to change humanity so it no longer *desired* to destroy itself?

The answer came into his mind with such clarity that he knew it was the answer of the Oversoul. No, it would not have been better.

But why? Nafai demanded.

An answer, many answers poured into his mind all at once, in such a burst that he could make no sense of them. But in the moments after, the moments of growing clarity, some of the ideas found language. Sentences as clear as if they had been spoken by another voice. But it was not another voice—it was Nafai's own voice, making a feeble attempt to capture in words some straggling remnant of what the Oversoul had said to him.

What the voice of the Oversoul said inside Nafai's mind was this: If I had taken away the desire for violence then humanity would not have been humanity. Not that human beings need to be violent in order to be human, but if you ever lose the will to control, the will to destroy, then it must be because you *chose* to lose it. My role was not to force you to be gentle and kind; it was to keep you alive while you decided for yourselves what kind of people you wanted to be.

Nafai was afraid to ask another question, for fear of drowning in the mental flood that might follow. And yet he couldn't leave the question unasked. Tell me slowly. Tell me gently. But *tell* me: What have we decided?

To his relief, the answer wasn't that same rush of pure unspeakable idea. This time it seemed to him as if a window had been opened in his mind, through which he could see. All the actual scenes, all the faces he saw, they were memories, things he had seen or heard of in Basilica, things that were already in his mind, ready for the Oversoul to draw on them, to bring them to the surface of his mind. But now he saw them with such clear understanding that they took on power and meaning beyond anything in his experience before. He saw memories of business dealings he had seen. He saw plays and satires he had watched. Conversations in the street. A holy woman being raped by a gang of drunken worshipers. The scheming of men who were trying to win a mating contract with a woman of note. The casual cruelty of women who played their suitors against each other. Even the way Elemak and Mebbekew had treated Nafai—and the way he had treated them. It all spoke of the willingness of people to hurt each other, the burning passion to control what other people thought and did. So many people, in secret, subtle ways, acted to destroy people—and not just their enemies, either, but also their friends. Destroying them for the pleasure of knowing that they had the power to cause pain. And so few who devoted their lives to building other people's strength and confidence. So few who were true teachers, genuine mates.

That's what Father and Mother are, thought Nafai. They stay together, not because of any gain, but because of the gift. Father doesn't stay with Mother because she is good for *him*, but rather because together they can do good for us, and for many others. Father entered into the politics of Basilica these last few weeks, not because he hoped to gain by it, the way Gaballufix did, but because he genuinely cared more about the good of Basilica than about his own fortune, his own life. He could walk away from his fortune without a second look. And Mother, her life is what she creates in the minds of her students. Through her girls, her boys, she is trying to create tomorrow's Basilica. Every word she breathes in the school is designed to keep the city from decay.

And yet they're losing. It's slipping away. The Oversoul would help them if it could, but it hasn't the power or influence that it once had; and anyway, it hasn't the freedom to act to make people goodhearted, only to keep their malice within fairly narrow boundaries. Spite and malice, that was the lifeblood of Basilica today; Gaballufix is only the man who happens to best express the poisonous heart of the city. Even those who hate him and fight against him are generally doing it, not because they are good and he is evil, but because they resent the fact that he is achieving dominance, when they had hoped for dominance for themselves.

I *would* help, said the silent voice of the Oversoul in Nafai's mind. I *would* help the good people of Basilica. But there aren't enough of them. The will of the city is for destruction. How then can I keep it from being destroyed? If Gaballufix fails in his plans, the city will raise up some other man to help it kill itself. The fire will come because the city craves it. They are far too few, those who love the living city instead of desiring to feed from its corpse.

Tears flowed from Nafai's eyes. I didn't understand. I never saw the city this way.

That's because you are your mother's son, your father's heir. Like all human beings, you assume that behind the masks of their faces, other people are fundamentally like yourself. But it isn't always so. Some of them can't see other people's happiness without wanting to destroy it, can't see the bonds of love between friends or mates without wanting to break them. And many others, who aren't malicious in themselves, become their tools in the hope of some short-term gain. The people have lost their vision. And I haven't the power to restore it. All that's left, Nafai, is my memory of Earth.

"Tell me about Earth," whispered Nafai.

Again a window opened in his mind, only now it was not memories of his own. Instead he was seeing things he had never seen before. It overwhelmed him; he could hardly make sense of the things he saw. Bright glass-and-metal caskets speeding along gray-ribbon highways. Massive metal houses that rose up in the air, skidding along the face of the sky on slender, fragile wedges of painted steel. Tall polyhedral buildings with mirrored faces, reflecting each other, reflecting the yellow sunlight. And there amid them, shacks made of paper and cast-off metal, where families watched their babies die with bloated bellies. People tossing balls of fire at each other, or great gouts of flame flowing out of hoses. And completely inexplicable things: one of the flying houses passing over a city, dropping something that seemed as insignificant as a turd, only suddenly it burst into a ball of flame as bright as the sun, and the entire city under it was flattened, and the rubble burned. A family sitting at a huge table, covered in food, eating ravenously, then leaning over and vomiting on ragged beggars that clung hopelessly to the legs of their chairs. Surely this vision was not literal, but figurative! Surely no one ever would be so morally bankrupt as to eat more than he needed, while others were dying of hunger before their eyes! Surely anyone who could think of a way to make the sky burst into flame so hot it could destroy a whole city at once, surely such a person would kill himself before he'd ever let anyone know the terrible secret of that weapon.

"Is this Earth?" he whispered to the Oversoul. "So beautiful and monstrous? Is this what we were?"

Yes, came the answer. It's what you were, and it's what you will be again, if I can't find a way to re-awaken the world to my voice. In Basilica there are many who eat their fill of food, and then eat more, while they know how many there are who haven't enough. There's a famine only three hundred kilometers to the north.

"We could use wagons to carry food there," said Nafai.

The Gorayni have such wagons. They carry food, too—but the food

is for the soldiers that came to conquer the famine-ravaged land. Only
when they had subdued the people and destroyed their government
did they bring food. It was the slops a swinekeeper brings to his herd.
You feed them now in order to hear them sizzle later.

The visions continued—for hours, it seemed at the time, though
later Nafai would realize that it could only have been a few minutes.
More and more memories of Earth, with ever more disturbing behavior, ever stranger machines. Until the great fire, and the spaceships
rising up from the smoke and ice and ash that remained behind.

"They fled because they had destroyed their world."

No, said the Oversoul. They fled because they longed to begin again.
At least those who came to Harmony came, not because Earth was no
longer fit for them, but because they believed they were no longer fit
for Earth. Billions had died, but there was still fuel and life enough on
Earth for perhaps a few hundred thousand humans to survive. But they
couldn't bear to live on the world they had ruined. We'll go away, they
said to each other, while the world heals itself. During our exile, we
will also learn healing, and when we return we'll be fit to inherit the
land of our birth, and care for it.

So they created the Oversoul, and brought it with them to Harmony,
and gave it hundreds of satellites to be its eyes, its voice; they altered
their own genes to give themselves the capacity to receive the voice of
the Oversoul inside their own minds; and they filled the Oversoul with
memories of Earth and left it to watch over their children for the next
twenty million years.

Surely in that time, they told each other, our children will have
learned how to live together in harmony. They will make the name of
this planet come true in their lives. And at the end of that time, the
Oversoul will know how to bring them home, to where the Keeper of
Earth is waiting for them.

"But we aren't ready," said Nafai. "After twice that time, we're as
bad as ever, except that you've kept us from developing the power to
turn all the life of this planet into ashes and ice."

The Oversoul put the thought into Nafai's mind: By now the Keeper
has surely done its part. The Earth is ready for our return. But the
people of Harmony aren't ready yet to come. I have kept all the knowledge of Earth for all these years, waiting to tell you how to build the
houses that fly, the starships that will bring you home to the world of

your birth; but I dare not teach you, because you'd use the knowledge to oppress and finally to obliterate each other.

"Then what are you doing?" asked Nafai. "What is your plan? Why have you brought us out here?"

I can't tell you yet, said the Oversoul. I'm not sure of you yet. But I've told you what you wanted. I've told you my purpose. I've told you what I've already accomplished, and what is yet to be accomplished. I haven't changed—I'm the same today as I was when your forebears first set me in place to watch over you. My plans are all designed to prepare humanity to return to the Keeper of Earth, who waits for you. It's all I live for, to make humankind fit to return. I am the memory of Earth, all that remains of it, and if you help me, Nafai, you will be part of accomplishing that plan, if it can be accomplished at all.

If it can be accomplished at all.

The overwhelming sense of the presence of the Oversoul in his mind was gone, suddenly; it was as if a great fire inside him had suddenly gone out, as if a great rushing river of life inside him had gone abruptly dry. Nafai sat there on the rock beside the river, feeling spent, exhausted, empty, with that last despairing thought still lingering in his heart: If it can be accomplished at all.

His mouth was dry. He knelt by the water, plunged in his hands, and drew the cupped water to his mouth to drink. It wasn't enough. He splashed into the water, his whole body, not with the reverent attitude of prayer, but with a desperate thirst; he buried his head under the water and drank deep, with his cheek against the cold stone of the riverbed, the water tumbling over his back, his calves. He drank and drank, lifted his head and shoulders above the water to gasp in the evening air, and then collapsed into the water again, to drink as greedily as before.

It was a kind of prayer, though, he realized as he emerged, freezing cold as the water evaporated from his skin in the breeze of the dark morning.

I am with you, he said to the Oversoul. I'll do whatever you ask, because I long for you to accomplish your purpose here. I will do all that I can to prepare us all to return to Earth.

He was chilled to the bone by the time he got back to the tent, not dripping wet anymore, but not dry, either. He lay trembling on his mat for a long time, warmed by the air in the tent, by the heat of Issib's body, until at last he was able to sleep.

*   *   *

There was a lot of work to do in the morning; tired though he was, Nafai had no chance to sleep late, but rather staggered through his jobs, slow and clumsy enough that Elemak and even Father barked at him angrily. Pay attention! Use your head! Not till the heat of the afternoon, when they took the nap that desert dwellers knew was as much a part of survival as water, did Nafai have a chance to recover from his night-walking, from his vision. Only then he couldn't bear to sleep. He lay on his mat and told Issib everything that he had seen, and what he had learned from the Oversoul. When he was finished, Issib had tears streaking his face, and he slowly and with great exertion reached out a hand to clasp Nafai's. "I knew there had to be some purpose behind it," whispered Issib. "This makes so much sense to me. It fits everything. How lucky you were, to hear the voice of the Oversoul. Even more clearly than Father did, I think. As clearly as Luet, I think. You are like Luet."

That made Nafai a little uncomfortable, for a moment at least. He had resented or ridiculed Luet in his own mind, and sometimes in his words. The contemptuous word *witch* had come so easily to his lips. Was this what she felt, when the Oversoul sent her a vision? How could I have ridiculed her for that?

He slept again, and woke, and they finished their work: a permanent corral for the camels, made of piled stones bonded with a gravitic field powered by solar collectors; refrigeration sheds for storing the dried food that would keep them for a year, if it took that long before they could return to Basilica; wards and watches placed around the perimeter of the valley, so that no one could come near enough to see them without them noticing him in return. They built no fires, of course—in the desert, wood was too precious to burn. They took it farther, though; they would cook nothing, because an inexplicable heat source might be detectable. The warmth of their bodies was all the infrared radiation they dared to give off, and the electromagnetic noise put out by their wards and watches, the gravitic field, the refrigeration, the solar collectors, and Issib's chair was not strong enough to be picked up much beyond their perimeter, except with instruments far more sensitive than anything passing marauders or caravans were likely to have. They were as safe as they could make themselves.

At dinner, Nafai commented on how unnecessary it all was. "We're on the errand of the Oversoul," he said. "The Oversoul has kept people away from here all these years, keeping it ready for us—it would have kept on keeping people away."

Elemak laughed, and Mebbekew hooted hysterically. "Well, Nafai the theologian," said Meb, "if the Oversoul's so capable of keeping us safe, why did it send us out here into the landscape of hell instead of letting us *safely* stay home?"

"How are you such an expert on the Oversoul, anyway, Nafai?" asked Elemak. "That mother of yours obviously had you spending too much time with witches."

For once, Nafai stifled his angry retorts. There was no point in arguing with them, he realized. But then, he had realized that many times before, and hadn't been able to hold his tongue. The difference now, Nafai realized, was that he was no longer just Nafai, the youngest of Wetchik's boys. Now he was the friend and ally of the Oversoul. He had more important concerns than arguing with Elya and Meb.

"Nafai," said Father, "your reasoning is faulty. Why should we make the Oversoul waste time watching over us, when we're perfectly capable of watching over ourselves?"

"Of course not, Father," said Nafai. His remark had been foolish. It would be wrong for them to burden the Oversoul, when the Oversoul needed them to help bear its burden. "I'm sorry."

Elemak smiled slightly, and Mebbekew rolled his eyes and laughed again. "Listen to them," he said. "Rational men, supposedly, talking about whether the Oversoul should tend our camels or not."

"It was the Oversoul that brought us here," said Father, rather coldly.

"It was *you* who made us go," said Mebbekew, "and Elemak who guided us."

"It was the Oversoul who warned me to leave," said Father, "and the Oversoul that brought us to this well-watered valley."

"Oh, yes, of course, I forgot," said Meb. "I thought that was a vulture circling, but instead it was the Oversoul, leading the way."

"Only a fool jokes about what he doesn't understand," said Father.

"Only an old *joke* goes around calling rational men *fools*," said Mebbekew. "*You're* the one who sees plots and conspiracies in shadows, Father."

"Shut up," said Elemak.

"Don't tell me to shut up."

"Shut up," said Elemak again. He turned slowly to meet Mebbekew's hot glare. Nafai could see that, though Elya's eyes were heavy lidded, as if he were barely awake, his eyes were afire as he stared Meb down.

"Fine," said Mebbekew, turning back to his dinner, smearing cold bean paste onto another cracker. "I guess I'm the only one who doesn't think camping trips are just the funnest thing."

"This isn't a camping trip," said Father. "It's exile."

"What I can't figure out," said Mebbekew, "is what *I* did to deserve exile."

"You're my son," said Father. "None of us were safe there."

"Come on," said Meb. "We were all safe."

"Drop it," said Elemak. Again he met Mebbekew's glare.

Now Nafai began to recognize the trend here. Elemak didn't like Mebbekew talking about whether there was really a plot against Father, or whether there had been any reason for the whole family to flee into the desert. It was a sensitive subject, and Nafai guessed that both of them knew more than they were willing to talk about. If they had some dark secret, it would be no surprise if Elemak chose to conceal it by never letting a conversation even come near it, while Mebbekew would be far more likely to try to hide it behind a smokescreen of casual denials and mocking lies.

"You *both* know that Father's life was in danger in Basilica," said Nafai.

The way they both looked at him told him that what he suspected was true. If they had been innocent, they would have taken his remark to mean only that he expected them to believe in Father's vision. Instead, they took it much more harshly.

"What makes you think you know what *other* people know?" demanded Elemak.

"If *you're* so sure Father's life was in danger," said Meb nastily, "maybe that means *you* were in on the conspiracy."

Again, their reactions were typical: Elemak, defending against Nafai's accusation by saying, in essence, You can't prove anything, while Mebbekew was defending himself by turning the accusation back on Nafai.

Now let them realize what they are confessing, thought Nafai. "What conspiracy?" he asked. "What are you talking about?"

Mebbekew immediately realized how much he had revealed. "I just assumed—that you were saying that we had some advance knowledge or something."

"If you *knew* of a plot against Father's life," said Nafai, "you would have *told* him, if you were any kind of decent human being. And you certainly wouldn't sit here whining about how we didn't really need to leave the city."

"I'm not the one who whines, little boy," said Mebbekew. His anger had lost all subtlety now. He wasn't sure how to interpret Nafai's words, which is why Nafai had spoken the way he did. Let Meb wonder—does Nafai know something, or not?

"Shut up, Meb," said Elemak. "And you, too, Nafai. Isn't it bad enough we're in exile here without you at each other's throats?"

Elya the peacemaker. Nafai wanted to laugh. But then—maybe it was true. Maybe Elemak *hadn't* known—maybe Gaballufix had never taken him into his confidence on that subject. Of course he hadn't, Nafai realized. Elya might be Gaballufix's half-brother, but he was still Wetchik's son and heir. Gaballufix would never be absolutely sure whose side Elemak was really on. He could use Elya as a go-between, a messenger to Father—but he could never trust him with real knowledge.

That would explain Elemak's effort to keep Meb silent, too; he wanted to hide his involvement with Gaballufix, yes, but there was no murder plot to keep secret. How could Nafai have imagined it? Besides, if they were out in the desert as part of the Oversoul's plan, didn't that mean that Elemak and Mebbekew were *also* part of the plan? Here I am, filled with suspicion about them, harboring exactly the kind of malice that is going to destroy Basilica. How can I claim to be on the Oversoul's side, if I let myself behave like the kind of person who doesn't trust even his own brother?

"I'm sorry," said Nafai. "I shouldn't have said that."

Now they all looked at him in true startlement. It took a moment for Nafai to realize that it was the first time in his life that he had ever actually apologized for some nasty thing he said to one of his brothers, without first being wrestled into submission and locked in some painful grip.

"That's all right," said Mebbekew. His voice was full of wonder—his eyes, though, radiated with triumphant contempt.

You think my apology means I'm weak, Nafai said silently to him. But it doesn't. It means I'm trying to learn how to be strong.

It was then that Nafai told Father and Elemak and Mebbekew something of the visions the Oversoul showed him during the night. He didn't get far into his account, though.

"I'm tired," said Elemak. "I don't have time for this."

Nafai looked at him in astonishment. Didn't have time to hear the plan of the Oversoul? Didn't have time to learn about the hope of humankind returning to Earth?

Mebbekew also yawned pointedly.

"You mean you don't even care?" asked Issib.

Elemak smiled at his crippled brother. "You're too trusting, Issya," he said. "Can't you see what's happening here? Nafai can't stand not to be the center of attention. He can't prove himself by being useful or even marginally competent—so he starts having visions. Next thing you know, Nyef's going to be giving us the Oversoul's orders and bossing us all around."

"No I'm not," said Nafai. "I saw the visions."

"Right," said Mebbekew. "I saw visions last night, too. Girls that you don't even have the gonads to dream of, Nafai. I'll believe in your dreams of the Oversoul as soon as you're willing to marry one of the girls from my dreams. I'll even give you one of the prettiest ones."

Elemak was laughing, and even Father smiled a little. But Mebbekew's taunts only filled Nafai with rage. "I'm telling you the truth," he insisted. "I'm telling you what the Oversoul is trying to accomplish!"

"I'd rather think about what the girls in my dreams were trying to accomplish," said Meb.

"That's enough of such vulgarity," said Father. But he was chuckling. It was the cruelest blow, that Father plainly believed Elemak about Nafai making up his visions.

So when Elemak and Mebbekew left to see to the animals, Nafai remained behind with Father and Issib.

"Why aren't you going?" said Father. "Issib can't help with chores like that, here where his floats don't work. But *you* can help."

"Father," said Nafai, "I thought that *you* would believe me."

"I do," said Father. "I believe you honestly want to be part of the work of the Oversoul. I honor you for it, and maybe some of your dreams *did* come from the Oversoul. But don't try to tell such things to your older brothers. They won't take it from you." He chuckled bitterly. "They barely endure it coming from me."

"I believe Nafai," said Issib. "They weren't dreams, either. He was awake, by the stream. I saw him come back to the tent, wet and cold." Nafai had never been so grateful to anyone, to have Issib back him up. He didn't have to do it, either. Nafai had half expected Issib to *stop* believing him, if Father wasn't taking him seriously.

"I believe him, too," said Father. "But the things you were saying were far more specific than anything the Oversoul tells us in visions. So I'm just saying that there's probably a kernel of truth in what you're saying. But most of it must have come from your own imagination, and I for one am not going to try to sort it out, not tonight."

"I believed *you*," said Nafai.

"Not at first," said Father. "And we don't trade belief like favors. We give belief and trust where they are earned. Don't expect me to be any quicker to believe *you* than you were to believe *me*."

Abashed, Nafai got up from the rug. Father's tent was so large that he didn't have to duck when he stood upright. "I was blind at first, when you told me what you saw. But now I see that you're deaf, so you can't possibly hear the things I've heard."

"Help your brother back into his chair," said Father. "And watch how you speak to your Father."

That night, in their tent, Issib tried to console Nafai. "Father's the *father*, Nafai. It can't be good news to him, to have his youngest son getting so much more information from the Oversoul than *he's* ever received."

"Maybe I'm more attuned to it or something," said Nafai. "I can't help it. But what difference does it make, who the Oversoul talks to? Wasn't Gaballufix supposed to believe Father, even though Father is below his station in the Palwashantu clan?"

"Below his office, maybe," said Issib, "but not below his *station*. If Father had wanted to be clan leader, he would have been chosen—he's the Wetchik by birth, isn't he? That's why Gaballufix has always hated him—because he knows that if Father hadn't despised politics, he could have wiped out Gaballufix's power and influence easily, right from the start."

But Nafai didn't want to talk about Basilican politics now. He fell silent, and in the silence spoke again to the Oversoul. You have to make Father believe me, he said. You have to show Father what's really happening. You can't show me a vision and then not help me persuade Father.

"*I* believe you, Nyef," Issib whispered. "And I believe in what the Oversoul is trying to do. Maybe that's all the Oversoul needs, did you think of that? Maybe the Oversoul doesn't need Father to believe you right now. So just accept it. Trust the Oversoul."

Nafai looked at Issib, but in the darkness of night inside the tent couldn't tell whether his brother's eyes were open or not. Had it really been Issib speaking, or was Issib asleep, and had Nafai heard the words of the Oversoul in Issib's voice?

"Someday, Nyef, it may come down to what Elemak said. You may have to give orders to your brothers. Even to Father. Do you think the Oversoul will leave you to yourself then?"

No, it couldn't be Issib. He was hearing the Oversoul in Issib's voice, saying things that Issib could never say. And now that he realized that he had his answer, he could sleep again. But before he slept, questions formed in his mind:

What if the Oversoul is telling me more than Father, not because it's part of a plan, but simply because I'm the only one who can hear and understand?

What if the Oversoul is counting on me to be able to figure out a way to persuade the others, because the Oversoul hasn't the power to convince them anymore?

What if I'm truly alone, except for this one brother who believes me —the one brother who is crippled, and therefore can do nothing?

Belief is not *nothing*, said the voice whispering in Nafai's mind. Issib's belief in you is the only reason you haven't yet started doubting it yourself.

Tell Father, Nafai pleaded as he drifted off to sleep. Speak to Father, so he'll believe me.

The Oversoul spoke to Father in the night, but not with any vision that Nafai had hoped for.

"I saw the four of you going back to Basilica," said Father.

"About time," said Mebbekew.

"Going back, but for a single purpose," said Father. "To get the Index and bring it back to me."

"The Index?" asked Elemak.

"It's been with the Palwashantu clan from the beginning. I believe that it might have been the reason the clan has preserved its identity for all these years. We were once called the Keepers of the Index, and my father told me that it was the right of the Wetchiks to use it."

"Use it for what?" asked Mebbekew.

"I'm not sure," said Father. "I've only seen it a few times. My grandfather left it with the clan council when he began traveling, and my father never made any serious effort to get it back after Grandfather died. Now it's in Gaballufix's house. But from the name of it, I'd guess it's a guide to a library."

"How useful," said Elemak. "And for *this* you're sending us back to Basilica? To get an object whose purpose you don't understand."

"To get it and bring it back to me. No matter the cost."

"Do you mean that?" said Elemak. "No matter the cost?"

"It's what the Oversoul wanted. I knew it—even though I—it's not my personal feeling. I want you back here, safe."

"Right," said Mebbekew. "It's as good as done. No problem."

"Should we bring back more supplies?" asked Nafai.

"There won't be more supplies," said Father. "I told Rashgallivak to sell all the caravaning supplies."

Nafai could see Elemak's face turn red under its dark tan. "So when our exile is over, Father, how do you propose we restore our business?"

It was a cusp of decision, Nafai could see that: Elemak was facing the fact that Father's actions were intended to be irrevocable. If Elya was going to rebel, it would be over this, which he could only see as the squandering of his inheritance. So Father spoke plainly in giving his reply.

"I don't propose to restore anything," said Father. "Do what I say, Elemak, or it won't matter to *you* what the Wetchik fortune is or is not."

There it was. It couldn't be more clear. If Elemak was ever to be Wetchik himself, he'd better obey the present Wetchik's commands.

Mebbekew cackled. "I never liked all those smelly animals anyway," said Mebbekew. "Who needs them?" His message was just as clear: I'll gladly become Wetchik in your place, Elemak—so please go ahead and get Father really really angry.

"I'll bring you your Index, Father," said Elemak. "But why send these others? Let me go alone. Or let me take Mebbekew, and keep the younger boys with you. Neither of them will be any use to me."

"The Oversoul showed me all four of you going," said Father. "So all four of you will go to Basilica, and all four of you will return. Do you understand me?"

"Perfectly," said Elemak.

"Last night you made fun of Nafai, because he claimed to be having visions," said Father. "But I tell you that you could learn a great deal from Nafai and Issib. *They,* at least, are making an effort to help. All I hear from my two elder sons is complaint."

Mebbekew glared pointedly at Nafai, but Nafai was more afraid of Elemak, who simply gazed steadily at Father through heavy-lidded eyes. Last night you wouldn't believe me, Father, Nafai said silently. Now today you make my brothers hate me even more than before.

"You know much, Elemak, Mebbekew," said Father, "but in all your learning you never seem to have mastered the concept of loyalty and obedience. Learn it from your younger brothers, and then you'll be worthy of the wealth and honors you aspire to."

That's it, Nafai said silently. I'm dead now. I might as well be a worm in their bread, the way they'll treat me on this whole trip. I'd rather stay home than go under these conditions, Father, thank you kindly.

"Father, I'll do all that you ask," said Elemak. But his voice was quiet and cold, and it made Nafai sick at heart to hear it.

Elemak sullenly set about preparing for the trip. As Nafai expected, Elya ignored him completely when he asked what he should do to help. And Mebbekew shot him such a look that Nafai felt a thrill of fear run through him. He wants me dead, he thought. Meb wants me to die.

Since he wasn't permitted to help, and since it would obviously be wiser for him to be as inconspicuous as possible for the next while, Nafai went back to the tent he shared with Issib and helped his brother pack up, which mostly consisted of wrapping his floats and stowing them in a bag. He could see in Issib's eyes as he looked hungrily at the floats that it didn't matter to Issib what Elemak or Mebbekew thought of him—he wanted to be back where his body was usable again, where he was free and didn't have to be dressed or taken outside to void himself like an infant or a pet. Such a prisoner he is, trapped in that body, thought Nafai. And then the job was done and Issib was in his chair, hovering over the ground looking like some ill-tempered monarch on his throne. He was impatient to go, impatient to return to Basilica.

All of them are, thought Nafai. But none for the right reason. None is eager to get there because of a desire to help with the Oversoul's plan.

Nafai found himself by the water's edge, gripping a bough that was ten centimeters thick, bending it between his hands, bending it like a horseshoe. It fought him, but it also gave under the strength of his grip.

"Don't break that," said Father.

Nafai turned, startled. He let go of the branch, and it whipped upward, out of control; some leaves slapped him in the face.

"It took so long for it to grow," said Father.

"I wasn't going to break it."

"It was on the verge," said Father. "I know plants. You don't. You were on the verge of breaking it."

"I'm not that strong."

"Stronger than you know." Father sized him up. "Fourteen." He laughed a little. "Your mother's genes, not mine, I fear. I look at you and I see—"

"Mother?"

"What Issib might have been, body as well as mind. Poor boy."

Poor boy. Why don't you look at me sometime, Father, and see *me*. Instead of some imaginary child. Instead of a little boy who makes up visions, why don't you see what I am: a man who heard the voice of the Oversoul, even more clearly than you.

"I'm afraid," said Father.

Nafai looked his father in the eye. Is he teasing me?

"I'm sending you into something more dangerous than I think your brothers understand. But *you* understand, don't you, Nafai."

"I think."

"After what you've seen," said Father. But it was as much a question as an answer. What was he asking, whether Nafai knew the truth about Elya and Meb? It couldn't be that, because Father didn't know about them himself. No, Father was asking whether Nafai really saw visions.

Nafai's first reaction was to be furious—hurt, offended. But then he realized that he was wrong to feel that way. Because Father had a right to ask, a right to let it take time to believe in his visions, just as Issib had said. He was *trying* to accept the idea of Nafai as a fellow servant of the Oversoul.

"Yes," said Nafai. "I've seen. But nothing about the Index."

"Gaballufix won't let it go," said Father. "In the vision he did, but the Oversoul can't see everything. The Index isn't just something you borrow. It's very powerful."

"Why? What can it do?"

"I don't know what it can do, of itself. But I know that it means power. I know that among the Palwashantu, the one who keeps the Index is the one who has the trust of the clan. The greatest honor. Gabya won't give it up. He'll kill first. And that's where I'm sending my sons."

The look on Father's face was angry. Nafai realized: He's furious at the Oversoul for requiring him to do this.

And then, as Nafai watched, Father mastered his rage, and his face grew calm. "I hope," said Father quietly, "I hope the Oversoul has really thought all this through."

"Father," Nafai said, "*I'll* go and do whatever the Oversoul has asked us to do. Because I know that the Oversoul wouldn't ask us to do it without preparing some way for it to be accomplished."

Father studied his face for the longest time. Then he smiled. Nafai had never seen such a smile on his father's face. The relief in it, the trust. "Not an act, is it," said Father. "You're not just saying what you think I want to hear."

"When have any of your sons said anything that they thought you wanted to hear?" asked Nafai.

Now Father laughed, tossed his head back and roared. "Never!" he cried. And then, just as suddenly, the laughter stopped. Father took Nafai's head between his hands, his large hands, calloused and wiry and horned and rough from years of handling bark and leather harnesses and raw stone, and holding those great palms on either side of Nafai's face, he leaned forward and kissed him on the mouth. "My son," he whispered. "My son."

For a moment they stood there together, beside the tree, beside the water, until they heard footsteps and turned. It was Elemak, his face still sour and angry. "Time to go," he said. "If we're going to make any kind of progress today, anyway."

"By all means go," said Father. "I wouldn't delay you for a moment."

In a few minutes they were on their camels again, heading back to the city.

11

Brothers

Basilica was not in sight yet, but Elemak knew the road. Knew it as well as he knew the skin of his own face in the mirror, every mole of the surface, every peak or declivity that snatched at the razor and bled. He knew the shadows of every hour of the day, where water might be waiting after a rain, where robbers might hide.

It was to one of those places that Elemak now led his brothers. They had not been on the road itself for some time, but till now had always kept it in sight. Now they left it behind, and soon the ground grew rough enough that he made them stop, dismount.

"Why are we stopping here?" asked Mebbekew.

"The floats are working," said Issib. "That's how close we are, I can move without the damn chair."

Elemak eyed his crippled brother and shook his head. "Not reliably. We'll dismount the chair—you'll have to use it."

Issib was usually so compliant, but not now. "Use it yourself, if you think it's so comfy."

"Look at you," said Elemak. "It's intermittent at best, with the float. You'll start losing it and fall over and we can't have that. Use the chair."

"It'll get better as we get closer."

"We aren't getting closer," said Elemak.

"Then what are we doing?" demanded Mebbekew.

"We're going down into this arroyo, where the magnetics of Basilica certainly do *not* reach, and there we're going to wait until nightfall."

"And then?" asked Mebbekew. "Since you seem to think you're in command here, I thought perhaps I'd ask."

Elemak had faced this kind of thing many times before from fellow travelers on the road, even sometimes from hired men. He knew how to handle it—brutal suppression, instant and public, so no doubt was left in anyone's mind of who was in charge. So instead of answering Mebbekew he took him by the arms—thin, womanly arms, an *actor*, by the Oversoul!—and slammed him back against a wall of rock. The sudden movement spooked one of the camels. It stamped, spat, blatted out a protest. For a moment Elemak was afraid he would have to go calm the animal—but no, Nafai had it, was calming it. The boy was actually useful for something besides sucking up to Father. Not like Mebbekew, who was reliable only in his unreliability. Why Gaballufix ever confided in him, Elemak never knew. Surely Gabya knew that Mebbekew would let something slip. Even if he didn't tell Father directly about the plot, he surely told *someone*—how else could Father have known?

There was raw panic in Meb's eyes, and pain, too—his head had smacked sharply against the stone. Well, good, thought Elemak. Think about pain a little bit. Think hard before you question my authority on the road.

"I *am* in command here," Elemak whispered.

Meb nodded.

"And I say that we'll wait until dark."

"I was joking," Meb whined. "You don't have to be so *serious* about everything, do you?"

Elemak almost hit him for that. Serious? Don't you realize that there inside Basilica, the most powerful, dangerous man in the city is almost certainly convinced that we betrayed him and warned Father to flee? To Mebbekew, Basilica was a city of pleasure and excitement. Well, there might be excitement indeed inside those walls, but of pleasure not a speck.

But Elemak did not hit Meb, because that would be excessive, and provoke resentment instead of respect among the others. Elemak knew how to lead men, and knew how to control his own feelings and not let them interfere with his judgment. He eased his grip on Mebbekew and then turned his back on him, to show his absolute confidence in his own leadership, and his contempt for Mebbekew. Meb would not dare attack him, even with his back turned.

"At nightfall, what will happen is simple enough. I will go inside the city, and I'll speak to Gaballufix, and I'll bring out the Index."

"No," said Issib. "Father said we should all go."

Another insubordination—but not a serious one, and it was Issib, the cripple, so a show of force was completely out of the question. "And we all *have* come. But I *know* Gaballufix. He's my half-brother—as much my brother as any of you. I have the best chance of talking him into giving us the Index."

"You mean we came all this way," said Issib, "and you're going to make me stay here, in this metal coffin of mine, and never get any closer to the city than this?"

"Better your chair than a real coffin," said Elemak. "I tell you that if you think going into the city will be fun, you're a fool. Gaballufix is dangerous."

"He *is*," said Nafai. "Elya is right. If we all go in together, then a failure might mean all of us killed—or imprisoned—or anything. If only one goes, then even if he fails the rest of us might still be able to accomplish something."

"If I fail, then go back to Father," said Elemak.

"Right," said Meb. "I'm sure we've all memorized the road."

"It can't be you," said Issib. "Of all of us, you're the only one necessary to lead us home."

"I'll go," said Nafai.

"Right," said Elemak, laughing. "*You* the one who looks most like Lady Rasa. I don't think you get the picture, Nyef—one look at you and Gaballufix is reminded of the one humiliation he's never been able to avenge—Lady Rasa lapsing his contract after two daughters and within a week making a new contract with Father—which she hasn't broken yet. Walk into Gaballufix's house alone, with no one in the city even knowing you're there, Nyef, and your life is over."

"Me, then," said Mebbekew.

"You'd only go get drunk or find some woman," said Elemak, "and then come back and lie and say you spoke to Gaballufix and he said no."

Mebbekew seemed to toy with the idea of getting angry, but then thought better of it. "Possibly," said Mebbekew. "But it's a better plan than I've heard from anyone else."

"What about mine?" said Issib. "*I* go and ask. What is Gaballufix going to do to a cripple?"

Elemak shook his head. "Break you in half with his bare hands, if he feels like it."

"And you were *friends* with him?" asked Mebbekew.

"Brothers. We're brothers. We don't get to choose our brothers, you know," said Elemak. "We just make do with what we get."

"He wouldn't hurt a cripple," Issib said again. "It would shame him in front of his own men."

Elemak knew that Issib was right. The cripple might be the best one to get into and out of an interview with Gaballufix alive. The trouble was that Elemak *couldn't* let Issib or Nafai talk to the man. Gaballufix might say something that would compromise Elemak. No, it had to be Elemak himself, so he could talk to Gabya alone, maybe smooth things over, persuade his brother that it wasn't him that warned Father of the plan to kill Roptat under circumstances that would implicate and discredit Wetchik. If they ever learned of this, Meb and Issya and Nyef wouldn't understand that in the long run it was the best plan for Father's own sake. If they didn't neutralize Father this way, then eventually it might be Father who died under mysterious circumstances.

"I'll tell you what," said Elemak. "Since we all disagree about who should go, let's let the Oversoul decide. A time-honored tradition—we draw lots."

He reached down and scooped up a handful of pebbles from the ground. "Three light ones, one dark one." But as he spoke, Elemak made sure a fourth light-colored stone was tucked out of sight between two of his fingers. "Dark stone goes into the city."

"All right," said Meb, and the others nodded.

"I'll hold the stones," said Nafai.

"Nobody holds the stones, my dear little boy," said Elemak. "Too much chance of cheating, yes?" Elemak reached up to a shelf in the rock, out of sight where they were standing. There he again made a show of mixing up the four stones. "When I'm through mixing them, though, you can mix them yourself, Nafai," he said. "That way we know that nobody knows which stone is which."

Nafai immediately strode forward, reached up to the shelf of stone, and mixed the stones. Four of them, of course—Elemak knew he would feel four stones and be satisfied. What he couldn't possibly know was that the dark stone was now between Elemak's fingers, and the four stones on the shelf were all light.

"While you've got your hand up there, Nyef, go ahead and choose a stone."

Nafai, poor fool, came away with a light-colored stone and frowned at it. What did he expect? He was playing at a man's game. None of these boys seemed to realize that a man with Elemak's responsibilities would never have lasted on the open road if he didn't know how to make sure that drawing lots always turned out the way he wanted.

"Me now," said Issib.

"No," said Elemak. "My draw." That was another rule of the game— Elemak had to draw early, or somebody might grow suspicious and check the rocks and see that there was no dark one there. He reached up, made a show of fumbling with the rocks, and then came away with the dark one, of course—but with the extra light one also tucked between his fingers. When they checked, they'd find only two stones left there on the shelf.

"You knew by the feel of it," said Mebbekew.

"Don't be a bad sport," said Elemak. "If all goes well, maybe we can all go into the city. It all depends on how Gaballufix reacts, yes? And he's my brother—if anyone can persuade him, I can."

"I'm going inside no matter what," said Issib. "I'll wait until you come back, but I'm not leaving here without going inside."

"Issya," said Elemak, "I can't promise that I'll let you go inside the walls of the city. But I *can* promise that before you leave here, you'll get close enough that you can use the floats. All right?"

Sullenly Issib nodded.

"Your word, though, that no one leaves this spot until I come back."

"What do we do if Gaballufix kills you?" asked Meb.

"He won't."

"What do we do," Meb insisted, "if you don't come back?"

"If I'm not back by dawn," said Elemak, "then I'm either dead or incapacitated. At that point, my dear brotherlets, I won't be in charge anymore and so I don't really care what you do. Go home, go back to Father, or go into the city and get laid or killed or lost, it will make not a speck of difference to me. But don't worry—I'll be back."

That gave them plenty to think about as he led them down the arroyo into a clear area where no one was likely to find them. "But look," said Elemak. "You can see the city walls from here. You can see High Gate."

"Is that the gate you'll be using?" asked Nafai.

"On the way in," said Elemak. "On the way out, I'll use any gate I can get to."

With that he left them, striding boldly away, wishing that he felt half as bold as the show he was putting on for them.

Entering the city through High Gate was nowhere near as difficult as it would have been at Market Gate—after all, there was no Gold Market to protect. Still, Elemak had to have his thumb scanned to prove his citizenship, and thus the city computer knew he had entered. Elemak had no doubt that even if Gabya's house computer wasn't tied directly to the city computers—which would be, of course, illegal—he certainly had informants in the city government, and if Gabya cared whether Elemak entered Basilica, he would know the information within moments.

Elemak was actually quite relieved not to be detained by the guard at the gate; it meant that Gaballufix had not put out his name for immediate arrest. Or else it meant that Gabya didn't yet have quite as much power in the city as he boasted about to his friends and supporters. Maybe it was still beyond his reach to issue orders to the gate guards to detain his personal enemies.

Am I his enemy? thought Elemak. His brother, yes. His friend, no. An ally of convenience for a while, yes. We both saw ways to get benefit from a closer relationship. But now will he see me as an old business deal gone sour, as a possibly useful friend, or as a traitor to be punished?

Elemak meant to go straight to Gaballufix's house, but once he was inside the city he couldn't bring himself to do it. He jogged from High Funnel up Library Street, then took Temple to Wing. Either Temple or Wing would have carried him near to Gabya's house, but by now Elemak was becoming more and more alarmed by the soldiers he was passing, or that were passing him. There were more of them, for one thing, than in the days before Father led them out into the desert, and even though he carefully avoided looking directly at them, he began to feel more and more uneasy about them. Finally, when he saw a group of a dozen turning onto Wing Street, he ducked into a doorway and then allowed himself to look at them directly as they passed.

Immediately he realized what was wrong. They were all identical—
the faces, the clothing, the weaponry, everything. "Impossible," he
whispered. There could not be so many identical people in the world at
the same time. The ancient stories of cloning flashed through his mind
—witches and wizards who tried to rule the world by creating genetically identical copies of themselves, which inevitably (in the stories, at
least) turned on their creators and killed them. But this was the real
world, and these were Gabya's soldiers; he had no more notion how to
clone than how to fly, and if he *could* make clones, he could certainly
have chosen a better model than this nondescript, stupid-looking hulk
that was going up and down the streets by dozens.

"It's all fakery," said a woman.

No one stood in the doorway with Elemak. Only when he stepped
out did he see the speaker, an ageless, filthy wilder, naked except for
the layers of grime and dust that covered her. Elemak was not one of
those who saw wilders as objects of desire, though some of his friends
used them as casually as if they were urinals for lust. He would have
ignored her, except she seemed to be answering his whispered comment, and besides, whom could he speak to more safely than to an
anonymous holy woman from the desert?

"How do they do it?" he asked. "Look all alike, I mean."

"They say it's an old theatre costume technique, much in vogue a
thousand years ago."

She didn't talk like a desert woman. "How does it work?"

"It's a fine netting, worn like a cloak. A control at the waist turns it
on and off. It automatically adjusts itself to the surrounding light—it
becomes very bright in sunlight, much more subtle in moonlight or
shadow. A very clever device."

Her voice sounded more and more refined the more she talked.

"Who are you?" he asked.

She looked into his face. "I am the Oversoul," she said. "And who
are you, Elemak? Are you my friend or my enemy?"

For a moment Elemak stood in terror. He had been so worried about
Gaballufix, so fearful that a soldier would recognize him, call out his
name, and carry him off or perhaps even kill him on the spot, that to
now be recognized by a madwoman in the street left him completely
empty-headed. How do you hide when even the street beggars know
your name? Only when *she* moved, inserting her index finger into her
navel and twiddling it around as if she were stirring some loathsome

mixture there, did his disgust overcome his fear and send him out into the street, running blindly away from her.

Thus his plan of casual, unobtrusive movement through the streets was ruined. He did have enough presence of mind, however, not to go directly to Gabya's house, not in *this* state of mind. Where else could he go, though? Habit would lead him to his mother's house—old Hosni kept a fine old house in The Wells, near Back Gate, where she meddled in politics and made and broke reputations of rising young men and women of government. But desire triumphed over custom, and instead of taking refuge with his mother, he found himself on the porch of Rasa's house.

He had studied here as a boy, of course, even before Father first mated with her; indeed, it was because his mother had placed him with Rasa that his father and his teacher first met. It had been vaguely embarrassing to have the other students gossip about the liaison between their mistress and Elya's father, and from then on he had never been fully comfortable there until he gratefully left off his schooling at the age of thirteen. Now, though, he came to Rasa's house, not as a student, but as a suitor—and one whose suit had long been welcomed.

For a moment, hesitating at the door, Elemak realized that he was doing exactly what he had forbidden his young brothers to do—he was conducting personal business when he was supposed to be on Father's errand. But whatever qualms he felt, he immediately dispelled them. His wooing of Eiadh was far more than pursuit of an advantageous match. Sometime in the last few months he had fallen in love with her; he desired her more than he had ever thought he could desire a woman. Her voice was music to him, her body an infinitely variable sculpture that astonished him with every movement. But as his devotion for her grew, he had become increasingly fearful that in her there was no matching increase of love for him. For all he knew, she still desired him only as the heir of the great Wetchik, who could provide her with enormous fortune and prestige. And if that was all she saw in him, all she felt for him, then recent events would turn her against him. There might be no advantage to her in marrying the Wetchik's heir *now*, with so much of the business being closed down and sold off. How would she respond to him now?

He pulled the cord; the bell rang. It was an old-fashioned bell, a deepish gong rather than the musical chimes that were all the fashion now. To his surprise, it was none other than Rasa herself who answered the door.

"A man comes to my door," she said. "A strong young man, with the dirt and sweat of the desert on his face. What am I to make of you? Are you bringing me word from my mate? Are you bringing more threats from Gaballufix? Are you here to carry off my niece Eiadh? Or have you come with fear in your heart, back to the house of your childhood schooling, hoping for a bath and a meal and four stout walls to keep you safe?"

All was said with such humor that Elemak's fear was dispelled. It felt good to have Rasa address him almost as an equal, and with genuine affection, too. "Father is well," he answered, "I haven't seen Gabya since I returned to the city, I hope to see Eiadh but have no plans for abduction at the moment, and as for the bath and the meal—I would accept such hospitality gratefully, but I would never have asked for it."

"I'm sure you wouldn't have," said Rasa. "You would have bounded in and expected Eiadh to be glad of your embrace when you smell like a camel and you spread dust with every step you take. Come in, Elemak."

As he luxuriated in the bath he again felt some guilt, thinking of his brothers waiting for him in the rocks through the heat of the day—but then, bathing and cleansing himself before seeing Gaballufix was the most sensible of plans. It would make him look far less desperate and give the clear message that he had friends in the city—a much better bargaining position. Unless Gaballufix saw it as further proof that Elemak had played a double game against him. Never mind, never mind. His clothing, freshly washed and aired, was laid out for him in the secator, and he slipped it on gratefully when he arose from the bath, letting the secator dry him off as he dressed. He disdained the hair oils—keeping the hair oil-free was one of the ways the pro-Potokgavan party identified themselves, refusing to resemble the Wetheads in any way.

Eiadh met him in Rasa's own salon. She seemed timid, but he took that as a good sign—at least she did not seem haughty or angry. Still, did he dare to take the liberties she had granted him at his last wooing? Or would that be too presumptuous now, seeing how his circumstances had changed. He strode toward her, but instead of seating himself beside her on the couch, he sank to one knee before her and reached for her hand. She let him—and then reached out her other hand and touched his cheek. "Are we strangers now?" she asked. "Are you unwilling to sit beside me?"

She had understood his hesitation, and this was the reassurance that he needed. Immediately he sat beside her, kissed her, put his hand at her waist and felt how she breathed so passionately, how she yielded to him so eagerly. They said little at first, at least in words; in actions she told him that her feelings for him were undiminished.

"I thought you were gone forever," she whispered, after long silence.

"Not from you," he said. "But I don't know what the future holds for me. The turmoil in the city, Father's exile—"

"Some say that your brother was plotting to kill your father—"

"Never."

"And others that your father was plotting to kill your brother—"

"Nonsense. Laughable. They're both strong-minded men, that's all."

"That's not *all*," said Eiadh. "Your father never came here with soldiers, threatening that he could come in whenever he wanted the way Gaballufix did."

"He came *here?*" said Elemak, angry. "For what?"

"He was Aunt Rasa's mate once, remember—they have two daughters. . . ."

"Yes, I think I've met them."

"Of course," she said, laughing. "They're your nieces, I know. And they're Nyef's and Issya's sisters, too—aren't families so complicated? But what I meant was, Gaballufix's coming wasn't what was strange. It's the *way* he came, with those soldiers in their horrible costumes so they all look so—inhuman."

"I heard it was holography."

"A very old theatrical device. Now that I've seen it, I'm glad that our actors use paint or, at the most, masks. Holographs are disturbing. Unnatural." She put her hand inside his shirt, slid it along his skin. It tickled. He trembled. "You see?" she said. "How could a holograph ever feel like that? How could anyone bear to be so *unreal.*"

"I imagine they're still real enough under the holograph. And they can make faces at you without your knowing it."

She laughed. "Imagine being an actor, though, with something like that. How would anyone ever know your facial expressions?"

"Maybe they only used them for non-speaking roles—so the same actors could play dozens of roles with instant costume changes."

Eiadh's eyes widened. "I didn't know you were so knowledgeable about the theatre."

"I once courted an actress," said Elemak. He did it deliberately, knowing how it bothered most women to hear about old loves. "I thought she was beautiful then. You see, I had never seen *you*. Now I wonder if she was anything but a holograph."

She kissed him as a reward for the pretty compliment.

Then the door opened and Rasa came in. She had allowed them the socially correct fifteen minutes—perhaps a little longer. "So nice of you to visit us, Elemak. Thank you, Eiadh, for conversing with our guest while I was detained." It was the delicate pretense of courting, this custom of acting as if the suitor had come to call on the lady of the house, while the young woman being wooed was merely helping the lady to entertain her guest.

"For all your hospitality, I am grateful beyond expression," said Elemak. "You have rescued a weary traveler, my Lady Rasa; I didn't know how near death I must have been, until your kindness made me so alive."

Rasa turned to Eiadh. "He's really very good at this, isn't he."

Eiadh smiled sweetly.

"Lady Rasa," said Elemak, "I don't know what the future will hold. I have to meet with Gaballufix today, and I don't know how that will turn out."

"Then *don't* meet with him," said Rasa, her expression turning quite serious. "He's become very dangerous, I think. Roptat is convinced that there was a plot to kill him in that meeting at the coolhouse, the day that Wetchik left. If Wetchik had been there, as agreed, Roptat would have walked right into a trap. I believe him—I believe Gaballufix has murder in his heart."

Elemak *knew* he had; but he also had no idea what might come if he confirmed Rasa's suspicions. For one thing, Rasa and Eiadh might wonder how Elemak could have known of such a plot, and if he did, why he didn't give warning to Roptat himself. Women didn't understand that sometimes to avoid the thousands of casualties of a bloody war, it was kindest and most peaceable to prevent the conflict with a single timely death. Good strategy could so easily be misunderstood as murder by the unsophisticated.

"Perhaps," said Elemak. "Does anyone really know someone else's heart?"

"I know someone's heart," said Eiadh. "And mine holds no secrets from him."

"If it isn't Elemak that you're referring to," said Rasa, "then poor Elemak might start contemplating some hot-blooded crime of passion himself."

"Of course I'm talking about Elya," said Eiadh. She took his hand and held it in her lap.

"Lady Rasa, I'm not going to Gaballufix unnecessarily. Father sent me. There's something he needs that only Gaballufix can give."

"There's something we *all* need that only Gaballufix can give," said Rasa, "and that is *peace*. You might mention that to him when you see him."

"I'll try," said Elemak, though of course they both knew he wouldn't.

"What is it that Wetchik wants? Did he send any message to me?"

"I don't think he expected me to see you," said Elemak. "It was a vision from the Oversoul that sent me. Actually, all four of us came—"

"Even Issib! Here!"

"No. I left them outside the city, in a safe place. No one but the two of you will know they're here, if I can help it. With any luck, I'll get the Index and be out of the city before night, and then I have no idea when we'll be back again."

"The Index," whispered Rasa. "Then he can never come back."

Elemak was disturbed to hear her say that. "Why? What *is* it?"

"Nothing," she said. "I mean, I don't know. Only that—let's just say that if the Palwashantu realize that it's gone . . ."

"How can it be that important? I never heard of it before Father sent us back for it."

"No, it's not much spoken of," said Rasa. "There hasn't been much need for it, I guess. Or perhaps the Oversoul didn't want it known."

"Why? There are lots of indexes—dozens in every library in the world, hundreds in Basilica alone. Why is this one *the* Index?"

"I'm not sure," said Rasa. "Really I'm not. I only know that it's the only artifact from the men's worship that is also mentioned in the women's lore."

"Worship? How is it used?"

"I don't know. It never *has* been used, to my knowledge. I've never seen it. I don't even know what it looks like."

"Oh, *that's* good news," said Elemak. "I assumed it would be like any other index, and now you're telling me that Gaballufix could hand me anything and call it the Index and I'd never even know if he was cheating me."

Rasa smiled. "Elemak, you must understand. Unless he wishes to lose his leadership of the Palwashantu, he will *never* give you the Index."

Elemak was worried, but not dismayed. She clearly meant what she was saying, but that did not necessarily mean that she was right. Nobody really knew what Gaballufix might do, and if he thought he could get some advantage out of it, he'd trade away anything. Even their mother, if Gabya ever thought old Hosni might have some value. No, the Index could be had, if the price was right.

And the more he realized how important this mysterious Index was, the more he wanted it, not just to humor Father, not just as part of the game he was playing to take possession of the future, but for the sake of having the Index himself. If so much power came to the one who had it, then why shouldn't it be Elemak's?

"Elemak," Rasa said, "if you do, somehow, get the Index, you must realize that Gaballufix won't let you keep it. Somehow he'll get it back. You'll be in terrible danger then. What I'm telling you is—if you or any of your brothers need refuge from Gabya, then trust no man. Do you understand? Trust no *man.*"

Elemak was unsure how to answer. He *was* a man; how did she expect him to respond to such advice?

"There are few women in this city," said Rasa, "who would not rejoice to see Gabya deprived of much of his power and prestige. They would gladly help the taker of the Index to escape the grasp of Gaballufix—even if the Index had been obtained by some means that ordinarily might be viewed as . . ."

"Criminal," said Elemak.

"I hate the thought of it," said Rasa. "But your Father is certainly right that it would be a harsh blow against Gaballufix, to lose the Index."

"It wasn't Father's idea, really," said Elemak. "He said it came to him in a dream. From the Oversoul."

"Then it might happen," she said. "It might. Perhaps . . . who knows whether the Oversoul might still have enough influence over Gaballufix to make him—what, temporarily stupid?"

"Stupid enough to give it to me?"

"And stupid enough not to find you and strike you down once you have it."

Elemak felt Eiadh's hand in his, her body leaning against him. I came here for refuge, and out of desire for you, Eiadh—but it was Rasa whose help I really needed. Imagine if I had gone into Gabya's house, not realizing how important this Index really is! "Lady Rasa, how can I thank you for all you've done for me."

"I fear that I've encouraged you to risk your life in an impossible endeavor," said Rasa. "I hate to think Gaballufix might really harm you, but the stakes in this gamble are very high. The future of Basilica is the prize—but I fear that the getting of the prize might harm the city so much that it isn't worth the game."

"Whatever happens," Elemak said, "you can be sure that I will return for Eiadh if I can, and if she'll have me."

"Even if you're a pariah and a criminal?" said Rasa. "Would you expect her to go with you even then?"

"Especially then!" cried Eiadh. "I don't love Elya for his money or his position in the city, I love him for himself."

"My dear," said Rasa, "you've never *known* him without his money or his position. How do you know who he'll be when he doesn't have them anymore?"

It was a cruel thing for her to say; Elemak could not believe that she had even thought such a thought, let alone brought it to her lips. "If Eiadh were the sort of woman whose heart followed her coveting, Lady Rasa, then she would not be a woman I could love, or even trust. But I *do* love her, and no woman is worthier of my trust."

Rasa smiled at him. "Oh, Eiadh, your suitor has such a beautiful vision of you. Do try to be worthy of it."

"The way my Aunt Rasa talks, you'd think she was trying to talk you *out* of loving me," said Eiadh. "Maybe she's the teensiest bit jealous of me for having such a fine man courting me."

"You forget," said Rasa. "I already have the father. What would I want with the son?"

It was a tense moment; things were being said that should not—*could* not—be said in polite company. Unless it was as a joke.

At last Rasa laughed. At last. They joined in her laughter eagerly, in relief.

"May the Oversoul go with you," said Rasa.

"Come back for me soon," said Eiadh. She pressed herself against him so tightly that he could feel where every part of her body touched him, as if she were imprinting herself on his flesh. Or perhaps taking the imprint of his body on herself. He embraced her back; she would have no doubt of his desire *or* his devotion.

It was midafternoon when Elemak got to Gaballufix's house. By habit he almost slipped down the alleyway to the private side entrance. But then he realized that his relationship with Gaballufix had changed in unpredictable ways. If Gaballufix regarded him as a traitor, then a secret arrival, completely unobserved, would give Gabya a perfect opportunity to be rid of him with no one the wiser. Besides, to come in the back way implied that Elemak was of a lower station than Gaballufix. He had had enough of that. He would come in openly, obviously, through the front entrance, like a man of importance in the city, an honored guest—with plenty of witnesses.

To his pleasure, Gaballufix's servants were deferential, ushering him inside immediately, and there was very little waiting before Elemak was led to the library, where he had always met with Gaballufix. Nothing seemed changed—Gabya arose from his chair and greeted Elemak with an embrace. They spoke like brothers, gossiping for a few minutes about people they both knew in Gaballufix's circle of friends and supporters. The only hint of tension between them was the way Gabya referred to Elemak's "hasty midnight departure."

"It wasn't my idea," said Elemak. "I don't know which of your people talked, but Father woke us up hours before dawn, and we were out on the desert before the meeting was to have taken place."

"I didn't like being taken by surprise," said Gaballufix. "But I know that sometimes these things are out of one's control."

Gabya was being understanding. Relief swept over him, and Elemak sat back more comfortably in his chair. "You can imagine how worried I was. I couldn't very well slip away and warn you what was happening —Father was on us the whole time, not to mention my little brothers."

"Mebbekew?"

"It was all I could do to keep him from loosing all his sphincters on the spot. You should never have brought him into the plan."

"Shouldn't I?"

"How do you know he wasn't the one who warned Father?"

"I don't know that," said Gaballufix. "All I know is that my dear cousin Wetchik left, and my brother Elemak with him."

"At least he's out of the city. He won't be interfering with you anymore."

"Won't he?"

"Of course not. What can he do from some secluded valley in the desert?"

"He sent *you* back," said Gaballufix.

"With a limited objective that has nothing to do with the whole debate over war wagons and Potokgavan and the Wetheads."

"The debate has moved far beyond those concerns anyway," said Gaballufix. "Or, perhaps I should say, it has moved far *closer* than those concerns. So tell me—what is your father's limited objective, and how can I thwart him?"

Elemak laughed, hoping that Gabya was joking. "The best way to thwart him, I think, is to give him what he wants—a simple thing, *nothing*, really—and then we'll go away and it'll be between you and Roptat, the way you wanted it."

"I never wanted it between me and anybody," said Gaballufix. "I'm a peaceable man. I want no conflict. I thought I had a plan whereby conflict could be avoided, but at the last moment the people I counted on fell through."

He was still smiling, but Elemak realized that things were not as steady between them as he had hoped.

"Now tell me, Elya, what is the little thing that you think I should do for your father, solely because your father asks for it?"

"There's some Index," said Elemak. "An old thing that's been in the family for generations."

"An Index? Why would I have one of Wetchik's family indexes?"

"I don't know. I assumed you'd know which one he meant. He just called it 'the Index' and so I thought you'd know."

"I have dozens of indexes. Dozens." Then, suddenly, Gaballufix raised an eyebrow, as if he had just realized something. Elemak had seen him put on that same performance before, however, so he knew he was being played with. "Unless you mean—but no, that's absurd, that's nothing that ever belonged to the Wetchik house."

Elemak dutifully played along. "What are you talking about?"

"The *Palwashantu* Index, of course," said Gaballufix. "The whole reason for the clan having been established in the first place, back at the dawn of time. The most precious artifact in all of Basilica."

Of course he would play up the value of it. Just like any merchant who was eager to sell. Pretend that what he's selling is the most valuable thing ever to exist on the planet, so you can set some absurdly high price, and then work your way down.

"That can't be the one, then," said Elemak. "Father certainly didn't think it had that much value. It was more of a sentimental thing. His grandfather owned it, and lent it to the clan council for safekeeping during his travels. Now Father wants to take it with him on his travels."

"Oh, that's the one, then. His grandfather had it, but only as a temporary guardian. It was delegated to the Wetchik by the Palwashantu clan; he wearied of the burden, and gave it back. Now another guardian has been appointed—me. And I'm not weary. So tell your father I'm grateful that he was willing to help me with my duties, but I'll struggle on without his help for another few years, I think."

It was time for the price to be mentioned. Elemak waited, but Gaballufix said nothing.

And then, when the silence had stretched on for several minutes, Gaballufix arose from behind his table. "Anyway, my dear brother, I'm glad to see you back in the city. I hope you'll be here for a long time—I can use your support. In fact, now that your father seems to have run off, I'll certainly use my influence to try to get you appointed Wetchik in his place."

This was not at all what Elemak had expected. It asserted a relationship between Elemak and his own inheritance that was completely intolerable. "Father is Wetchik," he said. "He hasn't died, and when he does, I'm Wetchik without any help from anyone."

"Hasn't died?" asked Gaballufix. "Then where is he? I don't see my old friend Wetchik—but I do see the son that stands to profit most from his death."

"My brothers will also witness that Father is alive."

"And where are *they*?"

Elemak almost blurted out the fact that they were hiding not very far from the city walls. Then he realized that this was almost certainly what Gaballufix wanted most to know—who Elemak's allies were, and where they were hiding. "You don't think I'd enter the city alone, do you, when my brothers are as eager to come back to Basilica as I am!"

Of course Gaballufix knew that Elemak was lying—or, at the least, he knew that Elemak's thumbprint was the only one that had shown up at any of the city gates. What Gabya couldn't know was whether Elemak was merely bluffing, and his brothers were all far away in the desert—or whether they had circumvented the guards at the gates and even now were in the city, plotting some mischief that Gaballufix would need to worry about. Yet Gaballufix couldn't say anything about the fact that he knew Elemak was the only one to enter the city legally —it would be as much as admitting that he had complete access to the city's computers.

"I'm glad they were able to return to the pleasures of the city," said Gabya. "I hope they're careful though. A rough element has been brought into the city—mostly by Roptat and his gang, I'm afraid—and even though I'm helping the city by letting a few of my employees put in extra duty hours patrolling the streets, it's still possible for young men wandering alone through the city to get involved in unfortunate incidents. Sometimes dangerous ones."

"I'll warn them to look out."

"And you, too, Elemak. I worry for you, my brother. There are those who think your father was involved in a plot against Roptat. What if they take out their resentment on *you*?"

At that moment Elemak realized that his mission had failed. Gabya clearly *did* believe that Elemak had betrayed him—or else had concluded that Elemak was no longer useful and might even be dangerous enough to be worth killing. There was no hope now of getting anything through a pretense of polite brotherliness. But it might be worth taking a different tack.

"Come now, Gabya," said Elemak, "you know that you're the one who's been putting out that story about Father plotting against Roptat. That was the plan, remember? For Father to be found in the coolhouse with Roptat's murdered corpse. He wouldn't be convicted, but he'd be implicated, discredited. Only Father didn't come, and therefore Roptat wouldn't get close enough for your thugs to kill him, and now you're trying to salvage as much of the plan as you can. We sat here and talked about it—why should we pretend now that we don't both know exactly what's going on?"

"But we *don't* both know what's going on," said Gaballufix. "I haven't the faintest idea what you're talking about."

Elemak looked at him with contempt. "And to think I once believed you were capable of leading Basilica to greatness. You couldn't even neutralize your opposition when you had the chance."

"I was betrayed by fools and cowards," said Gaballufix.

"That's the excuse that fools and cowards always give for their failures—and it's always true, as long as you realize that it's self-betrayal they're talking about."

"You call *me* a fool and a coward?" Gaballufix was angry now, losing control. Elemak had never seen him like this, except a flash of temper now and then. He wasn't sure that he could handle this, but at least it wasn't the suave indifference that Gabya had been showing him till now. "At least I didn't sneak off in the middle of the night," said Gaballufix. "At least I didn't believe every story I was told, no matter how idiotic it was."

"And I did?" asked Elemak. "You forget, Gabya, *you* were the only one telling me stories. So now, I'd like to know, which of the stories was I idiotic to believe? That you were only acting in the best interests of Basilica? I never believed that one—I knew you were out for your own profit and your own power. Or perhaps you think I believed the story that you really loved my father and were really trying to protect him from getting into the political situation over his head. Do you think I actually believed *that* one? You've hated him since Lady Rasa lapsed you and remated with him, and you've hated him more every year that they've stayed together."

"I never cared about that!" said Gaballufix. "She's nothing to me!"

"Even now she's the only audience you try to please—imagine, going to her house and strutting like some cockbird, showing off for her. You should hear how she laughs about you now." Elemak knew, of course, that saying such a thing put Rasa in great danger—but this was a game with high risks, and Elemak couldn't hope to win it unless he took some chances. Besides, Lady Rasa could handle Gaballufix.

"Laughs? She doesn't laugh. You haven't even spoken with her."

"Look at me—do you see any of the filth of travel on my clothing? I bathed in her house. I'm going to mate with her favorite niece. She told me that she would as soon have mated with a rabbit as to spend another night with you."

For a moment he thought Gaballufix would draw a weapon and kill him on the spot. Then Gabya's face relaxed a little, into something like a smile. "Now I *know* you're lying," he said. "Rasa would never say something so crude."

"Of course I made it up," said Elemak. "I just wanted you to see who was the fool, believing any story that he heard."

"It's one thing to believe for a moment," said Gaballufix. "It's another story to keep believing and believing in the stupidest ideas."

It was in that moment that it first dawned on Elemak what the lie was that Gaballufix was saying he still believed. And Gabya was right—Elemak was a fool ever to have believed it, and a worse fool to have kept on believing it until now. "You never meant to charge Father with killing Roptat, did you?"

"Of course I did," said Gabya.

"But not to bring him to trial."

"Oh, no, that would be silly—a waste of time. I told you that."

"You *said* it would be a waste of time because Father's prestige in the city meant he'd never be convicted. But the truth was he would never have come to trial because you meant people to discover both Roptat's *and* Father's bodies in the coolhouse."

"What a terrible accusation. I deny it all. You have such an evil imagination, *boy.*"

"You were using me to betray my own father so you could *kill* him."

"For the longest time," said Gaballufix, "I assumed you knew that. I assumed you understood that we were simply not speaking directly about it because it was such an unpleasant subject. I thought you realized that the only way I could get you your inheritance early was by arranging your father's death."

Elemak's fury at having almost been a conspirator in father-killing overwhelmed all his self-control. He lunged toward Gaballufix—and found himself staring at the pulse in Gaballufix's hand.

"Yes, yes, I see that you have some idea of what a pulse can do to a man at close range. You killed a man with a weapon just like this, didn't you? In fact," said Gaballufix, "it might have *been* this weapon, mightn't it!"

Elemak looked at the pulse and recognized the wear marks on it, where it had been laid down on stone, where it had been nicked and marked, where the color had been faded by the sunlight as it rested at his hip during countless hours of travel in the desert. "I lent that pulse to Mebbekew the day I got home from my last caravan," he said stupidly.

"And Mebbekew lent it to me. I told him—speaking of fools—that I wanted it to surprise you with later, at a party, to honor you for drawing blood. I told him I was going to use your story to inspire my soldiers." Gaballufix laughed. And laughed.

"That's why you brought Meb in. To get my pulse." But why? Elemak imagined his father lying there, dead, and then someone discovering Elemak's pulse not far away, abandoned perhaps in his haste to flee. He imagined Gaballufix explaining to the city council, tears in his eyes. "This is where greed in the younger generation leads—my own half-brother, willing to murder his father in order to get his inheritance."

"You're right," said Elemak quietly. "I *was* a fool."

"You were and you are," said Gaballufix. "You were seen in the city today—all over the city. My men tracked you through several neighborhoods. There are many witnesses—and it will be so delicious to see Rasa forced to testify against her beloved Volemak's oldest boy. Because someone is going to die tonight, killed with this very pulse, which will be found near the body, and then everyone will know that it was Wetchik's son who was the assassin, probably at his father's orders. And the best part of it is, I can tell you this, and then I can let you know, I can put you out of the city *alive* and there's still nothing you can do about it. If you start telling people about *my* plot to kill somebody—whoever I decide it should be—they'll all assume that you were simply trying to cover up your own crime in advance. You *are* a fool, Elemak, just like your father. Even when you knew I wasn't afraid to kill to accomplish my purposes, you somehow thought that you and your family would be immune, that somehow I'd be more tender with you because the same weary old womb bore you and me during our nine months sucking life out of a placenta."

Elemak had never seen such fury, such hatred, such *evil* in a human face, had never imagined it was possible. Yet there he stood, looking at Gabya's glee in describing a crime he meant to commit. It frightened Elemak, but it also made him feel an insane kind of confidence. As if Gaballufix's having revealed his true inner smallness made Elemak realize how much larger he was himself, after all.

"Who's the fool, Gabya," said Elemak. "Who's the fool."

"I think there's no doubt of that now," said Gaballufix.

"True enough," said Elemak. "You'll make it impossible for Father and me to return to the city, for a while at least, but the death of Roptat won't open the road for you. Are you so stupid, really? Nobody will believe for a moment that Father would kill Roptat, or that I would either."

"I'll have the weapon!" said Gaballufix.

"The weapon, but no witness to the killing, just *your* story bruited about by *your* people. They aren't so stupid that they can't add one and one. Who stands to gain from Roptat's death and Father's exile? Only you, Gabya. This city will rise up in bloody rebellion against you. Your soldiers will die in the streets."

"You overestimate the will of my feeble-hearted enemies," said Gaballufix. But his voice didn't sound so certain anymore, and the glee was gone.

"Your enemies aren't feeble-hearted, just because they're unwilling to kill in order to get their way. They *are* willing to kill to stop a man like *you.* A weak-brained, jealous, spiteful, malicious little parasitic roach like you."

"Do you want so much to die?"

"Yes, kill me here, Gabya. Hundreds of people know I'm here. Hundreds are waiting to hear what I tell them. Your whole plan stands revealed, and none of it will work. Because you were so stupid that you had to brag."

Elemak's words were all bluff, of course, but Gaballufix believed him. At least enough to make him pause. To make him wonder. Then Gabya smiled. "Elya, my brother, I'm proud of you."

Elemak recognized surrender when he heard it. He said nothing in reply.

"You *are* my brother after all—the blood of Volemak didn't weaken you after all. It may even have made you stronger."

"Do you really think I'll swallow your flattery *now?*"

"Of course not," said Gaballufix. "Of course you'll disregard it—but that doesn't stop me from admiring you, does it? It just stops you from believing in my admiration! The loss is yours, dear Elya."

"I came for the Index, Gaballufix," said Elemak. "A simple thing. Give it to me, and I'm gone. Wetchik and his family will never bother you again, and you can play your little games until somebody puts a knife in your back just to stop that squealing noise you make whenever you think you've been especially clever."

Gaballufix cocked his head to one side.

He's going to give it to me, thought Elemak, triumphantly.

"No," said Gaballufix. "I'd like to, but I can't. The disappearance of the Index—that would be hard to explain to the clan council. A lot of trouble, that's what it would cause, and why should I put myself to all that trouble just to get rid of Wetchik? After all, I'm already rid of him."

Now, at last, Elemak was where he wanted to be: bargaining like a merchant. "What else would it take to make it worth your while?" asked Elemak.

"Make me an offer. Enough money that it'll make up for all the extra effort I have to go through."

"Give me the Index, and Father will release funds to you. Whatever you want."

"I'm supposed to *wait* for the funds? Wait for *Wetchik* to pay me later for an Index I give you now? Oh—I get it—I see what's happening!" Gaballufix laughed in derision. "You can't give me money *now* because you don't have any. Wetchik still hasn't released any of his fortune to you! He sent you on this errand and he didn't even give you access to his money!"

It *was* humiliating. Father should have realized that in dealing with Gaballufix it would eventually come down to money; he should have given him password that would have let him access the Wetchik family funds. Rashgallivak, the steward, had more control over the Wetchik fortune than Elemak did. He was filled with fury and resentment against his father for putting him in such a position of weakness. The stupid short-sighted old man, always tripping over his own feet when it came to business!

"Tell me, Elya," said Gaballufix, interrupting his own laughter. "If your own father doesn't trust you with his money, why should I trust you with the Index?"

With that, Gaballufix reached under his table and apparently triggered some kind of switch, for three doors opened at once and identical-looking soldiers burst into the room. They took hold of Elemak and roughly thrust him out into the hall, then out the front door.

Nor was that enough. They quick-marched him to the nearest gate, which happened to be the Back Gate—right past his mother's house—and threw him into the dirt in front of the guards.

"This one's leaving the city!" shouted one of the soldiers.

"And never coming back!" cried another.

The guards, however, did not seem terribly impressed. "Are you a citizen?" asked one.

"Yes," said Elemak, dusting himself off.

"Thumb please." They presented the thumbscreen, and Elemak held his thumb over it. "Citizen Elemak son of Lady Rasa by the Wetchik. It is an honor to serve you." Whereupon the guards all stood at attention and saluted him.

It completely stunned him. Never, in all his passages into and out of the city of Basilica, had anyone done more than raise an eyebrow when the city computer reported his prestigious parentage. And now a salute!

Then Gaballufix's soldiers jeered again, boasting about what they'd do to him if he ever returned, and Elemak understood. The official city guards were letting him and everyone else near the gate see that *they* were not part of Gaballufix's little army. Furthermore, the very fact that the son of Wetchik was clearly the enemy of Gaballufix made city guards want to salute him. If Elemak could only figure out how to use this situation, he might very well be able to turn it to his advantage. What if I returned to the city as the deliverer, leading the guard and the militia in crushing Gabya and his hated army of costume clones. The city would then gladly give me all that Gabya is trying to win through trickery, intimidation, and murder. I'd have all the power Gaballufix ever imagined—and the city would love me for it.

12

Fortune

It was a miserable day in the desert, even allowing for the fact that except for about an hour and a half at noon, the canyon was in deep shade, with a steady breeze funneling through it. No place is comfortable, thought Nafai, when you're waiting for someone *else* to do a job you think of as your own. Worse than the heat, than the sweat dripping into his eyes, than the grit that got into his clothing and between his teeth, was the sick dread Nafai felt whenever he thought of *Elemak* being the one entrusted with the Oversoul's errand.

Nafai knew that Elemak had rigged the casting of lots, of course. He wasn't such a fool as to think Elemak would actually leave such a thing to chance. Even as he admired the deftness with which Elya handled it, Nafai was angry at him. Was he even *attempting* to get the Index? Or was he going into the city and meeting with Gaballufix in order to plan some further betrayal of Father and of the city and, finally, of the Oversoul's guardianship of humanity?

Would he even return?

Then, at last, in mid-afternoon, there came the clatter and rattle of stones tumbling, and Elemak clambered noisily down into their hiding place. His hands were empty, but his eyes were bright. We have been betrayed, thought Nafai.

"He said no, of course," said Elemak. "This Index is more important than Father told us. Gaballufix doesn't want to give it up—at least not for nothing."

"For what, then?" asked Issib.

"He didn't say. But he has a price. He made it clear that he's willing to hear an offer. The trouble is—we have to go back to Father and get access to his finances."

Nafai didn't like this at all. How did they know what Elemak and Gaballufix had promised each other?

"All the way back, empty-handed," said Mebbekew. "Tell you what, Elya. *You* go back, and the rest of us will wait here till you come back with the password to Father's accounts."

"Right," said Issib. "I'm not going to spend the night out here in the desert, when I can go into the city and use my floats."

"How stupid are you, really?" said Elemak. "Don't you realize that things are different now? You can't go wandering anonymously through the city anymore. Gabya's troops are all over it. And Gaballufix is not Father's friend. Therefore he's not *our* friend, either."

"He's your brother," said Mebbekew.

"He's nobody's brother," said Elemak. "He's got both the morals and the surface properties of slime. I know him better than any of you, and I can promise you that he'd just as soon kill any of us as look at us."

Nafai was amazed to hear Elemak talking this way. "I thought you wanted him to lead Basilica."

"I thought his plan was the best hope for Basilica in the coming wars," said Elemak. "But I never thought Gaballufix was out to get anything except his own advantage. His soldiers are all over the city— wearing some kind of holographic costume that covers their whole bodies, so all his soldiers look absolutely identical."

"Whole-body masks!" cried Mebbekew. "What a great idea!"

"It means," said Elemak, "that even when somebody sees one of Gaballufix's soldiers committing a crime—like kidnapping or killing a stray son of old Wetchik—no one can possibly identify the individual who did it."

"Oh," said Mebbekew.

"So," said Nafai, "even if Father gives us access to his money, what then? What makes you think Gaballufix would sell it?"

"Think, Nafai. Even a fourteen-year-old should be able to grasp *something* of the affairs of men. Gaballufix is paying hundreds and hundreds of soldiers. His fortune is large, but not large enough to keep that up forever, not without getting control of the tax money of Basilica to support them all. Father's money could make a huge difference. At the moment, Gaballufix probably needs money more than he needs the prestige of possessing this Index, which hardly anybody has even heard of anymore."

Swallowing Elemak's condescension, Nafai realized that Elemak's analysis was right. "The Index *is* for sale, then."

"*Could* be," said Elemak. "So we go back to Father and see whether the Index is worth spending money for, and how *much* money. Then he gives us access to his finances and we go back and bargain—"

"And I say *you* go home and let me take my chances in the city," said Mebbekew.

"I want to get away from my chair tonight," said Issib.

"When we come back," said Elemak, "*then* you can get into the city."

"Like this time? You make us wait again, just like this time, and we'll never get in," said Issib.

"Fine," said Elemak. "I'll go back alone and tell Father that you've abandoned him and his cause, just so you can go into the city and float around and get laid."

"I'm not going in to get laid!" protested Issib.

"And I'm not going in to float," said Mebbekew, grinning.

"Wait a minute," said Nafai. "If we go back to Father and get permission, then what? It'll be almost a week. Who knows how things might have changed by then? There could already be civil war in Basilica. Or by then Gaballufix might have arranged other financing, so that our money wouldn't mean anything to him. The time to make an offer is *now.*"

Elemak looked at him in surprise. "Well, yes, of course, that's true. But we don't have access to Father's money."

In answer, Nafai looked at Issib.

Issib rolled his eyes. "I promised Father," he said.

"You mean *you* have access to Father's password?" said Mebbekew.

"He said that somebody else ought to know it, in case of an emergency," said Issib. "How did *you* know about it, Nafai?"

"Come on," said Nafai, "I'm not an idiot. In your research you were getting access to city library files that they'd never let a kid like you get into without specific adult authorization. I didn't know Father had *given* it to you, though."

"Well," said Issib, "he only gave me the entry code. I kind of figured out the back half myself."

Mebbekew was livid. "All this time that I've been living like a beggar in the city, *you* had access to Father's entire fortune?"

"Think about it, Meb," said Elemak. "Who else could Father *trust* with his password? Nafai's a child, you're a spendthrift, and I was constantly disagreeing with him about where we ought to invest our money. Issib, though—what was *he* going to do with the money?"

"So because he doesn't *need* money, he gets all he wants?"

"If I had ever used his password to get money, he would have changed it and so of course I never used it," said Issib. "Maybe he has still another password for getting into the money—I never tried. And I'm not trying now, either, so you can forget it. Father didn't authorize us to go dipping into the family fortune."

"He told us that the Oversoul wanted us to bring him the Index," said Nafai. "Don't you see? The Index is so important that Father had to send us back to face his enemy, a man who planned to kill him—"

"Oh, come on, Nyef, that was Father's *dream*, not anything real," said Mebbekew. "Gaballufix wasn't planning to kill Father."

"Yes he was," said Elemak. "He was planning to kill Roptat *and* Father, and then put the blame on me."

Mebbekew's jaw hung open.

"He was going to arrange to have them find my pulse—the one I lent to *you*, Mebbekew—near Father's body. Clumsy of you to lose my pulse, Meb."

"How do you know all this?" asked Issib.

"Gaballufix told me," said Elemak. "While he was trying to impress me with my helplessness."

"Let's go to the council," said Issib. "If Gaballufix confessed—"

"He confessed—or rather *bragged*—to *me*, in a room alone. My word against his. There's no point in telling anybody. It wouldn't do any good."

"This is the opportunity," said Nafai. "Today, right now. We go down to the house, access Father's files through his own library, convert all the funds into liquid assets. We go to the gold market and pick it up as metal bars and negotiable bonds and jewels and what-not, and then we go to Gaballufix and—"

"And he steals it all from us and kills us and leaves the chopped-up bits of our bodies for the jackals to find in some ditch outside the city," said Elemak.

"Not so," said Nafai. "We take a witness with us—someone he won't dare to touch."

"Who?" said Issib.

"Rashgallivak," said Nafai. "He isn't just the steward of the house of Wetchik, you know. He's Palwashantu, and has a great deal of trust and prestige. We bring him along, he watches everything, he witnesses the exchange of Father's fortune for the Index, and we all walk out alive. Gaballufix might be able to kill *us*, because we're in hiding and Father's an exile, but he can't touch Rash."

"You mean all *four* of us go to Gaballufix?" asked Issib.

"Into the city?" asked Mebbekew.

"It's not a bad plan," said Elemak. "Risky, but you're right about this being the time to act."

"So let's go down to the house," said Nafai. "We can leave the animals here for the night, can't we? Issib and I can go to Father's library to do the funds transfer, while you and Meb find Rash and bring him there so we can go meet Gaballufix together."

"Will Rash go along with it?" asked Issib. "I mean, what if Gaballufix decides to kill us all anyway?"

"Yes," said Elemak. "He's a man of perfect loyalty. He will never swerve from his duty to the house of Wetchik."

It took only an hour or so. It was late afternoon when they walked into the Gold Market and began the final transactions. All of the funds that were not tied up in real property were all in spendable form in Issib's bank file—actually, like all the brothers' bank files, a mere subfile of Father's all-inclusive account. If anyone doubted that Issib was authorized to spend so much, there was Rashgallivak, silently observing. Everyone knew that if Rash was there, it had to be legitimate.

The amount involved was the largest single purchase of portable assets in the recent history of the Gold Market. No one broker had anything like enough ingots or jewels or bonds to handle even a large fraction of the buy. For more than an hour, until the sun was behind the red wall and the Gold Market was in shadow, the brokers scrambled among themselves until at last the whole amount was laid out on a single table. The funds were transferred; a staggering amount was moved from one column to another in all the computer displays—for all the brokers were watching now, in awe. The ingots then were rolled up in three cloth packages and tied, the jewels were rolled in cloth and bagged, and the bonds were folded into leather binders. Then all the parcels were distributed among the four sons of Wetchik.

One of the brokers had already arranged for a half-dozen of the city guards to accompany them wherever they were going, but Elemak sent them away. "If the guards are with us, then every thief in Basilica will see and take note of where we're going. Our lives will be worthless then," said Elemak. "We'll move swiftly and without guard, without notice."

Again the brokers looked at Rashgallivak, who nodded his approval.

Half an hour through the streets of the city, nervously aware of everyone who glanced at them, and then at last they were at the doors of Gaballufix's house. Nafai saw at once that both Elemak and Mebbekew were recognized here. So, too, was Rashgallivak—but Rash was widely known in the Palwashantu clan, so it would have been a surprise if he had *not* been recognized. Only Nafai and Issib had to be introduced as they stood before Gaballufix in the great salon of his— no, not *his*, but his *wife's* house.

"So you're the one who flies," said Gaballufix, looking at Issib.

"I float," said Issib.

"So I see," said Gaballufix. "Rasa's sons, the two of you." He looked Nafai in the eye. "Very large for one so young."

Nafai said nothing. He was too busy studying Gaballufix's face. So ordinary, really. A little soft, perhaps. Not young anymore, though younger than Father, who had, after all, slept with Gaballufix's mother —enough to produce Elemak. There was some slight resemblance between Elya and Gaballufix, but not very much, only in the darkness of the hair, and the way the eyes were perhaps a little close together under heavy-ridged brows.

It was in the eyes that they were alike, but also in the eyes that they differed most, for there was a rheuminess, a scarlet-rimmed look in Gaballufix's eyes that was the opposite of Elya's sharpness. Elemak was a man of action and strength, a man of the desert, who could face strangers and unknown places with courage and confidence and vigor. Gaballufix, by contrast, was a man who went nowhere and did nothing; rather he denned himself here and let others do his work for him. Elemak went out and penetrated the world, changing it where he would; Gaballufix stayed in one place and sucked the world dry, emptying it in order to fill himself.

"So the young one is speechless," said Gaballufix.

"For the first time in his life," said Meb. There was some nervous laughter.

"Why do the sons and the steward of Wetchik honor me with this visit?"

"Father wanted us to trade gifts with you," said Elemak. "We're living in a place where we need little in the way of money, yet Father has taken it into his heart—no, the Oversoul has commanded him—to bring the Index with him. While you, Gaballufix, have little use for the Index—have you even looked at it in all your years as leader of the clan council?—and might be able to turn some portion of the Wetchik estate to better advantage than Father ever could, being far from the city."

It was an eloquent, truthful, and completely deceptive speech, and Nafai admired it. There was no doubt in anyone's mind that a purchase was being attempted here, and yet it was delicately disguised as an exchange of gifts, so that no one could openly accuse Gaballufix of having sold the Index, or Father of having bought it.

"I'm sure my kinsman Wetchik is far too generous to me," said Gaballufix. "I can't imagine that I would be of much help to him, managing some trifling portion of his great fortune."

In answer, Elemak stepped forward and unrolled a heavy parcel of platinum ingots. Gaballufix picked up one ingot and hefted it in his hands. "This is a thing of beauty," he said. "And yet I know this is such a tiny part of the Wetchik fortune that I could not feel right about doing such a small favor for my kinsman, when he would bear in exchange the heavy burden of guarding the Palwashantu Index."

"This is only a sample," said Elemak.

"If I'm to be trusted with this, shouldn't I see the extent of my guardianship?"

Elemak removed all the rest of the treasure that he carried on his person, and laid it on the table. "Surely that is all that Father would dare ask you to be burdened with," he said.

"Such a slight burden," said Gaballufix. "I would be ashamed to have this be all the help I gave my kinsman." Yet Nafai could see that Gaballufix's eyes were shining at the sight of so much wealth all in one place. "I assume that it's only a quarter of what you carry." Gaballufix looked from Nafai to Issib and Mebbekew.

"I think that's enough," said Elemak.

"Then I couldn't agree to lay the burden of the Index on my kinsman," said Gaballufix.

"Very well," said Elemak. He reached out and started rolling up the ingots.

Is that all? thought Nafai. Do we give up so easily? Am I the only one who can see that Gaballufix hungers for the money? That if we offer just a little more, he'll sell?

"Wait," said Nafai. "We can add what I carry to this."

Nafai was aware that Elemak was glaring at him, but it was unthinkable to come so close and leave empty-handed. Didn't Elemak realize the Index was *important?* More important than mere money, that was certain. "And if that isn't enough, Issib has more," Nafai said. "Show him, Issib. Let me show him."

In moments, they had tripled the offer.

"I fear," said Elemak, his voice icy, "that my younger brother has inconsiderately offered to burden you with far more than I ever intended you to have to deal with."

"On the contrary," said Gaballufix. "It is your younger brother who has more correctly estimated how much of a burden I'm willing to bear. Indeed, I think that if the last quarter of what you carried into my house were upon this table, I'd feel right about weighing down my dear kinsman with the heavy responsibility of the Palwashantu Index."

"I say it's too much," said Elemak.

"Then you hurt my feelings," said Gaballufix, "and I can't see any reason for further discussion."

"We came for the Index," said Nafai. "We came because the Oversoul demands it."

"Your father is famous for his holiness and his visions," said Gaballufix.

"If you're willing to accept all that we have," said Nafai, "we'll gladly lay it before you in order to fulfil the will of the Oversoul."

"Such obedience will long be remembered in the Temple," said Gaballufix. He looked at Mebbekew. "Or is Nafai's holiness not matched by that of his brother Mebbekew?"

Anguished with indecision, Elemak looked back and forth between Elemak and Gaballufix.

But it was Elemak who acted. He reached down and again rolled up ingots into the cloth.

"No!" cried Nafai. "We won't turn back now!" He held out his hand to Mebbekew. "You know what Father would want you to do."

"I see that only the youngest has true understanding," said Gaballufix.

Mebbekew stepped forward and began laying parcels on the table. As he did, Nafai could feel Elemak grip his shoulder, the fingers biting deep, and Elemak whispered in his ear, "I told you to leave this to me. You've given him four times what we needed to pay, you little fool. You've left us with nothing."

Nothing but the Index, thought Nafai. But still, he vaguely realized that Elemak might in fact have known better how to handle the bargaining, and perhaps he should have kept his mouth shut and let Elya handle things. But at the time he acted, Nafai was so *sure* that he had to speak or they would never get the Index.

All the Wetchik fortune except the land and buildings themselves was on Gaballufix's table.

"Is *that* enough?" asked Elemak dryly.

"Exactly enough," said Gaballufix. "Exactly enough to prove to me that Volemak the Wetchik has completely betrayed the Palwashantu. This great fortune has been put into the hands of children, who have, with childish stupidity, resolved to waste it all on the purchase of that which every true Palwashantu knows can *never* be sold. The Index, the sacred, holy trust of the Palwashantu—did Volemak think it could be bought? No, impossible, it could not be! I can only conclude that he has either lost his mind or you have killed him and hidden his body somewhere."

"No!" cried Nafai.

"Your lies are obscene," said Elemak, "and we won't tolerate them." He stepped forward and reached out for a third time to gather up the treasure.

"Thief!" shouted Gaballufix.

Suddenly the doors opened, and a dozen soldiers entered the room.

"Do you think you can do this in the presence of Rashgallivak?" demanded Elemak.

"I *insist* on doing it in his presence," said Gaballufix. "Who do you think first came to me with the news that Volemak was betraying the trust of the Wetchiks? That Volemak's sons were gutting the Wetchik fortune for some mad whim?"

"I serve the house of Wetchik," said Rashgallivak. He looked at each of the brothers, his face a mask of sadness. "It could not possibly be in the interest of that great house to let the fortune be destroyed by one madman who thinks he sees visions. Gaballufix could hardly believe what I told him, but he agreed with me that the fortune of Wetchik had to be shifted into the care of another branch of the family."

"As chief of the Palwashantu clan," Gaballufix intoned, "I hereby declare that Volemak and his sons, having proven themselves unfit and unreliable as guardians of the greatest house in the clan, are therefore removed as heirs and possessors of the house of Wetchik for all time. And in recognition of years of loyal service, by himself and his ancestors for many centuries, I grant temporary guardianship of the Wetchik fortune, and the use of the name of Wetchik, to Rashgallivak, to care for all aspects of the Wetchik house until such time as the clan council shall dispose of them otherwise. As for Volemak and his sons, if they make any effort to protest or dispute this action, they will be regarded as blood-enemies of the Palwashantu, and shall be dealt with by laws more ancient than those of the city of Basilica." Gaballufix leaned forward across the table, smiling at Elemak. "Did you understand all that, Elya?"

Elemak looked at Rashgallivak. "I understand that the most loyal man in Basilica is now the worst traitor."

"You were the traitors," said Rash. "This sudden madness of visions, a completely unprofitable journey into the desert, selling off all the animals, dismissing all the workers, and now this—as steward of the house of Wetchik, I had no choice but to involve the clan council."

"Gaballufix isn't the clan council," said Elemak. "He's a common thief, and you've put our fortune in his hands."

"You were putting the fortune in his hands," said Rashgallivak. "Don't you see that I did this for you? For all four of you? The council will leave me as guardian for a few years, until all this blows over, and in that time if one of you proves himself to be a sober and completely reliable man, worthy of the responsibility, the Wetchik name and fortune will be returned to you."

"There'll be no fortune left," said Elemak. "Gabya will spend it on his armies before the year is out."

"Not at all," said Gaballufix. "I'm turning it all over to Rash, to continue as steward."

Elemak laughed bitterly. "As steward, required to use it as the council directs. And how will the council direct? You'll see, Rash. Very quickly indeed—because the council has incurred some pretty heavy expenses with all these soldiers they're paying."

Rashgallivak looked quite uncomfortable. "Gaballufix did mention that some small part of this might need to be deducted to meet present expenses, but your father would have contributed to clan expenses anyway, if he were still in his right mind."

"He's played you for the fool," said Elemak, "and me too. All of us."

Rash looked at Gaballufix, clearly concerned. "Maybe we ought to call in the council on this," he said.

"The council has already met," said Gaballufix.

"How heavy *are* the clan expenses?" asked Rashgallivak.

"A trifle," said Gaballufix. "Don't waste time worrying about it. Or are you going to prove yourself as unreliable as Volemak and his sons?"

"See?" said Elemak. "Already it begins—do as Gabya wants, or you won't be steward of the Wetchik fortune anymore."

"The law is the law," said Gaballufix. "And now it's time for these worthless young spendthrifts to leave my house before I charge them with the murder of their father."

"Before we say anything more to help Rash see the truth, you mean," said Elemak.

"We'll go," said Mebbekew. "But all this talk about the Palwashantu clan council and making Rashgallivak the Wetchik is rat piss. You're a thief, Gabya, a lying murdering thief who would have killed Roptat *and* Father if we hadn't left the city the day we did, and we're not leaving our family fortune in your bloody hands!"

With that Mebbekew lunged forward and seized a bag of jewels.

Immediately the soldiers were upon them, all four of them. The jewels were out of Meb's hands in a moment, and with no particular gentleness all four of them were out of the salon, out of the front doors, and thrown into the street.

"Away from here!" cried the soldiers. "Thieves! Murderers!"

Nafai hardly had a chance to think before Mebbekew was at his throat. "*You're* the one who had to lay all the treasure on the table!"

"He meant to have it all anyway," Nafai protested.

"Shut up, fools," said Elemak. "This isn't over. Our lives aren't worth dust—he probably has men waiting to kill us not fifty meters off. Our only hope is to split up and *run.* Don't stop for anything. And remember—something Rasa told me today—*trust no man.*" He said it again, changing the emphasis a little. "Trust no *man.* We'll meet tonight where the camels are. Anyone who isn't there by dawn we'll assume is dead. Now run—and *not* for any place that they'd expect you to go."

With that Elemak began to stride off toward the north. After only a few steps he turned back. "Now, fools! See—they're already signalling the assassins!"

Sure enough Nafai could see that one of the soldiers on Gaballufix's porch had raised one arm and was pointing at them with the other.

"How fast can you go with those floats?" Nafai asked Issib.

"Faster than you," he answered. "But not faster than a pulse."

"The Oversoul will protect us," said Nafai.

"Right," said Issib. "Now move, you fool."

Nafai ducked his head and plunged into the thickest part of the crowd. He had run a hundred meters south along Fountain Street when he turned back and saw why people were shouting behind him: Issib had risen some twenty meters into the air, and was just disappearing over the roof of the house directly across from Gaballufix's. I never knew he could do that, thought Nafai.

Then, as he turned to run again, it occurred to him that Issib probably hadn't known it, either.

"There's one," said a harsh voice. Suddenly a man appeared in front of him, a charged-wire blade in his hand. A woman gasped; people shied away. But almost without knowing that he knew it, Nafai could feel the presence of a man directly behind him. If he backed away from the blade in front, he would walk into the real assassin behind him.

So instead Nafai lunged forward. His enemy had not expected this unarmed boy to be aggressive—his swipe with the blade came nowhere near. Nafai put his knee sharply into the man's groin, lifting him off the ground. The man screamed. Then Nafai shoved him out of his way and ran in earnest now, not looking back, barely looking ahead except to dodge people and watch for the shimmering red glow of another blade, or the hot white beam of a pulse.

13

Flight

Issya had never tried to climb so high with his floats. He knew that they responded to his muscle tension, that whichever float he pressed down on the hardest remained fixed in its position in the air. But he had always thought that the position was somehow relative to the ground directly under the float. He was not entirely wrong—the higher he got, the more the floats tended to "slip" downward—but by and large he found that he could climb the air like a ladder until he was at roof height.

Naturally, everyone looked at him—but that's what he wanted. *Everybody* watch me, and talk about the young crippled boy who "flew" up to the roof. Gaballufix's goons wouldn't dare shoot him with so many witnesses, at least not directly in front of their leader's own house.

There was no one on the roofs, he saw that at once, and so he used them as a sort of highway, drifting low between vents and chimneys, cupolas and elevator housings, roofline ridges and the trees in rooftop gardens. Once he did surprise an old fellow who was repairing the masonry on the low wall around a widow's walk; the clattering sound of a broken tile worried Issib for a moment; when he turned, though, he saw that the man had not fallen, but rather stared gape-mouthed at

Issib. Will there be a story tonight, Issib wondered, about a young demigod seen drifting through the air over Basilica, perhaps on some errand of love with a mortal girl of surpassing beauty?

It was an exceptionally long block of houses, since several roads had been built over in this area. He was able to get more than halfway to Back Gate without descending to street level, and certainly he had made better time than any possible pursuers could have. There was always the chance, of course, that Gaballufix had assassins posted at all the city gates; certainly if he had an ambush at any gate it would be at Back Gate, the one nearest to his house. So Issib couldn't afford to be careless, once he was down at street level.

Before he left the roofs, though, he cast a longing gaze at the red wall of the city. High as he was, the sun was still up, split in half by the wall line. If only I could just fly over that. But he knew that the wall was loaded with complicated electronics, including the nodes that created the magnetic field that powered his floats. There was no crossing there—the tiny computer at his belt could never equalize the violently conflicting forces at the top of the wall.

He reached the end of a roof and drifted down into the crowd. This was the upper end of Holy Road, where men *were* allowed to go. Many noticed his descent, of course, but once he reached street level he immediately lowered himself to sitting position and scooted through the traffic at child-height. Let an assassin try to shoot me *now,* he thought. In minutes he was at the gate. The guards recognized his name the moment the thumb-scanner brought it up, and they clapped him on the back and wished him well.

It was not desert here at Back Gate, of course, but rather the fringes of Trackless Wood. To the right was the dense forest that made the north side of Basilica impassable; to the left, complicated arroyos, choked with trees and vines, led down from the well-watered hills into the first barren rocks of the desert. For a normal man, it would be a nightmare journey, unless he knew the way—as, he was sure, Elemak did. For Issib, of course, it was a matter of avoiding the tallest obstacles and floating easily down until the city was completely out of sight. He used the sun to steer by until he was down onto the desert plateau; then he bore south, crossing the roads named Dry and Desert, until, just at sunset, he reached the place where they had hidden his chair.

His floats were at the fringes of the magnetic field of the city now, and it was awkward maneuvering himself into the chair. But then everything to do with the chair was awkward and limiting. Still, it did have some advantages. Designed to be an all-purpose cripple's chair, it had a built-in computer display tied to the city's main public library when he was within range, with several different interfaces for people with different disabilities. He could even speak certain key words and it would understand them, and it could also produce a fair-sounding approximation of the commoner words in several dozen languages. If there were no such things as floats, the chair would probably be the most precious thing in his life. But there *were* floats. When he wore them, he was almost a regular human being, plus a few advantages. When he could not use them, he was a cripple with no advantages at all.

The camels were waiting outside the dependable influence of the city's magnetics, however, so use the chair he must. He got in, switched off the floats, and then guided the chair in its slow, hovering flight through narrow back canyons until at last he smelled, then heard the camels.

No one else was there; he was the first. He settled the chair onto its legs, leveled it, and then sat there alternately listening for anyone who might be approaching while scanning the library's news reports for word of any unexplained killings or other violent incidents. None yet. But then it might take time for word to reach the newswriters and the gossips. His brothers might be dying right now, or already dead, or captured and imprisoned and held for some sort of ransom. What would he do then? How could he hope to get home? The chair might carry him, though it was unlikely—it wasn't meant for long distance travel. He knew from experience that the chair could only move continuously for an hour or so before it needed several hours of solar recharging.

Mother will help me, thought Issib. If they don't come back tonight, Mother will help me. If I can get to her.

Mebbekew dodged through the crowd. He had seen several men trying to make their way toward him, but his experience as an actor— especially one who had to go through the audience collecting money— had given him a good sense of crowds, and he worked the traffic expertly against the men who were following him, heading always where the crowd was thickest, dodging through gaps that were about to be plugged by approaching groups of people. Soon the assassins—if that's what they were—were hopelessly far behind him. That was when Mebbekew began to *move*, a lazy, loping run that didn't give the impression of great haste but covered the ground very rapidly. It looked like he was running for the sheer joy of it, and in fact he was—but he never stopped watching. Whenever he saw soldiers, he headed straight for them, on the theory that Gaballufix wouldn't dare use men clearly identified as his own to conduct a public murder in the clear light of afternoon.

Within half an hour he had worked himself all the way east to Dolltown, the district that he knew best. The soldiers were rarer here, and while there were plenty of criminals for hire here, they were the sort who didn't stay bought for long. Meb also knew people who knew this part of town better than the city computer itself.

Trust no *man*, Elemak had said. Well, that was easy enough. Meb knew plenty of men, but his *friends* were all women. That had been an easy choice for him, from the time he was old enough to know the practical applications of the difference between men and women. He had almost laughed when Father got an auntie for him at the age of sixteen—he had enjoyed pretending to be new at lovemaking when he went to her, but within a few days she sent him away, laughingly saying that if he came back any more he'd be teaching *her* things that she had never particularly wanted to learn. Meb was good with women. They loved him, and they kept loving him, not because he was good at giving pleasure, though he was, but rather because he knew how to listen to women so they knew that he heard; he knew how to talk to them so they felt needed and protected, all at once. Not all women liked him, of course, but the ones that did liked him very much, and forever.

So it took only a few minutes in Dolltown before Mebbekew was in the room of a zither player on Music Street, and a few minutes more before he was in her arms, and a few minutes more before he was in her; then they talked for an hour, she went out and enlisted the help of some actresses they both knew, who were more than a little fond of Mebbekew themselves. Shortly after nightfall Mebbekew, in wig and gown and makeup, in voice and walk a woman, passed through Music Gate with a group of laughing, singing women. Only when he laid his thumb on the screen was his disguise revealed, and the guard, reading his name, merely winked at him and wished him a good night.

Mebbekew stayed in costume until he got to the rendezvous, and his only regret was that it was Issib who stared at him and didn't know him until he spoke, and not Elemak. It would have been nice to let his older brother see the joke. But then, given the fact that their entire fortune and Father's title as well had just been stolen from them, Elemak probably wouldn't have been in the mood for a joke anyway.

Elemak's passage from the city was the least eventful. He never saw an assassin, and had no problem getting to Hosni's house near the Back Gate. Fearing that perhaps the assassins were waiting at the gate itself, he ducked in to visit with his mother. She fed him a wonderful meal— she always hired the best cooks in Basilica—listened sympathetically to his story, agreed with him that if she had miscarried when pregnant with Gaballufix the world would be a better place, and finally sent him on his way several hours after dark with a bit of gold in his pocket, a sturdy metal-bladed knife at his belt, and a kiss. He knew that if Gaballufix came later that night, bragging about how he had tricked a fortune out of Volemak's sons, including Wetchik, Mother would laugh and praise him. She loved anything that was amusing, and was amused by almost anything. A cheerful woman, but utterly empty. Elemak was sure that Gaballufix got his morals from her, but certainly not his intelligence. Though, truth to tell, his teacher Rasa had told him once that his mother was actually very intelligent—much too intelligent to let others know how intelligent she was. "It's like being among dangerous foreigners," said Rasa. "It's much better to let them think you don't understand their language, so that they'll speak freely in front of you. That's how dear Hosni is when she's among those who fancy themselves very bright and well educated. She mocks them all unmercifully when they're gone."

Will she mock me to Gaballufix, as she mocked Gaballufix to me? Or ridicule us both to her womanfriends when we're gone?

At the gate, the guards recognized him at once, saluted him again, and offered to help him in any way they could. He thanked them, then plunged out into the night. Even by starlight he knew his way through the tangled paths leading down from Trackless Wood into the desert. Through all the dark journey he could think of nothing but his fury at Gaballufix, at the way he had outmaneuvered him by getting Rash on his side. He could hear in his mind their mother's laughter, as if it were all aimed at him. He felt so helpless, so utterly humiliated.

And then he remembered the most terrible moment of all, when

Nafai had so stupidly interfered with his bargaining and given away Father's entire fortune. If he hadn't done that, Rashgallivak might not have concluded that they were unworthy to have the Wetchik fortune. Then he wouldn't have acted against them, and they could have walked out with the treasure *and* Father's title intact. It was Nafai, really, who had lost the contest for them. If it had been up to Elemak alone, he might have done it. Gaballufix might have come through with the Index and settled for a quarter of Father's fortune—it was more money even so than Gaballufix could lay hands on any other way. Nafai, the stupid young jackass who could never keep his mouth shut, the one who pretended to have visions of his own so that Father would like him best, the one who, by the sheer act of being born, had made Gaballufix into Father's permanent enemy.

If I had him in my hands right now I'd kill him, thought Elemak. He has cost me my fortune and my honor and therefore my whole future. Easy for him to give away the Wetchik fortune—it would never have been his anyway. It would have been mine. I was born for it. I trained for it. I would have doubled it and doubled it again, and again and again, because I'm a far better man of business than Father ever was or ever could be. But now I'm an exile and an outcast, accused of theft and stripped of fortune, without even the respect of the man who should have been at my right hand, Rashgallivak.

All because of Nafai. All his fault.

Nafai ran in blind panic, with no thought of destination. It was not until he broke away from the crowds and found himself in an open space that he began to calm enough to think of where he was and what he ought to do next. He was in the Old Dance, once as large a dancing space as the Orchestra in Dolltown, which replaced it many centuries ago. Now, though, the buildings encroached the dance on every side. It had lost its roundness, and even the bowl shape of the amphitheatre was lost among the houses and shops. But an open space *did* remain, and that was where Nafai stood, looking at the sky, pink-tinged in the west, graying to black in the east. It was nearly full dark, and he had no idea whether assassins were still following him. One thing was certain —in the dark, in this part of town, the crowds would thin out, and murder would be much easier to accomplish unobserved. All his running had got him farther from safety than ever, and he had no idea what to do next.

"Nafai," said a girl's voice.

He turned. It was Luet.

"Hi," he greeted her. But he didn't have time to chat. He had to *think*.

"Quick," she said.

"Quick what?"

"Come with me."

"I can't," he said. "I have to do something."

"Yes," she said. "You have to come with me."

"I have to get out of the city."

She grabbed him by the front of his shirt and stood on tip-toe, which she no doubt intended to bring her eye-to-eye with him, but which succeeded only in making her hang from his shirt like a puppet. He laughed, but she didn't join him. "Listen, O thou busiest of men," she said, "have you forgotten that I'm a seer of the Oversoul?"

He *had* forgotten. Had forgotten even that it was her coming in the middle of the night that had saved Father from Gaballufix's plot. There were things she still didn't know about that, he realized. For some reason he thought he ought to explain. "Elemak and Mebbekew *were* involved in the plot," he said. "But I think Gaballufix lied to them about what he meant to do."

She had no patience for his confused babbling. "Do you think I care now? They're looking for you, Nafai. I saw it in a dream—a soldier with bloody hands stalking the streets. I knew that I had to find you. To save you."

"How can *you* save *me?*"

"Come with me," she said. "I know the way."

He had no better idea. In fact, when he tried to think of any alternative to following her, his mind went blank. He couldn't hold the thought. Finally it dawned on him that this was a message from the Oversoul. It wanted him to go with her. It had sent her to him, and so he must go with her, wherever she led him.

She took his hand and pulled him from the Old Dance down the street with the same name, until they reached the place where it narrowed, and then they took a fork to the left. "Our fortune is gone," said Nafai. "It was my fault, too. Except Rashgallivak betrayed us."

"Shut up," she said. "This isn't a good neighborhood."

She was right. It was dark here, and the road ran between old houses, dilapidated and dirty. There were few people there, and none of them seemed willing to look them in the eye.

They wound through a couple of sharp bends in the road, and then suddenly found themselves in Spring Street, near where it ran out into the holy wood. At that moment, Nafai saw ahead of him a group of soldiers, standing watch as if they had known he would emerge there. At once he turned to run, and then saw coming up the road they had just taken a couple of men with their charged-wire blades glowing slightly in the darkness.

"Good job, Nyef," Luet said contemptuously. "They probably wouldn't have noticed us. *Now* we look suspicious."

"*They* already know who we are," he said, pointing to the men approaching out of the dark street.

"Oh well," she said. "I had hoped to take the easy way in, but this one will have to do."

She grabbed his hand and half-dragged him the wrong way on Spring Street, away from the city and *toward* the holy forest. Nafai knew it was the stupidest thing she could possibly do. In the edges of the forest there'd be no witnesses at all. The assassins would have their way. If she imagined that Nafai had some particular skill at fighting and could somehow save them by disarming or killing the assassins, she would quickly discover the sad truth that he had never been interested in fighting and had no training along those lines at all. He couldn't even remember having hit someone in anger in his life, not even his older brothers, since fighting back against Meb or Elemak only made things worse in the end. Nafai might be large for his age, the tallest of Wetchik's sons, but it meant nothing when it came to battle.

As they moved into the darkness at the end of Spring Street, the assassins became bolder.

"That's right," one of them called out—softly, but audible enough to Nafai and Luet. "Into the shadows. That's where we'll have our conversation."

"We have nothing for you to steal." Luet's voice sounded panicked, trembling—but Nafai knew from her hand's steady grip that she was not trembling at all.

Nafai was trembling, however.

"Into the shadows," said the man again.

So they obeyed him. Plunged into the darkness under the trees. But to Nafai's surprise, they didn't stop, nor did they turn south, to skirt the forest and perhaps reenter the city at the next road. She led him almost straight east. Deeper into the forbidden country.

"I can't go here," he said.

"Shut up," she said. "Neither can they, unless they hear us talking and follow the sound."

He held his tongue, and followed her. After a while the ground began to fall away, not a slope anymore as much as a cliff, and it became very difficult to pick his way. The sky was fully dark now, and even though many leaves had fallen here, the shade of the trees was still quite deep. "I can't see," he whispered.

"Neither can I," she answered.

"Stop," he said. "Listen. Maybe they've stopped following us."

"They have," she said. "But we can't stop."

"Why not?"

"I've got to take you out of the city."

"If I'm caught here, the punishment is terrible."

"I know," she said. "As bad for me, though, for bringing you."

"Then take me back."

"No," she said. "This is where the Oversoul wants us to go."

It was too hard, however, to hold hands anymore—they both needed both hands to make their way down the ragged face of the cliff. It wouldn't have been that dangerous a climb in daylight, but in the darkness they might not see a drop-off that would kill them, so every step had to be tested. At least on this slope the trees were rarer, so the starlight could do a better job of helping them to see. At least, that's how it was until they reached the fog.

"Now we *have* to stop," he said.

"Keep climbing."

"In the fog? We'll get lost on the cliff face and fall and die."

"It's a good sign," said Luet. "It means that we're at least halfway down to the lake."

"You're not taking me to the lake!"

"Hush."

"Why don't I just throw myself down the quick way, then, and save them the effort of killing me?"

"Hush, you stupid man. The Oversoul will protect us."

"The Oversoul is a computer link with satellites orbiting Harmony. It doesn't have any magical machines to reach down and catch us if we fall."

"She is making us alert," said Luet. "Or she's helping *me*, at least, to find the way. If you'd only stop talking and let me listen to her."

They were hours climbing down through the fog, or so it seemed to Nafai, but at last they reached the bottom. Grass on a level plain, giving way to mud.

Warm mud. No, *hot* mud.

"Here we are," she said. "We can't go into the water here—it comes up from a rift deep in the crust of the world, where it's so hot that it boils and gives off steam. The water would cook the meat from our bones if we stayed in it for any length of time, even near the shore."

"Then how do women ever—"

"We do our worship nearer to the other end, where the lake is fed by ice-cold mountain streams. Some go into the coldest water. But the visions come to most of us when we float in the water at the place where the cold and hot waters meet. A turbulent place, the water endlessly rocking and swirling, freezing and searing us by turns. The place where the heart of the world and its coldest surface come together. A place where the two hearts of every woman are made one."

"I don't belong here," said Nafai.

"I know," said Luet. "But here is where the Oversoul led us, so here we'll stay."

And then what Nafai feared most. A woman, speaking not far off. "I *told* you I heard a man's voice. It came from *there*."

Lanterns came near, and many women. Their feet made splatting noises with each step in the hot mud, then sucking noises as they pulled them out again. How far have *I* sunk into the mud? wondered Nafai. Will they have trouble pulling me out? Or will they simply bury me alive right here, letting the mud decide whether to cook me or suffocate me?

"I brought him," said Luet.

"It's Luet," said an old woman. The name was picked up in a whisper and carried back through the gathering crowd.

"The Oversoul led me here. This man isn't like other men. The Oversoul has chosen him."

"The law is the law," said the old woman. "You have taken the responsibility on yourself, but that only moves the punishment from him to you."

Nafai saw how tense Luet looked. He realized: She doesn't understand the Oversoul any better than I do. For all she knows, the Oversoul doesn't care whether she lives or dies, and may be perfectly content to let her pay with her life for my safe passage here tonight.

"Very well," said Luet. "But you must take him to the Private Gate, and help him through the wood."

"You can't tell us what we *must* do, lawbreaker!" cried one woman. But others shushed her. Luet was held in great reverence, Nafai could see, even when she had committed an outrage.

Then the crowd parted, just a little, to let a woman pass, appearing like a ghost from the fog. She was naked, and because she was clean Nafai didn't realize for a moment that she must be a wilder. It was only when she came very close, plucking at Luet's sleeve, that Nafai could see how weathered and dry her skin was, how wrinkled and how gaunt her face.

"You," whispered Luet.

"You," echoed the wilder.

Then the holy woman from the desert turned to the old woman who seemed to be the leader of this band of justicers. "I have already punished her," she said.

"What do you mean?" asked the old woman.

"I am the Oversoul, and I say she has already borne my punishment."

The old woman looked at Luet, full of uncertainty. "Is this true speech, Luet?"

Nafai was amazed. Was their trust in Luet so complete that they would ask her to confirm or deny testimony that might cost her life or save it, depending on her own answer?

Their truth was justified, for Luet's answer contained no special pleading for herself. "This holy woman only slapped my face. How could it be punishment enough for this?"

"I brought her here," said the wilder. "I made her bring this boy. I have shown him great visions, and I will show him more. I will put honor in his seed, and a great nation shall arise. Let no one hinder him in his path through the water and the wood, and as for her, she has borne the mark of my hand upon her face. Who can touch her after I have done with her?"

"Truly this is the voice of the Mother," said the old woman.

"The Mother," whispered some.

"The Oversoul," whispered others.

The holy woman turned to face Luet again, and reached up and touched one finger to the girl's lips. Luet kissed that finger, gently, and for a moment Nafai ached for the sweetness of it. Then the wilder's expression changed. It was as if some brighter soul had been inside her face, and now it was gone; she looked distracted, vaguely confused. She looked around, recognizing nothing, and then wandered off into the fog.

"Was that your mother?" whispered Nafai.

"No," said Luet. "The mother of my body isn't holy anymore. But in my heart, all such women are my mother."

"Well spoken," said the old woman. "What a fairspoken child she is."

Luet bowed her head. When she lifted her face again, Nafai could see tears on her cheeks. He had no idea what was happening here, or what it meant to Luet; he only knew that for a while his life had been in danger, and then hers, and now the danger had passed. That was enough for him.

The wilder had said that no one should hinder him in his path through the water and the wood. After brief discussion, the women decided that this meant he had to traverse the lake from this point to the other end, from the hot to the cold; he had no idea how they discerned that from the holy woman's few words, but then he had often marveled at how many meanings the priests could wrest from the holy writings of the men's religion, too. They waited a few minutes until several women called out from the water. Only then did Luet lead him near enough for him to see the lake. Now it was clear where the fog came from—it rose as sheets of steam from the water, or so it appeared to him. Two women in a long low boat were bringing it to shore, the one rowing, the other at the tiller. The bow of the boat was square and low, but since there were no waves upon the lake, and the rowing was smooth, there seemed no danger of the boat taking water at the bow. They drew close, closer to shore, until at last they had run aground. Still there were several meters of water to cross between the boat and the mud flats where Nafai and Luet stood. The mud was painfully hot now, so that Nafai had to move his feet rather often to keep from burning them. What would it be like to walk through the water?

"Walk steadily," Luet whispered. "The less you splash, the better, so you mustn't run. You'll see that if you just keep going, you're in the boat soon, and the pain passes quickly."

So she had done this before. Very well, if Luet could bear it, so could he. He took a step toward the water. The women gasped.

"No," she said quickly. "In this place, where you're a child and a stranger, you must be led."

Me, a child? Compared to *you?* But then he realized that of course she was right. Whatever their ages might be, this was her place, not his; she was the adult and he the infant here.

She set the pace, brisk but not hurried. The water burned his feet, but it was shallow, and he didn't splash very much, though he was not as graceful and smooth in his movements as Luet. In moments they were at the boat, but it seemed like forever, like a thousand agonizing steps, especially the hesitation as she stepped into the boat. At last she was in, and her hand drew him in after her, and he walked on feet that stung so deep within the skin that he was afraid to look down at them for fear the flesh had been cooked off them. But then he *did* look, and the skin looked normal. Luet used the hem of her skirt to wipe his feet. The oarsman jammed the blade of an oar into the mud under the water and pushed them back, her muscles of her massive arms rippling with the exertion. Nafai faced Luet and clung to her hands as they glided through the water.

It was the strangest journey of Nafai's life, though not a long one. The fog made everything seem magic and unreal. Huge rocks loomed out of the water, they slipped silently between them, and then the stones were swallowed up as if they had ceased to be. The water grew hotter, and there were places where it bubbled; they steered around those spots. The boat itself was never hot, but the air around them was so hot and wet that soon they were drenched, their clothing clinging to their bodies. Nafai could see for the first time that Luet did, in fact, have a womanly shape to her; not much, but enough that he would never again be able to think of her as nothing but a child. Suddenly he was shy to be sitting there holding her hands, and yet he was more afraid to let go. He needed to be touching her, like a child holding his mother's hand in the darkness.

They drifted on. The air cooled. They passed through narrows, with steep cliffs on either hand, seeming to lean closer together the higher they went, until they were lost in the fog. Nafai wondered if perhaps this was a cave, or, if it wasn't, whether sunlight ever reached the base of this deep rift. Then the cliff walls receded, and the fog thinned just a little. At the same time, the water grew more turbulent. There were waves now, and currents caught the boat and made it want to spin, to yaw from side to side.

The oarsman lifted her oars; the steersman took her hand from the tiller. Luet leaned forward and whispered, "This is the place where the visions come. I told you—where the hot and the cold meet. Here is where we pass through the water in the flesh."

In the flesh apparently meant exactly that. Feeling even more shy to watch Luet undressing than to undress himself, he watched his own hands unfasten his clothing and fold it as Luet did hers and lay the pile in the boat. Trying to somehow watch her without seeing her, Nafai couldn't quite grasp how she managed to slip so noiselessly into the water, then lie motionless on her back. He could see that she made no move to swim, so when he—noisily—dropped himself into the water, he also lay still. The water was surprisingly buoyant. There was no danger of sinking. The silence was deep and powerful; only once did he speak, when he could see that she was drifting away from him.

"No matter," she answered quietly. "Hush."

He hushed. Now he was alone in the fog. The currents turned him— or perhaps they didn't, for in the fog he couldn't tell east from west or anything else having to do with location, except for up and down, and even *that* seemed to matter very little. It was peaceful here, a place where his eyes could see and yet not see, where his ears could hear and yet hear nothing. The current did not let him sleep, however. He could feel the hot and cold wash under him, sometimes very hot, sometimes very cold, so that sometimes he thought, I can't bear this another moment, I'll have to swim or I might die here—and then the current changed again.

He saw no vision. The Oversoul said nothing to him. He listened. He even spoke to the Oversoul, begging to know how he might somehow manage to get the Index that Father had sent him for. If the Oversoul heard him, it gave no sign.

He drifted on the lake forever. Or perhaps it was only a few minutes before he heard the soft touch of the oars in the water. A hand touched his hair, his face, his shoulder, then caught at his arm. He remembered how to turn his head and then he did it, and saw the boat, with Luet, now fully dressed, reaching out to him. It did not occur to him to be shy now; he was only glad to see her, and yet sad to think that he had to rise out of the water. He was not deft at climbing into the boat. He rocked it badly, and spilled water into it.

"Roll in," whispered Luet.

He lay on his side in the water, reached a leg and an arm into the boat, and rolled in. It was easy, almost silent. Luet handed him his clothing, still wet, but now very cold. He drew it on and shivered as the women propelled the boat on into the bone-chilling fog. Luet also shivered, but seemed undisturbed even so.

At last they came to a shoreline, where again a group of women were waiting. Perhaps another boat had gone directly across the lake, not waiting for the ritual of passing through the water in the flesh, or perhaps there was some road for runners bearing messages; whatever the reason, the women waiting for them already knew who they were. There was no need for explanations. Luet again led the way, this time through icy water that made Nafai's bones ache. They reached dry land —a grassy bank this time, instead of mud flats—and women's hands wrapped a dry blanket around him. He saw that Luet also was being warmed.

"The first man to pass through the water," said a woman.

"The man who passes through the waters of women," said another.

Luet explained to him, seeming a little embarrassed. "Famous prophecies," she said. "There are so many of them, it's hard not to fulfil one now and then."

He smiled. He knew that she took the prophecies much more seriously than she pretended. And so did he.

He noticed that no one asked her what had happened on the water; no one asked whether she had seen a vision. But they lingered, waiting, until finally she said, "The Oversoul gave me comfort, and it was enough." They drifted away then, most of them, though a few looked at Nafai until he shook his head.

"We're through the easy part now," she said.

He thought she was joking, but then she led him through the Private Gate, a legendary gap in the red wall that he had only half-believed was real. It was a curving passageway between a pair of massive towers, and instead of city guards, there were only women, watching. On the other side, he knew, lay Trackless Wood. Quickly he learned that it had earned its name. His face was streaked with cuts, and so was hers, and their arms and legs as well, by the time they emerged onto Forest Road.

"That way is Back Gate," said Luet. "And down any of these canyons you'll reach the desert. I don't know where you're going from there."

"That's good enough," said Nafai. "I can find my way."

"Then I've done what the Oversoul sent me to do."

Nafai didn't know what to say. He didn't even know the name for what he was feeling. "I think that I don't know you," said Nafai.

She looked at him, a little perplexed.

"No, that's wrong," Nafai said. "I think that I didn't know you before, even though I thought I knew you, and now that I finally know you, I don't really know you at all."

She smiled. "Those crossing currents do it to you every time," she said. "Tell no one, man or woman, what you did tonight."

"I'm not sure, when I remember it, whether I'll believe that it really happened myself."

"Will we see you again, at Aunt Rasa's house?"

"I don't know," said Nafai. "I only know this: that I don't know how I can get the Index without getting killed, and yet I have to get it."

"Wait until the Oversoul tells you what to do," said Luet, "and then do it."

He nodded. "That's fine, if the Oversoul actually tells me something."

"She will," said Luet. "When there's something to do, she'll tell you."

Then, impulsively, Luet reached out her hand and grasped his again, for just a moment. He remembered again, like an echo in his flesh, how it felt to cling to her on the lake. He was a little embarrassed now, though, and drew his hand away. She had seen him being weak. She had seen him naked.

"See?" she said. "You're forgetting already how it really was."

"No I'm not," he said.

She turned away and headed down the road toward Back Gate. He wanted to call out to her and say, You were right, I *was* forgetting how it really was, I was remembering it through common ordinary eyes, I was remembering it as the boy I was before, but now I remember that it wasn't me being weak or me being naked, or anything else that I should be ashamed of. It was me riding like a great hero out of prophecy across the magical lake, with you as my guide and teacher, and when we shed our clothing it wasn't a man and woman naked together, it was rather two gods out of ancient stories from faraway lands, stripping away their mortal disguises and standing revealed in their glorious immortality, ready to float over the sea of death and emerge unscathed on the other side.

But by the time he thought of all the things he wanted to say, she had disappeared around a bend.

14

Issib's Chair

Nafai didn't know what to expect when he got to the rendezvous. All the way across the desert in the starlight, he kept imagining terrible things. What if none of his brothers escaped? *They* didn't have the help of Luet and the women of Basilica. Or what if they *did* escape, but the soldiers followed one of them to their hiding place, and then slaughtered them? When he got there, would he find their mutilated bodies? Or would there be soldiers lying in wait for him, to take him as he made his way down the canyon?

He paused at the top of the canyon, the place where they had stopped to cast lots early that same morning. Oversoul, he said silently, should I go down there?

The answer he got was a picture in his mind—one of Gaballufix's inhuman soldiers walking through the empty nighttime streets of Basilica. He didn't know what sense to make of this. Was the Oversoul telling him that the soldiers were all in the city? Or was Nafai seeing this vision because the Oversoul was telling him that soldiers were waiting for him in the arroyo, and his brain had simply added irrelevant details of the city to the vision?

One thing was inescapable—the sense of urgency he was getting from the Oversoul. As if there was an opportunity he could not afford to miss. Or a danger he had to avoid.

When the message is so unclear, Nafai said silently, what can I go on except for my own judgment? If my brothers are in trouble I need to know it. I can't abandon them, even if there might be danger to myself. If I'm wrong, take this thought from me.

Then he started down the arroyo. There came no stupor, no distraction. Whatever else the Oversoul was trying to tell him, it certainly didn't mind him going down to the rendezvous with his brothers.

Or else it had given up on him. But no—it had just gone to so much trouble to bring him out of the city, through the Lake of Women, the Oversoul could hardly plan to abandon him now.

It was so dark in the canyon that he ended up stumbling, sliding down, until he finally came to rest on the gravelly shelf where his brothers were supposed to be waiting.

"Nafai."

It was Issib's voice. But Nafai hardly had time to hear it before he felt a harsh blow. Someone's sandal against his face, shoving him down into the rocks.

"Fool!" shouted Elemak. "I wish they'd caught you and killed you, you little bastard!"

Another foot, from the other side, smashing into his nose. And now Mebbekew's voice. "All gone, the whole fortune, everything, because of you!"

"He didn't take it, you fools!" cried Issib. "Gaballufix stole it!"

"You shut up!" shouted Mebbekew, advancing on Issib. Nafai was at last able to see what was happening. Though his face stung from the tiny rocks embedded in the bottoms of their sandals, they really hadn't hurt him seriously. Now, though, he could see that they truly were raging. But why at *Nafai*?

"Rash was the one who betrayed us," said Nafai.

Immediately they turned back to him. "Is that so?" said Elemak. "Didn't I tell you that *I* was going to do all the talking? I could have had the Index for a quarter of what we had, but no, *you* had to—"

"You were giving up!" cried Nafai. "You were walking out!"

Elemak roared in fury, pulled Nafai up by the shirt, lifting him partway from the ground. "Half of bargaining *is* walking out, you fool! Do you think I didn't know what I was doing? I, who have bargained in foreign lands and made great profit on few goods—why couldn't you trust me to know what I was doing? All you've ever bargained for is a few stupid myachiks in the market, little boy."

"I didn't know," said Nafai.

Elemak threw him down onto the ground. Nafai's elbows were scraped, and his head struck the stones hard enough that it hurt him. Without meaning to, he cried out.

"Leave him alone, you coward," said Issib.

"Calling me a coward?" said Elemak.

"Gaballufix was going to have our money no matter what we did. He already had Rash on his side."

"So now you're the expert on what *would* have happened," said Elemak.

"Sitting on your throne, judging us!" cried Mebbekew. "You think Nafai's so innocent, what about *you!* You're the one who got the money out of Father's accounts!"

Nafai stood up. He didn't like the way they were menacing Issib. It was one thing for them to take out their fury on him, but something else again when they seemed about to hurt Issya. "I'm sorry," said Nafai. There was nothing for it but to take the blame, and their anger. "I didn't understand, and I should have kept my mouth shut. I'm sorry."

"What is *sorry?*" said Elemak. "How many times have you said *sorry* when it was too late to undo the consequences? You never learn anything, Nafai. Father never taught you. His little baby, precious Rasa's little boy, who could do no wrong. Well, it's time you learned the lessons that Father should have taught you years ago."

Elemak pulled one of the rods out of a pack frame leaning against the canyon wall. It was designed to carry heavy loads on the back of a camel; it had some flex to it, and it wasn't terribly heavy, but it was sturdy and long. Nafai knew at once what Elemak intended. "You have no right to touch me," said Nafai.

"No, nobody has the right to touch you," said Mebbekew. "Sacred Nafai, Father's jewel-eyed boy, no one can touch him. He can touch *us,* of course. He can lose our inheritance for us, but no one can touch *him.*"

"It would never have been *your* inheritance, anyway," Nafai said to Mebbekew. "It was always for Elemak." Another thought came into Nafai's mind, thinking of who would have received the inheritance. He knew before he said it that it wasn't the wisest thing to say, when

Elemak and Mebbekew were already in a fury. But he said it anyway. "When it comes to what you *lost*, you both deserved to be disinherited anyway, plotting against Father."

"That is a lie," said Mebbekew.

"How stupid do you think I am?" said Nafai. "You might not have known Gaballufix meant to kill Father that morning, but you knew he meant to kill *somebody*. What did Gaballufix promise you, Elemak? The same thing he promised Rash—the Wetchik name and fortune, after Father was discredited and forced out of his place?"

Elemak roared and rushed at him, laying on with the rod. He was so angry that few of the blows actually landed true, but when they did, they were brutal. Nafai had never felt such pain, not even when he prayed, not even when his feet were in the scalding water of the lake. He ended up sprawled face-down in the gravel, with Elemak poised above him, ready to hit him—where, on his back? On his head?

"Please!" Nafai shouted.

"Liar!" roared Elemak.

"Traitor!" Nafai shouted back. He started to get to his knees to his feet.

The rod fell, knocking him back down to the ground. He's broken my back, thought Nafai. I'll be paralyzed. I'll be like Issib, crippled in a chair for the rest of my life.

It was as if the thought of Issib brought him into action. For as Elemak raised the rod again, Issib's chair swung across in front of him. The chair was turning as it went—it couldn't have been completely under control—and the rod caught Issib across one arm. He screamed in pain, and the chair lost control completely, spinning crazily and reeling back and forth. Its collision avoidance system kept it from banging into the stone walls of the arroyo, but it did bump into Mebbekew as he tried to run out of the way, knocking him down.

"Stay out of the way, Issib!" shouted Elemak.

"You coward!" cried Nafai. "You were *nothing* in front of Gaballufix, but now you can beat a cripple and a fourteen-year-old boy! Very brave!"

Again Elemak turned away from Issib to face Nafai. "You've said too much this time, boy," he said. He wasn't shouting this time. It was a colder, deeper anger. "I'm never going to hear that voice again, do you understand me?"

"That's right, Elya," said Nafai. "You couldn't get Gaballufix to kill

Father for you, but at least you can kill *me*. Come ahead, prove what a man you are by killing your little brother."

Nafai had been hoping to shame Elemak into backing off, but he miscalculated. Instead Elemak lost all self-control. As Issib spun by in front of him, Elemak seized an outflung arm and dragged Issib from the chair, throwing him to the ground like a broken toy.

"No!" screamed Nafai.

He rushed for Issib, to help him, but Mebbekew was between them, and when Nafai got near enough, Mebbekew shoved him to the ground. Nafai sprawled at Elemak's feet.

Elemak had dropped his rod. As he reached for it, Mebbekew ran to the pack frame and drew out another one. "Let's have done with him now. And if Issib can't keep his mouth shut, both of them."

Whether Elemak heard or not, Nafai couldn't tell. He only knew that the rod came whistling down, smashing into his shoulder. Elemak's aim still wasn't good, but this much was clear: He was striking high on Nafai's body. He was trying for the head. He meant Nafai to die.

Suddenly there was a blinding light in the canyon. Nafai lifted his head in time to see Elemak whirl around, trying to follow the source of the light. It was Issib's chair.

Only it couldn't be. Issib's chair had a passive switching system. When it was not being told explicitly what to do, it settled down, leveled itself on its legs, and waited for instructions. It had done just that the moment Elemak dragged Issib to the ground.

"What's happening?" asked Mebbekew.

"What's happening?" said a mechanical voice from the chair.

"You must have broken it," said Mebbekew.

"I am not the one who is broken," said the chair. "Faith and trust are broken. Brotherhood is broken. Honor and law and decency are broken. Compassion is broken. But I am not broken."

"Make it stop, Issya," said Mebbekew.

Nafai noticed that Elemak said nothing. He was eyeing the chair steadily, the rod still in his hands. Then, with a grunt, Elemak rushed forward and swung at the chair with the rod.

Lightning flashed, or so it seemed. Elemak screamed and fell back, as the rod flew into the air. It was burning, the whole length of it.

Carefully, slowly, Mebbekew slid his own rod back down into the pack frame.

"Why were you beating your younger brother with a rod, Elemak?" said the chair. "Why did you plan his death, Mebbekew?"

"Who's doing this?" Mebbekew said.

"Can't you guess, fool?" Issib spoke feebly, from where he lay in the rocks. "Who sent us on this errand in the first place?"

"Father," said Mebbekew.

"The Oversoul," said Elemak.

"Don't you understand yet, that because your younger brother Nafai was willing to hear my voice, I have chosen him to lead you?"

That silenced them both. But Nafai knew that in their hearts, their hatred of him had passed from hot anger to cold hard resentment that would never die. The Oversoul had chosen Nafai to lead them. Nafai, who couldn't even get through negotiations with Gaballufix without messing everything up. Oversoul, why are you doing this to me?

"If you had not betrayed your father, if you had believed in him and obeyed him, I would not have had to choose Nafai ahead of you," said the chair—said the Oversoul. "Now go up into Basilica again, and I will deliver Gaballufix into your hands."

With that, the chair's lights dimmed, and it settled slowly to the ground.

They all waited, dumbly, for a few silent moments. Then Elemak turned to Issib and gently, carefully lifted him back and put him into the chair. "I'm sorry, Issya," he said gently. "I was not in my right mind. I would never hurt you for the world."

Issib said nothing.

"It was Nafai we were angry at," said Mebbekew.

Issib turned to him and, in a whisper, repeated Meb's own words back to him. "Let's have done with him now. And if Issib can't keep his mouth shut, both of them."

Mebbekew was stung. "So I guess you're going to hold that against me forever."

"Shut up, Meb," said Elemak. "Let's think."

"Good idea," said Mebbekew. "Thinking has done us *so* much good up to now."

"It's one thing to see the Oversoul move a chair around," said Elemak. "But Gaballufix has hundreds of soldiers. He can kill each of us fifty times over—where are the soldiers of the Oversoul? What army is going to protect us now?"

Nafai was standing now, listening to them. He could hardly believe what he was hearing. "The Oversoul has just shown you some of its power, and you're still afraid of Gaballufix's soldiers? The Oversoul is stronger than these soldiers. If it doesn't want them to kill us, the soldiers won't kill us."

Elemak and Mebbekew regarded him in silence.

"You were willing to kill me because you didn't like my words," said Nafai. "Are you willing to follow me now, in obeying the words of the Oversoul?"

"How do we know you didn't rig the chair yourself?" said Mebbekew.

"That's right," said Nafai. "I knew before we ever went into the city today that you were going to blame me for everything and try to kill me, and so Issya and I rigged the chair to deliver exactly that speech."

"Don't be stupid, Meb," said Elemak. "We're going to get killed, but since we've lost everything else, it doesn't really make that much difference to me."

"Just because you're a fatalist doesn't mean *I* want to die," said Mebbekew.

Issib swung his chair forward. "Let's go," he said to Nafai. "It's the Oversoul I'm following, and you as his servant. Let's go."

Nafai nodded, then led the way up the canyon. For a while he heard only the sound of his own footfalls, and the faint whirring of Issib's chair. Then, at last, came the clatter of Elemak and Mebbekew, following him up the arroyo.

15

Murder

If we are to have any hope at all, thought Nafai, we have to stop trying to come up with our own plans. Gaballufix outmaneuvers us every time.

And now there was even less hope, since Elemak and Mebbekew were deliberately being uncooperative. Why did the Oversoul have to say what it did about Nafai leading them? How could he possibly take command over his own older brothers, who would be far gladder to see him fail than to help him succeed? Issib would be no problem, of course, but it was hard to see how he would be much help, either, even wearing his floats again. He was too conspicuous, too fragile, and too slow, all at once.

Gradually, as they made their way through the desert—Nafai leading, not because he wanted to, but because Elemak refused to help him pick out a path—Nafai came to an inescapable conclusion: He would have a much better chance alone than with his brothers.

Not that he thought his chances were very good on his own. But he would have the Oversoul to help him. And the Oversoul *had* got him out of Basilica before.

But when the Oversoul got him out of Basilica, it was because Luet held his hand. Who would be his Luet now? She was the seer, as familiar with the Oversoul as Nafai was with his own mother. Luet could feel the Oversoul showing her every step; Nafai only felt the guidance of the Oversoul now and then, so rarely, so confusingly. What was his vision of a bloody-handed soldier walking the streets of Basilica? Was this an enemy he would have to fight? Was it his death? Or his guide? He was so confused, how could he possibly come up with a plan?

He stopped.

The others stopped behind him.

"What now?" asked Mebbekew. "Enlighten us, O great leader anointed by the Oversoul."

Nafai didn't answer. Instead he tried to empty his mind. To relax the knot of fear in his stomach. The Oversoul didn't speak to him the way it spoke to Luet because Luet didn't *expect* herself to come up with a plan. Luet listened. Listened *first*, understood *first*. If Nafai was serious about trying to help the Oversoul, trying to be its hands and feet here on the surface of this world, then he had to stop trying to make up his own foolish plans and give the Oversoul a chance to talk to him.

They were near Dogtown, which stretched along the roads leading out from the gate known as the Funnel. Till now, he had assumed that he should go around Dogtown and pick his way through some canyon back up to Forest Road and enter Basilica through Back Gate. Now, though, he waited, tested the ideas. He thought of going on, around Dogtown, and his thoughts drifted aimlessly. Then he turned toward the Funnel, and at once felt a rush of confidence. Yes, he thought. The Oversoul is trying to lead me, if I'll just shut up and listen. The way I should have shut up and listened while Elemak was bargaining with Gaballufix this afternoon.

"Oh, good," said Mebbekew. "Let's go up to the second most closely watched gate. Let's go through the ugliest slum, where Gaballufix owns everybody that's for sale, which is everybody that's alive."

"Hush," said Issib.

"Let him talk," said Nafai. "It'll bring Gaballufix's men down on us and get us all killed right now, which is exactly what Mebbekew wants, because as we all die Meb can say, 'See, Nyef, you got us killed!' which will let him die happy."

Mebbekew started toward Nafai, but Elemak stopped him. "We'll be quiet," said Elemak.

Nafai led them on until they came to High Road, which ran from Gate Town to Dogtown. It was lined with houses much of the way, but at this time of night it wasn't too safe, and few people would be abroad on it. Nafai led them to the widest gap between houses on both sides of the road, scanned to the left and right, and then ducked down and scurried across. Then he waited in a dry ditch on the far side of the road, watching for the others.

They didn't come.

They didn't come.

They've decided to abandon me now, thought Nafai. Well, fine.

Then they appeared. Not scurrying, as Nafai had done, but walking. All three of them. Of course, thought Nafai. They had waited to get Issib out of his chair. I should have thought of that.

As they walked across the road, Nafai realized that instead of Issib floating, he was being helped by the other two, his arms flung across their shoulders, his feet being half-dragged. To anyone who didn't know the truth, Issib would look like a drunk being helped home by his friends.

Nor did they walk straight across the road. Rather they angled across, as if they were really going *with* the road, but losing their way in the dark, or being tipped in one direction by the drunk they were helping. Finally they were across, and slipped off into the bushes.

Nafai caught up with them as they were untangling Issib, helping him adjust his floats. "That was so good," he whispered. "A thousand people could have seen you and nobody would have thought twice about it."

"Elemak thought of it," said Issib.

"You should be leading," said Nafai.

"Not according to the Oversoul," said Elemak.

"Issib's chair, you mean," said Mebbekew.

"It was just as well, Nyef, you going across first," said Elemak. "The guards will be looking for four men, one of them floating. Instead they saw three, one of them drunk."

"Where now?" said Issib.

Nafai shrugged. "This way, I guess." He led the way, angling through the empty ground between High Road and the Funnel.

He got distracted. He couldn't think of what to do next. He couldn't think of anything.

"Stop," he said. He thought of leading them onward, and it felt wrong. What felt right was for him to go on alone. "Wait here," he said. "I'm going into the city alone."

"Brilliant," said Mebbekew. "We could have waited back with the camels."

"No," said Nafai. "Please. I need you *here*. I need to be sure I can come out of the gate and find you here."

"How long will you be?" asked Issib.

"I don't know," said Nafai.

"Well, what are you planning to *do*?"

He couldn't very well tell them that he hadn't the faintest idea. "Elemak didn't tell us what *he* was planning," said Nafai.

"Right," said Mebbekew. "Play at being the big man."

"We'll wait," said Elemak. "But if the sun rises with us here, we're out in the open and we'll be caught for sure. You understand that."

"At the first lightening of the sky, if I'm not back, get Issib's chair and head for the camels," said Nafai.

"We'll do it," said Elemak.

"If we feel like it," said Mebbekew.

"We'll feel like it," said Elemak. "Meb will be here, just like the rest of us."

Nafai knew that Elemak still hated him, still felt contempt for him— but he also knew that Elemak would do what he said. That even though Elemak was expecting him to fail, he was also giving him a reasonable chance to succeed. "Thank you," said Nafai.

"Get the Index," said Elemak. "You're the Oversoul's boy, get the Index."

Nafai left them then, walking toward the Funnel. As he got nearer, he could hear the guards talking. There were too many of them—six or seven, not the usual two. Why? He moved to the wall and then slipped closer, to where he could hear fairly well what they were saying.

"It's Gaballufix himself, *I* say," said one guard. "Probably killed Wetchik's boy first, so he couldn't leave the city, and then killed Roptat and put the blame where nobody could answer."

"Sounds like Gaballufix," another answered him. "Pure slime, him and all his men."

Roptat was dead. Nafai felt a thrill of fear. After all the failed plots, it had finally happened—Gaballufix had finally committed a murder. And blamed it on one of Wetchik's boys.

Me, Nafai realized. He blamed it on me. I'm the only one who didn't

leave the city through a monitored gate. So as far as the city computer
knows, I'm still inside. Of course Gaballufix would know that. So he
seized the chance, had Roptat killed, and put out the word that it was
the youngest son of Wetchik who did it.

But the women know. The women know he's lying. He doesn't realize it yet, but by tomorrow every woman in Basilica will know the truth
—that when Roptat was being killed I was at the lake with Luet. I
don't even have to go inside tonight. Gaballufix will be destroyed by
his own stupidity, and we can wait outside the walls and laugh!

Only he couldn't think of waiting outside. The Oversoul didn't want
that. The Oversoul didn't care about Gaballufix getting caught in his
lies. The Oversoul cared about the Index, and the fall of Gaballufix
wouldn't put the Index into Father's hands.

How do I get past the guards? Nafai asked.

In answer, all he felt was his own fear. He knew *that* didn't come
from the Oversoul.

So he waited. After a while, the guards' conversation lagged. "Let's
do a walk through Dogtown," said one of them. Five of them walked
out of the gate, into the darkness of the Dogtown streets. If they had
turned back to look at the gate, they would have seen Nafai standing
there, leaning against the wall not two meters from the opening. But
they didn't look back.

It was time, he knew that; his fear was undiminished, but now there
was also a hunger to act, to get moving. The Oversoul? It was hard to
know, but he had to do *something*. So, holding his breath, Nafai
stepped out into the light falling through the gate.

One guard sat on a stool, leaning against the gate. Asleep, or nearly
so. The other was relieving himself against the opposite wall, his back
to the opening. Nafai walked quietly through. Neither one stirred from
his position until Nafai was away from the gatelight. Then he heard
their voices behind him, talking—but not about him, not raising an
alarm. This must be how it was for Luet, he thought, the night she
came to give us warning. The Oversoul making the guards stupid
enough to let her pass as if she were invisible. The way I passed
through.

The moon was rising now. The night was more than half spent. The
city was asleep, except probably Dolltown and the Inner Market, and
even those were bound to be a bit subdued in these days of tension and
turmoil, with soldiers patrolling the streets. In this district, though, a

fairly safe one, with no night life at all, there was no one out and about. Nafai wasn't sure whether the emptiness of the streets was good or bad. It was good because there'd be fewer people to see him; bad because if he *was* seen, he'd be noticed for sure.

Except tonight the Oversoul was helping him *not* to be noticed. He kept to the shadows, not tempting fate, and once when a troop of soldiers did come by, he ducked into a doorway and they passed him without notice.

This must be the limit to the power of the Oversoul, thought Nafai. With Luet and Father and me, the Oversoul can communicate real ideas. And through a machine—through Issib's chair—but who can guess how much that cost the Oversoul? Reaching directly into the minds of these other people, it can't do much more than distract them, the way it steers people away from forbidden ideas. It can't turn the soldiers out of the road, but it *can* discourage them from noticing the fellow standing in the shadowed doorway, it *can* distract them from wanting to investigate, to see what he's doing. It can't keep the guards at the gate from doing their duty, but it *can* help the dozing guard to dream, so that the sound of Nafai's footsteps are part of the story of the dream, and he doesn't look up.

And even to do that much, the Oversoul must have its whole attention focused on this street tonight, thought Nafai. On this very place. On me.

Where am I going?

Doesn't matter. Turn off my mind and wander, that's what I have to do. Let the Oversoul lead me by the hand, the way Luet did.

It was hard, though, to empty his mind, to keep himself from recognizing each street he came to, keep himself from thinking of all the people or shops he knew of on that street, and how they might relate to getting the Index. His mind was too involved even now.

And why shouldn't it be? he thought. What am I supposed to do, stop being a sentient being? Become infinitely stupid so that the Oversoul can control me? Is my highest ambition in life to be a *puppet?*

No, came the answer. It was as clear as that night by the stream, in the desert. You're no puppet. You're here because you chose to be here. But now, to hear my voice, you have to empty your mind. Not because I want you to be stupid, but because you have to be able to hear me. Soon enough you'll need all your wits about you again. Fools are no good to me.

Nafai found himself leaning against a wall, gasping for breath, when the voice faded. It was no joke, to have the Oversoul *push* into his thoughts like that. What did our ancestors do to their children, when they changed us so that a computer could put things into our minds like this? In those early days, did all the children hear the voice of the Oversoul as I hear it now? Or was it always a rare thing, to be a hearer of that voice?

Move on. He felt it like a hunger. And he moved. Moved the way he had twice before in the last few weeks—going from street to street almost in a trance, uncertain of where he was, not caring. The way he had been only this afternoon, running from the assassins.

I don't even have a weapon.

The thought brought him up short. Pulled him out of his walking trance. He wasn't sure where he was. But there, half in shadow, there was a man lying in the street. Nafai came closer, curious. Some drunk, perhaps. Or it might be a victim of tolchocks, or soldiers, or assassins. A victim of Gaballufix.

No. Not a victim at all. It was one of Gaballufix's identical soldiers lying there, and from the stench of piss and alcohol, it wasn't any injury that put him on the ground.

Nafai almost walked away, until it dawned on him that here was the best disguise he could possibly hope for. It would be much simpler to get near Gaballufix if he was wearing one of the holographic soldier costumes—and here lay just such a costume, a gift that was his for the taking.

He knelt beside the man and rolled him over onto his back. It was impossible to *see* the box that controlled the holograph, but by running his hands through the image, he found it by touch, on a belt near the waist. He unfastened it, but even then it wouldn't come away from the man more than a few centimeters.

Oh, that's right, thought Nafai. Elemak said it was a kind of cloak, and the box was just a part of that.

Sure enough, when he pulled the box up the man's body, it slid easily. By half-rolling the man this way and that, he was finally able to get the holographic costume off his arms, out from under his body, and then off the man's head.

Only then did Nafai realize that the Oversoul had provided him with more than a costume. This wasn't a hired thug with a soldier suit. It was Gaballufix himself.

Drunk out of his mind, lying in his own urine and vomit, but never-theless, without any doubt, it was Gaballufix.

But what could Nafai *do* with this drunk? He certainly didn't have the Index with him. And Nafai harbored no delusion that by dragging him home he could win Gaballufix's undying gratitude.

The bastard must have been out celebrating the death of Roptat. A murderer lying here in the street, only he'll never be punished for it. In fact, he's trying to get *me* blamed for it. Nafai was filled with anger. He thought of putting his foot on Gaballufix's head and grinding his face down into the vomit-covered street. It would feel so good, so—

Kill him.

The thought was as clear as if someone behind him had spoken it.

No, thought Nafai. I can't do that. I can't kill a man.

Why do you think I brought you here? He's a killer. The law decrees his death.

The law decreed *my* death for seeing the Lake of Women, Nafai answered silently. Yet I was shown mercy.

I brought you to the lake, Nafai. As I brought you here. To do what must be done. You'll never get the Index while he's alive.

I can't kill a man. A helpless man like this—it would be murder.

It would be simple justice.

Not if it came from my hand. I hate him too much. I want him dead. For the humiliation of my family. For stealing my father's title. For taking our fortune. For the beating I got at my brother's hands. For the soldiers and the tolchocks, for the way he has blotted the light of hope out of my city. For the way he turned Rashgallivak, that good man, into a weak and foolish tool. For all those things I want him to die, I want to crush him under my foot. If I kill him now I'm a coward and an assassin, not a justicer.

He tried to kill you. His assassins had you marked for death.

I know it. So it would be private vengeance if I killed him now.

Think of what you're doing, Nafai. Think.

I'm not going to be a murderer.

That's right. You're going to *save* lives. There's only one hope of saving this world from the slaughter that destroyed Earth forty million years ago, and leaving this man alive will obliterate that hope. Should the billion souls of the planet Harmony all die, so that you can keep your hands clean? I tell you that this is not murder, not assassination, but justice. I have tried him and found him guilty. He ordered the death of Roptat, and your death, and your brothers' death, and the death of your father. He plots a war that will kill thousands and bring this city under subjugation. You aren't sparing him out of mercy, Nafai, because only his death will be merciful to the city and the people that you love, only his death will show mercy to the world. You're sparing him out of pure vanity. So that you can look at your hands and find them unstained with blood. I tell you that if you don't kill this man, the blood of millions will be on your head.

No!

Nafai's cry was all the more anguished for being silent, for being contained inside his mind.

The voice inside his head did not relent: The Index opens the deepest library in the world, Nafai. With it, all things are possible to my servants. Without it, I have no clearer voice than the one you hear now, constantly changed and distorted by your own fears and hopes and expectations. Without the Index, I can't help you and you can't help me. My powers will continue to fade, and my law will dwindle among the people, until at last the fires come again, and another world is laid waste. The Index, Nafai. Take from this man what the law requires, and then go and get the Index.

Nafai reached down and took the charged-wire blade that was hooked to Gaballufix's belt.

I don't know how to kill a man with this. It doesn't stab. I can't stab the heart with this.

His head. Take off his head.

I can't. I can't, I can't, I can't.

But Nafai was wrong. He could.

He took Gaballufix by the hair, and stretched out his neck. Gaballufix stirred—was he waking up? Nafai almost let go of his hair then, but Gaballufix quickly dropped back into unconsciousness. Nafai switched on the blade and then laid it lightly against the throat. The blade hummed. A line of blood appeared. Nafai pressed harder, and the line became an open wound, with blood spouting over the blade, sizzling loudly. Too late to stop now, too late. He pressed harder, harder. The blade bit deeper. It resisted at the bone, but Nafai twisted the head away and opened a gap between the vertebrae, and now the blade cut through easily, and the head came free.

Nafai's pants and shirt were covered with blood, as were his hands and face, spattered with it, dripping with it. I have killed a man, and this is his head that I'm holding in my hands. What am I now? Who am I now? How am I better than the man who lies here, torn apart by my hands?

The Index.

He couldn't bear to wear his blood-soaked clothes. Almost in a panic to be rid of them, he tore them off, then wiped his face and hands on the unbloodied back of his shirt. These were the clothes that Luet handed to me when I climbed back into the boat in the beautiful, peaceful place, and now see what I've done with them.

Now, kneeling beside the body, his own clothes cast down into the blood, he realized that because of the downhill slope of the street and the fact that the blood mostly poured upward out of the neck, away from the body, Gaballufix's own clothing was unstained with blood. Vomit and urine, yes, but not blood. Nafai had to wear something. The costume wouldn't be enough—underneath it he'd be cold and barefoot.

When he thought of putting on Gaballufix's clothing, it was abhorrent to him, yes, but he also knew that he had to do it. He dragged the body up away from the blood a little, then undressed it carefully, keeping the blood off. He almost gagged as he pulled the cold wet trousers on, but then he thought contemptuously that a man who could kill the way he had just killed should hardly feel squeamish about wearing another man's piss on his legs. The same with the stench of stomach acid in the shirt and the body armor that Gaballufix had been wearing underneath. Nothing is too horrible for me to do it now, thought Nafai. I'm already lost.

The only thing he could *not* bring himself to do was put the blade at his waist, the way Gaballufix had done. Instead he wiped his fingerprints from the handle and tossed it down near where the head was lying. Then he laughed. There are my clothes, which countless witnesses saw me wearing today. Why should I have tried to conceal myself, if I'm leaving those behind?

And I *am* leaving those behind, thought Nafai. Like my own dead body I'm leaving those. The costume of a child. I'm wearing a man's clothes now. And not just any man. The most vile, monstrous man I know. They fit me.

He pulled the cloak of the soldier costume over his head. He felt no different, but he assumed that the look was there. He stepped away from the body. He could not think of where to go now. He could not think of anything.

He turned back to the body. He had left something behind, he knew that. But all that was left was his old clothing, and the blade. So he picked up the blade again after all, wiped the blood from it with his old clothes, and put it on his belt.

Now he could go on. To Gaballufix's house, of course. He knew that now, very clearly. He could think very clearly now. The trousers froze on his legs, and chafed. The body armor was heavy. It was awkward walking with the charged-wire blade. This is how it felt to be Gaballufix, thought Nafai. Tonight I am Gaballufix.

I have to hurry. Before the body is found.

No. The Oversoul will keep them from noticing the body, for a while at least. Until there are so many people out in the morning that the Oversoul can't influence them all at once. So I do have time.

He came up Fountain Street, but then thought better of it. Instead he walked over to Long Street and came up to Gaballufix's house from behind. In the alley he found the door that he had seen Elemak use, so many—so few—days before. Would it be locked?

It was. What now? Inside there would be someone waiting. Keeping guard. How could he, in the guise of a common soldier, demand entrance at this hour? What if they made him switch off the costume once he got inside? They'd recognize him at once. Worse, they'd recognize Gaballufix's clothing and they'd know that there was only one way he could come in wearing their master's clothes.

No, *two* ways.

Gaballufix must have come home drunk before.

Nafai tried, silently at first, to think of how Gaballufix's voice sounded. Husky and coarse. Rasping in the throat. Nafai could get it generally right, he was sure—and it didn't have to be too perfect, because Gaballufix was *drunk*, of course—he reeked of it—and so his voice could be slurred and out of control, and he could stagger and fall and—

"Open up, open the door!" he bawled.

That was awful, that didn't sound like Gaballufix at all.

"Open the door you idiots, it's me!"

Better. Better. And besides, the Oversoul will nudge them a little, will encourage them to think of other things besides the fact that Gaballufix isn't really sounding like himself tonight.

The door opened a crack. Nafai immediately shoved it open and pushed his way through. "Locking me out of my own house, ought to send you home in a box, ought to send you back to your papa in pieces." Nafai had no idea how Gaballufix usually talked, but he guessed at general surliness and threats, especially when he was drunk. Nafai hadn't seen many drunks. Only a few times on the street, and then fairly often in the theatres, but those were actors *playing* drunk.

He thought: I'm an actor, after all. I thought that was what I might end up being, and here I am.

"Let me help you, sir," said the man. Nafai didn't look at him. Instead he deliberately stumbled and fell to his knees, then doubled over. "Going to puke, I think," he rasped. Then he touched the box at his belt and turned off the costume. Just for a moment. Just long enough that whoever else was in the room could see Gaballufix's clothing, while Nafai's face and hair were out of sight as he bent over. Then he turned the costume back on. He tried to produce the sound of dry heaves, and was so successful that he gagged and some bile and acid *did* come into his throat.

"What do you want, sir?" said the man.

"Who keeps the Index!" Nafai bawled. "Everybody wants the Index today—well now *I* want it."

"Zdorab," said the man.

"Get him."

"He's asleep, he . . ."

Nafai lurched to his feet. "When I'm off my ass in this house, *nobody* sleeps!"

"I'll get him, sir, I'm sorry, I just thought . . ."

Nafai swung clumsily at him. The man shied away, looking horrified. Am I carrying this too far? There was no way to guess. The man sidled along the wall and then ducked through a door. Nafai had no idea whether he would come back with soldiers to arrest him.

He came back with Zdorab. Or at least Nafai assumed it was Zdorab. But he had to be sure, didn't he? So he leaned close to the man and breathed nastily in his face. "Are you Zdorab?" Let the man imagine that Gaballufix was so drunk he couldn't see straight.

"Yes, sir," said the man. He seemed frightened. Good.

"My Index. Where is it?"

"Which one?"

"The one those bastards wanted—Wetchik's boys—*the* Index, by the Oversoul!"

"The *Palwashantu* Index?"

"Where did you put it, you rogue?"

"In the vault," said Zdorab. "I didn't know you wanted it accessible. You've never used it before, and so I thought—"

"I can look at it if I want!"

Stop talking so much, he told himself. The more you say, the harder it will be for the Oversoul to keep this man from doubting my voice.

Zdorab led the way down a corridor. Nafai made it a point to bump into a wall now and then. When he did it on the side where Elemak's rod had fallen most heavily, it sent a stab of pain through his side, from shoulder to hip. He grunted with the pain—but figured that it would only make his performance more believable.

As they moved on through the lowest floor of the house, fear began to overtake him again. What if he had to provide a positive identification to open the vault? A retina scan? A thumbprint?

But the vault door stood open. Had the Oversoul influenced someone to forget to close it? Or had it all come down to chance? Am I fortune's fool, Nafai wondered, or merely the Oversoul's puppet? Or, by some slim chance, am I freely choosing at least some portion of my own path through this night's work?

He didn't even know which answer he wanted. If he was freely choosing for himself, then he had freely chosen to kill a man lying helpless in the street. Much better to believe that the Oversoul had compelled him or tricked him into doing it. Or that something in his genes or his upbringing had forced him to that action. Much better to believe that there was no other possible choice, rather than to torment himself with wondering whether it might not have been enough to steal Gaballufix's clothing, without having to kill him first. Being responsible for what he did with his opportunities was more of a burden than Nafai really wanted to bear.

Zdorab walked into the vault. Nafai followed, then stopped when he saw a large table where the entire fortune that Gaballufix had stolen from them that afternoon was arranged in neat stacks.

"As you can see, sir, the assay is nearly done," said Zdorab as he wandered off among the shelves. "I have kept everything clean and organized there. It's very kind of you to visit."

Is he stalling me here in the vault, Nafai wondered, waiting till help can arrive?

Zdorab emerged from the shelves at the back of the room. He was a smallish man, considerably shorter than Nafai, and he was already losing his hair though he couldn't have been more than thirty. A comical man, really—yet if he guessed at what was really happening, he might cost Nafai his life.

"Is this it?" asked Zdorab.

Nafai hadn't the faintest idea what it was *supposed* to look like, of course. He had seen many indexes, but most of them were small free-standing computers with wireless access to a major library. This one had nothing that Nafai could recognize as a display. What Zdorab held was a brass-colored metal ball, about twenty-five centimeters in diameter, flattened a little at the top and the bottom. "Let me see," Nafai growled.

Zdorab seemed reluctant to part with it. For a moment, Nafai felt a wave of panic sweep over him. He doesn't want to give it to me because he knows who I really am.

Then Zdorab revealed his true concern. "Sir, you said we must always keep it very clean."

He was worried about how dirty Gaballufix might have got himself under his soldier costume. After all, he seemed falling-down drunk and smelled of liquor and worse. His hands could be covered with anything.

"You're right," said Nafai. "*You* carry it."

"If you wish, sir," said Zdorab.

"That's the one, isn't it?" said Nafai. He had to be sure—he could only hope that the drunk act was convincing enough that stupid questions wouldn't arouse suspicion.

"It's the Palwashantu Index, if that's what you mean. I just wondered if that's the one you really wanted. You've never asked for it before."

So Gaballufix hadn't even brought it out of the vault—he never, not for one moment, intended to give it to them, no matter how Elemak bargained or what they paid. It made Nafai feel a little better. There had been no missed opportunity. Every script would have led to the same ending.

"Where are we taking it?" asked Zdorab.

Excellent question, thought Nafai. I can't very well tell him that we're giving it to Wetchik's sons, who are waiting in the darkness outside the Funnel.

"Got to show it to the clan council."

"At this time of night?"

"Yes at this time of night! Interrupted me, the bastards. Having a party and they had to see the *Index* because they got some whim that maybe it got itself stolen by Wetchik's murdering lying thieving sons."

Zdorab coughed, ducked his head, and hurried on, leading Nafai down the corridor.

So Zdorab didn't like hearing Gaballufix lay such epithets on Wetchik's sons. Very interesting. But not so interesting that Nafai intended to take Zdorab into his confidence. "Slow down, you miserable little dwarf!" called Nafai.

"Yes sir," said Zdorab. He slowed down, and Nafai lurched after him.

They came to the door, where the same man stood on guard. The man looked at Zdorab, a question in his eyes. Here's the moment, thought Nafai. A signal passing between them.

"Please open the door for Master Gaballufix," said Zdorab. "We're going out again."

The only signal, Nafai realized, was that the doorkeeper was asking if this man in holographic soldier costume was Gaballufix, and Zdorab had answered by assuring him that the drunken lout inside the costume was the same one who had come in only a few moments before.

"Making merry, sir?" asked the doorkeeper.

"The council seems to be asserting itself tonight," said Zdorab.

"Want any escort?" asked the doorkeeper. "We've only got a couple of dozen close enough to lay hands on, but we can get some in from Dogtown in a few minutes, if you want them."

"No," barked Nafai.

"I just thought—the council might need a reminder, like last time—"

"They remember!" said Nafai. He wondered what "last time" was.

Zdorab led the way through the door. Nafai stumbled outside. The door latched behind them.

As they walked along the near-empty streets of Basilica, it began to dawn on Nafai what he had just accomplished. After all the day's failures, he had just come out of Gaballufix's house *with* the Index. Or at least with a man who was carrying the Index.

"The air is very invigorating, isn't it, sir," said Zdorab.

"Mm," said Nafai.

"I mean—your head seems to have cleared considerably."

It dawned on Nafai that he had forgotten to continue his drunk act. Too late to put it on again *now*, though—it would be stupid to stumble immediately after Zdorab had commented on how much less drunk he seemed. So instead, Nafai stopped, turned toward Zdorab, and glared. Not that Zdorab could see his facial expression. No, instead the man would have to imagine it.

Apparently Zdorab had a very good imagination. He immediately seemed to cower inside himself. "Not that your head wasn't clear to begin with. I mean, all along. That is, your head is *always* clear, sir. And you've got a meeting with the clan council tonight, so that's a good thing, isn't it!"

Wonderful, thought Nafai.

"Where *are* they meeting tonight?" asked Zdorab.

Nafai hadn't the faintest idea. He only knew that he had to meet his brothers outside the Funnel. "Where do you *think!*" he growled.

"Well, I mean, it's just—you seemed to be headed toward the Funnel, and . . . which isn't to say they couldn't hold a meeting out in Dogtown, it's just that usually they . . . not that anybody ever brings me along. I mean, for all I know you might hold the meetings in a different place every night, I just heard somebody talk about the clan council meeting at your mother's house near Back Gate, but that was just—it could have been just the once."

Nafai walked on, letting Zdorab talk himself into ever greater dread.

"Oh no!" cried Zdorab.

Nafai stopped. If I take the Index and run for the gate, can I make it before he can raise an alarm?

"I left the vault open," said Zdorab. "I was so concerned about the Index . . . Please forgive me, sir. I know that the door is supposed to be open only when I'm there, and I . . . goodness, I just realized that I left it open before, too, when I came to meet you at the back door. What's got into me? I'll understand if I lose my job over this, sir. I've never left the vault door unattended. Should I go back and lock it? All that treasure there—how can you be sure that none of the servants will . . . Sir, I can rush back and still rejoin you here in only a few minutes, I'm very fleet of foot, I assure you."

This was the perfect opportunity to rid himself of Zdorab—take the Index, let the man go, and then be out the Funnel before he can return. But what if this was just a subterfuge? What if Zdorab was trying to break free of him in order to give warning to Gaballufix's soldiers that an impostor in a holographic costume was making off with the Index?

He couldn't afford to let Zdorab go, not now. Not until he was safely outside the gate.

"Stay with me," said Nafai. He winced at how little his voice sounded like Gaballufix's now. Had Zdorab's eyebrows risen in surprise when Nafai spoke? Could he be wondering even now about the voice? Move on, thought Nafai. Keep moving, and say nothing. He hurried the pace. Zdorab, with his shorter legs, was jogging now to keep up.

"I've never been to a meeting like this, sir," said Zdorab. He was panting with the exertion now. "I won't have to say anything, will I? I mean, I'm not a member of the council. Oh, what am I saying! They probably won't let me into the actual meeting, anyway. I'll just wait for you outside. Please forgive me for being so nervous, I've just never . . . I spend my time in the vault and the library, of course, doing accounts and so on, you've got to realize that I just don't get out and about much, and since I live alone there's not much conversation, so most of what I know about politics is what I overhear. I know that *you're* very much involved, of course. All the people in the house are very proud to be working for such a famous man. Dangerous, though, isn't it—with Roptat murdered tonight. Aren't you just the tiniest bit afraid for yourself?"

Is he really such a fool as this? thought Nafai. Or is he, in fact, suspicious that Gaballufix might be Roptat's murderer, and this is his clumsy way of trying to extract information?

In any event, Nafai doubted Gaballufix would answer such questions, so he held his tongue. And there, at last, was the gate.

The guards were very much alert. Of course—Zdorab would be too curious if they were so strangely inattentive this time. Nafai cursed himself for having brought Zdorab along. He should have got rid of the man when he had a chance.

The guards got into position, holding out the thumbscreens. They looked belligerent, too—Nafai's soldier costume made him an enemy, or at least a rival. The thumbscreen would silently reveal his true identity, of course, but since Nafai was now under suspicion of having murdered Roptat, it wouldn't be much help.

As he stood there, frozen in indecision, Zdorab intervened. "You aren't actually going to insist that my master lay his thumb on your petty little screen, are you!" he blustered. Then he pressed his own thumb onto the scanner. "There, does that tell you who I am? The treasurer of Lord Gaballufix!"

"The law is, everybody lays his thumb here," said the guard. But he now looked a great deal less certain of himself. It was one thing to trade snubs with Gaballufix's soldiers, and quite another to face down the man himself. "Sorry, sir, but it's my job if I don't require it."

Nafai still didn't move.

"This is harassment," said Zdorab. "That's what it is." He kept glancing at Nafai, but of course he could read no approval or disapproval in the emotionless holographic mask.

"There's murderers out tonight," said the guard, apologetically. "You yourself reported the Wetchik's youngest son killed Roptat, and so we have to check everybody."

Nafai strode forward and reached out his hand toward the thumbscreen. As he did, however, he leaned his head close to the guard and said, quietly, "And what if the man who reported such an absurd lie was the murderer himself?"

The guard recoiled, surprised at the voice and hardly making sense of the words. Then he looked down at the screen and saw the name that the city computer showed there. He paused a moment, thinking.

Oversoul, give this man wit. Let him understand the truth, and act on it.

"Thank you for submitting to the law, Lord Gaballufix," said the guard. He pressed the clear button, and Nafai saw his name disappear. No one else could have seen it.

Without a backward glance, Nafai strode out through the gate. He heard Zdorab pattering along behind him. "Did I do right, sir?" asked Zdorab. "I mean, it seemed as though you were reluctant to give your thumb to it, and so I . . . Where are we going? Isn't it a little dark to be cutting through the brush here? Couldn't we stick to the road, Lord Gaballufix? Of course, there's a moon, so it's not *that* dark, but—"

With Zdorab's babbling, it was impossible to be subtle as they moved straight toward the spot where Nafai had left his brothers to wait for him. And now Zdorab had loudly called him by the name Gaballufix. It was hardly a surprise when Nafai saw a flurry of movement and heard footsteps, running away. Of course—they thought Nafai had been caught, that he had betrayed them, that Gaballufix had come to kill them. What could they see, except the costume?

Nafai fumbled with the controls. How could he tell whether it was off or not? Finally he yanked the costume off over his head, and then called out as loudly as he dared, and in his own voice. "Elemak! Issya! Meb! It's me—don't run!"

They stopped running.

"Nafai!" said Meb.

"In Gaballufix's clothing!" said Elemak.

"You did it!" cried Issib, laughing.

A tiny screech just behind him reminded Nafai that this sweet reunion scene would seem just a little less than happy to poor Zdorab, who had just discovered that he had been following the very man accused of murdering Roptat only a few hours before, and who had almost certainly done something quite similar to Gaballufix.

Nafai turned in time to see Zdorab turning tail and starting to run. "I'm very fleet of foot," Zdorab had said earlier, but now Nafai learned that it wasn't true. He outran the man in half a dozen steps, knocked him down, and wrestled with him on the stony ground for only a few moments before he had him pinned, with his hand over the poor man's mouth. The guards were no more than fifty meters away. No doubt the Oversoul had kept them from paying attention to the shouting that had just gone on, but there were limits to the Oversoul's ability to make people stupid.

"Listen to me," Nafai whispered fiercely. "If you do what I say, Zdorab, I won't kill you. Do you understand?"

Under his hand, Nafai felt the head nod up and down.

"I give you my oath by the Oversoul that I did not murder Roptat. Your master Gaballufix caused Roptat's death and gave orders for me and my brothers to be killed. *He* was the murderer, but now I've killed Gaballufix and that was justice. Do you understand me? I'm not one who kills for pleasure. I don't want to kill *you*. Will you be silent if I uncover your mouth?"

Again the nod. Nafai uncovered his mouth.

"I'm glad you don't want to kill me," Zdorab whispered. "I don't want to be dead."

"Do you believe my words?" Nafai asked.

"Would you believe my answer?" asked Zdorab. "I think we're in one of those situations where people will say pretty much whatever they think the other person wants to hear, wouldn't you say?"

He had a point. "Zdorab, I can't let you go back into the city, do you understand me? I guess what it comes down to is this—if you really are one of Gaballufix's men, one of the louts that he hires to do his dirty work in Basilica, then I can't trust anything you say and I might as well kill you now and have done. But I don't think that's who you are. I think you're a librarian, a record-keeper, a *clerk* who had no idea what working for Gaballufix entailed."

"I kept seeing things but nobody else seemed to think they were strange and no one would ever answer my questions so I kept to myself and held my tongue. Mostly."

"We're going out into the desert. If you go with us, and stay with us —if you give me your word by the Oversoul—then you'll be a free man, part of our household, the equal of any other. We don't want you for a servant; we'll only have you as a friend."

"Of course I'll give my oath. But how will you know whether to believe me?"

"Swear by the Oversoul, my friend Zdorab, and I'll know."

"By the Oversoul, then, I swear to stay with you and be your loyal friend forever. On the condition that you don't kill me. Though I guess if you killed me then the rest of it would be moot, wouldn't it."

Nafai could see that his brothers were now gathered around. They had heard the oath, of course, and had their own opinions. "Kill him," Meb said. "He's one of Gaballufix's men, you can't believe them."

"I'll do it, if it must be done," said Elemak.

"How can we know?" asked Issib.

But Nafai didn't hear them. He was listening for the Oversoul, and the answer was clear. Trust the man.

"I accept your oath," said Nafai. "And I swear by the Oversoul that neither I nor anyone in my family will harm you, as long as you keep your oath. All of you—swear it."

"This is absurd!" said Mebbekew. "You're putting us all at risk."

"For this night the Oversoul gave me the command," said Nafai, "and you promised to obey. I came out of the city with the Index, didn't I? And Gaballufix is dead. Swear to this man!"

They took the oath, all of them.

"Now," said Nafai to Zdorab, "give me the Index."

"I can't," said Zdorab.

"See?" said Meb.

"I mean—when you knocked me down, I dropped it."

"Wonderful," said Elemak. "All this way to get this precious Index, and now we're going to be picking up pieces of it all over the desert."

Issib found it, though, only a meter away, and when Elemak picked it up, it seemed unharmed. By moonlight, at least, there didn't seem to be even a scratch.

Mebbekew also took a close look at it, handled it, hefted it. "Just a ball. A metal ball."

"It doesn't even *look* like an index," said Issib.

Nafai reached out his hands and took the thing from Mebbekew. Immediately it began to glow. Lights appeared under it.

"You've got it upside down, I think," said Zdorab.

Nafai turned it over. In the air over the ball, a holographic arrow pointed southwest. Above the arrow were several words, but in a language Nafai didn't understand.

"That's ancient Puckyi," said Issib. "Nobody speaks it now."

The letters changed. It was a single word. *Chair.*

"The arrow," said Issib. "It's pointing toward where I left my chair."

"Let me see that," said Elemak.

Nafai handed him the Index. The moment it left Nafai's hands, the display disappeared.

Nafai reached out to take the Index back. Elemak looked at him steadily, his eyes like ice, and then he handed Nafai the metal ball. When Nafai touched it again, the display reappeared. Nafai turned to Zdorab. "What does this mean?"

"I don't know," said Zdorab. "It never did anything before. I thought it was broken."

"Let me try," said Issib.

"Please, no," said Nafai. "Let's wrap it up and carry it home to Father without looking at it again. Elemak knows the way. He should lead us."

"Right," said Mebbekew.

"Whatever," said Issib.

"Which one's Elemak?" asked Zdorab.

Elemak strode away toward High Road, toward the place where Issib's chair was waiting for them. By the time they got back to the camels, the sky was just beginning to lighten in the east. Nafai wrapped the Index and gave it to Elemak to stow it on a pack frame.

"*You* should give it to Father," Nafai said.

Elemak reached out and took a pinch of Nafai's—no, Gaballufix's— shirt between his thumb and forefinger. He leaned close and spoke softly. "Don't patronize me, Nafai. I see the way of things, and I'll tell you now. I won't be given power or honor or anything as a gift from *you.* Whatever I have I'll have because it's mine by right. Do you understand me?"

Nafai nodded. Elemak let go of his shirt and walked away. Only then did Nafai understand that there would be no healing this breach between him and his eldest brother. The Index had come to life under Nafai's hands. It had lain inert in Elemak's. The Oversoul had spoken, and Elemak would never forgive the message that it gave.

16

The Index of the Oversoul

Nafai and Father sat and Issib lay on a rug in Father's tent. The Index rested on the rug between them. Nafai touched the Index with his fingers. Father also reached out and touched it with one hand. Then, with the other, he lifted Issib's arm and brought his hand near, until it touched. With the three of them in contact with it at the same time, the Index spoke.

"Awake, after all this time," said the Index. It was a whisper. Nafai wasn't altogether sure whether he was hearing it with his ears, or whether his mind was transforming the ambient noises—the desert breeze, their own breathing—into a voice.

"You came to us at great cost," said Father.

"I waited for a long time to have this voice again," answered the Index.

It wasn't the Index speaking. Nafai knew that now. "This is the voice of the Oversoul."

"Yes," said the whisper.

"If this contains your voice," said Father, "why is it called an index?"

The answer came only after a long hesitation. "This is the index to *me,*" it finally said.

The Index of the Oversoul. An index was a tool created to make it easier for people to find their way through the labyrinthine memory of a complex computer. The Oversoul was the greatest of all computers, and this was the tool that would let Nafai and Issib and Father begin, at last, to understand it. "Now that we have the Index," said Nafai, "can you explain to us who you—*what* you are?" Nafai asked.

Again the pause, and then the whispering: "I am the Memory of Earth. I was never meant to last so long. I am weakening, and must return to the one who is wiser than I, who will tell me what to do to save this unharmonious world called Harmony. I have chosen your family to carry me back to the Keeper of Earth."

"*That* is where you're leading us?"

"The world that was buried in ice and hidden in smoke is surely alive and awake now. The Keeper who drove humankind from the planet they destroyed will surely not turn his face away from you now. Follow me, children of Earth, and I will take you back to your ancient home."

Nafai looked from Father to Issib and back again. "Do you realize what that means?" he said.

"A long journey," said Father, wearily.

"Long!" cried Nafai. "So long that it takes *light* a hundred years to reach us!"

"What are you talking about?" said Issib. "You'd think the Oversoul had promised to take us to another planet."

Issib's words hung in the air like music out of tune. Nafai sat there, stunned. Of *course* Oversoul had promised to take them to another planet. Those were its plain words. Except that this wasn't what Issib had heard. Or Father. Obviously, then, the Index did not make literal sounds, and they were in fact hearing with their minds, not their ears.

"What did *you* think the Oversoul said?" Nafai asked.

"That he was going to lead us to a beautiful land," said Father. "A good place, where crops would grow, and orchards thrive. A place where our children could be free and good, without the evils of Basilica."

"But *where?*" asked Nafai. "Where did it say that this beautiful land would be?"

"Nafai, you must learn to be more patient and trusting," said Father.

"The Oversoul will lead us one step at a time, and then, one day, one of those steps will be the last one in our journey, and we'll be home."

"It won't be a city," said Issib, "but it will be a place where I can use my floats again."

Nafai was deeply disappointed. He knew what he had heard, but he also knew that Father and Issib had not heard it. Why not? Either it meant that they simply couldn't comprehend the voice of the Oversoul as clearly as he could, or it meant that the Oversoul had given them a different message. Either way, he couldn't force his own understanding on them.

"What did *you* hear?" asked Father. "Was there more?"

"Nothing important for now," said Nafai. "What really matters is knowing that we're not going to wait around for Basilica to take us back. We're not exiles now, we're expatriates. Emigrants. Basilica is not our city anymore."

Father sighed. "And to think I was just about to retire and turn the business over to Elya. I didn't want to journey anymore! Now I'm about to take the longest journey of my life, I fear."

Nafai reached out and took the Index between his hands and drew it close. It trembled in his grasp. "As for you, my strange little Index, I hope you turn out to be worth all the trouble that was taken to get you. The price that was paid."

"Such a fortune," said Issib. "I never knew we were so rich until the day we weren't."

"We're richer than ever now," said Father. "We have a whole land promised to us, with no city or clan or enemy to take it away. And the Index to the Oversoul is here to lead the way."

Nafai hardly heard them. He was thinking of the blood that he had shed, of how it stained his clothing and his skin. I didn't want to do it, he thought, and it was simple justice, to take the life of a murderer. When Elemak thought he might have killed a man, from far off, with a pulse, he bragged about it. But I killed him close, under my own hand, as he lay drunken and helpless on the street. I did it, not in fear for my own life, and not to protect a caravan, but in cold blood, without anger. Because the Oversoul told me that it was right. And because I believed in my own heart that it was necessary.

But I also hated him. Will I ever be sure that I didn't do it because of that hatred, that longing for vengeance? I fear that I will always suspect that I am an assassin in my heart.

I can live with that, though. I can sleep tonight. With time I'm sure
that the pain of it will even fade. It's the price of the thing that I agreed
to be: a servant of the Oversoul. I'm not my own man anymore. I'm the
man the Oversoul has chosen to make of me. I hope I like at least a
small part of what I've become, when at last the Oversoul is through
with me.

He slept that night and dreamed. Not of murder. Not of Gaballufix's
head, nor of the blood on his own clothes. Instead he dreamed of
drifting on a sea whose currents ran hot and cold, as fog drifted endlessly in front of his face. And then, out of this lost and mysterious and
peaceful place, hands searched across his face, his shoulder, and then
took hold of his arm and pulled him close.

I'm not the first one here, he realized as he woke from the dream.
I'm not alone in this place, this kingdom of the Oversoul. Others have
been here before me, and are with me now, and *will* be with me
through all that is to come.

THE CALL
OF EARTH

To
Dave Dollahite
Teacher and dreamer
Husband and father
Friend and fellow citizen

Acknowledgments

I owe thanks to many for easing my way through the writing of this book. Clark and Kathy Kidd provided me with a refuge during the last week of the writing of this novel; half of it came forth under their roof, and with their good company.

A writer's life can so easily slip into undisciplined sloth; my body has long reflected the physical indolence of a mentally exhausting career. This book owes much to the fact that during the writing of it I woke my body up again: I owe thanks to Clark Kidd and Scott Allen for sweating with me as I tortured a new bicycle into submission on the roads and bikepaths of northern Virginia and on the streets and strands of North Myrtle Beach.

Several readers helped me reconcile this book with its predecessor, reading scraps of manuscript as they emerged from my printer, most notably Kathy Kidd and Russell Card. My editor on this series is Beth Meacham; my publisher is Tom Doherty; it is no accident that I have done the best work of my life so far for them. And my agent, Barbara Bova, has been a constant help and wise counselor during a turbulent time.

This novel was supposed to be easy, but it turned out not to be. Moozh complicated everything, and yet made it all worth doing. During the long struggle to make Moozh and the rest of the story fit together, I imagine that I was barely tolerable to live with, but still my wife, Kristine, and our children, Geoffrey, Emily, and Charlie Ben, were willing to keep me around; it is the joy of my life to find them always around me when I surface from immersion in my work. And, as always, Kristine has been my first and best editor and audience, reading my work with a sharp and trustworthy eye, then telling me what I have written so I can keep or alter it as need be.

Contents

Prologue

The master computer of the planet Harmony was not designed to interfere so directly in human affairs. It was deeply disturbed by the fact that it had just provoked young Nafai to murder Gaballufix. But how could the master computer return to Earth without the Index? And how could Nafai have got the Index without killing Gaballufix? There was no other way.

Or was there? I am old, said the master computer to itself. Forty million years old, a machine designed to last for nowhere near this long. How can I be sure that my judgment is right? And yet I caused a man to die for my judgment, and young Nafai is suffering the pangs of guilt because of what I urged him to do. All of this in order to carry the Index back to Zvezdakroog, so I could return to Earth.

If only I could speak to the Keeper of Earth. If only the Keeper could tell me what to do now. Then I could act with confidence. Then I would not have to doubt my every action, to wonder if everything I do might not be the product of my own decay.

The master computer needed so badly to speak to the Keeper; yet it could not speak to the Keeper except by returning to Earth. It was so frustratingly circular. The master computer could not act wisely without the help of the Keeper; it had to act wisely in order to get to the Keeper.

What now? What now? I need wisdom, and yet who can guide me? I have vastly more knowledge than any human can hope to master, and yet I have no minds but human minds to counsel me.

Was it possible that human minds might be enough? No computer could ever be so brilliantly dysorganized as the human brain. Humans made the most astonishing decisions based on mere fragments of data, because their brain recombined them in strange and truthful ways. It was possible, surely, that some useful wisdom might be extracted from them.

Then again, maybe not. But it was worth trying, wasn't it?

The master computer reached out through its satellites and sent images into the minds of those humans most receptive to its transmissions. These images from the master computer began to move through their memories, forcing their minds to deal with them, to fit them together, to make sense of them. To make from them the strange and powerful stories they called dreams. Perhaps in the next few days, the next few weeks, their dreams would bring to the surface some connection or understanding that the master computer could use to help it decide how to bring the best of them out of the planet Harmony and take home to Earth.

All these years I have taught and guided, shaped and protected them. Now, in the end of my life, are they ready to teach and guide, shape and protect *me*? So unlikely. So unlikely. I will surely be forced to decide it all myself. And when I do, I will surely do it wrong. Perhaps I should not act at all. Perhaps I should not act at all. I should not act. Will not. Must.

Wait.

Wait.

Again, wait. . . .

1
Betrayal

THE DREAM OF THE GENERAL

General Vozmuzhalnoy Vozmozhno awoke from his dream, sweating, moaning. He opened his eyes, reached out with his hand, clutching. A hand caught his own, held it.

A man's hand. It was General Plodorodnuy. His most trusted lieutenant. His dearest friend. His inmost heart.

"You were dreaming, Moozh." It was the nickname that only Plod dared to use to his face.

"Yes, I was." Vozmuzhalnoy—Moozh—shuddered at the memory. "Such a dream."

"Was it portentous?"

"Horrifying, anyway."

"Tell me. I have a way with dreams."

"Yes, I know, like you have a way with women. When you're through with them, they say whatever you want them to say!"

Plod laughed, but then he waited. Moozh did not know why he was reluctant to tell *this* dream to Plod. He had told him so many others. "All right, then, here is my dream. I saw a man standing in a clearing, and all around him, terrible flying creatures—not birds, they had fur, but much larger than bats—they kept circling, swooping down, touching him. He stood there and did nothing. And when at last they all had touched him, they flew away, except one, who perched on his shoulder."

"Ah," said Plod.

"I'm not finished. Immediately there came giant rats, swarming out of burrows in the Earth. At least a meter long—half as tall as the man. And again, they kept coming until all of them had touched him—"

"With what? Their teeth? Their paws?"

"And their noses. *Touched* him, that's all I knew. Don't distract me."

"Forgive me."

"When they'd all touched him, they went away."

"Except one."

"Yes. It clung to his leg. You see the pattern."

"What came next?"

Moozh shuddered. It had been the most terrible thing of all, and yet now as the words came to his lips, he couldn't understand why. "People."

"People? Coming to touch him?"

"To . . . to kiss him. His hands, his feet. To *worship* him. Thousands of them. Only they didn't kiss just the man. They kissed the—flying thing, too. And the giant rat clinging to his leg. Kissed them all."

"Ah," said Plod. He looked worried.

"So? What is it? What does it portend?"

"Obviously the man you saw is the Imperator."

Sometimes Plod's interpretations sounded like truth, but this time Moozh's heart rebelled at the idea of linking the Imperator with the man in the dream. "Why is that obvious? He looked nothing like the Imperator."

"Because all of nature and humankind worshipped him, of course."

Moozh shrugged. This was not one of Plod's most subtle interpretations. And he had never heard of animals loving the Imperator, who fancied himself a great hunter. Of course, he only hunted in one of his parks, where all the animals had been tamed to lose their fear of men, and all the predators trained to act ferocious but never strike. The Imperator got to act his part in a great show of the contest between man and beast, but he was never in danger as the animal innocently exposed itself to his quick dart, his straight javelin, his merciless blade.

If this was worship, if this was nature, then yes, one could say that all of nature and humankind worshipped the Imperator. . . .

Plod, of course, knew nothing of Moozh's thoughts in this vein; if one was so unfortunate as to have caustic thoughts about the Imperator, one took care not to burden one's friends with the knowledge of them.

So Plod continued in his interpretation of Moozh's dream. "What does it portend, this worship of the Imperator? Nothing in itself. But the fact that it *revolted* you, the fact that you recoiled in horror—"

"They were kissing a rat, Plod! They were kissing that disgusting flying creature . . ."

But Plod said nothing as his voice trailed off. Said nothing, and watched him.

"I am *not* horrified at the thought of people worshipping the Imperator. I have knelt at the Invisible Throne myself, and felt the awe of his presence. It wasn't horrible, it was . . . ennobling."

"So you say," said Plod. "But dreams don't lie. Perhaps you need to purge yourself of some evil in your heart."

"Look, *you're* the one who said my dream was about the Imperator. Why couldn't the man have been—I don't know—the ruler of Basilica."

"Because the miserable city of Basilica is ruled by women."

"Not Basilica, then. Still, I think the dream was about . . ."

"About what?"

"How should *I* know? I *will* purge myself, just in case you're right. I'm not an interpreter of dreams." That would mean wasting several hours today at the tent of the intercessor. It was so tedious, but it was also politically necessary to spend a certain amount of time there every month, or reports of one's impiety soon made their way back to Gollod, where the Imperator decided from time to time who was worthy of command and who was worthy of debasement or death. Moozh was about due for a visit to the intercessor's tabernacle anyway, but he hated it the way a boy hates a bath. "Leave me alone, Plod. You've made me very unhappy."

Plod knelt before him and held Moozh's right hand between his own. "Ah, forgive me."

Moozh forgave him at once, of course, because they were friends. Later that morning he went out and killed the headmen of a dozen Khlami villages. All the villagers immediately swore their eternal love

and devotion to the Imperator, and when General Vozmuzhalnoy
Vozmozhno went that evening to purge himself in the holy tabernacle,
the intercessor forgave him right readily, for he had much increased
the honor and majesty of the Imperator that day.

IN BASILICA, AND NOT IN A DREAM

They came to hear Kokor sing, came from all over the city of Basilica, and she loved to see how their faces brightened when—finally—
she came out onto the stage and the musicians began gently plucking
their strings or letting breath pass through their instruments in the soft
undercurrent of sound that was always her accompaniment. Kokor will
sing to us at last, their faces said. She liked that expression on their
faces better than any other she ever saw, better even than the look of a
man being overwhelmed with lust in the last moments before satisfaction. For she well knew that a man cared little who gave him the
pleasures of love, while the audience cared very much that it was
Kokor who stood before them on the stage and opened her mouth in
the high, soaring notes of her unbelievably sweet lyric voice that
floated over the music like petals on a stream.

Or at least that was how she wanted it to be. How she imagined it to
be, until she actually walked onstage and saw them looking at her. The
audience tonight was mostly men. Men with their eyes going up and
down her body. I should refuse to sing in the comedies, she told herself again. I should insist on being taken as seriously as they take my
beloved sister Sevet with her mannishly low, froggishly mannered
voice. Oh, they look at *her* with faces of aesthetic ecstasy. Audiences of
men and women together. *They* don't look *her* body up and down to
see how it moves under the fabric. Of course, that could be partly
because her body is so overfleshed that it isn't really a pleasure to
watch, it moves so much like gravel under her costume, poor thing. Of
course they close their eyes and listen to her voice—it's so much better
than *watching* her.

What a lie. What a liar I am, even when I'm talking only to myself!

I mustn't be so impatient. It's only a matter of time. Sevet is older—
I'm still barely eighteen. *She* had to do the comedies, too, for a time,
till she was known.

Kokor remembered her sister talking in those early days—more than
two years ago, when Sevet was almost seventeen—about constantly

having to dampen the ardor of her admirers, who had a penchant for entering her dressing room quite primed for immediate love, until she had to hire a bodyguard to discourage the more passionate ones. "It's all about sex," said Sevet then. "The songs, the shows, they're all about sex, and that's all the audience dreams of. Just be careful you don't make them dream too well—or too specifically!"

Good advice? Hardly. The more they dream of you, the greater the cash value of your name on the handbills advertising the play. Until finally, if you're lucky, if you're *good* enough, the handbill doesn't have to say the name of a show at all. Only *your* name, and the place, and the day, and the time . . . and when you show up they're all there, hundreds of them, and when the music starts they don't look at you like the last hope of a starving man, they look at you like the highest dream of an elevated soul.

Kokor strode to her place on the stage—and there *was* applause when she entered. She turned to the audience and let out a thrilling high note.

"What was that?" demanded Gulya, the actor who played the old lecher. "Are you screaming already? I haven't even touched you yet."

The audience laughed—but not enough. This play was in trouble. This play had had its weaknesses from the start, she well knew, but with a mere smattering of laughter like that, it was doomed. So in a few more days she'd have to start rehearsing all over again. Another show. Another set of stupid lyrics and stupid melodies to memorize.

Sevet got to decide her own songs. Songwriters came to her and begged her to sing what they had composed. *Sevet* didn't have to misuse her voice just to make people laugh.

"I wasn't screaming," Kokor sang.

"You're screaming now," sang Gulya as he sidled close and started to fondle her. His gravelly bass was always good for a laugh when he used it like that, and the audience was with him. Maybe they could pull this show out of the mud after all.

"But now you're *touching me!*" And her voice rose to its highest pitch and hung there in the air—

Like a bird, like a bird soaring, if only they were listening for beauty.

Gulya made a terrible face and withdrew his hand from her breast. Immediately she dropped her note two octaves. She got the laugh. The best laugh of the scene so far. But she knew that half the audience was laughing because Gulya did such a fine comic turn when he removed

his hand from her bosom. He was a master, he really was. Sad that his
sort of clowning had fallen a bit out of fashion lately. He was only
getting better as he got older, and yet the audience was slipping away.
Looking for the more bitter, nasty comedy of the young physical satirists. The brutal, violent comedy that always gave at least the illusion of
hurting somebody.

The scene went on. The laughs came. The scene ended. Applause.
Kokor scurried off the stage in relief—and disappointment. No one in
the audience was chanting her name; no one had even shouted it once
like a catcall. How long would she have to wait?

"Too pretty," said Tumannu, the stagekeeper, her face sour. "That
note's supposed to sound like you're reaching sexual climax. Not like a
bird."

"Yes yes," said Kokor, "I'm so sorry." She always agreed with everybody and then did what she wanted. This comedy wasn't worth doing if
she couldn't show her voice to best advantage at least now and then.
And it got the laugh when she did it her way, didn't it? So nobody
could very well say that her way was *wrong*. Tumannu just wanted her
to be obedient, and Kokor didn't intend to be obedient. Obedience was
for children and husbands and household pets.

"Not like a bird," said Tumannu again.

"How about like a bird reaching sexual climax?" asked Gulya, who
had come offstage right after her.

Kokor giggled, and even Tumannu smiled her tight sour little smile.

"There's someone waiting for you, Kyoka," said Tumannu.

It was a man. But not an aficionado of her work, or he'd have been
out front, watching her perform. She had seen him before. Ah, yes—he
showed up now and then when Mother's permanent husband,
Wetchik, came to visit. He was Wetchik's chief servant, wasn't he?
Manager of the exotic flower business when Wetchik was away on
caravan. What was his name?

"I am Rashgallivak," he said. He looked very grave.

"Oh?" she said.

"I am deeply sorry to inform you that your father has met with brutal
violence."

What an extraordinary thing to tell her. She could hardly make sense
of it for a moment. "Someone has injured him?"

"Fatally, madam."

"Oh," she said. There was meaning to this, and she would find it. "Oh, then that would mean that he's . . . dead?"

"Accosted on the street and murdered in cold blood," said Rashgallivak.

It wasn't even a surprise, really, when you thought about it. Father had been making such a bully of himself lately, putting all those masked soldiers on the streets. Terrifying everybody. But Father was so strong and intense that it was hard to imagine anything actually thwarting him for long. Certainly not *permanently.* "There's no hope of . . . recovery?"

Gulya had been standing near enough that now he easily inserted himself into the conversation. "It seems to be a normal case of death, madam, which means the prognosis isn't good." He giggled.

Rashgallivak gave him quite a vicious shove and sent him staggering. "That wasn't funny," he said.

"They're letting critics backstage now?" said Gulya. *"During* the performance?"

"Go away, Gulya," said Kokor. It had been a mistake to sleep with the old man. Ever since then he had thought he had some claim to intimacy with her.

"Naturally it would be best if you came with me," said Rashgallivak.

"But no," said Kokor. "No, that wouldn't be best." Who was *he?* He wasn't any kin to her at all, not that she knew of. She would have to go to Mother. Did Mother know yet? "Does Mother . . ."

"Naturally I told her first, and she told me where to find *you.* This is a very dangerous time, and I promised her that I would protect you."

Kokor knew he was lying, of course. Why should she need this stranger to protect her? From what? Men always got this way, though, insisting that a woman who hadn't a fear in the world needed watching out for. *Ownership,* that's what men always meant when they spoke of protection. If she wanted a man to own her, she *had* a husband, such as he was. She hardly needed this old pizdook to look out for her.

"Where's Sevet?"

"She hasn't been found yet. I must insist that you come with me."

Now Tumannu had to get into the scene. "She's going nowhere. She has three more scenes, including the climax."

Rashgallivak turned on her, and now there was some hint of majesty about him, instead of mere vague befuddlement. "Her father has been killed," he said. "And you suppose she will stay to finish a *play?*" Or

had the majesty been there all along, and she simply hadn't noticed it
until now?

"Sevet ought to know about Father," said Kokor.

"She'll be told as soon as we can find her."

Who is *we?* Never mind, thought Kokor. *I* know where to find her. I
know all her rendezvous, where she takes her lovers to avoid giving
affront to her poor husband Vas. Sevet and Vas, like Kokor and Obring,
had a flexible marriage, but Vas seemed less comfortable with it than
Obring was. Some men were so . . . territorial. Probably it was because Vas was a scientist, not an artist at all. Obring, on the other hand,
understood the artistic life. He would never dream of holding Kokor to
the letter of their marriage contract. He sometimes joked quite cheerfully about the men she was seeing.

Though, of course, Kokor would never actually insult Obring by
mentioning them herself. If he heard a rumor about a lover, that was
one thing. When he mentioned it, she would simply toss her head and
say, "You silly. You're the only man I love."

And in an odd sort of way it was true. Obring was such a dear, even
if he had no acting talent at all. He always brought her presents and
told her the most wonderful gossip. No wonder she had stayed married
to him through two renewals already—people often remarked on how
faithful she was, to still be married to her first husband for a third year,
when she was young and beautiful and could marry anyone. True,
marrying him in the first place was simply to please his mother, old
Dhel, who had served as her auntie and who was Mother's dearest
friend. But she had grown to like Obring, genuinely *like* him. Being
married to him was very comfortable and sweet. As long as she could
sleep with whomever she liked.

It would be fun to find Sevet and walk in on her and see whom she
was sleeping with tonight. Kokor hadn't pounced on her that way in
years. Find her with some naked, sweating man, tell her that Father
was dead, and then watch that poor man's face as he gradually realized
that he was all done with love for the night!

"*I'll* tell Sevet," said Kokor.

"You'll come with *me*," insisted Rashgallivak.

"You'll stay and finish the show," said Tumannu.

"The show is nothing but a . . . an *otsoss*," said Kokor, using the
crudest term she could think of.

Tumannu gasped and Rashgallivak reddened and Gulya chuckled his little low chuckle. "Now *that's* an idea," he said.

Kokor patted Tumannu on the arm. "It's all right," she said. "I'm fired."

"Yes, you are!" cried Tumannu. "And if you leave here tonight your career is *finished!*"

Rashgallivak sneered at her. "With her share of her father's inheritance she'll buy your little stage and your mother, too."

Tumannu looked defiant. "Oh, really? Who was her father, *Gaballufix?*"

Rashgallivak looked genuinely surprised. "Didn't you know?"

Clearly Tumannu had *not* known. Kokor pondered this for a moment and realized it meant that she must not ever have mentioned it to Tumannu. And that meant that Kokor had not traded on her father's name and prestige, which meant that she had got this part on her own. How wonderful!

"I knew she was the great Sevet's *sister,*" said Tumannu. "Why else do you think I hired her? But I never dreamed they had the same *father.*"

For a moment Kokor felt a flash of rage, hot as a furnace. But she contained it instantly, controlled it perfectly. It would never do to let such a flame burn freely. No telling what she would do or say if she ever let herself go at such a time as this.

"I must find Sevet," said Kokor.

"No," said Rashgallivak. He might have intended to say more, but at that moment he laid a hand on Kokor's arm to restrain her, and so of course she brought her knee sharply up into his groin, as all the comedy actresses were taught to do when an unwelcome admirer became too importunate. It was a reflex. She really hadn't even meant to do it. Nor had she meant to do it with such *force.* He wasn't a very heavy man, and it rather lifted him off the ground.

"I must find Sevet," Kokor said, by way of explanation. He probably didn't hear her. He was groaning too loudly as he lay there on the wooden floor backstage.

"Where's the understudy?" Tumannu was saying. "Not even three minutes' warning, the poor little bizdoon."

"Does it hurt?" Gulya was asking Rashgallivak. "I mean, what *is* pain, when you really think about it?"

Kokor wandered off into the darkness, heading for Dauberville. Her thigh throbbed, just above the knee, where she had pushed it so force-fully into Rashgallivak's crotch. She'd probably end up with a bruise there, and then she'd have to use an opaque sheen on her legs. Such a bother.

Father's dead. I must be the one to tell Sevet. Please don't let any-one else find her first. And *murdered*. People will talk about this for years. I will look rather fine in the white of mourning. Poor Sevet—her skin always looks red as a beet when she wears white. But she won't dare stop wearing mourning until *I* do. I may mourn for poor Papa for years and years and years.

Kokor laughed and laughed to herself as she walked along.

And then she realized she wasn't laughing at all, she was crying. Why am I crying? she wondered. Because Father is dead. That must be it, that must be what all this commotion is about. Father, poor Father. I must have loved him, because I'm crying now without having decided to, without anybody even watching. Who ever would have guessed that I loved him?

"Wake up." It was an urgent whisper. "Aunt Rasa wants us. Wake up!"

Luet could not understand why Hushidh was saying this. "I wasn't even asleep," she mumbled.

"Oh, you *were* sleeping, all right," said her sister Hushidh. "You were snoring."

Luet sat up. "Honking like a goose, I'm sure."

"Braying like a donkey," said Hushidh, "but my love for you turns it into music."

"That's why I do it," said Luet. "To give you music in the night." She reached for her housedress, pulled it over her head.

"Aunt Rasa wants us," Hushidh urged. "Come quickly." She glided out of the room, moving in a kind of dance, her gown floating behind her. In shoes or sandals Hushidh always clumped along, but barefoot she moved like a woman in a dream, like a bit of cottonwood fluff in a breeze.

Luet followed her sister out into the hall, still buttoning the front of her housedress. What could it be, that Rasa would want to speak to her and Hushidh? With all the troubles that had come lately, Luet feared the worst. Was it possible that Rasa's son Nafai had not escaped from the city after all? Only yesterday, Luet had led him along forbidden paths, down into the lake that only women could see. For the Oversoul had told her that Nafai must see it, must float on it like a woman, like a waterseer—like Luet herself. So she took him there, and he was not slain for his blasphemy. She led him out the Private Gate then, and through the Trackless Wood. She had thought he was safe. But of course he was not safe. Because Nafai wouldn't simply have gone back out into the desert, back to his father's tent—not without the thing that his father had sent him to get.

Aunt Rasa was waiting in her room, but she was not alone. There was a soldier with her. Not one of Gaballufix's men—his mercenaries, his thugs, pretending to be Palwashantu militia. No, this soldier was one of the city guards, a gatekeeper.

She could hardly notice him, though, beyond recognizing his insignia, because Rasa herself looked so . . . no, not frightened, really. It was no emotion Luet had ever seen in her before. Her eyes wide and glazed with tears, her face not firmly set, but slack, exhausted, as if things were happening in her heart that her face could not express.

"Gaballufix is dead," said Rasa.

That explained much. Gaballufix was the enemy in recent months, his paid tolchoks terrorizing people on the streets, and then his soldiers, masked and anonymous, terrifying people even more as they ostensibly made the streets of Basilica "safe" for its citizens. Yet, enemy though he was, Gaballufix had also been Rasa's husband, the father of her two daughters, Sevet and Kokor. There had been love there once, and the bonds of family are not easily broken, not for a serious woman like Rasa. Luet was no raveler like her sister Hushidh, but she knew that Rasa was still bound to Gaballufix, even though she detested all his recent actions.

"I grieve for his widow," said Luet, "but I rejoice for the city."

Hushidh, though, gazed with a calculating eye on the soldier. "This man didn't bring you *that* news, I think."

"No," said Rasa. "No, I learned of Gaballufix's death from Rashgallivak. It seems Rashgallivak was appointed . . . the new Wetchik."

Luet knew that this was a devastating blow. It meant that Rasa's husband, Volemak, who *had* been the Wetchik, now had no property, no rights, no standing in the Palwashantu clan at all. And Rashgallivak, who had been his trusted steward, now stood in his place. Was there no honor in the world? "When did Rashgallivak ascend to this honor?"

"Before Gaballufix died—Gab appointed him, of course, and I'm sure he loved doing it. So there's a kind of justice in the fact that Rash has now taken leadership of the Palwashantu clan, taking Gab's place as well. So yes, you're right, Rash is rising rather quickly in the world. While others fall. Roptat is also dead tonight."

"No," whispered Hushidh.

Roptat had been the leader of the pro-Gorayni party, the group trying to keep the city of Basilica out of the coming war between the Gorayni and Potokgavan. With him gone, what chance was there of peace?

"Yes, both dead tonight," said Rasa. "The leaders of both the parties that have torn our city apart. But here is the worst of it. The rumor is that my son Nafai is the slayer of them both."

"Not true," said Luet. "Not possible."

"So I thought," said Rasa. "I didn't wake you for the rumor."

Now Luet understood fully the turmoil in Aunt Rasa's face. Nafai was Aunt Rasa's pride, a brilliant young man. And more—for Luet knew well that Nafai also was close to the Oversoul. What happened to him was not just important to those who loved him, it was also important to the city, perhaps to the world. "This soldier has word of Nafai, then?"

Rasa nodded at the soldier, who had sat in silence until now.

"My name is Smelost," he said, rising to his feet to speak to them. "I was tending the gate. I saw two men approach. One of them pressed his thumb on the screen and the computer of Basilica knew him to be Zdorab, the treasurer of Gaballufix's house."

"And the other?" asked Hushidh.

"Masked, but dressed in Gaballufix's manner, and Zdorab called him Gaballufix and tried to persuade me not to make him press his thumb on the screen. But I had to make him do it, because Roptat was murdered, and we were trying to prevent the killer from escaping. We'd been told that Lady Rasa's youngest son, Nafai, was the murderer. It was Gaballufix who had reported this."

"So did you make Gaballufix put his thumb on the screen?" said Luet.

"He leaned close to me and spoke in my ear, and said, 'And what if the one who made this false accusation was the murderer himself?' Well, that's what some of us already thought—that Gaballufix was accusing Nafai of killing Roptat to cover up his own guilt. And then this soldier—the one that Zdorab was calling Gaballufix—put his thumb on the screen and the name the computer displayed for me was Nafai."

"What did you do?" Luet demanded.

"I violated my oath and my orders. I erased his name immediately and let him pass. I believed him . . . that he was innocent. Of killing Roptat. But his passage from the city was recorded, and the fact that I let him go, knowing who he was. I thought nothing of it—the original complaint came from Gaballufix, and here was Gaballufix's own treasurer with the boy. I thought Gaballufix couldn't protest if his man was along. The worst that would happen is that I'd lose my post."

"You would have let him go anyway," said Hushidh. "Even if Gaballufix's man hadn't been with him."

Smelost looked at her for a moment, then gave a little half-smile. "I was a follower of Roptat. It's a joke to think Wetchik's son might have killed him."

"Nafai's only fourteen," said Luet. "It's a joke to think he'd kill anybody."

"Not so," said Smelost. "Because word came to us that Gaballufix's body had been found. Beheaded. And his clothing missing. What should I think, except that Nafai got Gaballufix's clothing from his corpse? That Nafai and Zdorab almost certainly killed him? Nafai's big for fourteen, if that's his age. A man in size. He could have done it. Zdorab—not likely." Smelost chuckled wryly. "It hardly matters now that I'll lose my post for this. What I fear is that I'll be hanged as an accomplice to a murder, for letting him go. So I came here."

"To the widow of the murdered man?" asked Luet.

"To the mother of the supposed murderer," said Hushidh, correcting her. "This man loves Basilica."

"I do," said the soldier, "and I'm glad that you know it. I didn't do my duty, but I did what I thought was right."

"I need advice," said Rasa, looking from Luet to Hushidh and back again. "This man, Smelost, has come to me for protection, because he saved my son. And in the meantime, my son is named a murderer and I believe now that he might be guilty indeed. I'm no waterseer. I'm no raveler. What is right and just? What does the Oversoul want? You must tell me. You must counsel with me!"

"The Oversoul has told me nothing," said Luet. "I know only what you told me here, tonight."

"And as for raveling," said Hushidh, "I see only that this man loves Basilica, and that you yourself are tangled in a web of love that puts you at cross-purposes with yourself. Your daughters' father is dead, and you love them—and him, too, you love even *him*. Yet you believe Nafai killed him, and you love your son even more. You also honor this soldier, and are bound to him by a debt of honor. Most of all you love Basilica. Yet you don't know what you must do for the good of your city."

"I knew my dilemma, Shuya. It was the path out of it that I didn't know."

"I must flee the city," said Smelost. "I thought you might protect me. I knew of you as Nafai's mother, but I'd forgotten that you were Gaballufix's widow."

"Not his widow," said Rasa. "I let our contract lapse years ago. He has married a dozen times since then, I imagine. My husband now is Wetchik. Or rather the man who used to be Wetchik, and now is a landless fugitive whose son may be a murderer." She smiled bitterly. "I can do nothing about that, but I *can* protect *you*, and so I will."

"No you can't," said Hushidh. "You're too close to the center of all these mysteries, Aunt Rasa. The council of Basilica will always listen to you, but they won't protect a soldier who has violated his duty, solely on your word. It will simply make you both look all the guiltier."

"This is the raveler speaking?" asked Rasa.

"It's your student speaking," said Hushidh, "telling you what you would know yourself, if you weren't so confused."

A tear spilled out of Rasa's eye and slipped down her cheek. "What will happen?" said Rasa. "What will happen to my city now?"

Luet had never heard her so afraid, so uncertain. Rasa was a great teacher, a woman of wisdom and honor; to be one of her nieces, one of the students specially chosen to dwell within her household—it was the proudest thing that could happen to a young woman of Basilica, or so Luet had always believed. Yet here she saw Rasa afraid and uncertain. She had not thought such a thing was possible.

"Wetchik—my Volemak—he said the Oversoul was guiding him," said Rasa, spitting out the words with bitterness. "What sort of guide is this? Did the Oversoul tell him to send my boys back to the city, where they were almost killed? Did the Oversoul turn my son into a murderer and a fugitive? What is the Oversoul doing? Most likely it isn't the Oversoul at all. Gaballufix was right—my beloved Volemak has lost his mind, and our sons are being swallowed up in his madness."

Luet had heard enough of this. "Shame on you," she said.

"Hush, Lutya!" cried Hushidh.

"*Shame* on you, Aunt Rasa," Luet insisted. "Just because it looks frightening and confusing to you doesn't mean that the Oversoul doesn't understand it. I *know* that the Oversoul is guiding Wetchik, and Nafai too. All this will somehow turn to the good of Basilica."

"That's where you're wrong," said Rasa. "The Oversoul has no special love for Basilica. She watches over the whole world. What if the whole world will somehow benefit if Basilica is ruined? If my boys are killed? To the Oversoul, little cities and little people are nothing—she weaves a grand design."

"Then we must bow to her," said Luet.

"Bow to whomever you want," said Rasa. "I'm not bowing to the Oversoul if she's going to turn my boys into killers and my city into dust. If that's what the Oversoul is planning, then the Oversoul and I are enemies, do you understand me?"

"Lower your voice, Aunt Rasa," said Hushidh. "You'll waken the little ones."

Rasa fell silent for a moment, then muttered: "I've said what I have to say."

"You are not the Oversoul's enemy," said Luet. "Please, wait awhile. Let me try to find the Oversoul's will in this. That's what you brought me here to do, isn't it? To tell you what the Oversoul is planning?"

"Yes," said Rasa.

"I don't command the Oversoul," said Luet. "But I'll ask her. Wait here, and I'll—"

"No," said Rasa. "There's no time for you to go down to the waters."

"Not to the waters," said Luet. "To my room. To sleep. To dream. To listen for the voice, to watch for vision. If it comes."

"Then hurry," said Rasa. "We have only an hour or so before I have to do something—more and more people will come here, and I'll have to *act.*"

"I don't command the Oversoul," Luet said again. "And the Oversoul sets her own schedule. She does not follow yours."

Kokor went to Sevet's favorite hideaway, where she took her lovers to keep them from Vas's knowledge, and Sevet wasn't there. "She doesn't come here anymore," said Iliva, Sevet's friend. "Nor any of the other places in Dauberville. Maybe she's being faithful!" Then Iliva laughed and bade her good night.

So Kokor wouldn't be able to pounce after all. It was so disappointing.

Why had Sevet found a new hiding place? Had her husband Vas gone in search of her? He was far too dignified for that! Yet the fact remained that Sevet had abandoned her old places, even though Iliva and Sevet's other friends would gladly have continued to shelter her.

It could only mean one thing. Sevet had found a new lover, a real liaison, not just a quick encounter, and he was someone so important in the city that they had to find new hiding places for their love, for if it became known the scandal would surely reach Vas's ears.

How delicious, thought Kokor. She tried to imagine who it could be, which of the most famous men of the city might have won Sevet's heart. Of course it would be a married man; unless he was married to a woman of Basilica, no man had a right to spend even a single night in the city. So when Kokor finally discovered Sevet's secret, the scandal would be marvelous indeed, for there'd be an injured weeping wife to make Sevet seem all the more sluttish.

And I *will* tell it, thought Kokor. Because she hid this liaison from me and didn't tell me, I have no obligation to keep her secret for her. She didn't trust me, and so why should I be trustworthy?

Kokor wouldn't tell it *herself*, of course. But she knew many a satirist in the Open Theatre who would love to know of this, so he could be the first to dart sweet Sevet and her lover in a play. And the price she charged him for the story wouldn't be high—only the chance to play Sevet when he darted her. That would put a quick end to Tumannu's threat to blackball her.

I'll get to imitate Sevet's voice, thought Kokor, and make fun of her singing as I do. No one can sound as much like her as I can. No one knows all the flaws in her voice as I do. She will regret having hidden her secret from me! And yet I'll be masked when I dart her, and I'll deny it all, deny everything, even if Mother herself asks me to swear by the Oversoul, I'll deny it. Sevet isn't the only one who knows how to keep a secret.

It was late, only a few hours before dawn, but the last comedies wouldn't be over for another hour. If she hurried back to the theatre, she could probably even go back onstage and be there for the finale, at least. But she couldn't bring herself to play the scene she'd have to play with Tumannu—begging forgiveness, vowing never to walk away from a play again, weeping. It would be too demeaning. No daughter of Gaballufix should have to grovel before a mere stage manager!

Only now that he's dead, what will it matter if I'm his daughter or not? The thought filled her with dismay. She wondered if that man Rash had been right, if Father would leave her enough money to be very rich and buy her own theatre. That would be nice, wouldn't it? That would solve everything. Of course, Sevet would have just as much money and would probably buy her own theatre, too, just because she would have to overshadow Kokor as usual and steal any chance of glory, but Kokor would simply show herself to be the better promoter and drive Sevet's miserable imitative theatre into the dust, and, when it failed, *all* Sevet's inheritance would be lost, while Kokor would be the leading figure in Basilican theatre, and the day would come when Sevet would come to Kokor and beg her to put her in the starring role in one of her plays, and Kokor would embrace her sister and weep and say, "Oh, my darling sister, I'd love nothing better than to put on your little play, but I have a responsibility to my backers, my sweet, and I can't very well risk their money on a show starring a singer who is clearly *past her prime.*"

Oh, it was a delicious dream! Never mind that Sevet was only a single year older—to Kokor that made all the difference. Sevet might be ahead *now*, but someday soon youth would be more valuable than age to them, and then it would be Kokor who had the advantage. Youth and beauty—Kokor would always have more of both than Sevet. And she was every bit as talented as Sevet, too.

Now she was home, the little place that she and Obring rented in Hill Town. It was modest, but decorated in exquisite taste. That much, at least, she had learned from her Aunt Dhelembuvex—Obring's mother—that it's better to have a small setting perfectly finished than a large setting badly done. "A woman must present herself as the blossom of perfection," Auntie Dhel always said. Kokor herself had written it much better, in an aphorism she had published back when she was only fifteen, before she married Obring and left Mother's house:

> A perfect bud
> of subtle color
> and delicate scent
> is more welcome than a showy bloom,
> which shouts for attention but has nothing to show

that can't be seen in the first glance,
or smelled in the first whiff.

Kokor had been proudest of the way the lines about the perfect bud
were short and simple phrases, while the lines about the showy bloom
were long and awkward. But to her disappointment no noted melodist
had made an aria of her aphorism, and the young ones who came to her
with their tunes were all talentless pretenders who had no idea how to
make a song that would suit a voice like Kokor's. She didn't even sleep
with any of them, except the one whose face was so shy and sweet. Ah,
he was a tiger in the darkness, wasn't he! She had kept him for three
days, but he *would* insist on singing his tunes to her, and so she sent
him on his way.

What was his name?

She was on the verge of remembering who he was as she entered the
house and heard a strange hooting sound from the back room. Like the
baboons who lived across Little Lake, their pant-hoots as they babbled
to each other in their nothing language. "Oh. Hoo. Oo-oo. Hoooo."

Only it wasn't baboons, was it? And the sound came from the bedroom, up the winding stair, moonlight from the roof window lighting
the way as Kokor rushed upward, running the stairs on tiptoe, silently,
for she knew that she would find her husband Obring with some whore
of his *in Kokor's bed,* and that was unspeakable, a breach of all decency, hadn't he any consideration for her at all? She never brought
her lovers home, did she? She never let them sweat on *his* sheets, did
she? Fair was fair, and it would be a glorious scene of injured pride
when she thrust the little tartlet out of the house *without her clothes!* so
she'd have to go home naked and then Kokor would see how Obring
apologized to her and how he'd make it up to her, all his vows and
apologies and whimpering but there was no doubt about it now, she
would *not* renew him when their contract came up and then he'd find
out what happens to a man who throws his faithlessness in Kokor's
face.

In her moonlit bedroom, Kokor found Obring engaged in exactly the
activity she had expected. She couldn't see his face, or the face of the
woman for whom he was providing vigorous companionship, but she
didn't need daylight or a magnifying glass to know what it all meant.

"Disgusting," she said.

It worked just as she had hoped. They obviously had not heard her coming up the stair, and the sound of her voice froze Obring. For a moment he held his post. Then he turned his head, looking quite foolish as he gazed mournfully over his shoulder at her. "Kyoka," he said. "You're home early."

"I should have known," said the woman on the bed. Her face was still hidden behind Obring's naked back, but Kokor knew the voice at once. "Your show is so bad they closed it in mid-performance."

Kokor hardly noticed the insult, hardly noticed the fact that there wasn't a trace of embarrassment in Sevet's tone. All she could think of was, That's why she had to find a new hiding place, not because her lover was somebody famous, but to keep the truth from *me*.

"Hundreds of your followers every night would be glad for a yibattsa with you," Kokor whispered. "But you had to have my husband."

"Oh, don't take this personally," said Sevet, sitting up on her elbows. Sevet's breasts sagged off to the sides. Kokor loved seeing that, how her breasts sagged, how at nineteen Sevet was definitely older and *thicker* than Kokor. Yet Obring had wanted *that* body, had used that body on the very bed where he had slept beside Kokor's perfect body so many nights. How could he even be aroused by a body like that, after seeing Kokor after her bath so many mornings.

"You weren't using him, and he's very sweet," said Sevet. "If you'd ever bothered to satisfy him he wouldn't have looked at *me*."

"I'm sorry," Obring murmured. "I didn't mean to."

That was so outrageous, like a little child, that Kokor could not contain her rage. And yet she did contain it. She held it in, like a tornado in a bottle. "This was an accident?" whispered Kokor. "You stumbled, you tripped and fell, your clothes tore off and you just happened to bounce on top of my sister?"

"I mean—I kept wanting to break this off, all these months . . ."

"Months," whispered Kokor.

"Don't say any more, puppy," said Sevet. "You're just making it worse."

"You call him 'puppy'?" asked Kokor. It was the word they had used when they first reached womanhood, to describe the teenage boys who panted after them.

"He was so eager," said Sevet, sliding out from under Obring. "I couldn't help calling him that, and he likes the name."

Obring turned and sat miserably on the bed. He made no attempt to cover himself; it was obvious he had lost all interest in love for the evening.

"Don't worry about it, Obring," Sevet said. She stood beside the bed, bending over to pick up her clothing from the floor. "She'll still renew you. This is *one* story she won't be eager to have people tell about her, and so she'll renew you as long as you want, just to keep you from telling."

Kokor saw how Sevet's belly pooched out, how her breasts swung when she bent over. And yet *she* had taken Kokor's husband. After everything else, she had to have even *that*. It could not be borne.

"Sing for me," whispered Kokor.

"What?" asked Sevet, turning to face her, holding her gown in front of her.

"Sing me a song, you davalka, with that pretty voice of yours."

Sevet stared into Kokor's eyes and the look of bored amusement left her face. "I'm not going to sing right now, you little fool," she said.

"Not for me," said Kokor. "For Father."

"What *about* Father?" Sevet's face twisted into an expression of mock sympathy. "Oh, is little Kyoka going to tell on me?" Then she sneered. "He'll laugh. Then he'll take Obring drinking with him!"

"A *dirge* for Father," said Kokor.

"A dirge?" Sevet looked confused now. Worried.

"While you were here, boffing your sister's husband, somebody was busy killing Father. If you were human, you'd care. Even baboons grieve for their dead."

"I didn't know," said Sevet. "How could I know?"

"I looked for you," said Kokor. "To tell you. But you weren't in any of the places I knew. I left my play, I *lost my job* to search for you and tell you, and this is where you were and what you were doing."

"You're such a liar," said Sevet. "Why should I believe this?"

"I never did it with Vas," said Kokor. "Even when he begged me."

"He never asked you," said Sevet. "I don't believe your lies."

"He told me that just once he'd like to have a woman who was truly beautiful. A woman whose body was young and lithe and sweet. But I refused, because you were my sister."

"You're lying. He never asked."

"Maybe I'm lying. But he *did* ask."

"Not *Vas*," said Sevet.

"Vas, with the large mole on the inside of his thigh," said Kokor. "I refused him because you were my sister."

"You're lying about Father, too."

"Dead in his own blood. Murdered on the street. This is not a good night for our loving family. Father dead. Me betrayed. And you—"

"Stay away from me."

"Sing for him," said Kokor.

"At the funeral, *if* you're not lying."

"Sing *now*," said Kokor.

"Little *hen*, little *duck*, I'll never sing at *your* command."

Accusing her of cackling and quacking instead of singing, that was an old taunt between them, that was nothing. It was the contempt in Sevet's voice, the loathing that got inside her. It filled her, it overfilled her, it was more than she could contain. Not for another moment could she hold in the tempest that tore at her.

"That's right!" cried Kokor. "At my command, you'll *never* sing!" And like a cat she lashed out, but it wasn't a claw, it was a fist. Sevet threw up her hands to protect her face. But Kokor had no desire to mark her sister's face. It wasn't her face she hated. No, her fist connected right where she aimed, under Sevet's chin, on her throat, where the larynx lay hidden under the ample flesh, where the voice was made.

Sevet didn't make a sound, even though the force of the blow knocked her backward. She fell, clutching at her throat; she writhed on the floor, gagging, hacking. Obring cried out and leapt to her, knelt over her. "Sevet!" he cried. "Sevet, are you all right?"

But Sevet's only answer was to gurgle and spit, then to choke and cough. On blood. Her own blood. Kokor could see it on Sevet's hands, on Obring's thighs where he cradled her head on his lap as he knelt there. Glimmering black in the moonlight, blood from Sevet's throat. How does it taste in your mouth, Sevet? How does it feel on your flesh, Obring? Her blood, like the gift of a virgin, my gift to both of you.

Sevet was making an awful strangling sound. "Water," said Obring. "A glass of water, Kyoka—to wash her mouth out. She's bleeding, can't you see that? What have you done to her!"

Kyoka stepped to the sink—her own sink—and took a cup—her own cup—and brought it, filled with water, to Obring, who took it from her hand and tried to pour some of it into Sevet's mouth. But Sevet choked

on it and spat the water out, gasping for breath, strangling on the blood
that flowed inside her throat.

"A doctor!" cried Obring. "Cry out for a doctor—Bustiya next door is
a doctor, she'll come."

"Help," murmured Kokor. "Come quickly. Help." She spoke so
softly she almost couldn't hear the sound herself.

Obring rose up from the floor and looked at her in rage. "Don't
touch her," he said. "I'll fetch the physician myself." He strode boldly
from the room. Such strength in him now. Naked as a mythic god, as
the pictures of the Gorayni Imperator—the image of masculinity—that
was Obring as he went forth into the night to find a doctor who might
save his lady.

Kokor watched as Sevet's fingers scratched on the floor, tore at the
skin around her neck, as if she wanted to open up a breathing hole
there. Sevet's eyes were bugging out, and blood drooled from her
mouth onto the floor.

"You had everything else," said Kokor. "Everything else. But you
couldn't even leave me *him.*"

Sevet gurgled. Her eyes stared at Kokor in agony and terror.

"You won't die," said Kokor. "I'm not a murderer. I'm not a *be-
trayer.*"

But then it occurred to her that Sevet just *might* die. With so much
blood in her throat, she might drown in it. And then Kokor would be
held responsible for this. "Nobody can blame me," said Kokor. "Father
died tonight, and I came home and found you with my husband, and
then you taunted me—no one will blame me. I'm only eighteen, I'm
only a *girl.* And it was an accident anyway. I meant to claw out your
eyes but I missed, that's all."

Sevet gagged. She vomited on the floor. It smelled awful. This was
making such a mess—everything would be stained, and the smell
would never, never go. And they *would* blame Kokor for it, if Sevet
died. That would be Sevet's revenge, that the stain of this would never
go away. Sevet's way of getting even, to die and have Kokor called a
murderer forever.

Well, I'll show you, thought Kokor. I won't let you die. In fact, I'll
save your life.

So it was that when Obring returned with the doctor they found
Kokor kneeling over Sevet, breathing into her mouth. Obring pulled
her aside to let the doctor get to Sevet. And as Bustiya pushed the tube

down into Sevet's throat, as Sevet's face became a silent rictus of agony, Obring smelled the blood and vomit and saw how Kokor's face and gown were stained with both. He whispered to her as he held her there, "You do love her. You couldn't let her die."

She clung to him then, weeping.

"I can't sleep," Luet said miserably. "How can I dream if I can't sleep?"

"Never mind," Rasa said. "I know what we have to do. I don't need the Oversoul to tell us. Smelost has to leave Basilica, because Hushidh is right, I can't protect him now."

"I won't leave," said Smelost. "I've decided. This is my city, and I'll face the consequences of what I've done."

"Do you love Basilica?" said Rasa. "Then don't give Gaballufix's people somebody they can pin all the blame on. Don't give them a chance to put you on trial and use it as an excuse to take command of the guards so that his masked soldiers are the *only* authority in the city."

Smelost glared at her a moment, then nodded. "I see," he said. "For the sake of Basilica, then I'll go."

"Where?" asked Hushidh. "Where can you send him?"

"To the Gorayni, of course," said Rasa. "I'll give you provisions and money enough to make it north to the Gorayni. And a letter, explaining how you saved the man who—the man who killed Gaballufix. They'll know what that means—they must have spies who told them that Gab was trying to get Basilica to make an alliance with Potokgavan. Maybe Roptat was in contact with them."

"Never!" cried Smelost. "Roptat was no traitor!"

"No, of course he wasn't," said Rasa soothingly. "The point is that Gab was their enemy, and that makes you their friend. It's the least they can do, to take you in."

"How long will I have to stay away?" asked Smelost. "There's a woman that I love here. I have a son."

"Not long," said Rasa. "With Gab gone, the tumult will soon die down. He was the cause of it, and now we'll have peace again. May the Oversoul forgive me for saying so, but if Nafai killed him then maybe he did a good thing, for Basilica at least."

There was a loud knocking at the door.

"Already!" said Rasa.

"They can't know I'm here," said Smelost.

"Shuya, take him to the kitchen and provision him. I'll stall them at the door as long as I can. Luet, help your sister."

But it wasn't Palwashantu soldiers at the door, or city guards, or any kind of authority at all. Instead it was Vas, Sevet's husband.

"I'm sorry to disturb you at this hour."

"Me and my whole house," said Rasa. "I already know that Sevet's father is dead, but I know you meant well in coming to—"

"He's dead?" said Vas. "Gaballufix? Then maybe that explains . . . No, it explains nothing." He looked frightened and angry. Rasa had never seen him like this.

"What's wrong, then?" Rasa asked. "If you didn't know Gab was dead, why are you here?"

"One of Kokor's neighbors came to fetch me. It's Sevet. She's been struck in the throat—she almost died. A very bad injury. I thought you'd want to come with me."

"You *left* her? To come to me?"

"I wasn't with her," said Vas. "She's at Kokor's house."

"Why would Sevya be there?" One of the servants was already helping Rasa put on a cloak, so she could go outside. "Kokor had a play tonight, didn't she? A new play."

"Sevya was with Obring," said Vas. He led her out onto the portico; the servant closed the door behind them. "That's why Kyoka hit her."

"Kyoka hit her in the—*Kyoka* did it?"

"She found them together. That's how the neighbor told the story, anyway. Obring went and fetched the doctor stark naked, and Sevya was naked when they got back. Kyoka was breathing into her mouth, to save her. They have a tube in her throat and she's breathing, she won't die. That's all the neighbor knew to tell me."

"That Sevet is alive," said Rasa bitterly, "and who was naked."

"Her throat," said Vas. "It might have been kinder for Kokor simply to kill her, if this costs Sevet her voice."

"Poor Sevya," said Rasa. There were soldiers marching in the streets, but Rasa paid them no attention, and—perhaps because Vas and Rasa seemed so intent and urgent—the soldiers made no effort to stop them. "To lose her father and her voice in the same night."

"We've all lost something tonight, eh?" said Vas bitterly.

"This isn't about *you*," said Rasa. "I think Sevet really loves you, in her way."

"I know—they hate each other so much they'll do anything to hurt each other. But I thought it was getting better."

"Maybe now it will," said Rasa. "It can't get worse."

"Kyoka tried it, too," said Vas. "I sent her away both times. Why couldn't Obring have had the brains to say no to Sevet, too?"

"He has the brains," said Rasa. "He lacks the strength."

At Kokor's house, the scene was very touching. Someone had cleaned up: The bed was no longer rumpled with love; now it was smooth except where Sevet lay, demure in one of Kokor's most modest nightgowns. Obring, too, had managed to become clothed, and now he knelt in the corner, comforting a weeping Kokor. The doctor greeted Rasa at the door of the room.

"I've drained the blood out of the lungs," the physician said. "She's in no danger of dying, but the breathing tube must remain for now. A throat specialist will be here soon. Perhaps the damage will heal without scarring. Her career may not be over."

Rasa sat on the bed beside her daughter, and took Sevya's hand. The smell of vomit still lingered, even though the floor was wet from scrubbing. "Well, Sevya," whispered Rasa, "did you win or lose this round?"

A tear squeezed out between Sevet's eyelids.

On the other side of the room, Vas stood over Obring and Kokor. He was flushed with—what, anger? Or was his face merely red from the exertion of their walk?

"Obring," said Vas, "you miserable little bastard. Only a fool pees in his brother's soup."

Obring looked up at him, his face drawn, and then he looked back down at his wife, who wept all the harder. Rasa knew Kokor well enough to know that while her weeping was sincere, it was being played for the most possible sympathy. Rasa had almost none to give her. She was well aware how little her daughters had cared for the exclusivity clause in their marriage contracts, and she had no sympathy for faithless people who felt injured upon discovering that their mates were faithless, too.

It was Sevet who was suffering, not Kokor. Rasa could not be distracted from Sevet's need, just because Kokor was so noisy and Sevet was silent.

"I'm with you, my dear daughter," said Rasa. "It's not the end of the world. You're alive, and your husband loves you. Let that be your music for a while."

Sevet clung to her hand, her breath shallow, panting.

Rasa turned to the doctor. "Has she been told about her father?"

"She knows," Obring said. "Kyoka told us."

"Thank the Oversoul we have but one funeral to attend," said Rasa.

"Kyoka saved her sister's life," said Obring. "She gave her breath."

No, *I* gave her breath, thought Rasa. Gave her breath, but alas, I could not give her decency, or sense. I couldn't keep her out of her sister's sheets, or away from her sister's husband. But I did give her breath, and perhaps now this pain will teach her something. Compassion, perhaps. Or at least some self-restraint. Something to make good come out of this. Something to make her become *my* daughter, and not Gaballufix's, as they both have been till now.

Let this all turn to good, Rasa silently prayed. But then she wondered to whom she was praying. To the Oversoul, whose meddling had started so many other problems? I'll get no help from *her*, thought Rasa. I'm on my own now, to try to steer my family and my city through the terrible days to come. I have no power or authority over either of them, except whatever power comes from love and wisdom. I have the love. If only I could be sure I also had the wisdom.

2

Opportunity

THE DREAM OF THE WATERSEER

Luet had never tried to have an emergency dream before, and so it had never occurred to her that she couldn't just go to sleep and dream because she wished it. Quite the contrary—the sense of urgency was no doubt what had kept her awake and made it impossible for her to dream. She was furious and ashamed that she hadn't been able to learn anything from the Oversoul before Aunt Rasa had to make a decision about what to do with that soldier, Smelost. What made it worse was that, even though the Oversoul had told her nothing, she was certain that sending Smelost to the Gorayni was a mistake. It seemed too simple, to think that because Gaballufix had been an enemy of the Gorayni, the Gorayni would automatically welcome Gaballufix's enemy and give him sanctuary.

Luet had wanted to speak up and tell her, "Aunt Rasa, the Gorayni aren't necessarily our friends." She might even have said so, but Rasa had rushed out of the house with Vas and there was nothing to do but watch as Smelost gathered up the food and supplies the servants brought for him and then slipped out the back way.

Why couldn't Rasa have thought just a moment more? Wouldn't it have been better to send Smelost out into the desert to join Wetchik? But he wasn't the Wetchik anymore, was he? He was nothing but Volemak, the man who *had* been Wetchik until Gaballufix stripped him of the title—when?—only yesterday. Nothing but Volemak—yet Luet knew that Volemak, of all the great men of Basilica, was the only one who was part of the Oversoul's plans.

The Oversoul had begun all these problems by giving Volemak his vision of Basilica on fire. She had warned him that an alliance with Potokgavan would lead to the destruction of Basilica. She hadn't promised that Basilica could trust the Gorayni to be *friends*. And from what Luet knew of the Gorayni—the Wetheads, as they were called, from the way they oiled their hair—it was a bad idea to send Smelost to ask for refuge. It would give the wrong impression to the Gorayni. It would lead them to think that their allies were not safe in Basilica. Might that not entice them to do exactly what everyone wanted to keep them from doing—invade and conquer the city?

No, it was a mistake to send Smelost. But since Luet didn't reach this conclusion as a waterseer, but rather reached it through her own reasoning, no one would listen to her. She was a child, except when the Oversoul was in her, and so she only had respect when she was not herself. It made her angry, but what could she do about it, except hope that she was wrong about Smelost and the Gorayni, and then wait impatiently until she turned fully into a woman?

What worried her perhaps even more was that it was unlike Rasa to reach such a faulty conclusion. Rasa seemed to be acting out of fear, acting without thinking. And if Rasa's judgment was clouded, then what could Luet count on?

I want to talk to someone, she thought. Not her sister Hushidh—dear Shuya was very wise and kind and would listen to her, but she simply didn't care about anything outside Basilica. That was the problem with her being a raveler. Hushidh lived in the constant awareness of all the connections and relationships among the people around her. That web-sense was naturally the most important thing in her life, as she watched people connect and detach from each other, forming communities and dissolving them. And underlying all was Shuya's powerful awareness of the fabric of Basilica itself. She loved the city—but she knew it so well, focused so closely on it that she simply had no idea of how Basilica related to the world outside. Such relationships were too large and impersonal.

Luet had even tried to discuss this with her, but Hushidh fell asleep almost at once. Luet couldn't blame her. After all, it was nearly dawn, and they had missed hours of sleep in the middle of the night. Luet herself should be asleep.

If only I could talk with Nafai or Issib. Nafai especially—*he* can talk with the Oversoul when he's awake. He may not get the visions that I get, he may not see with the depth and clarity of a waterseer, but he can get *answers*. Practical, simple answers. And he doesn't have to be able to fall asleep to get them. If only he were here. Yet the Oversoul sent him and his father and all his brothers away into the desert. That's where Smelost should have gone, definitely. To Nafai. If only anyone knew where he was.

At last, at long last Luet's frenzied thoughts jumbled into the chaotic mentation of sleep, and from her fitful sleep a dream came, a dream that she would remember, for it came from outside herself and had meaning beyond the random firings of her brain during sleep.

"Wake up," said Hushidh.

"I *am* awake," said Luet.

"You've answered me that twice already, Lutya, and each time you stay asleep. It's morning, and things are even worse than we thought."

"If you said that every time I woke up," said Luet, "then no wonder I went back to sleep."

"You've slept long enough," said Hushidh, and then proceeded to tell her all about what happened at Kokor's house the night before.

Luet could hardly grasp that such things could actually happen—not to anyone connected with Rasa's house. Yet it wasn't just rumor. "That's why Vas took Aunt Rasa with him," said Luet.

"You have such a bright mind in the morning."

Her thoughts were coming so sluggishly that it took Luet a moment to realize that Hushidh was being ironic. "I was dreaming," she said, to explain her stupidness.

But Hushidh wasn't interested in her dream. "For poor Aunt Rasa the nightmare starts when she wakes up."

Luet tried to think of a bright spot. "At least she has the comfort of knowing Kokor and Sevet were auntied out to Dhelembuvex—it won't reflect on her house—"

"Won't reflect . . . ! They're her *daughters*, Lutya. And Auntie Dhel was over here with them all the time as they were growing up. This has nothing to do with how they were raised. This is what it means to be the daughters of Gaballufix. How deliciously ironic, that the very night he dies, one of his daughters strikes the other dumb with a blow to the throat."

"Sweet kindness flows with every word from your lips, Shuya."

Hushidh glared at her. "You've never loved Aunt Rasa's daughters, either, so don't get pure with me."

The truth was that Luet had no great interest in Rasa's daughters. She had been too young to care, when they last were in Rasa's house. But Hushidh, being older, had clear memories of what it was like to have them in the house all the time, with Kokor actually attending classes, and both of them surrounded by suitors. Hushidh liked to joke that the pheromone count couldn't have been higher in a brothel, but Hushidh's loathing for Kokor and Sevet had nothing to do with their attractiveness to men. It had to do with their vicious jealousy of any girl who had actually earned Rasa's love and respect. Hushidh was no rival to them, and yet they had both persecuted her mercilessly, taunting her whenever the teachers couldn't hear, until she became virtually a ghost in Rasa's house, hiding until the moment of class and rushing away afterward, avoiding meals, shunning all the parties and frolics, until Kokor and Sevet finally married at a mercifully young age—fourteen and fifteen, respectively—and moved out. Sevet was already a noted singer even then, and her practicing—and Kokor's—had filled the house like birdsong. But neither she nor Kokor had brought any true music to Rasa's house. Rather the music returned when they finally left. And Hushidh remained quiet and shy around everyone except Luet. So of course Hushidh cared more when Rasa's daughters played out some bitter tragedy. Luet only cared because it would make Aunt Rasa sad.

"Shuya, all this is only scandal. What's being said about that soldier? And about Gaballufix's death?"

Hushidh looked down in her lap. She knew that Luet was, in effect, rebuking her for having given false priority to trivial matters; but she accepted the rebuke, and did not defend herself. "They're saying that Smelost was Nafai's co-conspirator all along. Rashgallivak is demanding that the council investigate who helped Smelost escape from the city, even though he wasn't under a warrant or anything when he left. Rasa is trying to get the city guard put under the control of the Palwashantu. It's very ugly."

"What if Aunt Rasa is arrested as Smelost's accomplice?" said Luet.

"Accomplice in what?" said Hushidh. Now she was Hushidh the Raveler, discussing the city of Basilica, not Shuya the schoolgirl, telling an ugly story about her tormentors. Luet welcomed the change, even if it meant Hushidh's acting so openly astonished at Luet's lack of insight. "How insane do you think people actually are? Rashgallivak can try to whip them up, but he's no Gaballufix—he doesn't have the personal magnetism to get people to follow him for long. Aunt Rasa will hold her own against him on the council, and then some."

"Yes, I suppose so," said Luet. "But Gaballufix had so many soldiers, and now they're all Rashgallivak's. . . ."

"Rash isn't well-connected," said Hushidh. "People have always liked him and respected him, but only as a steward—as Wetchik's steward, particularly—and they aren't likely to give him the full honor of the Wetchik right away, let alone the kind of respect that Gaballufix was given as head of the Palwashantu. He doesn't have half the power he imagines he has—but he has enough to cause trouble, and it's very disturbing."

Luet was fully awake at last, and crawled off the foot of her bed. She remembered that there was something she must tell. "I dreamed," she said.

"So you said." Then Hushidh realized what she meant. "Oh. A little late, wouldn't you say?"

"Not about Smelost. About something—very strange. And yet it felt more important than any of what's going on around us."

"A true dream?" asked Hushidh.

"I'm never *sure*, but I think so. I remember it so clearly, it must come from the Oversoul."

"Then tell me as we go to breakfast. It's nearly noon, but Aunt Rasa told the cook to indulge us since we were up half the night."

Luet pulled a gown over her head, slipped sandals on her feet, and followed Hushidh down the stairs to the kitchen. "I dreamed of angels, flying."

"Angels! And what is that supposed to mean, except that you're superstitious in your sleep?"

"They didn't look like the pictures in the children's books, if that's what you mean. No, they were more like large and graceful birds. Bats, really, since they had fur. But with very intelligent and expressive faces, and somehow in the dream I knew they were angels."

"The Oversoul has no need of angels. The Oversoul speaks directly to the mind of every woman."

"And man, only hardly anybody listens anymore, just as you're not listening to *me*, Shuya. Should I tell you the dream or just eat bread and honey and cream and figure that the Oversoul has nothing to say that might interest you?"

"Don't be nasty with *me*, Luet. You may be this wonderful waterseer to everybody else, but you're just my stupid little sister when you get snippy like this."

The cook glared at them. "I try to keep a kitchen full of light and *harmony*," she said.

Abashed, they took the hot bread she offered them and sat at the table, where a pitcher of cream and a jar of honey already waited. Hushidh, as always, broke her bread into a bowl and poured the cream and honey on it; Luet, as always, slathered the honey on the bread and ate it separately, drinking the plain cream from her bowl. They both pretended to detest the way the other ate her food. "Dry as dust," whispered Hushidh. "Soggy and slimy," answered Luet. Then they both laughed aloud.

"Much better," said the cook. "You should both know better than to quarrel."

With her mouth full, Hushidh said, "The dream."

"Angels," said Luet.

"Flying, yes. Hairy ones, like fat bats. I heard you the first time."

"Not fat."

"Bats, anyway."

"Graceful," said Luet. "Soaring, that's how they were. And then I was one of them, flying and flying. It was so beautiful and peaceful. And then I saw the river, and I flew down to it and there on the riverbank I took the clay and made a statue out of it."

"Angels playing in the mud?"

"No stranger than bats making statues," Luet retorted. "And there's milk slobbering down your chin."

"Well, there's honey on the tip of your nose."

"Well, there's a big ugly growth on the front of your head—oh, no, that's your—"

"My face, I know. Finish the dream."

"I made the clay soft by putting it in my mouth, so that when I—as an angel, you understand—when I made the statue it contained something of me in it. I think that's very significant."

"Oh, *quite* symbolic, yes." Hushidh's tone was playful, but Luet knew she was listening carefully.

"And the statues weren't of people or angels or anything else. There were faces on them sometimes, but they weren't portraits or even *things*. The statues just took the shape that we needed them to take. No two of them were alike, yet I knew that at this moment, the statue I was making was the only possible statue I could make. Does that make sense?"

"It's a dream, it doesn't have to."

"But if it's a *true* dream, then it *must* make sense."

"Eventually, anyway," said Hushidh. Then she lifted another gloppy spoonful of bread and milk to her mouth.

"When we were done," said Luet, "we took them to a high rock and put them in the sun to dry, and then we flew around and around, and everyone looked at each other's statues. Then the angels flew off and now I wasn't with them anymore, I wasn't an angel, I was just there, watching the rocks where the statues stood, and the sun went down and in the dark—"

"You could see in the dark?"

"I could in my *dream*," said Luet. "Anyway, in the nighttime these giant rats came, and each one took one of the statues and carried it down, into holes in the ground, all the way to deep warrens and burrows, and each rat that had stolen a statue gave it to another rat and then together they gnawed at it, wet it down with their spit and rubbed it all over themselves. Covered themselves with the clay. I was so angry, Hushidh. These beautiful statues, and they wrecked them, turned them back into mud and rubbed it—even into their private parts, *everywhere*."

"Lovers of beauty," said Hushidh.

"I'm serious. It broke my heart."

"So what does it mean?" asked Hushidh. "Who do the angels represent, and who are the rats?"

"I don't know. Usually the meaning is obvious, when the Oversoul sends a dream."

"So maybe it was just a dream."

"I don't think so. It was so different and so clear, and I remember it so forcefully. Shuya, I think it's perhaps the most important dream I've ever had."

"Too bad nobody can understand it. Maybe it's one of those prophecies that everybody understands after it's all over and it's too late to do anything about it."

"Maybe Aunt Rasa can interpret it."

Hushidh made a skeptical face. "She's not at her best at the moment."

Secretly Luet was relieved that she wasn't the only one to notice that Rasa wasn't making the best decisions of her life right now. "So maybe I *won't* tell her, then."

Suddenly Hushidh smiled her tight little smile that showed she was really pleased with herself. "You want to hear a wild guess?" she said.

Luet nodded, then began taking huge bites of her long-ignored bread as she listened.

"The angels are the women of Basilica," said Hushidh. "All these millennia here in this city, we've shaped a society that is delicate and fine, and we've made it out of a part of ourselves, the way the bats in your dream made their statues out of spit. And now we've put our works to dry, and in the darkness our enemies are going to come and steal what we've made. But they're so stupid they don't even understand that they're statues. They look at them and all they see are blobs of dried mud. So they wet it down and wallow in it and they're so *proud* because they've got all the works of Basilica, but in fact they have *nothing* of Basilica at all."

"That's very good," said Luet, in awe.

"I think so, too," said Hushidh.

"So who are our enemies?"

"It's simple," said Hushidh. "Men are."

"No, that's *too* simple," said Luet. "Even though this is a city of women, the men who enter Basilica contribute as much as the women do to the works of beauty we make. They're part of the community, even if they can't own land or stay inside the walls without being married to a woman."

"I was sure it meant men the moment you said they were giant rats."

The cook chortled over the stew she was making for dinner.

"Someone else," insisted Luet. "Maybe Potokgavan."

"Maybe just Gaballufix's men," said Hushidh. "The tolchoks, and then his soldiers in those horrible masks."

"Or maybe something yet to come," said Luet. And then, in despair. "Or maybe nothing to do with Basilica at all. Who can tell? But that was my dream."

"It doesn't exactly tell us where we should have sent Smelost."

Luet shrugged. "Maybe the Oversoul thought we had brains enough to figure that out on our own."

"Was she right?" asked Hushidh.

"I doubt it," said Luet. "Sending him to the Gorayni was a mistake."

"I wouldn't know," said Hushidh. "Eating your bread dry—now *that's* a mistake."

"Not for those of us who have teeth," said Luet. "We don't have to sog our bread to make it edible."

Which led to a mock argument that got silly and loud enough that the cook threw them out of the kitchen, which was fine because they were finished with breakfast anyway. It felt good, for just a few minutes, to play together like children. For they knew that, for good or ill, they would both be involved in the events that were swirling in and near Basilica. Not that they wanted to be involved, really. But their gifts made them important to the city, and so they would do their best to serve.

Luet dutifully went to the city council and told her dream, which was carefully recorded and handed over to the wise women to be studied for meanings and portents. Luet told them how Hushidh had interpreted it, and they thanked her kindly and as much as told her that having dreams was fine—any idiot child could do *that*—but it took a real expert to figure out what they meant.

IN KHLAM, AND NOT IN A DREAM

It was a hot dry storm from the northwest, which meant it came across the desert, not a breath of moisture in it, just sand and grit and, so they said, the ground-up bones of men and animals that had got caught in the storm a thousand kilometers away, the dust of their flesh, and, if you listened closely, the howling of their souls as the wind bore them on and on, never letting go of them, either to heaven or to hell. The mountains blocked the worst of the storm, but still the tents of Moozh's army shuddered and staggered, the flaps of the tents snapped, the banners danced crazily, and now and then one of them would whip away from the ground and tumble, pole and all, along a dirty trampled avenue between the tents, some poor soldier often trying to chase it down.

Moozh's large tent also shuddered in the wind, despite its blessing from the Imperator. Of course the blessing was completely efficacious . . . but Moozh also made sure the stakes were pounded in hard and deep. He sat at the table by candlelight, gazing wistfully at the map spread out before him. It showed all the lands along the western shores of the Earthbound Sea. In the north, the lands of the Gorayni were outlined in red, the lands of the Imperator, who was of course the incarnation of God on Earth and therefore entitled to rule over all mankind, etc. etc. In his mind's eye Moozh traced the unmarked boundaries of nations that were at least as old as the Gorayni, and some of them much older, with proud histories—nations that now did not exist, that could not even be remembered, because to speak their names was treason, and to reach out and trace their old boundary on this map would be death.

But Moozh did not have to trace the boundary. He knew the borders of his homeland of Pravo Gollossa, the land of the Sotchitsiya, his own tribe. They had come across the desert from the north a thousand years before the Gorayni, but once they had been of the same stock, with the same language. But in the lush well-watered valleys of the Skrezhet Mountains the Sotchitsiya had settled down, had ceased both wandering and war, and become a nation of free men. They learned from the people around them. Not the Ploshudu or the Khlami or the Izmennikoy, for they were tough mountain people with no culture but hunger and muscle and a will to live despite all. Rather the Sotchitsiya, the people of Pravo Gollossa, had learned from the traders who came to them from Seggidugu, from Ulye, from the Cities of the Plain. And above all the caravanners from Basilica, with their strange songs and seeds, images in glass and cunning tools, impossible fabrics that changed colors with the hours of the day, and their poems and stories that taught the Sotchitsiya how wise and refined men and women spoke and thought and dreamed and lived.

That was the glory of Pravo Gollossa, for it was from these caravanners that they learned of the idea of a council, with decisions made by the vote of councilors who had themselves been chosen by the voice of the citizens. But it was also from these Basilican caravanners that they learned of a city ruled by women, where men could not even own land . . . and yet the city did not collapse from the incompetence of women to rule, and the men did not rebel and conquer the city, and women were able not only to vote but also to divorce their husbands at the end of every year and marry someone else if they chose. The constant pressure of those ideas wore down the Sotchitsiya and turned the once-strong warriors and rulers of the tribe into woman-hearted fools, so that in Moozh's great grandfather's day they gave the vote to women, and elected women to rule over them.

That was when the Gorayni came, for they knew that the Sotchitsiya had at last become women in their hearts, and so were no longer worthy to be free. The Gorayni brought their great army to the border, and the women of the council—as many males as females, but all women nonetheless—voted not to fight, but rather to accept Gorayni overlordship if the Gorayni would allow them to rule themselves in all but military matters. It was an unspeakable surrender, the final castration of the Sotchitsiya, their humiliation before all the world, and Moozh's own greatgrandfather was the delegate who worked out the terms of their surrender with the Gorayni.

For fifty years the agreement stood—the Sotchitsiya governed themselves. But gradually the Gorayni military began to declare more and more of Sotchitsiya affairs to be military matters, until finally the council was nothing but a bunch of frightened old men and women who had to petition the Imperator for permission to pee. Only then did any of the Sotchitsiya remember their manhood. They threw out the women who ruled them and declared themselves to be a tribe again, desert wanderers again, and swore to fight the Gorayni to the last man. It took three days for the Gorayni to defeat these brave but untrained rebels on the battlefield, and another year to hunt them down and kill them all in the mountains. After that there was no pretense that the Sotchitsiya had any rights at all. It was forbidden to speak the Sotchitsiya dialect; children who were heard speaking it had the privilege of watching their parents' tongues cut off, one centimeter for each offense. Only a few of the Sotchitsiya remembered their own language anymore, most of them old and many of them tongueless.

But Moozh knew. Moozh had the Sotchitsiya language in his heart. Even though he was the most successful, the most dangerous of the Imperator's generals, in his heart he knew his true language was Sotchitsiya, not Gorayni. And even though his many victories in battle had brought the great coastal nations of Uslavat and Ulye under the Imperator's dominion, even though his clever strategy had brought the thorny mountain kingdoms of Plosh and Khlam to obedience without a single pitched battle, Moozh's secret was that he loathed the Imperator and defied him in his heart.

For Moozh knew that the Imperator truly *was* God in the flesh, for better than most, Moozh could feel the power of God trying to control him. He had felt it first in his youth, when he sought a place in the Gorayni army. God didn't speak to him when he learned to be a strong soldier, his arms and thighs heavy with muscle, able to drive a battle-axe through the spine of his enemy and cleave him in half. But when Moozh imagined himself as an officer, as a general, leading armies, then came that heavy stupid feeling that made him want to forget such dreams. Moozh understood—God knew his hatred of the Imperator, and so was determined that one like Moozh would never have power beyond the strength of his arms.

But Moozh refused to capitulate. Whenever he sensed that God was making him forget an idea, he clung to it—he wrote it down and memorized it, he made a poem of it in the Sotchitsiya language so he could never forget. And thus, bit by bit, he built up in his heart his own rules of warfare, guided every step of the way by God, for whatever God tried to prevent him from thinking, that was what he knew that he must think of, deeply and well.

This secret defiance of God was what brought Moozh out of the ranks and made him a captain when his regiment was in danger of being overrun by the pirates of Revis. All the other officers had been killed, yet when Moozh thought of taking command and leading the few men near him in a counterattack against the flank of the uncontrolled, victorious Reviti, he felt that dullness of mind that always told him that God did not want him to pursue the idea. So he shouted down the voice of God and led his men in a foolhardy charge, which so terrified the pirates that they broke and ran, and the rest of the Gorayni took heart and followed Moozh in hot pursuit of them until they caught them on the riverbank and killed them all and burned their ships. They had brought Moozh for a triumph of the city of Gollod itself, where the Imperator had rubbed the camel-milk butter into his hair and declared him a hero of the Gorayni. But in his heart, Moozh knew that God had no doubt planned to have some loyal son of the Gorayni achieve the victory. Well, too bad for the Imperator—if the incarnation of God didn't understand that he had just oiled the hair of his enemy, then so much the worse for him.

Step by step Moozh had risen in command, until now he was at the head of a vast army. Most of his men were quartered in Ulye now, it was true, for the Imperator had commanded that they delay the attack against Nakavalnu until calm weather a month from now, when the chariots could be used to good advantage. Here in Khlam he had only a regiment, but that was all that was needed. Step by step he would lead the Gorayni onward, taking nation after nation along the coast until all the cities had fallen. Then he would face the armies of Potokgavan.

And then what? Some days Moozh thought that he would take his vengeance by orchestrating a complete and utter defeat for the armies of the Gorayni. He would gather all their military might into one place and then contrive to have them all slaughtered, himself among them. Then, with the Gorayni broken and Potokgavan having their will throughout the plain—then the Sotchitsiya would rise up and claim their freedom.

On other days, though, Moozh imagined that he would destroy the army of Potokgavan, so that along the entire western coast of the Earthbound Sea there was no rival to contest the supremacy of the Gorayni. Then he would stand before the Imperator, and when the Imperator reached out to smear the camelmilk butter on his hair, Moozh would slice off his head with a buck knife, then take the camelhump cap and put it on his own head, and declare that the empire that had been won by a Sotchitsiya would now be ruled by the Sotchitsiya. *He* would be Imperator, and instead of being the incarnation of God he would be the enemy of God, and the Sotchitsiya would be known as the greatest of men, and no longer as a nation of women.

These were his thoughts as he studied the map, while the storm flung sand at his tent and tried to tear it out of the ground.

Suddenly he came alert. The sound had changed. It wasn't just the wind; someone was scratching at his tent. Who would be so stupid as to walk about in this weather? He felt a sudden stab of fear—could it be the assassin sent by the Imperator, to prevent him from the treachery that God surely knew was in his heart?

But when he untied the flap and opened it, no assassin came in with a flurry of sand and hot wind. Instead it was Plod, his dear friend and comrade in arms, and another man, a stranger, in military garb that Moozh did not recognize.

Plod himself fastened the tent closed again—it would have been improper for Moozh to do it, with a junior officer present who could do it for him. So Moozh had a few moments to study the stranger. He was no soldier, not really—his breastplate was sturdy, his blade sharp, his clothing was fine, and he bore himself like a man. But his skin was soft-looking and his muscles lacked the hardness of a man who has wielded a sword in battle. He was the kind of soldier who stood guard at a palace or a toll road, bullying the common people but never having to face a charging horde of enemies, never having to run behind a chariot, hacking to death any who escaped the blades that whirred on the hubs of the chariot wheels.

"What portal do you guard?" asked Moozh.

The man looked startled, and he glanced back at Plod.

Plod only laughed. "No one told him anything, poor man. Did you think you could face General Vozmuzhalnoy Vozmozhno and keep anything secret from his eyes?"

"My name is Smelost," said the soft soldier, "and I bring a letter from Lady Rasa of Basilica."

He spoke the name as though Moozh should have heard of it. That's how these city people were, thinking that fame in their city must mean fame all over the world.

Moozh reached out and took the letter from him. Of course it was not written in the block alphabet of Gorayni—which they had stolen from the Sotchitsiya centuries ago. Instead it was the flowery vertical cursive of Basilica. But Moozh was an educated man. He could read it easily.

"It seems this man is our friend, dear Plod," said Moozh. "His life isn't safe in Basilica because he helped an assassin escape—but the assassin was *also* our friend, since he killed a man named Gaballufix who was in favor of Basilica forming an alliance with Potokgavan and leading the Cities of the Plain in war against us."

"Ah," said Plod.

"To think we never guessed how many dear and tender friends we had in Basilica," said Moozh.

Plod laughed.

Smelost looked more than a little ill at ease.

"Sit down," said Moozh. "You're among friends. No harm will come to you now. Find him some ale to drink, will you, Plod? He may be a common soldier, but he brings us a letter from a fine lady who has nothing but love and concern for the Imperator."

Plod unhooked a flagon from the back tentpole and gave it to Smelost, who looked at it in puzzlement.

Moozh laughed and took the flagon out of Smelost's hands and showed him how to rest it on his arm, tip it up, and let the stream of ale fall into his mouth. "No fine glasses for us in this army, my friend. You're not among the ladies of Basilica now."

"I knew that I was not," said Smelost.

"This letter is so cryptic, my friend," said Moozh. "Surely you can tell us more."

"Not much, I fear," said Smelost, swallowing a mouthful of ale. It was far sweeter than beer, and Moozh could see that he didn't like it much. Well, that hardly mattered, as long as Smelost got enough of the drug concealed in it that he'd speak freely. "I left before anything had come clear." He was lying, of course, thinking that he ought not to say more than Lady Rasa had said.

But soon Smelost overcame his reticence and told Moozh far more than he ever meant to. But Moozh was careful to pretend that he already knew most of it, so that Smelost would not feel he had betrayed any secrets when he thought back on the conversation and how much he had told.

There was obviously much confusion in Basilica at the moment, but the parts of the picture that mattered to Moozh were very clear. Two parties, one for alliance with Potokgavan, one against it, had been struggling for control of the city. Now the leaders of both parties were dead, killed on the same night, possibly by the same assassin, but, in Smelost's opinion, probably not. Accusations of murder were flying wildly; a weak man now controlled one group of hired soldiers who would now wander the streets uncontrolled, while the official city guard was under suspicion because this man, Smelost, had let the suspected assassin sneak out of the city two nights ago.

"What should we expect of a city of women?" said Moozh, when the story was done. "Of course there's confusion. Women are always confused when the violence begins."

Smelost looked at him warily. That was the sweet thing about the drug that Plod had given him—the victim was quite capable of believing that he was still being clever and deceptive, even as he poured out his heart on every subject. Moozh, of course, had immunized himself to the effects of the drug years ago, which was why he had no qualms about taking a mouthful of ale from the same flagon. He was also sure that Plod had no idea that Moozh was immune, and more than once he had suspected that Plod had given him some of the drug, whereupon Moozh always made a point of sharing a few harmless but indiscreet-sounding revelations—usually just his personal opinion of a few other officers. Never anything incriminating. Just enough to let Plod think the drug had worked its will on him.

"Oh, you know what I mean," said Moozh. "Nothing against the women, but they can't help their own biology, can they? It's the way they are—when the violence begins, they must rush to a male to find protection, or they're lost, wouldn't you say?"

Smelost smiled wanly. "You don't know the women of Basilica, then."

"Oh, but I do," said Moozh. "I know *all* women, and the women I don't know, Plod knows—isn't that right, Plod?"

"Oh, yes," said Plod, smiling.

Smelost glowered a little but said nothing.

"The women of Basilica are frightened right now, aren't they? Frightened and acting hastily. They don't like these soldiers running the streets. They fear what will happen if no strong man is there to control them—but they fear just as much what will happen if a strong man *does* come. Who knows how things will turn out, once the violence starts? There's blood on the street of Basilica. A man's head has drunk the dust of the street through both halves of his neck, as we say in Gollod. There's fear in every womanly heart in Basilica, yes, there is, and you know it."

Smelost shrugged. "Of course they're afraid. Who wouldn't be?"

"A *man* wouldn't be," said Moozh. "A *man* would smell the opportunity. A man would say, When others are afraid then anyone who speaks boldly has a chance to lead. Anyone who makes decisions, anyone who *acts* can become the focus of authority, the hope of the desperate, the strength of the weak, the soul of the spiritless. A *man* would *act*."

"Act," Smelost echoed.

"Act *boldly*," said Plod.

"And yet . . . you have come to us with a letter from a *woman* pleading for protection." Moozh smiled and shrugged.

Smelost immediately tried to defend himself. "Was I supposed to stand trial for having done what I knew was right?"

"Of course not. What—to be tried by women?" Moozh looked at

Plod and laughed; Plod took the cue and joined in. "For acting as a man must act, boldly, with courage—no, you shouldn't stand trial for *that.*"

"So I came here," said Smelost.

"For protection. So *you* could be safe, while your city is in fear."

Smelost rose to his feet. "I didn't come here to be insulted."

In an instant Plod's blade was poised at Smelost's throat. "When the General of the Imperator is seated, all men sit or they are treated as assassins."

Smelost gingerly lowered himself back into his chair.

"Forgive my dearest friend Plod," said Moozh. "I know you meant no harm. After all, you came to *us* to be *safe,* not to start a war!" Moozh laughed, staring in Smelost's eyes all the time, until Smelost also forced himself to laugh.

Smelost clearly hated it, to be forced to laugh at himself for seeking protection instead of acting like a man.

"But perhaps I've misunderstood you," said Moozh. "Perhaps you didn't come, as this letter says, just for yourself. Perhaps you have a plan in mind, some way that you can help your city, some stratagem whereby you can ease the fears of the women of Basilica and keep them safe from the chaos that threatens them."

"I have no plan," said Smelost.

"Ah," said Moozh. "Or perhaps you don't yet trust us enough to tell it to us." Moozh looked sad. "I understand. We're strangers, and this is your city at stake, a city that you love more than life itself. Besides, what you would need to ask of us is far greater than a common soldier would ordinarily dare to ask a general of the Gorayni. So I will not press you now. Go—Plod will show you to a tent where you can drink and sleep, and when this storm dies down you can bathe and eat, and by then perhaps you'll feel confident enough of me to tell me what you want us to do, to save your beautiful and beloved city from anarchy."

As soon as Moozh finished talking, he gave a subtle hand signal and then leaned his elbow on the arm of his chair, pretending to be a bit saddened by Smelost's reluctance to help. Plod caught the hand signal, of course, and immediately rushed Smelost out of the tent and back out into the storm.

As soon as they were outside, Moozh leapt to his feet and stood hunched over the table, studying the map. Basilica—so far to the south, but in the highest part of the mountains, right up against the desert, so that it would be possible to get there from here through the mountains. In two days, if he took only a few hundred men and pressed them hard. Two days, and he could easily be in possession of the greatest city of the Western Shore, the city whose caravanners have made their language the trading argot of every city and nation from Potokgavan to Gorayni. Never mind that Basilica had no meaningful army. What mattered was how it would seem to the Cities of the Plain—and to Potokgavan. *They* would not know how few and weak the Gorayni army would be. They would know only that the great General Vozmuzhalnoy Vozmozhno had stolen a march, conquered a city of legend and mystery, and now, instead of being a hundred and fifty kilometers north, beyond Seggidugu, now he loomed over them, could watch their every move from the towers of Basilica.

It would be a devastating blow. Knowing that Vozmuzhalnoy Vozmozhno would watch their fleet arrive and have plenty of time to bring his men down from Basilica and slaughter their army as it tried to land, Potokgavan would not dare to send an expeditionary force to the Cities of the Plain. And as for the cities themselves, they would surrender one by one, and soon Seggidugu would find itself surrounded, with no hope of succor from Potokgavan. They would make peace on any terms they could get. There probably wouldn't even be a battle—complete victory, at no cost, all because Basilica was in chaos and this soldier had come to tell Vozmuzhalnoy Vozmozhno of his glorious opportunity.

The tent flap reopened, and Plod came back in. "The storm is dying down," he said.

"Very good," said Moozh.

"What was all that about?" said Plod.

"What?"

"That nonsense you were saying to that Basilican soldier."

Moozh could not imagine what Plod was talking about. Basilican soldier? He had never seen a Basilican soldier in his life.

But Plod glanced at one of the chairs, and now Moozh vaguely remembered that not long ago *someone* had sat in that chair. Someone . . . a Basilican soldier? That would be important—how could he have forgotten?

I didn't forget, thought Moozh. I didn't forget. God has spoken, God has tried to make me stupid, but I refuse. I will not be forced into obedience.

"How do *you* assess the situation?" he asked. It would never do to let Plod think that Moozh was actually confused or forgetful.

"Basilica is far away," said Plod. "We can give this man sanctuary or kill him or send him back, it hardly matters. What is Basilica to us?"

Poor fool, thought Moozh. That's why you're merely the dear friend of the general, and not the general yourself, though I know you long to be. Moozh knew what Basilica was. It was the city of women whose influence had castrated his ancestors and cost them their freedom and their honor. It was also the great citadel poised above the Cities of the Plain. If Moozh could possess it, he wouldn't have to fight a single battle—his enemies would collapse before him. Was this the plan that he had had before, the one that God was trying to make him forget?

"Write this down," said Moozh.

Plod opened his computer and began to press the keys to record Moozh's words.

"Whoever is master of Basilica is master of the Cities of the Plain."

"But Moozh, Basilica has never exercised hegemony over those cities."

"Because it's a city of women," said Moozh. "If it were ruled by a man with an army, that would be a different story."

"We could never get there to take it," said Plod. "All of Seggidugu lies between us and Basilica."

Moozh looked at the map and another part of his plan came back to his mind. "A desert march."

"During the month of western storms!" cried Plod. "The men would refuse to obey!"

"In the mountains there's shelter. There are plenty of mountain roads."

"Not for an army," said Plod.

"Not for a *large* army," said Moozh, making up the plan as he went along.

"You could never hold Basilica against Potokgavan with the size army you could bring," said Plod.

Moozh studied the map for a moment longer. "But Potokgavan will never come, not if we already hold Basilica. *They* won't know how large an army we have, but they *will* know that we can see the whole coastline from there. Where would they dare to bring their fleet, knowing we could see them from far off and greet them at the shore, to cut them apart as they land?"

Plod finished typing, then studied the map himself. "There's merit in that," he said.

Why is there merit in it? Moozh asked silently. I haven't the faintest idea why I have this plan, except that a Basilican soldier apparently came here. What did he tell me? Why does this plan have merit?

"And with the present chaos in Basilica, you could probably take the city."

Chaos in Basilica. Good. So I wasn't wrong—the Basilican soldier apparently let me know of an opportunity.

"Yes," said Plod. "We have the perfect excuse for doing it, too. We aren't coming to invade, but rather to save the people of Basilica from the mercenary soldiers who are wandering their streets."

Mercenary soldiers? The idea was absurd—why would Basilica have mercenary soldiers running loose? Had there been a war? God had never made Moozh so forgetful that he couldn't remember a whole war!

"And the immediate provocation—the murders. The blood was already flowing—we had to come, to stop the bloodshed. Yes, that will be plenty of justification for it. No one can criticize us for attacking the city of women, if we come to save them from blood in the streets."

So that's my plan, thought Moozh. A very good one it is. Even God can't stop me from carrying it out. "Write it up, Plod, and have my aides draw up detailed orders for a thousand men to march in four columns through the mountains. Only three days' worth of supplies— the men can carry it on their backs."

"Three days!" said Plod. "And what if something goes wrong?"

"Knowing they have but three days' worth of food, dear Plod, the men will march very fast indeed, and they will allow nothing to delay them."

"What if the situation has changed at Basilica, when we arrive? What if we meet stout resistance? The walls of Basilica are high and thick, and chariots are useless in that terrain."

"Then it's a good thing we'll bring no chariots, isn't it? Except perhaps one, for my triumphal entry into the city—in the name of the Imperator, of course."

"Still, they might resist, and we'll arrive with scarcely any food to spare. We can't exactly besiege them!"

"We'll have no need to besiege them. We have only to ask them to open the gates, and the gates will open."

"Why?"

"Because I say so," said Moozh. "When have I been wrong before?"

Plod shook his head. "Never, my dear friend and beloved general. But by the time we get the Imperator's permission to go there, the chaos in the streets of Basilica may well have been settled, and it will take a much larger army than a thousand men to force the issue."

Moozh looked at him in surprise. "Why would we wait for the Imperator's permission?"

"Because the Imperator forbade you to make any attack until the stormy season is over."

"On the contrary," said Moozh. "The Imperator forbade me to attack Nakavalnu and Izmennik. I am not attacking them. I'm passing them by on their left flank, and marching as swift as horses through the mountains to Basilica, where again I will not attack anybody, but will rather enter the city of Basilica to restore order in the name of the Imperator. None of this violates any order of the Imperator."

Plod's face darkened. "You are interpreting the words of the Imperator, my general, and that is something only the intercessor has the right to do."

"Every soldier and every officer must interpret the orders he is given. I was sent to these southlands in order to conquer the entire western shore of the Earthbound Sea—that was the command the Imperator gave to me, and to me alone. If I failed to seize this great opportunity that God has given me"—ha!—"then I would be disobedient indeed."

"My dear friend, noblest general of the Gorayni, I beg you not to attempt this. The intercessor will not see it as obedience but as insubordination."

"Then the intercessor is no true servant of the Imperator."

Plod immediately bowed his head. "I see that I have spoken too boldly."

Moozh knew at once that this meant Plod intended to tell the intercessor everything and try to stop him. When Plod meant to obey, he did not put on this great pretense of obedience.

"Give me your computer," said Moozh. "I will write the orders myself."

"Don't shame me," said Plod in dismay. "I must write them, or I have failed in my duty to you."

"You will sit with me here," said Moozh, "and watch as I write the orders."

Plod flung himself to his knees on the carpets. "Moozh, my friend, I'd rather you kill me than shame me like this."

"I knew that you didn't intend to obey me," said Moozh. "Don't lie and say you did."

"I meant to delay," said Plod. "I meant to give you time to reconsider. Hoping that you'd realize the grave danger of opposing the Imperator, especially so soon after you dreamed a dream that was contemptuous of his holy person."

It took a moment for Moozh to remember what Plod was referring to; then his rage turned cold and hard indeed. "Who would know of that dream, except myself and my friend?"

"Your friend loved you enough to tell the dream to the intercessor," said Plod, "lest your soul be in danger of destruction without your knowing it."

"Then my friend must love me indeed," said Moozh.

"I do," said Plod. "With all my heart. I love you more than any man or woman on this Earth, excepting God alone, and his holy incarnation."

Moozh regarded his dearest friend with icy calm. "Use your computer, my friend, and call the intercessor to my tent. Have him stop on the way and bring the Basilican soldier with him."

"I'll go and get them," said Plod.

"Call them by computer."

"But what if the intercessor isn't using his computer right now?"

"Then we'll wait until he does." Moozh smiled. "But he *will* be using it, won't he?"

"Perhaps," said Plod. "How would I know?"

"Call them. I want the intercessor to hear my interrogation of the Basilican soldier. Then he'll know that we must go now, and not wait for word from the Imperator."

Plod nodded. "Very wise, my friend. I should have known that you wouldn't flout the will of the Imperator. The intercessor will listen to you, and *he'll* decide."

"We'll decide *together*," said Moozh.

"Of course." He pressed the keys; Moozh made no effort to watch him, but he could see the words in the air over the computer well enough to know that Plod was sending a quick, straightforward request to the intercessor.

"Alone," said Moozh. "If we decide not to act, I want no rumors to spread about Basilica."

"I already asked him to come alone," said Plod.

They waited, talking all the time of other things. Of campaigns in years past. Of officers who had served with them. Of women they had known.

"Have you ever *loved* a woman?" asked Moozh.

"I have a wife," said Plod.

"And you love her?"

Plod thought a moment. "When I'm with her. She's the mother of my sons."

"I have no sons," said Moozh. "No children at all, that I know of. No woman who has pleased me for more than a night."

"None?" asked Plod.

Moozh flushed with embarrassment, realizing what Plod was remembering. "I never loved *her*," he said. "I took her—as an act of piety."

"Once is an act of piety," said Plod, chuckling. "Two months one year, and then another month three years later—that's more than piety, that's *sainthood*."

"She was nothing to me," said Moozh. "I took her only for the sake of God." And it was true, though not in the way Plod understood it. The woman had appeared as if out of nowhere, dirty and naked, and called Moozh by name. Everyone knew such women were from God. But Moozh knew that when he thought of taking her, God sent him that stupor that meant it was *not* God's will for Moozh to proceed. So Moozh proceeded anyway, and kept the woman—bathed her, and clothed her, and treated her as tenderly as a wife. All the while he felt God's anger boiling at the back of his mind, and he laughed at God. He kept the woman with him until she disappeared, as suddenly as she had come, leaving all her fine clothing behind, taking nothing, not even food, not even water.

"So that wasn't love," said Plod. "God honors you for your sacrifice, then, I'm sure!" Plod laughed again, and for good fellowship Moozh also joined in.

They were still laughing when there came a scratching at the tent, and Plod leapt to open it. The intercessor came in first, which was his duty—and an expression of his faith in God, since the intercessor always left himself available to be stabbed in the back, if God did not protect him. Then a stranger came in. Moozh had no memory of ever having seen the man before. By his garb he was a soldier of a fine city; by his body he was a soft soldier, a gate guard rather than a fighting man; by his familiar nod, Moozh knew that this must be the Basilican soldier, and he must indeed have spoken with him, and left the conversation on friendly terms.

The intercessor sat first, and then Moozh; only then could the others take their places.

"Let me see your blade," Moozh said to the Basilican soldier. "I want to see what kind of steel you have in Basilica."

Warily the Basilican arose from his seat, watching Plod all the while. Vaguely Moozh remembered Plod with a blade at the Basilican's throat; no wonder the man was wary now! With two fingers the man drew his short sword from its sheath, and handed it, hilt first, to Moozh.

It was a city sword, for close work, not a great hewing sword for the battlefield. Moozh tested the blade against the skin of his own arm, cutting only slightly, but enough to draw a line of blood. The man winced to see it. Soft. Soft.

"I've thought about what you said, sir," the Basilican said.

Ah. So I gave him something to think about.

"And I can see that my city needs your help. But who am I to ask for it, or even to know what help would be right or sufficient? I'm only a gate guard; it's only the sheerest chance that I got caught up in these great affairs."

"You love your city, don't you?" asked Moozh, for now he knew what he must have told the man. "I *am* sharp enough even on my bad days," Moozh thought with some satisfaction. Sharp enough to lay God-proof plans.

"Yes, I do." Tears had suddenly come to the man's eyes. "Forgive me, but someone else asked me that, just before I left Basilica. Now I know by this omen that you are a true servant of the Oversoul, and I can trust you."

Moozh gazed steadily into the man's eyes, to show him that trust was appropriate indeed.

"Come to Basilica, sir. Come with an army. Restore order in the streets, and drive out the mercenaries. Then the women of Basilica will have no more fear."

Moozh nodded wisely. "An eloquent and noble request, which in my heart I long to fulfill. But I am a servant of the Imperator, and you must explain the situation in your city to the intercessor here, who is the eyes and ears and heart of the Imperator in our camp." As he spoke, Moozh rose to his feet, facing the intercessor, and bowed. Behind him he could hear Plod and the Basilican soldier also standing and bowing.

Surely Plod is clever enough to know what I plan to do, thought Moozh with a thrill of fear. Surely his knife is even now out of its sheath, to be buried in my back. Surely he knows that if he does not do this, the Basilican blade I hold in my hands will snake out and take his head clean off his shoulders as I rise.

But Plod was not that clever, and so in a moment his blood gouted and spattered across the tent as his body collapsed, his head flopping about on the end of the half-severed spine.

Moozh's blow had been so quick, so smooth, that neither the Basilican nor the intercessor quite understood how Plod came to be so abruptly dead. That gave Moozh plenty of time to drive the Basilican blade upward under the intercessor's ribs, finding his heart before the intercessor could speak a word or even raise himself from his chair.

Then Moozh turned to the trembling Basilican.

"What is your name, soldier?"

"Smelost, sir. As I told you. I've lied about nothing, sir."

"I know you haven't. Neither have I. These men were determined to stop me from coming to the aid of your city. That's why I brought them here together. If you wanted me to help you, I had to kill them first."

"Whatever you say, sir."

"No, not whatever I say. Only the truth, Smelost. These men were both spies set to watch every move I made, to hear every word I spoke, and judge my loyalty to the Imperator constantly. This one"—he pointed at Plod—"interpreted a dream I had as a sign of disloyalty, and told the intercessor. It would only have been a matter of time before they reported me and I lost my command, and then who would have come to save Basilica?"

"But how will you explain their deaths?" asked Smelost.

Moozh said nothing.

Smelost waited. Then he looked again at the bodies. "I see," he said. "The blade that killed them was mine."

"How much do you love your city?" asked Moozh.

"With all my heart."

"More than life?" asked Moozh.

Gravely Smelost nodded. There was fear in his eyes, but he did not tremble.

"If my soldiers think I killed Plod and the intercessor, they will tear me to pieces. But if they think—no, if they *know* that *you* did it, and I killed you for it—then they will follow me in righteous indignation. I'll tell them that you were one of the mercenaries. I will besmirch your name. I will say you were a traitor to Basilica, trying to prevent me from going to the city's aid. But because they believe those lies about you, they will follow me there and we will save your city."

Smelost smiled. "It seems that my fate is to be thought a worse traitor the better I serve my city."

"It is a terrible day when a man must choose between being thought loyal, and being loyal in fact, but that day has come to you."

"Tell me what to do."

Moozh almost wept with admiration for the courage and honor of the man, as he explained the simple play they would put on. If I did not serve a higher cause, thought Moozh, I would be too ashamed to deceive a man of such honor as yourself. But for the sake of Pravo Gollossa I will do any terrible thing.

A moment later, in a lull in the windstorm, Moozh and Smelost both began to bellow, and Moozh let out a high scream that witnesses would later swear was the death cry of the intercessor. Then, as soldiers stumbled out of their tents, they saw Smelost, already bleeding from a wound in his thigh, lurch from the general's tent, carrying a short sword dripping with blood. "For Gaballufix! Death to the Imperator!"

The name of Gaballufix meant nothing to the Gorayni soldiers, though soon enough it would be rich with meaning. What they cared about was the latter part of Smelost's shout—death to the Imperator. No one could say such a thing in a Gorayni camp without being flayed alive.

Before anyone could reach him, though, the general himself staggered from the tent, bleeding from his arm and holding his head where he must have been struck a blow. The general—the great Vozmuzhalnoy Vozmozhno, called Moozh whenever they thought he

could not hear—held a battle-ax in his left arm—his left, not his right!
—and struck downward into the base of the assassin's neck, cleaving
him to the heart. He should not have done it; everyone knew he should
have let the man be taken and tortured to punish him. But then, to
their horror, the general sank to his knees—the general with ice in his
veins instead of blood—he sank to his knees and wept bitterly, crying
out from the depths of his soul, "Plodorodnuy, my friend, my heart, my
life! Ah, Plod! Ah, Plod, God should have taken me and left you!"

It was a grief both glorious and terrible to behold, and without
speaking a word openly about it, the soldiers who heard his keening
resolved to tell no one of his blasphemous suggestion that perhaps God
might have ordered the world improperly. When they entered the tent
they understood perfectly why Moozh had forgotten himself and killed
the assassin with his own hand, for how could any mortal man see his
dearest friend and the intercessor both so cruelly murdered, and still
contain his rage?

Soon the story spread through the camp that Moozh was taking a
thousand fierce soldiers with him on a forced march through the mountains, to take the city Basilica and destroy the party of Gaballufix, a
group of men so daring and treacherous that they had dared to send an
assassin against the general of the Gorayni. Too bad for them that God
so dearly loved the Gorayni that he would not permit their Moozh to
be slain by treachery. Instead God had caused Moozh's heart to be
filled with righteous wrath, and Basilica would soon know what it
meant to have God and the Gorayni as their overlords.

3

Protection

THE DREAM OF THE ELDEST SON

The camels had all gathered under the shade of the large palm fronds that Wetchik and his sons had woven into a roof between a group of four large trees near the stream. Elemak envied them—the shade was good there, the stream was cool, and they could catch the breeze, so the air was never as stuffy as it was inside the tents. He was done with his work for the morning, and now there was nothing useful to do during the heat of the day. Let Father and Nafai and Issib drip their sweat all over each other as they huddled around the Index of the Oversoul in Father's tent. What did the Oversoul know? It was just a computer—Nafai himself said that, in his adolescent fanatic piety—so why should Elemak bother with a conversation with a machine? It had a vast library of information . . . so what? Elemak was done with school.

So he sat in the hot shade of the southern cliff, knowing that he would have at most an hour of rest before the sun rose high enough that the shade would disappear, and he would have to move. That didn't really bother Elemak—in fact, on his caravans he had counted on that to awaken him, so that he didn't sleep overlong during the day when they rested at oases. What made him so angry that he felt it like a pain in his stomach all the time was the fact that it was all so useless. They were not traveling, they were merely waiting here in the desert— and for what? For nothing. The Oversoul said that Basilica would be destroyed, that the world of Harmony was going to collapse in war and terror. It was laughably unlikely that any such thing would happen. The world had gone forty million years without being devastated by war. Now, for the first time, two great empires were on the verge of collision, and the Oversoul was treating it as if it were some cosmic event.

I could have understood leaving Basilica, he told himself, if we had taken our fortune with us and gone to another city and started over. What was vital in the plant trade was the knowledge inside Father's and my heads, not the buildings or the hired workers. We could have been rich. Instead we're here in the desert, we lost our entire fortune to my half-brother Gaballufix, and now Nafai has murdered *him* and we can never go back to Basilica again, or if we did, we'd be poor so why bother?

Except that even poverty in Basilica would be better than this meaningless waiting out here in the desert, in this miserable little valley that barely supported the troop of baboons downstream of them. Even now he could hear them barking and hooting. Beasts that couldn't decide whether to be men or dogs. That's exactly what we are now, only we didn't even have the sense to bring mates with us when we left, so we can't even form a reasonable tribe.

Despite the arrhythmic noises of the baboons and the occasional snorting of the camels, Elemak soon slept. He woke moments later, or so it felt; he could feel the burning heat of the sun on his clothing, so he assumed that the sun had wakened him. But no, it was something else; there was a shadow moving near him. With his eyes closed he thought of where his knife was and remembered how the ground was near him. Then, with a sudden rush of movement, he was on his feet, his long knife in his hand, squinting in the bright sunlight to see where his enemy was.

"It's only me!" squeaked Zdorab.

Elemak put away his knife in disgust. "You don't come up silently when a man is asleep in the desert. You can get yourself killed that way. I assumed you were a robber."

"But I wasn't all that quiet," said Zdorab reasonably. "In fact, you were noisy yourself. Dreaming, I expect."

That bothered Elemak, that he had not slept silently. But now that Zdorab mentioned it, he remembered that he *had* dreamed, and he remembered the dream with remarkable clarity. In fact he had never had such a clear dream, not that he remembered, anyway, and it made him think. "What was I saying?" asked Elemak.

"I don't know," said Zdorab. "It was more of a mumble. I came up here because your father asked to see you. I wouldn't have disturbed you otherwise."

It was true. Zdorab was the consummate servant, invisible most of the time, but always ready to help—even when he was completely incompetent, which was usually the case here in the desert, where the skills of a treasurer were quite useless. "Thanks," said Elemak. "I'll come in a minute."

Zdorab waited for just a moment—that hesitation that all good servants acquired sooner or later, that single moment in which the master could think of something else to tell before they left. Then he was gone, shambling clumsily down the shale slope and then across the dry stony soil to Wetchik's tent.

Elemak pulled up his desert robe and peed out in the open, where the sun would evaporate his urine in moments, before too many flies could gather. Then he headed for the stream, took a drink in his cupped hand, splashed water into his face and over his head, and only then made his way to where Father and all the others were waiting.

"Well," said Elemak as he entered. "Have you learned everything the Oversoul has to teach you?"

Nafai glared at him with his typical look of disapproval. Someday Elemak knew he'd have to give Nafai the beating of his life, just to teach him not to get that expression on his face, at least not toward Elemak. He had tried to give him that beating once before, and he had learned that *next* time he'd have to do it away from Issib's chair, so the Oversoul couldn't take control of it and interfere. But for now there was nothing to be gained by letting Nafai's snottiness get under his skin; so Elemak pretended not to notice.

"We need to start hunting for meat," said Father.

Elemak immediately let his eyes half close as he thought of what that meant. They had brought enough supplies for eight or nine months— for a year, if they were careful. Yet Father was talking about needing to hunt. That could only mean that he didn't expect to get anywhere civilized within a year.

"How about shopping for groceries in the Outer Market," said Meb.

Elemak agreed wholeheartedly, but said nothing as Father lectured Meb on the impossibility of returning to Basilica any time soon. He waited until the little scene had played itself out. Poor Meb—when would he learn that it's better to remain silent except to say what will accomplish your purpose?

Only when silence had returned did Elemak speak up. "We can hunt," he said. "This is fairly lush country, for desert, and I think we could probably bring in something once a week—for a few months."

"Can you do it?" asked Father.

"Not alone," said Elemak. "If Meb and I hunt every day, we'll find something once a week."

"Nafai too," said Father.

"No!" moaned Mebbekew. "He'll just get in the way."

"I'll teach him," said Elemak. "For that matter, I don't imagine Meb will be worth anything more than Nafai at first. But you have to tell them both—when we're hunting, my word is law."

"Of course," said Father. "They'll do exactly what you tell them, and nothing more."

"I'll take each of them every other day," said Elemak. "That way I won't have to put up with their arguing with each other."

Mebbekew glared at him with loathing—so subtle, Meb, no wonder you were such a successful actor—but Nafai only looked at the carpet on the floor of the tent. What was he thinking? No doubt conniving to find some way to turn this to his advantage.

Sure enough, Nafai lifted up his head and spoke solemnly to Elemak. "Elya, I'm sorry I've given you cause to think that's what I'd do, if you took Meb and me at once. If having us both come at once would be more efficient, I can promise I'll not say a word of argument, either to you or Meb."

Just like the little sneak, to make himself look so pious and cooperative, when Elemak knew that he would be snotty and argumentative the whole way, no matter what he promised now. But Elemak said nothing, as Father quietly praised Nafai's attitude, then told him that Elya's decision would stand. They would go hunting with Elya one at a time. "You'll learn better one on one, I assure you," said Father.

At times like this Elemak almost believed that Father saw through

Nafai's righteous act. But it wasn't so; in a moment Father would go off talking about what the Oversoul wanted, and then he and Nafai would be as thick as thieves.

Thinking of thieves made Elemak remember how Zdorab had wakened him a few moments ago; and thinking of waking up reminded him of his vivid dream. And it occurred to him that it might be amusing to play Nafai's game, and pretend that his dream was some vision from the Oversoul. "I was sleeping by the rocks," said Elemak into the silence, "and I dreamed a dream."

Immediately all eyes were on him, waiting. Elemak sized them up under heavy-lidded eyes; he saw the immediate joy on his father's face, and was almost ashamed of the sham he was going to play—but the consternation on Nafai's face and the utter horror on Meb's made it well worth doing. "I dreamed a dream," he said, "in which I saw all of us coming out of a large house."

"Whose house was it?" asked Nafai.

"Hush and let him tell the dream," said Father.

"A kind of house I've never seen before. And we didn't come out alone—the six of us, all six of us, each came out with a woman. And there were two other men, each with a woman as well. And many children. All of us had children."

There was silence for a long moment.

"Is that all?" asked Nafai.

Elemak said nothing, and the silence resumed.

"Elya," said Issib. "Did *I* have a wife?"

"In my dream," said Elemak, "you had a wife."

"Did you see her face?" asked Issib. "Did you know who she was?"

Now Elemak felt truly ashamed of himself, for he could see that Issib believed that this was a true vision, and for the first time in his life it occurred to him that poor Issib, palsied as he was, nevertheless yearned for a woman as any other man might yearn, and yet had no hope of finding one who would want him. In Basilica, where women had their pick of men, it would be one piss-poor specimen of womanhood who would choose a cripple like Issib for a mate. Even if he ever managed to have sex, it would be because some jaded female was curious about him—especially with his floats, that might interest some of the more adventurous ones. But to mate with him, to bear him children, to give him father's rights, no, that wouldn't happen, and Issib knew it. Which meant that by telling this dream, Elemak wasn't just manipulating Father, he was also setting Issib up for cruel disappointment. Elemak felt like shit.

"I didn't see her face," said Elemak. "It probably didn't mean anything. It was just a dream."

"It meant something," said Father.

"It means Elemak is ridiculing us," said Nafai. "He's making fun of us for having visions from the Oversoul."

"Don't call me a liar," said Elemak softly. "If I say I dreamed, I dreamed. Whether it means anything, I can't say. But I saw what I saw. Isn't that what Father said? Isn't that what *you* said? I saw what I saw."

"It meant something," said Father again. "Now an odd message I received through the Index makes perfect sense."

Oh no, thought Elemak. What have I done?

"I have thought for some time that we couldn't accomplish the Oversoul's purpose without wives. And yet where could we possibly find women who would join us here?"

Where could you find *men* who would join you here, for that matter, Father, except that you trapped your own sons into coming with you?

"But when I asked the Oversoul, the answer I got was to wait. That's all, just wait, which made no sense to me. Would wives sprout from the rocks? Would we mate with baboons?"

Elemak couldn't resist a jab. "Meb already has, from time to time."

Meb simpered.

"And now Elemak has dreamed," Father said. "I think that is what the Oversoul wanted me to wait for—Elemak's dream. For the answer to come to my eldest son, to my heir. So, Elya, you must think, you must remember—did you recognize *any* of the women in your dream?"

Father was taking this way too seriously, tying it with Elemak's status as his eldest. Elemak had been a fool to start this whole vision business today, he could see that now; how could he have forgotten that Father was willing to ruin everybody's lives for the sake of a vision? "No," said Elemak, to silence him, though it wasn't true.

"Think," said Father. "I know that you recognized at least one."

Elemak looked at him, startled. Had the old man started reading his mind now? "If the Oversoul has told you more about my dream than I know myself, then *you* tell us who they are," said Elemak.

"I know you recognized one because you said her name. If you think hard enough, you'll remember."

Elemak glanced at Zdorab, who was looking at the carpet. So, thought Elemak. When Zdorab said that he understood nothing of what I said in my sleep, it wasn't quite true. "What name?" asked Elemak.

"Eiadh," said Nafai. "Am I right?"

Elemak said nothing, but he hated Nafai for saying the name of the woman Elemak had been courting before Father dragged them out into the desert.

"It's all right," said Father. "I understand perfectly. You didn't want to tell us her name for fear that we would think that your dream was just an erotic wish for the woman you loved, and not a true dream."

Since that was exactly what Elemak thought his dream actually was, he couldn't argue with Wetchik's conclusion.

"But think, my sons. Would the Oversoul require you to choose strangers as your mates? You dreamed of Eiadh because the Oversoul intends her to be your mate," said Father. "And it makes sense, doesn't it? For you saw *me* with a mate as well, didn't you?"

"Yes," said Elemak, remembering. The dream was still *so* vivid in his mind that he could call it back, not just as a vague memory, but clearly. "Yes, and children. Young ones."

"There is only one woman I would take as my mate," said Father. "Rasa."

"She'd never leave Basilica," said Issib. "If you think she would, you don't know Mother."

"Ah," said Father. "But *I* would never have left Basilica, either, except that the Oversoul led me. Nor would Elemak and Mebbekew, except that the Oversoul brought them."

"Nor I," said Zdorab.

"Could the woman you saw in your dream, the woman who was *my* mate . . . she was Rasa, wasn't she?" asked Father.

Of course it was Rasa, but that didn't prove anything. Rasa had been Father's wife, year after year, so of course it was Rasa who would show up as his woman in Elemak's dreams. It would take no vision from the Oversoul for *that*. "Perhaps," said Elemak.

"And did you recognize any of the other women? For instance, the two other men who were strangers—could their mates have been Rasa's daughters?"

"I don't know your wife's daughters all that well," said Elemak. How far would this game have to go before he could have done with it?

"Don't be absurd," said Father. "They're your nieces, aren't they? Gaballufix's daughters."

"And one of them is famous," chimed in Meb. "Sevet, the singer—you've seen her."

"Yes," said Elemak. "The wives of the two strangers were Rasa's daughters." Of course he knew them, and their husbands, too, Vas and Obring.

"There, you see?" said Father. "The Oversoul has given you a true vision. The women you saw are all connected with Rasa. Her daughters, and Eiadh, one of the nieces of her household. I'm sure the others are all of her household, too. So this isn't some impossible dream that came to you because you had a hunger for venery, my son. This came from the Oversoul, because the Oversoul knows that to accomplish our purpose we must have wives who will bear us children. All of us."

"Well," said Elemak, "if it's really a vision, then *I'm* happy enough for the Oversoul to give me Eiadh. But I think there's a better chance of finding a falcon in a frog's mouth than of anyone *but* the Oversoul ever persuading Eiadh to come out into the desert to marry a penniless, homeless man like me, with no hope of wealth."

"You forget that the Oversoul has promised us a land of unspeakable richness," said Father.

"And you forget that we haven't found it yet," said Elemak. "We're not likely to find it, either, squatting in the desert like this."

"The Oversoul has shown us what we must do," said Father. "And as Nafai said to me before you left to seek the Index—if the Oversoul requires us to do something, he'll open a way for us to do it."

"Great idea," said Mebbekew. "Whom will Nafai kill to get us some women?"

"That's enough," said Father.

"Come on," said Mebbekew. "How else would Nafai ever get a wife, except by killing some drunk passed out on the street and stealing his blind, crippled daughter."

To Elemak's surprise, Nafai said nothing to Mebbekew's gibes. Instead, the boy got up and left the tent. So, thought Elemak. Nafai isn't entirely a child. Or else he was ashamed to have us see him cry.

"Meb," said Issib softly, "Nafai brought the Index, and you didn't."

"Oh, come on," said Mebbekew. "Can't anybody take a joke around here?"

"It isn't a joke to Nafai," said Issib. "Killing Gaballufix is the most terrible thing he ever did, and he thinks about it all the time."

"You were out of line to throw it up to him," said Father. "Don't do it again."

"What am I supposed to do," Mebbekew insisted, "pretend that Nafai got the Index by saying Pity Please?"

It was time for Elemak to get Mebbekew back in line—no one else could do it, and it needed to be done. "What you're supposed to do is shut up," said Elemak softly.

Meb looked at him defiantly. It was all an act, though, Elemak knew. All he had to do was meet Meb's gaze and hold it, and Meb would back down. It didn't take long, either.

"Elemak," said Father, "you must go back, you and your brothers."

"Don't put this on *me*," said Elemak. "If anyone can persuade Rasa, it's *you*."

"On the contrary," said Wetchik. "She knows me, she knows I love her, she loves me too—and that didn't bring her with me before. Do you think I didn't suggest it? No, if anyone persuades her it will be the Oversoul. All you have to do is go and suggest it to her, wait for the Oversoul to help her understand that she must come, and then provide safe escort for her and her daughters and the young women of her household who come with her."

"Oh, fine," said Elemak. He could wait a long cold time for the Oversoul to persuade anybody but Father to do something as idiotic as leaving Basilica for the desert. But at least he'd be waiting in Basilica, even if he had to do it in hiding. "Should I have her bring along a servant for Zdorab, too?"

Father's face went icy. "Zdorab isn't a servant now," he said. "He's a free man, and the equal of any man here. A woman of Rasa's household would do for him as well as for any of you, and as for that, a serving girl in Rasa's house would also do for any of you. Don't you understand that we're no longer in Basilica, that the society we form now will have no room for snobbery and bigotry, for castes and classes? We will be one people, all equals, with all our children equal in the eyes of the Oversoul."

In the eyes of the Oversoul, perhaps, but not in my eyes, thought Elemak. I'm the eldest son, and my firstborn son will be my heir as I am *your* heir, Father. Even if you gave up the lands and holdings that should have been my inheritance, I will still inherit your authority, and no matter where we end up settling, *I* will rule, or no one will. I may say nothing of this now, because I know when to speak and when not to speak. But be sure of this, Father. When you die, I will have your place—and anyone who tries to deprive me of it will follow you quickly into the grave.

Elemak looked at Issib and Meb, and knew that neither would resist him when that day came. But Nafai would cause trouble, bless his dear little heart. And Nafai knows it, thought Elemak. He knows that someday it will come down to him and me. For someday Father will try to pass his authority on to this miserable little toady of a boy, all because Nafai is so thick with the Oversoul. Well, Nafai, I've had a vision from the Oversoul, too—or at least Father thinks I have, which amounts to the same thing.

"Leave in the morning," Father said. "Come back with the women who will share the inheritance the Oversoul has prepared for us in another land. Come back with the mothers of my grandchildren."

"Mebbekew and I," said Elemak. "No others."

"Issib will stay home because his chair and his floats make him too conspicuous, and he increases your chances of being caught by our enemies there," said Father. "And Zdorab will stay."

Because you don't quite trust him yet, thought Elemak, no matter how much you claim that he's our equal and a free man.

"But Nafai goes with you."

"No," said Elemak. "He's even more dangerous to us than Issib. They're bound to have figured out that he killed Gaballufix—the city computer got his name on the way out of town, and the guards saw him wearing Gaballufix's clothing. And he had Zdorab with him, to clinch the connection between him and Gab's death. Bringing Nafai is like asking to have him killed."

"He goes with you," said Father.

"Why, when he only increases our danger?" demanded Elemak.

"Yes, *make* him say it, Elya," said Mebbekew. "Father doesn't want to insult you, but *I* don't mind. He wants Nafai there because, as someone recently pointed out, Nafai got the Index and none of the rest of us did. He wants Nafai there because he doesn't trust us not to just find some woman to take us in and stay in Basilica and never come back to this paradise by the sea. He wants Nafai there because he thinks Nafai will make us be good."

"Not at all," said Issib. "Father wants him to learn strength and wisdom by associating with his older brothers."

No one was ever sure whether Issib was being ironic or not. Nobody believed that this was Father's true purpose, but nobody—least of all Father—cared to deny it openly, either.

In the silence, the words that still rang in Elemak's ears were the last ones he himself had said: Bringing Nafai is like asking to have him killed.

"All right, Father," said Elemak. "Nafai can come with me."

IN BASILICA, AND NOT IN A DREAM

Kokor could not understand why *she* should be in seclusion. For Sevet it made sense—she was recuperating from her unfortunate accident. Her voice wasn't back yet; she was no doubt embarrassed to appear in public. But Kokor was in perfect health, and for her to have to hide out at Mother's house made it look as if she were ashamed to come out in public. If she had deliberately injured Sevet, then perhaps such isolation might be necessary. But since it was simply an unfortunate accident, the result of a psychological disturbance due to Father's death and the discovery of Sevet's and Obring's adultery, why, no one could blame Kokor. In fact, it would do her good to be seen in public. It would surely speed her recovery.

At least she should be able to go home to her own house, and not have to stay with Mother, as if she were a little girl or a mental incompetent who needed a guardian. Where was Obring? If he ever intended to make things up with her, he could begin by coming and getting her out of Mother's unbearably staid environment. There was nothing interesting going on here. Just endless classes in subjects that hadn't interested Kokor even when she was failing them years ago. Kokor was a woman of substance now. Father's inheritance probably would enable her to buy a house and keep her own establishment. And here she was living with mother.

Not that she saw that much of Mother. Rasa was constantly in meetings with councilors and other influential women of the city, who were making virtual pilgrimages to see her and talk to her. Some of the meetings seemed to be somewhat tense; Rasa began to gather the idea that some people, at least, were blaming Rasa for everything. As if Mother would try to kill Father! But they remembered that it was

Rasa's current husband, Wetchik, who had his inflammatory vision about Basilica in flames, and then her former husband, Gaballufix, who put tolchoks and then mercenary soldiers on the streets of the city. And now the word was that her youngest son, Nafai, was the killer of both Roptat and Gaballufix.

Well, even if all that was true, what did that have to do with Mother? Women can't very well control their husbands—didn't Kokor have proof of that herself? And as for Nafai killing Father—well, even if he did it, *Mother* wasn't there, and she certainly didn't *ask* the boy to do it. They might as well blame Mother for what happened to Sevet, when anyone could see it was Sevet's own fault. Besides, wasn't Father's death his own fault, really? All those soldiers—you don't bring soldiers into Basilica and expect not to have violence, do you? Men never understood these things. They could turn things loose, but they were always surprised when they couldn't tame them again at will.

Like Obring, poor fool. Didn't he know that it wasn't a clever thing to come between sisters? He was really more to blame for Sevet's injury than Kokor was.

And why doesn't anybody have any sympathy for *my* injury? The deep psychological harm that has come to me because of seeing Obring and my own sister like that! No one cares that *I'm* suffering, too, and that maybe I need to go out at night as *therapy*.

Kokor sat painting her face, practicing looks that might project well in her next play. For there would certainly be a next play *now*, once she got out of Mother's house. Tumannu's little attempt to blacklist her would certainly fail—there wasn't a comedy house in Dolltown that would refuse an actress whose name was on the lips of everyone in Basilica. The house would sell out every night just from curiosity seekers—and when they saw her perform and heard her sing, they'd be back again and again. Not that she would ever dream of deliberately hurting someone in order to advance her career; but since it had happened, why not make use of it? Tumannu herself would probably be in line to beg Kokor to take the lead in a comedy.

She had drawn a little pout on her mouth that looked quite fetching. She tried it out from several angles and liked the shape of it. It was too light, though. She'd have to redden it or no one would see it past the first row.

"If you make it any rounder it'll look as though somebody made a hole under your nose with a drill."

Kokor turned slowly to face the intruder who stood in her doorway. An obnoxious little thirteen-year-old girl. The younger sister of that nasty bastard girl Hushidh. Mother had taken them both in as infants, out of pure charity, and when Mother made Hushidh one of her nieces the girl obviously thought she should then be taken as seriously as if she were one of the nieces of high birth who would amount to something in Basilica. She and Sevet had had such fun cutting Hushidh down to size, back when they were still students here. And now the little sister, equally a bastard, just as ugly and just as uppity, dared to stand in the doorway of the bedroom of a *daughter* of the house, of a highborn woman of Basilica, and ridicule the appearance of one of the famous beauties of the city.

But it would be beneath Kokor to go to the effort of putting this child in her place as she so deserved. Enough to make her go away. "Girl, there is a door. It was closed. Please restore it to its previous condition, with yourself on the other side."

The child didn't move.

"Girl, if you were sent with a message, deliver it and vanish."

"Are you speaking to me?" asked the child.

"Do you see another girl here?"

"I am a niece in this house," said the child. "Only servants are addressed as 'girl.' I therefore assumed that since you are rumored to be a lady who would know correct forms of address, you must have been speaking to some invisible servant on the balcony."

Kokor rose to her feet. "I've had enough of you. I had enough before you came in here."

"What are you going to do?" asked the child. "Strike me in the throat? Or is that a sport you keep within your family?"

Kokor felt an unbearable rage rise within her. "Don't tempt me!" she cried. Then she controlled herself, penned in the anger. This girl was not worth it. If she wanted correct address, she would have it. "What's your business here, my dear young daughter-of-a-holy-whore?"

The girl did not seem abashed, not for a moment. "So you *do* know who I am," she said. "My name is Luet. My friends call me Lutya. You may call me Young Mistress."

"Why are you here and when will you leave?" demanded Kokor. "Have I come to my mother's house to be tormented by bastard children with no manners?"

"Have no fear of that," said Luet. "For as I hear it, you will not be in this house another hour."

"What are you talking about? What have you heard?"

"I came here as an act of kindness, to let you know that Rashgallivak is here with six of his soldiers to take you under the protection of the Palwashantu."

"Rashgallivak! That little pizdook! I showed him his place when he last tried to pull this stunt, and I'll do it again."

"He wants to take Sevet, too. He says that you're both in serious danger and you need protection."

"Danger? In Mother's house? I only need protection from obnoxious ugly little girls."

"You are so gracious, Mistress Kokor," said Luet. "I will never forget how you answered my thoughtfulness in bringing you this news." She turned and left the room.

What did the girl expect? If she had come in with dignity instead of with an insult, Kokor would have treated her better. A child of such low background could hardly be expected to understand how to behave, however, so Kokor would try not to hold it against her.

Mother was being so bossy lately that she might even think that sending her and Sevet to Rashgallivak would be a good idea. Kokor would have to take steps herself to ensure that nothing of the kind occurred.

She wiped off the pout and replaced it with daypaint, then chose a particularly fragile-looking housedress and put it on with the tiniest hint of disarray, so that it would seem that she was simply on her way to the kitchen when she was surprised to discover that Rashgallivak was here to try to kidnap her.

The plan was spoiled, though, by the fact that when she stepped into the hall, there was Sevet, leaning on the arm of that wretched Hushidh girl, Luet's older sister. How could Sevet—even with her injury—abase herself by leaning on a girl that she had once treated with such despite? Had she no shame? And yet her presence in the hall made it impossible for Kokor to ignore her. She would have to be solicitous. She would have to hover near her. Fortunately, since Sevet was already leaning on Hushidh, Kokor wouldn't have to offer *that* service. It would completely spoil her freedom of action, to have Sevet leaning on her.

"How are you, poor Sevet?" asked Kokor. "I've wept myself hoarse over what happened. We're so bad to each other sometimes, Sevet. Why do we do it?"

Sevet merely looked at the floor a meter ahead of her.

"Oh, I can understand why you're not speaking to me. You'll never forgive me for the accident. But I've forgiven *you* for what *you* did, and *that* was no accident, *that* was on purpose. Still, one can hardly expect you to feel forgiving yet, you're in such pain, you poor thing. Why are you even up? I can handle this thing with Rashgallivak. I jammed his balls into his spleen the other night, and I'll be glad to do it again."

At that Sevet actually smiled a little. Just a trace of a smile. Or perhaps she only winced as she started jolting down the stairs.

Mother hadn't even brought Rashgallivak into one of the sitting rooms. He was standing with his soldiers right at the door, which was still open. Mother turned and glanced at her daughters and Hushidh as they came down the hall from the stairs to the entryway.

"You can see that they are well," Mother said to Rashgallivak. "They are safe and in good hands here. In fact, no men have come here at all, except you and these superfluous soldiers."

"I'm not worried about what *has* happened," said Rashgallivak. "I'm concerned about what *might* happen, and I will not leave here without Gaballufix's daughters. They are under the protection of the Palwashantu."

"You are welcome to keep your soldiers out in the street," said Mother, "to prevent any tolchoks or marauders or assassins from entering our house, but you will not take my daughters. A mother's claim is superior to the claim of a clan of men."

While Mother and Rash continued arguing, Kokor leaned toward Sevet and, forgetting that her sister could not speak, asked her, "Why does Rashgallivak want us in the first place?"

Because Sevet couldn't answer, Hushidh did. "Aunt Rasa is at the center of resistance to Palwashantu rule in Basilica. He thinks if he has the two of you as hostages, she will behave."

"Then he doesn't know Mother," said Kokor.

"Rashgallivak is a weak man," whispered Hushidh. "And he's stupid at politics. If he were as smart as your father, he would have known that he could not get possession of the two of you without violence, and that violence would be against his best interests. Therefore he would never have made the request. But if for some reason he *did* decide to take you, he would have acted far more boldly. The two of you would already be in the grasp of two soldiers each, with the other two holding your mother at bay."

Hushidh was no fool, after all. That had never occurred to Kokor, that Hushidh might have some attribute worthy of respect. Her idea of Father was exactly true—yet Kokor herself would never have been able to express it so clearly.

Of course, Father would also have had some kind of right to try to take her and Sevet. Not a *legal* right, of course, not in the city of women, but people might have understood it if he tried. What claim did Rashgallivak have? "The Oversoul must have driven Rash mad, even to try this," whispered Kokor.

"He's afraid," said Hushidh. "People do strange things when they're afraid. Your mother already has."

Like keeping me in seclusion, thought Kokor.

Then she realized that if she had been at home with Obring, Rash would have had no trouble getting to her. Obring would have tried to fight with the soldiers, they would have knocked him down in an instant, and Kokor would have been carried off. So Mother *was* right to keep her in seclusion. Imagine that. "You mustn't criticize Mother," said Kokor. "She's doing very well, I think."

In the meantime, the argument between Rasa and Rash had continued, though now they were both repeating old arguments, and not always in new words. Hushidh had brought them to the very threshold of the foyer, so that they were as far as they could be from the soldiers and still be in the room. Till now Kokor had stayed with her and Sevet. Seeing the soldiers standing there, horribly identical in their holographic masks, took away her determination to show Rashgallivak what was what. He had seemed much smaller and weaker in the darkness backstage at the theatre. The soldiers made him much more menacing, and Kokor found herself admiring Mother's courage in facing them down like this. In fact, she wondered if Mother was not being just the tiniest bit foolish. For instance, why had she called Kokor and Sevet down here to be in plain sight, within easy reach of these soldiers? Why hadn't she kept them hidden away upstairs? Or warned them to sneak away into the woods? Perhaps this was what Hushidh meant about Mother already doing strange things because of fear.

Yet Mother didn't seem afraid.

"I think perhaps we should leave now," Kokor whispered to Hushidh.

"Not so," said Hushidh. "You must stay."

"Why?"

"Because if you tried to leave, it would alarm Rashgallivak and probably cause him to act. He would order the soldiers to detain you and all would be lost."

"He'll do that eventually anyway," whispered Kokor.

"Ah, but will he wait long enough?"

"Long enough for what?"

"Think," said Hushidh.

Kokor thought. What would mere delay profit them?

Unless someone was coming to help. But who could possibly stand against the soldiers of the Palwashantu?

"The city guard!" cried Kokor, delighted to have thought of it.

Could she help it if her words fell into a chance silence in the argument between Mother and Rash?

"What?" cried Rashgallivak. "What did you say?" He whirled and looked out the door. "There's no one there," he said. Then he looked at Rasa. "But they *are* coming, aren't they? That's what this is all about— delaying me until you can get the guard to come and stop me. Well, the delay is over. Take them!"

At once the soldiers strode toward the women in the hallway, and Kokor screamed.

"Run, you little fools!" cried Mother.

But Kokor could not run, because one of the soldiers already had her by the arm and another pair of soldiers had Sevet, too, and that bastard Hushidh wasn't doing *one thing* to help them.

"Do something, you little bitch!" cried Kokor. "Don't let them do this to us!"

Hushidh looked her in the eye for a moment as the soldiers dragged her toward the door. Then she seemed to make a decision.

"Stop, Rashgallivak!" cried Hushidh. "Stop this instant."

Rash only laughed. It chilled Kokor to the bone, his laugh. It was the laugh of a man who knew he had won. This pathetic man who had been the steward in the house of Wetchik only a few days ago now laughed in delight at the power his soldiers gave him.

"Order them to stop!" cried Hushidh. "Or you will never be able to order them to do anything again!"

"No, Hushidh!" cried Mother.

What in the world did Mother think that Hushidh could do *now*?

Kokor could see Sevet in the grasp of the soldiers, their blank faces so terrifying, so inhuman. It was wrong, for her sister to be in their grasp. Wrong for these hands to be gripping Kokor's arms and dragging her away. "Do it, Hushidh!" Kokor cried. Whatever it is Mother thinks you can do, do it.

To anyone but Hushidh, the scene was simple—Rash and two of his soldiers blocking anyone from interfering, as the other four soldiers were dragging Kokor and Sevet through the wide front door of Rasa's house. Aunt Rasa herself was shouting ineffectually—"It's *you* who's injuring Sevet! You'll be expelled from the city! Kidnapper!"—and other women and girls of the house were gathering, huddling in the hallway, listening, watching.

To Hushidh the Raveler, however, the scene was very different. For she could see not only the people, but also the webs that bound them together. To Hushidh, the frightened girls and women were not individuals or even little clumps—all of them were tightly bound to Rasa, so that instead of being helplessly alone as others would see her, Hushidh knew that she spoke from the strength of dozens of women, that their fear fed her fear, their anger her anger, and when she cried out in the majesty of her wrath, she was far larger than one mere woman. Hushidh even saw the powerful webs connecting Rasa to the rest of the city, great ropy threads like arteries and veins, pumping the lifeblood of Rasa's identity. When she cried out against Rashgallivak, it was the fury of the whole city of women in her voice.

Yet Hushidh could also see that Rasa, though she was surrounded by this vast web, also felt herself to be quite alone, as if the web came right up to her but didn't quite connect, or touched her only slightly. That was what Rash's exercise of raw power was doing to Rasa—making her feel as if her strength and power in the city amounted to nothing after all, for she could not resist the power of these soldiers.

At the same time, there was another web of influence—Rashgallivak's. And this one Hushidh knew was actually contemptible and weak. Where Rasa's links with her household were strong and real, her power in the city almost tangible to Hushidh, Rashgallivak had very little respect from his soldiers. He was able to command them only because he paid them, and then only because they rather liked what he was commanding them to do. Rashgallivak, compared to Rasa, was almost isolated. As for his men, their connections to each other were much stronger than their connections to *him*. And even then, they were nothing like the bonds among the women.

Most men were like this, Hushidh knew—relatively unconnected, unbound, alone. But these men were particularly untrusting and ungiving, and so the bonds that held them to each other were fragile indeed. It was not love at all, really, but rather a yearning for the honor and respect of the other men that held them. Pride, then. And at this moment they were proud of their strength as they dragged these women out of the house, proud to defy one of the great women of Basilica; they looked so grand in each other's eyes. Indeed, all their connection with each other at this moment was tied up with the respect they felt they were earning by their actions.

So fragile. Hushidh had only to reach out and she could easily snap the bonds between these men. She could leave Rashgallivak hopelessly alone. And even though Rasa was demanding that she *not* do it, at this moment Hushidh felt much more deeply her connection to Sevet and Kokor, for these girls had been her tormentors, her enemies, and now she had the chance to be their savior, to set them free, and they would *know she had done it*. It would undo one of the deepest injuries in her heart; what was Rasa's command compared to that need?

Hushidh knew exactly why she was acting even as she acted—so well did she understand herself, for as a raveler she could see even her own connections with the world around her—yet she acted anyway, because that was who she was at this moment, the powerful savior who had the power to undo these powerful men.

So she spoke, and undid them. It wasn't the words she said; this was no magical incantation that would disconnect the bonds that held them to each other. It was her tone of contempt, her face, her body, that gave her words the power to strike at the heart of each of the soldiers and make them believe that they were utterly alone, that other men would have only contempt for what they were doing. "Where is your honor in dragging this injured woman away from her mother," she said. "Baboons in the wild have more manhood than you, for mothers can trust their infants with the males of the tribe."

Poor Rash. He heard the words, and thought that he could counter Hushidh by arguing with her. He didn't realize that, with these men caught up in the story Hushidh was weaving around them, every word he said would drive these men farther away from him, for he sounded weaker and more cowardly with every sound he made. "You shut up, woman! These men are soldiers who do their duty—"

"A coward's duty. Look what this so-called man has led you to do. He's made you into filthy rodents, stealing bright and shining beauty and dragging it off to his hole where he will cover you with shit and call it glory."

First one, then another of the men let go of Kokor and Sevet. Sevet immediately sank to her knees, weeping silently. Kokor, for her part, put on a very convincing show of disgust and loathing, shuddering as she tried in vain to brush away the very memory of the soldiers' touch on her arms.

"See how you have disgusted the beautiful ones," said Hushidh. "That's what Rashgallivak has made of you. Slugs and worms, because you follow him. Where can you go to become men again? How can you find a way to be clean? There must be somewhere you can hide from your shame. Slither off and find it, little slugs; burrow deep and see if you can hide your humiliation! Do you think those masks make you look strong and powerful? They only mark you as servants of this contemptible gnat of a man. Servants of *nothing*."

One of the soldiers pulled off the cloak that created the holographic image that till now had hidden his face. He was an ordinary, rather dirty-looking man, unshaven, somewhat stupid, and very much afraid —his eyes were wide and filled with tears.

"There he is," Hushidh said. "That's what Rashgallivak has made of you."

"Put your mask back on!" cried Rashgallivak. "I order you to take these women back to Gaballufix's house."

"Listen to him," said Hushidh. "*He's* no Gaballufix. Why are you following *him?*"

That was the last push. Most of the other soldiers also swept off their masks, leaving the holo-cloaks on the porch of Rasa's house as they shambled off, running from the scene of their humiliation.

Rash stood alone in the middle of the doorway. Now the whole scene had changed. It didn't take a raveler to see that Rasa had all the power and majesty now, and Rash was helpless, weak, alone. He looked down at the cloaks at his feet.

"That's right," said Hushidh. "Hide your face. No one wants to see that face again, least of all you."

And he did it, he bent over and swept up one of the cloaks and pulled it across his shoulder; his body heat and magnetism activated the cloaks, which were still powered on, and suddenly he was no longer Rashgallivak, but rather the same uniform image of false masculinity that all the soldiers of Gaballufix had worn. Then he turned and ran away, just like his men, with that same defeated rounding of the shoulders. No baboon beaten by a rival could have shown more abjectness than Rash's body showed as he ran away.

Hushidh felt the web of awe that was forming around her; it made her tingle, knowing that she had the adulation of the girls and women of the house—and above all, the honor of Sevet and Kokor. Kokor, vain Kokor, who now looked at her with an expression stupid with awe. And Sevet, cruel in her mockery for so many years, now looking at her through eyes streaked with tears, her hands reaching out toward Hushidh like a supplicant, her lips struggling to say Thank you, thank you, thank you.

"What have you done," whispered Rasa.

Hushidh could hardly understand the question. What she had done was obvious. "I've broken Rashgallivak's power," she said. "He's no more threat to you."

"Foolish, foolish girl," said Rasa. "There are thousands of these villains in Basilica. Thousands of them, and now the one man who could control them, however weak he was, that man is broken and undone. By nightfall these soldiers will all be out of control, and who will stop them?"

All of Hushidh's sense of accomplishment slipped away at once. She knew that Rasa was right. No matter how clearly Hushidh saw in the present moment, she hadn't looked ahead to anticipate the larger consequences of her act. These men would no longer be bound by their hunger for honor, for it would no longer be seen as honorable to serve Rashgallivak. What would they do, then? They would be unbound in the city, soldiers starving to prove their strength and power, and no force could channel them to some useful purpose. Hushidh remembered the holos she had seen of apes displaying, shaking branches, charging each other, slapping at whoever was weak, whoever was near. Men on the rampage would be far, far more dangerous.

"Bring my daughters inside," Rasa said to the others. "Then all of you work to shutter the windows behind their bars. Tighten down the house. As if a tempest were coming. For it is."

Rasa then stepped onto the porch between her daughters.

"Where are you going, Mama!" wailed Kokor. "Don't leave us!"

"I must warn the women of the city. The monster is loose in the streets tonight. The Guard will be powerless to control them. They must secure what can be secured, and then hide from the fires that will burn here tonight in the darkness."

Moozh's troops were exhausted, but when, late in the afternoon, they crested a pass and saw smoke in the distance, it put new vigor into their steps. They knew as well as Moozh did that a city on fire is a city that is not about to defend itself. Besides, they knew that they had accomplished something remarkable, to cover such a distance on foot. And even though there were only a thousand of them, they knew that if they achieved a victory, their names would live forever, if not individually, then as a part of Moozh's Thousand. They could almost hear their grandchildren already asking them, Was it true you marched from Khlam to Basilica in two days, and took the city that night without resting, and without a man of you killed?

Of course, that last part of the story wasn't yet a foregone conclusion. Who knew what the condition inside Basilica really was. What if the soldiers of Gaballufix had already consolidated their position inside the city, and now were prepared to defend it? The Gorayni soldiers well knew they had barely food for another meal; if they didn't take the city tonight, in darkness, they would have to break their fast in the morning and take the city by daylight—or flee ignominiously down into the Cities of the Plain, where their enemies could see how few they really were, and cut them to pieces long before they could make it back north. So yes, victory was possible—but it was also essential, and it had to be now.

So why were they so confident, when desperation would have been more understandable? Because they were *Moozh's* Thousand, and Moozh had never lost. There was no better general in the history of the Gorayni. He was careful of his men; he defeated his enemies, not by expending his men in bloody assaults, but through maneuver and deft blows, isolating the enemy, cutting off supplies, dividing the enemy's forces, and so disorienting the opposing generals that they began taking foolish chances just to get the battle *over* with and stop the endless, terrifying ballet. His soldiers called it "Dancing with Moozh," the quick marches; they knew that by wearing out their feet, Moozh was saving their yatsas. Oh, yes, they loved him—he made them victors without sending too many of them home as a small sack of ashes.

There were even whispers in the ranks that their beloved Moozh was the *real* incarnation of God, and even though usually none would say it aloud—at least not where an intercessor could hear them—on this march, with no intercessor along, the whispers became a good deal more frequent. That fat-assed fellow back in Gollod was no incarnation of God, in a world that included a *real* man like Vozmuzhalnoy Vozmozhno!

A kilometer away from Basilica, they could hear some of the sounds coming out of the city—screams, mostly, carried by the wind, which was blowing smoke toward them now. The order came through the ranks: Cut down branches, a dozen or more per man, so we can light enough smoky bonfires to make the enemy think we are a hundred thousand. They hacked and tore at the trees near the road, and then followed Moozh down a winding trail from the mountains into the desert. Moonlight was a treacherous guide, especially burdened as they were with boughs, but there were few injuries though many fell, and in the darkness they fanned out across the desert, separating widely from each other, leaving vast empty spaces between the groups of men. There they built their piles of branches, and at the blare of a trumpet—who in the city could hear it?—they lit all the fires. Then, leaving one man at each bonfire to add boughs to keep the flames alive, the rest of the army gathered behind Moozh and marched, this time in four columns abreast, as if they were the bold advance guard for a huge army, up a wide flat road toward a gap in the high walls of the city.

Even before they reached the walls, they found themselves in the middle of a veritable city. There were men running and shouting there —many of them clearly oversatisfied with wine—but when they saw Moozh's army marching through their street, they fell silent and backed away into the shadows. If any of the Gorayni had lacked confidence before, they gained it now, for it was clear that the men of Basilica had no fight in them. What boldness they had was nothing but the bravado of drink.

As they drew near to the gate, they heard the clang of metal on metal that suggested a pitched battle. Cresting a rise they saw a battle in progress, between men clad in the same uniform as the assassin that Moozh had killed, and other men who were terrifyingly identical—not just their clothing, but even their faces were all the same!

Word passed down the columns: The men in the uniform of the Basilican guard will probably be our allies; our true enemies are the ones in masks. But slay no one until Moozh gives the order.

They reached the flat, clear area before the gate, and quickly split into two ranks left, two ranks right, until a semicircle formed surrounding the gate. In the middle of the semicircle stood Moozh himself.

"Gorayni, draw your weapons!" He bawled out the command—clearly he meant to be heard as much by the men fighting at the gate as by his own army, which normally would have received the command as a whisper down the ranks.

The fighting at the gate slackened. The men in the uniforms of the Basilican guard—few of them indeed to be making such a brave stand —saw the Gorayni troops and despaired. They fell back against the wall, uncertain which enemy to fight, but certain of this: That they would not live out the hour.

In the middle of the gate, their enemies withdrawn, the soldiers of identical faces also stood, uncertain of what to do next.

"We are the Gorayni. We have come to help Basilica, not to conquer her!" cried Moozh. "Look out in the desert and see the army we could bring to bear against the gates of your city!"

Moozh had chosen his gate well—from here all the Basilicans, guard and Palwashantu mercenaries alike, could see the bonfires, at least a hundred of them, stretching far across the desert.

"Yet only these five hundred have I brought to the gate!" Of course he lied about the number of men he had; his men smiled inwardly to know that for once he was only four hundred off, instead of forty thousand, which was the more usual lie. "We are here to ask if the City of Women, the City of Peace, might use our services to help quell a domestic disturbance. We will enter, serve the city at your pleasure, and leave when our task is accomplished. Thus do I speak in the name of General Vozmuzhalnoy Vozmozhno!" There was no reason to let them know that the most fearsome general on the western shores of the Earthbound Sea was standing before their gates with his sword sheathed and only nine hundred men to back him up. Let them think the general himself was out with the tens of thousands of troops tenting around the great bonfires in the desert!

"Sir," cried one of the guard. "You see how it is with us! We are the guard of the city, but how can we find out the will of our council, when we are fighting for our lives against these mad criminals!"

"*We* are the masters of Basilica now!" shouted one of the identical Palwashantu mercenaries. "No more taking the orders of women! No more being forced to stay outside the city that is ours by right! We rule this city now in the name of Gaballufix!"

"Gaballufix is dead!" shouted the officer of the guard. "And you are ruled by no man!"

"In the name of Gaballufix this city is ours!" And with that the mercenaries brandished their weapons and shouted.

"Men of Gaballufix!" cried Moozh. "We have heard the name of your fallen leader!"

The mercenaries cheered again.

"We know how to honor Gaballufix!" Moozh shouted. "Come out to us, and stand with us, and we will give you the city you deserve!"

With a cheer the mercenaries poured out from the gate toward the Gorayni. The Basilican guard shrank back against the walls, their weapons ready. Some few started slinking away to the left or the right, hoping to escape, but to their honor most of the guard remained in their places, prepared to end their lives doing their duty. Moozh's Thousand took note of this; they would treat the guard with respect, should a reckoning come between them.

As for the mercenaries, those closest to the Gorayni came with their guard down, prepared to embrace these newcomers as their brothers. But they found that swords and pikes and bows were pointed at them, and confusion spread from the rim to the center of the mob.

Moozh still stood where he had stood all along, only now he was surrounded by mercenaries, cut off from his own men. He seemed to show no alarm at all, though it made his men more than a little nervous. To their consternation, he began to push his way through the mob, not *toward* his men, but away from them and toward the gate. The mercenaries seemed content with this—it was a sign that he meant to lead them.

Moozh strode out into the open area in the middle of the gate, his back to the mercenaries. "Ah, Basilica," he said—loudly, but not in the voice of command. "How often I have dreamed of standing in your gate and seeing your beauty with my own eyes!" Then he turned to face the officer of the guard, who stood at the post of the gate, his weapon drawn. Moozh spoke softly to him. "Would Basilica regard it as a great service, my friend, if these hundreds of ugly twins were to die on this ground at this hour?"

"I think so, yes," said the officer, confused once again, but also glad with new hope.

Moozh turned back to face the mob—and his men behind them. "Every man who loves the name of Gaballufix, raise your sword high!"

Most of the mob—all but the wariest of them—raised their weapons. No sooner had they raised their arms, however, than Moozh drew his sword from its sheath.

That was the signal. Three hundred arrows were loosed at once, and every man at the periphery of the mob—their arms conveniently raised so that every arrow struck them in the body—fell, most of them pierced many times. Then, with a thunderous shout, the Gorayni fell on the remaining mercenaries and in only two or three minutes the carnage was over. The Gorayni immediately formed themselves into ranks again, standing before the bodies of their fallen enemies.

Moozh turned to the officer of the guard. "What is your name, sir?"

"Captain Bitanke, sir."

"Captain Bitanke, I ask again: Would Basilica welcome our intervention to help restore order in these beautiful streets? I have here a letter from the Lady Rasa; is her name known to you?"

"Yes it is, sir," said Bitanke.

"She wrote to me, asking for succor for her city. I came, and now respectfully ask your permission to bring these men within your gates, to serve as auxiliary troops in your effort to control the violence in your streets."

Bitanke bowed and then unlocked the guard booth in the gate and stepped inside. Moozh could see that he was typing into a computer. After a few moments he stepped back into the open. "Sir, I have told them what you did here. The situation of our city is desperate, and since you come in the name of the Lady Rasa, and you have proven your will to defeat our enemies, the city council and the guard invite you to enter. Temporarily you are placed under my immediate command, if you will accept one of my low rank, until a more orderly system can be arranged."

"Sir, it is not your rank but your courage and honor that make me salute you, and for that reason I will accept your leadership," said Moozh. "May I suggest that we deploy my men in companies of six, and authorize them to deal with any men they find who are behaving in a disorderly fashion. We will in all cases respect those who wear your uniform; any other men we find who have weapons drawn or who offer violence to us or to any woman of the city, we will slay on the spot and hang up on public display to quell any notion of further resistance by others!"

"I don't know about the hanging, sir," said Bitanke.

"Very well, we have our orders!" Ignoring Bitanke's hesitation, Moozh turned to his soldiers. "Men of the Gorayni, by sixes!"

Immediately the ranks shifted and suddenly there were a hundred and fifty squads of six men each.

"Harm no woman!" cried Moozh. "And whomever you see in that loathsome mask, hang him up, mask and all, until no man dares wear it by night or day!"

"Sir, I think . . ."

But Moozh had already waved his arm, and his soldiers now entered the city at a trot. Bitanke came closer to Moozh, to remonstrate perhaps, but Moozh greeted him with an embrace that stifled conversation. "Please, my friend—I know your men are exhausted, but couldn't they be usefully employed? For instance, I think this village outside the gate could profit from a little cleaning out. And as for you and me, we should make our way to those who are in authority, so I can receive the orders of the city council."

Whatever misgivings Captain Bitanke might have had were swept away by Moozh's embrace and his smile. Bitanke gave his orders, and his men spread out through Dogtown. Then Moozh followed him into the city. "While my men are restoring order, we must see about putting out some fires," said Moozh. "Can you call others of the city guard with your computer?"

"Yes, sir."

"It's not my place to tell you your business, but if your men can protect the firefighters, perhaps we can keep Basilica from burning down before dawn."

"Do you think the rest of your men might be able to come and help?"

Moozh laughed. "Oh, General Vozmuzhalnoy Vozmozhno would never allow that. If such a force came to your gates, someone in Basilica might fear that we meant to conquer the town. We are here to extend you our protection, not to rule over you, my friend! So we bring no more men than these five hundred."

"The Oversoul must have sent you, sir," said Captain Bitanke.

"You have only to thank the Lady Rasa," said Moozh. "Her and a brave man of your number named, I believe, Smelost."

"Smelost," whispered Bitanke. "He was a dear friend of mine."

"Then I am glad to tell you that he was received with honor by General Vozmuzhalnoy Vozmozhno, who lost no time in acting on his information and coming to the aid of your city."

"You came in good time," said Bitanke. "It began like this last night, and spread through the day, and I feared that tomorrow morning would find the city in ashes and all the good women of Basilica in despair or worse."

"I'm always glad to be a messenger of hope," said Moozh.

By now they were walking along a street with houses and shops on either side. Yet there was no one moving, and lights shone from many upper windows. The only sign that the rioting had been here was the broken glass in the street, the shattered windows of the shops, and the bodies of dead mercenaries, still wearing their holographic masks, dangling like beeves from upper-story balconies. Bitanke looked at them in faint dismay as they walked along the street.

"How long will those masks remain active?" asked Moozh.

"Until the—bodies cool, I imagine. I've heard that body heat and magnetism are the triggers."

"Ah," said Moozh.

"May I ask—what they are—how your men were able to hang them? I see no ropes and there are no—apparatuses for hanging men in the streets."

"I'm not sure," said Moozh. "Let's take the cloak off one of them and see."

Gingerly Bitanke reached up and tugged on the cloak of the nearest dangling corpse. When it came away, the holograph faded instantly and it was easy to see that the body had been pinned to the wall by a heavy knife through its neck. "His own knife, do you think?" asked Moozh.

"I think so," said Bitanke.

"Not a very secure job," said Moozh, pushing at the body a bit. "I daresay if we have any wind tonight most of these will be down by morning. We'll want to clean them up as quickly as possible, or we'll have quite a problem with the dogs."

"Yes sir," said Bitanke.

"Never seen a dead body?" asked Moozh. "You look a little ill."

"Oh, I've seen dead bodies, sir," said Bitanke. "I've just never heard of . . . treating them this way . . . I wish your men wouldn't . . ."

"Nonsense. These dangling bodies are like reinforcements. Any rioters that my soldiers happen to overlook—there are bound to be some using the toilet, don't you think?—they'll come out, see how quiet things are, notice the bodies, and most of the fight will go right out of them."

Bitanke chuckled a little. "I imagine so."

"You see?" said Moozh. "It's a way of letting these boys make up for a bit of the mischief they've caused, by policing the streets for us all night. Correct me if I'm wrong, Captain Bitanke, but no one is going to shed many tears, for them, right?"

Within the hour Moozh was meeting with the city council. In the meantime, the hundred soldiers who had been tending the bonfires were moving into position at every gate of the city, standing alongside the guard in those few cases where they were at the gate. There was no quarrel between them; no soldier of the Gorayni came to blows with any of the city guard.

Moozh's meeting with the city council was peaceful, and they concluded a firm agreement that Moozh would have full access to all the boroughs of the city—even those that normally were restricted to women only, since that was where the worst of the fires were burning and the marauders had been most out of control—but that after two and a half days, Moozh would withdraw his men to quarters outside the city, where they would be amply supplied and rewarded from the treasury of the city. It was a wonderful alliance, full of many compliments and much heartfelt gratitude.

Few in Basilica would realize it for several days, but by the time Moozh left the meeting his conquest of the city was complete.

Nafai said as little as possible to Elya and Meb as they set out on their journey back to Basilica. His silence did not make them any more cheerful toward him, but it meant that he didn't have to quarrel with them, or do some verbal dance to avoid quarreling. He could keep his own thoughts.

He could talk to the Oversoul.

As if it mattered what he said to the old computer. For a few days he had fancied that he and the Oversoul were working together. The Oversoul had shown him its memory of Earth, had explained its purpose in the world, to try to keep the planet Harmony from repeating the miserable, self-destructive history of Earth. Nafai had agreed to serve that purpose. Nafai had stood over a drunken man in the street—his enemy—and it never would have come to his own mind to kill the man as he lay there, helpless. But the Oversoul had told him to do it and Nafai had complied. Not because Gaballufix was a murderer himself who deserved to die. Why, then? Because Nafai believed the Oversoul, agreed with the Oversoul that by killing this one man, he could help preserve the whole world.

And, having done the crime, having put blood on his own hands for the sake of the Oversoul's cause, where was the Oversoul now? Nafai had imagined that there was now a special relationship between the Oversoul and himself. Hadn't there been that moment when the Index first spoke to him and Father and Issib? Father and Issib had only partly understood the Oversoul's message—they grasped the idea that the Oversoul meant to lead them on a long journey to a wonderful place where Issib could use his floats again and not be confined to his chair. But only Nafai had understood that the place the Oversoul meant to take them was not on the planet Harmony—that the Oversoul meant to take them back to Earth. After forty million years, home to Earth.

Since then, though, the Index had been nothing but a guide to a vast memory bank. Father and Issib studied, and Nafai with them, but all the time Nafai kept waiting for some word—to all of them, or perhaps to him alone. Perhaps some special private message, some word of encouragement. Something to fulfill the promise made that time when the Oversoul, speaking through Issib's chair, had said that it had chosen Nafai to lead his brothers.

Am I chosen, Oversoul? Why can't I see the results of your favor, then? I have made myself a murderer for you, and yet your vision of our wives came to Elemak. And what did he see? That you had chosen Eiadh for him! What has your favor brought me, then? Now you speak to Elemak, who plotted with Gaballufix, who tried to kill me; now you give him the woman that I have so long desired—why did he receive that dream, and not me? I have been humiliated now in front of all of them. I will have to eat dust, I will have to submit to Elya's orders and serve at his pleasure, I will have to watch Elya take that sweet and beautiful girl who has so long inhabited my dreams. Why do you hate me, Oversoul? What have I done, except to serve you and obey you?

The camels clambered with lazy strength up a slope, and Elemak led them along the edge of a precipice. Nafai looked out over the landscape and saw the savage knife-edged rocks and crags, with only here and there a bit of grey-green desert foliage. The Oversoul promised me life, promised me greatness and glory and joy, and here I am, in this desert, following my brothers, who plotted with Father's enemy and, wittingly or not, set Father up to be killed. I helped the Oversoul to save Father's life, and now here I am.

Yes, here you are.

It took a moment to realize that this was the voice of the Oversoul, for it spoke in Nafai's mind as if it were his own thought. But he knew, from his few experiences, that this thought was coming from outside himself, if only because it seemed to answer him.

In turn, he answered the Oversoul—and not with any particular respect. Oh, here *you* are, he said silently, sarcastically. Noticed me again? Hope I wasn't a bother.

I bother a great deal for you.

Like choosing Eiadh for my brother instead of me.

Eiadh is not for you.

Thanks for your help, said Nafai silently. Thanks for dealing me such a miserable hand in this game with my brothers.

I'm not doing too badly for you, Nafai.

Maybe I don't give you the same high marks you give yourself. I killed a man for you.

And every moment of this journey, I am saving your life.

The thought startled Nafai. Inadvertently he sat up straighter, looked around him.

Every moment of this journey, I am turning their thoughts away from their decision to kill you.

Fear and hatred, both at once, clawed their way down Nafai's throat and deep into his belly. He could feel them churning there, like small animals dwelling inside him.

It's good that you've been silent, said the Oversoul. It's good that you haven't provoked them, or even reminded them that you're along with them on this journey. For my influence in their minds, while strong, is not irresistible. If their anger flowed hotly against you, how would I stop them? I don't have Issib's chair to act through now.

Nafai was filled with fear, with a longing to go back to Father's tent.

At the same time, he was hurt and angry at his brothers. Why do they still hate me? How have I harmed them?

Foolish boy. Only a moment ago you were longing for me to reward you for your loyalty to me by giving you power over your brothers. Do you think they don't see your ambition? Every time I speak to you, they hate you more. Every time your father's face is filled with delight at your quick mind, at your goodness of heart, they hate you more. And when they see that you desire to have the privileges of the eldest son . . .

I don't! cried Nafai silently. I don't want to displace Elemak . . . I want him to love me, I want him to be a *true* older brother to me, and not this monster who wants me dead.

Yes, you want him to love you . . . *and* you want him to respect you . . . *and* you want to take his place. Do you think you are immune to the primate instincts within you? You are born to be an alpha male in a tribe of clever beasts, and so is he. But he is ruled by that hunger, while you, Nafai, can't you be civilized, can't you suppress the animal part of yourself, and work to help me achieve a far higher purpose than determining who will be the leading male in a troop of erect baboons?

Nafai felt as if he had been stripped naked in front of his enemies. If I am no better than Elemak, no better than any of the troop of baboons downstream from Father's tent, then why did you choose me?

Because you *are* better, and because you *want* to be better still.

Help me, then. Help me curb my own dark desires. And while you're at it, help Elemak, too. I remember him when he was younger. Playful, loving, kind. He's more than an ambitious animal, I know he is, even if he's forgotten it himself.

I know it, answered the Oversoul. Why do you think I gave that dream to Elemak? So he might have a chance to waken to my voice. He has much of the same sensitivity *you* have. But he has long chosen to hate me, to thwart my purposes if he can. So my voice has been nothing to him. This time, though, I could tell him something he wanted to hear. My purpose coincided with his own. What do you think your life would be worth, if I had shown *you* who his wife should be? Do you think he would have taken Eiadh at *your* hand?

I wouldn't have given him Eiadh.

So. You would have ignored me. You would have rebelled against me. You tell yourself that you killed Gaballufix only because you serve me and my noble purpose . . . but then you are willing to rebel against me and thwart my purpose, because you want a woman who would ruin your life.

You don't know that. You may be a very clever computer, Oversoul, but you can't tell the future.

I know her, as I know you, from the inside. And if you ever know her, you will understand that she could never be your wife.

Are you saying she's bad at heart?

I'm saying she lives in a world whose center of gravity is herself. She has no purpose higher than her own desires. But you, Nafai, will never be content unless your life is accomplishing something that will change the world. I am giving you that, if you have the patience to trust me until it comes to you. I will also give you a wife who will share the same dreams, who will help you instead of distracting you.

Who *is* my wife, then?

The face of Luet came into his mind.

Nafai shuddered. Luet. She had helped him escape, and saved his life at great risk to herself. She had taken him down to the lake of women and brought him through rituals that only women were allowed by law to receive. For bringing him there she might have been killed, right along with him; instead she faced down the women and persuaded them that the Oversoul had commanded it. He had floated with her in the mists at the boundary between the hot and cold waters of the lake, and she had brought him through Trackless Wood, beyond the private gate in the wall of Basilica that, until now, only women had known about.

And earlier, Luet had come in the middle of the night to Father's house far outside the city—had come at some risk to herself—solely to warn that Father's enemies planned to murder him. She had precipitated their departure into the wilderness.

Nafai owed her much. And he liked her, she was a good person, simple and sweet. So why couldn't he think of her as a wife? Why did he recoil at the thought?

Because she is the waterseer.

The waterseer—that's why he didn't want to marry her. Because she had been having visions from the Oversoul for far longer than he; because she had strength and wisdom that he couldn't even hope to have. Because she was better than Nafai in every way he could think of. Because if they became partners in this journey back to Earth, she would hear the voice of the Oversoul better than he; she would know the way when he knew nothing at all. When all was silent for him, she would hear music; when he was blind, she would have light. I can't bear it, to be tied to a woman who will have no reason to respect me, because whatever I do, she has done it first, she can do it better.

So . . . you didn't want a wife, after all. You wanted a worshipper.

This realization made him flush with self-contempt. Is that who I am? A boy who is so weak that he can't imagine loving a woman who is strong?

The faces of Rasa and Wetchik, his mother and father, came into his mind. Mother was a strong woman—perhaps the strongest in Basilica, though she had never tried to use her prestige and influence to win power for herself. Did it weaken Father because Mother was at least— at *least*—his equal? Perhaps that was why they had not renewed their marriage after Issib's birth. Perhaps that was why Mother had married Gaballufix for a few years, because Father had not been able to swallow his pride enough to remain happily married to a woman who was so powerful and wise.

And yet she returned to Father, and Father returned to her. Nafai was the child she bore to seal their re-marriage. And ever since then, they had renewed each other every year, not even questioning their commitment to each other. What had changed? Nothing—Mother did not have to diminish herself to be part of Father's life, and he did not have to dominate her in order to be part of *her* life. Nor did domination flow the other way; the Wetchik had always been his own man, and Rasa had never felt a need to rule over him.

In Nafai's mind, the faces of his father and mother flowed together and became one face. For a moment he recognized it as Father; then, without it changing at all, the face became clearly Mother's face.

I understand, he said silently. They are one person. What does it matter which of them happens to be the voice, whose hands happen to act? One is not above the other. They are together, and so there is no question of rivalry between them.

Can I find such a partnership with Luet? Can I bear it, to have her hear the Oversoul when I cannot? I seethed even now when it was Elya who dreamed a true dream; can I listen to Luet's dreams, and not be envious?

And what about *her?* Will she accept *me?*

Almost at once he was ashamed of the last question. She already *had* accepted him. She had brought him down to the lake of women. She had given him all that she was and all that she had, without hesitation, as far as he could tell. He was the one who was jealous and afraid. She was the one with courage and generosity.

The question is not, Can I bear to live as one with her. The question is, Am I worthy to be partnered with such a one as that?

He felt a trembling warmth suffuse through him, as if he were filled with light. Yes, said the Oversoul inside his mind. Yes, that is the question. That is the question. That is the question.

And then the trance of his communion with the Oversoul ended, and Nafai suddenly became aware of his surroundings again. Nothing had changed—Meb and Elya still led the way, the camels plodding along. Sweat still dripped on Nafai's body; the camel still lurched and rolled under him; the dry air of the desert still burned with every breath he drew into his body.

Keep me alive, said Nafai. Keep me alive long enough for me to conquer the animal in myself. Long enough for me to learn to partner myself with a woman who is better and stronger than me. Long enough for me to reconcile myself with my brothers. Long enough to be as good a man as my father, and as good as my mother, too.

If I can, I will. Like a voice in his head, that promise.

And if *I* can, I'll make it soon. I'll become worthy soon.

4

Wives

THE DREAM OF THE GENETICIST

Shedemei awoke from her dream, and wanted to tell someone, but there was no one there beside her. No one, and yet she had to tell the dream. It was too powerful and real; it had to be spoken, for fear that if she didn't say what she had seen, it would slip away from her memory the way most dreams slipped away. It was the first time she wished that she had a husband. Someone who would have to listen to her dream, even if all he did then was grunt and roll over and go back to sleep. It would relieve her so, to tell the dream aloud.

But where would a husband have slept, anyway, in the clutter of her rooms? There was barely room for her cot. The rest of the place was given over to her research. The lab tables, the basins and beakers, the dishes and tubes, the sinks and the freezers. And, above all, the great dryboxes lining the walls, filled with desiccated seeds and embryos, so she could keep samples of every stage of her research into redundancy as a natural mechanism for creating and controlling genetic drift.

Though she was only twenty-six years old, she already had a world-wide reputation among scientists in her field. It was the only kind of fame that mattered to her. Unlike so many of the other brilliant women who had grown up in Rasa's house, Shedemei had never been interested in a career that would win her fame in Basilica. She knew from childhood on that Basilica was not the center of the universe, that fame here was no better than fame in any other place—soon to be forgotten. Humanity had been forty million years on this world of Harmony, more than forty thousand times longer than all of recorded human history on the ancient home planet of Earth. If there was any lesson to be learned, it was that a singer or actress, a politician or soldier, all would be forgotten soon enough. Songs and plays were usually forgotten in a lifetime; borders and constitutions were redrawn within a thousand years at most. But science! Knowledge! If that was what you wrought, it might be remembered forever. That it was you who discovered something, *that* might be forgotten . . . but the thing you learned, it would be remembered, it would have echoes and reverberations down all the years to come. The plants you created, the animals you enhanced, *they* would endure, if you wrought well enough. Hadn't the plant trader Wetchik, dear Rasa's favorite husband, carried Shedemei's Dryflower plant throughout all the lands on the edges of the desert? As long as Dryflower bloomed, as long as its rich and heavy perfume could make a whole house in the desert smell like a jungle garden, Shedemei's works would be alive in the world. As long as scientists all over the world received copies of her reports from the Oversoul, she had the only fame that mattered.

So this was her husband: the works of her own hands. Her creations were a husband that would never betray her, the way Rasa's poor little daughter Kokor had been betrayed. Her research was a husband that would never rampage through the city, raping and looting, beating and burning, the way the men of the Palwashantu had done, until the Gorayni brought order. Her research would never cause any woman to cower in her rooms, all lights off, a pulse in her hands though she doubted she would even know how to use it against an intruder. No one had come, though twice the shouting seemed almost to be in her street. But she would have fought to protect her seeds and embryos. Would have fought and, if she could figure out how to do it, would have killed to protect her life's work.

Yet now this dream had come. A disturbing dream. A powerful dream. And she could not rest until she had told the dream to someone.

To Rasa. Who was there that she could tell, besides Aunt Rasa?

So Shedemei arose, made a half-hearted effort to straighten her hair from sleep, and headed out into the street. She did not think to change her clothing, though she had slept in it; she often slept in her clothing, and only thought to change what she wore on those occasions when she thought to bathe.

There were a good number of people in the street. It had not been so for many days; the fear and distrust that Gaballufix had brought upon the city had kept many indoors. Thus it was almost a relief to see the turbulent flow of pedestrians rushing hither and thither. Almost a pleasure to jostle with them. The dead bodies of the mercenaries no longer hung from the second stories of the buildings, no longer slumped in the streets. They had been hauled away and buried with more or less ceremony in the men's cemeteries outside the city. Only the occasional sight of a pair of men in the uniform of the Basilican guards reminded Shedemei that the city was still under military rule. And the council was set to vote today on how to repay the Gorayni soldiers, send them on their way, and put the city guard back at gate duty. No more soldiers on the streets, then, except when answering an emergency call. All would be well. All would be as before.

A proof of the restoration of peace was the fact that on the porch of Rasa's house were two classes of young girls, listening to teachers and occasionally asking questions. Shedemei paused for just a moment as she so often did, to hear the lessons and remember her own time, so long ago, as a pupil on this very porch, or in the classrooms and gardens within Rasa's house. There were many girls of aristocratic parentage here, but Rasa's was not a house for snobs. The curriculum was rigorous, and there was always room for many girls of ordinary family, or of no family at all. Shedemei's parents had been farmers, not even citizens; only her mother's distant cousinship with a Basilican servant woman had allowed Shedemei to enter the city in the first place. And yet Rasa had taken her in, solely because of an interview when Shedemei was seven. Shedemei couldn't even read at the time, because neither of her parents could read . . . but her mother had ambitions for her, and, thanks to Rasa, Shedemei had been able to fulfil them all. Her mother had lived to see Shedemei in her own rooms, and with her first money from the keen-eyed roach-killing shrew she had developed, Shedemei was able to buy her parents' farm from their landlord, so that they spent their last few years of life as freeholders instead of tenants.

All because Aunt Rasa would take in a poor, illiterate seven-year-old girl because she liked the way the girl's mind worked when she conversed with her. For this alone, Rasa would deserve to be one of the great women of Basilica. And this was why, instead of teaching classes in the higher schools, the only teaching Shedemei did was here in Rasa's house, where twice a year she taught a class of Aunt Rasa's most prized science students. Indeed, officially Shedemei was still a resident here in Rasa's house—she even had a bedroom here, though she hadn't used it since the last time she taught, and always half expected to find it occupied by someone else. It never was, though, no matter how consistently Shedemei slept on the cot in her rooms. Rasa always kept a place for her.

Inside the house, Shedemei soon learned that Rasa's very greatness meant that it would not be possible to see her till later in the day. Though Rasa was not at present a member of the city council, she had been asked to attend this morning's meeting. Shedemei had not expected this. It made her feel lost. For the dream still burned within her, and had to be spoken aloud.

"Perhaps," said the girl who had noticed her and spoken to her, "perhaps there's something I could help you with."

"I don't think so," said Shedemei, smiling kindly. "It was foolishness anyway."

"Foolishness is my specialty," the girl said. "I know you. You're *Shedemei.*" She said the name with such reverence that Shedemei was quite embarrassed.

"I am. Forgive me for not remembering your name. I've seen you here many times before, though."

"I'm Luet," said the girl.

"Ah," said Shedemei. The name brought associations with it. "The waterseer," she said. "The Lady of the Lake."

The girl was clearly flattered that Shedemei knew who she was. But what woman in Basilica had not heard of her? "Not yet," said Luet. "Perhaps not ever. I'm only thirteen."

"No, I imagine you have years yet to wait. And it isn't automatic, is it?"

"It all depends," said Luet, "on the quality of my dreams."

Shedemei laughed. "And isn't that true of all of us?"

"I suppose," said Luet, smiling.

Shedemei turned to go. And then realized again whom she was

talking with. "Waterseer," she said. "You must have some idea of the meanings of dreams."

Luet shook her head. "For dream interpretation you have to pay the truthmongers in the Inner Market."

"No," said Shedemei. "I don't mean that kind of dream. Or that kind of meaning. It was very strange. I never remember my dreams. But this time it felt . . . very compelling. Perhaps even . . . perhaps the kind of dream that I imagine one like *you* would have."

Luet cocked her head and looked at her. "If your dream might come from the Oversoul, Shedemei, then I need to hear it. But not here."

Shedemei followed the younger girl—half my age, she realized—into the back of the house and up a flight of stairs that Shedemei barely knew existed, for this region of the house was used for storage of old artifacts and furniture and classroom materials. They went up two more flights, into the attic space under a roof, where it was hot and dark.

"My dream was not so secret that we needed to come *here* to tell it," said Shedemei.

"You don't understand," said Luet. "There's someone else who must hear, if the dream is truly from the Oversoul." With that, Luet removed a grating from the gable wall and stooped through it, out into the bright air.

Shedemei, half blinded by the sunlight, could not see at first that there was a flat porch-like roof directly under the opening in the wall. She thought that Luet had stepped into nothingness and floated on the air. Then her eyes adjusted and, by squinting, she could see what Luet was walking on. She followed.

This flat area was invisible from the street, or from anywhere else, for that matter. A half dozen different sloping roofs came together here, and a large drainage hole in the center of the flat area made it clear why this place existed. In a heavy rain, it could fill up with roof runoff as much as four feet deep, until the drain could carry the water away. It was more of a pool than a porch.

It was also a perfect hiding place, since not even the residents of Rasa's house had any notion that this place existed—except, obviously, Luet and whoever was hiding here.

Her eyes adjusted further. In the shade of a portable awning sat an older girl who looked enough like Luet that Shedemei was not surprised to hear her introduced as Hushidh the Raveler, Luet's older sister. And across a low table from Hushidh sat a young man of large stature, but still too young to shave.

"Don't you know me, Shedemei?" said the boy.

"I think so," she said.

"I was much shorter when last you lived in Mother's house," he said.

"Nafai," she said. "I heard you had gone to the desert."

"Gone and come again too often, I fear," said Nafai. "I never thought to see a day when Gorayni soldiers would be keeping the gate of Basilica."

"Not for long," said Shedemei.

"I've never heard of the Gorayni giving up a city, once they had captured it," said Nafai.

"But they didn't capture Basilica," said Shedemei. "They only stepped in and protected us in a time of trouble."

"There are ashes from dozens and dozens of bonfires out on the desert," said Nafai, "and yet no sign of any encampment there. The story I hear is that the Gorayni leader pretended to have a huge army, led by General Moozh the Monster, when in fact he had only a thousand men."

"He explained it as a necessary ruse in order to psychologically overwhelm the Palwashantu mercenaries who were running wild."

"Or psychologically overwhelm the city guard?" said Nafai. "Never mind. Luet has brought you here. Do you know why?"

Luet interrupted at once. "No, Nafai. She's not part of that. She came on her own, to tell Mother a dream. Then she thought of telling me, and I wanted both of you to hear, in case it comes from the Oversoul."

"Why *him?*" asked Shedemei.

"The Oversoul speaks to him, as much as to me," Luet said. "He forced her to speak to him, and now they are friends."

"A man *forced* the Oversoul to speak to him?" asked Shedemei. "When did such things start happening in the world?"

"Only recently," said Luet, smiling. "There are stranger things on heaven and earth than are dreamt of in your philosophy, Shedemei."

Shedemei smiled back, but couldn't remember where the quotation came from, or why it should be amusing at this time.

"Your dream," said Luet's sister Hushidh.

"Now I feel silly," said Shedemei. "I've made too much of it, to tell it to such a large audience."

Luet shook her head. "And yet you walked all the way here from—where do you live? The Cisterns?"

"The Wells, but not far from the Cisterns district."

"You come all that way to tell Aunt Rasa," said Luet. "I think this dream may be more important to you than even *you* understand. So tell us the dream, please."

Glancing again at Nafai, Shedemei found she couldn't bring herself to speak.

"Please," said Nafai. "I won't mock your dream, or tell anyone else. I want to hear it only for whatever truth might be in it."

Shedemei laughed nervously. "I just . . . I'm not comfortable speaking in front of a man. It's nothing against you, Aunt Rasa's son, of course I trust you, I just . . ."

"He's *not* a man," said Luet. "Not *really.*"

"Thanks," murmured Nafai.

"He doesn't deal with women as men usually do. And not many days ago, the Oversoul commanded me to take him down to the lake. He sailed it, he floated it right along with me. The Oversoul commanded it, and he was not slain."

Shedemei looked at him in new awe. "Is this the time when all the prophecies come together?"

"Tell us your dream," said Hushidh softly.

"I dreamt—this will sound so silly!—I dreamt of myself tending a garden in the clouds. Not just the plants and animals I'm working with, but every plant and animal I'd ever heard of. Only it wasn't a large garden, just a small one. Yet they all fit within it, and all were alive and growing. I floated along in the clouds—forever, it seemed. Through the longest night in the world, a thousand-year night. And then suddenly it was daylight again, and I could look down off the edge of the cloud and see a new land, a green and beautiful land, and I said to myself—in the dream, you understand—This world has no need of my garden after all. So I left the garden and stepped off the cloud—"

"A dream of falling," said Luet.

"I didn't fall," said Shedemei. "I just stepped out and there I was, on the ground. And as I wandered through the forests and meadows, I realized that in fact many of the plants from my garden *were* needed, after all. So I reached up my hand, and the plants I needed *rained* down on me as seeds. I planted them, and they grew before my eyes. And then I realized that many of my animals were also needed. This was a world that had lost its birds. There were no birds at all, and few reptiles, and none of the beasts of burden or the domesticated meat animals. And yet there were billions of insects for the birds and reptiles to eat, and pastures and meadows to feed the ruminants. So again I lifted my hands toward the clouds, and down from the clouds rained the embryos of the animals I needed, and I watered them and they grew quickly, large and strong. The birds took flight, the cattle and sheep wandered off to the brooks and meadows, and the snakes and lizards all slithered and scampered away. And I heard the words as if someone else had spoken them in my ears, 'No one has ever had such a garden as yours, Shedemei, my daughter.' But it wasn't my mother's or father's voice. And I wasn't sure whether the voice was speaking of my garden in the clouds, or this new world where I was restoring the flora and fauna lost so many years before."

That was the dream, all she could remember of it.

At first they said nothing. Then Luet spoke. "I wonder how you knew that the plants and animals you called down to you from the clouds were flora and fauna that had once lived in that place, but had been lost."

"I don't know," said Shedemei. "But that's how I felt it to be. How I *knew* it to be. These plants and animals were not being introduced, they were being restored."

"And you couldn't tell whether the voice was male or female," said Hushidh.

"The question didn't come up. The voice made me think of my parents, until I realized it wasn't either of them. But I didn't think to notice whether the voice was actually female or male. I can't think which it was even now."

Luet and Hushidh and Nafai began to confer with each other, but they spoke loudly enough for Shedemei to hear—they were not excluding her at all. "Her dream has a voyage in it," said Nafai. "That's consistent with what I was told—and the flora and fauna were being restored. That says Earth to me, and no other place."

"It points that way," said Luet.

"But the clouds," said Hushidh. "What of that? Clouds go from continent to continent, perhaps, but never from planet to planet."

"Even dreams from the Oversoul don't come ready made," said Nafai. "The truth flows into our minds, but then our brain draws on our own mental library to find images with which to express those ideas. A great voyage through the air. Elemak saw it as a strange kind of house; Shedemei sees it as a cloud; I heard it as the voice of the Oversoul, saying we must go to Earth."

"Earth," said Shedemei.

"Father didn't hear it, nor Issib either," said Nafai. "But I'm as sure of it as I am that I'm alive and sitting here. The Oversoul plans to go to Earth."

"That makes sense with your dream, Shedemei," said Luet. "Humankind left the Earth forty million years ago. The deep winter that settled over the Earth may have killed off most species of reptiles and all the birds. Only the fish and the amphibians, and a few small warm-blooded animals would have survived."

"But it's been forty million years since then," said Shedemei. "Earth must have recovered long ago. There should have been ample time for new speciation."

"How long was the Earth encased in ice?" asked Nafai. "How slowly did the ice recede? Where have the landmasses moved in the millions of years since then?"

"I see," said Shedemei. "It's possible."

"But that magic trick," said Hushidh. "Raising her hands and the seeds and embryos coming down, and then watering the *embryos* to make them grow."

"Well, actually, that part made sense to me right off," said Shedemei. "The way we store our samples in the kind of research I do is to dry-crystallize the seeds and embryos. It essentially locks all their body processes into exactly the moment in which the crystallization took place. We store them bone dry, and then when it's time to restore them, we just add distilled water and the crystals decrystallize in a very rapid but non-explosive chain reaction. The whole organism, because it's so small, can be restored to full functions again within a fraction of a second. Of course, with the embryos we have to be able to put them immediately in a liquid growing solution and hook them up to artificial yolks or placentas, so we can't restore very many at a time."

"In order to carry with you enough samples to restore a significant amount of the flora and fauna most likely to have been killed off on Earth, how much equipment would it take?" asked Nafai.

"How much? A lot—a huge amount. A caravan."

"But what if you had to choose the most significant ones—the most useful birds, the most important animals, the plants we most need for food and shelter."

"Then any size would do," said Shedemei. "You just prioritize—if you have only one camel to carry it, then that's how many you take—two drycases per camel. Plus a camel to carry each set of restoration equipment and materials."

"So it could be done," said Nafai triumphantly.

"You believe the Oversoul will send you to Earth?" asked Shedemei.

"We believe it's the most important thing going on right now in the entire world of Harmony," said Nafai.

"My dream?"

"Your dream is part of it," said Luet. "So is mine, I think." She told Shedemei her dream of angels and diggers.

"It sounds plausible enough as a symbol of a world where new-life forms have evolved," said Shedemei. "What you're forgetting is that if your dream comes from the Oversoul, it can't possibly be literally true."

"Why not?" asked Luet. She seemed a little offended.

"Because how would the Oversoul know what's happening on Earth? How would it see a true picture of any species there? The Earth is a thousand lightyears away. There has never been an electromagnetic signal tight and true enough to carry significant transmissions that distance. If the Oversoul gave you that dream, she's only making it up."

"Maybe she's guessing," said Hushidh.

"Maybe he's only guessing about the need for Shedemei's seeds and embryos," said Nafai. "But we must still do what the dream commands. Shedemei must collect these seeds and embryos, and prepare to take them to Earth with us."

Shedemei looked at them in bafflement. "I came to tell Aunt Rasa a dream, not abandon my career on a mad impossible journey. How do you think you're going to Earth? By cloud?"

"The Oversoul has said we're going," said Nafai. "When the time comes, the Oversoul will tell us how."

"That's absurd," said Shedemei. "I'm a scientist. I know the Oversoul exists because our submissions are often transmitted to computers in faraway cities, something that can be done in no other way. But I've always assumed that the Oversoul was nothing more than a computer controlling an array of communications satellites."

Nafai looked at Luet and Hushidh in consternation. "Issib and I struggled to figure that out," he said, "and Shedemei knew it all along."

"You never asked me," said Shedemei.

"We would never have *spoken* to you," said Nafai. "After all, you're *Shedemei.*"

"Just another teacher in your mother's house," said Shedemei.

"Yes, like the sun is just another star in the sky," said Nafai.

Shedemei laughed and shook her head. It had never occurred to her that the young ones would hold her in such awe. She enjoyed knowing it—it felt good to think that someone admired her—but it also made her feel faintly shy and exposed. She had to live up to this image that they had of her, and she was nothing more than a hardworking woman who had been disturbed by a dream.

"Shedemei," said Hushidh, "whether it seems possible or not, the Oversoul is asking us to prepare for this voyage. We would never have dreamed of asking *you*, but the Oversoul has brought you to us."

"Coincidence brought me to you."

"Coincidence is just the word we use when we have not yet discovered the cause," said Luet. "It's an illusion of the human mind, a way of saying, 'I don't know why this happened this way, and I have no intention of finding out.'"

"That was in another context," said Shedemei.

"You had the dream," said Nafai. "You knew it mattered. It made you want to tell Mother. We were here when you arrived, and she was not. But we, too, were brought together by the Oversoul. Don't you see that you have been invited?"

Shedemei shook her head. "My work is here, not on some insane journey whose destination is a thousand lightyears away."

"Your work?" said Hushidh. "What is the value of your work, compared to the task of restoring lost species to Earth? Your work has been notable already, but to be the gardener for a planet . . ."

"*If* it's true," said Shedemei.

"Well," said Nafai, "we've all faced that same dilemma. *If* it's true. None of us can decide that for you, so when you make up your mind, let us know."

Shedemei nodded, but privately she knew that she would do everything within her power to avoid seeing these people again. It was too strange. They made too much of her dream. They demanded too much sacrifice of her.

"She has decided not to help us," said Luet.

"Nothing of the kind!" said Shedemei. But in her heart she wondered, guiltily, How did she know?

"Even if you decide not to go with us," said Nafai, "will you do this much? Will you gather a fair sampling of seeds and embryos—perhaps two camels' load? And the equipment we'll need to restore them? And train some of us in how to do the work?"

"Gladly," said Shedemei. "I should be able to find time over the next several months."

"We don't have *months,*" said Nafai. "We have hours. Or, perhaps, days."

"Don't make me laugh, then," said Shedemei. "What kind of garden am I supposed to assemble in hours?"

"Aren't there bio-libraries here in Basilica?" asked Hushidh.

"Well, yes—that's where I get my starting samples."

"Then couldn't you draw from them, and get most of what you'd need?"

"For two camels' load, I suppose I could get *all* of it. But the equipment to restore them, especially the animal embryos—the only equipment I have is my own set, and it would take months to build more."

"If you come with us," said Luet, "then you could bring your own. And if you don't come with us, you'll have the months to build more."

"You're asking me to give up my own equipment?"

"For the Oversoul," said Luet.

"So *you* believe."

"For Aunt Rasa's son," said Hushidh.

Of course the raveler would know how to break into my heart, thought Shedemei. "If Aunt Rasa asks me to do it for you," said Shedemei, "then I'll do it."

Nafai got a glint in his eye. "What if Mother asked you to go with us?"

"She never would," said Shedemei.

"What if Aunt Rasa was going herself?" asked Luet.

"She never will," said Shedemei.

"That's what Mother herself says," said Nafai, "but we'll see."

"Which of you will learn to use the equipment?" asked Shedemei.

"Hushidh and I," said Luet quickly.

"Then come this afternoon so I can teach you."

"You'll give us the equipment?" asked Hushidh.

Was she delighted, or merely surprised?

"I'll consider it," said Shedemei. "And teaching you how to operate it will cost nothing but time."

With that, Shedemei got up from the carpet and stepped out from under the awning. She looked for the grating through which she had come, but Luet must have replaced it, and she couldn't remember where she needed to go.

She didn't need to say anything, however, for Luet must have noticed her confusion instantly, and now the girl was leading her to the place. The grating hadn't been replaced, it had simply been out of sight behind the roofline. "I know the way from here," said Shedemei. "You needn't come with me."

"Shedemei," said Luet. "I dreamed of *you* once. Not many days ago."

"Oh?"

"I know you'll doubt me, and think I'm saying this only to try to persuade you to come, but it's not a coincidence. I was in the woods, and it was night, and I was afraid. I saw several women. Aunt Rasa, and Hushidh; Eiadh and Dol. And you. I saw you."

"I wasn't there," said Shedemei. "I never go into the woods."

"I know—I told you, it was a dream, though I was awake."

"I mean what I said, Luet. I *never* go into the woods. I never go down to the lake. I'm sure what you do is very important and fine, but it's not part of my life. It's no part of my life."

"Then perhaps," said Luet, "you should change your life."

To that Shedemei had nothing civil to say, so she stepped through the opening in the wall. Behind her she could hear the murmuring sound of their conversation resuming, but she couldn't make out any of the words. Not that she wanted to. This was outrageous, to ask her to do what they were asking her to do.

And yet it had felt so wonderful, in her dream, to reach up and bring down life from the clouds. Why hadn't she just left in that way—as a beautiful dream? Why had she told these children? Why couldn't she just forget what they had said, instead of having these thoughts that now whirled in her mind.

To return to Earth. Home to Earth.

What did that mean? In forty million years, human beings had been content on Harmony. Why now should Earth be calling to her? It was madness, contagious madness in these troubled times.

Still, instead of going home she went to the bio-library, and spent several hours poring over the catalogue, making up a plausible order for two camels' load of crystalized seeds and embryos that might restore the most useful plants and animals to an Earth that lost them long, long ago.

IN THE CITY COUNCIL, AND NOT IN A DREAM

Rasa had spent her life filled with confidence. There was nothing that could happen, she knew, that she could not handle with a combination of wit, kindness, and determination. People could always be persuaded, or if they could not, then they could be ignored and in time they would fade away. This philosophy had brought her to a point where her household was one of the most respected schools in Basilica, despite the fact that it was so new; it had also made her personally influential in every part of the city's life, though she had never held any office. She was consulted on most major decisions of the city council; she served on the governing boards of many of the arts councils; and, above all, she was privately consulted by the women—and, yes, even the men—who made most of the important decisions concerning Basilica's government and business. She was wooed by many men, but stayed happily married to the one man she had ever known who was neither threatened by nor covetous of her power. She had created a perfect role for herself within the city, and loved to live the part.

What had never occurred to her was how fragile it all was. The fabric of her life had been woven on the loom of Basilica, and now that Basilica was breaking apart, her life was fraying, snagging, tearing apart. Her former husband, Gaballufix, had begun the process, back while they were still married, when he attempted to get her to try to change the laws forbidding men to own property in the city. When she realized what his purpose in marrying her had been, she let the contract lapse and remarried Wetchik—permanently, as far as she was concerned. But Gaballufix hadn't given up, building support among the lowest sort of men in the villages outside the walls of the city. Then he brought them in as tolchoks, terrifying the women of the city, and then as mercenary soldiers in those hideous masks, supposedly to protect the city from the tolchoks—but as far as Rasa could tell, the mercenaries *were* the tolchoks in fancy holographic uniforms.

But Gaballufix might have been containable, if the Oversoul hadn't begun to act so strangely. She actually spoke to a man—and not just any man, but Wetchik himself. The problems this caused Rasa were incalculable. Not only was her former husband attacking the ancient laws of the city of women, but now her present husband was telling everyone who would listen that Basilica was going to be destroyed. Her dear friend Dhel remarked to her at the time—only a few weeks ago—that people were surprised that Rasa hadn't also been married to Roptat, the leader of the pro-Gorayni party. "Perhaps you ought to check your bed for some kind of madness-inducing parasite, my dear," said Dhel. She was joking, of course, but it was a painful joke.

Painful, but nothing compared to these past few days. Everything was falling apart. Gaballufix stole Wetchik's fortune and tried to kill his sons—including both of Rasa's own sons. Then the Oversoul commanded Luet to lead Nafai—of all people, *Nafai*, a mere child—down to the forbidden lake, where he floated on the water like a woman—like a waterseer. That same night, no doubt still wet from the lake of peace, Nafai had killed Gab. In one sense it was fair enough, for Gaballufix had tried to kill *him*. But to Rasa it was the most terrible thing she could imagine, her own son murdering her former husband.

Yet even that was only the beginning. For on that same night, she had found out exactly how monstrous her two daughters were. Sevya, sleeping with Kokor's husband—and Kokor then lashing out and nearly killing her. Civilization didn't even reach into my own home. My son a murderer, one daughter an adulterer and the other a murderer in her heart. Only Issib was still civilized. Issib the cripple, she thought bitterly. Perhaps that's what civilization is composed of—cripples who have banded together to try to control the strong. Wasn't that what Gaballufix said once? "In a time of peace, Rasa, you women can afford to surround yourselves with eunuchs. But when the enemy comes from outside, the eunuchs won't save you. You'll wish for real men, then, dangerous men, powerful men—and where will they be, since you've driven them all away?"

Rashgallivak—he was one of the foolish weaklings, wasn't he? One of the "eunuchs," in the sense that Gaballufix meant. He hadn't the strength to control the animals that Gaballufix had brought under harness. And then Hushidh cut loose that harness and the city began to burn. In my own house it happened! Why, again, am I the focal point?

The last insult was the coming of General Moozh, for Rasa knew now that it was he—it could be no one else. So audacious—to march to the city with only a thousand men, coming at a time when no enemy could be resisted, and when anyone willing to pretend to be a friend would be invited in. Rasa was not fooled by his promises. She was not deceived by the fact that his soldiers had withdrawn from the streets. They still held the walls and the gates, didn't they?

And even Moozh was tied to her, just as Wetchik and Gaballufix and Nafai and Rashgallivak had been tied. For he had come with her letter, and it was by using her name that he had first gained entry into the city.

Things could not possibly get any worse. And then, this morning, Nafai and Elemak had come into her house—from the forest side, which meant that they had both been creeping through lands that were forbidden to men. And why had they come? To inform her that the Oversoul required her to leave the city and join her husband in the desert, bringing with her whatever women she thought might be appropriate.

"Appropriate for what?" asked Rasa.

"Appropriate for marrying," said Elemak, "and bearing children in a new land far from here."

"I should leave the city of Basilica, taking some poor innocent women with me, and go out to live like a tribe of baboons in the desert?"

"Not like baboons," Nafai had said helpfully. "We still wear clothing, and none of us barks."

"I will not consider it," said Rasa.

"Yes you will, Mother," said Nafai.

"Are you threatening me?" asked Rasa—for she had heard too many men say such words recently.

"Not at all," said Nafai. "I'm predicting. I'll bet that before a half hour goes by, you'll be considering it, because you know the Oversoul wants you to do it."

And he was right. Not ten minutes. She couldn't get the idea out of her mind.

How did he know? Because he understood how the Oversoul worked. What he didn't know was that the Oversoul was already working on her. When Wetchik first left for the desert, he asked her to come with him. There was no talk of other women then, but when she prayed to the Oversoul, she was answered as clearly as if a voice had spoken in her heart. Bring your daughters, said the Oversoul. Bring your nieces, any who will come. To the desert, to be the mothers of my people.

To the desert! To be animals! In all her life, Rasa had tried to follow the teachings of the Oversoul. But now she asked too much. Who was Rasa, outside of Basilica, outside of her own house? She was no one there. Just Wetchik's wife. It would be men who ruled there—feral men, like Wetchik's son Elemak. He was one frightening boy, that Elemak; she couldn't believe that Wetchik couldn't see how dangerous he was. It would be Elemak the hunter that she'd depend on for food. And what influence would she have there? What council would listen to her? The men would hold the councils, and the women would cook and wash and care for the babies. It would be like primitive times, like animal times. She could not leave the city of women, for if she did, she would cease to be the Lady Rasa and would become a beast.

I only exist in this place. I am only human in this place.

And yet as she walked into the council chamber she knew that "this place" had ceased to be the city of women. As she looked at the frightened, solemn, angry faces in the council, she knew that Basilica as it once had been would never exist again. A new Basilica might rise in its place, but never again would a woman like Rasa be able to raise her daughters and nieces in perfect peace and security. Always there would be men trying to own, to control, to *meddle*. The best she could hope for would be a man like Wetchik, whose kindness would temper his instinct for power. But was there another Wetchik to be found in this world? And even his benign interference would be too much. All would be ruined. All would be poisoned and defiled.

Oversoul! You have betrayed your daughters!

But she did not cry out her blasphemy. Instead she took her place at one of the tables in the middle of the chamber, where non-voting counselors and clerks sat during the meetings. She could feel their eyes upon her. Many, she knew, blamed her for everything—and she could hardly disagree with them. Her husbands, her son, her daughters; her house where Rashgallivak lost control of his soldiers; and, above all, her letter in the hands of the Gorayni general when he came into the city.

The meeting began, and for the first time in Rasa's memory, the rituals of the opening were rushed, and some were eliminated entirely. No one complained. For they all knew that the deadline the council had imposed on the Gorayni to leave the city now loomed as a deadline on themselves—for it was clear now to all of them that the Gorayni did not intend to leave.

The argument soon raged. No one disputed the fact that the Gorayni now were masters of the city. The city debate was whether to defy the general—some called him Moozh, but only in ridicule, for he refused to answer to the name Vozmuzhalnoy Vozmozhno, and yet told them no other name to use for him—or give his occupation a legal gloss. They hated the idea of giving in to him, but if they did, there was a hope that he'd let them continue to govern the city in exchange for letting him use Basilica as a military base for his operations against the Cities of the Plain and, no doubt, Potokgavan. Yet by making his occupation legal, as he had requested, they gave him power in the long run to destroy them.

Still, what was the alternative? He had made no threats. In fact, all he had sent them was a very respectful letter: "Because my troops have not yet succeeded in abating the danger in Basilica, we are reluctant to abandon our dear friends to the return of such chaos as we found on our arrival. Therefore if you invite us to stay until such time as order is fully restored, we are willing to become your obedient servants for the indefinite future." On its face, the letter portrayed the Gorayni as being docile as lambs.

But they knew by now that nothing with the Gorayni was what it seemed. Oh, they bowed to every order or request of the city council, promising to obey. But only the orders that suited their purpose were actually carried out. And the city guard, too, was unreliable, for their officers had begun practically to worship the Gorayni general, and now were following his example of swearing obedience and then doing as they liked. Oh, the general was a clever man! He provoked no one, he argued with no one, he agreed with everything that was said . . . and yet he was immovable, doing all that he pleased, while never giving them anything they could attack him for. Everyone in the council chamber must have felt it as keenly as Rasa did, the slipping away of their own power, the centering of the city on the will of this one man, and all without any overt word or deed of his.

How does he do it? Rasa wondered. How does he master people without bluster or bullying? How does he make people fear him or love him, not in spite of his ruthlessness but because of it?

Maybe it is simply that he knows so clearly how he wants things to be, she thought. Maybe the fact that he believes in his vision of the world so intensely makes it impossible for those around him not to believe as well. Maybe we're all so hungry for someone to tell us what is true, what we can *count on*, that we'll accept even a vision that makes us weak and him strong, just for the sake of having a secure world at all.

"We are only a few minutes from the deadline," said old Kobe. "And in all our discussion this morning we have heard nothing from the Lady Rasa."

A murmur of approval arose, but it was immediately drowned in a growl of anger. "We shouldn't hear from her except at her trial!" cried one woman. "She brought all this on us!"

Rasa calmly turned and looked at the woman who spoke. It was Frotera, of course, the lady of another teaching household, who had long been envious of Rasa. "My Lady Frotera," Rasa said, "I fear you may be right."

That silenced them.

"Do you think I haven't also looked and seen what you all can see? Which of the calamities that has befallen us has not been tied to me? My son is accused of murder, my daughters have betrayed each other, Rashgallivak tried to drag them from my own house, my beloved city has been torn by riot and fire, and the army that squats in the gates of Basilica shows you a letter that I wrote. And I did write it, though I never dreamed that it would be used as he has used it. Sisters, all of this is true, but does it mean I have brought all of this upon us? Or does it mean that it has fallen more heavily on me than on any except those whose loved ones perished in the rioting?"

It made them think; ah, yes, she still had the power to tell them a story and make them see, at least for a moment, through her eyes.

"Sisters, if I believed that I was truly the cause of all the evil that has come to Basilica, I would leave at once. I love Basilica too much to be the cause of its downfall. But I am not the cause. The first cause was the greed of Gaballufix—and he married me as his first attempt to make an inroad against our ancient laws. Was it my husband who brought private soldiers into this city? No. It was a man whom I had *refused* to have as my husband. I repudiated Gaballufix while many of you on this council kept voting to tolerate his abuses! Do not forget that!"

Oh, they didn't forget, as they shrank back in their seats.

"Now the Gorayni have come with my letter. But I wrote that letter to help a young Basilican guard obtain refuge with the Gorayni. I knew he was in danger from Rashgallivak's mercenaries, and he had been kind to my son, so I gave him what small protection I could. Now I see that this was a terrible mistake. My letter alerted them to our weakness, and they came to exploit it. But I didn't create our weakness, and if the Gorayni hadn't come, would we be in *better* condition this morning than we are now? Would we even be holding this meeting, or would we all be victims of rape and plunder by the Palwashantu mercenaries? Would our city be in ashes? So tell me, sisters, which is better, to be in a bad situation, yet with *some* hope, or to be destroyed, powerless, utterly hopeless?"

Again a murmur, but she was carrying them. Only rarely had she spoken at such length or with such force—she had long since learned that she remained more powerful by never openly committing herself to anything, but rather working behind the scenes. Still, she had spoken often enough to know how to bend them, at least a little, to her will. It was a power that would be less effective every time she used it, but this was a time when she must use it or lose everything.

"If we defy him, what will happen then? Even if he keeps his word and leaves, can any of you say that our city guard will be as docile as they once were? And I don't believe that he *will* keep his word. Have you ever heard of General Vozmuzhalnoy Vozmozhno giving up one village, one field, one *pebble* that he has conquered?" A growing murmur. "Yes, it *is* General Moozh—we'd be fools to imagine otherwise for a moment. What other Gorayni general would have the audacity to do what he has done? Don't you see how daring and brilliant his plan has been? He came here with only a thousand men, but for a few crucial hours we believed he had a hundred times that number. He has been subservient and obsequious, and yet he has deployed his soldiers where he wanted them, seduced our city guard, and seized whatever supplies he needed. Always he apologizes and explains. Always he keeps us believing that he means well. But he is a liar with every breath he takes, and nothing that he says to us is true. He means to add Basilica to the Gorayni Empire. He will *never* let us go."

Loud muttering filled the room as she waited. Several of the women wept. "Defy him then!" one of the councilors cried.

"And what good would defiance do?" asked Rasa. "How many of us would die? And to what purpose? A fifth of our city is already in ashes. We have already huddled in terror as drunken men rampaged through our city. What would happen if now the plunderers were sober? If they were the same disciplined killers who nailed the rioters to the walls with their own knives? There'd be no refuge for us then!"

"So . . . what do you propose we do, Lady Rasa?"

"Give him what he has asked for. Permission to stay. Only make provision for his soldiers to be quartered outside the walls of the city. Make them take the same oaths that men are required to take when they become our husbands—to stay out of the forbidden parts of the city, to refrain from attempting to own any real property, and to leave when their term is up."

A murmur of approval.

"Will he accept it, Lady Rasa?"

"I have no idea," she said. "But so far, he has made an effort at least to *seem* to comply with our wishes. Let us make our offer as public as possible, and then hope he'll find it more convenient to adhere to its terms than not."

Rasa's exhortations were too successful by half. Yes, they approved her proposal, almost unanimously. But they also appointed her the ambassador to deliver their "invitation" to General Moozh. It was not an interview she looked forward to, but she had no time even to wonder what she ought to say or how she ought to act. The invitation had to be delivered personally and immediately; it was printed out, signed, and sealed on the spot, and the council watched as she left the chamber with the document in hand, minutes before the deadline that they themselves had set.

It was not Mebbekew's finest morning. He had dutifully trudged through the forbidden slopes of Basilica as Nafai led the way, just as he had followed Elemak all the way from the desert around the city to the northern woods. But when they came within sight of Rasa's house, Mebbekew slipped away. He had no intention of being a pawn in *their* plans. If they were here to do some wife-finding, Mebbekew would pick his own, thank you kindly. He would certainly *not* tag along behind his older brother, taking second choice forever; nor would he swallow the humiliation of going into his little brothers' mother's house and pleading with *her* to give up one of her precious nieces. Elemak had his heart set on that porcelain doll, Eiadh . . . well, that was his privilege. Mebbekew preferred women with blood in their veins, women who grunted and growled when they made love, women of vigor and strength. Women who loved Mebbekew.

Well, he found out about vigor and strength, right enough! The fires had been worst in Dolltown and Dauberville, so few of his old lovers were in the houses where he had known them. The few that he could find were *glad* to see him. They were all over him with tears and kisses, eager to have him stay with them. Stay with them *where?* In a half-burnt house with no running water? And *why* did they want him? So he could do all the brute man-labor required to rebuild, to repair; and so he could be their guardian. What a joke! Mebbekew, standing guard over some poor frightened girl! No doubt they would have rewarded him generously with their bodies if he had played the role they scripted for him, but it wasn't worth it—*no* woman was worth it right now, if her needs were even greater than his own. He wasn't here to be a protector or a provider, he was here to find protection and providence.

So he left them with a kiss and a promise, without even staying long enough to bathe or eat, because he knew that if he once got within their clinging embrace these women-in-need would make of him a husband. He had no intention of husbanding himself to women who had nothing to offer him but work and trouble!

As for suggesting to any of his old lovers that she give up everything in Basilica and come wander with him in the desert until they found a promised land, meanwhile having a passel of babies in order to populate their new home—it never seemed to come up in any of his conversations. Not that some of them wouldn't have done it. As they surveyed the ruin of their once-frivolous lives in Basilica, as they remembered the fear of that awful night of rioting, and then the horror of the dead bodies pinned to the walls by the Gorayni, the idea of striding out into the desert with a *real* man to lead and protect them would appeal to some of them. For the first few days, anyway; then they'd realize that the desert was lonely and no fun at all, and they'd be as eager to return to Basilica, ruined or not, as Mebbekew himself was.

It hardly mattered. He never intended to make such a proposal to any of his womenfriends. Let Elemak and Nafai play along with Father and have their stupid visions if they wanted to. All Mebbekew wanted was some woman to take him in to a nice, clean house and a nice clean bed, and hide him and console him for the loss of his fortune until Elemak and Nafai went away. Why should Mebbekew ever go out in the desert again? Basilica might be half-burnt and terrorized and occupied by Gorayni troops, but the toilets and baths still worked in *most* houses, and the food was fresh and there was plenty of pleasure and fun in the old town yet.

Yet even that limited plan wouldn't have worked for long, he gradually came to realize. During his early-morning wanderings through Dolltown, he realized that he couldn't hide in Basilica for long. For he had entered the city illegally, without being recorded, and somewhere along the line he'd get picked up and taken in. The city guard were quite active in the streets now, more than he'd ever seen, and they were demanding thumbscans and eyescans at checkpoints on several streets. He was bound to be picked up one of these days. Indeed, it wasn't easy getting from Dolltown to Rasa's house on Rain Street.

Yes, Rasa's house. It galled him, but he had tried everything else; so here he was, ready to surrender completely to his brothers and his father and their idiotic plans.

Standing in the street, looking at the front of Rasa's house, ready to give in—and yet not ready. It was unbearable. Humiliating. Knock, knock. Good morning, I'm Rasa's sons' half-brother, and I'm here because all my ex-lovers sent me packing and so I'd be grateful if Rasa and my half-brothers would take me in and give me something to eat and drink, not to mention a long hot shower, before I die.

It was a hideous scene to imagine, and even though he knew he had to do it, Mebbekew had never acquired much practice in doing unpleasant things just because he knew he had to do them. So instead he did what he *usually* did under such circumstances. He waited, just within reach of his painful goal, and then proceeded to do nothing.

He did nothing—suffering imagined torments all the while—for at least twenty minutes, watching the classes of young girls and boys that were meeting on the porch. Now and then he could even catch a word that was said, and so he tried to guess the subjects being taught and what the particular lesson was. It took his mind off his troubles for a moment or two, at least. The nearer class, he decided, was studying either geometry or organic chemistry or building with blocks.

A young woman left one of the classes, jogged down the steps of the porch, and then strode purposefully toward him. No doubt she had seen him watching the porch and decided he was a would-be child molester or burglar. He thought of turning and leaving before she reached him—which was what she almost certainly expected him to do —but instead he studied her face and realized that he recognized her.

"Good morning," she said icily, as soon as she was close enough to say it without shouting.

Mebbekew wasn't worried about the prospect of an argument. He had never yet met a young and beautiful woman he couldn't warm up quickly enough, if he tried hard enough to find out what she hungered for, and then gave it to her. It was always a pleasure dealing with a woman he had never worked on before. Especially because he recognized her at once—or at least saw a resemblance.

"Didn't you used to be Dolya?" he asked.

Her face turned scarlet, but her expression became colder and angrier. So he was right—she *was* Dol. "Shall I send for the Guard to send you away?"

"I saw you in *Pirates* and *West Wind*. You were brilliant," he said.

Her blush deepened and her expression softened.

"You had the talent," he went on. "It wasn't just looks. It wasn't just that you were young and sweet. I never understood why they didn't give you adult parts as you got older. I know you could have carried it off. It was damned unfair."

And now her expression wasn't angry at all, but rather bemused. "I have never heard anyone engage in such transparent, cynical flattery," she said.

"Ah, but I meant every word. Dolya—I suppose you go by the adult name, Dol, now?"

"To my friends, I do. Others call me ma'am."

"Ma'am, I hope that someday I can earn the right to be your friend. In the meantime, I was hoping you might tell me if my half-brothers Elemak and Nafai are in Rasa's house."

She eyed him up and down. "I don't see that you look all that much like either of them."

"Ah, but now you flatter *me*," he said.

She laughed a little and stepped toward him, offering her hand. "I'll take you in, if you're really Mebbekew."

He withdrew a pace from her. "Don't touch me! I'm filthy. Two days' traveling in the desert isn't the best perfume, and if my body's stench didn't kill you my breath would."

"I didn't expect you to be a bouquet," she said. "I'll risk taking your hand to lead you in."

"Then you have courage to match your beauty," he said, taking her hand. "By the Oversoul," he whispered, "your hand is cool and soft to touch."

She laughed again—an actress with as much experience as Dol had had, back when she was famous, could never be fooled by flattery. But Mebbekew figured that it had been years now since anyone had bothered to flatter her at all, so the very fact that he thought it was worth trying would be a sort of meta-flattery against which she wouldn't be able to protect herself. And, indeed, it seemed to be working quite well.

"You don't have to say such things," she said. "Aunt Rasa left instructions for you to be admitted as soon as you—how did she say it—as soon as you 'bothered to show up.'"

"If I had known I'd find you here, ma'am, I'd have come much sooner. And as you say, I don't have to flatter anybody to get into Rasa's house this morning. So what I say to you now isn't flattery. It's my own heart. When I was a boy I fell in love with the image of Dolya on the stage. Now I see you with a man's eyes. I see you as a woman. And I know that your beauty has only increased. I never knew you were one of Rasa's nieces or I would have stayed in school."

"I *was* her niece. I'm a teacher here now. Comportment, that sort of thing. I've been teaching Eiadh in particular. You know, the one your brother Elemak is wooing."

"It's just like Elemak to woo the pale copy, while he ignores the original." Mebbekew deliberately kept his eyes on her face, but not on her eyes—instead he studied her lips, her hair, all her features, knowing that she would see how his eyes moved, how he was drinking her in. "Elemak's only my half-brother, by the way," said Mebbekew. "When I'm all cleaned up you'll see that I'm much better looking."

She laughed, but he knew he had won her interest—he had long since learned that flattery always works, and that even the most outrageously dishonest praise is believed, if you repeat it and elaborate on it enough. In this case, though, he really didn't have to lie. Dol *was* beautiful, though of course nowhere near as lovely as she had been when she was an ethereal child of thirteen. Still, she had grace and poise and a smile that dazzled, and, now that he had been working on her for a few minutes, her eyes were bright and wide whenever she looked at him. It was desire. He had kindled desire in her. It wasn't the desire for passion, of course; rather it was the desire to hear more of his praise for her beauty, more of his verbal petting. Yet he knew from experience that it would be easy enough to get from here to there, if he wasn't too tired after breakfast and a bath.

She showed him to her own bedroom—a good sign—where the servants ran a bath for him. He was still in the water, luxuriating in his cleanliness, when she came back in with a tray of food and a pitcher of water. She had brought it with her own hands, and they were alone. All the time she chattered—not nervously, either, but comfortably. That was Mebbekew's greatest talent, that women so easily became comfortable with him that they talked to him with the kind of candor they usually had only with their girlfriends.

As she talked, he rose up out of the water; when she turned around from setting the tray on her dresser, she saw him toweling himself down, quite naked. She gasped prettily and looked away.

"I'm sorry," he said. "It didn't occur to me that you'd be startled. You must have seen so many men in your days as an actress—I've been on the stage, too, and no one is shy or modest backstage."

"I was young," said Dol. "They always protected me in those days."

"I feel like some kind of beast, then," said Mebbekew. "I didn't mean to shock you."

"No," she said. "No, I'm not shocked."

"The trouble is that I haven't anything to wear. I don't think it would be helpful to put my dirty clothes back on."

"The servants already took your clothes to be washed. I have a robe for you, though."

"One of yours? I doubt it will fit *me.*" All this time, of course, he had continued toweling, still making no effort to cover himself. And as they talked, she had turned back around and now was looking at him quite frankly. Since things were going so smoothly and he anticipated making love to this woman very soon, his body had become quite alert. As soon as he caught her looking at his crotch, he pretended to notice for the first time and made a show of putting the towel in front of himself. "I'm sorry," he said. "I've been alone on the desert so long, and you're so beautiful—I meant no insult."

"I'm not insulted," she said. And he could see the desire in *her* eyes, too. She wanted more than pretty words from him now. As he had guessed, she probably didn't get many suitors these days. With her beauty, she'd have had no lack of lovers in Dolltown, but as a teacher in Rasa's house the opportunities would be much more limited. So she was almost certainly as eager as he was.

This was what he had come back to Basilica for. Not those frightened, hungry women in Dolltown, who needed him to be strong and dependable, but *this* woman, who needed him only to be passionate and flattering and fun. Dol felt herself to be safe and comfortable enough in Rasa's house that she could still be what Basilican women were *supposed* to be—self-supporting providers for men, needing nothing more from their lovers than a little pleasure and attention.

She brought him her robe. It probably could have fit well enough, but he made a show of jamming his arm so far in the sleeve that it barely passed his elbow. "Oh, that won't do," she said.

"It hardly matters by now," he said. "I don't exactly have any secrets from you anymore!"

Of course, he had dropped the towel to try on the robe. He bent over to pick it up, even as he was taking the robe off his arm. But when he stood again, she took both the towel and the robe away from him. "You're right," she said. "There's little point in trying for modesty now." She tossed the robe and towel into a corner and then brought him a handful of grapes from the food tray on the dresser. "Here," she said.

She held out the grape, not to his hand, but to his lips. He leaned forward farther than he needed to, and got her fingers into his mouth along with the grape. She let her fingers linger in his mouth as he slowly pulled the grape away. At last he bit down on the grape and felt the juice of it squirt inside his mouth. It was tart and sweet and delicious. He sat on the bed and she fed him another, and then another. But the rest of the grapes ended up on the floor.

Moozh had waited with great anticipation to meet Lady Rasa at last, and she did not disappoint him. He had installed himself in Gaballufix's house—the symbolism was deliberate—and he knew that she would certainly see the true meaning of his residence here. Lady Rasa would not be a *complete* fool, that much he was sure of, from what he had heard about her. All that remained now was to see which of several plans he ought to follow with her. She might be turned into an ally. She might be turned into a dupe. She might, of course, be an implacable enemy. No matter which, he would make use of her.

She did not carry herself with any particular majesty; she made no

attempt to entice or intimidate him. But that was just about the only
way a woman could impress him anymore. He had been worked on by
the finest court women in Gollod, but it was plain that Rasa had no
interest in working on him. Rather she spoke with him as with an
equal, and he liked it. He liked *her*. It would be a good game.

"Of course I want to accept the invitation of the city council," he
said. "We are only too happy to help this beautiful city maintain order
and security while rebuilding from these unfortunate events of the past
weeks. But I have a problem that perhaps you can help me with."

He could see from the look on her face that she had expected more
demands from him—and he knew, too, that she had no illusions about
the fact that he was in a position to make demands, and make them
stick, too.

"You see," he said, "the traditional way for a Gorayni general to
reward his men after a great victory is to divide up the conquered
territory and give them land and wives."

"But you have not conquered Basilica," said Rasa pointedly.

"Exactly!" he said. "You see my dilemma. My men performed with
extraordinary heroism and discipline in this campaign, and their victory over the ruffians and rioters was complete. And yet I lack a means
to reward them!"

"Our treasury is deep," said Rasa. "I'm sure the city council can
make each of your thousand men as rich as you please."

"Money?" asked Moozh. "Oh, you hurt me deeply. Me and my men
alike. We are not mercenaries!"

"You accept land, but not the money with which to buy land?"

"Land is a matter of title and honor. A landed man is a lord. But
money—that would be like calling my soldiers *tradesmen.*"

She gazed at him for a moment, and then said, "General
Vozmuzhalnoy Vozmozhno, does the Imperator know that you call
these men *your* soldiers? *Your* men?"

Moozh felt a sudden thrill of fear. It was delicious indeed—it had
been a long time since he had sat across a table from someone who
knew how to take the initiative away from him. And she had struck
immediately at his weakest point. For not only had he defied the Imperator's orders about not making any offensive maneuvers, he had also
left behind the corpses of the Imperator's public and private spies to
come here. His greatest danger at the moment came from the Imperator, who would surely by now have heard of his venture. Moozh knew

the Imperator well enough to know that he would not act rashly—
indeed, that was the Imperator's primary fault, that he was terrified of
risk—but already a new intercessor would certainly be on his way
southward, and not without temple troops to back him up. Either
Moozh would be able to put a good face on things and win back the
Imperial trust, or he would have to commit himself to open rebellion
with only a thousand troops and a hundred kilometers deep in hostile
territory. It was not a good moment for him to face an opponent who
understood exactly what his weakness was.

"When I call them mine," said Moozh, "of course I recognize that
they are mine only as long as the Imperator permits me to be his
servant."

"I notice that you don't deny that you *are* Vozmuzhalnoy
Vozmozhno."

He shrugged. "I recognize that you are far too clever for me. Why
should I try to conceal my identity from *you?*"

She frowned. His flattery and his frank admission had set her back a
bit. Now she would no doubt be wondering why he so willingly admitted his true name, and why he was calling her clever. She would
assume that because he called her clever, it must mean she had *not*
been clever at all. Thus she would no longer trust her belief that the
way to get at him was by exploiting differences between him and the
Imperator. He had long since learned that one of the best ways to
disarm a genuinely clever opponent was to make him mistrust his own
strengths, and it seemed to be working well enough with Rasa.

"Cleverness doesn't enter into it," she said. "Truth is what matters. I
don't believe there's a word of truth in what you say. You don't usually
reward your soldiers with land, or you'd have no soldiers left. Your
officers, perhaps. But this talk of land is just your first bid in an effort to
destroy the land law of the city of women. Let me guess how the game
goes: I return to the council with your humble request, and they send
me back with an offer to settle your men outside the city. You praise
our generosity, and then point out that your men could never be content as second-class citizens of a land they had rescued from destruction. How could he explain to Gorayni soldiers that they could never
own land inside the city? Then you would propose a compromise—just
to allow them and us to both save face. Your compromise would be that
Gorayni soldiers who married Basilican women would be allowed to
hold half-ownership with them of their land inside the city. The

women would, of course, remain completely in control of the land, but your soldiers could keep their self-respect."

"You have a gift of prescience," said Moozh.

"Not so—I'm only improvising," she said. "Half-rights in property would lead within weeks to a series of opportune marriages, and then there'd be pressure for an equal vote—especially since you will have proved that your men are meek and obedient husbands who make no effort to control the property in which they have a titular half-interest. How many steps from there to the day when women have *no* vote, and all the property of Basilica is owned by men?"

"My dear lady, you misjudge me."

"You don't have much time," said Rasa. "Your Imperator will certainly have representatives here within two weeks at the latest."

"All Gorayni armies travel with Imperial representatives."

"Not yours," said Rasa. "Or the city guard would know it. We've read accounts here of how your army works, and there is no intercessor's tent. Some of your soldiers feel the lack of confession quite keenly."

"I have nothing to fear from the coming of an intercessor."

"Then why did you try to fool me into thinking you had one here already? No, General Vozmuzhalnoy Vozmozhno, I think you have to move swiftly indeed to consolidate your position here before you face the challenge of the Imperator. I think you don't have time to deal with any kind of uprising, either—it has to be settled peacefully and at once."

So she had not been deflected at all by his flattery. The thrill of fear once again pulsed through him. "Ma'am, you are wise indeed. It is possible that the Imperator will misconstrue my actions, even though my motive was purely to serve him. But you're mistaken to think it will take many gradual steps to consolidate my position here."

"You think not?" asked Rasa.

"It won't take many marriages, I think, but only one." He smiled. "Mine."

At last he had succeeded in startling *her*. "Aren't you already married, sir?" she asked.

"As a matter of fact I am not," said Moozh. "I have never been married. Until now it has always been politically preferable."

"And you think that your marriage to a Basilican woman will solve everything for you? Even if they grant you a special exception and let you share in your wife's property, there's no one woman in Basilica who controls so much property that it would make any difference to you."

"I don't intend to marry for property."

"For what, then?"

"For influence," he said. "For prestige."

She studied his face for a moment. "If you think *I* have that kind of influence or prestige, you're a fool."

"You are a striking woman, and I confess that you are of the right age for me—mature and accomplished. To marry you would make life a dangerous and engrossing game, and you and I would both enjoy it. Alas, though, *you* are already married, even if your husband is rumored to be a mad prophet hiding in the desert. I don't believe in breaking up happy families. Besides, you have too many opponents and enemies in this city for you to be a useful consort."

"Imperators have consorts, General Vozmuzhalnoy Vozmozhno; generals have wives."

"Please, call me Moozh," he said. "It's a nickname that I only permit my friends to use."

"I am not your friend."

"The nickname means 'husband,'" he said.

"I know what it means, and neither I nor any woman of Basilica will ever call you that to your face."

"Husband," said Moozh, "and Basilica is my bride. I will wed her, I will bed her, and she will bear me many children, this fair city. And if she doesn't take me willingly as her husband, I will have her anyway, and in the end she *will* be docile."

"In the end this city will have your balls on a plate, General," she retorted. "The last lord of this house discovered that, when he tried to do what you are doing."

"But he was a fool," said Moozh. "I know it, because he lost *you.*"

"He didn't lose *me*," said Rasa. "He lost himself."

He smiled at her. "Farewell, ma'am," he said. "Till we meet again."

"I doubt we will," she said.

"Oh, I'm sure we'll converse again."

"After I return and tell them what you really are, there'll be no more emissaries from the city council."

"But my dear lady," said Moozh, "did you think I'd have spoken to you so freely, if I intended to let you speak again to the council?"

Her face blanched. "So you *are* no different from any of the other bullies. Like Gaballufix and Rashgallivak, you love to hear your own bluster. You think it makes you manly."

"Not so," said Moozh. "Their posturing and boasting came to nothing—they did it because they feared their own weakness. I never posture and I never boast, and when I decide what is necessary I do it. You will be escorted from here to your own house, which is already surrounded by Gorayni troops. All the non-resident children in your house have been sent safely home; the others will be kept indoors, since from this point on no one will be allowed to enter or leave your house. We will, of course, deliver food to you, and I believe your water supply is entirely provided by wells and a clever rain collection system."

"Yes," she said. "But the city will never stand for your arresting me."

"You think not?" asked Moozh. "I have already sent one of the Basilican guard to inform the city council that I have arrested you in their name, in order to protect the city from your plotting."

"My *plotting!*" she cried, rising to her feet.

"You came to me and suggested that I abolish the city council and establish one man as king of Basilica. You even had a candidate in mind —your husband, Wetchik, who already had his sons murder his chief rivals and even now is waiting in the desert for me to call for him to come and rule the city as a vassal of the Imperator."

"Monstrous lies! No one will believe you!"

"You know that your statement is false, even as you make it," said Moozh. "You know that there are many on that council who will be only too happy to believe that all your actions have been inspired by private ambition, and that you have been involved in causing all your city's misfortunes from the start."

"You'll see that the women of Basilica are not so easily fooled."

"You have no idea, Lady Rasa, how happy I would be if the women of Basilica proved to be so wise that I could not deceive them. I have longed all my life to find people of such exemplary wisdom. But I think I have not found them here, with the single exception of yourself. And *you* are completely under my control." He laughed merrily. "By the Incarnation himself, ma'am, after conversing with you this morning it terrifies me to know that you are even *alive*. If you were a man with an army I would be afraid to campaign against you. But you are not a man with an army, and so you pose no threat to me—not anymore."

She rose from her chair. "Are you finished?"

"Do your household a favor—don't try to send anyone out with secret messages. I *will* catch anyone you send, and then I'll probably have to do something grisly like delivering the next day's rations to your house sewn up inside your would-be messenger's skin."

"You are exactly the reason why Basilica banned men from the city in the first place," she said coldly.

"And you are exactly the reason why the city of women is an abomination in the sight of God," he answered. But his voice was warm with admiration—even affection—for the truth was that this woman alone had taught him that the city of women was not as weak and effeminate as he had imagined all these years.

"God!" she said. "God means nothing to you. The way you think, the way you live—I daresay that you spend every moment of your life trying to flout the will of the Oversoul and unmake all her works in this world."

"You are close to the mark, dear lady," he said. "Closer than you ever imagined. Now do please bow to the inevitable and make no trouble for my poor soldiers who have the unpleasant duty of taking you home under public arrest through the streets of Basilica."

"What trouble could I make?"

"Well, for one thing, you could try to shout some ridiculous revolutionary message to the people you pass. I would recommend silence."

She nodded gravely. "I will accept your recommendation. You can be sure that I'll despise you in silence all the way home."

It took six of them to walk her home. His lies about her had been so persuasive that crowds gathered in many places to vilify her as a traitor to her city. That was bad enough, to be unjustly loathed by her beloved city, but it didn't gall her half as much as the other shouts—the cheers for General Moozh, the savior of Basilica.

5

Husbands

Her name was Torstiga in the language of her homeland, but she had been so long away from *that* place, far in the east, that she didn't even remember the language of her childhood. She had been sold into slavery by her uncle when she was seven years old, was carried west to Seggidugu, and there was sold again. Slavery was not intolerable—her mistress was strict but not unfair, and her master kept his hands to himself. It could have been much worse, she well knew—but it was not freedom.

She prayed constantly for freedom. She prayed to Fackla, the god of her childhood, and nothing happened. She prayed to Kui, the god of Seggidugu, and still she was a slave. Then she heard stories of the Oversoul, the goddess of Basilica, the city of women, a place where no man could own property and every woman was free. She prayed and prayed, and one day when she was twelve, she went mad, caught up in the trance of the Oversoul.

Since many slaves pretended to be god-mad in order to win their freedom, Torstiga was locked up and starved during her frenzy. She did not mind the darkness of the tiny cubicle where they confined her, for she was seeing the visions that the Oversoul put into her mind. Only when the visions ended at last did she notice her own physical discomfort. Or at least, that was how it seemed to her mistress, for she cried out again and again from her cubicle: "Thirsty! Thirsty! Thirsty!"

They did not understand that she was crying out that one word, not because she needed to drink—though indeed she was far along with dehydration—but because it was her name, Torstiga, translated into the language of Basilica. The language of the Oversoul. She called her own name because she had lost herself in the midst of her visions; she hoped that if she called out loud enough and long enough, the girl she used to be might hear her, and answer, and perhaps come back and live in her body once again.

Later she came to understand that her true self had never left her, but in the confusion and ecstasy and terror of her first powerful visions she was transformed and never again would she be the twelve-year-old girl she once had been. When they let her out of her confinement, warning her not to pretend to be god-mad again, she didn't argue with them or protest that she had been sincere. She simply drank what they gave her to drink, and ate until the food they set before her was gone, and then returned to her labor.

But soon they began to realize that for once a slave was *not* pretending. She looked at her master one day and began to weep, and would not be comforted. That afternoon, as he oversaw construction of a fine new house for one of the richest men of the city, he was knocked down by a stone that got away from the crew that was trying to manhandle it into place. Two slaves suffered broken bones in the mishap, but Thirsty's master fell into the street and a passing horse stamped on his head. He lingered for a month, never regaining consciousness, taking small sips that his wife gave him every half hour, but vomiting any food she managed to get down his throat. He starved to death.

"Why did you weep that day?" his widow demanded.

"Because I saw him fallen in the street, trampled by a horse."

"Why didn't you warn him?"

"The Oversoul showed it to me, mistress, but she forbade me to tell it."

"Then I hate the Oversoul!" cried the woman. "And I hate you, for your silence!"

"Please don't punish me, mistress," said Thirsty. "I wanted to tell you, but she wouldn't let me."

"No," said the widow. "No, I won't punish you for doing what the goddess demanded of you."

After the master was buried, his widow sold most of the slaves, for she could no longer maintain a fine household in the city, and would have to return to her father's estate. Thirsty she did not sell. Instead she gave her her freedom.

Her freedom, but nothing else. Thus Thirsty began her time as a wilder, not because she was driven into the desert by the Oversoul, but because she was hungry, and in every town the other beggars drove her away, not because her small appetite would have deprived them of anything, but rather because she was slight and meek and so she was one of the few creatures in the world they had the power to drive away.

Thus she found herself in the desert, eating locusts and lizards and drinking from the rank pools of water that lingered in the shade and in caves after each rainstorm. Now she lived her name indeed, but in time she became a wilder in fact, and not just in appearance and habits of life. For she *was* dirty, and she *was* naked, and she starved in the desert like any proper holy woman—but she raged against the Oversoul in her heart, for she was bitterly angry at the way the Oversoul had answered her prayer. I asked for freedom, she howled at the Oversoul. I never asked you to kill my good master and impoverish my good mistress! I never asked you to drive me out into the desert, where the sun burns my skin except where I've managed to produce enough sweat that the dust will cling to my naked body and protect me. I never asked for visions or prophecies. I asked only to be a free woman, like my mother was. Now I can't even remember her name.

The Oversoul was not done with her, though, and so she could not yet have peace. When she was only fourteen years old, by her best reckoning, she had a dream of a place that was mountainous and yet so lush with life that even the face of the sheerest cliff was thickly green with foliage. She saw a man in her vision, and the Oversoul told her that this was her true husband. She cared nothing for that news—what she saw was that this man had food in his hand, and a stream of water ran at his feet. So she headed north until she found the green land, and found the stream. She washed herself, and drank and drank and drank. And then one day, clean and satisfied, she saw him leading his horse down to the water.

Almost she ran away. Almost she fled from the will of the Oversoul, for she didn't want a husband now, and there had been berries enough by the riverbank that she hungered for nothing that he might offer.

But he saw her, and gazed at her. She covered her breasts with her hands, knowing vaguely that this was what men desired, for that was what they looked at; she had no experience of men, for the Oversoul had protected her from desert wanderers until now.

"God forbids me to touch you," he said softly. He spoke in the language of Basilica, but with an accent very different from the speech of Seggidugu.

"That is a lie," she said. "The Oversoul has made me your wife."

"I have no wife," he answered. "And if I did, I wouldn't take a puny child like you."

"Good," she said. "Because, *I* don't want *you*, either. Let the Oversoul find you an *old* woman if she wants you to have a wife."

He laughed. "Then we're agreed. You're safe from me."

He took her home, and clothed her, and fed her, and for the first time in her life she was happy. In a month she fell in love with him, and he with her, and he took her the way a man takes a wife, though without a ceremony. Oddly, though, *she* was convinced that marrying him was exactly what the Oversoul required of him, while *he* was convinced that taking her into his bed was pure defiance of the will of God. "I will defy God every chance I get," he said. "But I would never have taken you against your will, even for the sake of defying my enemy."

"Is God your enemy, too?" she whispered.

For a month they were together. Then the madness came upon her and she fled into the desert.

It happened once again, several years later, only this time there was no month of waiting, and she didn't find him in his homeland, but rather in a cold foreign land with pine trees and a trace of snow on the ground, and this time there was no month of chastity before they were together as man and wife. And again, after a month she became god-mad and fled again into the desert.

Both times she conceived a child. Both times she longed to take her daughter to him, and lay the babe at his feet, and claim her right as his wife. But the Oversoul forbade it, and instead she brought the baby into the city of women, into Basilica, to the house that the Oversoul had shown her in a dream, and both times she gave her child into the arms of a woman that the Oversoul truly loved.

Thirsty envied that woman so much, for when you have the love of the Oversoul, you are given a house, and freedom, and happiness, and you are surrounded by daughters and friends. But Thirsty had only the hatred of the Oversoul, and so she lived alone in the desert.

Until, at last, ten years ago, the madness left her for good—or so she thought. She came down out of the desert then, into the land of Potokgavan, where kind strangers took her in. She was not beautiful or desirable, but she was striking in a strange way, and a good plain farmer with a strong house that stood on thick stilts asked for her to be his wife. She said yes, and together they had seven children.

But she never forgot her days as a holy woman, when the Oversoul hated her, and she never forgot the two daughters she bore to the strange man who was the husband the Oversoul gave her. The elder daughter she had named Hushidh, which was also the name of a desert flower which smelled sweet, but often held the larvae of the poisonous saberfly. The younger daughter she had named Luet, after the lyuty plant, whose leaves were ground up and soaked to make the sacred tea that helped the women who worshipped the Oversoul to enter a trance that sometimes, they said, gave them true visions. She never forgot her daughters, and prayed for them every morning, though she never told her husband or their children about the two she had been compelled to give into the hands of another.

Then one night she dreamed again, a god-mad dream. She saw herself once again walking into the presence of the husband the Oversoul had given her, the father of her first two daughters. Only now he was older, and his face was terrible and sad. In the dream he had his two daughters, the younger one beside him, the elder kneeling before him, and Thirsty saw herself walk to him and take him by the hand and say, "Husband, now that you have claimed your daughters, will I be your wife in the eyes of men, as well as in the eyes of the Oversoul?"

She hated this dream. Hated it deeply, for it denied the husband she had now, and repudiated the children they had together. Why did you set me free to have this life in Potokgavan, O cruel Oversoul, if you meant to tear me away from them? And if you meant me to be with my first two daughters, why couldn't you have let me keep them from the start? You are too cruel to me, Oversoul! I will not obey you!

But every night she dreamed the same dream. Again and again, all night long, until she thought she would go mad with it. Yet still she did not go.

Then, on one morning, at the end of the same relentless vision, there came something new into her dream. A sweet high keening sound. And in her dream she looked around and saw a furred creature flying through the air, and she knew that the sweet high song was this angel's song. The angel came to her in the dream, and landed on her shoulder, and clung to her, wrapping his leathery wings around her and his song was piercing and brilliant in her ear.

"What should I do, sweet angel?" she asked him in the dream.

In answer, the angel threw himself backward onto the ground before her, and lay there in the dust. And as he lay there, exposed and helpless, his wings useless and vulnerable and slack, there came creatures that at first seemed to be baboons, from their size, but then seemed to be rats, from their teeth and eyes and snout. They came to the angel, and sniffed at him, and when he did not move or fly, they began to gnaw at him. Oh, it was terrible indeed, and all the time his eyes looked at Thirsty, so sadly.

I must save him, thought Thirsty. I must shoo away these terrible enemies. Yet in the dream she could not save him. She could not act at all.

When the fell creatures finally left, the angel was not dead. But his wings had been chewed away, and in their place were left only two spindly, fragile arms, with barely a fringe under them to show where once the wings had been. She knelt by him, then, and cradled him up into her arms, and wept for him. Wept and wept and wept.

"Mother," said her middle son. "Mother, you're weeping from a dream, I think. Wake up."

She woke up.

"What was it?" asked the boy. He was a good boy, and she did not want to leave him.

"I must take a journey," she said.

"Where?"

"To a far place, but I'll come home, if the Oversoul will let me."

"Why must you go?"

"I don't know," she said. "The Oversoul has called me, and I don't know why. Your father is already working in the fields. Don't tell him until he comes home for his noon meal. By then I'll be gone too far for him to pursue me. Tell him that I love him and that I'll return to him. If he wants to punish me when I come back, then I will submit to his punishment gladly. For I would rather be here with him, and with our children, than to be a queen in any other country."

"Mama," said the boy, "I've known for a month that you would go."

"How did you know?" she asked. And for a moment she feared that he, too, might be cursed with the voice of the Oversoul in his heart.

But it was no god-madness the boy had—instead it was common sense. "You kept looking to the northwest, and Father tells us sometimes that that was where you came from. I thought I saw you wishing to go home."

"No," she said. "Not wishing to go home, because I *am* home, right here. But there's an errand I must tend to, and then I'll come back to you."

"If the Oversoul will let you."

She nodded. Then, taking a small bundle of food and a leather bottle filled with water, she set out on foot.

I had no intention of obeying you, Oversoul, she said. But when I saw that angel, with his wings torn away because I did nothing to help him in his moment of need, I did not know if that angel represented my daughters or the man who gave them to me, or even perhaps yourself—I only knew that I could not stand in my place and let some terrible thing happen, though I don't know what the terrible thing will be, or what I must do to stop it. All I know is that I will go where you lead me, and when I get there I will try to do good. If that ends up serving your purpose, Oversoul, I will do it anyway.

But when it's done, please, oh! Please, let me go home.

IN BASILICA, AND NOT IN A DREAM

It had come now to getting permission from Rasa, and Elemak was by no means certain she would grant it. Word throughout the house was that she had come home from her meeting with the Gorayni general in a foul humor, and no one could miss the fact that there were Gorayni soldiers in the street outside the house. Yet no matter what happened in Basilica, Elemak would not go back into the desert without a wife. And since she was willing, it would be Eiadh, with or without Rasa's permission.

But better *with* her permission. Better if Rasa herself performed the ceremony.

"This is an inauspicious time," said Rasa.

"Don't speak like an old woman, please, Aunt Rasa," said Eiadh. Her voice was so soft and sweet that Rasa showed no sign of being offended at what could only be regarded as sauciness. "Remember that *young* women are not timid. We marry most readily when our men are about to go to war, or when times are hard."

"You know nothing of desert life."

"But *you* have gone out into the desert with Wetchik, from time to time."

"Twice, and the second time was because I failed to trust my memory of how much I loathed the first time. I can promise you that after a week in the desert you'd be willing to come back to Basilica as a bondservant, just so you could come back."

"My lady Rasa," began Elemak.

"If you speak again, dear Elemak, I will send you from the room," said Rasa, in her gentlest tones. "I'm trying to talk sense to your beloved. But you needn't worry. Eiadh is so besotted with love of—what, your strength? I suspect she has visions of perfect manhood in her heart, and you fulfill all those fantasies."

Eiadh blushed. It was all Elemak could do to keep from smiling. He had hoped this from the start—that Eiadh was not a girl who looked for wealth or position, but rather one who looked for courage and strength. It would be boldness, not ostentation, that would win her heart: So Elemak had determined at the outset of his wooing, and so it had turned out in the end. Rasa herself confirmed it. Elemak had chosen a girl who, instead of loving him as the Wetchik's heir, would love him for those very virtues that were most evident in Elemak out in the desert—his ability to command, to make quick, bold decisions; his physical stamina; his wisdom about desert life.

"Whatever dreams she has in her heart," Elemak said, "I will do my best to make them all come true."

"Be careful what you promise," said Rasa. "Eiadh is quite capable of sucking the life out of a man with her adoration."

"Aunt Rasa!" said Eiadh, genuinely horrified.

"Lady Rasa," said Elemak, "I can't imagine what cruel intent you must have, to say such a thing about this woman."

"Forgive me," said Rasa. She looked genuinely sorry. "I thought my words would be taken as teasing, but I haven't the heart for levity right now, and so it became an insult. I didn't intend it that way."

"Lady Rasa," said Elemak, "all things are forgiven when Wethead soldiers stand watch in the street outside your house."

"Do you think I care about that?" said Rasa. "When I have a raveler and a waterseer in my house? The soldiers are nothing. It's my city that I fear for."

"The soldiers are *not* nothing," said Elemak. "I've been told how Hushidh unbound poor Rashgallivak's soldiers from their loyalty to him, but you must remember that Rashgallivak was a weak man, newly come into my brother's place."

"Your father's place, too," said Rasa.

"Usurping both," said Elemak. "And the soldiers that Shuya unbound were mercenaries. General Moozh is said to be the greatest general in a thousand years, and his soldiers love and trust him beyond understanding. Shuya wouldn't find it easy to unweave *those* bonds."

"Suddenly you're an expert on the Gorayni?"

"I'm an expert on how men love and trust a strong leader," said Elemak. "I know how the men of my caravans felt about me. True, they all knew they would be paid. But they also knew that I wouldn't risk their lives unnecessarily, and that if they followed me in all things they would live to *spend* that money at journey's end. I loved my men, and they loved me, yet from what I hear of General Moozh, his soldiers love him ten times more than that. He has made them the strongest army of the Western Shore."

"And masters of Basilica, without one of them being killed," said Rasa.

"He hasn't mastered Basilica yet," said Elemak. "And with you as his enemy, Lady Rasa, I don't know if he ever will."

Rasa laughed bitterly. "Oh, indeed, he removed *me* as a threat from the start."

"What about our marriage?" asked Eiadh. "That *is* what we're meeting about, isn't it?"

Rasa looked at her with—what, pity? Yes, thought Elemak. She hasn't a very high opinion of this niece of hers. That remark she let slip, that insult, it was no joke. Suck the life out of a man with her adoration—what did that mean? Am I making a mistake? All my thought was to make Eiadh desire me; I never questioned my desire for *her*.

"Yes, my dear," said Rasa. "You may marry this man. You may take him as your first husband."

"Technically," said Elemak, "it wasn't permission we were seeking, since she's of age."

"*And* I will perform the ceremony," said Rasa wearily. "But it will have to be in this house, for obvious reasons, and the guest list will have to consist of all those who find themselves in residence here. We must all pray that Gorayni soldiers do not also choose to attend the ceremony."

"When?" asked Eiadh.

"Tonight," said Rasa. "Tonight will be soon enough, won't it? Or does your clothing itch so much you want it to come off at noon?"

Again, an insult beyond bearing, and yet Rasa plainly did not see that she was being crude. Instead she arose and walked from the room, leaving Eiadh flushed and angry on the bench where she sat.

"No, my Edhya," said Elemak. "Don't be angry. Your Aunt Rasa has lost much today, and she can't help being a little mean about also losing you."

"It sounds as though she'd be *glad* to get rid of me, she must hate me so," said Eiadh. And a tear slipped from Eiadh's eye and dropped, twinkling for a moment in the air, onto her lap.

Elemak took her in his arms then, and held her; she clung to him as if she longed to become a part of him forever. This is love, he thought. This is the kind of love that songs and stories are made of. She will follow me into the desert and with her beside me I will fashion a tribe, a kingdom for her to be the queen. For whatever this General Moozh can do, *I* can do. I am a truer husband than any Wethead could ever be. Eiadh hungers for a man of mastery. I am that man.

Bitanke was not happy with all that had happened in Basilica these past few days. Especially because he could not get free of the feeling that perhaps it was all his fault. Not that he had had much choice in those moments at the gate. His men had fought valiantly, but they were too few, and the mob of Palwashantu mercenaries was bound to win. What hope, then, would he have had, standing against the Gorayni soldiers who came out of nowhere and promised alliance with him?

I could have called to the Palwashantu mercenaries and begged them to make common cause with me against the Gorayni—it might have worked. Yet at the time the Gorayni general had seemed so earnest. And there were all those firelights out on the desert. It looked like an army of a hundred thousand men. How was I to know that their entire army was the men standing at the gate? And even then, we could not have stood against them.

But we could have fought. We could have cost them soldiers and time. We could have alerted all the other guards, and sent the alarm through the city. I could have died there, with a Gorayni arrow through my heart, rather than having to live and see how they have conquered my city, my beloved city, without even one of them suffering a wound serious enough to keep him from marching boldly wherever he pleases.

And yet. And yet even now, as he was called into the presence of General Moozh for still another interview, Bitanke could not help but admire the man for his audacity, his courage, his brilliance. To have marched so far in such a short time, and to essay to take a city with so few men, and then to have his way when even now the guard outnumbered his army significantly. Who could say that Basilica might not be better off with Moozh as its guardian? Better him than that swine Gaballufix would have been, or the contemptible Rashgallivak. Better even than Roptat. And better than the women, who had proven themselves weak and foolish indeed, for the way they now believed Moozh's obvious lies about Lady Rasa.

Couldn't they see how Moozh manipulated them to divide against each other and ignore the one woman who might have led them to effective resistance? No, of course they couldn't see—any more than Bitanke himself could see that first night that, far from helping, the Gorayni stranger was controlling him and making him betray his own city without even realizing it.

We are all fools when one wise man appears.

"My dear friend," said General Moozh.

Bitanke did not take the offered hand.

"Ah, you're angry with me," said Moozh.

"You came here with Lady Rasa's letter, and now you have her under arrest."

"Is she so dear to you?" asked Moozh. "I assure you that her confinement is only temporary, and is entirely for her protection. Terrible lies about her are circulating through the city right now, and who can tell what might happen to her if her house was not cordoned off?"

"Lies invented by you."

"My lips have said nothing about Lady Rasa except my great admiration for her. She is the best of the women of this city, with the wit and courage of a man, and I will never permit a hair of her head to be harmed. If you don't know that about me, Bitanke, my friend, you know nothing about me at all."

Which was almost certainly true, thought Bitanke. I know nothing about you. No one knows anything about you.

"Why did you summon me?" asked Bitanke. "Are you going to strip away yet one more power from the Basilican guard? Or do you have some vile work for us to do that will humiliate and demoralize us all the more?"

"So angry," said Moozh. "But think hard, Bitanke. You feel free to say such things to me, and without fear that I'll strike your head off. Does that seem like tyranny to you? Your soldiers all have their arms, and they are the ones keeping the peace in this city now—does that sound as though I'm a treacherous enemy?"

Bitanke said nothing, determined not to let himself be taken in again by Moozh's smooth talking. And yet he felt the stab of doubt in his heart, as he had so many times before. Moozh *had* left the guard intact. He had done no violence against any citizen. Perhaps all he meant to do was use Basilica as a staging area and then move on.

"Bitanke, I need your help. I want to restore this city to its former strength, before Gaballufix's meddling."

Oh, yes, I'm certain that's all you desire—Moozh the altruist, going to all this trouble just so you can help the city of women. Then you'll march your men away, rewarded with a warm glow in your heart because you know you leave so much happiness behind you.

But Bitanke said nothing. Better to listen than to speak, at a time like this.

"I won't pretend to you that I don't intend to turn things here to my own purposes. There is a great struggle ahead between the Gorayni and the miserable puddle swimmers of Potokgavan. We know that they were maneuvering to take control of Basilica—Gaballufix was their man. He was prepared to overthrow the city of women and let his thugs rule. And now here I am, with my soldiers. Have I or my men ever done anything to make you think our intentions are as ruthless or brutal as Gaballufix?

Moozh waited, and at last Bitanke answered, "You have never been so obvious, no."

"I will tell you what I need from Basilica. I need to know, securely, that those who rule her are friends of the Gorayni, that with Basilica at

my back I don't have to fear any treachery from this city. Then I can
bring supply lines through the desert to this place, completely bypass-
ing Nakavalnu and Izmennik and Seggidugu. *You* know that this is
good strategy, my friend. Potokgavan counted on our having to fight
our way south to the Cities of the Plain; they counted on having at least
a year, perhaps several years, to strengthen their position here—perhaps to bring an army here to try to stand against our chariots. But now
we will command the Cities of the Plain—with my army in Basilica,
none of them will resist. And then Nakavalnu and Izmennik and Seggidugu will not dare to make any alliance with Potokgavan. Without
conquest, without war, we will have secured the entire Western Shore
for the Imperator, years before Potokgavan would have imagined possible. That is what I want. That is *all* I want. And to accomplish it, I don't
need to break Basilica, I don't need to treat you as a conquered people.
All I need is to be certain that Basilica is loyal to me. And that purpose
is better accomplished through love than through fear."

"Love!" said Bitanke derisively.

"So far," said Moozh, "I have not had to do anything that was not
gratefully received by the people of Basilica. They have more peace
and security now than in the past several years. Do you think they
don't understand that?"

"And do you think the worse men of Dogtown and Gate Town and
the High Road aren't hoping that you'll let them come into the city and
rule here? Then you'd have your loyal allies—if you give them what
Gaballufix promised, a chance to dominate these women who have
barred them from citizenship for all these thousands of centuries."

"Yes," said Moozh. "I could have done that. I could do it still." He
leaned forward across the table, to look Bitanke in the eye. "But you
will help me, won't you, so that I don't have to do such a terrible
thing?"

Ah. So this was the choice, after all. Either conspire with Moozh or
watch the very fabric of Basilica be destroyed. All that was beautiful
and holy in this place would now be hostage to the threat of turning
loose the covetous men from outside the walls. Hadn't Bitanke seen
how terrible that would be? How could he let it happen again?

"What do you want from me?"

"Advice," said Moozh. "Counsel. The city council is not a reliable
instrument of control here. It's fine for passing laws governing local
matters, but when it comes to making a firm alliance with the army of

the Imperator, who's to say a faction won't arise within a week to strike down that policy? So I need to set up a single individual as . . . what . . .

"Dictator?"

"Not at all. This person would merely be the face that Basilica turns to the outside world. He, she—whoever it is—will be able to promise that Gorayni armies may pass through here, that Gorayni supplies can be stored here, and that Potokgavan will find no friends or allies here."

"The city council can do this."

"You know better."

"They will keep their word."

"You have seen this very day how treacherously and unfairly they dealt with Lady Rasa, who has done nothing but serve them loyally all her life. How then will they deal with the stranger? My men's lives, my Imperator's power, all will depend on the loyalty of Basilica—and this city council has proven itself incapable of being loyal even to their own worthiest sister."

"*You* started those rumors about her," said Bitanke, "and now you use them to show how unworthy the council is?"

"Before God I deny that I started any slander about Lady Rasa—I admire her above any other woman I have met. Yet no matter who started the rumor, Bitanke, what matters is that it was *believed*. By this city council, which you tell me I can trust with the lives of my men. What is to stop Potokgavan from starting rumors of their own? Tell me honestly, Bitanke, if you were in *my* place, with *my* needs, would you trust this city council?"

"I have served this council all my life, sir, and I trust them," said Bitanke.

"That's not what I asked you," said Moozh. "I am here to accomplish the purpose of the Imperator. Traditionally we have done this by slaughtering the ruling class of the lands we conquer, and replacing them with men of some long-disfranchised oppressed people. Because I love this city, I wish to find another way here. I am taking great risks to do so."

"You have only a thousand men," said Bitanke. "You want to subdue Basilica without bloodshed because you can't afford to suffer *any* losses."

"You see half the truth," said Moozh. "I have to *win* here. If I can do it without bloodshed, then the Cities of the Plain will say that I must have the power of God with me, and they will submit to my orders. But I can also achieve the same end by terror. If their leaders are brought here and find this city desolate, burned to the ground, house and forest, and the lake of women thick with blood, they will also submit to me. But one way or another, Basilica will serve my purpose."

"You are truly a monster," said Bitanke. "You speak of sacrilege and massacre of innocents, and then ask me to trust you."

"I speak of necessity," said Moozh, "and ask you to help me keep from being a monster. You have served a higher purpose—the will of the council. Sometimes, in their name, you have done that which you, of yourself, would not wish to do. Is that not so?"

"That's what it means to be a soldier," said Bitanke.

"I also am a soldier," said Moozh. "I also must accomplish the purpose of my master, the Imperator. And so I will even be a monster if I must, to accomplish it. As you have had to arrest men and women you thought were innocent."

"Arrest is not slaughter."

"Bitanke, my friend, I keep hoping that you will be what I thought you were when first I met you bravely fighting at that gate. I imagined that night that you fought, not for some institution, not for that feeble city council that believes any slander that flies through the city, but rather for something higher. For the city itself. For the *idea* of the city. Wasn't *that* what you were prepared to die for at the gate?"

"Yes," said Bitanke.

"Now I offer you the chance to serve the city again. You know that long before there *was* a council, Basilica was a great city. Back when Basilica was ruled by the priestesses, it was still Basilica. Back when Basilica had a queen, it was still Basilica. Back when Basilica put the great general Snaceetel in charge of its army and fought off the Seggidugu warriors, and then let him drink of the waters of the lake of women, it was still Basilica."

Against his will Bitanke saw that Moozh was right. The city of women was not the council. The form of government had changed many times before, and would change again. What mattered was that it remain the holy city of women, the one place on the planet Harmony where women ruled. And if, for a short time, because of great events sweeping through the Western Shore, Basilica had to be subservient to the Gorayni, then what of that—as long as the rule of women was preserved within these walls?

"While you consider," said Moozh, "consider *this*. I could have tried to frighten you. I could have lied to you, pretended to be something other than the calculating general that I am. Instead I have spoken to you as a friend, openly and freely, because what I want is your willing help, not your mere obedience."

"My help to do what?" asked Bitanke. "I will *not* arrest the council, if that's what you hope for."

"Arrest them! Haven't you understood me at all? I need the council to continue—without replacing a single member of it! I need the people of Basilica to see that their internal government is unchanged. But I also need a consul of the people, someone to set in place *above* the council, to handle the foreign affairs of Basilica. To make an alliance with us that will be adhered to. To command the guards at the city gates."

"Your men already perform that office."

"But I *want* it to be *your* men who do it."

"I'm not the commander of the guard."

"You're one of the leading officers," said Moozh. "I wish you *were* commander, because you're a better soldier than any of the men above you. But if I promised you the office of commander, you would think I was trying to bribe you and you would reject me and leave this house as my enemy."

Bitanke felt a great relief inside. Moozh knew, after all, that Bitanke was no traitor. That Bitanke would never act for his own self-interest. That Bitanke would act only for the good of the city.

"The men of the guard will be reluctant," said Bitanke, "to take their orders from anyone but their own commander, appointed by the city council."

"Imagine, though, that the city council has unanimously appointed someone to be consul of the city, and has asked the guard to obey that consul."

"It would mean nothing if they thought for a moment that the consul was a mere puppet of the Gorayni. The guard are not fools, and we are not traitors, either."

"So. You see my dilemma. I must have someone who will understand the necessity of Basilica remaining loyal to the Imperator, and yet this consul will only be effective if the people of Basilica trust her—or him—to be a loyal Basilican, and not a puppet."

Bitanke laughed. "I hope you don't imagine for a moment that *I*

would do for that purpose. There are already plenty of people whispering that I must be your puppet for having let you into the city in the
first place."

"I know," said Moozh. "You were the first one I thought of, but I
realized that you can only serve Basilica—and my purposes, too—by
remaining where you are, with *no* obvious advantage coming to you
because of my influence in the city."

"Then why am I here?"

"To advise me, as I told you before. I need you to tell me who in this
city, if she—or he—were appointed as consul, the guard and the city as
a whole would follow and obey."

"There *is* no such creature."

"Say this, and you might as well ask me to pour the blood and ashes
of the city into the lake of women."

"Don't threaten me!"

"I'm not threatening you, Bitanke, I'm telling you what I have done
before and what I do not want to do again. I beg you, help me to find a
way to avoid that dreadful outcome."

"Let me think."

"I ask for nothing more."

"Let me come to you tomorrow."

"I must act today."

"Give me an hour."

"Can you do your thinking here? Can you do it without leaving the
house?"

"Am I under arrest, then?"

"This house is watched by a thousand eyes, my friend. If you are
seen leaving and then returning in an hour, it will be said that you
make too many visits to General Vozmuzhalnoy Vozmozhno. But if you
want to leave, you may."

"I'll stay."

"I'll have you shown to the library, then, and given a computer to
write on. It will help my thinking, if you write down the names and
your reasons why they might or might not be good for this purpose. In
an hour, come to me again with your list of names."

"For Basilica I do this, and not for you." And not for any advantage
to myself.

"It's for Basilica that I ask it," said Moozh. "Even though my first loyalty is to the Imperator, I hope to save this city from destruction if I can."

The interview was over. Bitanke left the room, and was immediately joined by a Gorayni soldier who led him to the library. Moozh had said nothing to this soldier, and yet he knew where to take him. Knew to assign him a computer to use. Either this meant that the general let his junior officers listen in to his negotiations, which was almost unthinkable, or it meant that Moozh had given these orders before Bitanke even arrived.

Could it be that Moozh had planned it all, every word that passed between them? Could it be that Moozh was so good at manipulation that he could determine all outcomes in advance? Then in that case Bitanke might just be another dupe, betraying his city because he had been twisted into believing whatever Moozh wanted.

No. No, that was not it at all. Moozh simply counted on being able to persuade me to act intelligently in the best interest of Basilica. And so I will find candidates for him, if it is possible to imagine anyone serving as consul, appointed because of the Gorayni and yet holding the loyalty of the people, the council, and the guard. If it is possible, I will bring the name to the General.

"I need to speak to my children," said Rasa. *"All* of them."

Luet looked at her for a moment, uncertain what to do; this was the sort of thing a lady might say to her servants, giving orders without seeming to. But Luet was not a servant in this house, and never had been, and so she was supposed to ignore such expressions of desire. Yet Rasa seemed not to realize she had spoken as if to a servant, when no servant was present. "Madam," she said, "are you sending me on this errand?"

Rasa looked at her almost in surprise. "I'm sorry, Luet. I forgot who was with me. I'm not at my best. Would you please go find my children and my husband's children for me, and tell them I want to see them now?"

Now it was a request, a favor, and asked directly of her, so of course Luet bowed her head and left in search of servants to help her. Not that Luet wouldn't willingly have done the task herself, but Rasa's house was large, and if there was any urgency in Rasa's request—as there seemed to be—it would be better to have several people searching. Besides, the servants were more likely to know exactly where everyone was.

It was easy enough to find out where Nafai, Elemak, Sevet, and Kokor were, and send servants to summon them. Mebbekew, however, had not been seen for several hours, not since he first came into the house. Finally Izdavat, a youngish maid of more eagerness than sense, reluctantly mentioned that she had brought Mebbekew breakfast in Dol's room. "But that was some time ago, lady."

"I'm only sister, or Luet, please."

"Do you want me to see if he's still there, sister?"

"No, thank you," said Luet. "It would be improper for him still to be there, and so I'll go ask Dolya where he went." She headed off to the stairs in the teachers' wing of the house.

Luet was not surprised that Mebbekew had already managed to attach himself to a woman, even in this house where women were taught to see through shallow men. However, it *did* surprise her that Dolya was giving the boy the time of day. She had been worked over by champion flatterers and sycophants in her theatre days, and shouldn't have noticed Mebbekew except to laugh discreetly at him.

But then, Luet was quite aware that she saw through flatterers more easily than most women, since the flatterers never actually tried to work their seductive magic on *her*. Waterseers had a reputation for seeing through lies—though, truth to tell, Luet could only see what the Oversoul showed her, and the Oversoul was not noted for helping a daughter with her love life. As if I had a love life, thought Luet. As if I needed one. The Oversoul has marked my path for me. And where my path touches others' lives, I will trust the Oversoul to tell them her will. My husband will discover me as his wife when he chooses to. And I will be content.

Content . . . she almost laughed at herself. All my dreams are tied up in the boy, we've been to the edge of death together, and still he pines for Eiadh. Are men's lives nothing but the secretions of overactive glands? Can't they analyze and understand the world about them, as women can? Can't Nafai see that Eiadh's love will be as permanent as rain, ready to evaporate as soon as the storm passes? Edhya *needs* a man like Elemak, who won't tolerate her straying heart. Where Nafai would be heartbroken at her disloyalty, Elemak would be brutally angry, and Eiadh, the poor foolish creature, would fall in love with him all over again.

Not that Luet saw all this herself, of course. It was Hushidh who saw all the connections, all the threads binding people together; it was Hushidh who explained to her that Nafai seemed not to notice Luet because he was so enamored of Eiadh. It was Hushidh who also understood the bond between Elemak and Eiadh, and why they were so right for each other.

And now Mebbekew and Dol. Well, it was another piece of the puzzle, wasn't it? When Luet had seen her vision of women in the woods behind Rasa's house, that night when she returned from warning Wetchik of the threat against his life, it had made no sense to her. Now, though, she knew why she had seen Dolya. She would be with Mebbekew, as Eiadh with Elemak. Shedemei would also be coming out to the desert, or at least would be involved with their journey, gathering seeds and embryos. And Hushidh also would come. And Aunt Rasa. Luet's vision had been of the women called out into the desert.

Poor Dolya. If she had known that taking Mebbekew into her room would take her on a path leading out of Basilica, she would have kicked him and bit him and hit him, if need be, to get him out of her room! As it was, though, Luet fully expected to find them together.

She knocked on Dol's door. As she expected, there was the sound of a flurry of movement inside. And a soft thump.

"Who is it?" asked Dol.

"Luet."

"I'm not conveniently situated at the moment."

"I have no doubt of it," said Luet, "but Lady Rasa sent me with some urgency. May I come in?"

"Yes, of course."

Luet opened the door to find Dolya lying in bed, her sheets up over her shoulders. There was no sign of Mebbekew, of course, but the bed had been well-rumpled, the bath was full of grey water, and a bunch of grapes had been left on the floor—not the way Dolya usually arranged things before taking a midday nap.

"What does Aunt Rasa want of me?" asked Dol.

"Nothing of *you*, Dol," said Luet. "She wants all her children and Wetchik's children to join her at once."

"Then why aren't you knocking at Sevet's or Kokor's door? They aren't here."

"Mebbekew knows why I'm here," said Luet. Remembering the

thump she heard, and the brief amount of time before she opened the door, she reached a conclusion about his present whereabouts. "So as soon as I close the door, he can get up off the floor beside your bed, put some kind of clothing on, and come to Lady Rasa's room."

Dol looked stricken. "Forgive me for trying to deceive you, Waterseer," she whispered.

Sometimes it made Luet want to scream, the way everyone assumed that when she showed any spark of wit it must be a revelation from the Oversoul—as if Luet would be incapable of discerning the obvious on her own. And yet it was also useful, Luet had to admit. Useful in that people tended to tell her the truth more readily, because they believed she would catch them in their lies. But the price of this truthfulness was that they did not like her company, and avoided her. Only friends shared such intimacies, and only freely. Forced, or so they thought, to share their secrets with Luet, they withheld their friendship, and Luet was not part of the lives of most of the women around her. They held her in such awe; it made her feel unworthy and filled her with rage, both at once.

It was that anger that led Luet to torment Mebbekew by forcing him to speak. "Did you hear me, Mebbekew?"

A long wait. Then: "Yes."

"I'll tell Lady Rasa," said Luet, "that her message was received."

She started to back out the door and draw it closed behind her, when Dol called out to her. "Wait . . . Luet."

"Yes?"

"His clothes . . . they were being washed . . ."

"I'll send them up."

"Do you think they'll be dry by now?"

"Dry enough," said Luet. "Don't you think so, Mebbekew?"

Mebbekew sat upright, so his head appeared on the other side of the bed. "Yes," he said glumly.

"Damp clothes will cool you off," said Luet. "It's such a hot day, at least in this room." It was a fine joke, she thought, but nobody laughed.

Shedemei strode vigorously along the path to Wetchik's coldhouse, which was nestled in a narrow valley and shaded by tall trees just outside the place where the city wall curved around the Old Orchestra. It was the last and, she feared, the hardest part of her task of assembling the flora and fauna for the mad project of a voyage through space, back to the legendary lost planet Earth. I am going to all this trouble because I had a dream, and took it for interpretation to a dreamer. A journey on camels, and they think it will lead them to Earth.

Yet the dream was still alive within her. The life she carried with her on the cloud.

So she came to the door of Wetchik's coldhouse, not certain whether she really hoped to find one of his servants acting as caretaker.

No one answered when she clapped her hands. But the machines that kept the house cold inside might well mask her loudest clapping. So she went to the door and tried it. Locked.

Of course it was. Wetchik had gone into the desert weeks ago, hadn't he? And Rashgallivak, his steward and, supposedly, the new Wetchik, had been in hiding somewhere ever since. Who would keep the place running, with both of them gone?

Except that the machines here *were* running, weren't they? Which meant *somebody* was still caring for the place. Unless they carelessly left them on, and the plants untended inside.

That was quite possible, of course. The cold air would keep the specialized plants thriving for many days, and the coldhouse, drawing its power from the solar scoops on the poles rising high above the house, could run indefinitely without even drawing on the city's power supply.

And yet Shedemei knew that someone was still taking care of this place, though she could not have said *how* she knew it. And further-more, she knew that the caretaker was inside the coldhouse right now, and knew she was there, and wanted her to go away. Whoever was in here was hiding.

And who was it who needed to hide?

"Rashgallivak," called Shedemei. "I'm only Shedemei. You know me, and I'm alone, and I will tell no one you are here, but I must talk to you." She waited, no response. "It's nothing about the city, or the things going on in there," she called out loudly. "I simply need to buy a couple of pieces of equipment from you."

She could hear the door unbolting from the inside. Then it swung open on its heavy hinges. Rashgallivak stood there, looking forlorn and wasted. He held no weapon.

"If you've come to betray me, then I welcome it as a relief."

Shedemei declined to point out that betrayal would only be pure justice, after the way Rashgallivak had betrayed the Wetchik's house, allying himself with Gaballufix in order to steal his master's place. She had business to do here; she was not a justicer.

"I care nothing for politics," she said, "and I care nothing for you. I simply need to buy a dozen drycases. The portable ones, used for caravans."

He shook his head. "Wetchik had me sell them all."

Shedemei closed her eyes for a weary moment. He was forcing her to say things she had not wanted to throw in his face. "Oh, Rashgallivak, please don't expect me to believe that you actually sold them, knowing that you intended to take control of the house of Wetchik and would need to continue in the business."

Rashgallivak flushed—in shame, Shedemei hoped. "Nevertheless, I sold them, as I was told to do."

"Then who bought them?" asked Shedemei. "It's the drycases I want, not you."

Rashgallivak didn't answer.

"Ah," said Shedemei. "*You* bought them."

After a moment's pause, he said, "What do you need them for?"

"You're asking *me* to account for myself?" asked Shedemei.

"I ask, because I know you have plenty of drycases at your laboratory. The only conceivable use of the portable ones is for a caravan, and that's a business you know nothing about."

"Then no doubt I will be killed or robbed. But that's no concern of yours. And perhaps I won't be killed or robbed."

"In which case," said Rashgallivak, "you would be selling your plants in far-off countries, in direct competition with me. So why should I sell my competitor the portable drycases she needs?"

Shedemei laughed in his face. "What, do you think that there is any business as usual in this place? I'm not going on a trading journey, you poor foolish man. I'm removing my entire laboratory, *and* myself, to a place where I can safely pursue my research without being interrupted by armed madmen burning and looting the city."

Again he flushed. "When they were under my command, they never harmed anyone. I was no Gaballufix."

"No, Rash. You are no Gaballufix."

That could be taken two ways, but Rash apparently decided to take it as a confirmation of her belief in his fundamental decency. "You're not my enemy, are you, Shedya."

"I just want drycases."

He hesitated a moment more, then stepped back and beckoned her inside.

The entry of the coldhouse wasn't chilled like the inner rooms, and Rash had turned it into a pathetic sort of apartment for himself. A makeshift bed, a large tub that had once held plants, but which he no doubt used now for bathing and washing his clothes. Very primitive, but resourceful, too. Shedemei had to admire that in the man—he had not despaired, even when everything worked against him.

"I'm alone here," he said. "The Oversoul surely knows I need money more than I need drycases. And the city council has cut me off from all my funds. You can't even pay me, because I haven't an account anymore to receive the money."

"That shouldn't be a problem," said Shedemei. "As you might imagine, a lot of people are pulling their money out of the city accounts. I can pay you in gems—though the price of gold and precious stones has tripled since the recent disturbances."

"Do you think I imagine myself to be in a position to bargain?"

"Stack the drycases outside the door," said Shedemei. "I'll send men to load them and bring them to me inside the city. I'll give you fair payment separately. Tell me where."

"Come alone, afterward," said Rash. "And put them into my hand."

"Don't be absurd," said Shedemei. "I'll never come here again, and we'll never meet, either. Tell me where to leave the jewels for you."

"In the traveler room of Wetchik's house."

"Is it easy to find?"

"Easy enough."

"Then it will be there as soon as I have received the drycases."

"It hardly seems fair, that I must trust you completely, and you don't have to show any trust in me at all."

Shedemei could think of nothing to say that would not be cruel.

After a while he nodded. "All right," he said. "There are two houses on Wetchik's estate. Put the jewels in the traveler room of the smaller, older house. On top of one of the rafters. I'll find it."

"As soon as the drycases are at my laboratory," said Shedemei.

"Do you think I have some network of loyal men who will ambush you?" asked Rashgallivak, bitterly.

"No," said Shedemei. "But knowing you will soon have the money, there'd be nothing to stop you from hiring them now."

"So you'll decide when to pay me, and how much, and I get no voice in the matter."

"Rash," said Shedemei, "I will treat you far more fairly than you treated Wetchik and his sons."

"I'll have a dozen drycases outside within a half hour."

Shedemei got up and left. She heard him close the door behind her, and imagined him timidly drawing the bolts closed, fearful that someone might discover that the man who had, for a day, ruled the petty empires of Gaballufix and Wetchik both, now cowered inside these heavy shaded walls.

Shedya passed through Music Gate, where the Gorayni guards checked her identity with dispatch and let her through. It still bothered her to see that uniform in the gates of Basilica, but like everyone else she was growing accustomed to the soldier's perfect discipline, and the new orderliness that had come to the chaotic entrances of the city. Everyone waited patiently in line now.

And something else. There were now more people waiting to get into the city than waiting to get out. Confidence was returning. Confidence in the strength of the Gorayni. Who would have imagined how quickly people would come to trust the Wethead enemy?

After walking the long passage along the city wall to Market Gate, Shedemei found the muleteer she had hired. "Go ahead," Shedemei said. "There should be a dozen of them." The muleteer bowed her head and set off at a jog. No doubt that show of speed would stop the moment Shedemei could no longer see her, but Shedemei nevertheless appreciated the attempt at *pretending* to be fast. It showed that the muleteer knew what speed *was*, and thought it worthwhile to give the illusion of it.

Then she found a messenger boy in the queue waiting just inside the Market Gate. She scribbled a note on one of the papers that were kept there at the messenger station. On the back of the note she wrote directions to Wetchik's house, and instructions about where to leave the note. Then she keyed in a payment on the station computer. When the boy saw the bonus she was giving him for quick delivery, he grinned, snatched the note, and took off like an arrow.

Rashgallivak would be angry, of course, to find a draft against one of the Market Gate jewelers, instead of the jewels themselves. But Shedemei had no intention of either carrying or sending an enormous sum of completely liquid funds to some lonely abandoned place. It was

Rash who needed the money—let *him* take the risk. At least she had drawn the draft on one of the jewelers who kept a table outside Market Gate, so he wouldn't have to pass any guards to get his payment.

Rasa looked at her son and daughters, and Wetchik's two boys by other wives. Not the world's finest group of human beings, she thought. I'd be a bit more contemptuous of Volemak's failure with his two older boys, if I didn't have my two prize daughters to remind me of my own lack of brilliance as a parent. And, to be fair, all these young people have their gifts and talents. But only Nafai and Issib, the two children Volya and I had together, have shown themselves to have integrity, decency, and love of goodness.

"Why didn't you bring Issib?"

Elemak sighed. Poor boy, thought Rasa. Is the old lady making you explain again? "We didn't want to worry about his chair or his floats on this trip," he said.

"It's just as well we don't have him locked up in here with us," said Nafai.

"I don't think the general will keep us under arrest for long," said Rasa. "Once I'm thoroughly discredited, there'd be no reason to do something as clearly repressive as this. He's trying to create an image of himself as a liberator and protector, and having his soldiers in the streets here isn't helpful."

"And then we leave?" asked Nafai.

"No, we put down roots here," said Mebbekew. "Of course we leave."

"I want to go home," said Kokor. "Even if Obring is a wretched miserable excuse for a husband, I miss him."

Sevet said nothing.

Rasa looked at Elemak, who had a half-smile on his face. "And you, Elemak, are you also eager to leave my house?"

"I'm grateful for your hospitality," he said. "And we'll always remember your home as the last civilized house we lived in for many years."

"Speak for yourself, Elya," said Mebbekew.

"What is he talking about?" said Kokor. "*I* have a civilized house waiting for me right now."

Sevet gave a strangled laugh.

"I wouldn't boast about how civilized my house is, if I were you," said Rasa. "I see, too, that Elemak is the only one who understands your true situation here."

"I understand it," said Nafai.

Of course Elemak glared at Nafai under hooded eyes. Nafai, you foolish boy, thought Rasa. Must you always say the thing that will most provoke your brothers? Did you think I had forgotten that you have heard the voice of the Oversoul, that you understand far more than your brothers or sisters do? Couldn't you trust me to remember your worthiness, and so hold silence?

No, he couldn't. Nafai was young, too young to see the consequences of his actions, too young to contain his feelings.

"Nevertheless, it is Elemak who will explain it to us all."

"We can't stay in the city," said Elemak. "The moment the soldiers leave their watch, we have to escape, and quickly."

"Why?" asked Mebbekew. "It's Lady Rasa who's in trouble, not us."

"By the Oversoul, you're stupid," said Elemak.

What a refreshingly direct way of saying it, thought Rasa. No wonder your brothers worship you, Elya.

"As long as Lady Rasa is under arrest, Moozh has to see to it that no harm comes to anyone here. But he's set it up so that Rasa will have plenty of enemies in the city. As soon as his soldiers step out of the way, some very bad things will start to happen."

"All the more reason for us to get out of Mother's house," said Kokor. "Mother can flee if she wants, but they've got nothing against *me.*"

"They've got something against *all* of us," said Elemak. "Meb and Nafai and I are fugitives, and Nafai in particular has been accused of two murders, one of which he actually committed. Kokor can be charged with assault and attempted murder against her own sister. And Sevet is a flagrant adulterer, and since it was with her own sister's husband, the incest laws can be dredged up, too."

"They wouldn't dare," said Kokor. "Prosecute *me!*"

"And why wouldn't they dare?" asked Elemak. "Only the great respect and love people had for Lady Rasa protected you from arrest in the first place. Well, *that's* gone, or at least weakened."

"They'd never convict me," said Kokor.

"And the adultery laws haven't been enforced for centuries," said Meb. "And people are disgusted by incest between in-laws, but as long as they're at the age of consent . . ."

"Is *everyone* here criminally dumb?" asked Elemak. "No, I forget—*Nafai* understands *everything.*"

"No," said Nafai. "I know we need to go out to the desert because the Oversoul commanded it, but I don't have any idea what *you're* talking about."

Rasa couldn't stop herself from smiling. Nafai could be foolish sometimes, but his very honesty and directness could also be disarming. Without meaning to, Nafai had pleased Elemak by humbling himself and acknowledging Elya's greater wisdom.

"Then I'll explain," said Elemak. "Lady Rasa is a powerful woman—even now, because the wisest people in Basilica don't believe the rumors about her, not for a moment. It won't be enough for Moozh just to discredit her. He needs her to be either completely under his control, or dead. To accomplish the former, all he needs to do is put one or all of Rasa's children on trial for murder—or Father's sons, too for that matter—and she'll be helpless. Lady Rasa is a brave woman, but I don't think she has the heart to let her children or Father's sons go to prison just so she can play politics. And if she *did* have that degree of ruthlessness, Moozh would simply up the stakes. Which of us would he kill first? Moozh is a deft man—he'd do only enough to communicate his message clearly. He'd kill *you*, I think, Meb, since you're the one who is most worthless and whom Father and Lady Rasa would miss the least."

Meb leaped to his feet. "I've had enough of you, fart-for-breath!"

"Sit down, Mebbekew," said Lady Rasa. "Can't you see he's goading you for sport?"

Elemak grinned at Mebbekew, who wasn't mollified. Mebbekew glowered as he sat back down.

"He'd kill *somebody*," said Elemak, "just as a warning. Of course, it wouldn't be *his* soldiers. But he'd know that Lady Rasa would see his hand in it. And if holding us as hostages for her good behavior didn't work, Moozh has already laid the groundwork for murdering Lady Rasa herself. It would be easy to find some outraged citizen eager to kill her for her supposed treachery; all Moozh would have to do is set up an opportunity for such an assassin to strike. It would be simple. It's when the soldiers *leave* the streets outside this house that our true danger begins. So we have to prepare to leave immediately, secretly, and permanently."

"Leave Basilica!" cried Kokor. Her genuine dismay meant that she had finally grasped the idea that their situation was serious.

Sevet understood, that was certain. Her face was tilted downward, but Rasa could still see the tears on her cheeks.

"I'm sorry that your close association with me is costing you so much," said Rasa. "But for all these years, my dear daughters, my dear son, my beloved students, you have all benefitted from the prestige of my house, as well as the great honor of the Wetchik. Now that events have turned against us in Basilica, you must share in paying the price, as well. It is inconvenient, but it is not unfair."

"Forever," murmured Kokor.

"Forever it is," said Elemak. "But I, for one, will not go out into the desert without my wife. I hope my brothers have made some provision for themselves. It *is* the reason we came here."

"Obring," said Kokor. "We must bring Obring!"

Sevet lifted her chin and looked into her mother's face. Sevet's eyes were swimming with tears, and there was a frightened question in her face.

"I think that Vas will come with you, if you ask him," said Rasa. "He's a wise and a forgiving man, and he loves you far more than you deserve." The words were cold, but Sevet still took them as comfort.

"But what about *Obring*," insisted Kokor.

"He's such a weak man," said Rasa, "I'm sure you can persuade him to come along."

In the meantime, Mebbekew had turned to Elemak. "Your *wife?*" he asked.

"Lady Rasa is going to perform the ceremony for Eiadh and me tonight," said Elemak.

Mebbekew's face betrayed some powerful emotion—rage, jealousy? Had Mebbekew also wanted Eiadh, the way poor Nafai had?

"You're marrying her *tonight?*" demanded Mebbekew.

"We don't know when Moozh will lift our house arrest, and I want my marriage to be done properly. Once we're out in the desert, I don't want any question about who is married to whom."

"Not that we can't change around as soon as our terms are up," said Kokor.

Everyone looked at her.

"The desert isn't Basilica," said Rasa. "There'll only be a handful of us. Marriages will be permanent. Get used to that idea right now."

"That's absurd," said Kokor. "I'm not going, and you can't make me."

"No, I can't make you," said Rasa. "But if you stay, you'll soon discover how different life is when you're no longer the daughter of Lady Rasa, but merely a young singer who is notorious for having silenced her much more famous sister with a blow from her own hand."

"I can live with that!" said Kokor defiantly.

"Then I'm sure I don't want you with me," said Rasa angrily. "What good would a girl with no conscience be on the terrible journey that lies ahead of us?" Her words were harsh, but Rasa could taste her disappointment in Kokor like a foul poison on her tongue. "I've said all I have to say. You all have work to do and choices to make. Make them and have done."

It was a clear dismissal, and Kokor and Sevet got up and left at once, Kokor sweeping past, her nose in the air in a great show of hauteur.

Mebbekew sidled up to Rasa—couldn't the boy walk naturally, without looking like a sneak or a spy?—and asked his question. "Is Elya's wedding tonight an exclusive affair?"

"Everyone in the house is invited to attend," said Rasa.

"I meant—what if I were to marry someone, too. Would you do the ceremony tonight?"

"Marry *someone?* I assure you, Dolya may have been indiscreet, but I'll be surprised if she takes you on as a husband, Mebbekew."

Meb looked furious. "Luet told you."

"Of course she told me," said Rasa. "Half a dozen servants and Dolya herself would have told me before nightfall. Do you actually imagine anyone can keep a secret like *that* from me in my own house?"

"*If* I can persuade her to accept a piece of unworthy slime like myself," said Meb, his voice dripping with sarcasm, "will you condescend to include us in the ceremony?"

"It would be dangerous to bring you out into the desert without a wife," said Rasa. "Dolya would be more than enough woman for *you,* though she could hardly do worse for herself."

Mebbekew's face was red with fury. "I have done nothing to deserve such scorn from you."

"You have done nothing *but* to earn it," said Rasa. "You seduced my niece under my own roof, and now you contemplate marrying her— and don't think I'm fooled, either. You want to marry her, not to join your father in the desert, but to use her as your license to remain in Basilica. You'll be unfaithful to her the moment we're gone and you have your papers."

"And I swear to you in the eyes of the Oversoul that I will bring Dolya out into the desert, as surely as Elya is bringing Eiadh."

"Be careful when you make the Oversoul the witness of your oath," said Rasa. "She has a way of making you hold to your word."

Mebbekew almost said something else, but then thought better of it and stalked out of Rasa's private receiving room. No doubt off to flatter Dolya into proposing marriage to *him*.

And it will work, thought Rasa bitterly. Because this boy, who has so little else going for him, *is* good with women. Haven't I heard of his exploits from the mothers of so many girls in Dolltown and Dauberville? Poor Dolya. Has life left you so hungry that you'll swallow even the poor imitation of love?

Only Elemak and Nafai remained.

"I don't want to share my ceremony with Mebbekew," said Elemak coldly.

"It's tragic, isn't it, that we don't always get what we want in this world," said Rasa. "Anyone who wants to be married tonight, will be. We don't have time to satisfy your vanity, and you know it. You'd tell me so yourself, if you were giving me impartial counsel."

Elemak studied her face for a few moments. "Yes," he said. "You're very wise." Then he, too, left.

But Rasa understood him, too, better than he imagined. She knew that he had sized her up and decided that, while she might be powerful in Basilica, she would be nothing in the desert. He would bow to her rule tonight, but once they got out into the desert he would delight in subjugating her. Well, I am not afraid to be humiliated, thought Rasa. I can bear much more than you imagine. What will your torments mean to me, when I will feel the agony of my beloved city, and know that in my exile I can do nothing to save it after all?

Only Nafai was with her now.

"Mother," he said, "what about Issib? And Gaballufix's treasurer, Zdorab? They'll need wives. And Elemak saw wives for all of us, in his dream."

"Then the Oversoul must provide wives for them, don't you think?"

"Shedemei will come," he said. "She had a dream, too. The Oversoul is bringing her. And Hushidh. She's part of this, isn't she? The Oversoul will surely bring her. For Issib, or for Zdorab."

"Why don't you ask her?" said Rasa.

"Not *me*," said Nafai.

"You told me that the Oversoul said you would lead your brothers someday. How will that happen, if you haven't the strength inside yourself to face even a sweet and generous girl like Shuya?"

"To you she seems sweet," said Nafai. "But to *me*—and asking her such a thing—"

"She knows you boys came back here for wives, you foolish child. Do you think she hasn't counted heads? She's a raveler—do you think she doesn't already see the connections?"

He was abashed. "No, I didn't think of that. She probably knows more than I do about everything."

"Only about some things," said Rasa. "And you're still hiding from the most important question of all."

"No, I'm not," said Nafai. "I know that Luet is the woman I should marry, and I know that I will ask her. I didn't need your advice about that."

"Then I have nothing to fear for you, my son," said Rasa.

The soldiers brought Rashgallivak into his room and, as Moozh had instructed them beforehand, cast him down brutally onto the floor. When the soldiers had left, Rashgallivak touched his nose. It wasn't broken, but it was bleeding from its impact with the floor, and Moozh offered him nothing to wipe the blood. Since the soldiers had stripped Rashgallivak naked before bringing him here, there was nothing for Rashgallivak to do but let the blood flow into his mouth or down his chin.

"I knew I'd see you sooner or later," said Moozh. "I didn't have to search. I knew there'd come a time when you imagined that you had something I'd want from you, and then you'd come to me and try to bargain for your life. But I can assure you, I need nothing that you have."

"So kill me and have done," said Rashgallivak.

"Very dramatic," said Moozh. "I say I *need* nothing that you have, but I might *want* something, and I might even want it enough not to put your eyes out or castrate you or some other small favor before you are burned to death as a traitor to your city."

"Yes, so deeply you care for Basilica," said Rashgallivak.

"You gave me this city, you poor fool. Your stupidity and brutality gave it to me as a gift. Now it's the brightest jewel in my possession. Yes, I care deeply for Basilica."

"Only if you can keep it," said Rashgallivak.

"Oh, I assure you, I'll keep this jewel. Either by wearing it to adorn me, or by grinding it to powder and swallowing it down."

"So fearless you are, brave General. And yet you've got Lady Rasa under house arrest."

"I still have many paths that I can follow," said Moozh. "I can't think why any of them lead to anything but your immediate death. So you'll have to do better than tell me what I already know."

"Like it or not," said Rashgallivak, "I *am* the legal Wetchik and the head of the Palwashantu clan, and while no one has much love for me right now, if the disfranchised men outside the walls saw that I was in your favor and had some power to bestow, they would rally to me. I could be useful to you."

"I see that you harbor some pathetic dreams of being my rival for power here."

"No, General," said Rashgallivak. "I was a steward all my life, working to build and strengthen the house of Wetchik. Gaballufix talked me into acting on ambitions that I never had until he made me feel them. I've had plenty of time to regret believing him, to scorn myself for strutting around as if I were some great leader, when in fact what I am is a born steward. I was only happy when I served a stronger man than myself. I was proud that I always served the strongest man in Basilica. That happens to be yourself, and if you kept me alive and used me, you would find I am a man of many good gifts."

"Including unquestionable loyalty?"

"You will never trust me, I know that. I betrayed Wetchik, to my shame. But I only did it when Volemak was already exiled and powerless. You will *never* weaken or fail, and so you can trust me implicitly."

Moozh couldn't help laughing. "You're telling me that I can trust you to be loyal, because you're too much of a coward to betray a strong man?"

"I've had plenty of time to know myself, General Vozmuzhalnoy Vozmozhno. I have no desire to deceive either myself or you."

"I can put anyone in charge of the rabble of men who call themselves Palwashantu," said Moozh. "Or I can lead them myself. Why would I need you alive, when I can gain so much more from your public confession and execution?"

"You're a brilliant general and leader of men, but you still don't know Basilica."

"I know it well enough to rule here without losing the life of a single man of mine."

"Then if you're so all-knowing, General Vozmuzhalnoy Vozmozhno, perhaps you'll understand immediately why it is important that Shedemei bought a dozen drycases from me today."

"Don't play games with me, Rashgallivak. You know that I have no notion of who this Shedemei is, or what his buying drycases might mean."

"Shedemei is a woman, sir. A noted scientist. Very clever with genetics—she has developed some popular new plants, among other things."

"If you have a point . . ."

"Shedemei is also a teacher in Rasa's house, and one of her most beloved nieces."

Ah. So Rashgallivak *might* have something worth learning. Moozh waited to hear more.

"Drycases are used to transport seeds and embryos across great distances without refrigeration. She told me that she was moving her entire research laboratory to a faraway city, and that's why she needed drycases."

"And you don't believe her."

"It is unthinkable that Shedemei would move her laboratory *now*. The danger is clearly over, and ordinarily she would simply bury herself in her work. She is a very focused scientist. She barely notices the world around her."

"So her plan to leave comes from Rasa, you think."

"Rasa has been faithfully married to Wetch—to Volemak, the former Wetchik—for many years. He exiled himself from the city several weeks ago, ostensibly in obedience to some vision from the Oversoul. His sons came back to the city and tried to buy the Palwashantu Index from Gaballufix."

Rashgallivak paused, as if waiting for Moozh to make some connection; but of course Rashgallivak would know that Moozh lacked the information necessary to make this connection. It was Rashgallivak's way of trying to assert Moozh's need for him. But Moozh had no intention of playing this game. "Either tell me or don't," he said. "Then

I'll decide whether I want you or not. If you continue to imagine you can manipulate my judgment, you only prove yourself to be worthless."

"It's clear that Volemak still dreams of ruling here in Basilica. Why else would he want the Index? Its only value is as a symbol of authority among the Palwashantu men; it reminds them of that ancient, ancient day when they were not ruled by women. Rasa is his wife and a powerful woman in her own right. Alone she is dangerous to you—in combination with her husband, they would be formidable indeed. Who else could unite the city against you? Shedemei would not be preparing for a journey like this unless Rasa asked her to. Therefore Rasa and Volemak must have some plan that requires drycases."

"And what kind of plan would that be?"

"Shedemei is a brilliant geneticist, as I said. What if she could develop some mold or fungus that would spread like a disease through Basilica? Only Rasa's and Volemak's supporters would have the fungicide to kill it."

"A fungus. And you think this would be a weapon against the soldiers of the Gorayni?"

"No one's ever used such a thing as a weapon, sir," said Rashgallivak. "I could hardly think of it myself. But imagine how well your soldiers would fight if their bodies were covered with an excruciating, unbearable itch."

"An *itch*," echoed Moozh. It sounded absurd, laughable. And yet it might work—soldiers distracted by an itching, ineradicable fungus would not fight well. Nor would the city be easily governed, if people were suffering from such a plague. Governments were never less imposing than when they showed themselves impotent against disease or famine. Moozh had used this fact against the enemies of the Imperator many times. Was it possible that Rasa and Volemak were so clever, so evil-hearted, that they could conceive of such an inconceivable weapon? To use a scientist as a weapon maker—how could God allow such a vile practice to come into the world?

Unless . . .

Unless Rasa and Volemak have, like me, learned to resist God. Why should I be the only one with the strength to ignore God's efforts to turn men stupid when they attempted to walk on the road leading to power?

But then, couldn't Rashgallivak also be a tool God was using to mislead him? It had been many days since God had attempted to block him from any action. Was it possible that God, having failed to dominate Moozh directly, might now be trying to control Moozh by leading him after foolish imagined conspiracies? Many generals had been destroyed by just such fancies as the one Rashgallivak had now brought to him.

"Couldn't the drycases be for something else?" asked Moozh, testing.

"Of course," said Rashgallivak. "I only pointed out the most extreme possibility. Drycases also work very well for transporting supplies through the desert. Volemak and his sons—his oldest boy, Elemak, in particular—are more familiar with the desert than most. It holds no fear for them. They could be planning to build an army. You *do* have only a thousand men here."

"The rest of the army of the Gorayni will be here soon."

"Then perhaps that's why Volemak needed only twelve drycases—he won't need to supply his little army for very long."

"Army," said Moozh scornfully. "Twelve drycases. You were found with a draft for jewels of very high value. How do I know you haven't been bribed to tell me foolish lies and waste my time?"

"I wasn't *found,* sir. I turned myself over to your soldiers deliberately. And I brought the draft instead of the jewels because I wanted you to see that it was Shedemei's own hand that wrote the note. This amount is far more than the drycases are worth. She is clearly trying to buy my silence."

"So. This is where you are now, Rashgallivak. A few days ago you thought you were master of the city. And now you betray your former master once again, in order to ingratiate yourself with a new one. Explain to me why I shouldn't retch at the sight of you."

"Because I can be useful to you."

"Yes, yes, I can imagine, like a vicious but hungry dog. So tell me, Rashgallivak, what bone do you want me to toss you?"

"My life, sir."

"Your life will never be your own again, as long as you live. So again I ask you to tell me what bone you want to gnaw on."

Rashgallivak hesitated.

"If you pretend to have some altruistic desire to serve me or the Imperator or Basilica, I'll have you gutted and burned in the marketplace within the hour."

"We don't burn traitors here. It would make you look monstrous to the Basilicans."

"On the contrary," said Moozh. "It would make them very happy to see such treatment meted out to *you*. No one is so civilized as not to relish vengeance, even if later they're ashamed of how they loved to see their enemy suffer before he died."

"Stop threatening me, General," said Rashgallivak. "I've lived in terror and I've come out of it. Kill me or not, torture me or not, it doesn't matter to me. Just decide what to do."

"Tell me first what you want. Your secret desire. Your dream of the best thing that might come to you from all of this."

Again he hesitated. But this time he found the strength to name his desire. "Lady Rasa," he whispered.

Moozh nodded slightly. "So ambition isn't dead in you," he said. "You still have dreams of living infinitely above your station."

"I told you because you insisted, sir. I know it could never happen."

"Get out of here," said Moozh. "My men will take you to be bathed. And then dressed. You will live at least another night."

"Thank you, sir."

The soldiers came in and took Rashgallivak away—but this time without dragging him, without any brutality. Not that Moozh had decided to use Rashgallivak. His death was still an attractive possibility— it would be the most decisive way for Moozh to declare himself the master of Basilica, to mete out justice so publicly, so popularly, and so clearly in violation of all Basilican law and custom and decency. The citizens would love it, and in loving it they would cease to be the old Basilica. They would become something new. A new city.

My city.

Rashgallivak married to Rasa. That was a nasty thought, conceived in a nasty little mind. Yet it would certainly humiliate Rasa, and clinch the image of her in many people's minds as a traitor to Basilica. And yet she would still be a leading citizen of Basilica, with an aura of legitimacy. After all, she *was* on Bitanke's list. As was Rashgallivak.

It was a fine list, too. Well thought out, and quite daring. Bitanke was a bright man, very useful. For example, he was wise enough not to underestimate Moozh's powers of persuasion. He didn't leave people off his list just because he fancied that they'd never be willing to serve Moozh by ruling Basilica for him.

So the names that led the list were, unsurprisingly, the very names that Rashgallivak had mentioned as possible rivals: Volemak and Rasa. Rashgallivak's name, too, was there. And Volemak's son and heir, Elemak, because of both his ability and his legitimacy. Volemak's and Rasa's youngest, too—Nafai, because he linked those two great names and because he had killed Gaballufix with his own hands.

Was everyone who might serve Moozh's need linked to Rasa's house? That was no surprise to him—in most cities he'd conquered, there were at most two or three clans that had to be either eliminated or co-opted in order to control the populace. Almost everyone else on Bitanke's list was far too weak to rule well without constant help from Moozh, as Bitanke himself pointed out: They were too closely linked with certain factions, or too isolated from any support at all.

The only two who weren't tied by blood to Volemak or Rasa were nevertheless nieces in Rasa's house: The waterseer Luet and the raveler Hushidh. They were still only girls, of course, hardly ready to handle the difficult work of governance. But they had enormous prestige among the women of Basilica, especially the waterseer. They would be only figureheads, but with Rashgallivak to actually run things, and Bitanke to watch Rashgallivak and protect the figurehead from being manipulated against Moozh's best interest, the city could run very well while Moozh turned his attention to his real problems— the Cities of the Plain, and the Imperator.

Rashgallivak married to Rasa. It sounded so pleasantly dynastic. No doubt Rash's dreams included supplanting Moozh one day and ruling in his own right. Well, Moozh could hardly begrudge him those dreams. But there would soon be a dynasty that would surpass Rash's poor dreams. Rash might take the Lady Rasa, but how would that compare with the glorious marriage of the waterseer or the raveler with General Moozh himself? That would be a dynasty that could stand for a thousand years. That would be a dynasty that could topple the feeble house of that pathetic little man who dared to call himself the incarnation of God—the Imperator, whose power would be nothing when Moozh decided to move against him.

And, best of all, by marrying and using one of these chosen vessels of the Oversoul, Moozh would have the triumph that pleased him most: The triumph over God. You were never strong enough to control me, O Almighty One. And now I'll take your chosen daughter, filled with your visions, and make her the mother of a dynasty that will defy you and destroy all your plans and works.

Stop me if you can! I am far too strong for you.

Nafai found Luet and Hushidh together, waiting for him in the secret place on the roof. They looked very grave, which did nothing to calm the fear in Nafai's heart. Until now, Nafai had never felt himself to be young; he had always felt himself to be a person, equal to any other. But now his youth pressed in on him. He had not thought to marry now, or even really to *decide* whom to marry. Nor was it the easy, temporary union that he had expected his first marriage to be. His wife would probably be his only wife, and if he did badly in this marriage, he'd have no recourse. Seeing Luet and Hushidh, both looking at him solemnly as he made his way across the brightly sunlit roof, he wondered again if he could do this: If he could marry this girl Luet, who was so perfect and wise in the eyes of the Oversoul. She had come to the Oversoul with love, with devotion, with courage—he had come like a bratty child, taunting and testing his unknown parent. She had years of experience in speaking with the Oversoul; perhaps more important, she had had years in speaking *for* the Oversoul, to the women of Basilica. She knew how to dominate others—hadn't he seen it there on the shores of the lake of women, when she faced them down and saved his life?

Will I be coming to you as a husband or a child? A partner or a student?

"So the family council is over," said Hushidh, when at last he was near enough for easy speech.

He seated himself on the carpet under the awning. The shade gave him little enough respite from the heat. Sweat dripped under his clothing. It made him aware of his own naked body, hidden from view. If he married Luet, he would have to offer that body to her tonight. How often had he dreamed of such an offering? And yet never once had he thought of coming to a girl who filled him with awe and shyness, and yet who was herself utterly without experience; always in his dreams the woman was eager for him, and he was a bold and ready lover. There would be nothing like that tonight.

He had a wrenching thought. What if Luet wasn't ready yet? What if she wasn't even a *woman* yet? He quickly spoke a prayer in his heart to the Oversoul, but couldn't finish it, because he wasn't sure whether he hoped she *was* a woman, or hoped that she was *not.*

"How thickly woven are the bonds already," said Hushidh.

"What are you talking about?" asked Nafai.

"We're tied to the future by so many cords. The Oversoul has always told dear Luet, here, that she wants human beings to follow her freely. But I think she has caught us in a very tight-woven net, and we have about as much choice as a fish that's been dragged up from the sea."

"We have choices," said Nafai. "We always have choices."

"Do we?"

I don't want to talk to *you,* Hushidh. I came here now to talk to Luet.

"We have the choice to follow the Oversoul or not," said Luet, her voice coming soft and sweet, compared to Hushidh's harsher tone. "And if we choose to follow, then we are not caught in her net, but rather carried in her basket into the future."

Hushidh smiled wanly. "Always so cheerful, aren't you, Lutya."

A lull in the conversation.

If I am to be a man and a husband, I must learn to act boldly, even when I'm afraid. "Luet," he began. Then: "Lutya."

"Yes?" she said.

But he could not ignore Hushidh's eyes boring into him, seeing in him things that he had no desire for her to see.

"Hushidh," he said, "could I speak to Luet alone?"

"I have no secrets from my sister," said Luet.

"And will that be true, even when you have a husband?" asked Nafai.

"I have no husband," said Luet.

"But if you did, I would hope that he would be the one you shared your inmost heart with, and not your sister."

"If I had a husband, I would hope that he would not be so cruel as to require me to abandon my sister, who is my only family in the world."

"If you had a husband," said Nafai, "he should love your sister as if she were his own sister. But still not as much as he loved *you,* and so you should not love your sister as much as you loved *him.*"

"Not all marriages are for love," said Luet. "Some are because one has no choice."

The words stung him to the heart. She knew, of course—if the Oversoul had told *him,* it would certainly have told *her,* as well. And she was telling him that she didn't love him, that she was marrying him only because the Oversoul commanded it.

"True," said Nafai. "But that doesn't mean that the husband and the wife can't treat each other with gentleness and kindness, until they learn trust for each other. It doesn't mean they can't resolve to love each other, even if they didn't choose the marriage freely, for themselves."

"I hope that what you've said is true."

"I promise to make it true, if you'll promise me the same."

Luet looked at him with a chagrined smile on her face. "Oh. Is this how I'm to hear my husband ask me to be his wife?"

So he had done it wrong. He had offended her, perhaps hurt her, certainly disappointed her. How she must loathe the idea of being married to him. Didn't she see that he would never have chosen to force such a thing on her? As the thought formed in his mind, he blurted it out. "The Oversoul chose us for each other, and so yes, I'm asking you to marry me, even though I'm afraid."

"Afraid of *me?*"

"Not that you mean me any harm—you've saved my life, and my father's life before that. I'm afraid—of your disdain for me. I'm afraid that I'll always be humiliated before you and your sister, the two of you, seeing everything weak about me, looking down on me. The way you see me now."

In all his life, Nafai had never spoken with such brutal frankness about his own fear; he had never felt so exposed and vulnerable in front of anyone. He dared not look up at her face—at their faces—for fear of seeing a look of wondrous contempt.

"Oh, Nafai, I'm sorry," whispered Luet.

Her words came as the blow that he had most dreaded. She pitied him. She saw how weak and frightened and uncertain he was, and she felt sorry for him. And yet even in the pain of that moment of disappointment, he felt a small bright fire of joy inside. I can do this, he thought. I have shown my weakness to these strong women, and still I am myself, and alive inside, and not defeated at all.

"Nafai, I only thought of how frightened I was," said Luet. "I never imagined that you might feel that way, too, or I would never have asked Shuya to stay here when you came to me."

"It's no great pleasure to *be* here, I assure you," added Hushidh.

"It was wrong of me to make you say these things in front of Shuya," said Luet. "And it was wrong of me to be afraid of you. I should have known that the Oversoul wouldn't have chosen you if you weren't a good-hearted man."

She was afraid of *him?*

"Won't you look at me, Nafai?" she asked. "I know you never looked at me before, not with hope or longing, anyway, but now that the Oversoul has given us to each other, can't you look at me with—with kindness, anyway?"

How could he lift his face to her now, with his eyes full of tears; and yet, since she asked him, since it would mean disappointment to her if he did not, how could he refuse? He looked at her, and even though his eyes swam with tears—of joy, of relief, of emotions even stronger that he didn't understand—he saw her as if for the first time, as if her soul had been made transparent to him. He saw the purity of her heart. He saw how fully she had given herself to the Oversoul, and to Basilica, and to her sister, and to him. He saw that in her heart she longed only to build something fine and beautiful, and how readily she was willing to try to do that with this boy who sat before her.

"What do you see, when you look at me like that?" asked Luet, her voice timid, yet daring to ask.

"I see what a great and glorious woman you are," he said, "and how little reason I have to fear you, because you'd never harm me or any other soul."

"Is that all you see?" she asked.

"I see that the Oversoul has found in you the most perfect example of what the human race must all become, if we are to be whole, and not destroy ourselves again."

"Nothing more?" she asked.

"What can be more wonderful than the things I've told you that I see?"

By now his eyes had cleared enough to see that *she* was now on the verge of crying—but not for joy.

"Nafai, you poor fool, you blind man," said Hushidh, "don't you know what she's hoping that you see?"

No, I don't know, thought Nafai. I don't know any of the right things to say. I'm not like Mebbekew, I'm not clever or tactful, I give offense to everybody when I speak, and somehow I've done it again, even though everything I said was what I honestly feel.

He looked at her, feeling helpless; what could he do? She looked at him so hungrily, aching for him to give her—what? He had praised her honestly, with the sort of praise that he could have spoken to no other woman in the world, and it was nothing to her, because she wanted something more from him, and he didn't know what it was. He was hurting her with his very silence, stabbing her to the heart, he could see that—and yet was powerless to stop doing it.

She was so frail, so young—even younger than he. He had never realized that before. She had always been so sure of herself, and, because she was the waterseer, he had always been in awe. He had never realized how . . . how *breakable* she was. How thinly her luminous skin covered her, how small her bones were. A tiny stone could bruise her, and now I find her battered with stones that I cast without knowing. Forgive me, Luet, tender child, gentle girl. I was so afraid for myself, but I turned out not to be breakable at all, even when I thought you and Hushidh had scorned me. While you, whom I had thought to be strong . . .

Impulsively he knelt up and gathered her into his arms and held her close, the way he might hold a weeping child. "I'm sorry," he whispered.

"Don't be sorry, please," she said. But her voice was high, the voice of a child who is trying not to be caught crying, and he could feel her tears soaking into his shirt, and her body trembling with silent weeping.

"I'm sorry that it's only me you get as a husband," he said.

"And I'm sorry that it's only me you get as a wife," she said. "Not the waterseer, not the glorious being you imagined that you saw. Only me."

Finally he understood what she had been asking for all along, and couldn't help but laugh, because without knowing it he had just now given it to her. "Did you think that I said those things to the *waterseer?*" he asked. "No, you poor thing, I said those things to *you*, to Luet, to the girl I met in my mother's school, to the girl who sassed me and anybody else when she felt like it, to the girl I'm holding in my arms right now."

She laughed then—or sobbed harder, he wasn't sure. But he knew that whatever she was doing now, it was better. That was all she had needed—was for him to tell her that he didn't expect her to be the waterseer all the time, that he was marrying the fragile, imperfect human being, and not the overpowering image that she inadvertently wore.

He moved his hands across her back, to comfort her; but he also felt the curve of her body, the geometry of ribs and spine, the texture and softness of skin stretched taut over muscles. His hands explored, memorizing her, discovering for the first time how a woman's back felt to a man's hands. She was real and not a dream.

"The Oversoul didn't give you to me," he said softly. "You are giving yourself to me."

"Yes," she said. "That's right."

"And I give myself to you," he said. "Even though I, too, belong to the Oversoul."

He drew back a little, enough to cup the back of her head in his right hand as she looked up at him, enough to touch her cheek with the fingers of his left.

Then, suddenly, as if they both had the same thought at the same moment—which, quite certainly, they did—they looked away from each other, and toward the spot where Hushidh had been sitting through this whole conversation.

But Hushidh wasn't there. They turned back to each other then, and Luet, dismayed, said, "I shouldn't have made her come with me to—"

She never finished the sentence, because at that moment Nafai began to learn how to kiss a woman, and she, though she had never kissed a man before, became his tutor.

6

Weddings

THE DREAM OF THE RAVELER

Hushidh saw nothing joyful about the wedding. Not that anything went wrong. Aunt Rasa had a way with rituals. Her ceremony was simple and sweet, without a hint of the false portentousness that so many other women resorted to in their desperate desire to seem holy or important. Aunt Rasa had never needed to pretend. And yet she still took great care that when the public passages of life—weddings, comings-of-age, graduations, embarkations, divinations, deathwatches, burials—were under her care, they took place with an easy grace, a gentleness that kept people's minds focused on the occasion, and not on the machinery of celebration. There was never a hint of anyone hurrying or bustling; never a hint that everything had to be *just so,* and therefore you'd better watch your step so you don't do anything wrong . . .

No, Rasa's wedding for her son Nafai and his two brothers—or, if you looked at it the other way, Rasa's wedding for her three nieces, Luet, Dol, and Eiadh—was a lovely affair on the portico of her house, bright and aromatic with flowers from her greenhouse and the blossoms that grew on the portico. Eiadh and Dol were astonishingly beau-

tiful, their gowns clinging to them with the elegant illusion of simplicity, their facepaint so artfully applied that they seemed not to be
painted at all. Or *would* have seemed so, had it not been for Luet.

Sweet Luet, who had refused to be painted at all, and whose dress
really *was* simple. Where Eiadh and Dol had all the elegance of
women trying—very successfully—to seem bright and young and gay,
Luet really *was* young, her gown artlessly covering a body that was still
more the promise than the reality of womanhood, her face bright with
a grave and timid sort of joy that made Eiadh and Dol look older and
far too experienced. In a way, it was almost cruel to make the older
girls have their weddings in the presence of this girl who rebuked
them by her very naivete. Eiadh had actually noticed, before the ceremony began—Hushidh overheard her urging Aunt Rasa to "send
somebody up with Luet to help her choose a dress and to do something
with her face and hair" but Aunt Rasa had only laughed and said, "No
art will help that child." Eiadh took that, of course, to mean that Aunt
Rasa thought Luet to be too plain to be helped by costume and
makeup; but Hushidh caught Aunt Rasa's eye the moment afterward,
and Aunt Rasa winked at her and rolled her eyes to let her know that
they both understood that poor Eiadh hadn't a clue about what would
happen at the wedding.

And it did happen, though fortunately Eiadh and Dol had no idea
that when the watching servants and students and teachers whispered,
"Ah, she is so lovely"; "Ah, so sweet"; "Look, who knew she was so
beautiful," they were all speaking of Luet, only of Luet. When Nafai, as
the youngest man, came forward to be claimed by his bride, the sighs
were like a song from the congregation, an improvised hymn to the
Oversoul, for having brought this boy of fourteen, who had the stature
and strength of a man and the bright fire of the Oversoul in his eyes, to
marry the Oversoul's chosen daughter, the waterseer, whose pure
beauty grew from the soul outward. He was the bright gold ring in
which this jewel of a girl would glow with unreflected luster.

Hushidh saw better than anyone how the people belonged to Luet in
their hearts. She saw the threads between them, sparkling like the
dew-covered strands of a spider's web in the first sunlight of morning;
how they love the waterseer! But most of all Hushidh saw the firming
bonds between the husbands and wives as the ceremony progressed.
Unconsciously she took note of each gesture, each glance, each facial

expression, and in her mind she was able to understand the connection.

Between Elemak and Eiadh, it would be a strange sort of unequal partnership, in which the less Eiadh loved Elemak, the more he would desire her; and the more he treated her gently and lovingly, the more she would despise him. It would be a painful thing to watch, this marriage, in which the agony of coming apart was the very thing that would hold them together. But she could say nothing of this—neither one would understand this about themselves, and would only be furious if she tried to explain it.

As for poor Dolya and her precious new lover, Mebbekew, it was an ill-considered marriage indeed—and yet there was no reason to suppose it would be less viable than Elemak's and Eiadh's. At the moment, flushed with the glory of being, as they supposed, the center of attention, they were happy with the new bonds between them. But soon enough the reality would settle in. If they stayed in the city, they would hate each other within weeks—Dol because of Mebbekew's betrayals and unfaithfulness, Mebbekew because of Dol's clinging, possessive need for him. Hushidh imagined their domestic life. Dol would be forever throwing her arms around him in wonderfully enthusiastic hugs, thinking she was showing her love when really she was asserting her ownership; and Meb, shuddering under her profuse embraces, slipping away at every opportunity to find new bodies to possess, new hearts to ravish. But in the desert, it would be very different. Meb would find no woman who desired him except Dolya, and so his own lusts would throw him back into her arms again and again; and the very fact that he *could* not betray her would ease Dol's lonely fears, and she would not oppress him so much with her need for him. In the desert, they could make a marriage of it, though Mebbekew would never be happy with the boredom of making love with the same woman, night after night, week after week, year after year.

Hushidh imagined, with a pleasure she wasn't proud of, what Elemak would do the first time Meb made some flirting advance toward Eiadh. It would be discreet, so as to avoid weakening Elemak's public position by hinting that he feared being cuckolded. But Meb would never so much as look at Eiadh again afterward . . .

The bonds between Elemak and Eiadh, between Dol and Mebbekew, they were the sort of links that Hushidh saw every day in the city. These were Basilican marriages, made more poignant—and perhaps more viable—by the fact that soon the Oversoul would bring them out into the desert where they would need each other more and have fewer alternatives than in the city.

The marriage between Luet and Nafai, however, was not Basilican. For one thing, they were too young. Luet was only thirteen. It was almost barbaric, really—like the forest tribes of the Northern Shore, where a girl was bought as a bride before her first blood had stopped trickling. Only Hushidh's sure knowledge that the Oversoul had brought them together kept her from recoiling from the ceremony. Even at that, she felt a deep anger that she did not fully understand as she watched them join hands, make their vows, kiss so sweetly with Aunt Rasa's hands on their shoulders. Why do I hate this marriage so much, she wondered. For she could see that Luet was full of hope and joy, that Nafai was in awe of her and eager to please her—what more could Hushidh have hoped for, for her dear sister, her only kin in this world?

Yet when the wedding ended, when the newly married couples made their laughing, flower-strewn procession back into the house and up the stairways to their balcony rooms, Hushidh could not contain herself long enough even to watch her sister out of sight. She fled into a servants' corridor, and ran, not to her room, but to the rooftop where she and Luet had so often retreated together.

Even here, though, it was as if she could still see, in the gathering dark of evening, the shadow of Luet's and Nafai's first embrace, their first kiss. It filled her with rage, and she threw herself down onto the rug, beating on the thick fabric with her fists, weeping bitterly and sobbing, "No, no, no, no."

To what was she saying no? She didn't understand it herself. There she lay and there she wept until, weary with knowing too much and understanding not enough, she fell asleep in the cooling air of a Basilican night. Late in spring the breezes blew moist and cool from the sea, dry and warm from the desert, and met to do their turbulent dance in the streets and on the rooftops of the city. Hushidh's hair was caught in these breezes, and swirled and played as if it had a life of its own, and longed for freedom. But she did not wake.

Instead she dreamed, and in her dreams her unconscious mind brought forth the questions of fear and rage that she could not voice when she was awake. She dreamed of her own wedding. On a desert pinnacle, herself standing on the very tip of a high spire of rock, with no room for anyone else; yet there was her husband, floating in the air beside her: Issib, the cripple, blithely flying as she had seen him fly through the halls of Rasa's house during all his student years. In her dream she screamed the question that she had not dared to voice aloud: Why am I the one who must marry the cripple! How did you come up with my name for that life, Oversoul! How have I offended you, that I will never stand as Luet stood, sweet and young and blossoming with love, with a man beside me who is strong and holy, capable and good?

In her dream, she saw Issib float farther away from her, still smiling, but *she* knew that his smile was merely his own kind of courage, that her cries had broken his heart. As she watched, his smile faded; he crumpled, he fell like a bird taken out of the sky by a cruel miraculous arrow. Only then did she realize in the dream that he had been flying only by the power of his love for her, his need for her, and when she recoiled from him he had lost his power of flight. She tried to reach for him, tried to catch him, but all that happened then was that she herself lost her footing on the spire of rock and tumbled after him, downward to the ground.

She woke, panting, trembling in the cold. She gathered the free end of the carpet and pulled it over her and huddled under it, her cheeks cold from the tears drying there, her eyes puffy and sore from crying. Oversoul! she cried out silently with all her heart. O Mother of the Lake, tell me that you don't hate me so! Tell me that this is not your plan for me, that it was only accident that left me so bereft of hope on my sister's wedding night!

And then, with the perfect illogic of grief and self-pity, she prayed aloud, "Oversoul, tell me why you planned this life for me. I have to understand it if I'm going to live it. Tell me that it means something. Tell me why I am alive, tell me if some plan of yours brought me into this life as I am. Tell me why this power of understanding you gave me is a blessing, and not a curse. Tell me if I'll ever be as happy as Luet is tonight!" And then, ashamed of having put her jealousy and longing in such naked words, Hushidh wept again and drifted back into sleep.

Under the carpet she grew warm, for the night was not so cold yet, when she was covered. Her tears were replaced by sweat, drips of it tickling across her body like tiny hands. And again she dreamed.

She saw herself in the doorway of a desert tent. She had never seen a pitched tent before, except in holograms, yet this was not a tent she had seen in any picture. There she stood, holding a baby in her arms, as four other children, like stepstairs in height, rushed forth from the tent, and in the dream she thought it was as though the tent had just given birth to them, as though they were just now exploding into the world. If I had to, I would bear them all over again, and bring them here just to see them living so, brown and laughing in the desert sunlight. Around and around the children ran, chasing each other in some childish game while Hushidh watched. And then in her dream she heard the baby in her arms begin to fuss, and so she bared a breast and let the baby suckle; she could feel the milk flowing gratefully out of her nipple, could feel the sweet tingling of the baby's lips, kissing and sucking and smacking for life, warm life, wet life, a mingling of milk and saliva making a froth of tiny bubbles at the corners of the baby's mouth.

Then, through the door of the tent, there floated a chair, and in the chair a man. Issib, she knew at once. But there was no anger in her heart when she saw him, no sense that she had been cheated out of some good thing in life. Instead she could see herself bound to him, heart to heart, by great ropes of glowing silk; she took the baby from her breast and laid it in Issib's lap, and he talked to the baby, and made her laugh as Hushidh lazily dried her breast and covered it again. All of them bound together, mother, father, children . . . she saw that this was what mattered, not some imagined ideal of what a husband ought to be. The children ran to their father and circled his chair, and he spoke to them, and they listened raptly, laughed when he laughed, sang with him when he sang. This Issib-of-dreams was not a burden for her to bear, he was as true a friend and husband as any she had ever seen.

Oversoul, she prayed in her dream, how did you bring me here? Why did you love me so much that you brought me to this time, to this place, to this man, to these children?

At once the answer came, with threads of gold and silver. The children connected to Hushidh and Issib, and then threads reaching out from them, backward, to other people. A rush, a haze of people, a billion, a trillion people, she saw them milling around, marching forward on some unknowable quest, or perhaps a migration. It was a fearful vision, so many people all at once, as though Hushidh were being shown every man and woman who had ever lived on Harmony.

And among them, here and there, those same silver and golden threads.

All at once she understood: These are the ones in whom the connection with the Oversoul bred true. These are the ones who are best able to hear the voice of the Oversoul, in whom the genetic alteration of Harmony's founding has been doubled, redoubled, so that instead of receiving only vague feelings, a stupor of thought when they venture onto some forbidden avenue of invention or action, these special ones, these gold and silver ones can receive clear ideas, images, even words.

At first the gold and silver threads were short and thin, only glimpses here and there—mutations, chance connections, random variations in the genetic molecules. But here and there they found each other, these people, and married; and when they mated, gold to gold or silver to silver, some of their children were also linked to the Oversoul. Two different strains, two different kinds of genetic link, Hushidh understood; when gold mated with silver, the children were almost never gifted this way. Over the centuries, over the uncountable multitudes, she could see that now the Oversoul was nudging gifted people, trying to bring them together, and after millions of years the gold and silver were no longer threads, they were strong cords, passing from generation to generation with much more regularity.

Until at last there came a time when one parent alone could pass the gold thread on to all his children; and then, many generations later, a time when the silver thread, too, became a dominant trait, that one parent could pass on regardless of whether the other parent was gifted or not.

Now the Oversoul grew more eager, and nudges became intricate plots as people were drawn together over thousands of kilometers, improbable marriages and matings. She saw a woman rise naked out of a stream to couple with a man she had come a thousand kilometers to find, the woman never knowing that this was the Oversoul's purpose. The man had in him both the gold and silver, strong and true, and so did the woman, and their daughter was born with cords of the brightest metal, shining as if with its own light.

In her dream Hushidh saw the mother take her baby and lay it in the arms of Rasa, who was herself linked to generations past with strands of gold and silver. And then the same woman, the same mother, laying yet another daughter, brighter still, in Rasa's arms. Before her eyes the second baby grew and became Luet, and now Hushidh saw what she had seen this very night, Luet and Nafai being bound together, but now she could see that, more than the cords of love and loyalty, of need and passion that Hushidh always saw, there were also these gold and silver cords, brighter in Luet and Nafai than in any others in the room. No wonder their eyes shone with such grace and beauty, thought Hushidh. They were created by the Oversoul, as surely as if she had come and smelted them out of perfect ore and touched them with the magic of life from her own hand.

Then Hushidh rose up as if she were flying over the portico, and she could see that all the couples being married there had these threads in them. Not as bright and strong as in Luet and Nafai, but they had them. Mebbekew and Elemak both had silver and gold in them; Dol had the silver only, and Eiadh the gold, with just a trace of silver.

Who else? How many others have you brought together, Oversoul?

Higher and higher she rose over the city, but because this was a dream she could still clearly see the people on the streets and in their houses. There were many bright traces of gold and silver here, far more than in any other place in all the world. Here in this city of women, many traders had come and brought, not just their goods, but their seed; many women had come on pilgrimage and stayed, at least long enough to bear a child; many families had sent their daughters and their sons to be educated; and now there was hardly a person in Basilica who was not touched with the gift to feel the influence of the Oversoul, to one degree or another. And those who were so touched could feel, not only the Oversoul, but also each other, though they never realized how much they understood. No wonder this is a holy city, thought Hushidh in her dream. No wonder it is known throughout the world for beauty and for truth.

Beauty and truth, but also darker things. The connection with the Oversoul did not mean that a person would be kinder or more generous. And unconscious knowledge of another person's heart could easily be turned to exploitation, manipulation, cruelty, or domination. Hushidh saw Gaballufix and realized that the threads in him were almost as bright as in Rasa or Wetchik. No wonder he knew so well how to lead the men of the Palwashantu, how to intimidate the women of Basilica, how to dominate those close to him.

Then Gaballufix as she saw in her dream stepped forth from his house, flailing about himself with his charged-wire blade as if a thousand invisible enemies attacked him. Hushidh understood that this was his own madness, and the Oversoul grieved at what he was doing. So she made Gaballufix stumble. He fell to the ground and lay there, still bright with gold and silver, but helpless and harmless for the moment.

As he lay there, another came: Nafai, she knew. She was being shown Luet's husband in his most terrible moment, for she could see how he stood over the body and pleaded with the Oversoul not to require him to do what he was being asked to do. Yet when he sliced off Gaballufix's head, he was not being controlled by the Oversoul. He had freely chosen to follow the Oversoul's path. Gaballufix was extinguished, and Nafai stood alone in the street, shining and ashamed.

Hushidh fairly flew over the city, catching glimpses of the brightest ones. Shedemei, alone in her laboratory, filling portable drycases with seeds and embryos. A man walking with Nafai toward the city gate, carrying a globe wrapped in a cloth—it had to be Zdorab, the one Nafai had told them about—and Zdorab was also bright with gold and silver. Sevet's husband, Vas. Kokor's husband, Obring. Both almost as bright as Rasa's and Gaballufix's daughters themselves. All these people brought together in this city, at this moment, and all the best of them were coming out into the desert to join Wetchik. The Oversoul had bred them for this, and now was calling them forth out of the world to take them to another place.

What will our children be? And our grandchildren?

Again she rose up over the city, rejoicing now to understand the Oversoul's plan, when she caught a glimpse of yet another gold and silver cord, as bright as any she had seen. She wanted to look, and because it was a dream she immediately swooped down and saw that the light came from Gaballufix's house, but the man was not Gaballufix. Instead he wore a strange uniform, and his hair was oiled and hung in wet-looking ringlets.

General Vozmuzhalnoy Vozmozhno, she realized. Moozh. He, too, has been brought here! He, too, is one that the Oversoul desires!

But as she watched, she saw Moozh stand up and draw his metal sword. Was he like Gaballufix, then? Would he flail about himself in a frenzy of killing?

No. He turned and saw the gold and silver cords that bound him to the Oversoul, and hacked at them with the blade. He cut them off, and then fled from them. Yet in a moment the cords grew back again, and once again he chopped them away and ran from where the cords had once led him. Again and again it happened, and Hushidh knew that he hated his connection with the Oversoul.

Yet he was here. However it had happened, the Oversoul had brought him here. And then she understood: The Oversoul, knowing how he hated her, how Moozh rebelled against her, had simply pushed him *not* to do whatever she actually wanted him to do. So easily he had been fooled! So easily he had been guided. And in her sleep she laughed.

Laughed and began to waken; she could feel the sleep falling away from her, could feel her body now, the real one, wrapped in a carpet, sweating even though the air was chill around her.

In that moment, as wakefulness drove away the dream, there came a sudden flash of vision that seemed different from all that had come before. She saw the image from her earlier dream, the one where she stood on the spire of rock and Issib floated in the air beside her, and he tumbled and fell and she also fell after him; it passed through her mind in a single flash, and then she saw something new: Winged creatures, hairy as animals and yet able to soar and fly; they swooped out of the sky and caught Issib and Hushidh by the arms and legs as they tumbled toward the ground, and with a great beating and pounding of their wings, they kept them from striking the rocks below, and instead carried them upward into the sky.

It terrified her, this sudden unexpected dream, for Hushidh knew that she was not really asleep, and no dream should have come at all, especially not one as clear and frightening as this. Hadn't the Oversoul already shown her everything she asked for? Why now did she bring her back to this old image?

And again, she flashed on a former moment in this night's dreams: She stood with Issib in the doorway of the tent, with the baby in Issib's lap and the children gathered around his floating chair. No sooner had she recognized the scene than it changed; they were no longer in the desert, but instead in lush forest, in the doorway of a wooden house in a clearing, and all at once giant rats rose up out of holes in the ground and dropped from the limbs of trees and rushed at them, and Hushidh knew they meant to steal their children, to carry them off and eat them, and she screamed in terror. Yet before the sound could even reach her lips, there came those flying creatures again, tumbling out of the sky to catch her children and lift them up out of the jaws and hands of the huge ravenous rats. Seeing what was happening, she snatched her own baby from Issib's lap and held it high above her head, and one of the flying creatures swooped down and snatched it from her hands and carried it away. And she stood there and wept, because she did not know if she had simply given her children from one predator to another . . . and yet she *did* know. She had made her choice, and when they came again she took Issib's arms and held them upward for the flying creatures to take him, to carry him away. Only before they could come, the rats were on them, tumbling them down, and a hundred tiny savage hands fumbled and seized at her, tugged at her—

She awoke with the sound of her own scream in her ears, and an unsoothable fear clawing at her heart. She was drenched in sweat, and the night was dark around her, the breeze chilling her, but her trembling was not from cold. She threw off the carpet that covered her and ran, stumbling, still half-blind from the sleep in her eyes and awkward from the stiffness of uncomfortable rest, to the gap in the gable that led her into an attic of the house.

By the time she got to her own room, she could see well enough, and walked smoothly and quietly, but she was still weak and terrified, and she could not bear the thought of being alone. For there was Luet's bed —Luet, who should be there to soothe her now—but it was empty, because Luet had gone to another bed, and held someone who needed her far less than Hushidh did tonight. Hushidh huddled on her own bed, alternating between silent trembling and great, gasping sobs, until she feared that someone in another room might hear her.

They'll think I'm jealous of Luet, if they hear me weeping. They'll think I hate her for marrying before me, and that isn't so . . . not now, anyway, not since the Oversoul showed me the meaning of it all. She tried to bring that dream back into her memory—of herself and her children and her husband at the door of the tent—but the moment she did, it transformed again and she was possessed by the terror of the rats coming out of their holes, out of the trees, and her only hope the desperate strangeness of the flying beasts—

And she found herself in the corridor outside her room, running away from a fear that she carried with her as she ran. Ran and ran until she hurled open the door to the room where she knew that Luet would be, for she couldn't bear this, she had to have help, and it could only be Luet, only Luet could help her . . .

"What is it?" The fear in Luet's voice was an echo of the terror in Hushidh's own. Hushidh saw her sister, sitting bolt upright on the bed, holding a sheet up to her throat as if it were a shield. And then Nafai, awakened more by her voice than by the door, sleepily rising from the bed, standing on the floor, coming toward Hushidh, not yet understanding who it was but knowing that if an intruder came it was his job to block the way . . .

"Shuya," said Luet.

"Oh, Luet, forgive me," Hushidh sobbed. "Help me. Hold me!"

Before Luet could reach her, Nafai was there, helping her, leading her into the room from the doorway. Then Luet was with her and brought her to sit on the rumpled bed, and now Hushidh could let out her sobs as her sister held her. She was vaguely aware of Nafai moving through the room; he closed the door, then found clothing enough for himself and Luet that they didn't need to be embarrassed when Hushidh stopped crying and came to herself.

"I'm sorry, I'm so sorry," Hushidh said again and again as she wept.

"No, please, it's all right," said Luet.

"Your wedding night, I never would have . . . but I dreamed, it was so terrible—"

"It's all right, Shuya," said Nafai. "Only I wish you could cry a little softer, because if anybody hears you they're going to think it's Luet sobbing her heart out on her wedding night and then who knows what they'll think of me." He paused. "Of course, come to think of it, maybe you should cry a little louder."

There was laughter and calm in Nafai's voice, and Luet also laughed a little at his jest. It was what Hushidh needed, to take away her terror: She could think of Luet and Nafai instead of her dream.

"No one has ever done anything as wretched as this," said Hushidh, miserable and ashamed and yet so deeply relieved. "Bursting in on my own sister's wedding night."

"It's not as if you interrupted anything," said Nafai, and then he and Luet both burst into laughter—no, *giggling* was what it was. Like little children with a ridiculous secret.

"I'm sorry to laugh when you're so unhappy," said Luet, "but you have to understand. We were both so bad at it." They both burst into giggles again.

"It's an acquired skill," said Nafai. "Which we haven't acquired."

Hushidh felt herself enfolded by their laughter, included in the calm that they created between them. It was unthinkable, that a young husband and his bride, interrupted in their first night together, should so willingly include and comfort an intruding sister; yet that was who they were, Lutya and her Nyef. She felt herself filled with love and gratitude for them, and it spilled out in tears, but glad ones, not the desperate tears born of loneliness and terror in the night.

"I wasn't weeping for myself," she said—for now she could speak. "I *was* jealous and lonely, I admit it, but the Oversoul sent me a kind dream, a good one, and it showed me and . . . my husband, and our children . . ." Then she had a thought that had not occurred to her before. "Nafai, I know that I am meant for Issib. But I have to ask—he *is* . . . capable, isn't he?"

"Shuya, he could hardly be *less* capable than I was tonight."

Luet playfully slapped at Nafai's hand. "She's asking a real question, Nafai."

"He's as much a virgin as I am," said Nafai, "and away from the city he has scant use of his hands. But he isn't paralyzed, and his . . . involuntary responses, well, *respond.*"

"Then the dream *was* true," said Hushidh. "Or it can be, anyway. I dreamed of my children. With Issib. That could be true, couldn't it?"

"If you want it to be," said Nafai. "If you're willing to accept him. He's the best of us, Shuya, I promise you that. The smartest and the kindest and the wisest."

"You didn't tell me that," said Luet. "You told me *you* were the best."

Nafai only grinned at her with stupid joy.

Hushidh felt better now, and also knew that it wasn't right for her to remain between them like this; she had received all that she could hope for from her sister, and now she could return to her room and sleep alone. The shadow of the evil dream had passed from her. "Thank you both," she whispered. "I will never forget how kind you were to me tonight." And she arose from the edge of the bed and started for the door.

"Don't go," said Nafai.

"I must sleep now," said Hushidh.

"Not until you tell us your dream," he said. "We need to hear it. Not the sweet dream, but the one that made you so afraid."

"He's right," said Luet. "It may be our wedding night, but the whole world is dark around us and we must know everything the Oversoul says to any of us."

"In the morning," said Hushidh.

"Do you think that we can sleep, wondering what terrible dream could strike so hard at our sister?" said Nafai.

Even though Hushidh knew how carefully he had chosen his words, she was grateful for the good and loving impulse behind them. In his heart he might very well fear or resent her close connection with his new wife, but instead of trying to resist that closeness or drive them apart, Nafai was deliberately working to include himself in their sisterhood, and include Hushidh in the closeness of their marriage. It was a generous thing to do, on this night of all nights, when it must have seemed to him that his worst fears about Hushidh were true, what with her plunging into their bridal chamber sobbing her eyes out in the middle of the night! If he was willing to try so hard, could she do any less than accept the relationship he wanted to create? She was a raveler, after all. She knew about binding people together, and was glad to help him tie this knot.

So she came back and they sat together on the bed, making a triangle with their crossed legs, knee to knee, as she told her dreams, from beginning to end. She spared herself nothing, confessing her own resentments at the beginning so that they could understand how glad she was for the Oversoul's assurances.

Twice they interrupted her with their astonishment. The first time was when she told of seeing Moozh, and how the Oversoul was ruling him through his very rejection of her. Nafai laughed in wonderment. "Moozh himself—the bloody-handed general of the Gorayni, running away from the Oversoul into the very path the Oversoul laid out for him. Who could have guessed it!"

The second time was when Hushidh told of the winged beasts that caught her and Issib as they fell. "Angels!" cried Luet.

At once Hushidh remembered the dream that Luet had told her days before. "Of course," Hushidh said. "That's why they came into my dream—because I remembered your telling me about those angels and the giant rats."

"Don't reach conclusions now," said Luet. "Tell us the rest of the dream."

So she did, and when it was done, they sat in silence, thinking for a while.

"The first dream, of you and Issib, I think that was from yourself," said Luet at last.

"I think so, too," said Hushidh, "and now that I remember your telling me that dream of hairy angels . . ."

"Quiet," said Luet. "Don't get ahead of the dream. After that first vision that came from your fears about marrying Issib, you begged the Oversoul to tell you her purpose, and she showed you that wonderful dream of the gold and silver cords binding people together—"

"Breeding us like cattle," said Nafai.

"Don't be irreverent," said Luet.

"Don't be too reverent," said Nafai. "I sincerely doubt that the Oversoul's original programming told it to start a breeding program among the humans of Harmony."

"I know that you're right," said Luet, "that the Oversoul is a computer established at the dawn of our world to watch over human beings and keep us from destroying ourselves, but still in my heart I feel the Oversoul as a woman, as the Mother of the Lake."

"Woman or machine, it's developed purposes of its own, and I'm not comfortable with this one," said Nafai. "Bringing us together to make a journey to Earth, I accept that, I'm glad of it—it's a glorious undertaking. But this breeding thing. My mother and father, coupling like a ewe and a ram brought together to keep the bloodlines pure . . ."

"They still love each other," said Luet.

He reached out a hand to her and cupped her fingers gently in his. "Lutya, they *do*, as we will love each other. But what we've done, we've done willingly, knowing the Oversoul's purpose and consenting to it, or so we thought. What other plots and plans does the Oversoul have in mind for us, which we'll only discover later?"

"The Oversoul told me this because I asked," said Hushidh. "If she *is* a computer, as you say—and I believe you, I really do—then perhaps she simply can't tell us what we haven't yet asked to know."

"Then we must ask. We must know *exactly* what she—what *he*— what *it* is planning," said Nafai.

Luet smiled at his confusion but did not laugh. Hushidh was not his loyal wife; she could not suppress a small hoot.

"However we think of the Oversoul," Nafai said patiently, "we have to ask. What it means for Moozh to be here, for instance. Are we supposed to try to bring him out into the desert, too? Is that why the Oversoul brought him here? And these strange creatures, these angels and rats—what do they mean? The Oversoul has to tell us."

"I still think the rats and angels came because Lutya dreamed them and told me about them and there they were, ready to give a face to my fears," said Hushidh.

"But why did they come into Lutya's dream?" asked Nafai. "*She* didn't fear them."

"And the rats weren't terrible or dangerous in my dream," said Luet. "They were just—themselves. Living their lives. They had nothing to do with human beings in my dream."

"Let's stop guessing," said Nafai, "and ask the Oversoul."

They had never done this before. Men and women did not pray together in the rituals of Basilica—the men prayed with blood and water in their temple, or in their private places, and the women prayed in water at the lake, or in *their* private places. So they were shy and uncertain. Nafai impulsively reached out his hands to Hushidh and Luet, and they took his hands and joined to each other as well.

"I speak to the Oversoul silently," said Nafai. "In my mind."

"I, too," said Luet, "but sometimes aloud, don't *you?*"

"The same with me," said Hushidh. "Luet, speak for us all."

Luet shook her head. "It was you who saw the dream tonight, Hushidh. It was you the Oversoul was speaking to."

Hushidh shuddered in spite of herself. "What if the bad dream comes back to me?"

"What does it matter which of us speaks?" said Nafai, "as long as we ask the same questions in our hearts? Father and Issib and I speak to the Oversoul easily, when we have the Index with us, asking questions and getting answers as if we spoke with the computer at school. We'll do the same here."

"We don't have the Index," Luet pointed out.

"No, but we are bound to the Oversoul with threads of gold and silver," said Nafai, glancing at Hushidh. "That should be enough, shouldn't it?"

"Speak for us then, Luet," said Hushidh.

So Luet spoke their questions, and then spoke aloud her own worries, and those Nafai had expressed, and the terror Hushidh had experienced. It was to that question that the first answer came.

I don't know, said the Oversoul.

Luet fell silent, startled.

"Did you hear what I heard?" asked Nafai.

Since no one knew what Nafai had heard, no one could answer.

Until Hushidh dared to say the thing *she* had heard inside her mind. "She doesn't know," whispered Hushidh.

Nafai gripped their hands tighter, and spoke to the Oversoul, his voice now and not Luet's speaking for them all. "What don't you know?"

I sent the dream of the gold and silver threads, said the Oversoul. I sent the dream of Issib and the children at the door of the tent. But I never meant you to see the general. I never showed you the general."

"And the . . . the rats?" asked Hushidh.

"And the angels?" asked Luet.

I don't know where they came from or what they mean.

"So," said Hushidh. "It was just a strange chance dream in your mind, Luet. And then because you told your dream it became a memory in *my* mind, and that's it."

No!

It was as if the Oversoul had shouted into her mind, and Hushidh shuddered under the force of it.

"What, then!" cried Hushidh. "If you don't know where it came from, how do you know that it isn't just an ordinary frightening dream?"

Because the general had it too.

They looked at each other in amazement.

"General *Moozh?*"

To Hushidh's mind there came a fleeting image of a man with a flying creature on his shoulder, and a giant rat clinging to his leg, and many people—humans, rats, and angels—approaching, touching the three of them, worshipping. As quickly as it came, the image receded.

"The general saw this dream?" asked Hushidh.

He saw it. Weeks ago. Before any of you dreamed of these creatures.

"Three of us then," said Luet. "Three of us, and we have never met the general, and he has never met us, and yet we all dreamed of these creatures. He saw worship, and I saw art, and you saw war, Hushidh, war and salvation."

"If it didn't come from you, Oversoul," said Nafai, urgently pressing the question, holding tightly to their hands. "If it didn't come from you, then where could such a dream have come from?"

I don't know.

"Is there some other computer?" asked Hushidh.

Not here. Not in Harmony.

"Maybe you just didn't know about it," suggested Nafai.

I would have known.

"Then why are we having these dreams?" demanded Nafai.

They waited, and there was no answer. And then there *was* an answer, but one that they did not wish for.

I'm afraid, said the Oversoul.

Hushidh felt the fear return to her own heart, and she gripped her sister's hand more tightly, and Nafai's hand as well. "I hate this," said Hushidh. "I hate it. I didn't want to know it."

I'm afraid, said the Oversoul, as clear as speech in Hushidh's mind—and, she hoped, in the minds of the other two as well. I'm afraid, for fear is the name I have for uncertainty, for impossibility that is nevertheless real. Yet I also have a hope, for that is another name for the impossible that might be real. I have a hope that what you have been given is from the Keeper of Earth. That across these many lightyears the Keeper of Earth is reaching out to us.

"Who is the Keeper of Earth?" asked Hushidh.

"The Oversoul has mentioned it before," said Nafai. "It's never been clear, but I think it's a computer that was set up as guardian of Earth when our ancestors left forty million years ago."

Not a computer, said the Oversoul.

"What is it then?" asked Nafai.

Not a machine.

"What, then?"

Alive.

"What could possibly be alive after all these years?"

The Keeper of Earth. Calling to us. Calling to you. Maybe my desire to bring you back to Earth is also a dream from the Keeper. I have also been confused, and did not know what I should do, and then ideas came into my mind. I thought they were the result of the randomizer routines. I thought they were my programming. But if you and Moozh can dream strange dreams of creatures never known in this world, can't I also be given thoughts that were never programmed into me, that do not come from anything in this world?

They had no answer for the Oversoul's question.

"I don't know about you," said Hushidh, "but I was definitely counting on the Oversoul to be in charge of everything, and I really don't like the idea of her not knowing what's going on."

"Earth is calling to us," said Nafai. "Don't you see? Earth is calling to us. Calling the Oversoul, but not *just* the Oversoul. *Us.* Or you two, anyway, and Moozh. Calling you to come home to Earth."

Not Moozh, said the Oversoul.

"How do you know, not Moozh?" asked Hushidh. "If you don't know why or how or even *whether* the Keeper of Earth gave us these dreams, then how do you know that Moozh is not supposed to come out onto the desert with us?"

Not Moozh, said the Oversoul. Leave Moozh alone.

"If you didn't mean Moozh to join us, then why did you bring him here?" asked Nafai.

I brought him here, but not for you.

"He has the same gold and silver threads as we do," said Luet. "And the Keeper of Earth has spoken to him."

I brought him here to destroy Basilica.

"That tears it," said Nafai. "That really tears it. The Oversoul has one idea. The Keeper of Earth has another. And what are *we* supposed to do?"

Leave Moozh alone. Don't touch him. He's on his own path.

"Right," said Nafai. "A minute ago you tell us that you don't know what's going on, and now we're supposed to take your word for it that Moozh isn't part of what we're doing! We're not puppets, Oversoul! Do you understand me? If you don't know what's going on, then why should we follow your orders in this? How do you know you're right, and we're wrong?"

I *don't* know.

"Then how do you know I shouldn't go to him and ask him to come with us?"

Because he's dangerous and terrible and he might use you and destroy you and I can't stop him if he decides to do it.

"Don't go," said Luet.

"He's one of *us,*" said Nafai. "If our purpose is a good one in the first place, then it's a good one *because* there's something right about *us,* the people that the Oversoul has bred, going back to Earth. If it's good it's good because the Keeper of Earth is calling us."

"Whatever sent me that terrible dream," said Hushidh, "I don't know if it's good or not."

"Maybe the dream was a warning," said Nafai. "Maybe there's some danger we'll face, and the dream was warning you."

"Or maybe the dream was a warning for you to stay away from Moozh," said Luet.

"How in the world could the dream possibly mean *that?*" he asked. He was shucking off the odd clothing he had thrown on in a hurry a short while before, and dressing seriously now, dressing to go out into the city.

"Because that's what I want it to mean," said Luet, and suddenly she was crying. "You've only been my husband for half a night, and suddenly you want to go to a man that the Oversoul says is dangerous and terrible, and for what? To invite him to come out into the desert? To invite him to give up his armies and his kingdoms and his blood and violence and travel with us in the desert on a journey that will somehow end with us on Earth? He'll kill you, Nafai! Or imprison you and keep you from coming with us. I'll *lose you.*"

"You won't," said Nafai. "The Oversoul will protect me."

"The Oversoul warned you not to go. If you disobey . . ."

"The Oversoul won't punish me because the Oversoul doesn't even know that I'm not right. The Oversoul will bring me back to you because the Oversoul wants me with you almost as much as *I* want me with you."

I don't know if I can protect you.

"Yes, well, there's an awful lot that you don't know," said Nafai. "I think you've made that clear to us tonight. You're a very powerful computer and you have the best intentions in the world, but you don't know what's right any more than *I* do. You don't know whether all your plans for Moozh might have been influenced by the Keeper of Earth, do you—you don't know whether the *Keeper's* plan is for me to do exactly what I'm doing, and let your plot to destroy Basilica go hang. To *destroy Basilica*, of all things! It's your chosen city, isn't it? You've brought together all the people who are closest to you in this one place, and you want to destroy it?"

I brought them together to create *you*, foolish children. Now I'll destroy it to spread my people out again throughout the world. So that whatever influence I have left in this world will reach into every land and nation. What is the city of Basilica, compared to the world?

"The last time you talked that way, I killed a man," said Nafai.

"Please," said Luet. "Stay with me."

"Or let me come with you," said Hushidh.

"Not a chance," said Nafai. "And Lutya, I *will* come back to you. Because the Oversoul *will* protect me."

I don't know if I can.

"Then do your best," said Nafai. With that he was out the door and gone.

"They'll arrest him the minute he tries to go anywhere in the street," said Hushidh.

"I know," said Luet. "And I understand why he's doing it, and it's a brave thing to do, and I even think it's the right thing to do, and I *don't want him to do it!*"

Luet wept, and now it was Hushidh's turn to hold and comfort *her.* What a dance this has been tonight, she thought. What a wedding night for you, what a night of dreams for me. And now, what morning will it be? You could be left a widow without even his child inside you. Or—why not?—the great general Moozh might come with Nafai, renounce his army, and disappear with us into the desert. Anything could happen. Anything at all.

IN GABALLUFIX'S HOUSE, AND NOT IN A DREAM

Moozh spread out his map of the Western Shore on Gaballufix's table, and let his mind explore the shape of things. The Cities of the Plain and Seggidugu were spread out before him like a banquet. It was hard to guess which way to move. By now they all must have heard that a Gorayni army held the gates of Basilica. No doubt the hotheads in Seggidugu were urging a quick and brutal response, but they would not prevail—the northern border of Seggidugu was too close to the main Gorayni armies in Khlam and Ulye. It would take so many soldiers to take Basilica, even if they knew there were only a thousand Gorayni to defend it, that it would leave Seggidugu vulnerable to counterstrike.

Indeed, many faint hearts in Seggidugu would already be wondering if it might not be best to come before the Imperator now, as supplicants, begging him to take their nation under his beneficent protection. But Moozh was sure that these would have no more luck than the hotheads. Instead the coolest minds, the most careful men would prevail. They would wait and see. And that was what Moozh was counting on.

In the Cities of the Plain, there was no doubt already a movement

afoot to revive the old Defense League, which had driven off the Seggidugu invaders nine times. But that was more than a thousand years
ago, when the Seggidugu had first stormed over the mountains from
the desert; it was unlikely that more than a few of the cities would
unite, and even in supposed unity they would be quarreling and stealing from each other and weakening each other more than if each stood
alone.

What was in Moozh's power to make happen? At this moment, if he
sent a delegation with a sternly worded demand for the surrender of
the nearest cities, they would no doubt receive quick compliance. But
the refugees would gout out of those cities like blood from a
heartwound, and the other Cities of the Plain *would* unite then. They
might even ask Seggidugu to lead them, and in that case Seggidugu
might well act.

Instead he might demand Seggidugu's surrender. If they complied,
then the Cities of the Plain would all roll over and play dead. But it was
too big a gamble, if he could find a better way. He really *could* force
the surrender of any one or even two of the Cities of the Plain, but he
had far too few men—and far too tenuous a link with the main Gorayni
armies—to make his ultimatum stick if Seggidugu decided to defy him.
Great wars had been avoided, great empires had been created by just
such dangerous bluffs, and Moozh was not afraid to take the chance if
there was no better way.

And if there *was* a better way, he would have to find it soon. By now
the Imperator himself would know that both Plod and the intercessor
assigned to Moozh's army had been killed—by a Basilican assassin, of
course, but no one had been able to question him because Moozh had
killed the man with his own hands. Then Moozh took off with a thousand men and no one knew where he was. That bit of news would
strike terror into the heart of the Imperator, for he knew quite well
how fragile the power of a ruler is, when his best generals become too
popular. The Imperator would be wondering how many of his own
men would flock to Moozh if he raised a flag of rebellion in the mountains; and how many others, too loyal to defect, would nevertheless be
terrified to fight against the greatest general of the Gorayni. All these
fears would prompt the Imperator to put his armies in motion, and to
have them moving south and west, toward Khlam and Ulye.

All well and good . . . that would frighten the Seggidugu even
more, and increase the chance that bluffing them into submission

might work. And these army movements would *not* get far before the next news reached the Imperator—that Moozh's bold movement had succeeded brilliantly, that the fabled city of Basilica was now in Gorayni hands.

Moozh smiled in pleasure at the thought of how that news would strike terror in the hearts of all the courtiers who had been whispering to the Imperator that Moozh was a traitor. A traitor? A man who has the wit and courage to take a city with a thousand men? To march past two powerful enemy kingdoms and take a mountain fortress perched in their rear? What kind of traitor is this? the Imperator would ask.

But still, he would be afraid, for boldness in his generals always terrified him. Especially boldness in Vozmuzhalnoy Vozmozhno. So the Imperator would send him a legate or two—certainly an intercessor, probably a new friend, and also a couple of close and trusted family members. They would not have the authority to overrule Moozh—the Gorayni would never have conquered so many kingdoms if the impera-tors had allowed their underlings to countermand the orders of gener-als in the field. But they *would* have the ability to interfere, to question, to protest, to demand explanations, and to send word back to the Impe-rator of anything they didn't like.

When would these legates arrive? They would have to take the same desert route that Moozh had taken with his men. But now that road would be closely watched by Seggidugu and Izmennik, so there would have to be a ponderous bodyguard, and supply wagons, and many scouts and tents and all sorts of livestock. Thus the legates would have neither the desire nor the ability to move even half as quickly as Moozh's army had moved. So it would be at least a week before they arrived, probably longer. But when they came, they would have many soldiers—perhaps as many as Moozh had already brought—and these soldiers would almost certainly not be men who had fought under Moozh, men he had trained, men he could count on.

A week. Moozh had at least a week in which to set in motion the course he was going to follow. He could try his bluff against Seggidugu now, and risk deep humiliation if he was defied—the Cities of the Plain would certainly unite against him then, and he'd soon be defending Basilica from a siege. This would not lead to his ouster as general, but it would take the luster off his name, and it would put him back under the thumb of the Imperator. These last few days had been so delicious, not to have to play the games of deception and subterfuge that consumed half his life when he had to deal with a friend appointed by the Imperator, not to mention some career-advancing, meddlesome intercessor. Moozh had killed relatively few people with his own hands, but he certainly relished the memory of those deaths—the surprise on their faces, the exquisite relief that Moozh felt then. Even the necessity of killing that good soldier of Basilica, Smelost, even *that* did not take away the sheer joy of his new freedom.

Am I ready?

Am I ready to make the move of my life, to strike in vengeance against the Imperator in the name of Pravo Gollossa? To risk all on my ability to unite Basilica, Seggidugu, and the Cities of the Plain, along with every Gorayni soldier who will follow me and whatever support we can eke out from Potokgavan?

And if I am not ready for that, am I ready to set my neck back into the collar that the Imperator forces all his generals to wear? Am I ready to bow to the will of God's incarnation here on Harmony? Am I ready to wait years, decades for an opportunity that may never be closer than it is right now?

He knew the answer even as he asked the question. Somehow he must turn this week, this day, this hour into his opportunity, his chance to bring down the Gorayni and replace their cruel and brutal empire with a generous and democratic one, led by the Sotchitsiya, whose vengeance was long delayed but not one whit less sure for all that. Here Moozh stood with an army—a small one, but *his*—in the city that symbolized all that was weak and effete and cringing in the world. I longed to destroy you, Basilica, but what if instead I make you strong? What if I make you the center of the world—but a world ruled by men of power, not these weak and cringing women, these politicians and gossips and actors and singers. What if the greatest story told about Basilica was not that it was the city of women, but that it was the city of the Sotchitsiya ascendancy?

Basilica, you city of women, your husband is here for you, to master you and teach you the domestic arts that you have so long forgotten.

Moozh looked again at Bitanke's list of names. If he was looking for someone to rule Basilica in the name of the Imperator, then he would have to choose a man as consul: One of Wetchik's sons, if they could be found, or perhaps Rashgallivak himself, or some weaker man who might be propped up by Bitanke.

But if Moozh wanted to unite Basilica and the Cities of the Plain and

Seggidugu as well against the Imperator, then what he needed was to become a citizen of Basilica by marriage, and to gain a place for himself at the head of the city; he needed, not a consul, but a bride.

So the names that intrigued him most were the two girls, the waterseer and the raveler. They were young—young enough that it would offend many if he married either of them, especially the waterseer—thirteen! And yet these two had the right kind of prestige, the kind that could include him in its aura if he married one or the other of them. Moozh, the great general of the Gorayni, marrying one of the most holy women of Basilica—humbling himself to enter the city as a mere husband instead of as a conqueror. It would win their hearts, not just those who were already grateful to him for the peace he had imposed, but all of them, for they would see that he desired, not to conquer them, but to lead them to greatness.

With the raveler or the waterseer as his wife, Moozh would not longer merely *hold* Basilica. He would *be* Basilica, and instead of issuing ultimata to the southern kingdoms and cities of the Western Shore, he would issue a battlecry. He would arrest the spies of Potokgavan and send them home to their lazy waterlogged empire with presents and promises. And the word would sweep like wildfire through the north: Vozmuzhalnoy Vozmozhno has declared himself the new incarnation, the true Imperator. He calls upon all loyal soldiers of God to come south to him, or to rise up against the usurper where they are! In the meantime the word would be whispered in Pravo Gollossa: The Sotchitsiya will rule. Rise up and take what has belonged to you for all these years!

In the chaos that would result in the northlands, Moozh would march northward, gathering allies with him as he went. The Gorayni armies would retreat before him; the natives of the conquered nations would welcome him as their liberator. He would march until the Gorayni were thrown back into their own lands, and there he would stop—for one long winter in Pravo Gollossa, where he would train his motley army and weld it into a worthy fighting force. Then in the spring of next year he would move into the hillfast land of the Gorayni and utterly destroy their capacity to rule. Every man of fighting age would have his thumbs cut off, so he could never wield either sword or bow, and with every thumb that was sheared off, the Gorayni would understand again the pain of the tongueless Sotchitsiya.

Let God try to stop him now!

But he knew that God would not. In these last few days, ever since he defied God and came south to seize Basilica, God had not tried to move against him, had not tried to block him in any way. He had half expected that God would make him forget these plans that he was laying out. But God must know now that it wouldn't matter if he did, for the plans were so true and obvious that Moozh would simply think of them again—and again and again, if it were necessary.

For me will be the overthrow of the Gorayni and the uniting of the Western Shore. For my son will be the conquest of Potokgavan, the civilizing of the northern forest tribes, the subduing of the northshore pirates. My son, and the son of my wife.

Which of you will it be? The waterseer was the more powerful of the two, the one with more prestige; but she was younger, too young, really. There would be a danger of people pitying her for such a marriage, unless Moozh could truly persuade her to come of her own free will.

The other one, though, the raveler, even though her prestige was less, would still do, and she was sixteen. Sixteen, a good age for a political marriage, for she had no former husbands and, if Bitanke was right, not even any lovers that anyone had heard about. And some of the prestige of the waterseer would still come to the marriage, because the raveler was her sister, and Moozh would see to it that the waterseer was well treated—and closely tied to the new dynastic house that Moozh would soon establish.

It was a very attractive plan. All that remained now was for Moozh to be sure—sure enough to act. Sure enough to go to Rasa's house and maneuver for the hand of one of these girls in marriage.

A single knock on the door. Moozh rapped once on the table. The door opened.

"Sir," said the soldier. "We have made an interesting arrest on the street in front of Lady Rasa's house."

Moozh looked up from the map on the table and waited for the rest of the message.

"Lady Rasa's youngest son. The one who killed Gaballufix."

"He escaped into the desert," said Moozh. "Are you sure it's not an impostor?"

"Quite possible," said the soldier. "But he did walk out of Rasa's house and straight up to the sergeant in charge and announce who he

was and that he needed to speak to you at once about matters that
would determine your future and the future of Basilica."

"Ah," said Moozh.

"So he's either the boy with balls of brass who cut off Gaballufix's
head and wore his clothes out of the city, or he's a madman with a
deathwish."

"Or both," said Moozh. "Bring him to me, and be prepared with an
escort of four soldiers to take him directly back to Lady Rasa's house
afterward. If I slap his face when you open the door to take him back,
then you will kill him on Lady Rasa's front porch. If I smile at him,
then you will treat him with courtesy and honor. Otherwise, he is
under arrest and will not be permitted to leave the house again."

The soldier left the door open behind him. Moozh sat back in his
chair and waited. Interesting, he thought, that I don't have to search
for the key players in this city's bloody games. They all come to me,
one by one. Nafai was supposed to be safely in the desert, beyond my
reach—but he was in Lady Rasa's house all the time. What other surprises have we pent up in her house? The other sons? How had
Bitanke summed them up . . . Elemak, the sharp and dangerous
caravanner; Mebbekew, the walking penis; Issib, the brilliant cripple.
Or why not Wetchik, the visionary plantseller himself? They might all
be waiting within Lady Rasa's walls for Moozh to decide how to use
them.

Was it possible—barely possible—that God really *had* decided to
favor Moozh's cause? That instead of opposing him, God might now be
aiding Moozh, bringing into his hands every tool he needed to accomplish his purpose?

I am certainly not the incarnation of anything but myself, thought
Moozh; I have no desire to play at holiness, the way the Imperator
does. But if God is willing at long last to let me have some help in my
cause, I will not refuse it. Perhaps in God's heart the hour of the
Sotchitsiya has arrived.

Nafai was afraid, but also he was not afraid. It was the strangest feeling.
As if there was a terrified animal inside him, aghast that he was walking
into a place where death was only a word away, and yet Nafai himself,
that part of him that *was* himself and not the animal, was simply fascinated to find out what he might say, and whether he would meet
Moozh, and what would happen next. It was not that he was unaware

of the perpetual immanence of death among the Gorayni; rather he had simply decided, at some deep level of his mind, that personal survival was an irrelevant issue.

The soldiers had seemed, if anything, more perplexed than alarmed at his accosting them on the street with the words, "Take me to the general. I'm Wetchik's son Nafai, and I killed Gaballufix." With those words he put his very life into this conversation, since Moozh now had witnesses of his confession of a crime that could lead to his execution; Moozh wouldn't even have to fabricate a pretext to have him killed if he wanted to.

Gaballufix's house had not changed, and yet it was entirely changed. None of the wall hangings, none of the furniture had been altered. All the lazy opulence was still intact, the plushness, the overdecoration in detail, the bold colors. And yet instead of being overpowering, the effect of all this ostentation was rather pathetic, for the simple discipline and brisk, unhesitating obedience of the Gorayni soldiers had the effect of diminishing everything around them. Gaballufix had chosen these furnishings to intimidate his visitors, to overawe them; now they looked weak, effete, as if the person who bought them had been frightened that people might see how weak his soul was, and so he had to hide it behind this barricade of bright colors and gold trim.

Real power, Nafai realized, does not demonstrate itself in anything that can be purchased for mere money. Money only buys the illusion of power. Real power is in the force of will—will strong enough that others bend to it for its own sake, and follow it willingly. Power that is won through deception will evaporate under the hot light of truth, as Rashgallivak had found; but real power grows stronger the more closely you look at it, even when it resides only in a single person, without armies, without servants, without friends, but with an indomitable will.

Such a man waited for him, sitting at a table behind an open door. Nafai knew this room. It was here that he and his brothers had faced Gaballufix, here that Nafai had blurted out some word or other that destroyed Elemak's delicate negotiations for the Index. Not that Gaballufix ever intended anything but to cheat them. The fact remained that Nafai had spoken carelessly, not realizing that Elemak, the sharp businessman, was holding back key information.

For a moment Nafai resolved inside himself to be more careful now, to hold back information as Elemak would have done, to be canny in this conversation.

Then General Moozh looked up and Nafai looked into his eyes and saw a deep well of rage and suffering and pride and, at the bottom of that well, a fierce intelligence that would see through all sham.

Is this what Moozh really is? Have I seen him true?

And in his heart, the Oversoul whispered, I have shown him to you as he truly is.

Then I can't lie to this man, thought Nafai. Which is just as well, because I'm not good at lying. I don't have the skill for it. I can't maintain the deep self-deception that successful lying requires. The truth keeps rising to the surface in my mind, and so I confess myself in every word and glance and gesture.

Besides, I didn't come here to play some game, to try my wits in some contest with General Vozmuzhalnoy Vozmozhno. I came here to give him the chance to join with us in our journey back to Earth. How could he do that if I tell him anything less than the truth?

"Nafai," said Moozh. "Please sit down."

Nafai sat down. He noticed that a map was spread out on the table before the general. The Western Shore. Somewhere on that map, deep in the southwest corner, was the stream where Father and Issib and Zdorab waited in their tents, listening to a troop of baboons hooting and barking at each other. Is the Oversoul showing Father what I'm doing now? Does Issib have the Index, and is he asking where I am?

"I assume that you didn't turn yourself in because your conscience overwhelmed you and you wanted to be put on trial for the murder of Gaballufix in order to expunge your guilt."

"No sir," said Nafai. "I was married last night. I have no desire to be imprisoned or tried or killed."

"Married last night? And out on the street confessing felonies before dawn? My boy, I fear you have not married well, if your wife can't hold you for even one night."

"I came because of a dream," said Nafai.

"Ah—*your* dream, or your bride's?"

"*Your* dream, sir."

Moozh waited, expressionless.

"I believe you dreamed once of a man with a hairy flying creature on his shoulder, and a giant rat clinging to his leg, and men and rats and angels came and worshipped them, all three of them, touching them with . . ."

But Nafai did not go on, for Moozh had risen to his feet and was boring into him with those dangerous, agonizing eyes. "I told this to Plod, and he reported it to the intercessor, and so it was known," said Moozh. "And the fact that you know it tells me that you have been in contact with someone from the Imperator's court. So stop this pretense and tell me the truth!"

"Sir, I don't know who Plod or the intercessor might be, and your dream wasn't told to me by anyone from the Imperator's court. I heard it from the Oversoul. Do you think the Oversoul doesn't know your dreams?"

Moozh sat back down, but his whole manner had changed. The certainty, the easy confidence was gone.

"Are you the form that God has taken now? Are you the incarnation?"

"Me?" asked Nafai. "You see what I am—I'm a fourteen-year-old boy. Maybe a little big for my age."

"A little young to be married."

"But not too young to have spoken to the Oversoul."

"Many in this city make a career of speaking to the Oversoul. You, however, God apparently answers."

"There's nothing mystical about it, sir. The Oversoul is a computer —a powerful one, a self-renewing one. Our ancestors set it in place forty million years ago, when they first reached the planet Harmony as refugees from the destruction of Earth. They genetically altered themselves and all their children—to us, all these generations later—to be responsive, at the deepest levels in the brain, to impulses from the Oversoul. Then they programmed the computer to block us from any train of thought, any plan of action that would lead to high technology or rapid communications or fast transportation, so that the world would remain a vast and unknowable place to us, and wars would remain a local affair."

"Until me," said Moozh.

"Your conquests have indeed ranged far beyond the area that the Oversoul would normally allow."

"Because I am not a slave to God," said Moozh. "Whatever power God—or, if you're right, this computer—whatever power it might have over other men is weaker in me, and I have withstood it and over-whelmed it. I am here today because I am too strong for God."

"Yes, he told us that you thought so," said Nafai. "But actually the influence of the Oversoul is even stronger in you than in most people. Probably about as strong as it is in me. If it was appropriate, if you opened yourself to its voice, the Oversoul could talk to you and you wouldn't need me to tell you what I'm here to tell you about."

"If the Oversoul told you that it is *stronger* in me than in most people, then your computer is a liar," said Moozh.

"You have to understand—the Oversoul isn't really concerned with individual people's lives, except insofar as it's been running some kind of breeding program to try to create people like me—and you, of course. I didn't like it when I learned about it, but it's the reason I'm alive, or at least the reason my parents were brought together. The Oversoul manipulates people. That's its job. It has manipulated you almost constantly."

"I'm aware that it has tried. I called it God, you call it the Oversoul, but it has not controlled me."

"As soon as it became aware that you intended to resist it, it simply turned things backward," said Nafai. "Whatever it wanted you to do, it forbade you to do. Then it made sure you remembered to do it and you obeyed almost perfectly."

"A lie," whispered Moozh.

It made Nafai afraid, to see how emotions were seizing this man. The general clearly was not accustomed to feelings he could not con-trol; Nafai wondered if perhaps he ought to let him calm down before proceeding. "Are you all right?" Nafai asked.

"Go on," said Moozh acidly. "I can hear anything that dead men say."

That was such a weak thing to say that Nafai was disgusted. "Oh, am I supposed to change my story because you threaten me with death?" he asked. "If I was afraid to die, do you think I would have come here?"

Nafai could see a change come over Moozh. As if he visibly reined himself in. "I apologize," said Moozh. "For a moment I behaved like the kind of man I most despise. Blustering a threat in order to change the message of a messenger who believes, at least, that he is telling me the truth. But I can assure you, whatever I might feel, if you die today it will not be because of any words you might say. Please go on."

"You must understand," said Nafai, "if the Oversoul really wants you to forget something, you *will* forget it. My brother Issib and I thought we were very clever, forcing our way through its barriers. But we didn't really force it. We simply became more trouble than it was worth to resist us. The Oversoul would rather have us go along with its plans knowingly than to have to control us and manipulate us. That's why I'm here. Because my wife's sister saw in a dream how strong your link with the Oversoul is, and how you waste yourself in a vain effort to resist. I came to tell you that the only way to break free of its control is to embrace its plan."

"The way to win is to surrender?" Moozh asked wryly.

"The way to be *free* is to stop resisting and start talking," said Nafai. "The Oversoul is the servant of humanity, not its master. It can be persuaded. It will listen. Sometimes it needs our help. General, *we* need you, if you'll only come with us."

"Come with you?"

"My father was called out to the desert as the first step in a great journey."

"Your father was driven out onto the desert by the machinations of Gaballufix. I have spoken with Rashgallivak, and I can't be deceived."

"Do you honestly believe that speaking with Rashgallivak is a way to ensure that you *won't* be deceived?"

"I would know if he lied to me."

"But what if he believed what he told you, and yet it still wasn't true?"

Moozh waited, unspeaking.

"I tell you that, regardless of the immediate impetus that caused our departure at a certain hour of a certain day, it was the Oversoul's purpose to get Father and me and my brothers out into the desert, as the first step to a journey."

"And yet here you are in the city."

"I told you," said Nafai. "I was married last night. So were my brothers."

"Elemak and Mebbekew and Issib."

Nafai was surprised and a little frightened that Moozh knew so much about them. But he had set out to tell the truth, and tell it he would. "Issib is with Father. He wanted to come. I wanted him to come. But Elemak wouldn't have it, and Father went along. We came for wives. And for Father's wife. When we arrived, Mother laughed and said that she would never go out onto the desert, no matter what mad project Wetchik had in mind. But then you put her under arrest and spread those rumors about her. In effect, you cut her off from Basilica, and now she understands that there's nothing for her here and so she, too, will go with us into the desert."

"You're saying that what I did was all part of the Oversoul's plan to get your mother to join her husband in a tent?"

"I'm saying that your purposes were bent to serve the Oversoul's plans. They always will be, General. They always have been."

"But what if I refuse to allow your mother to leave her house? What if I keep you and your brothers and your wives under arrest there? What if I send soldiers to stop Shedemei from gathering up seeds and embryos for your journey?"

Nafai was stunned. He knew about Shedemei? Impossible—she would never have told anyone. What was this Moozh capable of, if he could come into a strange city and be so aware of things so quickly that he could realize that Shedemei's gathering of seeds had something to do with Wetchik's exile?

"You see," said Moozh. "The Oversoul does not have power where I rule."

"You can keep us under arrest," said Nafai. "But when the Oversoul determines that it's time for us to go, you will find that you have a compelling reason to let us go, and so you'll let us go."

"If the Oversoul wants you to go, my boy, you may be sure that you will *not* go."

"You don't understand. I haven't told you the most important part. Whatever this war is that you think you're having with whatever version of the Oversoul it is that you call God, what matters is that dream you had. Of the flying beasts, and the giant rats."

Moozh waited, but again Nafai could see that he was deeply disturbed.

"The Oversoul didn't send that dream. The Oversoul didn't understand it."

"So. Then it was a meaningless dream, a common sleeping dream."

"Not at all. Because my wife also dreamed of those same creatures, and so did her sister. All three of you, and these were not common dreams. They felt important to all of you. You knew that they had a meaning. Yet they didn't come from the Oversoul."

Again Moozh waited.

"It has been forty million years since human beings abandoned the Earth they had almost completely destroyed," said Nafai. "There has been time enough for Earth to heal itself. For there to be life there again. For there to be a place for humankind. Many species were lost—that's why Shedemei is gathering seeds and embryos for our journey. We are the ones that have the gift of speaking easily with the Oversoul. We are the ones who have been gathered together, here in Basilica, this day, this hour, so that we can go forth on a journey that will lead us back to Earth."

"Apart from the fact that Earth, if it exists, is a planet orbiting a faraway star, to which even birds can't fly," said Moozh, "you have still said nothing about what this journey might have to do with my dream."

"We don't *know* this," said Nafai. "We only guess it, but the Oversoul also thinks it might be true. Somehow the Keeper of Earth is calling us. Across all the lightyears between us and Earth, it has reached out to us and it's calling us back. For all we know, it even altered the programming of the Oversoul itself, telling it to gather us together. The Oversoul thought it knew why it was doing this, but it only recently learned the real reason. Just as you are only now learning the real reason for everything you've done in your life."

"A message in a dream, and it comes from someone thousands of lightyears away from here? Then the dream must have been sent thirty generations before I was born. Don't make me laugh, Nafai. You're far too bright to believe this. Doesn't it occur to you that maybe the Oversoul is manipulating *you?*"

Nafai considered this. "The Oversoul doesn't lie to me," he said.

"Yet you say that it has lied to me all along. So we can't pretend that the Oversoul is rigidly committed to truthfulness, can we?"

"But it doesn't lie to *me.*"

"How do you know?" asked Moozh.

"Because what it tells me . . . *feels* right."

"If it can make *me* forget things—and it can, it's happened so many times that . . ." His voice petered out as Moozh apparently decided not to delve into those memories. "If it can do *that,* why can't it also make *you,* as you say, 'feel right'?"

Nafai had no ready answer. He had not questioned his own certainty, and so he didn't know why Moozh's reasoning was false. "It's not just me," said Nafai, struggling to find a reason. "My wife also trusts the Oversoul. And her sister, too. They've had dreams and visions all their lives, and the Oversoul has never lied to them."

"Dreams and visions all their lives?" Moozh leaned forward on the table. "Whom, exactly, did you marry?"

"I thought I told you," said Nafai. "Luet. She's one of my mother's nieces in her teaching house."

"The waterseer," said Moozh.

"I'm not surprised that you've heard of her."

"She's thirteen years old," said Moozh.

"Too young, I know. But she was willing to do what the Oversoul asked of her, as was I."

"You think you're going to be able to take the waterseer away from Basilica on some insane journey into the desert in order to find an ancient legendary planet?" asked Moozh. "Even if *I* did nothing to stop you, do you think the people of this city would stand for it?"

"They will if the Oversoul helps us, and the Oversoul *will* help us."

"And your wife's sister, which of your brothers did *she* marry? Elemak?"

"She's going to marry Issib. He's waiting for us at my father's tent."

Moozh leaned back in his chair and chuckled merrily. "It's hard to see who has been controlling whom," he said. "According to *you*, the Oversoul has a whole set of plans that I'm a small part of. But the way it looks to me, God is setting things up so that everything plays into my hands. I thought before you came in here that it looked as though God had finally stopped being my enemy."

"The Oversoul was never your enemy," said Nafai. "It was *your* decision to make a contest of it."

Moozh got up from the table, walked around it, sat down beside Nafai, and took him by the hand. "My boy, this has been the most remarkable conversation of my life."

Mine, too, thought Nafai, but he was too astonished to say anything.

"I'm sure you're very earnest about your desire to make this journey, but I can assure you that you've been seriously misled. You're not leaving this city, and neither is your wife or her sister, and neither are any of the other people you plan to take along. You'll realize that sooner or later. If you realize it sooner—if you realize it *now*—then I have another plan for you that I think you'll like a little better than puttering around among the rocks and scorpions and sleeping in a tent."

Again, Nafai wanted to be able to explain to him why he *wanted* to follow the Oversoul. Why he knew that he was freely following the Oversoul, and perhaps the Keeper of Earth as well. Why he knew that the Oversoul wasn't lying to him or manipulating him or controlling him. But because he couldn't find the words or even the reasons, he remained silent.

"Your wife and her sister are the keys to everything. I'm not here to conquer Basilica, I'm here to win Basilica's loyalty. I've watched you now for an hour, I've listened to your voice, and I'll tell you, lad, you're a remarkable boy. So earnest. So *honest*. And eager, and you mean well, it's plain to anyone with half an eye that you mean no harm to anyone. And yet you're the one who killed Gaballufix, and so freed the city from a man who *would* have been tyrant, if he had lived another day or two. And it happens that you've just married the most prestigious figure in Basilica, the girl who commands the most universal love and respect and loyalty and hope in this city."

"I married her to serve the Oversoul."

"Please, keep saying that, I want everyone to believe that, and when you say it it's amazingly truthful-sounding. It will be a simple matter for me to spread this story about how the Oversoul commanded you to kill Gaballufix in order to save the city. And you can even bruit it about that the Oversoul brought *me* here, too, to save the city from the chaos that came after your wife's sister, the raveler, destroyed Rashgallivak's power. It's all such a neat little package, don't you see? You and Luet and Hushidh and me, sent by the Oversoul to save the city, to lead Basilica to greatness. We all have a mission from the Oversoul . . . it's a story that will make the Imperator's nonsense about being God incarnate look pathetic."

"Why would you do this?" asked Nafai. It made no sense to him, for Moozh to propose making Nafai look like a hero instead of a killer, for Moozh to want to link himself with three people he was keeping prisoner in Rasa's house. Unless . . .

"What do you think?" asked Moozh.

"I think you imagine you can set *me* up as tyrant of Basilica instead of Gaballufix."

"Not tyrant," said Moozh. "Consul. The city council would still be there, quarreling and arguing and doing nothing important as usual. You'd just handle the city guard and the foreign relations; you'd just control the gates and make sure that Basilica remained loyal to me."

"Do you think they wouldn't see through this and realize I was a puppet?"

"They would if I didn't become a citizen of Basilica myself, and your good friend and close kin. But if I become one of them, a *part* of them, if I become the general of the Basilican army and do all that I do in your name, then they won't care who is puppet to whom."

"Rebellion," said Nafai. "Against the Gorayni."

"Against the most cruel and corrupt monsters who ever walked on Harmony's poor face," said Moozh. "Avenging their monstrous betrayal and enslavement of my people, the Sotchitsiya."

"So this is how Basilica will be destroyed," said Nafai. "Not *by* you, but because of your rebellion."

"I assure you, Nafai, I *know* the Gorayni. They're weak in the core, and their soldiers love me better than they love their pathetic Imperator."

"Oh, I have no doubt of it."

"If Basilica is my capital, the Gorayni won't destroy it. Nothing will destroy it, because I will be victorious."

"Basilica is nothing to you," said Nafai. "A tool of the moment. I can imagine you in the north, with a vast army, poised to destroy the army defending Gollod, the city of the Imperator, and at that moment you hear that Potokgavan has taken this opportunity to land an army on the Western Shore. Come back and defend Basilica, your people will beg. *I* will beg you. Luet will beg you. But you'll decide that there's plenty of time to deal with Potokgavan later, after you've defeated the Gorayni. And so you'll stay and finish your work, and the next year you'll sweep south and punish Potokgavan for their atrocities, and you'll stand in the ashes of Basilica and weep for the city of women. Your tears may even be sincere."

Moozh was trembling. Nafai could feel it in the hands that held his.

"Decide," said Moozh. "Whatever happens, either you will rule Basilica for me or you will die in Basilica—also for me. One thing is certain: You will never again *leave* Basilica."

"My life is in the hands of the Oversoul."

"Answer me," said Moozh. "Decide."

"If the Oversoul wanted me to help you subjugate this city, then I would be consul here," said Nafai. "But the Oversoul wants me to journey back to Earth, and so I will not be consul."

"Then the Oversoul has fooled you again, and this time you may well die for it," said Moozh.

"The Oversoul has never fooled me," said Nafai. "Those who follow the Oversoul willingly are never lied to."

"You never catch the Oversoul in his lies, is what you mean," said Moozh.

"No!" cried Nafai. "No. The Oversoul doesn't lie to me because . . . because everything that it has promised me has come true. All of it has been true."

"Or it has made you forget the ones that *didn't* come true."

"If I wanted to doubt, then I could doubt endlessly," said Nafai. "But at some point a person has to stop questioning and *act*, and at that point you have to trust something to be true. You have to act as if something is true, and so you choose the thing you have the most reason to believe in, you have to live in the world that you have the most hope in. I follow the Oversoul, I *believe* the Oversoul, because I want to live in the world that the Oversoul has shown me."

"Yes, Earth," said Moozh scornfully.

"I don't mean a planet, I mean—I want to live in the *reality* that the Oversoul has shown me. In which lives have meaning and purpose. In which there's a plan worth following. In which death and suffering are not in vain because some good will come from them."

"All you're saying is that you want to deceive yourself."

"I'm saying that the story the Oversoul tells me fits all the facts that I see. *Your* story, in which I'm endlessly deceived, can also explain all those facts. I have no way of knowing that your story is not true—but you have no way of knowing that *my* story isn't true. So I will choose the one that I love. I'll choose the one that, if it's true, makes this reality one worth living in. I'll act as if the life I hope for is real life, and the life that disgusts me—*your* life, your *view* of life—is the lie. And it *is* a lie. You don't even believe in it yourself."

"Don't you see, boy, that you've told me exactly the same story I told you? That the Oversoul has been fooling me all along? All I did was turn back on you the mad little tale you turned on me. The truth is that the Oversoul has played us both for fools, so all we can do is make the best life for ourselves that we can in this world. If you think that the best life for you and your new wife is to rule Basilica for me, to be part of the creation of the greatest empire that Harmony has ever known, then I'm offering it to you, and I will be as loyal to you as you are to me. Decide now."

"I've decided," said Nafai. "There will be no great empire. The Oversoul won't allow it. And even if there were such an empire, it would mean nothing to me. The Keeper of Earth is calling us. The Keeper of Earth is calling *you*. And I ask you again, General Vozmuzhalnoy Vozmozhno, forget all this meaningless pursuit of empire or vengeance or whatever it is that you've been chasing all these years. Come with us to the world where humanity was born. Turn your greatness into a cause that's worthy of you. Come with us."

"Come with you?" said Moozh. "You're going nowhere." Moozh arose and walked to the door and opened it. "Take this boy back to his mother."

Two soldiers appeared, as if they had been waiting by the door. Nafai got up from his chair and walked to where Moozh stood, half-blocking the door. They looked into each other's eyes. Nafai saw rage there still, unslaked by anything that had transpired here this morning. But also he saw fear, which had not been in his eyes before.

Moozh raised his hand as if to strike Nafai across the face; Nafai did not wince or shrink from the blow. Moozh hesitated, and the blow, when it came, was upon Nafai's shoulder, and then Moozh smiled at him. In his mind Nafai heard the voice that he knew as that of the Oversoul: A slap on the face was the soldiers' signal to murder you. I have this much power in the mind of this rebellious man: I have turned Moozh's slap into a smile. But in his heart, he wants you dead.

"We are not enemies, boy," said Moozh. "Tell no one what I've said to you today."

"Sir," said Nafai, "I will tell my wife and my sisters and my mother and my brothers anything that I know. There are no secrets there. And even if I didn't tell them, the Oversoul would; my secrecy would accomplish nothing but my loss of their trust."

At the moment he refused to agree to secrecy, Nafai saw that the soldiers stiffened, ready to strike out at him. But whatever the signal was that they waited for, it didn't come.

Instead Moozh smiled again. "A weak man would have promised not to tell, and then told. A fearful man would have promised not to tell, and then would not have told. But you are neither weak nor fearful."

"The general praises me too highly," said Nafai.

"It will be such a shame if I have to kill you," said Moozh.

"It would be such a shame to die." Nafai could hardly believe it when he heard himself answer so flippantly.

"You truly believe that the Oversoul will protect you," said Moozh.

"The Oversoul has already saved my life today," said Nafai.

Then he turned and left, one soldier ahead of him, and one behind. "Wait," said Moozh.

Nafai stopped, turned. Moozh strode down the hall. "I'll come with you," said Moozh.

Nafai could feel it in the way the soldiers nervously shifted their weight, though they didn't so much as glance at each other: This was not expected. This was not part of the plan.

So, thought Nafai. I may not have accomplished what I hoped for. I may not have convinced Moozh to come with us to Earth. But *something* has changed. Somehow things are different because I came.

I hope that means they're better.

The Oversoul answered in his mind: I hope so, too.

7
Daughters

THE DREAM OF THE LADY

Rasa slept badly after the weddings. She had, as a Basilican teacher should, kept her misgivings to herself, but it was emotionally grueling to give her dear weak Dolya to a young man that Rasa disliked as much as Wetchik's son Mebbekew. Oh, the boy was handsome and charming —Rasa wasn't blind, she knew exactly how attractive he could be—and she wouldn't have minded him as Dolya's first husband under ordinary circumstances, for Dolya was no fool and would certainly decide not to renew Meb after a single year. But there would be no question of renewals once they got into the desert. Wherever this journey would take them—Nafai's unlikely theory of Earth or some more possible place on Harmony—there would be no casual Basilican attitude toward marriage there, and even though she had warned them more than once, she knew that Meb and Dolya, at least, did not give her warnings even the slightest heed.

For, of course, Rasa was sure that Meb did not intend to leave Basilica. Married to Dol, he was now entitled to stay—he had his citizenship, and so he intended to laugh at any attempt by anyone to get him out of the city. If there weren't Gorayni soldiers outside the house, Meb would have taken Dolya and left tonight, never to show his face again until the rest of them had given up on him and left the city. So it was only the fact that Rasa was under house arrest that kept Meb in line. Well, so be it. The Oversoul would order things as she saw fit, and Mebbekew was hardly the one to thwart her.

Meb and Dolya, Elya and Edhya. . . . Well, she had seen nieces of hers marry miserably before. Hadn't she watched her own daughters marry badly? Well, actually, it was Kokor who married badly—Obring was a more moral man than Mebbekew only because he was too weak and timid and stupid to deceive and exploit women on Mebbekew's scale. Sevet, for her part, had actually married rather well, and Vas's behavior during the past few days had quite impressed Rasa. He was a good man, and maybe now that her voice had been taken from her Sevet would finally let pain turn her into a good woman. Stranger things had happened.

Yet when Rasa went to bed after the weddings, and could not sleep, it was the marriage between her son Nafai and her dearest niece, Luet, that troubled her and kept her awake. Luet was too young, and so was Nafai. How could they be thrust so early into manhood and womanhood, when their childhood was far from complete? Something precious had been stolen from both of them. And their very sweetness about the whole thing, the way they were trying so hard to fall in love with each other, only served to break Rasa's heart all the more.

Oversoul, you have so much to answer for. Is it worth all this sacrifice? My son Nafai is only fourteen, but for your sake he has a man's blood on his hands, and now both he and Luet share a marriage bed when at their age they should still be glancing at each other shyly, wondering if someday the other might fall in love with them.

She tossed and turned in her bed. The night was hot and dark—the stars were out, but there was little moonlight, and the streetlights shone dimly in the curfewed city. She could see almost nothing in her room, and yet did not want to turn on a light; a servant would see it, and think she might need something, and discreetly enter and inquire. I must be alone, she thought, and so she lay in darkness.

What are you plotting, Oversoul? I'm under arrest, no one can come or go from my house. Moozh has cut me off so that I can't begin to guess whom I might or might not be able to trust in Basilica, and so I must wait here for his plots and yours to unfold. Which will triumph here, Moozh's malevolent scheming or your own, Oversoul?

What do you want from my family? What will you *do* to my family, to my dearest ones? Some of it I consent to, however reluctantly: I consent to the marriage of Nyef and Lutya. As for Issib and Hushidh, when that time comes, if Shuya is willing then I am content, for I always dreamed of Issib finding some sweet woman who would see past his frailty and discover the man he is, the husband he might be— and who better than my precious raveler, my quiet, wise Shuya?

But this journey in the wilderness—we aren't prepared for it, and can't very well *get* prepared here in this house. What are you doing about *that*, in all your scheming? Aren't you perhaps a little over your head in all that's going on? Have you really planned ahead? Expeditions like this take a little planning. Wetchik and his boys could go out into the desert on a moment's notice because they had all the equipment they needed and they had some experience with camels and tents. I hope you don't expect me or my girls to be able to do that!

Then, a little bit ashamed of herself for having told the Oversoul off so roundly, Rasa uttered a much more humble prayer. Let me sleep, she prayed, dipping her fingers into the prayer basin beside the bed. Let me have rest tonight, and if it wouldn't be too much bother, show me some vision of what it is you plan for us. Then she kissed the prayer water off her fingers.

As she did so, more words passed through her mind, like a flippant addendum to her prayer. While you're telling me your plans, dear Oversoul, don't be afraid to ask for some advice. I've had some experience in this city and I love and understand these people more than you do, and you haven't been doing all that well up to now, or so it seems to me.

Oh, forgive me! she cried silently, abashed.

And then: Oh, forget it. And she rolled over and went to sleep, letting her fingers dry in the faint drafts coming in at the windows of her chamber.

She slept at last; she dreamed.

In her dream she sat in a boat on the lake of women, and opposite her—at the helm—sat the Oversoul. Not that Rasa had ever seen the Oversoul before, but after all, this was a dream, and so she recognized her at once. The Oversoul looked rather like Wetchik's mother had looked—a stern woman, but not unkind.

"Keep rowing," said the Oversoul.

Rasa looked down and saw that she was at the oars. "But I don't have the strength for this."

"You'd be surprised."

"I'd rather not be," said Rasa. "I'd rather be doing *your* job. You're the deity here, *you're* the one with infinite power. *You* row. *I'll* steer."

"I'm just a computer," said the Oversoul. "I don't have arms and legs. You have to do the rowing."

"I can see your arms and legs, and they're a great deal stronger than mine. Furthermore, I don't know where you're taking us. I can't see where we're going because I'm sitting here facing backward."

"I know," said the Oversoul. "That's how you've spent your whole life, facing backward. Trying to reconstruct some glorious past."

"So, if you disapprove of that, have the cleverness if not the decency to trade places with me. Let me look into the future while you do the rowing for a change."

"You all push me around so," said the Oversoul. "I'm beginning to regret breeding you all. When you get too familiar with me, you lose your respect."

"That's hardly *our* fault," said Rasa. "Here, we can't pass side by side, the boat's too narrow and we'll tip over. You crawl between my legs, and that way the boat won't spill."

The Oversoul grumbled as she crawled. "See? No respect."

"I *do* respect you," said Rasa. "I just don't have any illusions that you're always right. Nafai and Issib say that you're a computer. A program, in fact, that lives in a computer. And so you're no wiser than those who programmed you."

"Maybe they programmed me to learn wisdom. After forty million years, I may even have picked up a few good ideas."

"Oh, I'm sure you have. Someday you must show me one of them— you certainly haven't done so well till now."

"Maybe you just don't *know* all that I've done."

Rasa settled herself in the stern of the boat, her hand on the prow, and she saw to her satisfaction that the Oversoul had a good grip on the oars and was able to give a good strong pull.

However, the boat merely lurched forward and then stopped dead. Rasa looked around to see why, and she realized that they weren't on water at all, they were in the middle of a waste of wind-rippled sand.

"Well, *this* is a miserable turn of events," said Rasa.

"I'm not terribly impressed with your helmsmanship," said the

Oversoul. "I hope you don't expect me to do any serious rowing in *this.*"

"*My* helmsmanship," said Rasa. "It's *you* that got us out into the desert."

"And you could have done better?"

"I should hope so. For instance, where are the camels? We need camels. And tents! Enough for—oh, how many of us are there? Elemak and Eiadh, Mebbekew and Dol, Nafai and Luet—and Hushidh, of course. That's seven. And me. And then we'd better take Sevet and Kokor, and their husbands if they'll come—that's twelve. Am I forgetting something? Oh, of course—Shedemei and all her seeds and embryos—how many drycases? I can't remember—at least six camels for her project alone. And our supplies? I'm not even sure how to estimate this. Thirteen of us, and that's a lot of us to feed and shelter along the way."

"Well, why are you telling *me?*" asked the Oversoul. "Do you think I keep some sort of binary camels and tents in my memory?"

"So, just as I thought. You haven't even prepared a thing for the journey. Don't you know that these things can't be done suddenly? If you can't help me, take me to somebody who can."

The Oversoul began to lead her toward a distant hill. "You're so bossy," said the Oversoul. "*I'm* the one who's supposed to be the guardian of humanity, if you'll be so good as to remember that."

"That's fine, you keep doing that job, while I look out for the people I love. Who's going to take care of my household after I'm gone? Did you ever think of that? So many children and teachers who depend on me."

"They'll all go home. They'll find other teachers or other jobs. You're not indispensable."

They had reached the crest of the hill—as with all dreams, they were able to move very quickly sometimes, and sometimes very slowly. Now, at the top of the hill, Rasa saw that she was in the street in front of her own house. She had never known there was a way right down the hill to the desert from her own street. She looked around to see which way the Oversoul had brought her, only to find herself face-to-face with a soldier. Not a Gorayni, to her relief. Instead he was one of the officers of the Basilican guard.

"Lady Rasa," he said, in awe.

"I have work for you to do," she said. "The Oversoul would have told you all this already, only she's decided to leave this particular job up to me. I hope you don't mind helping."

"All I want to do is serve the Oversoul," he said.

"Well, then, I hope you'll be very resourceful and do all these jobs properly, because I'm not an expert and I'll have to leave a good many things to your judgment. To start with, there'll be thirteen of us."

"Thirteen of you to do *what?*"

"A journey in the desert."

"General Moozh has you under house arrest."

"Oh, the Oversoul will take care of that. I can't do *everything.*"

"All right, then," said the officer. "A journey into the desert. Thirteen of you."

"We'll need camels to ride on and tents to sleep in."

"Large tents or small ones?"

"How large is large, and how small is small?"

"Large can be up to a dozen men, but those are very hard to pitch. Small can be for two men."

"Small," said Rasa. "Everybody will sleep in couples, except one tent for three, for me and Hushidh and Shedemei."

"Hushidh the raveler? Leaving?"

"Never mind the roster, that's none of your business," said Rasa.

"I don't think Moozh will want Hushidh to leave."

"He doesn't want *me* to leave, either—*yet,*" said Rasa. "I hope you're taking notes."

"I'll remember."

"Fine. Camels for us to ride, and tents for us to sleep in, and then camels to carry the tents, and also camels to carry supplies enough for us to travel—oh, how far? I can't remember—ten days should be enough."

"That's a lot of camels."

"I can't help that. You're an officer, I'm sure you know where the camels are and how to get them."

"I do."

"And something else. An extra half-dozen camels to carry Shedemei's drycases. She might already have arranged for those herself—you'll have to check with her."

"When will you need all this?"

"Right away," said Rasa. "I have no idea when this journey will begin—we're under house arrest right now, you might have heard—"

"I heard."

"But we must be ready to leave within an hour, whenever the time comes."

"Lady Rasa, I can't do these things without Moozh's authority. He rules the city now, and I'm not even the commander of the guard."

"All right," said Rasa. "I hereby give you Moozh's authority."

"You can't give that to me," said the officer.

"Oversoul?" said Rasa. "Isn't it about time you stepped in and did something?"

Immediately Moozh himself appeared beside the officer. "You've been talking to Lady Rasa," he said sternly.

"She's the one who came to *me*," said the officer.

"That's fine. I hope you paid attention to everything she said."

"So you authorize me to proceed?"

"I can't right at the moment," said Moozh. "Not officially, because at the moment I don't actually know that I'm going to want you to do this. So you have to do it very quietly, so that even I don't find out about it. Do you understand?"

"I hope I won't be in too much trouble if you find out."

"No, not at all. I *won't* find out, as long as you don't go out of your way to tell me."

"That's a relief."

"When the time comes for me to want this journey to begin, I'll order you to make preparations. All you have to say is, Yes sir, it can be done right away. Please *don't* embarrass me by pointing out that you've had it ready since noon, or anything like that to make it look as though my orders aren't spur-of-the-moment. Understand?"

"Very good, sir."

"I don't want to have to kill you, so please don't embarrass me, all right? I may need you later."

"As you wish, sir."

"You may leave," said Moozh.

Immediately the officer of the guard disappeared.

Moozh immediately turned into Rasa's dream image of the Oversoul. "I think that about takes care of it, Rasa," she said.

"Yes, I think so," said Rasa.

"Fine," said the Oversoul. "You can wake up now. The real Moozh will soon be at your door, and you want to be ready for him."

"Oh, thanks so very much," said Rasa, more than a little put out.

"I've hardly had any sleep at all, and you're making me wake up already?"

"I wasn't responsible for the timing," said the Oversoul. "If Nafai hadn't run off half-cocked in the wee hours of the morning, demanding an interview with Moozh before the sun came up, you could have slept in to a reasonable hour."

"What time *is* it?"

"I told you, wake up and look at the clock."

With that the Oversoul disappeared and Rasa was awake, looking at the clock. The sky was barely greying with dawn outside, and she couldn't see what time it was without getting out of bed and looking closely. Wearily she groaned and turned on a light. Too, too early to get up. But the dream, strange as it was, had been this much true: Someone was ringing the bell.

At this hour, the servants knew they had no consent to open the door until Rasa herself had been alerted, but they were surprised to see her come into the foyer so quickly.

"Who?" she asked.

"Your son, Lady Rasa. And General Vozmoozh . . . the General."

"Open the door and you may retire," said Rasa.

The night bell was not so loud that the whole house heard it, so the foyer was nearly empty anyway. When the door opened, Nafai and Moozh entered together. No one else. No soldiers—though no doubt they waited on the street. Still, Rasa could not help remembering two earlier visits by men who thought to rule the city of Basilica. Gaballufix and Rashgallivak had both brought soldiers, holographically masked, in an attempt not so much to terrify *her* as to bolster their own confidence. It was significant that Moozh felt no need for accompaniment.

"I didn't know my son was out wandering the streets at this hour," said Rasa. "So I certainly appreciate your kindness in bringing him home to me."

"Surely now that he's married," said Moozh, "you won't be watching his comings and goings so carefully, will you?"

Rasa showed her impatience to Nafai. What was he doing, blurting out the fact that he had just married the waterseer last night? Had he no discretion at all? No, of course not, or he wouldn't even have been outside to be picked up by Moozh's soldiers. What, had he been trying to escape?

But no, hadn't there been something . . . in the dream, yes, the

Oversoul had said something about Nafai going off half-cocked, demanding an interview with Moozh. "I hope he hasn't been any trouble to you," said Rasa.

"A little, I will confess," said Moozh. "I had hoped he might help me bring to Basilica the greatness that this city deserves, but he declined the honor."

"Forgive me for my ignorance, but I fail to see how anything my son could do might bring greatness to a city that is already a legend through all the world. Is there any city still standing that is older or holier than Basilica? Is there any other that has been a city of peace for so long?"

"A solitary city, madam," said Moozh. "A lonely city. A city for pilgrims. But soon, I hope, a city for ambassadors from all the great kingdoms of the world."

"Who will no doubt sail here on a sea of blood."

"Not if things work well. Not if I have significant cooperation."

"From whom?" asked Rasa. "From me? From my son?"

"I would like to meet, though I know the honor is inconvenient, with two nieces of yours. One of them happens to be Nafai's young bride. The other is her unmarried sister."

"I do not wish you to meet with them."

"But they will wish to meet with me. Don't you think? Since Hushidh is sixteen, and free to receive visitors under the law, and Luet is also married, and thus also free to receive visitors, then I hope you will respect both law and courtesy and inform them that I wish to meet with them."

Rasa could not help but admire him even as she feared him—for, at a moment when Gabya or Rash would have blustered or threatened, Moozh simply insisted on courtesy. He did not bother reminding her of his thousand soldiers, of his power in the world. He simply relied on her good manners, and she was helpless before him, for right was not yet clearly on her side.

"I dismissed the servants. I will wait with you here, while Nafai goes for them."

When Moozh nodded, Nafai left, walking briskly toward the wing of the house where the bridal couples had spent the night. Rasa vaguely wondered at what hour Elemak and Eiadh, Mebbekew and Dol would rise, and what they would think of the fact that Nafai had gone to General Moozh. They ought perhaps to admire the boy's courage, but

Elemak would no doubt resent him for his very intrusiveness, meddling always in affairs that shouldn't concern him. Whereas Rasa didn't resent Nafai's failure to remember that he was only a boy. Rather she feared for him because of it.

"The foyer is not a comfortable place," said Moozh. "Perhaps there might be some private room, where early risers will not interrupt us."

"But why would we have need of a private room, when we don't yet know whether my nieces will receive you?"

"Your niece and your daughter-in-law," said Moozh.

"A new relationship; it could hardly bring us closer than we already were."

"You love the girls dearly," said Moozh.

"I would lay down my life for them."

"And yet cannot spare a private room for their meeting with a foreign visitor?"

Rasa glowered at him and led him out to her private portico—the screened-off area, where there was no view of the Rift Valley. But Moozh made no pretense of sitting in the place on the bench that she patted. Instead he made for the balustrade beyond the screens. It was forbidden for men to stand there, to see that view; and yet Rasa knew that it would weaken her to attempt to forbid him. It would be . . . pathetic.

So instead she arose and stood beside him, looking out over the valley.

"You see what few men have seen," said Rasa.

"But your son has seen it," said Moozh. "He has floated naked on the waters of the lake of women."

"It wasn't my idea," said Rasa.

"The Oversoul, I know," said Moozh. "He takes us down so many twisted paths. Mine perhaps the most twisted one of all."

"And which bend will you take now?"

"The bend towards greatness and glory. Justice and freedom."

"For whom?"

"For Basilica, if the city will accept it."

"We *have* greatness and glory. We *have* justice and freedom. How can you imagine that any exertion of yours will add one whit to what we have?"

"Perhaps you're right," said Moozh. "Perhaps I'm only using Basilica to add luster to my *own* name, at the beginning, when I need it. Is

Basilican glory so rare and dear that we can't find a bit of it to share with me?"

"Moozh, I like you so much that I almost regret the terror that fills my heart whenever I think of you."

"Why? I mean no harm to you, or to anyone you love."

"The terror is not for that. It's for what you mean to my city. To the world at large. You are the thing that the Oversoul was set in place to prevent. You are the machineries of war, the love of power, the lust for enlargement."

"You could *not* have made me prouder than to praise me thus."

There were footsteps behind them. Rasa turned to find Luet and Hushidh approaching. Nafai hung back.

"Come with your wife and sister-in-law, Nafai," said Rasa. "General Moozh has decreed our ancient custom to be abrogated, at least for this morning, with the sun preparing to rise behind the mountains."

Nafai walked more briskly then, and they took their places. Moozh easily and artfully arranged them, simply by taking his place leaning against the balustrade, so that as they sat on the arc of benches, their focus, their center was Moozh.

"I have come here this morning to congratulate the waterseer directly on her wedding last night."

Luet nodded gravely, though Rasa was reasonably sure that Luet knew Moozh had no such purpose. In fact, Rasa rather hoped that Nafai had some idea of what he had in mind, and had briefed the girls before they got here.

"It was an astonishing thing, for one so young," said Moozh. "And yet, having met young Nafai here, I can see that you have married well. A fitting consort for the waterseer, for Nafai is a brave and noble young man. So noble, in fact, that I begged him to let me place his name in nomination for the consulship of Basilica."

"There is no such office," said Rasa.

"There will be," said Moozh, "as there was before. An office little called for in times of peace, but needful enough in times of war."

"Of which we would have none, if you would only go away."

"It hardly matters, for your son declined the honor. In a way, it's almost fortunate. Not that he wouldn't have made a splendid consul. The people would have accepted him, for not only is he the bridegroom of the waterseer, but also he hears the voice of the Oversoul himself. A prophet and a prophetess, together in the highest chamber of the city. And for those who feared he might be a weakling, a puppet of the Gorayni overmaster, we need only point out the fact that long before old General Moozh arrived, Nafai himself, under the orders of the Oversoul, boldly ended a great menace to the freedom of Basilica and carried out a just execution of the penalty of death already owed by one Gaballufix, for ordering the murder of Roptat. Oh, the people would have accepted Nafai readily, and he would have been a wise and capable ruler. Especially with Lady Rasa to advise him."

"But he declined," said Rasa.

"He did."

"So what point is there in flattering us further?"

"Because there is more than one way for me to achieve the same end," said Moozh. "For instance, I could denounce Nafai for the cowardly murder of Gaballufix, and bring forth Rashgallivak as the man who heroically tried to hold the city through a time of turmoil. Had it not been for the vicious interference of a raveler named Hushidh, he might have succeeded—for everyone knew that Rashgallivak's hands were not stained with any man's blood. Instead he was the capable steward, struggling to hold together the households of both Wetchik and Gaballufix. While Nafai and Hushidh go on trial for their crimes, Rashgallivak is made consul of the city. And, of course, he quite properly takes Gaballufix's daughters under his protection, as he will also do with Nafai's widow after his execution, and the raveler after she is pardoned for her crime. The city council would not want these poor women under the influence of the dangerous, self-serving Lady Rasa for another day."

"So you *do* make threats, after all," said Rasa.

"Lady Rasa, I am describing serious possibilities—choices that I can make, which will lead me to the end that, one way or another, I *will* achieve. I *will* have Basilica freely allied with me. It will be *my* city before I go on to challenge the tyrannical rule of the Gorayni Imperator."

"There is another way?" asked Hushidh quietly.

"There is, and it is perhaps the best of all," said Moozh. "It is the reason why Nafai brought me home with him—so I could stand before the raveler and ask for her to marry me."

Rasa was aghast. "Marry *you!*"

"Despite my nickname, I have no wife," said Moozh. "It isn't good for a man to be alone too long. I'm thirty years old—I hope not too old for you to accept me as your husband, Hushidh."

"She is intended for my son," said Rasa.

Moozh turned on her, and for the first time his sweet manners were replaced by a biting, dangerous anger. "A cripple who is hiding in the desert, a manlet whom this lovely girl has never desired as a husband and does not desire now!"

"You're mistaken," said Hushidh. "I *do* desire him."

"But you have not married him," said Moozh.

"I have not."

"There is no legal barrier to your marrying me," said Moozh.

"There is none."

"Enter this house and slay us all," said Rasa, "but I will not let you take this girl by force."

"Don't make a drama of this," said Moozh. "I have no intention of forcing anything. As I said, I have several paths open to me. At any point Nafai can say, 'I'll be the consul,' whereupon Hushidh will find the onerous burden of my marriage proposal less pressing—though not withdrawn, if she would like to share my future with me. For I assure you, Hushidh, that come what may, my life will be glorious, and the name of my wife will be sung with mine in all the tales of it forever."

"The answer is no," said Rasa.

"The question is not asked of you," said Moozh.

Hushidh looked from one to another of them, but not asking them anything. Indeed, Rasa was quite sure that Hushidh was seeing, not their features, but rather the threads of love and loyalty that bound them together.

"Aunt Rasa," said Hushidh at last, "I hope you will forgive me for disappointing your son."

"Don't let him bully you," said Rasa fiercely. "The Oversoul would never let him have Nafai executed—it's all bluster."

"The Oversoul is a computer," said Hushidh. "She is not omnipotent."

"Hushidh, there are visions tying you to Issib. The Oversoul has chosen you for each other!"

"Aunt Rasa," said Hushidh, "I can only beg you to keep your silence and respect my decision. For I have seen threads that I never guessed were there, connecting me to this man. I did not think, when I heard his name was Moozh, that I would be the one woman with the *right* to use that name for him."

"Hushidh," said Moozh, "I decided to propose to you for political reasons, having never seen you. But I heard that you were wise, and I saw at once that you are lovely. Now I have seen the way you think and heard the way you speak, and I know that I can bring you, not just power and glory, but also the tender gifts of a true husband."

"And I will bring you the devotion of a true wife," said Hushidh, rising to her feet and walking to him. He reached for her, and she accepted his gentle embrace and his kiss upon her cheek.

Rasa, devastated, could say nothing.

"Can my Aunt Rasa perform the ceremony?" asked Hushidh. "I assume that for . . . political reasons . . . you'll want the wedding to be soon."

"Soon, but it can't be Lady Rasa," said Moozh. "Her reputation is none too good right now, though I'm sure that situation can be clarified soon after the wedding."

"Can I have a last day with my sister?"

"It's your wedding, not your funeral that you're going to," said Moozh. "You'll have many days with your sister. But the wedding will be today. At noon. In the Orchestra, with all the city as witnesses. And your sister Luet will perform the ceremony."

It was too terrible. Moozh understood too well how to turn this all to his advantage. If Luet performed the marriage, then her prestige would be on it. Moozh would be fully accepted as a noble citizen of Basilica, and he would have no need of any stand-in to be his puppet consul. Rather he would easily be named consul himself, and Hushidh would be his consort, the first lady of Basilica. She would be glorious in her role, worthy of it in every way—except that the role should not be played by anyone, and Moozh would destroy Basilica with his ambition.

Destroy Basilica . . .

"Oversoul!" cried Rasa from her heart. "Is that what you planned from the beginning?"

"Of course it is," said Moozh. "As Nafai himself told me, I was maneuvered here by God himself. For what other purpose, than to find a wife?" He turned again to Hushidh, who still looked up to him, still touched him, her hand on his arm. "My dear lady," said Moozh, "will you come with me now? While your sister prepares to perform the ceremony, we have many things to talk about, and you should be with me when we announce our wedding to the city council this morning."

Luet stood and strode forward. "I haven't agreed to play any part in this abominable farce!"

"Lutya," said Nafai.

"You can't force her!" cried Rasa triumphantly.

But it was Hushidh, not Moozh, who answered. "Sister, if you love me, if you have ever loved me, then I beg you, come to the Orchestra prepared to perform this wedding." Hushidh looked at them all. "Aunt Rasa, you must come. And bring your daughters and their husbands, and Nafai, bring your brothers and their wives. Bring all the teachers and the students of this house, even those who live away. Will you bring them to see me take a husband? Will you give me that one courtesy, in memory of all my happy years in this good house?"

The formality of her speech, the distance of her manner broke Rasa's heart, and she wept even as she agreed. Luet, too, promised to perform the ceremony.

"You will release them from this house for the wedding, won't you?" Hushidh asked Moozh.

He smiled tenderly at her. "They will be escorted to the Orchestra," he said, "and then escorted home."

"That's all I ask," said Hushidh. And then she left the portico on Moozh's arm.

When they were gone, Rasa sank to the bench and wept bitterly. "Why have we served her all these years?" Rasa demanded. "We are nothing to her. Nothing!"

"Hushidh loves us," said Luet.

"She's not talking about Hushidh," said Nafai.

"The Oversoul!" cried Rasa. Then she shouted the word, as if she were crowing it to the rising sun. "Oversoul!"

"If you've lost faith in the Oversoul," said Nafai, "at least have faith in Hushidh. She still has hope of turning this the way we want it to go, don't you realize? She took Moozh's offer because she saw some plan in it. Perhaps the Oversoul even *told* her to say yes, did you think of that?"

"I thought of it," said Luet, "but I can hardly believe it. The Oversoul has hinted nothing of this to us."

"Then instead of talking to each other," said Nafai, "and instead of getting resentful about it, perhaps we should listen. Perhaps the Oversoul is only waiting for us to spare it some scrap of our attention to tell us what's going on."

"I'll wait then," said Rasa. "But this better be a good plan."

They waited, all three with their own questions in their hearts.

From the look on Nafai's and Luet's faces, they received their answer first. And as Rasa waited, longer and longer, she realized that she would get no answer at all.

"Did you hear?" asked Nafai.

"Nothing," said Rasa. "Nothing at all."

"Perhaps you're too angry with the Oversoul to hear anything from her," said Luet.

"Or perhaps she's punishing me," said Rasa. "Spiteful machine! What did she have to say?"

Nafai and Luet glanced at each other. So the news wasn't good.

"The Oversoul isn't exactly in control of this," said Luet finally.

"It's my fault," said Nafai. "My going to the general put things at least a day ahead of schedule. He was already planning to marry one of them, but he would have studied it for another day at least."

"A day! Would that have made so much difference?"

"The Oversoul isn't sure that she can bring off her best plan, so quickly," said Luet. "But we can't blame Nafai for it, either. Moozh is impetuous and brilliant and he might have done it this quickly without Nafai's . . ."

"Stupidity," offered Nafai.

"Boldness," said Luet.

"So we're condemned to stay here as Moozh's tools?" asked Rasa. "Well, he could hardly misuse us more carelessly than the Oversoul has."

"Mother," said Nafai, and his tone was rather sharp. "The Oversoul has not misused us. Whether Hushidh marries Moozh or not, we will still take our journey. If she does end up as Moozh's wife, then she'll use her influence to set us free—he'll have no need for us once his position in the city is secured."

"*Us?*" asked Rasa. "Set *us* free?"

"All of us that we already planned for the journey, even Shedemei."

"And what about Hushidh?" asked Rasa.

"That's what the Oversoul can't do," said Luet. "If she can't prevent the wedding, then Hushidh will stay."

"I will hate the Oversoul forever," said Rasa. "If she does this to sweet Hushidh, then I'll never serve the Oversoul again. Do you hear me?"

"Calm yourself, Mother," said Nafai. "If Hushidh had refused him, then I would have agreed to be consul, and it would have been Luet and I who stayed behind. One way or another, it was going to happen."

"Is that supposed to comfort me?" Rasa asked bitterly.

"Comfort *you?*" asked Luet. "Comfort *you*, Lady Rasa? Hushidh is my sister, my only kin—you'll have all the children you ever bore with you, *and* your husband. What are you losing, compared with what I'm going to lose? Yet do you see me weeping?"

"You *should* be weeping," said Rasa.

"All the way through the desert I'll do my weeping," said Luet. "But for now we have very few hours to prepare."

"Oh, am I supposed to teach you the ceremony?"

"That will take five minutes," said Luet, "and the priestesses will help me anyway. The time we have must be spent in packing for the journey."

"The *journey*," said Rasa bitterly.

"We must have everything ready so it can be loaded onto camels in five minutes," said Luet. "Isn't that so, Nafai?"

"There's still a chance that all will work well," said Nafai. "Mother, now is not the time for you to give up. All my life, you've held firm no matter what the provocation. Are you collapsing now, when we need you most to bring the others into line?"

"Do you expect *us* to get Sevet and Vas, Kokor and Obring to pack up for a desert journey?" asked Luet.

"Do you think Elemak and Mebbekew will take these instructions from *me?*" asked Nafai.

Rasa dried her eyes. "You ask too much of me," said Rasa. "I'm not as young as you. I'm not as resilient."

"You can bend as much as you need to," said Luet. "Now please, tell us what to do."

So Rasa swallowed, for now, her grief, and stepped back into her old familiar role. Within minutes the whole house was set in motion, the servants packing and preparing, the clerks drafting letters of recommendation for every teacher who would be left behind, and reports on the progress of every pupil, so that they could all find new schools easily after Rasa left and the school was closed.

Then Rasa walked the long corridor to Elemak's bridal chamber, to begin the grueling process of informing the reluctant travelers that they *would* attend the wedding, since soldiers would be marching them there, and they *would* prepare for a desert journey, since for some reason the Oversoul had decided that they would not have suffered enough until they were out among the scorpions.

AT THE ORCHESTRA, AND NOT IN A DREAM

This was hardly the way Elemak would have wanted to spend the morning after his wedding. It was supposed to be a leisurely time of dozing and lovemaking, talking and teasing. Instead it had been a flurry of preparations—hopelessly inadequate preparations, too, since they were supposedly preparing for a desert journey and yet had neither camels nor tents nor supplies. And it was disturbing how badly Eiadh had adjusted to the situation. Where Mebbekew's Dol was immediately cooperative—more so than Meb himself, the slug—Eiadh kept wasting Elemak's time with protests and arguments. Couldn't we stay behind and join them later? Why do *we* have to leave just because Aunt Rasa is under arrest?

Finally Elemak had sent Eiadh to Luet and Nafai to get her questions answered while he supervised the packing, to eliminate needless clothing—which meant bitter arguments with Rasa's daughter Kokor, who could not understand why her light and provocative little frocks were not going to be particularly useful out on the desert. Finally he had blown up, in front of her sister Sevet and both their husbands, and said, "Listen, Kokor, the only man you're going to be able to have out there is your husband, and when you want to seduce *him,* you can take your clothes *off.*" With that he picked up her favorite dress and tore it down the middle. Of course she screamed and wept—but he saw her later, magnanimously giving away all her favorite gowns—or perhaps trading them for more practical clothing, since it was likely that Kokor had owned nothing serviceable at all.

If the ordeal of packing had not been enough, there was the mortifying passage through the city. True, the soldiers had done a fair job of being discreet—no solid phalanx of brutish men marching in step. But they were still Gorayni soldiers, and so passersby—most of them also heading for the Orchestra—cleared a space around them and then gawked at them as they passed. "They look at us like we're criminals," Eiadh said. But Elemak reassured her that most bystanders probably

assumed they were guests of honor with a military escort, which made
Eiadh preen. It bothered Elemak just a little, in the back of his mind,
that Eiadh was so childish. Hadn't Father warned him that young
wives, while they had sleeker, lighter bodies, also had lighter minds?
Eiadh was simply young; Elemak could hardly expect her to take serious matters seriously, or even to understand what was serious in the
first place.

Now they sat in places of honor, not up among the benches on the
upward slopes of the amphitheatre, but down on the Orchestra itself,
to the righthand side of the low platform that had been erected in the
center for the ceremony itself. They were the bride's party; on the
other side, the groom's party consisted of many members of the city
council, along with officers of the Basilican guard and a few—only a
handful—of Gorayni officers. There was no sign of Gorayni domination
here. Not that there needed to be. Elemak knew that there were plenty
of Gorayni soldiers and Basilican guards discreetly out of sight, but
close enough to intervene if something unexpected should happen. If,
for instance, some assassin or other curiosity-seeker should attempt to
cross the open space between the benches and the wedding parties
around the platform, he would find himself sporting a new arrow somewhere in his body, from one of the archers in the prompters' and
musicians' boxes.

How quickly things change, thought Elemak. Only a few weeks ago
I came home from a successful caravan, imagining that I was ready to
take my place as a man in the affairs of Basilica. Gaballufix seemed to
be the most powerful man in the world to me then, and my future as
the Wetchik's heir and Gabya's brother seemed bright indeed. Since
then nothing had stayed the same for two days at a time. A week ago,
dehydrating mind and body on the desert, would he have believed he
might be married to Eiadh in Rasa's house not a week thence? And
even last night, when he and Eiadh had been the central figures in the
wedding ceremony, could he have imagined that at noon the next day,
instead of Nafai and Luet being the childish, pathetic hangers-on at
Elemak's wedding, they would now sit on the platform itself, where
Luet would perform the ceremony and Nafai would stand as General
Moozh's sponsor?

Nafai! A fourteen-year-old boy! And General Moozh had asked *him*
to stand as his sponsor for citizenship in Basilica, offering him to
Hushidh as if Nafai were some important figure in the city. Well, he

was an important figure—but only as the husband of the waterseer. Nobody could possibly think that he deserved any such honor in and of himself.

Waterseer, raveler . . . Elemak had never paid much heed to such things. It was all priestcraft, a profitable business but one he didn't have much patience with. Like the foolish dream that Elemak had had out on the desert—it was such an easy matter to turn a meaningless dream into a plan of action, because of the gullible fools who believed that the Oversoul was some noble being instead of a mere computer program responsible for pressing data and documents from city to city by satellite. Even Nafai himself was saying that the Oversoul was just a computer, and yet he and Luet and Hushidh and Rasa were all full of tales about how the Oversoul was trying to arrange things so the marriage wouldn't take place and they would all end up out on the desert, ready for the journey, before the day was over. What, could a computer program make camels appear out of nothing? Make tents rise up out of the dust? Turn rocks and sand into cheeses and grain?

"Doesn't he look brave and fine?" asked Eiadh.

Elemak turned to her. "Who? Is General Moozh here?"

"I mean your brother, silly. Look."

Elemak looked toward the platform and did not think Nafai looked particularly brave or fine. In fact, he looked silly, all dressed up like a boy pretending to be a man.

"I can hardly believe he would walk right up to one of the Gorayni soldiers," said Eiadh. "And go speak to General Vozmuzhalnoy Vozmozhno himself—while everyone was still asleep!"

"What was brave about that? It was dangerous and foolish, and look what it led to—Hushidh having to marry the man."

Eiadh looked at him in bafflement. "Elya, she's marrying the most powerful man in the world! And Nafai will stand as his sponsor."

"Only because he's married to the waterseer."

Eiadh sighed. "She *is* such a plain little thing. But those dreams— I've tried to have dreams myself, but no one takes them seriously. I had the strangest dream last night, in fact. A hairy flying monkey with ugly teeth was throwing doo-doo on me, and a giant rat with a bow and arrow shot him out of the sky—can you believe anything so silly? Why can't *I* have dreams from the Oversoul, can you tell me that?"

Elemak was hardly listening. Instead he was thinking of how Eiadh had clearly been envious because Hushidh was marrying the most

powerful man in the world. And how she had admired Nafai for his
damnable cheek, in going out and accosting General Moozh in the
middle of the night. What could he possibly have accomplished, except
to infuriate the man? Pure stupid luck that it had ended up with Nafai
on that platform. But it galled Elemak all the same, that it was Nafai
who was sitting there, with all the eyes of Basilica upon him. Nafai who
was being whispered about, Nafai who would be seen as the husband
of the waterseer, the brother-in-law of the raveler. And as Moozh installed himself as king—oh, yes, the official word for it would be *consul*, but it would *mean* the same—Nafai would be the brother-in-law of
majesty and the husband of greatness and Elemak would be a desert
trader. Oh, of course they would restore Father to his place as Wetchik,
once Father realized that the Oversoul wasn't going to be able to get
anybody out of Basilica after all. And Elemak would again be his heir,
but what would *that* title mean anymore? Worst of all would be the fact
that he would receive his rank and his future back as a gift from *Nafai*.
It made him seethe inside.

"Nafai is so *impetuous*," said Eiadh. "Aren't you proud of him?"

Couldn't she stop talking about him? Until this morning, Elemak
had known that Eiadh was the finest marriage a man could make for
himself in this city. But now he realized that in the back of his mind he
had really been thinking that she was the finest *first* marriage a *young*
man could make. Someday he would need a real wife, a consort, and
there was no reason to think that Eiadh would grow up into such a one.
She would probably always be shallow and frivolous, the very thing
that he had found so endearing. Last night when she had sung to him,
her throaty voice full of rehearsed passion, he had thought he could
listen to her sing forever. Now he looked at the platform and realized
that it was Nafai, after all, who had made a marriage that would be
worth having thirty years from now.

Well, fine, thought Elemak. Since we *won't* get away from Basilica,
I'll keep Eiadh for a couple of years and then gently ease her away.
Who knows? Luet may not stay with Nafai. When she gets older she
may begin to wish for a *strong* man beside her. We can look back on
these first marriages as childish phases we went through in our youth.
Then *I* will be the brother-in-law of the consul.

As for Eiadh, well, with luck she'll bear me a son before we're
through. But would that truly be luck? Should my eldest son, my heir,
be a boy with such a shallow woman for his mother? In all likelihood, it

will be the sons of my later marriages, my mature marriages, who will
be the worthiest to take my place.

Then, like a sudden attack of indigestion, there came the realization
that Father, too, might feel that way. After all, Lady Rasa was *his*
marriage of maturity, and Issib and Nafai the sons of that marriage.
Wasn't Mebbekew walking, talking proof of the unfortunate results of
early marriages?

But not me, thought Elemak. I was not the son of some frivolous
early marriage. I was a son he couldn't have dared to ask for—his
Auntie's son, Hosni's son, born only because she so admired the boy
Volemak as she introduced him to the pleasures of the bed. Hosni was
a woman of substance, and Father trusts and admires me above his
other children. Or *did*, anyway, until he started having visions from the
Oversoul and Nafai was able to parlay that into an advantage by pretending to have visions, too.

Elemak was filled with rage—old, deep-burning rage and hot new
jealousy because of Eiadh's admiration for Nafai. Yet what burned hot-
test and deepest was his fear that Nafai was not pretending, that for
some unknowable reason the Oversoul had chosen Father's youngest
instead of his eldest to be his true heir. When Issib's chair was taken
over by the Oversoul and stopped Elemak from beating Nafai in that
ravine outside the city, hadn't the Oversoul as much as said so? That
Nafai would one day lead his brothers, or something to that effect?

Well, dear Oversoul, not if Nafai is dead. Ever think of that? If you
can speak to *him* then you can speak to me, and it's about time you
started.

I gave you the dream of wives.

The sentence came into Elemak's mind as clearly as speech. Elemak
laughed.

"What are you laughing at, Elya, dear?" asked Eiadh.

"At how easily a person can deceive himself," said Elemak.

"People always talk about how a person can lie to himself, but I've
never understood that," said Eiadh. "If you tell yourself a lie, then you
know you're lying, don't you?"

"Yes," said Elemak. "You know you're lying, and you know what the
truth is. But some people fall in love with the lie and let go of the truth
completely."

As you're doing now, said the voice in his head. You prefer to believe the lie that I cannot speak to you or anyone else, and so you will deny me.

"Kiss me," said Elemak.

"We're in the middle of the Orchestra, Elya!" she said, but he knew she wanted to.

"All the better," he said. "We were married last night—people expect us to be oblivious to everything but each other."

So she kissed him, and he let himself fall into the kiss, blanking his mind to everything but desire. When at last the kiss ended, there was a smattering of applause—they had been noticed, and Eiadh was delighted.

Of course, Mebbekew immediately proposed an identical kiss to Dol, who had the good sense to decline. Still, Mebbekew persisted, until Elemak leaned across Eiadh and said, "Meb. Anticlimax is always bad theatre—didn't you tell me that yourself?"

Meb glowered and dropped the idea.

I am still in control of things, Elemak thought. And I am *not* about to start believing voices that pop into my mind just because I wish for them. I'm not like Father and Nafai and Issib, determined to believe in a fantasy because it feels so warm and cuddly to think that some superior being is in charge of things. I can deal with the cold hard truth. That's always enough for a *real* man.

The horns began. From all the minarets around the amphitheatre, the horners began their wailing cries. These were ancient instruments, not the finely-tuned horns of theatre or concert, and there was no attempt to create harmony between them. Each horn produced one note at a time, held long and loud, then fading as the horner lost breath. The notes overlaid each other, sometimes with winsome dissonance, sometimes with astonishing harmonies; always it was a haunting, beautiful sound.

It silenced the citizens gathered in the benches, and it filled Elemak with a trembling anticipation, as he knew it did with every other person in the Orchestra. The wedding was about to begin.

Thirsty stood at the gate of Basilica and wondered why the Oversoul had failed her now. Hadn't she been helped every step of the way from Potokgavan? She had come upon a canal boat and asked them to let her ride, and they had taken her aboard without question, though she could give them no fare. At the great port, she had boldly told the captain of the corsair that the Oversoul required her to have the fastest passage to Redcoast ever achieved, and he had laughed and boasted that as long as he took no cargo, he could make it in a day, with such a fair wind. In Redcoast a fine lady had dismounted from her horse and offered it to Thirsty on the street.

It was on that horse that Thirsty arrived at the Low Gate, expecting to be admitted easily, as all women always were, citizens or not. Instead she found the gate tended by Gorayni soldiers, and they were turning everyone away.

"There's a great wedding going on inside," a soldier explained to her. "General Moozh is marrying some Basilican lady."

Without knowing how, Thirsty knew at once that this wedding was the reason she had come.

"Then you must let me in," she said, "because I am an invited guest."

"Only the citizens of Basilica are invited to attend, and only those who were already inside the walls. Our orders allow no exceptions, not even for nursing mothers whose babes are inside the walls, not even for physicians whose dying patients are within."

"I am invited by the Oversoul," said Thirsty, "and by that authority I revoke any orders you were given by a mortal man."

The soldier laughed, but only a little, for her voice had carried, and the crowd at the gate was watching, listening. They had also been turned away, and were liable to turn surly at the slightest provocation.

"Let her in," said one of the soldiers, "if only to keep the crowd from turning."

"Don't be a fool," said another. "If we let her in we'll have to let them all in."

"They all want me to enter," said Thirsty.

The crowd murmured their assent. Thirsty wondered at this—that the crowd of Basilicans should heed the Oversoul so readily, while the Gorayni soldiers were deaf to her influence. Perhaps this was why the Gorayni were such an evil race, as she had heard in Potokgavan: because they could not hear the voice of the Oversoul.

"My husband is waiting for me inside," said Thirsty, though not until she heard herself say the words did she realize it was true.

"Your husband will have to wait," said a soldier.

"Or take a lover," said another, and they laughed.

"Or satisfy himself," said the first, and they hooted.

"We should let her in," said one of the soldiers. "What if God has chosen her?"

Immediately one of the other soldiers drew his lefthand knife and put it to the throat of the one who had spoken. "You know the warning we were given—that it's the very one that we *want* to allow inside who must be prevented!"

"But she needs to be there," said the soldier who was sensitive to the Oversoul.

"Say another word and I'll kill you."

"No!" cried Thirsty. "I'll go. This is not the gate for me."

Inside her she felt the urgency to enter the city increase; but she would not have this man be killed when it would not get her through the gate in any case. Instead she wheeled the horse and made her way back through the crowd, which parted for her. Quickly she made her way up the steep trail that led to the Caravan Road, but she did not bother trying the Market Gate; she made her way along the High Road, but she did not try to enter at High Gate or Funnel Gate, either. She hurried her mount along the Dark Path, which wound among deep ravines sloping upward into the forested hills north of the city until she reached the Forest Road—but she did not follow it down to Back Gate, either.

Instead she dismounted and plunged into the dense underbrush of Trackless Wood, heading for the private gate that only women knew of, that only women used. It had taken an hour for her to go around the city, and she had gone the long way, too—but there was no horsepath around the east wall, which dropped straight down to crags and precipices, and to clamber that route on foot would have taken far longer. Now the wood itself seemed to snag at her, to hold her back, though she knew that the Oversoul was guiding every step she took, to find the quickest path to the private gate. Even when she entered there, however, it would take time to make her way up into the city, and already she could hear the horns beginning their plaintive serenade. The ceremony would begin in moments, and Thirsty would not be there.

Luet moved and spoke as slowly as she could, but as she stepped and spoke her way through the ceremony, she did not have the option of doing what she desired in her heart—to stop the wedding and denounce Moozh to the gathered citizens. At best she would merely be hustled from the platform before she could say a word, as a more responsible priestess took over; at worst, she might actually speak, might be stopped by an arrow, and then riot and bloodshed would ensue and Basilica could easily be destroyed before another morning came. What would that accomplish?

So she walked through the ceremony—with deliberation, with long pauses, but never stopping altogether, never ignoring the whispered promptings of the priestesses who were with her at every turning, at every speech.

For all the turmoil inside of Luet, though, she could not see that Hushidh felt anything but perfect calm. Was it possible that Hushidh actually welcomed this marriage, as a way of avoiding life as a cripple's wife? No—Shuya had been sincere when she said that the Oversoul had reconciled her to that future. Her calm must come from utter trust in the Oversoul.

"She is right to trust," said a voice—a whisper, really. For a moment she thought it was the Oversoul, but instead she realized that it was Nafai, who had spoken as she passed near him during the processional of flowers. How had he known what words he needed to say just then, to answer so perfectly her very thoughts? Was it the Oversoul, forging an ever-closer link between them? Or was it Nafai himself, seeing so deeply into her heart that he knew what she needed him to say?

Let it be true, that Shuya is right to trust the Oversoul. Let it be true that we will not have to leave her here when we make our journey to the desert, to another star. For I could not bear it to lose her, to leave her. Perhaps I would know joy again; perhaps my new husband could be a companion to me as Hushidh has been my dear companion. But there would always be an ache, an empty place, a grief that would never die, for my sister, my only kin in the world, my raveler who when I was an infant tied the knot that will bind us to each other forever.

And then, at last, the moment came, the taking of the oaths, Luet's hands on their shoulders—reaching up to Moozh's shoulder, so hard and large and strange, and to Hushidh's shoulder, so familiar, so frail by comparison to Moozh's. "The Oversoul makes one soul from the woman and the man," said Luet. A breath. An endless pause. And then the words she could not bear to say, yet had to say, and so said. "It is done."

The people of Basilica rose from their seats as if they were one, and cheered and clapped and called out their names: Hushidh! Raveler! Moozh! General! Vozmuzhalnoy! Vozmozhno!

Moozh kissed Hushidh as a husband kisses a wife—but gently, Luet saw, kindly. Then he turned and led Hushidh down to the front of the platform. A hundred, a thousand flowers filled the air, flying forward; those thrown from the back of the amphitheatre were picked up and tossed again, until the flowers filled the space between the platform and the first row of benches.

Amid the tumult, Luet became aware that Moozh himself was shouting. She could not hear the words he said, but only the fact that he was saying something, for his back was toward her. Gradually the people on the front row realized what he was saying, and took up his words as a chant. Only then did Luet understand how he was turning his own wedding now to clear political advantage. For what he said was a single word, repeated over and over again, spreading through the crowd until they all shouted with the same impossibly loud voice.

"Basilica! Basilica! Basilica!"

It went on forever, forever.

Luet wept, for she knew now that the Oversoul had failed, that Hushidh was married to a man who would never love *her*, but only the city that he had taken as her dowry.

At last Moozh raised his hands—his left hand higher, palm out to silence them, his right still holding Hushidh's hand. He had no intention of breaking his link to *her*, for this was his link to the city. Slowly the chanting died down, and at last a curtain of silence fell on the Orchestra.

His speech was simple but eloquent. A protestation of his love for this city, his gratitude at having been privileged to restore it to peace and safety, and now his joy at being welcomed as a citizen, the husband of the sweet and simple beauty of a true daughter of the Oversoul. He mentioned Luet, too, and Nafai, how honored he felt to be kinsmen of the best and bravest of Basilica's children.

Luet knew what came next. Already the delegation of councilors had risen from their seats, ready to come forward and ask that the city accept Moozh as consul, to lead Basilica's military and foreign relations. It was a foregone conclusion that the vast majority of the people, overwhelmed with the ecstasy and majesty of the moment, would acclaim the choice. Only later would they realize what they had done, and even then most would think it was a wise and good change.

Moozh's speech was winding toward its end—and it would be a glorious end, well received by the people despite his northern accent, which in other times would have been ridiculed and despised.

He hesitated. In an unexpected place in his speech. An inappropriate place. The hesitation became a pause, and Luet could see that he was looking at something or someone that *she* could not see. So she stepped forward, and Nafai was instantly beside her; together they took the few steps necessary for both of them to be on Moozh's left, behind him still but able now to see whom he was looking at.

A woman. A woman dressed in the simple garb of a farmer of Potokgavan—a strange costume indeed for this time and place. She was standing at the foot of the central flight of steps leading up into the amphitheatre; she made no move to come forward, so neither the Gorayni archers nor the two Basilican guards had made any move to stop her till now.

Because the general said nothing, the soldiers did not know what to do—should they seize the woman and hustle her away?

"You," said Moozh. So he knew her.

"What are you doing?" she asked. Her voice was not loud, and yet Luet heard it clearly. How could she hear so clearly?

Because I am speaking her words again in the mind of every person here, said the Oversoul.

"I am marrying," said Moozh.

"There has been no marriage," she said—again softly, again heard perfectly by all.

Moozh gestured at the assembled multitude. "All these have seen it."

"I don't know what they have seen," said the woman. "But what *I* see is a man holding his daughter by the hand."

A murmur arose in the congregation.

"God, what have you done," whispered Moozh. But now the Oversoul also carried *his* softest voice into their ears.

Now the woman stepped forward, and the soldiers made no effort to stop her, for they saw that what was happening was far larger than a mere assassination.

"The Oversoul brought me to you," she said. "Twice she brought me, and both times I conceived and bore daughters. But I was not your wife. Rather I was the body that the Oversoul chose to use, to bear *her* daughters. I took the daughters of the Oversoul to the Lady Rasa, whom the Oversoul had chosen to raise them and teach them, until the day when she chose to name them as her own."

The woman turned to Rasa, pointed at her. "Lady Rasa, do you know me? When I came to you I was naked and filthy. Do you know me now?"

Aunt Rasa shakily rose to her feet. "You are the one who brought them to me. Hushidh first, and then Luet. You told me to raise them as if they were my daughters, and I did."

"They were not your daughters. They were not my daughters. They are the daughters of the Oversoul, and this man—the one called Vozmuzhalnoy Vozmozhno by the Gorayni—he is the man that the Oversoul chose to be her Moozh."

Moozh. Moozh. The whisper ran through the crowd.

"The marriage you saw today was not between this man and this girl. She only stood as proxy for the Mother. He has become the husband of the Oversoul! And insofar as this is the city of the Mother, he has become the husband of Basilica! I say it because the Oversoul has put the words into my mouth! Now *you* must say it! All of Basilica must say it! Husband! Husband!"

They took up the chant. Husband! Husband! Husband! And then, gradually, it changed, to another word with the same meaning. Moozh! Moozh! Moozh!

As they chanted, the woman came forward to the front of the low platform. Hushidh let go of Moozh's hand and came forward, knelt before the woman; Luet followed her, too stunned to weep, too filled with joy at what the Oversoul had done to save Hushidh from this marriage, too filled with grief at having never known this woman who was her mother, too filled with wonder at discovering that her father had been this northern stranger, this terrifying general all along.

"Mother," Hushidh was saying—and *she* could weep, spilling her tears on the woman's hand.

"I bore you, yes," said the woman. "But I am not your mother. The woman who raised you, *she* is your mother. And the Oversoul who caused you to be born, *she* is your mother. I'm just a farmer's wife in the wetlands of Potokgavan. That is where the children live who call *me* mother, and I must return to them."

"No," whispered Luet. "Can we only see you once?"

"I will remember you forever," said the woman. "And you will remember me. The Oversoul will keep these memories fresh in our hearts." She reached out one hand and touched Hushidh's cheek, and another to touch Luet, to stroke her hair. "So lovely. So worthy. How she loves you. How your mother loves you now."

Then she turned from them and left—walked from the platform, walked down into the ramp leading to the dressing rooms under the amphitheatre, and she was gone. No one saw her leave the city, though stories of strange miracles and odd visions quickly sprang up, of things she supposedly did but could not possibly have done on her way out of Basilica that day.

Moozh watched her turn and leave, and with her she took all his hopes and plans and dreams; with her she took his life. He remembered so clearly the time he had spent with her—she was the reason he had never married, for what woman could make him feel what he had felt for her. At the time he had been sure that he loved her in defiance of God's will, for hadn't he felt that strong forbidding? When she was with him, hadn't he woken again and again with no memory of her, and yet he had overcome God's barriers in his mind, and kept her, and loved her? It was as Nafai said—even his rebellion was orchestrated by the Oversoul.

I am God's fool, God's tool, like everyone else, and when I thought to have my own dreams, to make my own destiny, God exposed my weakness and broke me to pieces before the people of the city. *This* city of all cities—Basilica. Basilica.

Hushidh and Luet arose from their knees at the front of the stage; Nafai joined them as they came to face Moozh. They had to come very close to him to be heard above the chanting of the crowd.

"Father," said Hushidh.

"Our father," echoed Luet.

"I never knew that I had children," said Moozh. "I should have known. I should have seen my own face when I looked at you." And it was true—now that the truth was known, the resemblance was obvious. Their faces had not followed the normal pattern of Basilican beauty because their Father was of the Sotchitsiya, and only God could guess where their mother might be from. Yet they *were* beautiful, in a strange exotic way. They were beautiful and wise, and strong women as well. He could be proud of them. In the ruins of his career, he could be proud of them. As he fled from the Imperator, who would certainly know what he had meant to attempt with this aborted marriage, he could be proud of them. For they were the only thing he had created that would last.

"We must go into the desert," said Nafai.

"I won't resist it now."

"We need your help," said Nafai. "We must go at once."

Moozh cast his eyes across the party he had assembled on his side of the platform. Bitanke. It was Bitanke who must help him now. He beckoned, and Bitanke arose and bounded onto the platform.

"Bitanke," said Moozh, "I need you to prepare for a desert journey." He turned to Nafai. "How many of you will there be?"

"Thirteen," said Nafai, "unless you decide to come with us."

"Come with us, Father," said Hushidh.

"He can't come with us," said Luet. "His place is here."

"She's right," said Moozh. "I could never go on a journey for God."

"Anyway," said Luet, "he'll be with us because his seed is part of us." She touched Nafai's arm. "He will be the grandfather of all our children, and of Hushidh's children, too."

Moozh turned back to Bitanke. "Thirteen of them. Camels and tents, for a desert journey."

"I will have it ready," said Bitanke. But Moozh understood, in the tone of his voice, in the confident way he held himself, and from the fact that he asked no questions, that Bitanke was not surprised or worried by this assignment.

"You already knew," said Moozh. He looked around at the others. "You all planned this from the start."

"No sir," said Nafai. "We knew only that the Oversoul was going to try to stop the marriage."

"Do you think that we would have been silent," asked Luet, "if we had known we were your daughters?"

"Sir," said Bitanke, "you must remember that you and Lady Rasa told me to prepare the camels and the tents and the supplies."

"When did I tell you such a thing?"

"In my dream last night," Bitanke said.

It was the crowning blow. God had destroyed him, and even went so far as to impersonate him in another man's prophetic dream. He felt his defeat like a heavy burden thrown over his shoulders; it bent him down.

"Sir," said Nafai, "why do you imagine that you've been destroyed? Don't you hear what they're chanting?"

Moozh listened.

Moozh, they said. Moozh. Moozh. Moozh.

"Don't you see that even as you let us go, you're stronger than you were before? The city is yours. The Oversoul has given it to you. Didn't you hear what their mother said? You are the husband of the Oversoul, and of Basilica."

Moozh had heard her, yes, but for the first time in his life—no, for the first time since he had loved her so many years before—he had not immediately thought of what advantage or disadvantage her words might bring to him. He had only thought: My one love was manipulated by God; my future has been destroyed by God; he has owned me and ruined me, past and future.

Now he realized that Nafai was right. Hadn't Moozh felt for the past few days that perhaps God had changed his mind and was now working *for* him? That feeling had been right. God meant to take his newfound daughters out into the desert on his impossible errand, but apart from that Moozh's plans were still intact. Basilica was his.

Moozh raised his hands, and the crowd—whose chanting had already been fading, from weariness if nothing else—fell silent.

"How great is the Oversoul!" Moozh shouted.

They cheered.

"My city!" he shouted. "Ah, my bride!"

They cheered again.

He turned to the girls and said, softly, "Any idea how I can get you out of the city without it looking like I'm exiling my own daughters, or that you're running away from me?"

Hushidh looked at Luet. "The waterseer can do it."

"Oh, thanks," said Luet. "Suddenly it's up to me?"

"Pretty much, yes," said Nafai. "You can do it."

Luet set her shoulders, turned, and walked to the front of the platform. The crowd was silent again, waiting. She was still hooked up to the amplification system of the Orchestra, but it hardly mattered—the crowd was so united, so attuned to the Oversoul that whatever she wanted them to hear, they would hear.

"My sister and I are as astonished as any of you have been. We never guessed our parentage, for even as the Oversoul has spoken to us all our lives, she never told us we were hers, not in this way, not as you have seen today. Now we hear her voice, calling us into the wilderness.

We must go to her, and serve her. In our place she leaves her husband, our father. Be a true bride to him, Basilica!"

There was no cheering, only a loud hum of murmuring. She looked back over her shoulder, clearly afraid that she was handling it badly. But that was only because she was unaccustomed to manipulating crowds—Moozh knew that she was doing well. So he nodded, indicated with a gesture that she must go on.

"The city council was prepared to ask our father to be consul of Basilica. If it was wise before, it is doubly wise now. For when the deeds of the Oversoul are known, all nations of the world will be jealous of Basilica, and it will be good to have such a man as this to be our voice before the world, and our protector from the wolves that will come against us!"

Now the cheering came, but it faded quickly.

"Basilica, in the name of the Oversoul, will you have Vozmuzhalnoy Vozmozhno to be your consul?"

That was it, Moozh knew. She had finally given them a clear moment to answer her, and the answer came as he knew it would, a loud shout of approbation from a hundred thousand throats. Far better than to have a councilor propose it, it was the waterseer who asked them to accept his rule, and in the name of God. Who could oppose him now?

"Father," she said, when the shouting died away. "Father, will you accept a blessing from your daughters' hands?"

What was this? What was she doing now? Moozh was confused for a moment. Until he realized that she wasn't doing this for the crowd now. She wasn't doing this to manipulate and control events. She was speaking from her heart; she had gained a father today, and would lose him today, and so she wanted to give him some parting gift. So he took Hushidh by the hand and they stepped forward; he knelt between them, and they laid their hands upon his head.

"Vozmuzhalnoy Vozmozhno," she began. And then: "Our father, our dear father, the Oversoul has brought you here to lead this city to its destiny. The women of Basilica have their husbands year to year, but the city of women has stayed unmarried all this time. Now the Oversoul has chosen, Basilica has found a worthy man at last, and you will be her only husband as long as these walls stand. But through all the great events that you will see, through all the people who will love and follow you through years to come, you will remember us. We bless you that you will remember us, and in the hour of your death you will see

our faces in your memory, and you will feel your daughters' love for
you within your heart. It is done."

They passed through Funnel Gate, and Moozh stood beside Bitanke
and Rashgallivak to salute them as they left. Moozh had already decided to make Bitanke commander of the city guard, and Rash would
be the city's governor when Moozh was away with his army. They
passed in single file before him, before the waving, weeping, cheering
crowd that gathered there—three dozen camels in their caravan,
loaded with tents and supplies, passengers and drycases.

The cheering died away in the distance. The hot desert air stung
them as they descended onto the rocky plain where the black chars of
Moozh's deceiving fires were still visible like pockmarks of some dread
disease. Still they all kept their silence, for Moozh's armed escort rode
beside them, to protect them on their way—and to be certain that none
of the reluctant travelers turned back.

So they rode until near nightfall, when Elemak determined where
they would pitch the tents. The soldiers did the labor for them, though
at Elemak's command they carefully showed those who had never
pitched a tent how the job was done. Obring and Vas and the women
looked terrified at the thought of having to do such a labor themselves,
but Elemak encouraged them, and all went smoothly.

Yet when the soldiers left, it was not Elemak that they saluted, but
rather Lady Rasa, and Luet the waterseer, and Hushidh the raveler—
and, for reasons Elemak could not begin to understand, Nafai.

As soon as the soldiers had ridden off, the quarreling began.

"May beetles crawl into your nose and ears and eat your brain out!"
Mebbekew screamed at Nafai, at Rasa, at everyone within earshot.
"Why did you have to include *me* in this suicidal caravan?"

Shedemei was no less angry, merely quieter. "I never agreed to
come along. I was only going to *teach* you how to revive the embryos.
You had no *right* to force me to come."

Kokor and Sevet wept, and Obring added his grumbling to Mebbekew's screams of rage. Nothing that Rasa, Hushidh, or Luet could
say would calm them, and as for Nafai, when he tried to open his
mouth to speak, Mebbekew threw sand in his face and left him gasping
and spitting—and silent.

Elemak watched it all and then, when he figured the rage had about
spent itself, he stepped into the middle of the group and said, "No

matter what else we do, my beloved company, the sun is down and the desert will soon be cold. Into the tents, and be silent, so you don't draw robbers to us in the night."

Of course there was no danger of robbers here, so close to Basilica and with so large a company. Besides, Elemak suspected that the Gorayni soldiers were camped only a little way off, ready to come at a moment's notice to protect them, if the need arose. And to prevent anyone from returning to Basilica, no doubt.

But they weren't desert men, as Elemak was. If I decide to return to Basilica, he said silently to the unseen Gorayni soldiers, then I will go to Basilica, and even *you*, the greatest soldiers in the world, won't stop me, won't even know that I have passed you by.

Then Elemak went to his tent, where Eiadh waited for him, weeping softly. Soon enough she forgot her tears. But Elemak did not forget his anger. He had not screamed like Mebbekew, had not howled or whined or grumbled or argued. But that did not mean he was any less angry than the others. Only that when he acted, it would be to some effect.

Moozh might not have been able to stand against the plots and plans of the Oversoul, but that doesn't mean that *I* can't, thought Elemak. And then he slept.

Overhead a satellite was slowly passing, reflecting a pinpoint of sunlight from over the horizon. One of the eyes of the Oversoul, seeing all that happened, receiving all the thoughts that passed through the minds of the people under its cone of influence. As one by one they fell asleep, the Oversoul began to watch their dreams, waiting, hoping, eager, for some arcane message from the Keeper of Earth. But there were no visions of hairy angels tonight, no giant rats, no dreams but the random firings of thirteen human brains asleep, made into meaningless stories that they would forget as soon as they awoke.

Epilogue

General Moozh succeeded as he had hoped. He united the Cities of the Plain and Seggidugu, and thousands of Gorayni soldiers deserted and joined with him. The Imperator's troops melted away, and before the summer was out, the Sotchitsiya lands were free. That winter the Imperator huddled in the snows of Gollod, while his spies and ambassadors worked to persuade Potokgavan to put an army like a dagger in Moozh's back.

But Moozh had foreseen this, and when the Potoku fleet arrived, it was met by General Bitanke and ten thousand soldiers, men and women of a militia he had trained himself. The Potoku soldiers died in the water, most of them, their ships burning, their blood leaving red foam with every wave that broke upon the beach. And in the spring, Gollod fell and the Imperator died by his own hand, before Moozh could reach him. Moozh stood in the Imperator's summer palace and declared that there *was* no incarnation of God on Harmony, and never had been—except for one unknown woman who came to him as the body of the Oversoul, and bore two daughters for the husband of the Oversoul.

Moozh died the next year, poisoned by a Potoku dart as he besieged the floodbound capital of Potokgavan. Three Sotchitsiya kinsmen, a half-dozen Gorayni officers, and Rashgallivak of Basilica all claimed to be his successor. In the course of the civil wars that followed, three armies converged on Basilica and the inhabitants fled. Despite Bitanke's brave defense, the city fell. The walls and buildings all were broken down, and the teams of war captives cast the stones into the lake of women until all were gone, and the lake was wide and shallow.

The next summer there was nothing but old roads to show that once there had been a city in that place. And even though some few priestesses returned, and built a little temple beside the lake of women, the hot and cold waters now mixed far below the new surface of the lake, and so the thick fogs no longer rose and the place was not so holy anymore. Few pilgrims came.

The former citizens of Basilica spread far and wide throughout the world, but many of them remembered who they were, and passed the stories on, generation after generation. We were of Basilica, they told their children, and so the Oversoul is still alive within our hearts.

THE SHIPS
OF EARTH

To Bill and Laraine Moon
with fond memories of temples and malls,
of copy machines and newsletters,
of great kids and good company;
of love freely given and honor unyielding.

Acknowledgments

This was the novel that fate did not want me to write. I had set aside a good part of the summer to write it—even canceled a free trip to Australia because it would have come right in the middle of this project. Then, because that's how the world works, I suddenly found myself touring America signing copies of *Xenocide*, which for various excellent reasons had been released a couple of months early. Then, when I got home, we were caught up in the process of getting ready to move across town into a new house—we were going to be renters no more! Add to that the seductive details of remodeling the new house to contain not so much us as our computers, and I could see there was no way I'd be able to concentrate on writing *Ships of Earth* unless I went into hiding.

Which is precisely what I did. Poor Clark and Kathy Kidd! They must have thought that somehow, accidentally, back in the Pleistocene, they had spawned a child who now had come home to live with them! I descended on their house in Sterling, Virginia, took over their dining-room table, and then buried myself in writing. I surfaced only when two different computers failed on me and I had to whine and beg for Northgate to replace them. And when Clark and Kathy got a free weekend at Rehoboth Beach, there I was, tagging along—the first draft of Chapter 6 has Delaware sand in it. Yet through it all, the Kidds pretended they were having a wonderful time, and I'm grateful to them.

Much as I owe Clark and Kathy, though, I owe as much again to my wife, Kristine, and our assistant, Erin Absher, who kept our home running, our children alive, and the remodeling of the new house on track despite a plethora of disasters, major and minor. Kristine managed to *read* this book and comment on it, making me take out the really icky parts—which greatly improved the novel, you may be sure! I can't write without peace of mind, and that was the gift that, among them, Kristine and Erin and Clark and Kathy gave to me, each in their own way.

I must also tip my hat to Shirley Strum, author of *Almost Human*, the book that gave me the baboons in *Ships of Earth*, which are some of my favorite characters; and to Beth Meacham, my editor, and Barbara Bova, my agent: Thank you for enduring all my whimpering, and helping me in so many ways that the public will never know about and that I will never forget.

Contents

Prologue

The master computer of the planet Harmony was full of hope at last. The chosen human beings had been drawn together and removed from the city of Basilica. Now they were embarked on the first of two journeys. This one would take them through the desert, through the Valley of Fires, to the southern tip of the island once called Vusadka, to a place where no human being had set foot for forty million years. The second journey would be from that place across a thousand lightyears to the home planet of the human species, Earth, abandoned forty million years ago and ready now for human beings to return.

Not just any human beings. *These* human beings. The ones born, after a million generations of guided evolution, with the strongest ability to communicate with the master computer, mind to mind, memory to memory. However, in encouraging people with this power to mate and therefore enhance it in their offspring, the master computer had not made any attempt to choose only the nicest or most obedient, or even the most intelligent or skillful. That was not within the purview of the computer's program. People could be more difficult or less difficult, more or less dangerous, more or less useful, but the master computer had not been programmed to show preference for decency or wit.

The master computer had been set in place by the first settlers on the planet Harmony for one purpose only—to preserve the human species by restraining it from the technologies that allowed wars and empires to spread so far that they could destroy a planet's ability to sustain human life, as had occurred on Earth. As long as men could fight only with hand weapons and could travel only on horseback, the world could endure, while the humans on it would remain free to be as good or evil as they chose.

Since that original programming, however, the master computer's hold on humanity had weakened. Some people were able to communicate with the master computer more clearly than anyone had ever imagined would be possible. Others, however, had only the weakest of connections. The result was that new weapons and new methods of transportation were beginning to enter the world, and while it might yet be thousands or tens of thousands of years before the end, the end would still come. And the master computer of Harmony had no idea of how to reverse the process.

This made it urgent enough for the master computer to attempt to return to Earth, where the Keeper of Earth could introduce new programming. But in recent months the master computer and some of its human allies discovered that the Keeper of Earth was already, somehow, introducing change. Different people had dreamed clear and powerful dreams of creatures that had never existed on Harmony, and the master computer itself discovered subtle alterations in its own programming. It should have been impossible for the Keeper of Earth to influence events so far away . . . and yet that entity which had dispatched the original refugee ships forty million years before was the only imaginable source of these changes.

How or why the Keeper of Earth was doing this, the master computer of the planet Harmony could not begin to guess. It only knew that forty million years had not been kind to its own systems, and it needed replenishment. It only knew that whatever the Keeper of Earth asked for, the master computer of Harmony would try to supply. It asked now for a group of human beings to recolonize the Earth.

So the master computer chose sixteen people from the population of Basilica. Many were kin to each other; all had unusual ability to communicate with the master computer. However, they were not all terribly bright, and not all were particularly trustworthy or kind.

Many of them had strong dislikes or resentments toward others, and while some of them were committed to the master computer's cause, some were just as committed to thwarting it. The whole enterprise might fail at any time, if the darker impulses of the humans could not be curbed. Civilization was always fragile, even when strong social forces inhibited individual passions; now, cut off from the larger world, would they be able to forge a new, smaller, harmonious society? Or would the expedition be destroyed from the beginning?

The master computer had to plan and act as if the expedition would survive, would succeed. In a certain place the master computer triggered a sequence of events. Machinery that had long been silent began to hum. Robots that had long been in stasis were awakened and set to work, searching for machines that needed repair. They had waited a long, long time, and even in a stasis field they could not last forever.

It would take several years to determine just how much work would be needed, and how it should or even could be done. But there was no hurry. If the journey took time, then perhaps the people could use that time to make peace with each other. There was no hurry; or rather, no hurry that would be detectable to human beings. To the master computer, accomplishing a task within ten years was a breathless pace, while to humans it could seem unbearably long. For though the master computer could detect the passage of milliseconds, it had memories of forty million years of life on Harmony so far, and on that scale, compared to the normal human lifespan, ten years was as brief a span of time as five minutes.

The master computer would use those years well and productively, and hoped the people could manage to do the same. If they were wise, it would be a time in which they could create their families, bear and begin to raise many children, and develop into a community worthy to return to the Keeper of Earth. However, that would be no easy achievement, and at the moment all the master computer could really hope for was to keep them all alive.

1

The Law of
the Desert

Shedemei was a scientist, not a desert traveler. She had no great need for city comforts—she was as content sleeping on a floor or table as on a bed—but she resented having been dragged away from her laboratory, from her work, from all that gave her life meaning. She had never agreed to join this half-mad expedition. Yet here she was, atop a camel in the dry heat of the desert wind, rocking back and forth as she watched the backside of the camel in front of her sway in another rhythm. It made her faintly sick, the heat and the motion. It gave her a headache.

Several times she almost turned back. She could find the way well enough; all she had to do was get close enough to Basilica and her computer would link up with the city and show her the rest of the way home. Alone, she'd make much better time—perhaps she could even be back before nightfall. And they would surely let her into the city—she wasn't kin by blood or marriage to anyone else in this group. The only reason she had been exiled with them was because she had arranged for the dryboxes full of seeds and embryos that would reestablish some semblance of the old flora and fauna on Earth. She had done a favor for her old teacher, that's all—they could hardly force her into exile for *that*.

Yet that cargo was the reason she did not turn back. Who else would understand how to revive the myriad species carried on these camels? Who else would know which ones needed to go first, to establish themselves before later species came that would have to feed on them?

It's not fair, thought Shedemei for the thousandth time. I'm the only one in this party who can begin to do this task—but for me, it's not a challenge at all. It's not *science*, it's *agriculture*. I'm here, not because the task the Oversoul has chosen me for is so demanding, but because all the others are so deeply ignorant of it.

"You look angry and miserable."

Shedemei turned to see that it was Rasa who had brought her camel up beside Shedemei's on the wide stony path. Rasa, her teacher—almost her mother. But not *really* her mother, not by blood, not by *right*.

"Yes," said Shedemei.

"At me?" asked Rasa.

"Partly you," said Shedemei. "You maneuvered us all into this. I have no connection with any of these people, except through you."

"We all have the same connection," said Rasa. "The Oversoul sent you a dream, didn't she?"

"I didn't ask for it."

"Which of us did?" said Rasa. "No, I do understand what you mean, Shedya. The others all made choices that got them into this. Nafai and Luet and Hushidh and I have come willingly . . . more or less. And Elemak and Meb, not to mention my daughters, bless their nasty little hearts, are here because they made some stupid and vile decisions. The others are here because they have marriage contracts, though for some of them it's merely compounding the original mistake to come along. But you, Shedemei, all that brings you here is your dream. And your loyalty to me."

The Oversoul had sent her a dream of floating through the air, scattering seeds and watching them grow, turning a desert land into forest and meadow, filled with greenery, abounding with animals. Shedemei looked around at the bleak desert landscape, seeing the few thorny plants that clung to life here and there, knowing that a few lizards lived on the few insects that found water enough to survive. "*This* is not my dream," said Shedemei.

"But you came," said Rasa. "Partly for the dream, and partly out of love for me."

"There's no hope of succeeding, you know," said Shedemei. "These aren't colonizers here. Only Elemak has the skill to survive."

"He's the one who's *most* experienced in desert travel. Nyef and Meb are doing well enough, for their part. And the rest of us will learn."

Shedemei fell silent, not wanting to argue.

"I hate it when you back away from a quarrel like that," said Rasa.

"I don't like conflict," said Shedemei.

"But you always back off at exactly the moment when you're about to tell the other person *exactly* what she needs to hear."

"I don't know what other people need to hear."

"Say what you had on your mind a moment ago," said Rasa. "Tell me why you think our expedition is doomed to failure."

"Basilica," said Shedemei.

"We've *left* the city. It can't possibly harm us now."

"Basilica will harm us in a thousand ways. It will always be our memory of a gentle, easier life. We'll always be torn with longing to go back."

"It's not homesickness that worries you, though, surely," said Rasa.

"We carry half the city with us," said Shedemei. "All the diseases of the city, but none of its strengths. We have the custom of leisure, but none of the wealth and property that made it possible. We have become used to indulging too many of our appetites, which can never be indulged in a tiny colony like ours will be."

"People have left the city and gone colonizing before."

"Those who want to adapt *will* adapt, I know," said Shedemei. "But how many want to? How many have the will to set aside their own desires, to sacrifice for the good of us all? *I* don't even have that degree of commitment. I'm more furious with every kilometer we move farther away from my work."

"Well, then, we're fortunate," said Rasa. "Nobody else here *had* any work worth mentioning. And those who did have lost everything so they couldn't go back anyway."

"Meb's work is waiting for him there," said Shedemei.

Rasa looked baffled for a moment. "I'm not aware that Meb *had* any work, unless you mean his sad little career as an actor."

"I meant his lifelong project of coupling with every female in Basilica who wasn't actually blood kin of his, or unspeakably ugly, or dead."

"Oh," said Rasa, smiling wanly. "*That* work."

"And he's not the only one," said Shedemei.

"Oh, I know," said Rasa. "You're too kind to say it, but my own daughters are no doubt longing to take up where they left off on their own versions of that project."

"I don't mean to offend you," said Shedemei.

"I'm not offended. I know my daughters far too well. They have too much of their father in them for me not to know what to expect from them. But tell me, Shedya, which of these men do you honestly expect them to find attractive?"

"After a few weeks or a few days, *all* the men will start looking good to them."

Rasa laughed lightly. "I daresay you're right, my dear. But all the men in our little party are married—and you can bet that their wives will be looking out to make sure no one intrudes in their territory."

Shedemei shook her head. "Rasa, you're making a false assumption. Just because *you* have chosen to stay married to the same man, renewing him year after year since—well, since you gave birth to Nafai —that doesn't mean that any of the *other* women here are going to feel that possessive and protective of their husbands."

"You think not?" said Rasa. "My darling daughter Kokor almost killed her sister Sevet because she was sleeping with Kokor's husband Obring."

"So . . . Obring won't try to sleep with Sevet again. That doesn't stop him from trying for Luet, for instance."

"Luet!" said Rasa. "She's a wonderful girl, Shedya, but she's not beautiful in the way that a man like Obring looks for, and she's also *very* young, and she's plainly in love with Nafai, and most important of all, she's the waterseer of Basilica and Obring would be scared to death to approach her."

Shedemei shook her head. Didn't Rasa see that *all* these arguments would fade to unimportance with the passage of time? Didn't she understand that people like Obring and Meb, Kokor and Sevet lived for the hunt, and cared very little who the quarry might be?

"And if you think Obring might try for Eiadh, I'd laugh out loud," said Rasa. "Oh, yes, he might *wish*, but Eiadh is a girl who loves and admires only strength in a man, and that is one virtue that Obring will never have. No, I think Obring will be quite faithful to Kokor."

"Rasa, my dear teacher and friend," said Shedemei, "before this month is out Obring will even have tried to seduce *me.*"

Rasa looked at Shedemei with a startlement she could not conceal. "Oh, now," she said. "You're not his—"

"His type is whatever woman hasn't told him *no* recently," said Shedemei. "And I warn you—if there's one thing our group is too small to endure, it's sexual tension. If we were like baboons, and our females were only sexually attractive a few times between pregnancies, we could have the kind of improvised short-term matings that baboons have. We could endure the periodic conflicts between males because they would end very quickly and we'd have peace the rest of the year. But we're human, unfortunately, and we bond differently. Our children need stability and peace. And there are too few of us to take a few murders here and there in stride."

"Murders," said Rasa. "Shedemei, what's got into you?"

"Nafai has already killed one man," said Shedemei. "And he's probably the *nicest* of this group, except perhaps Vas."

"The Oversoul told him to."

"Yes, so Nafai's the one man in this group who obeys the Oversoul. The others are even more likely to obey *their* god."

"Which is?"

"It dangles between their legs," said Shedemei.

"You biologists have such a cynical view of human beings," said Rasa. "You'd think we were the lowest of animals."

"Oh, not the lowest. Our males don't try to eat their young."

"And our females don't devour their mates," said Rasa.

"Though some have tried."

They both laughed. They had been talking fairly quietly, and their camels were well separated from the others, but their laughter bridged the distance, and others turned to look at them.

"Don't mind us!" called Rasa. "We weren't laughing at you!"

But Elemak *did* mind them. He had been riding near the front of the caravan. Now he turned his animal and came back along the line until he reached them. His face was coldly angry.

"Try to have a little self-control, Lady Rasa," said Elemak.

"What," said Rasa, "my laughter was too loud?"

"Your laughter—and then your little jest. All at top volume. A woman's voice can be carried on this breeze for miles. This desert isn't thickly populated, but if anybody *does* hear you, you can find yourself raped, robbed, and killed in a remarkably short time."

Shedemei knew that Elemak was right, of course—he was the one who had led caravans through the desert. But she hated the condescension in his tone, the sarcasm. No man had a right to speak to Lady Rasa that way.

Yet Rasa herself seemed oblivious to the insult implied by Elya's attitude. "A group as large as ours?" asked Rasa innocently. "I thought robbers would stay away."

"They *pray* for groups like ours," said Elemak. "More women than men. Traveling slowly. Heavily burdened. Talking carelessly aloud. Two women drifting back and separating from the rest of the group."

Only then did Shedemei realize how vulnerable she and Rasa had been. It frightened her. She wasn't used to thinking this way—thinking about how to avoid getting attacked. In Basilica she had always been safe. *Women* had always been safe in Basilica.

"And you might take another look at the men of our caravan," said Elemak. "Which of them do you expect can fight for you and save you from a band of even three or four robbers, let alone a dozen?"

"*You* can," said Rasa.

Elemak regarded her steadily for a moment or two. "Here in the open, where they'd have to show themselves for some distance, I suppose I could. But I'd rather not have to. So keep up and shut up. Please."

The *please* at the end did little to ameliorate the sternness of his tone, but that did not keep Shedemei from deciding wholeheartedly to obey him. She did not have Rasa's confidence that Elemak could single-handedly protect them from even small numbers of marauders.

Elemak glanced briefly at Shedemei, but his expression carried no meaning that she could interpret. Then he wheeled his camel and it lurched on ahead toward the front of the little caravan.

"It'll be interesting to see whether it's your husband or Elemak who rules once we reach Wetchik's camp," said Shedemei.

"Pay no attention to Elya's bluster," said Rasa. "It will be my husband who rules."

"I wouldn't be too sure. Elemak takes to authority quite naturally."

"Oh, he likes the feel of it," said Rasa. "But he doesn't know how to maintain it except through fear. Doesn't he realize that the Oversoul is protecting this expedition? If any marauders so much as think of passing this way, the Oversoul will make them forget the idea. We're as safe as if we were home in bed."

Shedemei did not remind her that only a few days ago they had felt quite unsafe in their beds. Nor did she mention that Rasa had just proved Shedemei's own point—when Rasa thought of home and safety, it was Basilica she had in mind. The ghost of their old life in the city was going to haunt them for a long time to come.

Now it was Kokor's turn to stop her beast and wait for Rasa to catch up. "You were bad, weren't you, Mama?" she said. "Did nasty old Elemak have to come and tell you off?"

Shedemei was disgusted at Kokor's little-girl silliness—but then, Kokor usually disgusted her. Her attitude always seemed false and manipulative; to Shedemei the wonder of it was that these pathetically obvious ploys must work on people fairly often, or Kokor would have found new ones.

Well, whoever Kokor's little-girl act worked on, it *wasn't* her own mother. Rasa simply fixed Koya with an icy stare and said, "Shedya and I were having a private conversation, my dear. I'm sorry if you misunderstood and thought we had invited you to join us."

It took just a moment for Kokor to understand; when she did, her face darkened for a moment—with anger? Then she gave a prim little smile to Shedemei and said, "Mother is perpetually disappointed that I didn't turn out like *you* Shedya. But I'm afraid neither my brain nor my body had enough *inner* beauty." Then, awkwardly, Kokor got her camel moving faster and soon she was ahead of them again.

Shedemei knew that Kokor had meant to insult her by reminding her that the only kind of beauty she would ever have was the inner kind. But Shedemei had long since grown out of her adolescent jealousy of pulchritudinous girls.

Rasa must have been thinking the same thoughts. "Odd, isn't it, that physically plain people are perfectly able to see physical beauty in others, while people who are morally maimed are blind to goodness and decency. They honestly think it doesn't exist."

"Oh, they know it exists, all right," said Shedemei. "They just never know which people have it. Not that my feelings at this moment would prove me to be a moral beauty."

"Having thoughts of murder, were you?" said Rasa.

"Oh, nothing so direct or final," said Shedemei. "I was just wishing for her to develop truly awful saddle sores."

"And Elemak? Did you wish some uncomfortable curse on him?"

"Not at all," said Shedemei. "Perhaps, as you say, he didn't need to try to frighten us into obedience. But I think he was right. After all, the Oversoul hasn't had exactly a perfect record in keeping us out of danger. No, I harbor no resentment toward Elya."

"I wish I were as mature as you, then. I found myself resenting the way he spoke to me. So condescending. I know *why*, of course—he feels my status in the city is a threat to *his* authority out here, so he has to put me in my place. But he should realize that I'm wise enough to follow his leadership without his having to humiliate me first."

"It isn't a question of what *you* need," said Shedemei. "It never is. It's a question of what *he* needs. He needs to feel superior to you. For that matter, so do I, you silly old woman."

For a moment Rasa looked at her in horror. Then, just as Shedemei was about to explain that she was *joking*—why didn't anybody ever understand her humor?—Rasa grinned at her. "I'd rather be a silly old woman than a silly young one," she said. "Silly *old* women don't make such spectacular mistakes."

"Oh, I don't know about that," said Shedemei. "Coming on this expedition, for instance . . ."

"A mistake?"

"For me it certainly is. My life is genetics, but the closest I'm going to come to it for the rest of my life is if I manage to reproduce my *own* genes."

"You sound so despairing. Having children isn't all that awful. They aren't *all* Kokor, and even she may grow up to be human someday."

"Yes, but you *loved* your husbands," said Shedemei. "Whom will I end up with, Aunt Rasa? Your crippled son? Or Gaballufix's librarian?"

"I think Hushidh plans to marry Issib," said Rasa. Her voice was cold, but Shedemei didn't care.

"Oh, I know how you've got us sorted out. But tell me, Aunt Rasa, if Nafai hadn't happened to drag the librarian along with him when he was stealing the Index . . . would you have arranged to bring *me*?"

Rasa's face was positively stony. She didn't answer for a long time.

"Come now, Aunt Rasa. I'm not a fool, and I'd rather you not try to fool me."

"We needed your skills, Shedya. The Oversoul chose you, not me."

"You're sure it wasn't *you*, counting up males and females and making sure we came out even?"

"The Oversoul sent you that dream."

"The sad thing is," said Shedemei, "that except for you there's not a one of us that's a proven reproducer. For all you know, you've set up one of these men with a sterile wife. Or perhaps you've put one of us women with a sterile husband."

Rasa's anger was beginning to turn from cold to hot now. "I told you, it wasn't *my* choice . . . Luet had a vision, too, and—"

"*Are* you going to set the example? *Are* you going to have' more children, Aunt Rasa?"

Rasa seemed completely nonplussed. "Me? At my age?"

"You've still got a few good eggs in you. I know you haven't reached menopause, because you're flowing now."

Rasa looked at her in consternation. "Why don't I just lie down under one of your microscopes?"

"You'd never fit. I'd have to slice you razor thin."

"Sometimes I feel as if you already had."

"Rasa, you make us stop several times a day. I *know* you have better bladder control than that. We *all* know you're shedding the tears of the moon."

Rasa raised her eyebrows briefly, a sort of facial shrug. "More children indeed."

"I think you must. To set an example for all of us," said Shedemei. "Don't you understand that we're not just taking a trip. We're a *colony*. The first priority of colonists is reproduction. Anyone who isn't having babies is next to worthless. And no matter how envious Elemak is of your authority, you *are* the leader of the women here. You must set the pattern for us all. If *you* are willing to get pregnant during this trip, the others will fall into line, particularly since their husbands will feel the need to demonstrate that they can get a woman just as pregnant as old Wetchik can."

"He's not Wetchik anymore," said Rasa irrelevantly. "He's Volemak."

"He can still perform, can't he?"

"Really, Shedemei, is there anything you won't ask? Would you like us to provide stool samples for you next?"

"Before this journey is over I imagine I'll be looking at samples of almost everything. I'm the closest thing to a physician we have."

Rasa suddenly chuckled. "I can just see Elemak bringing you a se-
men sample."

Shedemei had to laugh, too, at the very idea of asking him. Such an
assault on his dignity as leader of the caravan!

They rode together in silence for a few minutes. Then Rasa spoke.
"Will you do it?" she asked.

"Do what?"

"Marry Zdorab?"

"Who?"

"The librarian, Zdorab."

"Marry him," sighed Shedemei. "I never meant to marry anyone."

"Marry him and have his babies."

"Oh, I suppose I will," said Shedemei. "But *not* if we live under
baboon law."

"Baboon law!"

"Like Basilica—with a competition for new mates every year. I'll
take this middle-aged man that I've never seen, I'll let him bed me, I'll
bear his children, I'll raise them with him—but not if I have to fight to
keep him. Not if I have to watch him court Eiadh or Hushidh or Dolya
or—or *Kokor*—every time our marriage contract is about to expire, and
then come crawling back to me and ask me to renew his contract for
another year *only* because none of the truly desirable women would
have him."

Rasa nodded. "I see now what you were trying to say before. It
wasn't about Kokor's infidelity, it was about the customs we all grew up
with."

"Exactly," said Shedemei. "We're too small a group to keep the old
marriage customs of Basilica."

"It's really just a matter of scale, isn't it," said Rasa. "In the city
when a woman doesn't renew a man, or when he doesn't ask, you can
avoid each other for a while until the pain wears off. You can find
someone else, because there are so many thousands to choose from.
But we'll have exactly sixteen people. Eight men, eight women. It
would be unbearable."

"Some would want to kill, the way Kokor tried to do," said
Shedemei. "And others would wish to die."

"You're right, you're right, you're right," murmured Rasa, thinking
aloud now, it seemed. "But we can't tell them now. Some of them
would turn back—desert or no desert, bandits or no bandits. Lifelong

monogamy—why, I doubt that Sevet and Kokor have ever been faithful
for a whole week. And Meb hadn't married till now for the good reason
that he has no intention of being faithful but lacks my daughters' ability
to behave with complete dishonesty. And now we're going to tell them
that they *must* remain faithful. No one-year contracts, no chance to
change."

"They're not going to like it."

"So we won't tell them until we're at Volemak's camp. When it's far
too late for them to turn back."

Shedemei could hardly believe she had heard Rasa say such a thing.
Still, she answered mildly. "Except it occurs to me," she said, "that if
they want to turn back, perhaps we should let them. They're free
people, aren't they?"

Rasa turned fiercely to her. "No, they aren't," she said. "They were
free until they made the choices that brought them here, but now
they're *not* free because our colony, our *journey* can't succeed without
them."

"You're so certain you can hold people to their commitments," murmured Shedemei. "No one's ever made them do that before. Can you
now?"

"It's not just for the sake of the expedition," said Rasa. "It's for their
own good. The Oversoul has made it clear that Basilica is going to be
destroyed—and them with it, if they're still there when the time
comes. We're saving their lives. But the ones most likely to turn back
are also the ones least likely to believe in the visions the Oversoul has
shown us. So to save their lives we must—"

"Deceive them?"

"Withhold some explanations until later."

"Because you know so much better than they do what's good for
them?"

"Yes," said Rasa. "Yes, I do."

It infuriated Shedemei. All that Rasa had said was true enough, but
it didn't change Shedemei's conviction that people had the right to
choose even their own destruction, if they wanted. Maybe that was
another luxury of living in Basilica, having the right to destroy yourself
through your own stupidity or shortsightedness, but if so it was a luxury that Shedemei was not yet ready to give up. It was one thing to tell
people that faithful monogamy was one of the conditions of staying
with the group. Then they could choose whether to stay and obey or

leave and live by another rule. But to lie to them until it was too late to choose . . . it was *freedom* that was at stake here, and it was freedom that made survival worthwhile. "Aunt Rasa," said Shedemei, "*you* are not the Oversoul."

And with that remark, Shedemei urged her camel to move faster, leaving Rasa behind her. Not that Shedemei had nothing more she could have said. But she was too angry to stay there; the idea of quarreling with Aunt Rasa was unbearable. Shedemei hated to argue with anyone. It always set her to brooding for days. And she had enough to brood about as it was.

Zdorab. What kind of man becomes an archivist for a power-hungry killer like Gaballufix? What kind of man lets a boy like Nafai manipulate him into betraying his trust, giving up the precious Index, and then *follows* the thief right out of the city? What kind of man then lets Nafai wrestle him into submission and extract an oath from him to go out into the desert and never see Basilica again?

Shedemei knew *exactly* what kind of man: a tedious stupid weakling. A shy dull-witted coward who will formally ask my permission before each of his studious attempts to impregnate me. A man who will neither take nor give joy in our marriage. A man who will wish he had married any one of the other women here rather than me, but who will stay with me only because he knows that none of them would have him.

Zdorab, my husband-to-be. I can't wait to meet you.

The tents went up more smoothly their third night in the desert. Everyone knew well now which jobs they had to do—and which they could avoid. Rasa noticed with contempt that both Meb and Obring managed to spend more than half their time "helping" their wives do jobs that were already childishly easy—they *had* to be, or neither Dolya nor Kokor would have done them. Not that Dol wasn't willing to work sometimes, but as long as Kokor and Sevet weren't doing much that was worthwhile, she would not put herself beneath them. After all, Dol had been a starring actress when Kokor and Sevet were still chirping out their little children's songs. Rasa knew how Dol's mind worked. Status first, *then* human decency.

But at least decency was on her list! Who *are* these people I have raised and taught? The ones who are too selfish to endure threaten our peace, and yet some of the others are so compliant with the Oversoul that I fear even more for them.

I am not in charge of their lives now, Rasa reminded herself. I am in charge of getting the tent lines taut enough that it won't collapse in the first wind.

"It *will* collapse in a bad wind, no matter what you do," said Elemak. "So you don't have to make it strong enough to withstand a hurricane."

"Just a sandstorm?" Rasa felt a drop of sweat slip into her eye and sting, just as he spoke. She tried to wipe it away with her sleeve, but her arm was sweatier than her face, even under the light muslin.

"It's sweaty close work, no matter what the weather outside," said Elemak. "Let me."

He held the guyline tight while she cinched the knot into place. She well knew that he could just as easily have done the knot himself, without help holding the line. She saw at once what he was doing, making sure she learned her job, showing confidence in her, and letting her feel a sense of accomplishment when the tent held up. "You're good at this," she said.

"There's nothing hard about tying knots, once you learn them."

She smiled. "Ah, yes, knots. Is that what you're tying together here?"

He smiled back—and she could see that he *did* appreciate her praise. "Among other things, Lady Rasa."

"You are a leader of men," said Rasa. "I say this not as your stepmother, or even as your sister-in-law, but as a woman who has had some occasion of leadership myself. Even the lazy ones are ashamed to be too obvious about it." She did not mention that so far he had only succeeded in centering authority in himself—that no one had internalized anything yet, so that when he wasn't around, nothing happened. Perhaps that was all he had ever needed to learn about leadership during his years leading caravans. But if he meant to rule over this expedition (and Rasa was not such a fool as to think Elemak had any intention of allowing his father to have more than titular authority) he would have to learn how to do much more than make people dependent on him. The essence of leadership, my dear young ruler, is to make people *independent* and yet persuade them to follow you freely. Then they will obey the principles you've taught them even when your back is turned. But she could not say this to him aloud; he wasn't able yet to hear such counsel. So instead she continued to praise him, hoping to build his confidence until he *could* hear wise counsel. "And I've heard less argument and complaint from my daughters than I ever heard back when their lives were easy."

Elemak grimaced. "You know as well as I do that half of them would rather head back to Basilica this moment. I'm not sure that I'm not one of them."

"But we're not going back," said Rasa.

"I imagine it would be rather anticlimactic, returning to Moozh's city after he sent us away in such glory."

"Anticlimactic and dangerous," said Rasa.

"Well, Nafai *has* been cleared of the charge of killing my beloved half-brother Gaballufix."

"He's been cleared of nothing," said Rasa. "Nor, for that matter, have you, son of my husband."

"Me!" His face became hard and a little flushed. Not good, that he showed his emotion so easily. Not what a leader needed.

"I just want you to realize that returning to Basilica is out of the question."

"Be assured, Lady Rasa, that if I wanted to return to Basilica before seeing my father again, I would do so. And may *yet* do so after I see him."

She nodded slightly. "I'm glad that it cools off in the desert at night. So that we can bear the brutal heat of day, knowing the night will be gentle."

Elemak smiled. "I arranged it just for you, Lady Rasa."

"Shedemei and I were talking today," said Rasa.

"I know."

"About a very serious matter," said Rasa. "Something that could easily tear our colony apart. Sex, of course."

Elemak was instantly alert. "Yes?" he asked—but his voice was calm.

"In particular," said Rasa, "the matter of marriage."

"Everyone is paired up well enough for now," said Elemak. "None of the men are sleeping unsatisfied, which is better than the way it is with *most* of my caravans. As for you and Hushidh and Shedemei, you'll soon be with your husbands, or the men who will be their husbands."

"But for some it is not the coupling itself they desire, but rather the chase."

"I know," said Elemak. "But the choices are limited."

"And yet some are still choosing, even though their choice seems to be made."

She could see how he stiffened his back and his neck, pretending to be calm, refusing to lean toward her and ask her the question in his heart. He worries about Eiadh, his bride, his beloved. She had not realized he was so perceptive about her, that he would already worry.

"They must be held faithful to their spouses," said Rasa.

Elemak nodded. "I can't say that I've had the problem—on my caravans, the men are alone until we reach cities, and then it's whores for most of them."

"And for you?" said Rasa.

"I'm married now," said Elemak. "To a young wife. A good wife."

"A good wife for a young man," said Rasa.

A smile flickered at the corners of his mouth. "No one is young forever," he said.

"But will she be a good wife in five years? In ten?"

He looked at her strangely. "How should *I* know?"

"But you must think about it, Elya. What kind of wife will she be in fifty years?"

He looked dumbfounded. He had not thought ahead on this issue, and did not even know how to *pretend* he had thought ahead, it took him so much by surprise.

"Because what Shedemei was pointing out—confirming my own thoughts on the matter—is that there's no chance that we can continue the marriage customs of Basilica out here in the desert. Basilica was very large, and we will be but sixteen souls. Eight couples. When you abandon Eiadh for another, whom will she marry then?" Of course, Rasa knew—and knew that Elemak *also* knew—that it was far more likely that it would be Eiadh deciding not to renew her marriage contract with Elemak, and not the other way around. But the question was still the same—whom would Eiadh marry?

"And children," said Rasa. "There'll be children—but no schools to send them to. They'll stay with their mothers, and another man—other men—will rear them."

She could see that her account of the future was getting to him. She knew exactly what would worry him most, and Lady Rasa wasn't ashamed to use that knowledge. After all, the things she was warning him about were true.

"So you see, Elemak, that as long as we're just sixteen souls who must stay together in order to survive in the desert, marriage must be permanent."

Elemak did not look at her. But his thoughts were visible on his face as he sank down on the carpet that had been spread to make a floor for the tent, covering the sandy soil.

"We can't survive the quarreling," she said, "the hurt feelings—we'll be too close to each other all the time. They must be told. Your spouse now is your spouse forever."

Elemak lay back on the carpet. "Why would they listen to *me* on such a subject?" he said. "They'll think I'm saying that in order to try to keep Eiadh for myself. I happen to know that others have already looked with longing, expecting to court her when we've had our few years of marriage."

"So you must persuade them to accept the reasons for lifelong monogamous marriage—so they'll understand that it *isn't* a self-serving plan on your part."

"Persuade them?" Elemak hooted once, a single bitter laugh. "I doubt I could persuade Eiadh."

She could see that he regretted at once having said that last remark. It confessed too much. "Perhaps then persuasion isn't the term I want. They must be helped to understand that this is a law we must obey in order to keep this family from coming apart in an emotional and physical bloodbath, as surely as we must keep quiet during each traveling day."

Elemak sat up and leaned toward her, his eyes alight with—what, anger? Fear? Hurt? Is there something more to this than I understand? Rasa wondered.

"Lady Rasa," said Elemak, "is this law you want important enough to *kill* for?"

"Kill? Killing is the very thing that I most fear. It's what we must *avoid*."

"This is the desert, and when we reach Father's encampment it will still be the desert, and in the desert there is only one punishment for crime of any kind. Death."

"Don't be absurd," said Rasa.

"Whether you cut off his head or abandon him in the desert, it's all the same—out here exile *is* death."

"But I wouldn't dream of having a penalty so severe as *that*."

"Think about it, Lady Rasa. Where would we imprison somebody as we journey day to day? Who could spare the time to keep someone under guard? There's always flogging, of course, but then we would have to deal with an injured person and we couldn't travel safely anymore."

"What about withdrawing a privilege? Taking something away? Like a fine, the way they did it in Basilica."

"What do you take away, Lady Rasa? What privileges do any of us have? If we take away something the lawbreaker really *needs*—his shoes? his camel?—then we injure him anyway, and have to travel slower and put the whole group at risk. And if it isn't something he needs, but merely treasures, then you fill him with resentment and you have one more person you have to deal with but can't trust. No, Lady Rasa, if shame isn't strong enough to keep a man from breaking a law, then the only punishment that means anything is death. The lawbreaker will never break the law again, and everybody else knows you're serious. And any punishment short of death has the opposite result—the lawbreaker will simply do it again, and no one else will respect the law. That's why I say, before you decide that this should be the law during our travels, perhaps you ought to consider, is it worth killing for?"

"But no one will believe you'd kill anyway, would they?"

"You think not?" said Elemak. "I can tell you from experience that the hardest thing about punishing a man on a journey like that is telling his widow and his orphaned children why you didn't bring him home."

"Oh, Elemak, I never dreamed . . ."

"No one does. But the men of the desert know. And when you abandon a man instead of killing him outright, you don't give him any chance, either—no camel, no horse, not even any water. In fact, you tie him up so he can't even move, so the animals will get him quickly— because if he lives long enough, bandits might find him, and then he'll die far more cruelly, and in the process of dying he'll tell the bandits where you are, and how many you are, and how many you leave on watch, and where all your valuables are stored. He'll tell other things, too—the pet name he calls his woman, the nicknames of the guards, so the bandits'll know what to say in the darkness to confuse your party, to put them off their guard. He'll tell them—"

"Stop it!" cried Rasa. "You're doing this on purpose."

"You think that life in the desert is a matter of heat and cold, of camels and tents, of voiding your bowel in the sand and sleeping on

rugs instead of on a bed. But I tell you that what Father and you and
Nafai, bless his heart, what you've all chosen for us—"

"What the *Oversoul* has chosen!"

"—is the hardest life imaginable, a dangerous and brutal world
where death is breathing into the hair on the back of your head, and
where you have to be ready to kill in order to maintain order."

"I'll think of something else," said Rasa. "Some other way of handling marriages . . ."

"But you won't," said Elemak. "You'll think and think, and in the
end you'll come to the only conclusion. *If* this insane colony is to
succeed, it must succeed in the desert and by desert law. That means
that women will be faithful to their men, or they will die."

"And men, if *they're* unfaithful," said Rasa, sure that he couldn't
possibly mean that only women would be punished.

"Oh, I see. If two people break this marriage law, you want them
both to die, is that it? Who's the bloodthirsty one now? We can spare a
woman more easily than a man. Unless you propose that I train Kokor
and Sevet to fight. Unless you think Dol and Shedemei can really
handle lifting the tents onto the camel's backs."

"So in your man-ruled world the woman bears the brunt of . . ."

"We're not in Basilica now, Lady Rasa. Women thrive where civilization is strong. Not here. No, if you think about it you'll see that punishing the woman alone is the surer way to keep the law. Because which
man can whisper, 'I love you,' when they both know that what he really
means is, 'I want to tup you so badly that I don't care if you die.' How
much success will his seduction have then? And if he tries to force his
way, she'll scream—because she'll know that it's her life at stake. And
if he's taken for raping her, as she screams, why, then it *is* the man who
dies. You see? It takes so much of the romance out of flirting."

Elemak almost laughed aloud at the stricken look on Rasa's face when
he turned and left her tent. Oh, yes, she still fancied herself a leader,
even out here in the desert where she knew less than nothing about
survival, where she was a constant danger to everyone, with her chat,
with her supposed wisdom that she was always *so* willing to share, with
her air of command. She could bring off the illusion of power in Basilica, where women had men so fenced around with custom and manners that she could make decisions and people would comply. But here
she would soon find—was already finding—that she lacked the true

will to power. She wanted to rule, but didn't want to do the hard things that rule required.

Permanent marriage indeed. What woman could possibly satisfy a man of any strength for more than a year or two? He had never intended Eiadh to be anything more than a *first* wife. She would have been a great success at that role—she'd adorn him in his first Basilican household, bear him his firstborn, and then they'd both move on. Elemak even planned that Rasa herself would be his children's teacher —she did a fine job of schooling youngsters; Elemak knew what her true value was. But now to think that he would be willing to endure having Eiadh clinging to him when she was fat and old . . .

Except that in his heart he knew that he was lying to himself. He could pretend that he didn't want Eiadh forever, but in fact the only thing he felt for her was desire. A powerful, possessive desire that showed no signs of slackening. It was Eiadh, not Elemak, who was changeable. She was the one who had so admired Nafai when he stood against Moozh and refused the warlord's offer of the consulship. So pathetic, that she would admire Nyef more for refusing power than she admired her own new husband for having and using it. But Eiadh *was* a woman, after all, and had been raised with the same mystical dependence on the Oversoul, and since the Oversoul had so clearly "chosen" Nafai, it made him all the more attractive in her eyes.

As for Nafai . . . Elemak had known for many months that Nafai had his eye on Eiadh. That was part of what had made Eiadh so attractive to Elemak from the start—that marrying her would put his snotty little brother in his place. Let him marry her later, when she had already had Elemak's first child or two. That would let Nafai know where he stood. But now Eiadh was casting an eye toward the boy— damn him for being the one who killed Gaballufix! That's what was seducing her! She loved the delusion that Nafai was strong. Well, Eiadh, my darling, Edhya my pet, *I* have killed before, and not a drunkard lying in the street, either. I killed a bandit who was charging my caravan, bent on murder and robbery. And I can kill again.

I can kill again, and Rasa has already consented to the justification. The law of the desert, yes, *that* is what will bring Nafai's interference to an end. Rasa is so sure that her dear sweet youngest boy would *never* break the law that she'll agree—they'll *all* agree—that the penalty for disobedience is death. And then Nafai will disobey. It will be so simple, so symmetrical, and I can then kill him on exactly the same pretext Nyef himself used for killing Gabya—I'm doing it for the good of all!

That night, when the cold supper was heavy in their bellies, when the chill night breeze had driven them all inside their tents, Elemak set Nafai to keep the first watch. He knew that Nafai, poor fellow, was keenly aware of who was waiting for Elemak inside his tent. He knew that Nafai was sitting there in the cold starlight imagining how Elya gathered Eiadh's naked body into his arms, how hot and humid they made their tent. He knew that Nafai heard, or imagined that he heard, the soft low cries that Eiadh made. And when Elemak emerged from his tent, the sweat and smell of love still on him, he knew that Nafai could taste the bitterness of going to his own tent, where the awkward shapeless body of Luet the waterseer was the only solace the poor boy would find. It was almost tempting to take Rasa's law and make it real, for then it would be Nafai who would grow old watching Eiadh always and knowing that she was Elemak's, and he could never, never, never have her for his own.

2

Binding and Unbinding

Nafai stood his watch as he always did, by conversing with the Oversoul. It was easier now than it had been at first, back when he and Issib had practically forced the Oversoul to talk to them. Now he would form thoughts carefully in his mind, almost as if he were speaking them, and then, almost without trying, he could feel the Oversoul's answers come to him. They came as if they were Nafai's own thoughts, of course, so that at times he still had trouble distinguishing between the Oversoul's actual ideas and the ideas that came from his own mind; to be sure, he often asked the same question again, and the Oversoul, since it was a computer and therefore never felt a sense of hurry, willingly repeated as often as he liked.

Tonight, because he was on watch, he first asked the Oversoul if any danger was near.

(A coyote, tracking the scent of a hare.)

No, I meant danger to *us*, said Nafai silently.

(The same bandits I told you about before. But they keep hearing noises in the night, and now they're hiding in a cave, trembling.)

You enjoy doing this to them, don't you? asked Nafai.

(No, but I sense *your* delight. This is what you call a game, isn't it?)

More like what we call a trick. Or a joke.

(And you love the fact that only you know that I am doing this.)

Luet knows.

(Of course.)

Any other danger?

(Elemak is plotting your death.)

What, a knife in the back?

(He is full of confidence. He believes he can do it openly, with the consent of all. Even your mother.)

And how will he do it? Blast me with his pulse and pretend it's an accident? Can he frighten my camel into throwing me from a cliff?

(His plan is more subtle than that. It has to do with marriage laws. Rasa and Shedemei realized today that marriages must be made permanent, and Rasa has now persuaded Elemak.)

Good. That will work much better than if the idea had come from Luet and me.

(But it *did* come from you and Luet.)

But only we and you are aware of that, and no one else will guess. They'll see the sensibleness of the law. And besides, I had to do something to stop Eiadh from trying to start something with me. I find it disgusting that it's only since I killed Gaballufix and refused to be Moozh's puppet that she finds me interesting. I think I was much nicer before . . . before all this started.

(You were a boy then.)

I'm still a boy.

(I know. That's one of our problems. Worse yet, you're a boy who's not very good at deception, Nafai.)

But you're a whiz at it.

(You can't lead these people by relying on me to plant your ideas in their minds. On the voyage from Harmony to Earth I won't have the same power to reach into their minds that I have here. You will have to learn how to speak with them directly. Teach them to look to you for decisions.)

Elya and Meb will *never* be willing to accept my lead.

(Then they are expendable.)

Like Gaballufix? I'll never do that again, Oversoul. You can be sure of that—I killed once for you, but never again, never, never, don't even make me think of it, *no!*

(I hear you. I understand you.)

No, you don't understand. You never felt the blood on your hands. You never felt the sword cut through the flesh and hack apart the cartilage between the vertebrae. You never heard his last gasping breaths through the bloody gap in his throat.

(Through your eyes I saw, through your arms I felt, through your ears I heard.)

You never felt the . . . that terrible irrevocability. That there's no turning back. That he's *gone*, and no matter how terrible a man he was, I had no right to cut him off like that . . .

(You had the right because I gave it to you, and I had the right because humankind built me in order to protect the entire species, and the death of that man was necessary for the preservation of humanity on this world.)

Yes, I know, again and again you tell me.

(Again and again you reject the truth and insist on remaining in this meaningless agony of guilt.)

I ended the life of a helpless drunken man. There was no glory in that act. There was no decency. There was no cleverness or wisdom. I was not a good man when I did that.

(You were my hands, Nafai. What I needed to do, you did for me.)

They were my own hands, Oversoul. I could have said no. As I say no *now*, when you hint of my killing Elemak and Mebbekew. It will not happen. I will take no more lives for you.

(I'll keep that in mind as I make my plans for the future. But you *can* establish leadership. You *must*. Your father is too old and tired, and he relies on Elemak too much. He'll give in to your brother far too often, again and again he'll surrender to him, until he has no will left at all.)

So it's better that he surrenders to me?

(You won't make him surrender anything. You'll always lead *through* him, with great respect for him. If you lead, your father will remain a proud and powerful man. I've told you this. Now stand up and take your place.)

Not yet. This is not the time for me to challenge Elemak. We need him to lead us through the desert.

(And I tell you that he has no such qualms. At this very moment, even though he's making love to Eiadh, he is picturing you tied up and abandoned in the desert, where you'll soon discover, Nafai, that while I can influence bandits I can't do a thing about the beasts and birds of prey, the insects that think of anything that doesn't walk or fly or slither away as their next meal. They don't listen to *me*, they simply act out what their genes require them to do, and you *will* die, and what will I do then without you?)

Does he mean to act now, before we get to Father's camp?

(At last you're listening.)

What is his plan, then?

(I don't know. He never thinks of it plainly. I'm searching as best I can, but it's hard. I can't just ransack a human's memories, you know. He fears his own murderous heart so much that he won't let himself think of his whole plan openly.)

Perhaps when he's not distracted by lovemaking.

(Distracted? He's even doing *this* for your benefit. He thinks that you still want Eiadh, so he's hoping you notice the movement in the tent, and the noises she's making.)

It only makes me long for my watch to end, so I can go back to Luet.

(He can't conceive of a man not desiring the woman he desires.)

I did. I fancied that Eiadh was exactly what I needed and wanted. But I understood nothing then. Luet believes she's already pregnant. Luet and I can talk about everything. We've only been married for a few days, yet she understands my heart even better than you do, and I can speak her thoughts almost before she thinks them. Does Elemak imagine that I could desire a mere woman, when Luet is my *wife*?

(He knows that Eiadh is attracted to you. He remembers that you were once attracted to her. He also knows that I have chosen you to lead. He's mad with jealousy. He hungers for your death. It consumes him so that even the act of making love to her is a kind of murder in his heart.)

Don't you realize that this is the most terrible thing of all? If there's anything I want in my life, it's for Elemak to love me and respect me. What did I do, to turn him away!

(You refused to let him own your will.)

Love and respect have nothing to do with controlling what other people do.

(To Elemak, if he doesn't control you, you either don't exist or you're his enemy. For many years you didn't exist. Then he noticed you, and you weren't as easy to manipulate or intimidate as Mebbekew, and so you became a rival.)

Is it really that simple?

(I glossed over the hard parts.)

His tent isn't bouncing. Does that mean he's coming out soon?

(He's getting dressed. He's thinking of you. So is Eiadh.)

At least she doesn't want to kill me.

(If she ever got what she's wishing for, it would end the same, with you dead.)

Don't tell Luet that Elemak is planning to kill me.

(I'll tell Luet everything, exactly as I tell *you*. I don't lie to the humans who serve my cause.)

You lie to us whenever you think it's necessary. And I don't want you to lie to her, anyway—I just don't want her to worry.

(I *do* want her to worry, since you refuse to. I think sometimes you want to die.)

You can relieve your mind on that score. I like being alive and intend to continue.

(I think sometimes you look forward to death, because you think that you deserve to die for having killed Gaballufix.)

Here he comes.

(Notice how he makes sure you smell his hands.)

Nafai didn't appreciate the Oversoul's calling attention to that—he might not have noticed, otherwise. But, truth to tell, that was unlikely, because Elemak made a point of putting both hands on his shoulders, and even of brushing his fingers across Nafai's cheek as he said, "So you *did* stay awake. Maybe you'll amount to something in the desert after all."

"You didn't leave me on watch all that long," Nafai answered.

The womanly smell was plain enough. It was vaguely disgusting that Elemak would use his intimacy with his own wife this way. It was as if she had become nothing to him. A tool. Not a wife at all, but just a *thing* that he owned.

But if the Oversoul was right, then that was how Elemak experienced love—as ownership.

"Did you see anything?" asked Elemak.

"Darkness," said Nafai. He did not tell Elemak about the bandits only a few hundred meters away. First, it would only make him furious that Nafai was getting information from the Oversoul. And second, it would humiliate him that he chose as his campsite a place where bandits could conceal themselves so close. He would probably insist on searching for them, which would mean battle and bloodshed, or wak-

ing everybody up and moving on, which would be pointless, since the
Oversoul was having no trouble keeping this spineless group of cut-
purses under control.

"If you ever looked up, you'd notice there are stars," said Elemak.

Elemak was baiting him, of course, and Nafai knew that he should
just ignore him, but he was filled with anger already, knowing that
Elemak was plotting to kill him and yet still pretended to be his
brother, knowing that Elemak had just made love to his wife in order
to try to make Nafai suffer from jealousy. So Nafai could not contain
himself. He flung a hand upward. "And that one is Sol, the Sun. Barely
visible, but you can always find it if you know where to look. That's
where we're going."

"Are we?" asked Elemak.

"It's the only reason the Oversoul brought us out of Basilica," said
Nafai.

"Maybe the Oversoul won't necessarily get his way," said Elemak.
"He's just a computer, after all—you said so yourself."

Nafai almost answered again, some snide comment to the effect that
if the Oversoul was "just" a computer then Elemak himself was "just" a
hairless baboon. Six months ago Nafai *would* have said it, and Elemak
would have thrown him against a wall or knocked him down with a
blow. But Nafai had learned a little since then, and so he held his
tongue.

Luet was waiting for him in the tent. She had probably been dozing
—she had worked hard since they started laying camp, and unlike the
lazy ones she would be up early again in the morning. But she greeted
him wordlessly with open eyes and a smile that warmed him in spite of
the chill that Elemak had put in his heart.

Nafai undressed quickly and gathered her to him under the blankets.
"You're warm," he said.

"I think the technical term is *hot,*" she answered.

"Elemak is planning to kill me," he whispered.

"I wish the Oversoul would just *stop* him," she whispered.

"I don't think it can. I think Elemak's will is too strong for the
Oversoul to make him change his mind once he's set on doing something." He didn't tell her that the Oversoul had hinted that somewhere
along the line Nafai might have to kill his brother. Since Nafai had no
intention of ever doing it, there was no reason to put the idea in Luet's

mind. He would be ashamed to say it anyway, for fear she would then think he might consider such a thing.

"Hushidh thinks she senses Elemak bonding more closely with the ones who want to turn back—Kokor and Sevet, Vas and Obring, Meb and Dol. They're forming a sort of community now, and separating almost completely from the rest of us."

"Shedemei?"

"She wants to turn back, but there's no bond between her and the others."

"So only you and I and Hushidh and Mother want to go on into the desert."

"And Eiadh. *She* wants to go wherever *you* go."

They both laughed, but Nafai understood that Luet needed reassurance that Eiadh's desire for him was not reciprocated. So he reassured her thoroughly, and then they slept.

In the morning, with the camels packed, Elemak called them together. "A couple of things," he said. "First, Rasa and Shedemei have proposed it and I agree with them completely. While we're living in the desert, we can't afford to have the kind of sexual freedom we had in Basilica. It would only cause rancor and disloyalty, and that's a death sentence for a caravan. So as long as we remain in the desert—and that includes at Father's camp, and anywhere else that our population consists of just us and the three who are waiting for us—this is the law: There'll be no sleeping with anyone except your own husband or wife, and all marriages as they presently stand are permanent."

Immediately there was a gasp of shock from several; Luet looked around and saw that it was the predictable ones—Kokor and Obring and Mebbekew—who were most upset.

"You have no right to make a decision like that," said Vas mildly. "We're all Basilicans, and we live under Basilican law."

"When we're in Basilica we live under Basilican law," said Elemak. "But when you're in the desert you live under desert law, and desert law has it that the word of the caravan leader is final. I'll listen to any ideas until I have to make a decision, but once the decision is made *any* resistance is mutiny, do you understand me?"

"No one tells me who I *must* sleep with and who I may *not*," said Kokor.

Elemak walked up to her and faced her; she looked so frail compared to the sheer mass of Elemak's tall, well-muscled body. "And I tell you that in the desert, I won't have anyone creeping from tent to tent. It will lead to murder one way or another, and so instead of letting you improvise the dying, I'll let you know right now: If anyone is caught in a position that even *looks* like you're getting sexually involved with someone you aren't married to, I will personally kill the woman on the spot."

"The *woman!*" cried Kokor.

"We need the men to help load the camels," said Elemak. "Besides, the idea shouldn't seem strange to *you,* Koya, since you made exactly the same decision the last time *you* decided that somebody should die for the crime of adultery."

Luet could see how both Kokor and her sister Sevet immediately touched their throats—for it was in the throat that Kokor had struck Sevet, nearly killing her and leaving her almost voiceless ever since. While Kokor's husband, Obring, who had been bouncing away just as merrily when Kokor found the two of them, was unscathed. It was viciously unkind and exactly appropriate for Elemak to remind them all of that event, because it completely silenced any kind of opposition to the new law from three of the four people most likely to oppose it: Kokor, Sevet, and Obring had nothing to say at all.

"You don't have the right to decide this," said Mebbekew. He was, of course, the fourth—but Luet knew that Elemak would have no trouble bringing him into line. He never did, with Meb.

"I not only have the right," said Elemak, "I have the duty. This is a law necessary for the survival of our little company in the desert, and so it will be obeyed or I will enforce the only penalty that I *can* enforce here, so many kilometers from civilization. If you can't grasp this idea, then I'm sure Lady Rasa can explain it to you."

He turned and faced Rasa, in a silent demand that she back him up. She did not disappoint him. "I tried and tried all night to think of another way to handle this," she said, "but we can't live without this law, and as Elya says, in the desert the only penalty that means anything at all is . . . what he said. But not killing outright!" she said, clearly hating the whole idea of it. "Only binding and leaving a person."

"*Only?*" said Elemak disdainfully. "It's by far the crueler death."

"It leaves her in the hands of the Oversoul," Rasa said. "Perhaps to be rescued."

"You should pray not," said Elemak. "The animals are kinder than any rescuers she'd find out here."

"A lawbreaker is to be bound and abandoned, *not* killed!" Rasa insisted.

Luet thought: She fears it will be a daughter of hers who will first break this law. As for Elemak's rule that having only the woman die will better restrain the man, he has it backward. Few men think of consequences when they're filled with desire, but a woman can put off her own desires if a man she loves would be at risk.

"As the lady wishes," said Elemak. "The law of the desert leaves the choice up to the leader of the caravan. I would normally choose a quick, clean death by pulse, but let us hope that no such choice ever has to be made." He looked around at the whole group, turning to include in his gaze the ones who were behind him. "I don't ask for your consent in this," he said. "I simply tell you that this is the way it will be. So now raise your hand if you understand the law we will live by."

They all raised their hands, though clearly some were furious.

No, not quite all. "Meb," said Elemak. "Raise your hand. You're embarrassing your dear wife Dol. She's no doubt beginning to wonder who is the woman here whose love you consider so desirable that you would cause an imperfectly virtuous lady's certain death by pursuing it."

Now Meb raised his hand.

"Good," said Elemak. "And now for the other matter. We have a decision to make," he said.

The sun had not yet risen, so it was still bitterly cold—especially for the ones who had done very little of the work of striking the tents and loading the camels. So it might have been just the cold that made Mebbekew's voice tremble when he said, "I thought *you* were making all the decisions now."

"I make all the decisions that have to do with keeping us alive and moving," said Elemak. "But I don't fancy myself some kind of tyrant. The decisions that *don't* have to do with survival belong to the whole group, not to me. We can't survive unless we all stay together, so I'll tolerate *no* divisions among us. At the same time, I don't recall a point where anybody actually decided where it was we were going."

"We're going back to Father and Issib," said Nafai immediately. "You know they're counting on us to return."

"They have plenty of water as long as they stay put. They need someone to go and fetch them sometime in the next few months—they've got years of supplies, for that matter," said Elemak. "So let's not turn this into a life and death matter unless we have to. If the majority wants to go on until we reach Volemak in the desert, fine. That's where we'll *all* go."

"We can't go back to Basilica," said Luet. "My father made that very clear." Her father, of course, was Moozh, the great general of the Gorayni, though she had not known that until a few days ago. But by reminding the others of this newfound family connection, she hoped to make her words carry more weight. She wasn't skilled at persuasion; she had always simply told the truth, and because the women of Basilica knew her to be the waterseer, her words were taken seriously. It was a new thing, talking to a group that included men. But she knew that asserting one's family status was one of the ways people got their way in Basilica, and so she tried it now.

"Yes," said Kokor, "your tender loving father who tried to marry his own daughter and then threw us all out of the city when he couldn't."

"That's not the way it happened," said Luet.

Hushidh touched Luet's hand to still her. "Don't try," Hushidh whispered softly. "Koya's better at it than you are."

No one else heard Hushidh's words, but when Luet fell silent they understood the effect of what she said, and Kokor smirked.

"Luet is right enough that we probably can't go back to Basilica," said Elemak, "at least not right away—I think that was the message we were meant to understand from the fact that he sent an escort of soldiers to make sure we got safely away from the city."

"I'm so tired of hearing how *none* of us can get back to Basilica," said Mebbekew, "when it's only *those* who embarrassed him in front of everybody." He was pointing at Hushidh and Luet and Nafai.

"Do shut up, Meb," said Elemak with genial contempt. "I don't want us to be standing here talking when the sun comes up. We're in exactly the kind of country that bandits like to hole up in, and if there are some hiding from the darkness in caves nearby, they're bound to come out by daylight."

Luet wondered if in fact Elemak *had* picked up some intimation of the bandits that the Oversoul had been controlling. Perhaps Elemak knew all along that such men were only brave in the sunlight, and hid at night. Besides, it was possible that Elemak was receiving the Oversoul's messages subliminally, not realizing where the thoughts and ideas were coming from. After all, Elemak was as much a result of the Oversoul's secret breeding program as any of the rest of them were, and he *had* received a dream not long ago. If only Elemak would simply admit that he could communicate with the Oversoul and follow her plans willingly—it would uncomplicate everything. As it was, she and Hushidh had been working on plans to try to thwart Elemak in whatever it was he was planning to do.

"Even though we really can't go back to Basilica immediately," Elemak went on, "that doesn't mean we have to go join Father at once. There are many other cities that would take in a caravan of strangers, if only because Shedemei has an extremely valuable cargo of embryos and seeds."

"They're not for sale," said Shedemei. Her voice was harsh enough, her answer abrupt enough, that everyone knew she had no intention of arguing about it.

"Not even to save our lives?" said Elemak sweetly. "But never mind —I don't propose selling them anyway. They're only valuable when they come along with the knowledge that Shedya has in her head. What matters is that they *will* let us in if they know that, far from being a band of penniless wanderers recently expelled from Basilica by General Moozh of the Gorayni, we are instead accompanying the famous geneticist Shedemei, who is moving her laboratory away from strife-torn Basilica to some peaceful city that will guarantee her a place to do her work without disturbance."

"Perfect," said Vas. "There's not a City of the Plain that would refuse us entry on those terms."

"They'd offer us money, in fact," said Obring.

"They'd offer *me* money, you mean," said Shedemei. But clearly she was flattered—she hadn't really thought of the fact that her presence would convey a certain amount of prestige on any city she settled in. Luet could see that Elemak's flattery was having its effect.

(He's going to put it to a vote.) The Oversoul spoke in Luet's mind.

That much is obvious by now, said Luet. What is his *plan?*

(When Nafai opposes the decision to return to the city, it will be mutiny.)

Then he must not oppose.

(Then my work would be thwarted.)

Then control the vote.

(Whose vote should I change? Which of them would Elemak believe if he suddenly voted to go on?)

Then don't let the vote happen.

(I have no such influence with Elemak.)

Then tell Nafai not to oppose!

(He must oppose, or there will be no voyage to Earth.)

"No!" cried Luet.

Everyone looked at her. "No what?" asked Elemak.

"No vote," she said. "There will be *no* vote."

"Ah yes," said Elemak. "We have another freedom-lover here who realizes that she doesn't approve of democracy after all, when she thinks the vote will go against her."

"Who said anything about voting?" asked Dol, who was never terribly sharp about what was going on around her.

"I vote we go back to civilization," said Obring. "Otherwise we're slaves to marriage—and to Elemak, for that matter!"

"But I said nothing about putting things to a vote," said Elemak. "I said only that we must make a decision about where to go. A vote might be interesting, but I won't be bound by it. It's your counsel that I need, not your governance."

So they counseled him, eloquently—or tried to. But if anyone even began to advance an argument that someone else had already stated, Elemak would silence them at once. "I've already heard that. Anything new to add?" As a result, the discussion didn't last very long at all. Sooner than Luet would have thought possible, Elemak asked, "Anything else?" and no one answered.

He waited, looked around at them. The sun was coming over the tops of the distant mountains now, and his eyes and hair glowed with reflected light. This is his finest moment, thought Luet. This is what he has planned for—a whole community, including his father's wife, including his brother Nafai, including the waterseer and the raveler of Basilica, including his own bride, all waiting for the decision that will change their lives. Or end them.

"Thank you for your wise counsel," said Elemak gravely. "It seems to me that we don't have to choose one way *or* another. Those who want to return to civilization may, and soon enough those who want to go on into the desert on this errand for the Oversoul may do so as well. We can call it a rescue of my father or we can call it the beginning of a voyage to Earth—that's not at issue now. What matters is that all can be satisfied. We'll go south a little way and then come over the mountains and down into the Cities of the Plain. There we can leave those who can't bear to live under the harsh law of the desert, and I can take the stronger ones with me."

"Thanks so much!" said Mebbekew.

"I don't care what he calls me, as long as I have my freedom," said Kokor.

"Fools," said Nafai. "Don't you see that he's only pretending?"

"What did you say?" said Elemak.

"He intended to take us back to civilization all along," said Nafai.

"Don't, Nafai," said Luet, for she knew what was coming next.

"Listen to your brideling, Brother," said Elemak. His voice was deceptively mild.

"I will listen to the Oversoul," said Nafai. "The only reason we're alive right now is because the Oversoul has been influencing a band of robbers to stay holed up in their cave not three hundred meters away. The Oversoul can lead us perfectly well across the desert, with or without Elemak and his stupid desert law. It's a game for boys that he's playing—who can make the boldest threats—"

"Not threats," said Elemak. "Laws that every desert traveler knows."

"If we trust in the Oversoul we will be perfectly safe on this journey. If we trust in Elemak we'll return to the Plain and be destroyed in the wars that are coming."

"Trust in the Oversoul," said Meb with a sneer. "What you mean is do whatever *you* say."

"Elemak knows that the Oversoul is real enough—he had a dream that led us back to the city to marry our wives, didn't he?"

Elemak only laughed. "Babble on, Nafai."

"It's as Elemak said. This isn't a matter for democracy. It's a matter for each of us to decide. Go on with the journey as the Oversoul has directed, and we'll take the greatest voyage in forty million years and inherit a world for us and our children. Or go back to the city where you can betray your spouse as some of you are already planning. As for me and Luet, we will never go back to the city."

"Enough," said Elemak. "Not another word or you're dead this instant." A pulse was in his hand. Luet had not noticed he was carrying it, but she knew what it meant. This was exactly what Elemak had been waiting for. He had set it up very carefully, and now he could kill Nafai and no one would dare condemn him for it. "I know the desert and you don't," said Elemak. "There are no bandits where you *claim* there are, or we'd already be dead. If that's what passes for wisdom in your fevered little brain, Brother, then anyone who stayed with you would surely be doomed. But no one *will* stay with you, because I'm not about to let this group split up. That would mean certain death for anyone who went with you."

"A lie," said Nafai.

"Please, speak again so I can kill you as the mutineer you are."

"Hold your tongue, Nafai, for my sake!" said Luet.

"You've all heard him, haven't you?" said Elemak. "He has proclaimed rebellion against my authority and attempted to lead a group away to their destruction. That's mutiny, which is far more serious than adultery, and the penalty is death. You are all witnesses. There's not one of you but would have to confess it in court, should it ever come to that."

"Please," said Luet. "Let him be, and he'll say no more."

"Is that true, Nafai?" asked Elemak.

"If you continue to head back to the city," said Nafai, "the Oversoul will have no reason to restrain the bandits any further, and you will all be killed."

"You see?" said Elemak. "Even now he tries to frighten us with these fantasies of nonexistent bandits."

"That's what you've been doing all along," said Shedemei. "Making us do what you want for fear of bandits finding us."

Elemak turned to her. "I never claimed they were a few meters away, hiding in a cave, only that there was a chance that some would come upon us. I've said nothing but the truth to you—but this boy thinks you're such fools that you'll believe his obvious lies."

"Believe what you like," said Nafai. "You'll see the proof soon enough."

"Mutiny," said Elemak, "and all of you—even his own mother—will be my witnesses that I had no choice, because he would not desist in his rebellion. If he were not my own brother, I wouldn't have waited this long. He'd be dead already."

"And if you didn't carry genes that the Oversoul regards as precious ones," said Nafai, "Gaballufix would have killed you when you failed to lead Father into his trap."

"Accusing me does nothing but compound your crime," said

Elemak. "Say good-bye to your mother and your wife—from where you are, and no nearer!"

"Elemak, you can't mean this," said Rasa.

"You yourself agreed with me, Rasa, that our survival depends on obedience to the law of the desert, and what the penalty had to be."

"I see that you maliciously—"

"Careful, Lady Rasa. I'll do what must be done, even if it includes leaving you to your death as well."

"Don't worry, Mother," said Nafai. "The Oversoul is with us, and Elemak is helpless."

Luet began to catch a glimmer of what Nafai was doing. He seemed quite calm—unbelievably calm. Therefore he must be quite sure that the Oversoul would be able to protect him after all. He must have a plan of his own, and so Luet would do best to be silent and let it unfold, no matter how frightened she was.

It would be nice if you would share the plan with me, though, she said to the Oversoul.

(Plan?) answered the Oversoul.

Luet's hands began to tremble.

"We'll see how helpless you are," said Elemak. "Mebbekew, take a length of packing cord—the light line, and a good length, several meters—and tie his hands. Use the cinching knot, so it binds tight, and don't worry about cutting off the circulation in his hands."

"You see?" said Nafai. "He has to kill a bound man."

Don't! cried Luet in her heart. Don't provoke him into shooting you! If you let him tie you, then you have a chance.

Elemak glanced at Mebbekew, at which Meb took a few steps to one of the waiting camels and came back with a cord.

As he was tying Nafai's hands behind his back, twining the cords around and around his wrists, Hushidh stepped forward.

"Stay where you are," said Elemak. "I'm binding him and abandoning him out of respect for Lady Rasa, but I'll be just as happy to give him the pulse and have done with it."

Hushidh stayed where she was; she had what she wanted anyway, which was the group's attention. "Elemak planned this all along," said Hushidh to the others, "because he wanted to kill Nafai. He knew that if he decided to turn back, Nafai would have no choice but to oppose him. He set it up to provide him with a legal excuse for murder."

Elemak's eye twitched. Luet could see the rage building out of control in him. What are you doing, Hushidh, my sister! Don't talk him into killing my husband as we stand here!

"Why would Elya do that?" said Eiadh. "You're saying my Elemak is a murderer, and he's not!"

"Eiadh, you poor dear," said Hushidh. "Elemak wants Nafai dead because he knows that if you had the choice today, you'd leave him and choose Nafai."

"A lie!" cried Elemak. "Don't answer her, Eiadh! Say nothing!"

"Because he can't bear to hear the truth," said Hushidh. "He'll hear it in your voice."

Now Luet understood. Hushidh was using her talent from the Oversoul, just as she did when Rashgallivak stood in the foyer of Rasa's house, planning to use his soldiers to kidnap Rasa's daughters. Hushidh was saying the words that would destroy the loyalty of Elemak's followers, that would remove all support from him. She was unbinding them, and if she could just say a few more sentences, she would succeed.

Unfortunately, Luet wasn't the only one who realized this. "Silence her!" said Sevet. Her voice was harsh and husky, for she had not yet recovered well from the injury Kokor gave her. But she could speak well enough to be heard, and the very painfulness of her voice brought her all the more attention. "Don't let Hushidh speak. She's a raveler, and if she says enough she can turn everyone against everybody else. I saw her do it to Rashgallivak's men, and she can do it now, if you let her."

"Sevet is right," said Elemak. "Not another word from you, Hushidh, or I'll kill him."

Almost she opened her mouth to speak again, Luet could see it. But something—perhaps the Oversoul—restrained her. She turned and stepped back to where she had stood before, on the far side of Rasa and Shedemei. It was the last hope gone, as far as Luet could see. The Oversoul could make weak-willed people stupid or afraid for a short while, but she hadn't the strength to stop a man determined on murder. She hadn't the strength to make the bandits turn suddenly kind in their dealings with Nafai, should they find him. She certainly couldn't keep the animals of the desert from finding him and devouring him. Hushidh's ploy had been the last possibility, and it was gone.

No, I will *not* despair, thought Luet. Perhaps if we abandon him here I can slip away from the party and come back and untie him. Or perhaps I can kill Elemak in his sleep and . . .

No, no. She hadn't murder in her, and she knew it. Not even if the Oversoul commanded it, as she had commanded Nafai to kill Gaballufix. She couldn't do it even then. Nor would she be able to slip away and help Nafai in time. It was over. There was no hope.

"He's tied," said Mebbekew.

"Let me check the knot," said Elemak.

"Do you think I don't know how to tie it?" asked Mebbekew.

"This computer they worship supposedly has the power to make people stupider than usual," said Elemak. "Isn't that right, Nafai?"

Nafai said nothing. Luet was proud of him for that, but still frightened for him. For she knew that the Oversoul's power was very great over a long period of time, but very slight at any one moment.

Elemak was now standing close behind Nafai, with the pulse pointed at his back. "Kneel down, little brother."

Nafai didn't kneel, but as if by reflex Meb began to.

"Not you, fool. Nyef."

"The condemned man," said Nafai.

"Yes, you, little brother. Kneel."

"If you're going to use the pulse, I prefer to die standing up."

"Don't make such a show of this," said Elemak. "I want your hands tied to your ankles, so kneel down."

Slowly, carefully, Nafai sank to one knee, then to both.

"Sit on your heels," said Elemak. "Or near them. Yes. Now, Meb, pass the ends of the rope down between his ankles, bring them up and over his legs, and tie them together—in front of his wrists—yes, like that, where his fingers can't possibly reach them. Very good. Can you feel anything in your hands, Nafai?"

"Only the throbbing of my blood, trying to get past the ropes around my wrists."

"Strings, not ropes, Nafai, but they might as well be steel."

"You're not cutting off *my* blood, Elemak, you're cutting off your own," said Nafai. "For your blood will be unknown on Earth, while my blood will live on for a thousand generations."

"Enough," said Elemak.

"I'll say what I like now," said Nafai, "since you've already determined to kill me—what difference will it make now, for me to say the truth? Should I be afraid that you'll kick me or spit on me, when I already stare death in the face?"

"If you're trying to provoke me into shooting you, it won't work. I promised Lady Rasa, and I'll keep my word."

But Luet could see that Nafai's words *were* having an effect. The tension in the whole group was rising higher and higher, and it was clear that in everyone's eyes the showdown between them was yet to come, even when Elemak thought he had already won.

"We'll get on our camels now," said Elemak. "And no one will turn back to try to save this mutineer, or whoever tries will share his fate."

If Luet had not been sure that Nafai and the Oversoul must have some kind of plan, she would have insisted then on dying beside her husband. But she knew him well enough, even after only these few days, to know that Nafai felt no fear at all right now. And while he was a brave young man, she knew that if he truly believed he was going to die, *she* at least would be able to sense his fear. His mother must feel the same way, too, Luet realized, because she was not protesting, either. Instead they both waited and watched as the little play unfolded.

Elemak and Mebbekew started to walk away from Nafai. Then Mebbekew turned, put his foot on Nafai's shoulder, and pushed him over sideways to lie in the sand. With his hands tied to his ankles, he could do nothing to cushion his fall. But now Luet could see behind him, could see clearly that instead of being tied tightly, the strings were only loosely gathered.

So that was what the game was. The Oversoul was doing all she could to influence Mebbekew and Elemak to see tightly bound ropes where in fact the strands were only loops. She normally did not have the power to make them stupid—or at least not enough to make *Elemak* so unobservant. But between Hushidh and Nafai, with their dangerous, infuriating talk, they had managed to make Elemak so angry that the Oversoul had more power to confuse him. Indeed, there must be others who could see that Nafai was not firmly tied, though fortunately those in the best position to see were also those least likely to point it out—Lady Rasa, Hushidh, and Shedemei. As for the others, with the Oversoul's help they no doubt saw what they expected to see, what Elemak and Mebbekew had led them to *expect* to see.

"Yes," said Lady Rasa. "Let's go to the camels." She strode boldly toward the waiting animals. Luet and Hushidh followed her. The others also turned and moved.

All except Eiadh. She stood motionless, looking at Nafai. The others, standing beside their kneeling camels, could not help but turn and watch as Elemak walked up to her, put his hand on her back. "I know this hurts your tender heart, Edhya," said Elemak. "But a leader must sometimes act harshly, for the good of all."

She did not even glance at him. "I never thought a man could face death with such perfect calm," she said.

Wonderful, Luet said silently to the Oversoul. You're making her love Nafai all the more? How helpful of you, to guarantee that we'll never have peace, even if Nafai gets out of this alive.

(Have a little trust, will you? I can't do everything at once. Which would you rather have, Eiadh out of love with your husband, or your husband alive and the caravan headed toward Volemak?)

I trust you. I just wish you wouldn't cut it so close.

"Hear me!" cried Nafai.

"Pleading will get you nowhere now," said Elemak. "Or do you want to make one last speech of mutiny?"

"He wasn't speaking to us," said Eiadh. "He was speaking to her. To the Oversoul."

"Oversoul, because I have put my trust in you, deliver me from the murdering hands of my brothers! Give me the strength to burst these cords that bind my hands!"

How did it look to the others? Luet could only guess. What *she* saw was Nafai easily pulling one hand, then the other out of the cords, then clambering without much grace to his feet. But the others surely saw what they feared most—Nafai tearing the cords apart with his hands, then springing to his feet with majesty and danger gathering about him. No doubt the Oversoul was focusing all her influence on the others, sparing none for those who already accepted her purpose. Luet, Hushidh, and Lady Rasa were seeing the facts of what happened. The others were no doubt seeing something, not factual, but filled with truth: that Nafai had the power of the Oversoul with him, that he was the chosen one, the true leader.

"You will not turn those camels toward any city known to human-kind!" cried Nafai. His voice was tense and harsh-sounding as he strained to be heard across the broad expanse between him and the farthest camels, where Vas had been helping Sevet to mount. "This mutiny of yours against the Oversoul has ended, Elemak. Only the Oversoul is more merciful than you. The Oversoul will let you live—

but only as long as you vow never again to lay one hand upon me. Only as long as you promise to fulfil the journey we began—to join with Father, and then to voyage onward to the world that the Oversoul has prepared for us!"

"What kind of trick is this!" cried Elemak.

"The only trick is the one you used to fool yourself," said Nafai. "You thought that by binding me with cords you could also bind the Oversoul, but you were wrong. You could have led this expedition if you had been obedient and wise, but you were filled with your own lust for power and your own envy, and so you have nothing left now but to obey the Oversoul or die."

"Don't threaten me!" cried Elemak. "I have the pulse, you fool, and I've passed a sentence of death on you!"

"Kill him!" shouted Mebbekew. "Kill him now, or you'll regret it forever!"

"So brave of you," said Hushidh, "to urge your brother to do what you would never have the heart for yourself, little Meb." Her voice had such sting to it that he stepped back as if he had been slapped.

But Elemak did not step back. Instead he strode forward, holding the pulse. Luet could see that he was terrified—he absolutely believed that Nafai had done something miraculous by breaking free so easily from his bonds—yet terrified or not, he was determined to kill his youngest brother, and the Oversoul could not possibly stop him. It hadn't the power to turn Elemak away from his firm purpose.

"Elya, no!" The cry was from Eiadh. She ran forward, clutched at him, plucked at the sleeve that held the pulse. "For my sake," she said. "If you touch him, Elya, the Oversoul will kill you, don't you know that? It's the law of the desert—what you yourself said. Mutiny is death! Don't rebel against the Oversoul."

"This isn't the Oversoul," Elemak said. His voice trembled with fear and uncertainty, though—and no doubt the Oversoul was seizing on every scrap of doubt in his heart, magnifying it as Eiadh pled with him. "This is my arrogant little brother."

"It should have been you," said Nafai. "You should have been the one who made the others go along with the Oversoul's plan. The Oversoul would never have chosen *me*, if you had only been willing to obey."

"Listen to *me*," said Eiadh. "Not to *him*. You're the one who is the father of the child within me—how do you know I don't have a child within me? If you hurt him, if you disobey him, then you'll die, and my child will be fatherless!"

At first Luet feared that Elemak would interpret Eiadh's pleading for Nafai's life as yet another proof that his wife loved Nafai more than him. But no. Her pleading was that he must save his *own* life by not harming Nafai. Therefore he could only take it as proof that she loved *him*, for it was his life she was trying to save.

Vas had also come back to Elemak, and now laid a hand on his other shoulder. "Elya, don't kill him. We won't go back to the city—none of us will, none of us!" He turned back to face the others. "Will we! We're all content to go on to join Volemak, aren't we!"

"We've seen the power of the Oversoul," said Eiadh. "None of us would have asked to return to the city if we had understood. Please, we all agree. Our purpose is one now, no division among us. Please, Elemak. Don't make me a widow over this. I'm your wife forever, if you turn away from killing him. But what am I if you rebel against the Oversoul and die?"

"You're still our travel leader," said Lady Rasa. "Nothing changes that. Only the destination, and you said yourself that the destination wasn't yours to choose alone. Now we see that the choice belongs to none of *us*, but only to the Oversoul."

Eiadh wept, and the tears were hot and real. "Oh, Elya, my husband, why do you hate me so much that you want to die!"

Luet could almost have predicted what would happen next. Dol, seeing how affecting Eiadh's tears were, could not bear to have her performance hold the center of everyone's attention. So she now clung to *her* husband, and wailed loudly—with very real-seeming tears indeed—that he, too, must refrain from harming Nafai. As if Mebbekew would ever have dared to act alone! As if her tears would ever have moved him! Luet would have laughed aloud, if she hadn't been so aware of the fact that Nafai's life depended now on how Elemak reacted to all the wailing.

She could almost see the change happening on his face. His determination to kill Nafai, which had not yielded to the influence of the Oversoul, now melted before the pleas of his wife. And as that will to murder faded, the Oversoul had more and more opportunity to seize upon and magnify his fears. So from being a dangerous killer, in only a few moments he turned into a trembling wreck of a man, appalled at what he had almost done. He looked down at the pulse in his hands and shuddered, then threw it away from him. It landed at Luet's feet.

"Oh, Nafai, my brother, what was I doing!" Elemak cried.

Mebbekew was even more abject. He flung himself belly-down on the ground. "Forgive me, Nafai! Forgive me for tying you up like an animal—don't let the Oversoul kill me!"

You're overdoing this, Luet said silently to the Oversoul. They're going to be deeply humiliated when they remember how they acted, no matter whether they figure out it was you making cowards of them or not.

(What, do you think I have some kind of fine control over this? I can shout fear at them, and they don't hear me and they don't hear me and then suddenly they hear me and collapse like this. I think I'm doing pretty well, for not having done this before.)

I'm just suggesting that you lighten up on them a little. The job is done.

"Elemak, Mebbekew, of course I forgive you," said Nafai. "What does it matter what happens to *me?* It's the Oversoul whose forgiveness matters, not mine."

"Kneel to the Oversoul," said Eiadh, urgently pulling Elemak downward. "Kneel and beg for forgiveness, please. Don't you see that your life is in danger?"

Elemak turned to her, and spoke almost calmly, despite the fear that Luet knew was gnawing at him. "And do you care so much whether I live or die?"

"You're my life," said Eiadh. "Haven't we all sworn an oath to stay married forever?"

As a matter of fact, they hadn't, thought Luet. All they had done was listen to Elemak's edict and raise their hands to show they *understood* it. But she prudently said nothing.

Elemak sank to his knees. "Oversoul," he said, his voice trembling. "I'll go where you want me to go."

"Me too," said Mebbekew. "Count me in." He didn't raise his head from the sand.

"As long as Eiadh is mine," said Elemak, "I'm content, whether I'm in the desert or the city, on Harmony or on Earth."

"Oh, Elya!" cried Eiadh. She flung her arms around him and wept into his shoulder.

Luet bent over and picked up the pulse from the sand at her feet. It wouldn't do to risk losing a precious weapon. Who knew when they might need it for hunting?

Nafai walked over to her. It meant more than Luet could say, that he came first to her, his wife of only a few days, rather than to his mother. He embraced her, and she held him. She could feel his trembling. He *had* been afraid, despite his confidence in the Oversoul. And it had been a near thing, too.

"Did you know how it would all come out?" she whispered.

"The Oversoul wasn't sure it could bring off the rope thing," he murmured back to her. "Especially when he actually walked up to inspect the knot."

"He had to do that, if he was going to believe it was miraculous when you broke free."

"You know what I was thinking, when I was kneeling there with the pulse at my head, saying those things that were goading him to kill me? I was thinking—I'll never know what our baby looks like."

"And now you will."

He pulled away from her, then reached out and took the pulse out of her hand.

Hushidh stepped close and put her hand on the pulse. "Nyef," she said, "if you hold that, there's no hope of healing."

"What if I give it back to him?"

Hushidh nodded. "The best thing," she said.

No one understood better than Hushidh the Raveler what bound and unbound people. Nafai at once strode to Elemak and held out the pulse to him. "Please," he said. "I don't even know how to use this. We need you to lead us back to Father's camp."

Elemak paused just a moment before taking the pulse. Luet knew that he hated receiving it from Nafai's hand. But at the same time he also knew that Nafai didn't have to give it to him. That Nafai didn't have to give him back his place of leadership. And he needed that place, needed it so much that he would even take it from Nafai.

"Glad to," said Elemak. He took the pulse.

"Oh, thank you, Nafai," said Eiadh.

Luet felt a stab of fear through her heart. Does Elemak hear it in her voice? Can he see it in her face? How she looks with such awe at Nafai? She's a woman who loves only strength and courage and power —it is the alpha male in the tribe who attracts her. And in her eyes, Nafai is clearly that most desirable of men. She was the best actress of all today, thought Luet. She was the one who was able to convince Elemak of her love for him, in order to save the man she *really* loved. I can't help but admire her for that, thought Luet. She's really something.

Those thoughts of admiration were themselves lies, though, and Luet could not long fool herself. Beautiful Eiadh is still in love with my husband, and even though his love for me is strong right now, there'll come a day when the primate male in him overcomes the civilized man, and he'll look at Eiadh with desire, and she'll see it and in that moment I will surely lose him.

She shook the jealous thought from her, and walked with Lady Rasa, who was trembling with relief, in order to help her clamber onto her camel. "I thought he was dead," said Rasa softly, clinging to Luet's hand. "I thought I had lost him."

"So did I, for a few moments there," said Luet.

"I can tell you this," said Lady Rasa. "Elemak would have died before nightfall, if he had gone through with it."

"I was plotting his death in my own heart, too," said Luet.

"That's how close we are to animals. Did you ever dream of such a thing? That we would be ready to do murder all so suddenly?"

"Just like baboons, protecting the troop," said Luet.

"I think it's rather a grand discovery, don't you?"

Luet grinned at her and squeezed her hand. "Let's not tell anybody, though," she said. "It would make the men so nervous, to know how dangerous we really are."

"It doesn't matter now," said Rasa. "The Oversoul was stronger than I thought possible. It's all over and done with now."

But as Luet walked back to find her own camel, she knew it was *not* finished. It had only been postponed. The day would come again when there would be a struggle for power. And next time there was no guarantee that the Oversoul would be able to bring off such a sweet little trick. If Elemak had once decided to fire off the pulse, it would have been over; next time he might realize that, and not let himself be sidetracked by something so foolish as Lady Rasa's plea that he only tie Nafai up and abandon him. It was *that* close, such a near thing. And at the end, Luet knew that Elemak's hatred for Nafai was stronger than ever, even though for a time at least he would deny it, would pretend even to himself that his hate was gone. You can fool the others, Elemak, but I'll be watching you. And if anything happens to my husband, you can be sure of it, you'd better kill me too. You'd better be sure I'm dead, and even then, if I can find a way, I'll come back and wreak some vengeance on you from the grave.

"You're trembling, Lutya," said Hushidh.

"Am I?" Perhaps that was why she was having so much trouble making certain of the cinch on her camel's saddle.

"Like a dragonfly's wing."

"It was a very emotional thing," said Luet. "I suppose that I'm still upset."

"Still jealous of Eiadh, that's what you are," said Hushidh.

"Not even a speck," said Luet. "He loves me absolutely and completely."

"Yes, he does," said Hushidh. "But still I see such rage in you toward Eiadh."

Luet knew that she *did,* yes, feel some jealousy toward Eiadh. But Hushidh had called it rage, and that was a far stronger feeling than she had been aware of in herself. "I'm not angry because she loves Nafai," said Luet, "truly I'm not."

"Oh, I know that," said Hushidh. "Or rather, I see that *now.* No, I think you're angry at her and jealous of her because she was able to save your husband's life, when you couldn't do it."

Yes, thought Luet. That was it. And now that Hushidh had named it, she could feel the agonizing frustration of it wash through her, and hot tears of rage and shame flooded out of her eyes and down her cheeks.

"There," said Hushidh, holding her. "It's good to let it out. It's good."

"That's nice," said Luet. "Because apparently I'm going to cry like a ninny whether it's good to let it out or not, so it might as well be good."

She was still crying when Nafai came back to find her and help her on her beast. "You're the last one," said Nafai.

"I think I just needed to feel you touch me one more time," she said. "To be sure you were alive."

"Still breathing," he said. "Are you going to cry like that for long? Because all that moisture on your face is bound to attract flies."

"Whatever happened to those bandits?" she said, wiping her tears with her sleeve.

"The Oversoul managed to put them to sleep just before it started getting serious about influencing the others. They'll wake up in a couple of hours. Why did you think about *them?*"

"I was just thinking how stupid we would all have felt, if they had come running up and hacked us all to pieces while we stood there bickering about whether or not to kill you."

"Yes," said Nafai. "I know what you mean. To face death, that's nothing much. But to feel *really stupid* when you die, well, that would be insufferable."

She laughed and held his hand for just a moment. Just another moment, and then another long, long moment.

"They're waiting for us," said Nafai. "And the bandits *will* wake up eventually."

So she let go of him, and as soon as he headed toward his own camel, hers lurched to its feet and she rose high above the desert floor. It was like riding atop an unsteady tower in an earthquake, and she didn't usually like it. But today it felt as lovely as she had ever imagined it might be to sit upon a throne. For there, on the camel before her, sat Nafai, her husband. Even if it had not been Luet herself who saved him, what of it? It was enough that he was alive, and he was still in love with her.

3

Hunting

They came down into Volemak's camp in the evening. They had traveled longer than usual that day, because they were close; yet still there was all the evening work to do, for Volemak had not known they were coming that night, and there were no extra tents pitched, and Zdorab had already washed up from the supper he prepared for himself and Volemak and Issib. The evening work went slower than usual, because they felt safer, and because, having arrived, it seemed so unfair to have as much work to do as during the journey.

Hushidh stayed as close to Luet and Nafai as she could. She caught glimpses of Issib now and then as he floated somewhere on his chair. There was nothing surprising to her about his appearance—she had known him for years, since he was Lady Rasa's oldest son and had studied at Rasa's house as long as Hushidh had been there herself. But she had always thought of him as the crippled one, and paid him little mind. Then, back in Basilica, as she came to realize that she was going out onto the desert with Nafai and Luet, it came clear to her—for she could always see the connections between people—that in the pairings of male and female in the Oversoul's expedition, she would end up with Issib. The Oversoul wanted his genes to go on, and hers as well, and for good or ill they would be making that effort together.

It had been a hard thing to accept. Especially on the wedding night, as Luet and Nafai, Elemak and Eiadh, Mebbekew and Dolya all were married by Lady Rasa and then went, two by two, to their bridal beds, Hushidh could hardly bear the rage and fear and bitter disappointment in her heart, that *she* could not have the kind of love that her sister Luet had.

In answer, the Oversoul—or so she had thought at first—sent her a dream that night. In it she saw herself linked with Issib; she saw him flying and flew with him; she understood from that that his body did not express his true nature, and that she would find that marriage with him was not something that would grind her down but rather would lift her up. And she saw herself bearing children with him, saw herself standing in the door of a desert tent with him, watching their children play, and she saw that in that future scene she would love him, would be bound with him by gold and silver threads tying them back through generations, and leading them also forward into the future, year by year, child by child, generation by generation. There were other parts of the dream, some of them terrifying, but she clung to the comfort of it all these days. As she had stood with General Moozh, forced to marry the conqueror of Basilica, she had thought about the dream and knew that she would not really end up with him, and sure enough, the Oversoul brought Hushidh's and Luet's mother, the woman named Thirsty, who named them as her daughters—with Moozh as their father. No marriage then, and within hours they were in the desert, on their way to join Volemak in the desert.

But since then she had had time to think—time to remember her fears. Of course she tried not to, tried instead to cling to the comfort of the dream, or to Nafai's reassurances, for he had told her that Issib was very bright and funny, a man of good company, which of course she had never had much chance to see at school.

Yet despite the dream, despite Nafai, her old impressions, the ones she had held for so many years, remained. All the way through the desert she kept seeing the almost macabre way his arms and legs used to move in the city, where he could wear lifts under his clothing, so that he always seemed to be bouncing through the air like gamboling ghost, or like a—what was it that Kokor had once called him?—like a rabbit under water. How they had laughed! And now, how disloyal she felt, although it had been Issib's own sister who made the joke. Hushidh could not have guessed that someday the cripple, the ghost, the underwater rabbit would be her husband. The old fear and strangeness remained as an undercurrent, despite all her attempts to reassure herself.

Until now, seeing him, she realized that she was not afraid of *him*. The dream had given her too much hope. No, she was afraid of what *he* would think of *her*—an even older and darker fear. Did Issib know yet what Aunt Rasa and the Oversoul had planned for him? Was he already eyeing her as she worked at tent-pitching, sizing her up? No doubt that if he was, he would be bitterly disappointed. She could imagine him thinking, Of course the *cripple* gets the plain one, the one too tall, the sour-faced one whose body has never caused a man to take a second glance. The studious one, who has no gift for causing anyone to laugh, except sometimes her younger sister Luet (ah, so bright! but *she* belongs to Nafai). He must be thinking: I'll have to make the best of it, because I'm a cripple and have no choice. Just as I'm thinking, I'll have to make do with the cripple, because no other man would have me.

How many marriages have begun with such feelings as these? Were any of them ever happy, in the end?

She delayed as long as she could, lingering over supper—which *was* better than anything they had eaten while traveling. Zdorab and Volemak had found wild greens and roots in this valley and simmered them down into a stew, so much better than handfuls of raisins and jerky, and the bread was fresh and leavened, instead of the crackers and hard biscuits they had made do with while traveling. Soon it would be better still, for Volemak had planted a garden here, and within a few weeks there would be melons and squashes, carrots and onions and radishes.

Everyone was tired and awkward with each other through supper. The memory of Nafai's near-execution still lingered in their minds, all the more embarrassing to them now that they had returned to Volemak and could see how easily he held command over all of them, being a man of *true* leadership, so much more powerful than Elemak's swaggering, bullying style. It made them all dread some kind of accounting with the old man, for how many of them, except perhaps Eiadh—and of course Nafai himself—were truly proud of how they acted? So, good as the food was, no one but Hushidh had much desire to stay and chat. There were no fond reminiscences of the journey, no amusing tales to recount to those who had waited here for them. As quickly as the supper was cleared away, the couples went to their tents.

They went so suddenly that despite her anxiousness to avoid exactly this moment, Hushidh returned from the stream with the last of the pots she had washed to find that only Shedemei remained of the women, and only Zdorab and Issib of the men. There was already a dreadful silence, for Shedemei had no gift of chat, and both Zdorab and Issib seemed painfully shy. How hard for all of us, thought Hushidh. We know we are the leftovers of the group, thrown together only because we weren't wanted by anyone but the Oversoul. And some of us not even by *her*, for poor Zdorab was here only because Nafai had extracted an oath from him instead of killing him at the gate of Basilica, on the night Nafai cut off Gaballufix's head.

"What a miserable group you are," said Volemak.

Hushidh looked over in relief to see Volemak and Rasa returning to the cookfire. They must have realized that something needed to be said —introductions needed to be made, at least, between Shedya and the librarian, who had never even met.

"I was entering my husband's tent," said Rasa, "thinking how good it was to be back with him, when suddenly I realized how much I missed my traveling companions, Shuya and Shedya, and *then* I remembered that I had failed in my duty as lady of this house."

"House?" said Issib.

"The walls may be stone and the roof may be sky, but this is my house, a place of refuge for my daughters and safety for my sons," said Rasa.

"*Our* house," said Volemak gently.

"Indeed—I spoke of it as *my* house only because of the old habits of Basilica, where the houses belonged only to women." Rasa lifted her husband's hand to her lips and kissed it and smiled at him.

"Out here," said Volemak, "the houses belong to the Oversoul, but he is renting this one to us at a very reasonable fee: When we leave here, the baboons downstream of us get to keep the garden."

"Hushidh, Shedemei, I believe you know my son Issib," said Rasa.

"*Our* son," said Volemak, as gently as before. "And this is Zdorab, who was once Gaballufix's archivist, but now serves our way station as gardener, librarian, and cook."

"Miserable at all three, I fear," said Zdorab.

Rasa smiled. "Volya tells me that both Issib and Zdorab have explored the Index while they've been waiting here. And I know both of my dear nieces, Shuya and Shedya, will have profound interest in what they've found there."

"The Index of the Oversoul is the pathway into all the memory of Earth," said Volemak. "And since Earth is where we are going, it's just as important for us to study in that great library as it is for us to do the work that keeps our bodies alive in this desert."

"You know we'll do our duty," said Shedemei.

Hushidh knew that she was not referring to studies alone.

"Oh, hang the courteous obliquities," said Lady Rasa. "You all know that you're the unmarried ones, and that everybody *has* to marry if this is going to work at all, and that leaves only the four of you. I know that there's no particular reason why you shouldn't at least have the freedom to sort things out among yourselves, but I'll tell you that because of age and experience I rather imagined that it would be Hushidh who ended up with Issib and Shedemei who ended up with Zdorab. It doesn't have to be that way, but I think it would be helpful if you at least explored the possibilities."

"The Lady Rasa speaks about experience," said Zdorab, "but I must point out that I am a man of no experience whatsoever when it comes to women, and I fear that I will offend with every word I say."

Shedemei gave one hoot of derisive laughter.

"What Shedemei meant, with her simple eloquence," said Rasa, "is that she cannot conceive of your having less experience of women than she has of men. She, too, is quite certain of her ability to offend *you* with every word, which is why she chose to respond to you without using any."

The absurdity of the whole situation combined with Shedemei's gracelessness and Zdorab's awkward courtesy was too much for Hushidh. She burst out laughing, and soon the others joined in.

"There's no hurry," said Volemak. "Take your time to become acquainted."

"I'd rather just get it over with," said Shedemei.

"Marriage is not something you get over with," said Rasa. "It's something you begin. So as Volemak was saying, take your time. When you're ready, come to either me or my husband, and we can arrange new tent assignments, along with the appropriate ceremonies."

"And if we're never ready?" asked Issib.

"None of us will live long enough to see never," said Volemak. "And for the present, it will be enough if you try to know and like each other."

That was it, except for a few pleasant words about the supper Zdorab had prepared. They quickly divided, and Hushidh followed Shedemei to the tent they would share for now.

"Well, *that* was reassuring," said Shedemei.

It took a moment for Hushidh to realize that Shedya was being ironic; it always did. "*I'm* not much reassured," Hushidh answered.

"Oh, you didn't think it was sweet of them to let us take our time about deciding whether to do the inevitable? Rather like giving a condemned murderer the lever of the gallows trap and telling him, 'Whenever you're ready.'"

It was a surprise to realize that Shedemei seemed far angrier about this than Hushidh was. But then, Shedemei was not a willing participant in the journey, the way Hushidh had been. Shedemei had not thought of herself as belonging to the Oversoul, not the way Hushidh had ever since she realized she was a raveler, or Luet, ever since she discovered she was a waterseer. So of course *everything* seemed out of kilter to her; all her plans were in disarray.

Hushidh thought to help her by saying, "Zdorab is as much a captive on this journey as you are—he never asked for this, and *you* at least had your dream." But she saw at once—for Hushidh *always* saw the connections between people—that her words, far from giving comfort, were driving a wedge between her and Shedemei, and so she fell silent.

Fell silent and suffered, for she well remembered that it was Issib who had asked, What if we're never ready? That was a terrible thing to hear your future husband say, a terrible thing, for it meant that he did not think he could ever love her.

Then a thought came abruptly into her mind: What if Issib said that, not because he thought *he* could never desire *her*, but because he was certain that *she* could never be ready to marry *him?* Now that she thought about it, she was certain that was what he meant, for she knew Issib to be a kind young man who was not likely to say something that he thought might hurt someone else. She suddenly found a floodgate of memory opened inside her mind, and saw all the images she had of Issib. He was quiet, and bore his infirmity without complaint. He had great courage, in his own way, and his mind was bright indeed—he had always been quick in class, the times they had been together, and his ideas were never the obvious ones, but always showed him thinking a step or two beyond the immediate question.

His body may be limited, she thought, but his mind is at least a match for mine. And plain as I am, I can't possibly be as worried about my own body as he is about his. Nafai may have assured me that Issib is physically capable of fathering children, but that doesn't mean he has any notion of lovemaking—indeed, he's probably terrified that I will be disgusted by him, or at least frustrated at how little he imagines he can give me in the way of pleasure. I am not the one who needs reassurance, *he* is, and it would only be destructive if I entered into our courtship with the idea that he must somehow reassure *my* self-doubting heart. No, I must make him confident of my acceptance of *him*, if we're to build a friendship and a marriage.

This insight filled Hushidh with such great relief that she almost wept with the joy of it. Only then did she realize that ideas that came to her so suddenly, with such great clarity, might not be her ideas at all. Indeed, she noticed now that she had been imagining a picture of Issib's body as it appeared to *him*, only it hadn't been imagination at all, had it? The Oversoul had shown her the thoughts and fears inside Issib's mind.

As so many times before, Hushidh wished she had the same easy communication with the Oversoul that Luet and Nafai had. Occasionally the Oversoul was able to put thoughts as words inside her mind, as always happened with them, but it was never a comfortable dialogue for her, never easy for her to sort out which were her own thoughts and which were the Oversoul's. So she had to make do with her gift of raveling, and then sometimes these clear insights that always felt like her own ideas when they came, and only afterward seemed to be too clear to be anything but visions from the Oversoul.

Still, she was certain that what she had seen was, not her imagination, but the truth: The Oversoul had shown her what she needed to see, if she was to get past her own fears.

Thank you, she thought, as clearly as she could, though she had no way of knowing if the Oversoul heard her thoughts, or was even listening at the moment. I needed to see through his eyes, at least for a moment.

Another thought came to her: Is he also seeing through *my* eyes at this moment? It disturbed her, to think that Issib might be seeing her body as she saw it, complete with her fears and dissatisfactions.

No, fair is fair. If he is to have confidence in himself, and if he is to be a kind husband to me, he must know that I am as fearful and uncertain as he is. So do, if you haven't already, *do* show him who I am, help him to see that even though I am no beauty, I'm still a woman, I still long to love, to be loved, to make a family with a man who is bound into my heart and I into his as tightly as Rasa and Volemak are woven through each other's souls. Show him who I am, so he will pity me instead of fearing me. And then we can turn pity into compassion, and compassion into understanding, and understanding into affection, and affection into love, and love into life, the life of our children, the life of the new self that we will become together.

To Hushidh's surprise, she was sleepy now—she had feared that she'd get no sleep at all tonight. And from Shedemei's slow and heavy breathing, she must already be asleep.

I hope you showed her what *she* needed to see, too, Oversoul. I only wonder how other men and women manage to love each other when they don't have your help to show them what is in the other's heart.

Rasa woke up angry, and it took her a while to figure out why. At first she thought it was because when Volemak had joined her in bed last night he offered her no more than an affectionate embrace, as if her long fast did not deserve to be broken with a feast of love. He was not blind; he knew that she was angry, and he explained, "You're wearier than you think, after such a journey. There'd be little pleasure in it for either of us." His very calmness had made her angry beyond reason, and she curled up to sleep apart from his arms; but this morning she knew that her pique last night had been clear proof that he was right. She had been too tired for anything but sleep, like a fussy little child.

Almost no light got into the tent from outside. It could be high noon or even later, and from the stiffness of her body and the lack of a wind outside the tent, she could well have slept late into the morning. Still, to lie abed was delicious; no need to rise in a hurry, eat a scant breakfast in the predawn light, strike the tents, pack the beasts and be underway by sunrise. The journey was over; she had come home to her husband.

With that thought she realized why she had come awake this morning with so much anger in her. Coming home was not supposed to be to a tent, even one with double walls that stayed fairly cool through the day. And it was not *she* who ought to come home to *him*, but rather her husband who should come home to *her*. That's how it had always been. The house had been hers, which she had kept ready for him, and offered to him as a gift of shade in the summer, shelter in the storm, refuge from the tumult of the city. Instead *he* was the one who had prepared this place, and the more comfortable it was the angrier it made her, for in this place she would have no idea how to prepare anything. She was helpless, a child, a student, and her husband would be her teacher and her guardian.

No one had directed her in her own affairs since she first came into her own house, which she had done young, using money she inherited from her mother to buy the house that her great-grandmother had made famous, then as a music conservatory; Rasa had made it still more famous as a school, and from that foundation she had risen to prominence in the City of Women, surrounded by students and admirers and envious competitors—and now here she was in the desert where she did not even know how to cook a meal or how toileting was handled in a semi-permanent encampment like this. No doubt it would be Elemak who explained it to her, in his oh-so-offhanded way, the elaborate pretense that he was telling you what you already knew—which *would* have been gracious except that there was always the undertone of studiedness that made it plain that both you and he knew that you did *not* already know and in fact you depended on him to teach you how to pee properly.

Elemak. She remembered that terrible morning when he stood there with a pulse pointed at Nafai's head and thought: I must tell Volemak. He must be warned about the murder in Elemak's heart.

Except that the Oversoul had clearly shown that murder would not be tolerated, and Elemak and Mebbekew both had begged forgiveness. The whole issue of going back to Basilica was closed now, surely. Why bring it up again? What would Volemak do about it now, anyway? Either he'd repudiate Elemak, which would make the young man useless through the rest of the journey, or Volemak would uphold him in his right to make such a vile decision, in which case there'd be no living with Elemak from then on, and Nafai would shrink to nothing in this company. Elemak would never let Nafai rise to his natural position of leadership. That would be unbearable, for Rasa knew that of her own children, only Nafai was suited to lead well, for only he of the men of his generation had both the wit to make wise decisions and the close communication with the Oversoul to make informed ones.

Of course, Luet was every bit as well qualified, but they were now in a primitive, nomadic setting, and it was almost inevitable that males would take the lead. Rasa hadn't needed Shedemei's instruction about primate community formation to know that in a wandering tribe, the males ruled. Soon enough the women would all be pregnant, and then they would turn inward; when the children were born, their circle would enlarge only enough to include the little ones. Food and safety and teaching would be their concern then, in such a fearful, hostile place as the desert. There would be neither reason nor possibility of challenging the leadership of men here.

Except that if the leader were a man like Nafai, he would be compassionate to the women and listen to good counsel. While Elemak would be what he had already shown himself to be—a jealous tyrant, slow to listen to advice and quick to twist things to his own advantage, unfair and conniving . . .

I can't let myself hate him. Elemak is a man of many fine gifts. Much like his half-brother, Gaballufix, who was once my husband. I loved Gabya for those gifts; but, alas, he passed few of them to our daughters, Sevet and Kokor. Instead they got his self-centeredness, his inability to bridle his hunger to possess everything that seemed even faintly desirable. And I see that in Elemak also, and so I hate and fear him as I came to hate and fear Gaballufix.

If only the Oversoul had been just the teeniest bit fussier about whom she brought along on this journey.

Then Rasa stopped in the middle of dressing herself and realized: I'm thinking of how selfish and controlling Elemak is, and yet I'm angry this morning because *I'm* not the one in charge here. Who is the controlling one! Perhaps if I had been deprived of real control as long as Elemak has, I'd be just as desperate to get it and keep it.

But she knew that she would not. Rasa had never undercut her mother as long as she lived, and Elemak had already acted to thwart his father several times—to the point of almost killing Volemak's youngest son.

I must tell Volya what Elemak did, so that Volemak can make his decisions based on complete information. I would be a bad wife indeed if I didn't give my husband good counsel, including telling him everything I know. He has always done the same for me.

Rasa pushed aside the flap and stepped into the air trap, which was much hotter than the inside of the tent. Then, after closing the flap behind her, she parted the outer curtain and stepped out into the blazing sun. She felt herself immediately drenched in sweat.

"Lady Rasa!" cried Dol in delight.

"Dolya," said Rasa. What, had Dol been waiting for Rasa to emerge? There was *nothing* productive for her to do? Rasa could not resist giving her a little dig. "Working hard?"

"Oh, no, though I might as well be, with this hot sun."

Well, at least Dol wasn't a hypocrite . . .

"I volunteered to wait for you to come out of the tent, since Wetchik wouldn't let anybody waken you, not even for breakfast."

It occurred to Rasa that she was a little hungry.

"And Wetchik said that when you woke up you'd be starving, so I'm to take you to the kitchen tent. We keep everything locked up so the baboons don't ever find it, or Elemak says we'd have no peace. They can't ever learn to find food from us, or they'd probably follow us farther into the desert and then die."

So Dolya *did* absorb information from other people's conversation. It was so hard to remember sometimes that she was quite a bright girl. It was the cuteness thing she did that made it almost impossible to give her credit for having any wit.

"Well?" asked Dol.

"Well what?"

"You haven't said a thing. Do you want to eat now, or shall I call everyone together to hear Wetchik's dream?"

"Dream?" asked Rasa.

"He had a dream last night, from the Oversoul, and he wanted to tell us all together. But he didn't want to waken you, so we all started doing other things, and I was supposed to watch for you."

Now Rasa was deeply embarrassed. It was a bad precedent for Volya to set, making everyone else get up and work while Rasa slept. She did *not* want to be the pampered wife of the ruler, she wanted to be a full participant in the community. Surely Volemak understood that.

"Please, call everyone together. Point me to the kitchen tent first, of course. I'll bring a little bread to the gathering."

She heard Dol as she wandered off, calling out at the top of her lungs—with full theatrical training in projecting her voice—"Aunt Rasa's up now! Aunt Rasa's up!"

Rasa cringed inwardly. Why not announce to everybody *exactly* how late I slept in?

She found the kitchen tent easily enough—it was the one with a stone oven outside, where Zdorab was baking bread.

He looked up at her rather shamefacedly. "I must apologize, Lady Rasa. I never said I was a baker."

"But the bread smells wonderful," said Rasa.

"Smells, yes. I can do smells. You should catch a whiff of my favorite —I call it 'burning fish.'"

Rasa laughed. She liked this fellow. "You get fish from this stream?"

"Your husband thought of doing some shore fishing down there." He pointed toward where the stream flowed into the placid waters of the Scour Sea.

"So you had some luck?"

"Not really," said Zdorab. "We caught fish, but they weren't very good."

"Even the ones that didn't get turned into your favorite smell . . ."

"Even the ones we stewed. There just isn't enough life on the land here. The fish would gather at the stream mouth if there were more organic material in the sediment being deposited by the stream."

"You're a geologist?" asked Rasa, rather surprised.

"A librarian, so I'm a little bit of everything, I guess," said Zdorab. "I was trying to figure out why this place doesn't have a permanent human settlement, and the reason came from the Index, some old maps from the last time there was a major culture in this area. They always grow up on the big river just over that mountain range." He pointed east. "Right now there are still a couple of minor cities there. The reason they don't use this spot is because there isn't enough plantable land. And the river fails one year in five. That's too often to maintain a steady population."

"What do the baboons do?" asked Rasa.

"The Index doesn't really track baboons," said Zdorab.

"I guess not," said Rasa. "I guess the baboons will have to build their own Oversoul someday, eh?"

"I guess." He looked mildly puzzled. "It'd help if they'd just build their own latrine."

Rasa raised an eyebrow.

"We have to keep an eye on them, so one of them doesn't wander upstream of us and then foul our drinking water."

"Mm," said Rasa. "That reminds me. I'm thirsty."

"And hungry too, I'll bet," said Zdorab. "Well, help yourself. Cool water and yesterday's bread in the kitchen tent, locked up."

"Well, if it's locked up . . ."

"Locked to *baboons*. For humans, it should be easy enough."

When Rasa got into the kitchen tent she found he was right. The "lock" was nothing but a twist of wire holding the solar-powered cold chest closed. So why did they stress the fact that it was locked? Perhaps just to remind her to close it after her.

She opened the lid and found several dozen loaves of bread, as well as quite a few other cloth-wrapped parcels of food—frozen meat, perhaps? No, it couldn't be frozen, it wasn't cold enough inside. She reached down and opened one of the packages and found, of course, camel's milk cheese. Nasty stuff—she had eaten it once before, at Volemak's house, when she was visiting him once between the two times they were married. "See how much I loved you?" he had teased her. "The whole time we were married, and I never made you taste this!" But she knew now that she'd need the protein and the fat—they'd be on lean rations through most of the journey, and they had to eat everything that had nutritional value.

Taking a flat round bread, she tore off half, rewrapped the rest, and then stuffed the part she meant to eat with a few chunks from the cheese. The bread was dry and harsh enough to mask much of the taste of the cheese, so all in all it wasn't as nauseating a breakfast as it could have been. Welcome to the desert, Rasa.

She closed the lid and turned toward the door.

"Aaah!" she screeched, quite without meaning to. There in the doorway was a baboon on all fours, looking at her intently and sniffing.

"Shoo," she said. "Go away. This is *my* breakfast."

The baboon only studied her face a little longer. She remembered then that she had *not* locked the cold box. Shamefaced, she turned her back on the baboon and, hiding what she was doing with her body, she retwisted the wire. Supposedly the baboon's fingers weren't deft enough to undo the wire. But what if his teeth were strong enough to bite through it, what then? No point in letting him know that it was the wire keeping him out.

Of course, it was quite possible he could figure it out on his own. Didn't they say that baboons were the closest things to humans on Harmony? Perhaps that's why the original settlers of this planet brought them—for they were from Earth, not native to this place.

She turned back around and again let out a little screech, for the baboon was directly behind her now, standing up on his hind legs, regarding her with that same steady gaze.

"This is *my* breakfast," Rasa said mildly.

The baboon curled his lip as if in disgust, then dropped down to all fours and started out of the tent.

At that moment Zdorab entered the tent. "Ha," he said. "We call this one Yobar. He's a newcomer to the tribe, and so they don't really accept him yet. He doesn't mind because he thinks it makes him boss when they all run away from him. But the poor fellow's randy half the time and he can't ever get near the females."

"Which explains his name," said Rasa. *Yobar* was an ancient word for a man who is insatiable in lovemaking.

"We call him that to sort of encourage him," said Zdorab. "Get on out of here now, Yobar."

"He was already leaving, I think, after I declined to share my bread and cheese with him."

"The cheese is awful, isn't it?" said Zdorab. "But when you consider that the boons eat baby keeks alive when they can catch them, you can understand that to them, camel cheese is really good stuff."

"We humans *do* eat it, though, right?"

"Reluctantly and constantly," said Zdorab. "And you never get used to the aftertaste. It's the chief reason we drink so much water and then have to pee so much. Begging your pardon."

"I have a feeling that city rules of delicate speech won't be as practical out here," said Rasa.

"But I ought to try more, I think," said Zdorab. "Well, enjoy your meal, I'm trying not to create the aroma of burnt bread."

He backed on out of the kitchen tent.

Rasa took her first bite of bread and it was good. So she took her second and nearly gagged—this time there was cheese in it. She forced herself to chew it and swallow it. But it made her think with fondness of the recent past, when the only camel product she had to confront was manure and no one expected her to eat it.

The tent door opened again. Rasa half expected to see Yobar again, back for another try at begging. Instead it was Dol. "Wetchik says we won't gather until the shadows get long, so it won't be so miserably hot. Good idea, don't you think?"

"I'm only sorry you had to waste half the day waiting for me."

"Oh, that's all right," said Dol. "I didn't want to work anyway. I'm not much at gardening. I think I'd probably kill the flowers right along with the weeds."

"I don't think it's a flower garden," said Rasa.

"You know what I mean," said Dol.

Oh, yes, I understand exactly.

I also understand that I must find Volemak and insist that he put me to work at once. It will never do for me to get days of rest when everyone else is working hard. I may be the second oldest here, but that doesn't mean I'm *old.* Why, I can still have babies, and I certainly will, if I can get Volya to greet me as his long-lost wife, instead of treating me like an invalid child.

What she could not say to herself, though she knew it and hated it, was the fact that she would have to have babies to have any role at all here in the desert. For they were reverting to a primitive state of human life here, in which survival and reproduction were at the fore-front, and the kind of civilized life that she had mastered in Basilica would never exist again for her. Instead she would be competing with younger women for position in this new tribe, and the coin of the competition would be babies. Those who had them would be some-body; those who didn't, wouldn't. And at Rasa's age, it was important to begin quickly, for she wouldn't have as long as the younger ones.

Angry again, though with no one but poor frivolous Dol to be angry *at,* Rasa left the kitchen tent, still eating her bread and cheese. She looked around the encampment. When they had come down the steep incline into the canyon, there had been only four tents. Now there were ten. Rasa recognized the traveling tents, and felt vaguely guilty that the others were still living in such cramped quarters, when she and Volya shared so much space—a large, double-walled tent. Now, though, she could see that the tents were laid out in a couple of con-centric circles, but the tent she shared with Volemak was not the cen-ter; nor was the kitchen tent. Indeed, at the center was the smallest of the four original tents, and after a moment's thought Rasa realized that that was the tent where the Index was kept.

She had simply assumed that Volemak would keep the Index in his own tent, but of course that would not do—Zdorab and Issib would be using the Index all the time, and could hardly be expected to arrange their schedule around such inconveniences as an old woman whose husband let her sleep too late in the morning.

Rasa stood outside the door of the small tent and clapped twice. "Come in."

From the voice she knew at once that it was Issya. She felt a stab of guilt, for last night she had hardly spoken to the boy—the man—that was her firstborn child. Only when she and Volya had spoken to the four unmarried ones all at once, really. And even now, knowing that he was inside the tent, she wanted to go away and come back another time.

Why was she avoiding him? Not because of his physical defects— she was used to *that* by now, having helped him through his infancy and early childhood, having fitted him for chairs and floats so he could move easily and have a nearly normal life—or at least a life of freedom. She knew his body almost more intimately than he knew it himself, since until he was well into puberty she had washed him head to toe, and massaged and moved his limbs to keep them flexible before he slowly, painfully learned to move them himself. During all those sessions together they had talked and talked—more than any of her other children, Issib was her friend. Yet she didn't want to face him.

So of course she parted the door and walked into the tent and faced him.

He was sitting in his chair which had linked itself to the solar panel atop the tent so he wasn't wasting battery power. The chair had picked up the Index and now held it in front of Issib, where it rested against his left hand. Rasa had never seen the Index but knew at once that this had to be it, if only because it was an object she had never seen.

"Does it speak to you?" she asked.

"Good afternoon, Mother," said Issib. "Was your morning restful?"

"Or does it have some kind of display, like a regular computer?" She refused to let him goad her by reminding her of how late she had arisen.

"Some of us didn't sleep at all," said Issib. "Some of us lay awake wondering how it happened that our wives-to-be were brought in and dumped on us with only the most cursory of introductions."

"Oh, Issya," said Rasa, "you know that this situation is the natural consequence of the way things are, and nobody planned it. You're feeling resentful? Well, so am I. So here's an idea—I won't take it out on you, and you don't take it out on me."

"Who else *can* I take it out on?" said Issib, smiling wanly.

"The Oversoul. Tell your chair to throw the Index across the room."

Issib shook his head. "The Oversoul would simply override my command. And besides, the Index isn't the Oversoul, it's simply our most powerful tool for accessing the Oversoul's memory."

"How much does it remember?"

Issib looked at her for a moment. "You know, I never thought you'd refer to the Oversoul as *it.*"

Rasa was startled to realize she had done so, but knew at once why she had done so. "I wasn't thinking of *her*—the Oversoul. I was thinking of *it*—the Index."

"It remembers everything," said Issib.

"How much of everything? The movements of every individual atom in the universe?"

Issib grinned at her. "Sometimes it seems like that. No, I meant everything about human history on Harmony."

"Forty million years," said Rasa. "Maybe two million generations of human beings. A world population of roughly a billion most of the time. Two quadrillion lives, with thousands of meaningful events in every life."

"That's right," said Issib. "And then add to those biographies the histories of every human community, starting with families and including those as large as nations and language groups and as small as childhood friends and casual sexual liaisons. And then include all natural events that impinged on human history. And then include every word that humans ever wrote and the map of every city we ever built and the plans for every building we ever constructed . . ."

"There wouldn't be room to contain all the information," said Rasa. "Not if the whole planet were devoted to nothing but storing it. We should be tripping over the Oversoul's data storage with every step."

"Not really," said Issib. "The Oversoul's memory isn't stored in the cheap and bulky memory we use for ordinary computers. Our computers are all binary, for one thing—every memory location can carry only two possible meanings."

"On or off," said Rasa. "Yes or no."

"It's read electrically," said Issib. "And we can only fit a few trillion bits of information into each computer before they start getting too bulky to carry around. And the *space* we waste inside our computers— just to represent simple numbers. For instance, in two bits we can only hold four numbers."

"A-1, B-1, A-2, and B-2," said Rasa. "I *did* teach the basic computer theory course in my little school, you know."

"But now imagine," said Issib, "that instead of only being able to represent two states at each location, on or off, you could represent *five* states. Then in two bits—"

"Twenty-five possible values," said Rasa. "A-1, B-1, V-1, G-1, D-1, and so on to D-5."

"Now imagine that each memory location can have thousands of possible states."

"That certainly does make the memory more efficient at containing meaning."

"Not really," said Issib. "Not yet anyway. The increase is only geometric, not exponential. And it would have a vicious limitation on it, in that each *single* location could only convey one state *at a time*. Even if there were a billion possible messages that a single location could deliver, each location could only deliver one of those at a time."

"But if they were paired, that problem disappears, since between them any two locations could deliver millions of possible meanings," said Rasa.

"But still only *one* meaning at any one time."

"Well, you can't very well use the same memory location to store contradictory information. Both G-9 *and* D-9."

"It depends on how the information is stored. For the Oversoul, each memory location is the interior edge of a circle—a very tiny, tiny circle —and that inside edge is fractally complex. That is, thousands of states can be represented by protrusions, like the points on a mechanical key, or the teeth on a comb—in each location it's either got a protrusion or it doesn't."

"But then the memory location is the tooth, and not the circle," said Rasa, "and we're back to binary."

"But it can stick out farther or not as far," said Issib. "The Oversoul's memory is capable of distinguishing hundreds of different degrees of protrusion at each location around the inside of the circle."

"Still a geometric increase, then," said Rasa.

"But now," said Issib, "you must include the fact that the Oversoul can also detect teeth *on* each protrusion—hundreds of different values from each of hundreds of teeth. And on each tooth, hundreds of barbs, each reporting hundreds of possible values. And on each barb, hundreds of thorns. And on each thorn, hundreds of hairs. And on each hair—"

"I get the idea," said Rasa.

"And then the meanings can change depending on *where* on the circle you start reading—at the north or the east or south-southeast. You see, Mother, at every memory location the Oversoul can store trillions of *different* pieces of information at once," said Issib. "We have nothing in our computers that can begin to compare to it."

"And yet it's not an infinite memory," said Rasa.

"No," said Issib. "Not infinite. Because eventually we get down to the minimum resolution—protrusions so small that the Oversoul can no longer detect protrusions *on* the protrusions. About twenty million years ago the Oversoul realized that it was running out of memory—or that it *would* run out in about ten million years. It began finding shorthand ways of recording things. It devoted a substantial area of memory to storing elaborate tables of *kinds* of stories. For instance, table entry ZH-5-SHCH might be, 'quarrels with parents over degree of personal freedom they permit and runs away from home city to another city.' So where a person's biography is stored, instead of explaining each event, the biographic listing simply refers you to the vast tables of possible events in a human life—it'll have the value ZH-5-SHCH and then the code for the city he ran away to."

"It makes our lives seem rather sterile, doesn't it. Unimaginative, I mean. We all keep doing the same things that others have done."

"The Oversoul explained to me that while ninety-nine percent of every life consists of events already present in the behavior tables, there's always the one percent that has to be spelled out because there's no pre-existing entry for it. No two lives have ever been duplicates yet."

"I suppose that's a comfort."

"You've got to believe that *ours* is following an unusual path. 'Called forth by the Oversoul to journey through the desert and eventually return to Earth'—I bet there's no table entry for *that.*"

"Oh, but since it has happened now to sixteen of us, I'll bet the Oversoul *makes* a new entry."

Issib laughed. "It probably already has."

"It must have been a massive project, though, constructing those tables of possible human actions."

"If there's one thing the Oversoul has had plenty of, it's time," said Issib. "But even *with* all that, there's decay and loss."

"Memory locations can become unreadable," said Rasa.

"I don't know about that. I just know that the Oversoul is losing satellites. That makes it harder for it to keep an eye on us. So far there aren't any blind spots—but each satellite has to bring in far more information than it was originally meant to. There are bottlenecks in the system. Places where a satellite simply *can't* pass through all the information that it collects fast enough not to miss something going on among the humans it's observing. In short, there are events happening now that aren't getting remembered. The Oversoul is controlling the losses by guessing to fill in the gaps in its information, but it's only going to get worse and worse. There's still plenty of memory left, but soon there'll be millions of lives that are remembered only as vague sketches or outlines of a life. Someday, of course, enough satellites will fail that some lives will never be recorded at all."

"And eventually all the satellites will fall."

"Right. And, more to the point, when those blind spots occur, there will also be people who are not under the influence of the Oversoul in any way. At that point they'll begin to make the weapons again that can destroy the world."

"So—why not put up more satellites?"

"Who? What human society has the technology to build the ships to carry satellites out into space? Let alone building the satellites in the first place."

"We make computers, don't we?"

"The technology to put satellites into space is the same technology that can deliver weapons from one side of Harmony to the other. How can the Oversoul teach us how to replenish its satellites without also teaching us how to destroy each other? Not to mention the fact that we could probably then figure out how to reprogram the Oversoul and control it ourselves—or, failing that, we could build our own *little* Oversouls that key in on the part of our brain that the Oversoul communicates with, so that we'd have a weapon that could cause the enemy to panic or get stupid."

"I see the point," said Rasa.

"It's the quandary the Oversoul is in. It must get repaired or it will stop being able to protect humanity; yet the only way it can repair itself is to give human beings the very things that it's trying to prevent us from getting."

"How circular."

"So it's going home," said Issib. "Back to the Keeper of Earth. To find out what to do next."

"What if this Keeper of Earth doesn't know either?"

"Then we're up to our necks in kaka, aren't we?" Issib smiled. "But I think the Keeper knows. I think it has a plan."

"And why is that?"

"Because people keep getting dreams that aren't from the Oversoul."

"People have always had dreams that aren't from the Oversoul," said Rasa. "We had dreams long before there *was* an Oversoul."

"Yes, but we didn't have the *same* dreams, carrying clear messages about coming home to Earth, did we?"

"I just don't believe that some computer or whatever that's many lightyears from here could possibly send a *dream* into our minds."

"Who knows what's happened back on Earth?" said Issib. "Maybe the Keeper of Earth has learned things about the universe that we don't begin to understand. That wouldn't be a surprise, either, since *we've* had the Oversoul making us stupid whenever we tried to think about really advanced physics. For forty million years we've been slapped down whenever we used our brains too well, but in forty million years the Keeper of Earth, whoever or whatever it is, might well have thought of some really useful new stuff. Including how to send dreams to people lightyears away."

"And all this you learned from the Index."

"All this I dragged kicking and screaming from the Index, with Zdorab's and Father's help," said Issib. "The Oversoul doesn't like talking about itself, and it keeps trying to make us forget what we've learned about it."

"I thought the Oversoul was cooperating with us."

"No," said Issib. "We're cooperating with *it*. In the meantime, it's trying to keep us from learning even the tiniest bit of information that isn't directly pertinent to the tasks it has in mind for us."

"So how did you learn all that you just told me? About how the Oversoul's memory works?"

"Either we got around its defenses so well and so persistently that it finally gave up on trying to prevent us from knowing it, or it decided that this was harmless information after all."

"Or," said Rasa.

"Or?"

"Or the information is wrong and so it doesn't matter whether you know it or not."

Issib grinned at her. "But the Oversoul wouldn't *lie*, would it, Mother?"

Which brought back a conversation they had had when Issib was a child, asking about the Oversoul. What had the question been? Ah, yes —Why do men call the Oversoul *he* and women call the Oversoul *she?* And Rasa had answered that the Oversoul permitted men to think of her as if she were male, so they'd be more comfortable praying to her. And Issib had asked that same question: But the Oversoul wouldn't lie, would it, Mother?

As Rasa recalled it, she hadn't done very well answering that question the first time, and she wasn't about to embarrass herself by trying to answer it again now. "I interrupted your work, coming here like this," said Rasa.

"Not at all," said Issib. "Father said to explain anything you asked about."

"He knew I'd come here?"

"He said it was important that you understand our work with the Index."

"What *is* your work with the Index?"

"Trying to get it to tell us what *we* want to know instead of just what the Oversoul wants us to know."

"Are you getting anywhere?"

"Either yes or no."

"What do you mean?"

"We're finding out a lot of things, but whether that's just because the Oversoul wants us to know them or not is a moot point. Our experience is that the Index does different things for different people."

"Depending on what?"

"That's what we haven't figured out yet," said Issib. "I have days when the Index practically sings to me—it's like it lives inside my head, answering my questions before I even think of them. And then there are days when I think the Oversoul is trying to torture me, leading me on wild goose chases."

"Chasing after what?"

"The whole history of Harmony is wide open to me. I can give you the name of every person who ever came to this stream and drank from it. But I can't find out where the Oversoul is leading us, or how we're going to get to Earth, or even where the original human settlers of Harmony first landed, or where the central mind of the Oversoul is located."

"So she's keeping secrets from you," said Rasa.

"I think it *can't* tell us," said Issib. "I think it would like to tell, but it can't. A protective system built into it from the start, I assume, to prevent anybody from taking control of the Oversoul and using it to rule the world."

"So we have to follow it blindly, not even knowing where it's leading us?"

"That's about it," said Issib. "Just one of those times in life when things don't go your way but you still have to live with it."

Rasa looked at Issib, at the steady way he regarded her, and knew that he was reminding her that nothing the Oversoul was doing to her right now was even close to being as oppressive as Issib's life in a defective body.

I know that, foolish boy, she thought. I know perfectly well that your life is awful, and that you complain about it very little. But that was unpreventable and remains incurable. Perhaps the Oversoul's refusal to tell us what's going on is *also* unpreventable and incurable, in which case I'll try to bear it with at least as much patience as you. But if I *can* cure it, I will—and I won't let you shame me into accepting something that I may not have to accept.

"What the Oversoul can't tell us for the asking," said Rasa, "we might be able to find out on the sly."

"What do you think Zdorab and I have been working on?"

Ah. So Issib wasn't really being fatalistic about it, either. But then another thought occurred to her. "What does your *father* think you've been working on?"

Issib laughed. "Not *that*," he said.

Of course not. Volemak wouldn't want to see the Index used to subvert the Oversoul. "Ah. So the Oversoul isn't the only one that doesn't tell others what she's doing."

"And what do *you* tell, Lady Mother?" asked Issib.

What an interesting question. Do I tell Volemak what Issib is doing and run the risk of Volya trying to ban his son from using the Index? And yet I have never kept secrets from Volemak.

Which brought her back to the decision she had made earlier that day, to tell Volemak about what happened in the desert—about Elemak passing a sentence of death on Nafai. That could also have awful consequences. Did she have the right to cause those consequences by telling? On the other hand, did she have the right to deprive Volemak of important information?

Issib didn't wait for her answer. "You know," he said, "the Oversoul already knows what we're trying to do, and hasn't done a thing to stop us."

"Or else has done it so well you don't know she's doing it," said Rasa.

"If the Oversoul felt no need to tell Father, then is it so urgent, really, for you to do so?"

Rasa thought about that for a moment. Issib thought he was asking only about his own secret, but she was deciding about both. This *was* the Oversoul's expedition, after all, and if anyone knew and understood human behavior, it was the Oversoul. *She* knows what happened on the desert, just as she knows what Issib and Zdorab are doing with the Index. So why not leave it up to the Oversoul to decide what to tell?

Because that's exactly what Zdorab and Issib are trying to find a way to circumvent—the Oversoul's power to make all these decisions about telling or not telling. I don't want the Oversoul deciding what I can or cannot know—and yet here I am contemplating treating my husband exactly as the Oversoul treats me. And yet the Oversoul really *did* know better than Rasa whether Volemak should be informed about these things.

"I really hate dilemmas like this," said Rasa.

"So?"

"So I'll decide later," she said.

"That's a decision, too," said Issib.

"I know that, my clever firstborn," said Rasa. "But that doesn't mean it's a permanent one."

"You haven't finished your bread," said Issib.

"That's because there's camel cheese in it."

"Really vile stuff, isn't it," said Issib. "And you wouldn't believe how it constipates you."

"I can't wait."

"That's why none of the rest of us ever eat it," said Issib.

Rasa glared at him. "So why is there so much in the coldbox?"

"Because we share it with the baboons. They think it's candy."

Rasa looked at her half-eaten sandwich. "I've been eating baboon food." Then she laughed. "No wonder Yobar came into the kitchen tent! He thought I was preparing a treat for *him!*"

"Just wait till you actually *give* him a piece of cheese, and he tries to mate with your leg."

"I get goose bumps just thinking about it."

"Of course, I've only seen him do it with Father and Zdorab. He might be a zhop, in which case he'll just ignore you."

Rasa laughed, but Issib's crude little joke about the baboon being a homosexual made her think. What if the Oversoul had brought someone along in their company who wasn't going to be able to perform his siring duties? And then another thought—did the Oversoul send this idea to her? Was it a warning?

She shuddered and laid her hand on the Index. Tell me now, she said silently. Is one of our company unable to take part? Will one of the wives be disappointed?

But the Index answered her not at all.

It was late afternoon and the only one who had killed any game today was Nafai, which annoyed Mebbekew beyond endurance. So Nafai was better at climbing quietly on rocks than Mebbekew was—so what? So Nafai could aim a pulse like he'd been born with it in his hands—all that proved was that Elemak should have fired the thing when he had the chance out on the desert.

Out on the desert. As if they weren't *still* in the desert. Though in truth this place *was* lush compared to some of the country they had gone through. The green of the valley where they lived was like a drink of cool water for the eyes—he had caught a glimpse of the trees from a promontory a few minutes ago, and it was delicious to his eyes, such a *relief* after the bleak pale grey and yellow of the rocks and sand, the greyish green of the dryplants that Elemak persisted in naming whenever he saw them, as if anybody cared that he knew every plant that grew around here by its full name. Maybe Elemak really *did* have cousins among the desert plants. It would hardly have been surprising to know that some distant ancestor of Elemak's had mated with a prickly grey bush somewhere along the way. Maybe I peed on a cousin of Elya's today. That would be nice—to show exactly what I think of people who love the desert.

I didn't even *see* the hare, so how could I possibly aim at it? Of course Nafai shot it—he *saw* it. Of course, Meb had fired his pulse, because everybody else was, too. Only it turned out not to have been everybody else after all. Just Vas, who aimed too low and his pulse set on too diffuse a setting anyway, and Nafai, who actually hit the thing and burned a smoky little hole right in its head. And, of course, Mebbekew, aiming at nothing in particular, so that Elemak had said, "Nice shot, Nafai. You're aiming low and raggedly, Vas, and tighten the beam. And you, Mebbekew, were you trying to *draw* a hare on that rock with your pulse? This isn't an etchings class. Try to aim toward the same planet that the quarry is on."

Then Elemak and Nafai headed down to retrieve the hare.

"It's getting late," Mebbekew had said. "Can't the rest of us go home without waiting for you to find the bunny-body?"

Elemak had looked at him coldly then. "I thought that you'd want to know how to gut and clean a hare. But then, you'll probably never *need* to know how to do it."

Oh, very clever, Elemak. That's how to build up confidence in your poor struggling pupils. At least I *fired*, unlike Obring, who treats his pulse as if it were another man's hooy. But Meb said none of that, just glared back at Elya and said, "Then I can go?"

"Think you can find the way?" asked Elemak.

"Of course," said Mebbekew.

"I'm *sure* you can," said Elemak. "Go ahead, and take anybody with you who wants to go."

But nobody wanted to go with him. Elemak had made them afraid that Mebbekew would lose his way. Well, he *hadn't* lost his way. He had gone in just the right direction, retracing their path quite easily, and when he clambered up to the crest of that hill just to be sure, there was the valley, exactly where he had expected to see it. I'm not *completely* incompetent, O wise elder brother. Just because I didn't sweat my way across the desert a few dozen times like you, toting fancy plants on camelback from one city to another, doesn't mean that I have no sense of direction.

If only he could figure out exactly when and where he tore his tunic and split the crotch of his breeches. . . . He really hated it when his clothes weren't at their best, and these were now soaked with sweat and caked with dust. He'd never be clean again.

He came to the edge of the canyon and looked down, expecting to see the tents. But there wasn't a tent in sight.

For a moment he panicked. They've left without me, he thought. They hurried past me, struck the camp and left me behind, all because I couldn't see the stupid *hare.*

Then he realized that he was simply downstream from the camp. There were the tents, up there to the left. And of course he was much closer to the sea. If the Scour Sea had had any waves like the ones on the shore of the Earthbound Sea, he'd have been able to hear the surf from here. And there were the baboons, eking out their miserable supper from the roots and berries and plants and insects and warty little animals that lived near the river and the seashore.

How did I end up here? So much for my sense of direction.

Oh, yes. We did walk down this way this morning, when we left Daddy's lazy wife asleep in the camp and all the lazy women, *especially* my completely useless stupid lazy wife, lolling around the tents and the garden. That's the only part of the route that I missed, just that one turn, so big deal, I *still* have a good sense of direction.

But he had a really bad taste in his mouth, and he wanted to kick something, he wanted to break something, he wanted to *hurt* someone.

And there were the baboons, right down there, stupid doglike animals that thought they were human. One of the females was showing red right now, and so the males were cuffing each other and maneuvering to get a quick poke. Poor stupid males. That's how we live our lives.

Might as well go down the canyon wall here and walk up the valley to the camp. And on the way maybe I can get a clear shot at whichever male ends up plugging her siggle. He'll die happy, right? And Nafai won't be the only one going home with a dead animal to his credit.

About halfway down the rugged slope, after scuffing a knee and sliding a couple of times, Meb realized that the lower he got, the worse his line of sight would be toward the baboons. Already there were rocks and bushes blocking his view of some of them, including the ones who were busy trying to mate. However, a smallish one was in plain sight, considerably closer than the others had been. It would be an easier shot anyway.

Meb remembered what Elemak had taught them earlier in the day and braced his elbows on a boulder as he took aim. Even so, his hands kept trembling, and the more he tried to hold them steady, the worse the sight on the pulse seemed to bounce. And when he pressed his finger against the button to fire, it jostled the pulse again, so that a small jet of smoke erupted from a bush more than six meters from the baboon he had been aiming at. The baboon must have heard something, too, because it whipped around to look at the burning shrub and then backed away in fear.

But not for long. A moment later it moved in again, and watched the flame as if trying to learn some secret from it. The bush was dry, but not dead, and so it burned only slowly, and with a great deal of smoke. Meb aimed again, this time a little to the right to compensate for the movement that pushing the button would cause. He also found that his hands were a bit more steady this time, and now he remembered that Elemak had stressed the need to relax. So . . . now Mebbekew was doing it just as Elemak had said, and this boon would soon be history.

Just as he was about to pull the trigger, he was startled by a sharp cracking sound only a meter from his head. His own shot went wild as he turned sharply to look at the place the sound had come from. A small plant growing from a crack in the rock a couple of meters above his head had been burnt to nothing, and smoke was rising from the spot. Since he had just seen the same thing happen to the shrub near the baboon, Meb recognized immediately what had happened. Someone was firing a pulse at *him*. Bandits had come—the camp was in danger, and he was going to die, off by himself, because the bandits had no choice but to kill him to keep him from giving the alarm. But I won't give the alarm, he thought. Just let me live and I'll hide here and be very quiet until it's all over, just don't kill me . . .

"What were you doing, shooting at baboons!"

With a clatter of small stones, Nafai slid down the last slope to stand in on the stone where Meb was standing. Meb saw with some pleasure that Nafai had slipped down just as he had; but then realized that Nafai had somehow done it without losing control, and ended up on his feet instead of sitting on the stone.

Only then did Meb realize that it was Nafai who had shot at him, and missed him by only a couple of meters. "What were you trying to do, kill me?" demanded Meb. "You're not *that* good a shot that you should be shooting so close to humans!"

"We don't kill baboons," said Nafai. "They're like people—what are you thinking of!"

"Oh, since when do people sit around digging for grubs, looking for a chance to tup every woman with a red butt?"

"It pretty much describes your life, Meb," said Nafai. "Did you think we were going to *eat* baboon meat?"

"I didn't really care," said Meb. "I wasn't shooting for meat, I was going for the kill. You're not the only one who can shoot, you know."

With those words, it occurred to Meb that he and Nafai were alone now, with no one else watching, and Meb had a pulse. It could be an accident. I didn't mean to touch the button. I was just shooting at a target and Nafai came down out of nowhere. I didn't hear him, I was concentrating. Please, please forgive me, Father, I feel so terrible, my own brother, I deserve to die. Oh, you're forgiven, my son. Just let me grieve for my youngest boy, who just got his balls shot off in a terrible hunting accident and bled to death. Why don't you go get laid while I'm weeping here?

That'd be the day, Father actually wishing Mebbekew something he wanted!

"You don't waste pulsefire on nothing shots," said Nafai. "Elemak said so—they don't last forever. And we don't eat baboon. Elemak said that, too."

"Elemak can fart into a flute and play it as a tune, it doesn't mean *I* have to do it *his* way." I have the pulse in my hand. Already sort of half-aimed at Nafai. I can show how I turned around, startled, and the pulse sort of fired and blew out Nafai's chest. At this range, it might blow him up entirely, spattering little Nafai bits all over. I'll come home with blood on my clothes no matter what.

Then he felt a pulse pressed against his head. "Hand me your pulse," said Elemak.

"Why!" demanded Meb. "I wasn't going to do it!"

Nafai piped up. "You already fired at the baboon once. If you were a better shot it would already be *done.*" So Nafai, of course, misunderstood completely what Meb had meant that he wasn't going to do. But Elemak understood.

"I said give me your pulse, handle first."

Meb sighed dramatically and handed the pulse to Elemak. "Let's make a big deal about it, shall we. *I'm* forbidden to shoot at a baboon, but *you* can point your pulse at the head of whichever brother you feel like pointing at, and it's all *right* when you do it."

Elemak clearly didn't appreciate Meb's reminder about the supposed execution of Nafai for mutiny in the desert. But Elemak merely left his pulse pressed to Meb's temple as he spoke to Nafai. "Never let me see you aim your pulse at another human again," said Elemak.

"I wasn't aiming at him. I was aiming at the plant above his head and I hit it."

"Yes, you're a wonderful shot. But what if you sneeze? What if you stumble? It's quite possible for you to take your own brother's head off with one little slip. So you *never* aim at another person or anywhere near, do you understand me?"

"Yes," said Nafai.

Oh, yes, yes, Big Brother Elemak, I'll suck up to you just the way I've always sucked up to Papa. It made Meb want to puke.

"It *was* a good shot, though," said Elemak.

"Thanks."

"And Meb is lucky it was you who saw him, and not me, because I might have aimed for his foot and left him with a stump to help him remember that you don't shoot baboons."

This wasn't right, Elemak attacking him like this in front of Nafai of all people. Oh, and of course, here come Vas and Obring, they *have* to be here to see Elemak showing him such disdain as to rag him in front of Nafai. "So suddenly baboons are the sacred animal?" asked Meb.

"You don't kill them, you don't eat them," said Elemak.

"Why *not?*"

"Because they do no harm, and eating them would be like cannibalism."

"I get it," said Meb. "You're one of those people who believe that boons are magical. They've got a pot of gold hidden away somewhere, every tribe of them, and if you're really nice and feed them, then, after they've stripped your land bare of every edible thing and torn apart your house looking for more, they'll rush off to their hiding place and bring the pot of gold to *you.*"

"More than one lost wanderer on the desert has been led to safety by baboons."

"Right," said Meb. "So that means we should let them all live forever? Let me tell you a secret, Elya. They'll all die eventually, so why not now, for target practice? I'm not saying we have to *eat* it or anything."

"And I'm saying you're through hunting. Give me your pulse."

"Oh, swell," said Meb. "I'm supposed to be the only man without a pulse?"

"The pulses are for hunting. Nafai's going to be a good hunter, and you're not."

"How do you know? It's only the first day of serious work on it."

"You're not because you're never going to have a pulse in your hands again as long as I live."

It stung Mebbekew to the heart. Elemak was stripping away all his dignity, and for what? Because of a stupid baboon. How could Elya do this to him? And in front of Nafai, no less. "Oh, I get it," said Meb. "This is how you show your *worship* for King Nafai."

There was a moment's pause in which Meb wondered if he might have goaded Elya just a speck too far and maybe this was the time Elemak was going to kill him or beat him to a pulp. Then Elemak spoke. "Head back to camp with the hare, Nafai," he said. "Zdorab will want to get it into the coldbox until he starts the stew in the morning."

"Yes," said Nafai. Immediately he scampered down the hill to the valley floor.

"You can follow him," Elemak said to Vas and Obring, who had just clattered down the slope, both of them landing on their butts.

Vas arose and dusted himself off. "Don't do anything stupid, Elya," said Vas. Then he turned and started down the nontrail that Nafai had used.

Since Meb figured these words from Vas were all the support he was going to get, he decided to make the most of it. "When you get back to camp, tell my father that the reason I'm dead is because Elya's little accident with his pulse wasn't an accident at all."

"Yes, tell Father that," said Elemak. "It'll prove to him what he's long suspected, that Meb is out of his dear little mind."

"I'll tell him nothing at all, for now—*unless* you two don't get back to camp right away," said Vas. "Come on, Obring."

"I'm not your puppy," said Obring.

"All right then, stay," said Vas.

"Stay and do *what?*" asked Obring.

"If you have to ask, you'd better come with me," said Vas. "We don't want to interfere in this little family quarrel."

Meb didn't want them to go. He wanted witnesses to whatever it was Elya was planning to do. "Elemak's just superstitious!" he called after them. "He believes those old stories about how if you kill a baboon, his whole troop comes and carries off your babies! Eiadh must be pregnant, that's all! Come on back, we can all walk to camp together!"

But they didn't come back.

"Listen, I'm sorry," said Meb. "You don't need to make such a fuss about it. It's not as if I hit the boon or anything."

Elemak leaned in close to him. "You'll never take a pulse in your hands again."

"Nafai was the one who shot at *me*," said Meb. "You'll take away my pulse for shooting at a boon, and Nafai shoots at *me* and he gets to *keep* his?"

"You don't kill animals you don't plan to eat. That's a law of the desert, too. But you know why I'm taking your pulse, and it isn't the baboon."

"What, then?"

"Your fingers were itching," said Elemak. "To kill Nafai."

"Oh, you can read my mind now, is that it?"

"I can read your body, and Nafai's no fool, either, he knows what you were planning. Don't you realize that the second you started to move your pulse he would have blown your head off?"

"He doesn't have the spine for it."

"Maybe not," said Elemak. "And maybe neither do you. But you aren't going to get the chance."

This was the stupidest thing Meb had ever heard. "A couple of days ago on the desert you tried to tie him up and leave him for the animals!"

"A couple of days ago I thought I could get us back to civilization," said Elemak. "But that isn't going to happen now. We're stuck out here, together whether we like it or not, and if Eiadh isn't pregnant yet she will be soon."

"If you can just figure out how it's done."

He had pushed a bit too far, he discovered, for Elemak swung his left arm around and smacked him square on the nose with his palm.

"Gaah! Aah!" Mebbekew grabbed at his nose, and sure enough his hands came away bloody. "You peedar! Hooy sauce!"

"Yeah, right," said Elemak. "I love how pain makes you eloquent."

"Now I've got blood all over my clothes."

"It'll only help you bring off the illusion of being manly," said Elemak. "Now listen to me, and listen close, because I mean this. I will *break* your nose next time, and I'll go on breaking it every day if I see you plotting anything against anybody. I tried one time to break free of this whole sickening thing, but I couldn't do it, and you know why."

"Yeah, the Oversoul is better with ropes than I am," said Meb.

"So we're stuck with it, and our wives are going to have babies, and they're going to grow up to be our children. Do you understand that? This company, these sixteen people we've got here, that's going to be the whole world that our children grow up in. And it's not going to be a world where a little ossly-ope like you goes around murdering people because they didn't let him shoot a baboon. Do you understand me?"

"Sure," said Meb. "It'll be a world where big tough he-men like *you* get their jollies by smacking people around."

"You won't get smacked again if you behave," said Elemak. "There'll be no killing, period. Because no matter how smart you think you are, I'll be there before you, waiting for you, and I'll tear you apart. Do you understand me, my little actor friend?"

"I understand that you're sucking up to Nafai for all you're worth," said Mebbekew. He half expected Elemak to hit him again. Instead Elya chuckled.

"Maybe so," said Elemak. "Maybe I am, for the moment. But then, Nafai is also sucking up to *me*, too, in case you didn't notice. Maybe we'll even make peace. What do you think of that?"

I think you've got camel kidneys where your brains should be, which is why your talk is nothing but hot piss in the dirt. "Peace sounds just wonderful, my dear kind gentle older brother," said Meb.

"Just remember that," said Elemak, "and I'll try to make your loving words come true."

Rasa saw them come straggling home—Nafai first, with a hare in his poke, full of the triumph of making a kill, though of course, being Nafai, he tried vainly to conceal his pride; then Obring and Vas, looking tired and bored and sweaty and discouraged; and finally Elemak and Mebbekew, smug and jocular, as if *they* were the ones who had taken the hare, as if *they* were co-conspirators in the conquest of the universe. I'll never understand them, thought Rasa. No two men could be more different—Elemak so strong and competent and ambitious and brutal, Mebbekew so weak and flimsy and lustful and sly—and yet they always seemed to be in on the same jokes, sneering at everyone else from the same lofty pinnacle of private wisdom. Rasa could see how Nafai might annoy others, with his inability to conceal his own delight in his accomplishments, but at least he didn't make other people feel dirty and low just by being near them, the way Mebbekew and Elemak did.

No, I'm being unfair, Rasa told herself. I'm remembering that dawn on the desert. I'm remembering the pulse pointed at Nafai's head. I'll never forgive Elemak for that. I'll have to watch him every day of the journey, to make sure of the safety of my youngest son. That's one good thing about Mebbekew—he's cowardly enough that you don't really have to fear anything from him.

"I know you're hungry," said Volemak. "But it's early yet for supper, and the time will be well spent. Let me tell you the dream that came to me last night."

They had already gathered, of course, and now they sat on the flat stones that Zdorab and Volya had dragged into place days ago for just this purpose, so all would have a place to sit off the ground, for meals, for meetings.

"I don't know what it means," said Volemak, "and I don't know what it's for, but I know that it matters."

"If it matters so much," said Obring, "why doesn't the Oversoul just tell you what it means and have done?"

"Because, son-in-law of my wife," said Volemak, "the dream didn't come from the Oversoul, and he is just as puzzled by it as I am."

Rasa noted with interest that Volya still spoke of the Oversoul as *he;* so Nafai's and Issib's custom of calling her *it* had not yet overtaken him. She liked that. Perhaps it was just because he was getting old and unimaginative, but she liked it that Volemak still thought of the Oversoul in the old manly way, instead of thinking and speaking of her as a mere computer—even one with fractal-like memory that could hold the lives of every human who ever lived and still have room for more.

"So I'll begin, and tell the dream straight through," said Volemak. "And I'll warn you now, that because the dream didn't come from the Oversoul, it gives me more reason to rejoice—for Nafai and Issib, anyway—and yet also more reason to fear for my first sons, Elemak and Mebbekew, for you see, I thought I saw in my dream a dark and dreary wilderness."

"You can see *that* wide awake," murmured Mebbekew. Rasa could see that Meb's jest was nothing but a thin mask for anger—he didn't like having been singled out like that before the dream began. Elemak didn't like it either, of course—but Elemak knew how to hold his tongue.

Volemak gazed at Mebbekew placidly for a moment or two, to silence him, to let him know that he would brook no more interruption. Then he began again.

4

The Tree of Life

"**I** thought I saw in my dream a dark and dreary wilderness," said Volemak, but he knew as he said it that they would not understand what his words meant to him. Not the hot desert that they knew so well by now, dreary as *that* wilderness was. Where he walked in his dream was dank, chill and dirty, with little light, barely enough to see each step he took. There might have been trees not far off, or he might have been underground for all he knew. He walked on and on, with no hope and yet unable to stop hoping that by moving he would eventually escape this desolate place.

"And then I saw a man, dressed in a white gown." Like a priest of Seggidugu, only those are ordinary men, sweating as they perform their rites. This man seemed so at ease with himself that I thought at once that he must be dead. I was in a place where dead men waited, and I thought perhaps that *I* was dead. "He up came to me, and stood there in front of me, and then he spoke to me. Told me to follow him."

Volemak could tell that the others were getting bored—or at least the most childish of them. It was so frustrating, to have only words to tell them what the dream was like. If they could know how that voice sounded when the man spoke, how warm and kind he seemed, as if the very sound of him was the first light in this dark place, then they'd know why I followed him, and why it *mattered* that I followed him. Instead, to them, it's only a dream, and this is clearly the dull part. Yet to me it was not dull.

"I followed him for many hours in the darkness," said Volemak. "I spoke to him but he didn't answer. So, since by now I was convinced that this man was sent by the Oversoul, I began to speak to the Oversoul in my mind. I asked him how long this had to go on, and where I was going, and what it was all about. I got no answer. So I became impatient, and told him that if this was a dream it was time for me to wake up, and if there was going to be some point to this maybe he should get to it before dawn. And there was no answer. So I began to think that maybe it was real, that it would go on forever, that this is what happens to us after death, we go to a dreary wasteland and walk forever behind some man who won't tell us anything that's going on."

"Sounds like life, lately," murmured Mebbekew.

Volemak paused, not looking at Meb, waiting for the others to glare him into silence. Then he went on. "Thinking it might be real, I began to plead with the Oversoul or whoever was in charge of this place to have a little mercy and tell me something or let me see something, let me *understand* what was happening. It was only then, after I began to plead for relief, that the place lightened—not like sunrise or coming near a campfire, I couldn't see any source of the light, I could simply *see*, like bright daylight, and I came out of the stony place to a vast field of tall grass and flowers, bending slightly in the breeze. It was such a relief—to see *life*—that I can't describe it to you. And a little way off— perhaps three hundred meters or so—there was a tree. Even at that distance I could see that amid the bright green of the leaves there were spots of white—fruit, I knew at once. And suddenly I could smell the fruit, and I knew that whatever it was, it was delicious, the most perfect food that ever existed, and if I could only taste that fruit, I'd never be hungry again."

He paused for just a moment, waiting for Mebbekew's obligatory smart remark about how hungry they all were right now, waiting for this dream to end. But Meb had apparently been chastened, because he was silent.

"I walked—I *ran* to the tree—and the fruit was small and sweet. Yes, I tasted it, and I can tell you that no food I've ever had in life was as good."

"Yeah, like sex in dreams," said Obring, who apparently thought that he could fill in for Meb. Volemak bowed his head for a moment. He could hear a movement—yes, Elemak rising to his feet. Volemak knew the scene without looking, for Elemak had learned this technique from him. Elemak was standing, looking at Obring, saying nothing at all, until Obring withered before him. And yes, there it was, Obring's mumbled apology, "Sorry, go on, go on." Volemak waited a moment more, and there was the sound of Elemak sitting back down. Now he could go on, perhaps without another interruption.

But it had been spoiled. He had thought he might be on the verge of finding exactly the right words to explain how the taste of the fruit had been in his mouth, how it made him feel alive for the first time. "It *was* life, that fruit," he said, but now the words sounded empty and inadequate, and he knew the moment of lucidity had passed, and they would never understand. "The joy I felt when I tasted it—was so perfect—I wanted my family to have it. I couldn't bear the thought that I had this perfect fruit, this taste of life in my mouth, and my family didn't know about it, wasn't sharing it. So I turned to look for you, to see where I might find you. You weren't back in the direction I had come from, and as I turned around I saw that a river ran near the tree, and when I looked upriver, I saw Rasa and our two sons, Issib and Nafai, and they were looking around as if they didn't know where they were supposed to go. So I called to them, and waved, and finally they saw me and came to me, and I gave them the fruit and they ate it and felt what I had felt and I could see it in them, too, that when they ate the fruit it was as if life came into them for the first time. They had been alive all along, of course, but now they knew *why* they were alive, they were *glad* to be alive."

Volemak couldn't help the tears that flowed down his cheeks. The memory of the dream was so fresh and strong inside him that telling it was to relive it, and the joy he felt could not be contained even now, after a day of work in the garden, even with the sweat and dirt of the desert on him. He could still taste the fruit in his mouth, could still see the look on their faces. Could still feel the longing he felt then, for Elemak and Mebbekew to taste it, too.

"I thought then of Elemak and Mebbekew, my first two sons, and I looked for them, wanting them to come and taste the fruit as well. And there they were, too, toward the head of the river where Rasa and Issib and Nafai had been. And again I called to them, and beckoned, but they wouldn't come. I tried to tell them about the fruit, shouting to them, but they acted as if they couldn't hear me, though I thought at the time that perhaps they really could. Finally they turned away from me and wouldn't even pretend to listen. There I stood with that perfect fruit in my hand, that taste in my mouth, that scent in my nose, knowing that they would be as filled with joy as I was if only they would come and taste it, and yet I was powerless to bring them."

Before his tears had been of joy; now they flowed for Elemak and Mebbekew, and they tasted bitter to him. But there was nothing more to be said about their refusal—he went on with the dream.

"It was only then, after my two oldest sons had refused to come to the tree, that I realized we weren't the only people there in that huge meadow. You know how it is in dreams—there aren't any people, and now there are thousands of them. In fact, not just people, but others—some that flew, some that scurried along—but I knew that they were people too, if you know what I mean. A lot of them had seen the tree. I thought maybe they had heard me shouting to Elya and Meb about what the fruit was like, how it tasted and all, and now they were trying to get to the tree. Only the distance was much farther now than it had been before, and it was as if they couldn't actually see the tree itself, but only knew generally where it was. I thought, How are they going to find it if they can't see it?

"That was when I saw that there was a kind of railing along the bank of the river, and a narrow little path running right along the river's edge, and I could see that that was the only route they could follow to reach the tree. And the people who were trying to find the tree caught hold of the iron rail and began to follow the path, clinging to the rail whenever the ground was slippery, so they didn't fall into the water. They pressed forward, but then they came into a fog, a thick and heavy fog drifting up from the river, and those that didn't hold on to the rod got lost, and some of them fell into the river and drowned, and others wandered off into the mist and got lost in the field and never found the tree.

"But the ones who held on to the railing managed to find their way through the fog, and finally they came out into the light, near enough to the tree that now they could see it with their own eyes. They came on then, in a rush, and gathered around me and Rasa and Issib and Nafai, and they reached up and took the fruit, and those that couldn't reach high enough, we plucked fruit for them and handed it down, and when there weren't enough to reach from the ground, Nafai and Issib climbed the tree—"

"I climbed . . ." whispered Issib. All of them heard him, but no one said a thing about it, knowing or guessing what he must think, to imagine himself climbing a tree alongside Nafai.

"Climbed the tree and brought down more of the fruit to give to them," said Volemak. "And I saw in their faces that they all tasted what I had tasted, and felt what I had felt. Only then I noticed that after eating the fruit, many of them began to look around them furtively, as if they were ashamed of having eaten the fruit, and they were afraid to be seen. I couldn't believe that they could feel that way, but then I looked in the direction that many of them had looked and there on the other side of the river I could see a huge building, like the buildings of Basilica only larger, with a hundred windows, and in every window we could see rich people, extravagant people, stylish and beautiful people, laughing and drinking and singing, the way it is in Dolltown and Dauberville, only more so. Laughing and having a wonderful time. Only I knew that it wasn't real, that it was the wine making them think they were having fun—or rather, they *were* having fun, but the wine made them think it *mattered* to have fun, when here, just across the river, I had the fruit that would give them the kind of joy that they were pretending they already had. It was so sad, in a way. But then I realized that many of the people who were there with me, people who were actually *eating the fruit*, were looking at the people in that huge building and they were envious of them. They wanted to go *there*, give up the fruit of the tree and join the ones who were laughing so loudly and singing so merrily."

Volemak didn't tell them that for a moment he also felt a faint sting of envy, for seeing them laughing and playing across the river made him feel old, not to be at the party. Made him remember that when he was young, he had been with friends who laughed with him; he had loved women whose kisses were a game, and caressing them was like gamboling and rolling in soft grass and cool moss, and he had laughed, too, in those days, and sung songs with them, and had drunk the wine, and it was real enough, oh yes, it was real. Real, but also out of reach, because the first time was always the best time, and anything he repeated was never as good as it had been before, until finally it all slipped out of his reach, all became nothing but memory, and that was when he knew that he was old, when the joys of youth were completely unrecoverable. Some of his friends had kept trying, had pretended that it never faded for them—but those men and women faded themselves, became painted mannequins, badly made worn-out puppets made in a mockery of youth.

So Volemak envied the people in the building, and remembered having been one of them, or having tried at least to be one of them— was anyone ever really a true part of this transient community of pleasure, which evaporated and re-formed itself over and over again in a single night, and a thousand times in a week? It never quite existed, this family of frolickers, it only seemed about to exist, always on the verge of becoming real, and then it retreated always just out of reach.

But here at this tree, Volemak realized, here is the real thing. Here with the taste of this fruit in our mouths, we are part of something that isn't just illusion. We're part of *life*, wives and husbands, parents and children, the vast onward passage of genes and dreams, bodies and memories, generation after generation, time without end. We are making something that will outlast us, that's what this fruit is, that's what *life* is, and what they have across the river, their mad pursuit of every sensation their bodies can experience, their frantic avoidance of anything painful or difficult, it all misses the point of being alive in the first place. Nothing that is new is ever new twice. While things that are true are still true the next time; truer, in fact, because they have been tested, they have been tasted, and they are always ripe, always ready . . .

Yet Volemak could explain none of this to the people gathered around him, because he knew that these feelings were his own. Not really part of the dream itself, but rather his own responses to the dream, and perhaps not even what the dream was supposed to mean.

"The people in the building looked out at us who were gathered by the tree, and they pointed and laughed, and I could hear them ridiculing us for having been duped into standing around eating fruit when we could really experience life if we would only come over the river and join them. Join the party."

"Yes," whispered Obring sharply.

"I saw a lot of the ones who had tasted the fruit drop what was left of it onto the grass and head for the river, to cross it and get to the building, and many who had never tasted it or even come near the tree also headed for the endless party going on there. Some of them drowned in the river, were swept away downstream, but many of them made it across and went to the building, dripping wet, and went inside, and I saw them come to the windows and point at us and laugh. But I wasn't angry with them, because now I saw something I hadn't seen before. The river was filthy, you see. Raw sewage floating in it. All the garbage of an unfastidious city was flowing downstream, and when they got out of the water, that's what was dripping from their clothing, that's what they smelled like when they entered the party, and inside the building, everybody there was covered with the sludge from the river, and the smell was unspeakable. And when you looked into the building you could see that no one actually enjoyed being near anybody else, because of the filth and the stench. They'd come together for a short time, but then the vileness of the other person's clothing would drive them away. And yet nobody seemed to realize that—they all seemed so eager to cross the river and get into the party. They all seemed to be afraid that they'd be turned away if they didn't hurry and get there *now*."

Volemak sat straighter, leaned back on the rock he was sitting on. "That was all. Except that even at the end, I found myself looking for Elemak and Mebbekew, hoping they'd come join me at the tree. Because I still had that fruit in my hand, the taste of it in my mouth. And it was still delicious and perfect, and it didn't fade away; each bite of it was better than the one before, and I wanted all my family, all my *friends* to have it. To be part of the *life* of it. And then I knew that I was waking up—you know how it is in a dream—and I thought, I can still taste it. I can still feel the fruit in my hands. How wonderful—now I'll be able to bring it to Elya and Meb and they can taste it for themselves, because if they once taste it they'll join the rest of us at the tree. And then I really woke up and found that my hands were empty, and Rasa was asleep beside me having her own dream and so she hadn't tasted the fruit after all, and Nafai and Issib were still in their tents, and it hadn't happened."

Volemak leaned forward again. "But I could still taste it. I can taste it now. That's why I had to tell you. Even though the Oversoul denies that he sent the dream to me, it felt more real, more true than any dream I've ever had before. No, it felt—it *feels*—more real than reality, and while I ate the fruit I was more alive than I've ever been in life. Does this mean anything to you?"

"Yes, Volya," said Rasa. "More than you know."

There was a general murmur of assent, and Volemak could see, look-

ing around the group, that most of them looked thoughtful, and many
of them had been moved—perhaps more by Volemak's own emotions
than by the tale of the dream itself, but at least something about it had
touched them. He had done what he could to share his experience with
them.

"In fact it's made me really hungry," said Dol. "All that talk about
fruit and stuff."

"And the sewage in the river. Mm-mmmm," said Kokor. "What's for
supper?"

They laughed. The seriousness of the mood was broken. Volemak
couldn't be angry, though. He couldn't expect that they would spend
the rest of their lives transformed by his dream.

But it *does* mean something. Even if it didn't come from the Oversoul, it's true, and it matters, and I'll never forget it. Or if I do, I'll be
the poorer for it.

Those who had worked on supper got up to check on the food and
begin to serve it. Rasa came and sat beside Volemak and put her arm
around him. Volemak looked for Issib and saw that he had tearstains
down his cheeks, and Nafai and Luet were walking arm-in-arm,
thoughtful and tender with each other—so good, so right, the two of
them. Most of the others Volemak barely knew. His gaze instinctively
glided over and past them, searching for Mebbekew and Elemak. And
when he saw them he was surprised, for they looked neither moved
nor angry. In fact, if Volemak could have put a name on what he saw in
their faces, he would have called it fear.

How could they hear this dream and be afraid?

"He's setting us up for later," whispered Mebbekew. "This whole
dream thing, with us cut off from the family—he's going to disinherit
us both."

"Oh, shut up," said Elemak. "He's just letting us know that he
knows about what happened on the desert, and he isn't going to make a
big fuss about it, but he *knows*. So this is probably the end of it—
unless one of us does something really stupid."

Meb looked at him coldly. "As I recall, it was *you* who pointed the
pulse at Nafai on the desert, not *me*. So let's not point the finger and
call people stupid."

"I seem to remember a more recent incident," said Elemak.

"Of which you were the only witness. Even darling Nyef had no idea, and in fact it isn't even true, you made it all up, you sorry pizdook."

Elemak ignored the epithet. "I hope I never look as stupid as Father did, crying in front of everybody—about a dream."

"Yes, everybody's stupid except Elemak," said Mebbekew. "You're so smart you fart through your nose."

Elemak could not believe how disgustingly childish Meb could be. "Are we still twelve, Meb? Do we still think rhyming *smart* with *fart* is clever?"

"That was the irony of it, you poor thick-headed lummox," said Meb in his most charming voice. "Only you're so smart you never understand irony. No wonder you think everybody around you is dumb— you never understand what they're saying, so you think they must not be speaking intelligibly. Let me tell you the secret that everybody else in this camp knows, Elya, my pet brother. You may know how to get through the desert alive, but it's the only thing you *do* know. Even Eiadh jokes with the other women that you finish with her so quickly she doesn't even have time to notice you've started. You don't even know how to please a woman, and Elya, let me tell you, they're all *very* easy to please."

Elemak let the insults and the innuendos slide off him. He knew Meb when he was in these moods. When they were both boys, Elemak used to beat him up when he got this way—but then it finally dawned on him that this was exactly what Mebbekew wanted. As if he didn't mind the pain as long as he got to see Elemak so angry and red-faced, sweating, with sore hands from pounding on Mebbekew's bones. Because then Meb knew he was in control.

So Elemak didn't let himself be goaded. Instead he left Meb and joined the others getting their supper at the cookfire. Eiadh was serving from the stewpot—there hadn't been time to cook the hare, so the only meat in it was jerky, but Rasa had made sure to pack plenty of spices so at least there'd be some flavor to the soup tonight. And Eiadh looked so lovely ladling it out into the bowls that Elemak was filled with longing for her. He knew well that Meb was lying—Eiadh had nothing to complain about in their lovemaking—and if there wasn't a baby in her there would be soon. That knowledge tasted sweet indeed to Elemak. This is what I was searching for in all those journeys. And if that's what Father meant by his tree of life—taking part in the great enterprise of love and sex and birth and life and death—then Elemak had indeed tasted of the fruit of that tree, and it *was* delicious, more than anything else that life had to offer. So if Father thought that Elemak would be shamed because he didn't come to the tree in Father's dream, then he'd be disappointed, because Elemak was already at the tree and didn't need Father to show him the way.

After supper, Nafai and Luet headed for the Index tent. They would have gone before eating, they were that eager—but they knew that there'd be no stock of food for snacking later. They had to eat when meals were served. So now, as darkness fell, they parted the door and stepped inside—only to find Issib and Hushidh already there, their hands together on the Index.

"Sorry," said Luet.

"Join us," said Hushidh. "We're asking for an explanation of the dream."

Luet and Nafai laughed. "Even though it's perfectly clear what it means?"

"So Father told you that, too," said Issib. "Well, I suppose he's right—it's sort of a general moral lesson about taking care of your family and ignoring the fun life and all that—like the books they give to children to persuade them to be good."

"But," said Nafai.

"But why *now?* Why *us?*" said Issib. "That's what we're asking."

"Don't forget that he saw what the rest of us have seen," said Luet. "What General Moozh saw."

"What do you mean?" asked Issib.

"He wasn't there," Hushidh reminded them. "I haven't told him yet—about my dream."

"We saw dreams," said Luet. "And even though all our dreams were different, they all had something in common. We all saw these hairy flying creatures—I thought of them as angels, though they don't look particularly sweet. And the Oversoul told us that General Moozh saw them also—Hushidh's and my father. And our mother, too, the woman called Thirsty who stopped Hushidh from being married to General Moozh. And the ones on the ground, too . . ."

Hushidh spoke up. "I saw the ratlike ones eating—someone's children. Or trying to."

"And Father's dream is part of all that," said Luet, "because even though it's different from the others, it still has the rats and the angels in it. Remember that he said he saw some flying, and some scurrying along the ground? But he knew they were people, too."

"I remember that now," said Issib. "But he skipped right over it."

"Because he didn't realize that that was the sign," said Luet.

"Of what?"

"That the dream didn't come from the Oversoul," said Luet.

"But Father already said that," said Issib. "The Oversoul told him."

"Ah, but whom *did* it come from?" asked Nafai. "Did the Oversoul tell him *that?*"

"The Keeper of Earth," said Luet.

"Who is *that?*" asked Issib.

"That's the one that the Oversoul wants to go back to Earth to see," said Luet. "That's the one we're *all* going to go back there to see. Don't you understand? The Keeper of Earth is calling us all in our dreams, one by one, telling us things. And what happened in Father's dream *is* important because it really does come from the Keeper. If we could just put it together and understand it . . ."

"But something coming from Earth—it would have to travel faster than light," said Issib. "Nothing can do that."

"Or it sent these dreams a hundred years ago, at lightspeed," said Nafai.

"Sent dreams to people who aren't even born?" said Luet. "I thought you had dropped that idea."

"I still think that the dreams might be sort of—in the air," said Nafai. "And whichever of us is sleeping when the dream arrives, has the dream."

"Not possible," said Hushidh. "My dream was far too specific."

"Maybe you just worked the Keeper's stuff into your own dream," said Nafai. "It's possible."

"No it isn't," said Hushidh. "It was all of a piece, my dream. If any of it came from the Keeper of Earth, it all did. And the Keeper knew me. Do you understand what that means? The Keeper knew me and she knew . . . everything."

Silence fell over the group for a moment.

"Maybe the Keeper is only sending these dreams to the people it *wants* to have come back," said Issib.

"I hope you're wrong," said Nafai. "Because I haven't had one like that yet. I haven't seen these rats and angels."

"Neither have I," said Issib. "I was thinking that maybe—"

"But you were in *my* dream," said Hushidh, "and if the Keeper is calling to me, she wants you, too."

"And we were both in Father's dream," said Nafai. "Which is why we have to find out what it meant. It's obviously more than just telling us to be good. In fact, if that's what it was for it did a pretty lousy job, since it made Elemak and Mebbekew furious to be singled out in the dream because they refused to come to the tree."

"So join us," said Issib. "Touch the Index and ask."

The longer arm of Issib's chair held the Index so he could rest his hand on it; the others gathered near and touched it, too. Touched it and questioned it, asking over and over again, silently in their minds . . .

"No," said Issib, "nothing's happening. It doesn't work this way. We have to be clear."

"Then speak for us," said Hushidh. "Ask the question for all of us."

With their hands all on the Index, Issib put voice to their questions. He asked; they waited. He asked again. They waited again. Nothing.

"Come on," said Nafai. "We've done everything you asked. Even if all you can tell us is that you're as confused as we are, at least tell us *that.*"

The voice of the Index came at once: "I'm as confused as you are."

"Well, why didn't you say so from the start?" asked Issib in disgust.

"Because you weren't asking me what *I* thought of it, you were asking what it means. I was trying to figure it out. I can't."

"You mean you haven't yet," said Nafai.

"I mean I can't," said the Index. "I don't have enough information. I can't intuit the way you humans do. My mind is too simple and direct. Don't ask me to do more than I'm capable of. I know everything that is knowable by observation, but I can't guess what the Keeper of Earth is trying to do, and you exhaust me when you demand that I try to do it."

"All right," said Luet. "We're sorry. But if you learn anything . . ."

"I'll tell you if I think it's appropriate for you to know."

"Tell us even if you don't," demanded Issib.

But the Index's voice did not come again.

"It can be so *infuriating* dealing with the Oversoul!" said Nafai.

"Speak of her with respect," said Hushidh, "and perhaps she'll be more cooperative with you."

"Show it *too* much respect and the computer starts thinking that it's really a god," said Issib. "Then it's *really* hard to deal with."

"Come to bed," said Luet to Nafai. "We'll talk of this again tomorrow, but tonight we need our sleep."

It took little persuasion to get Nafai to follow her to their tent, leaving Hushidh and Issib alone.

They sat in silence for a while. Issib felt the uncomfortableness as if it were smoke in the air; it made it hard to breathe. It was Father's dream that had brought them together here, to speak to the Oversoul through the Index. It was an easy thing to show Hushidh how comfortably he dealt with the Index; he was confident of himself, when it came to the Index, even when the Oversoul was itself confused and couldn't answer aright. But now there was no Index between them—it rested voiceless in its case, where Nafai had placed it, and now only Hushidh and Issib remained, and they were supposed to marry each other and yet Issib couldn't think of anything to say.

"I dreamed of you," said Hushidh.

Ah! She had spoken first! At once the pent-up need to speak brought words to Issib's lips. "And you woke screaming?" No, that was a stupid thing to say. But he had said it, and—yes, she was smiling. She knew it was a joke, so he didn't have to be embarrassed.

"I dreamed of you flying," she said.

"I do that a lot," he said. "But only in other people's dreams. I hope you didn't mind."

And she laughed.

He should have said something else then, something serious, because he knew she was doing all the hard part—she was saying serious things, and he was deflecting them with jokes. That was fine to make them comfortable with each other, but it also kept turning away from the hard things she was trying to say. So he knew he should help her say the hard things, and yet he couldn't think of what they were, not now, sitting here with her in the Index tent, alone. Except that he knew he was afraid, for she needed a husband and it was going to have to be him except he had no idea if he could do any of the husbandly things for her. He could talk, of course, and he knew Hushidh well enough to know that she was a talker, when she knew you—he'd heard her speak passionately in class, and also in private conversations that he'd overheard. So they'd probably be able to talk, except that for talking they wouldn't need to marry, would they? What kind of father will I be? Come here right now, son, or I'll mash you with my chair! Not to mention the question of how he'd get to be a father in the first place. Oh, he had worked out the mechanics of it in his own mind, but he couldn't imagine any woman actually wanting to go through with her part of it. And so that was the hard question that he couldn't bring himself to ask. Here is the script for how we'll make babies—are you willing to consider taking the starring role? The only drawback is that you'll have to do everything, while I lie back and give you no pleasure whatsoever, and then you'll have the babies while I help you not at all, and finally when we get old you'll have to nurse me till I die except that it won't make much difference since you'll probably have been nursing me all along, since once I have a wife everybody will expect to leave off helping me, so it'll be you, performing personal services that will disgust you, and then you'll be expected to receive my seed and bear me babies after *that* and there's no words I can bring to my lips that could persuade you to do that.

Hushidh looked at him steadily in the silence. "You're breathing rather heavily," she said.

"Am I?" he asked.

"Is that passion or are you as scared of all this as I am?" she asked.

Yes. More scared. "Passion," he said.

It wasn't very light inside the tent, but it wasn't very dark, either. He could see her make a decision, then reach up under her blouse and do something or other, and when she brought out her hands again, he could see that her breasts now moved freely under the cloth. And because she did that, he was more scared than ever, but he also felt just a touch of desire, because no woman had ever done such a thing in front of him, and certainly not *for* him, for him to *see* on *purpose*. Only he was probably expected to do something now and he had no idea what to do.

"I'm not very experienced at this sort of thing," said Hushidh.

What sort of thing? he wanted to ask, but then decided not to, since he understood exactly what she meant and it wasn't a good moment to joke.

"But I thought we ought to perform a kind of experiment," she said. "Before we decide anything. To see if you could possibly be attracted to me."

"I could," he said.

"And to see if you can give anything to me," she said. "It'll be better if we can both enjoy it, don't you think?"

Her words were so matter-of-fact. He could hear, though, from the trembling in her voice, that it wasn't matter-of-fact to her. And for the first time it occurred to him that she probably didn't think of herself as a beautiful woman. She was never one that the young men in the school had drooled over behind her back; now it occurred to Issib that she might be perfectly aware of that, probably *was* aware, and that she might be as frightened about whether he would desire her as he was about whether he could please her. It put them on something closer to equal terms. And instead of worrying about whether she'd be disgusted, he could give some thought to what she might enjoy.

She moved closer to him. "I asked my sister Luet," she said. "What men do for women that she thought you might be able to do for me." Her hands now rested on the arms of the chair. And now her right hand dropped down and rested on his leg. His thin, thin leg; he wondered how it felt to her, this thigh that barely had muscle on it. Then she pressed closer to him and he realized that his hand was now touched by the cloth of her blouse. "She said that you could do buttons."

"Yes," he said. It was hard, but he had learned to button and unbutton clothing that fastened that way.

"And I assumed that meant you could also undo them."

Only then did he realize that he was being invited.

"An experiment," he said.

"A midterm exam," she said, "in unbuttoning and opening, with an extra credit question later."

He lifted his hand—it was such hard work—lifted it and took hold of her blouse's top button. It was a bad angle—back-handed.

"Not a good angle, is it," she said. Then she moved her right hand to his other thigh, and higher, and then leaned in front of him. Now he could use both hands, and unbuttoning her blouse was almost easy, even though he had never had to unbutton someone else's clothing before. It occurred to him that this would be a useful skill with children who hadn't learned to dress themselves yet.

"Perhaps you can improve your time on the next one," she said.

He did. And now as he worked the skin of his hands brushed against her breasts. He had dreamed, day and night, of touching a woman's breasts, but had always believed that it would never be more than a dream. And now, as he unbuttoned each button, she lifted herself higher, so the next lower button would be in reach, and this moved her breasts closer to his face, until finally, by turning his head just a little, he would be able to kiss her skin.

His fingers unbuttoned the last button, and now the two sides of her blouse swung free, too. I can't I can't, he said, and then he did anyway, turned his head and kissed her. The skin was a little sweaty, but also soft and smooth, not like skin that had been weathered—not like his own hands, smooth as *they* were, or even his mother's smooth cheek, which he had often kissed; this was such skin as had never touched his lips before, and he kissed her again.

"You only got an average mark for unbuttoning and opening," she said, "but your extra credit work seems promising. You don't always have to be *that* gentle."

"I'm actually being as rough and brutal and manly as I can," he said.

"Then it's fine," she said. "You can't do it wrong, you know. As long as I know you're doing it because you want to."

"I do," he said. And then, because he realized that she needed to hear it, he said, "I want to very much. You're so . . . perfect."

She seemed to wince a little.

"Like what I imagined," he said. "Like a dream."

Then *her* hand moved, and tested him as well, to see how he was responding, and though his first instinct was to hide, to shy away, for once he was glad that his body wouldn't allow him to move away that quickly, because she needed also to know that he had been aroused.

"I think the experiment was a success, don't you?" asked Hushidh.

"Yes," said Issib. "Does that mean you want me to stop now?"

"No," she said. "But someone might come into this tent at any moment." She drew away and rebuttoned her blouse. She was breathing rather heavily, though. He could hear her despite his own heavy breathing. "That was a lot of exercise, for me," he said.

"I hope to wear you out."

"Can't unless you marry me," he said.

"I thought you'd never ask."

"Will you?"

"Is tomorrow soon enough?"

"No," he said. "I don't think so."

"Then maybe I should go and get your parents." Her blouse was buttoned by now, and she got up and left the tent. Only then did he realize that whatever the underwear was that had bound her breasts before, it was lying in the middle of the carpet, a little white pile. He dropped his right hand to the controls of his chair and made the chair's long arm go out and pick it up, then bring it close to him. He could see how the undergarment was made, and thought it was rather ingenious, but at the same time resented the way the elasticized fabric must hold a woman's breasts close to her body all the time. Maybe the women wore such things only for riding camels. It would be sad if they were confined like that all the time. Especially for him, because he liked very much the way Hushidh's body moved under her blouse when this had been removed.

He told his chair to stow it in the small case under the chair; it complied. Only just in time—Hushidh came back in at once with Father and Mother. "I can't very well complain that it's too sudden," said Father. "We've been expecting this and hoping it would come sooner rather than later."

"Do you want us to call everyone together for the ceremony?" asked Mother.

And have them spend a half hour being alternately bored by the ceremony and curious about how Hushidh and Issib would handle sex? "No thanks," he said. "All the important people are here."

"Well, too bad," said Hushidh. "I asked Luet and Nafai to come in, too, as soon as they've notified Zdorab and Shedemei about the new sleeping arrangements."

Issib hadn't thought of that—Hushidh had been sharing a tent with Shedemei, just as Issib had with Zdorab. The two of them would be forced together before they were ready, and . . .

"Don't worry," said Father. "Zdorab will sleep here with the Index, and Shedemei will stay where she is. Hushidh will move in with you, because your tent is already . . . equipped."

Equipped with his private latrine arrangements, the pans for his sponge baths, his bed with the mattress of air bubbles so he didn't get bedsores. And in the morning, he'd need to void his bladder and his bowels, and he'd say, Shuya, darling, would you mind bringing me my jar and my pan? And then wipe up after me, there's a dear . . .

"And Nafai and Zdorab will come in the morning, to help you get ready for the day," said Father.

"And to teach me," said Hushidh. "That's not going to be a barrier between us, Issib, if you're to be my husband. I refuse to let it bother me, and you must refuse to let it bother you."

Easier said than done, thought Issib, but he nodded his agreement, hoping that it would be true.

The ceremony took only a few moments, once Nafai and Luet got there. Nafai stood with Issib and Luet with Hushidh, while Mother and Father took turns saying the parts of the ceremony. It was really the women's marriage ceremony, which was the usual way in Basilica, and so Father had to be prompted now and then to say his part right, but that was just part of the ceremony, or so it felt, to have Father's voice repeating the words Mother had just spoken, so gently, to remind him. At last it was done, and Rasa joined their hands. Hushidh bent to him in his chair, and kissed him. It was the first time his lips had touched hers, and it surprised him. It also pleased him very much, and besides, during the kiss she knelt down beside the chair and as she did, her breasts came to press against his arm, and all he really wanted was for everyone else to leave them alone so he could see how the rest of the experiment would go.

It was another half hour, with some teasing and joking from Nafai and Luet, but at last they were alone in Issib's tent, and they took up the experiment where they left off. When Hushidh was naked, she lifted him out of the chair—he knew that she was surprised at how very light he was, though Nafai had no doubt assured her that she'd have no difficulty lifting him, tall as he was. She undressed him and then brought her body near him, so he could give to her as much as she would give to him. He thought that he could not bear how powerful the feelings were as he could see the pleasure he was giving her, and feel the pleasures she was giving him; his body spent itself almost the very moment she eased herself upon him. But that was all right, too, for she still held him, and moved upon him, and kissed him, and he kissed her cheek, her shoulder, her chest, her arm, whenever a part of her came near his lips; and when he could, he pulled his arms around her so that when she moved atop him she could feel his hands also on her back, her thighs; gently, weakly, capable of nothing, really—but there. Was that truly enough for her? Was it something she could enjoy, again and again, forever?

Then, instead of wondering, it occurred to him to ask.

"Yes," she said. "You're done, then?"

"The first time, anyway," he said. "I hope it didn't hurt you too much."

"A little," she said. "Luet told me that I shouldn't expect to be overwhelmed the first time anyway."

"How not-overwhelmed were you."

"I wasn't *over*whelmed," she said. "But it's not like I wasn't whelmed at all, either. In fact, I'd say that on my wedding night I was well and thoroughly whelmed, and I rather look forward to our next whelming, to see how much better it can get."

"How about first thing in the morning?" he asked.

"Perhaps," she said. "But don't be surprised if you wake up and find yourself being taken advantage of in the middle of the night."

"Are you just pretending, or do you really mean all this?" said Issib.

"Are *you* just pretending?" she asked.

"No," he said. "This is the most wonderful night of my life. Mostly because . . ."

She waited.

"Because I never thought it would happen."

"It did though," she said.

"I answered," he said. "Now you."

"I thought I might have to pretend, and I *would* have pretended if I'd had to, because I know our marriage can work in the long run—I know it because I saw it in my dream from the Keeper of Earth. So if it meant I had to pretend to make it work well at the start, then I would have done it."

"Oh."

"But I didn't have to pretend. I showed you what I really felt. It wasn't as good as it's going to be, but it was good. *You* were good to me. Very gentle. Very kind. Very . . ."

"Loving?"

"Was that what you meant to be?"

"Yes," he said. "I meant that part most of all."

"Ah," she said.

But then in a moment he realized that she hadn't said *ah* at all, but rather had let a sound escape her mouth without meaning to, and he saw in the dim light that she was crying, and it occurred to him that he had said exactly the right things to her, as she had said exactly the right things to him.

And as he drifted toward sleep, her body close to his, his arm resting lightly on her side, he thought: I have tasted of the fruit in Father's dream. Not when we coupled, not when my body first gave its seed into a woman's body, but rather when I let her see my fear, and my gratitude, and my love, and she let me also see hers. Then we both reached up and tasted just the first bite of that fruit, and now I know the secret from Father's dream, the thing that even he didn't understand—that you can never taste the fruit by reaching for it yourself. Rather you only taste it when you pick it from the tree for someone else, as Shuya gave the fruit to me, and I, though I never thought it possible, plucked and gave a taste of it to her.

5

The Face
of the Keeper

Luet sat watching the baboons. The female that she thought of as
Rubyet, because of a livid scar on her back, was in estrus, and it was
interesting to watch the males compete for her. The most blustering
male, Yobar, the one who spent so much time in camp with the humans, was the least effective at getting Rubyet's attention. In fact, the
more aggressive he got, the less progress he made. He would display
his rage, stamping and snarling, even snapping his teeth and taking
swipes with his hands, to try to intimidate one of the males who was
courting Rubyet. Every time, the one he was intimidating would give
up very quickly and run away from him—but while Yobar was chasing
his victim, other males would approach Rubyet. So when Yobar returned to Rubyet from his "victory," he would find other males there
before him, and the whole play was enacted again.

Finally, Yobar got really angry and began to attack one of the males
in earnest, biting and tearing at him. It was a male that Volemak had
pointed out once with the name Salo, because he had once smeared
grease all over his face while stealing food from the cookfire. Salo
immediately became submissive, showing his backside to Yobar, but

Yobar was too angry to accept the submission. The other males looked on, perhaps amused, as Yobar continued to pummel and nip at his victim.

Salo at last managed to break free, howling and whining as he ran away from Yobar, who, still raging, followed after him at a furious pace, knocking him this way and that whenever he got within reach.

Then Salo did the most extraordinary thing. He ran straight for a young mother called Ploxy, who had a nursing infant that Salo often played with, and tore the infant from Ploxy's arms. Ploxy hooted once in annoyance, but the baby immediately started to act happy and excited—until Yobar, still furious, came charging up and started pummeling Salo again.

This time, however, the infant Salo was holding started screeching in terror, and now, instead of watching complacently, the other males immediately became agitated. Ploxy began screaming, too, calling for help, and within a few moments the entire troop of baboons had assembled around Yobar and were beating him and screaming at him. Confused, frightened, Yobar tried to grab the infant out of Salo's hands, perhaps thinking that if *he* held the infant, everybody would be on *his* side, but Luet realized that it wouldn't work. Sure enough, the moment he grabbed for the baby, the others became downright brutal in their beating of him, finally ejecting him from the group and chasing him away. Several of the males chased him quite a distance and then stayed nearby to watch and make sure he didn't come near. Luet wondered if that would be the end of Yobar's attempt to be part of the troop.

Then she looked for Salo, trying to spot him somewhere near Ploxy and the baby—but he wasn't there, though most of the other baboons were still there, chattering and bobbing up and down and otherwise showing how agitated they were.

Salo, however, was off in the brush upstream of the main group. He had got Rubyet away from the rest and now was mounting her. She had the most comically resigned look on her face, which now and then gave way to a look of eyes-rolled-back pleasure—or exasperation. Luet wondered if human faces gave that same weirdly mixed signal under similar circumstances . . . a sort of distracted intensity that might mean pleasure or might mean perplexity.

In any event, Yobar, the aggressive one, had been completely defeated—might even have lost his place in the tribe. And Salo, who wasn't particularly large, had lost the skirmish but won the battle *and* the war.

All because Salo had grabbed a baby away from its mother.

"Lucky Salo," said Nafai. "I wondered who would win sweet Rubyet's heart."

"He did it with flowers," said Luet. "I didn't mean to be off here so long."

"I wasn't looking for you to *do* anything," said Nafai. "I was looking for you because I wanted to be with you. There isn't anything for me to do now anyway, till supper. I got my prey early this morning and brought the bloody thing home to lay at my mate's feet. Only she was busy throwing up and didn't give me my customary reward."

"Wouldn't you know that *I'd* be the one who'd get sick all the time," said Luet. "Hushidh burped once and that was it for her. And Kokor *tries* to throw up but she just can't bring it off, so she ends up *not* getting the sympathy she wants and I end up having it when I don't want it."

"Who would have thought that it would be a race between you and Hushidh and Kokor for the first baby in the colony."

"A good thing for you," said Luet. "It'll give you an infant to grab, in case there's trouble."

He hadn't seen Salo's strategem, so he didn't understand.

"Salo—he grabbed Ploxy's baby."

"Oh, yes, they do that," said Nafai. "Shedemei told me. The males who are fully accepted in the tribe make friends with an infant or two, so the infant likes them. Then, in combat, they grab the infant, who *doesn't* scream when his *friend* takes him. The other male *isn't* his friend, so when he keeps attacking the baby gets scared and screams, which brings the whole tribe down on the poor pizdook's head."

"Oh," said Luet. "So it was routine."

"I've never seen it. I'm jealous that you did and I didn't."

"There's the prize," said Luet, pointing to Salo, who still hadn't finished with Rubyet.

"And where's the loser? I'll bet it's Yobar." Luet was already pointing, and sure enough, there was Yobar, looking forlorn off in the distance, watching the troop but not daring to come closer because of the two males who were browsing halfway between him and the rest of the troop.

"You'd better make friends with my baby, then," said Luet. "Or you won't ever get your way in this tribe we're forming."

Nafai put his hand on Luet's stomach. "No bigger yet."

"That's fine with me," said Luet. "Now, what did you really come out here for?"

He looked at her in consternation.

"You didn't know I was down here because nobody knew I was down here," said Luet, "so you didn't come looking for me, you came here to be alone."

He shrugged. "I'd rather be with you."

"You're so impatient," said Luet. "The Oversoul already said there's no hurry—she won't even be ready for us at Vusadka for years yet."

"This place can't sustain us—it's already getting harder to find game," said Nafai. "And we're too close to that settled valley over the mountains to the east."

"That isn't what you're anxious about, either," said Luet. "It's driving you crazy that the Keeper of Earth hasn't sent you a dream."

"*That* doesn't bother me at all," said Nafai. "What bothers me is the way you keep throwing it up to me. That you and Shuya and Father and Moozh and Thirsty all saw these angels and rats, and I didn't. What, does that mean that some computer orbiting a planet a hundred or so lightyears away somehow judged me a century before I was born and decided that I wasn't worthy to receive his neat little menagerie dreams?"

"You really *are* angry," said Luet.

"I want to *do* something, and if I can't then at least I want to *know* something!" cried Nafai. "I'm sick of waiting and waiting and *nothing* happens. It's no good for me to work with the Index because Zdorab and Issib are constantly using it and they're more familiar with how it works than I am—"

"But it still speaks more clearly to you than anybody."

"So while it tells me nothing it does it with greater clarity, how excellent."

"And you're a good hunter. Elemak even says so."

"Yes, that's about all anybody's found for me to do—kill things."

Luet could see the shadow of the memory of Gaballufix's death pass over Nafai's face. "Aren't you ever going to forgive yourself for that?"

"Yes. When Gaballufix comes down out of the baboons' sleeping caves and tells me he was just pretending to be dead."

"You just don't like waiting, that's all," said Luet. "But it's like my being pregnant. I'd like to have it over with. I'd like to have the baby. But it takes time, so I wait."

"You wait, but you can feel the change in you."

"As I vomit everything I eat."

"Not everything," said Nafai, "and you know what I mean. I don't feel any changes, I'm not needed for anything . . ."

"Except the food we eat."

"All right, you win. I'm vital, I'm necessary, I'm busy all the time, so I must be happy." He started to walk away from her.

She thought of calling after him, but she knew that it would do no good. He wanted to be miserable, and so all she would do by trying to cheer him up was thwart him in his mood of the day. Aunt Rasa had told her a few days ago that it wouldn't hurt for her to remember that Nafai was still just a boy, and that she shouldn't expect him to be a mature tower of strength for her. "You were both too young to marry," said Rasa then, "but events got away from us. You've come up to the challenge—in time, Nyef will too."

But Luet wasn't sure at all that she had come up to any challenge. She was terrified at the thought of giving birth out here in the wilderness, far from the physicians of the city. She had no idea whether they'd even have food in a few months—everything depended on their garden and the hunters, and it was really only Elemak and Nafai who were any good at *that*, though Obring and Vas sometimes went out with pulses, too. The food supply could fail at any time, and soon she'd have a baby and what if they suddenly decided they had to travel? Bad as her sickness was right now, what if she had to ride atop a swaying camel? She'd rather eat camel cheese.

Of course, the thought of camel cheese made the nausea come back in a wave, and she knew that this time it might well come out, so down she went on her knees again, sick of the pain of the acidy stuff that came up from her gut into her mouth. Her throat hurt, her head hurt, and she was tired of it all.

She felt hands touch her, gathering her hair away from her face, twisting it and holding it out of the way, so none of the flecks of vomitus would get in it. She wanted to say thank you, knowing it was Nafai; she also wanted him to go away, it was so humiliating and awful and painful to be like this and have somebody *watching*. But he was her husband. He was part of this, and she couldn't send him away. Didn't even *want* to send him away.

At last she was through puking.

"Not too effective," said Nafai, "if we judge these things by quantity."

"Please shut up," said Luet. "I don't want to be cheered up, I want my baby to be a ten-year-old child already so that I remember all of this as an amusing event from my childhood long ago."

"Your wish is granted," said Nafai. "The baby is here and aged ten. Of course, she's incredibly obnoxious and bratty, the way *you* were at ten."

"I wasn't."

"You were the waterseer already, and we all knew you bossed and sassed grownups all the time."

"I told them what I saw, that's all!" Then she realized that he was laughing. "Don't tease me, Nafai. I know I'd be sorry later, but I still may lose control and kill you now."

He gathered her into his arms and she had to twist away to keep him from kissing her. "Don't!" she said. "I've got the most awful taste in my mouth, it would probably kill you!"

So he held her and after a while she felt better.

"I think about Keeper of Earth all the time," said Nafai.

I would, too, if I weren't thinking about the baby, Luet said silently.

"I keep thinking that maybe it *isn't* just another computer," said Nafai. "That maybe it *isn't* calling us through hundred-year-old dreams, that maybe it knows us, and that it's just waiting for . . . for *something* before it speaks to me."

"It's waiting for the message that only you can receive."

"I don't care," said Nafai. "About it being only me. I'd take *Father's* dream, if only I could experience what it feels like inside my head. How the Keeper is different from what the Oversoul does inside me. I want to *know.*"

I know you do. You keep coming back to it, day after day.

"I've been trying to talk to the Keeper of Earth. That's how crazy I'm getting, Luet. Show me what you showed Father! I say it over and over."

"And she ignores you."

"It's a hundred lightyears away!" said Nafai. "It doesn't know I exist!"

"Well if all you want is the same dream as Volemak, why not get the Oversoul to give it to you?"

"It isn't *from* the Oversoul."

"But she must have recorded the whole experience inside your father's mind, right? And she can retrieve it, and show it to you. And the way you get everything so much more clearly through the Index—"

"Just like experiencing it myself," said Nafai. "I can't believe I never thought of that. I can't believe the *Oversoul* never thought of that."

"She's not very creative, you know that."

"She's creatively *inert*," said Nafai. "But *you're* not." He kissed her on the cheek, gave her one last hug, and bounded to his feet. "I have to go talk to the Oversoul."

"Give her my love," said Luet mildly.

"I—oh, I see. I can wait—let's walk back together."

"No, really—I wasn't hinting. I want to stay here a while longer. Maybe just to see if they let Yobar back."

"Don't miss supper," said Nafai. "You're eating for—"

"Two," said Luet.

"Maybe three!" said Nafai. "Who knows?"

She groaned theatrically, knowing that was what he wanted to hear. Then he ran off, back up the valley toward the camp.

He really is just a boy, as Aunt Rasa said. But what am I? His mother now? Not really—*She's* his mother. I shouldn't expect more of him— he works hard and well, and more than half the meat we eat is from his hunting. And he's kind and gentle with me—I don't know how Issib could be any sweeter and more tender than Nafai, no matter what Shuya says. And I'm his friend—he comes to me to talk about things that he says to no one else, and when I want to talk he listens and answers, unlike some of the other husbands, or so *their* wives say. By any standard I ever heard of, he's a fine husband, and mature beyond his years—but it isn't what I thought it was going to be. When I took him through the Lake of Women, I thought it meant that he and I were going to do great and majestic things together. I thought we would be like a king and a queen, or at least like a great priestess and her priest, doing powerful and majestic things to change the universe. Instead I throw up a lot and he bounds around like a fifteen-year-old who is really hurt because some computer from another planet won't send dreams to him . . .

Oh, I'm too tired to think. Too sick to care. Maybe someday my image of our marriage will come true. Or maybe that'll be his second wife, after I puke to death and get buried in the sand.

Shedemei had spent her whole life knowing that people looked at her oddly. At first it was because she was so intelligent as a child, because she cared about things that children weren't supposed to care about. Adults would look at her strangely. So would other children, but sometimes the adults smiled and nodded their approval, while the children never did. Shedemei had thought this meant that when she was an adult, she would be fully accepted by everyone, but instead the opposite was true. When she became an adult it only meant that all the other adults were the same age now and treated her as the children had. Of course, now she was able to recognize what she was seeing. It was fear. It was resentment. It was envy.

Envy! Could she help it that she had been given a combination of genes that gave her an extraordinary memory, an enormous capacity for grasping and understanding ideas, and a mind that was able to make connections that no one else could see? It's not as if she *chose* to be able to do mental gymnastics beyond the reach of anyone she had ever met in person. (There were people just as intelligent as she, and some perhaps more intelligent, but they were in far cities, even on other continents, and she knew of them only through their published works, distributed by the Oversoul from city to city.) She had no malicious intent. She certainly didn't have the ability to share her ability with the envious ones—she could only share the products of her ability. They gladly took those, and then resented her for being able to produce them.

Most human beings, she concluded long ago, love to worship from afar people with extraordinary ability, but prefer to have their friends be genial incompetents. And, of course, most of them get their preference.

But now she was permanently attached to this little society of sixteen people, and unable to avoid meeting them day by day. She did her work—her time weeding in the garden, her water turn, her hours of baboon-watching during the day to make sure they didn't leave their area and get into the food. She gladly covered for Luet when she was throwing up, and uncomplainingly did the tasks that Sevet was too lazy and Kokor too pregnant and Dol just generally too precious a being to do. Yet still she did not fit, was not accepted, was not *part* of the group, and it only got worse, day by day.

It didn't help a bit that she understood exactly what was happening. The bonding between husband and wife triggers a need for others also to be bonded in the same pattern, she knew that, she had studied it. The old courtship patterns, the loose and easy friendships, those now make the married ones feel uneasy, because they don't want anything around them that threatens the stability of the monogamous marriage bond, while the essence of unmarried society is always to be off balance, always to be free and random and unconnected and playful.

Admittedly, that was precisely the way some of them still wished to behave—Shedemei could see how monogamy chafed at Mebbekew and Obring, Sevet and Kokor. But they were *acting* the role of spouse right now, perhaps even more aggressively than the ones who actually meant it. In any event, the result was that Shedemei was even more cut off from others around her than she had ever been before. Not that she was shunned. Hushidh and Luet were as warm to her as ever, and Eiadh in her way was decent, while Aunt Rasa was utterly unchanged —she would never change. However, the men were all universally . . . what, *civil?* And Dol's, Sevet's, and Kokor's attitudes ranged from ice to acid.

Worst of all, this little company of humans was taking a shape that systematically excluded her from any influence in it. Why had they stopped saying, "The men will do *this* while the women do *that*"? Now it was, "The *wives* can stay here while the men go off and" do whatever it was that the men wanted to do. It drove her crazy sometimes that the women were lumped together as *wives,* while the men never called themselves *husbands*—they were still men. And, as if they were as stupid as baboons, the other women seemed not to know what Shedemei was talking about when she pointed it out.

Of course, they *did* notice, at least the brighter ones did, but they chose not to make an issue of it because . . . because they were all becoming so *wifelike.* All these years in Basilica, where women did *not* have to submerge their identity in order to have husbands, and now, six weeks into the journey, and they were acting like nomadic tribeswomen. The coding for getting along without making waves must be so deep in our genes that we can never get it out, thought Shedemei. I wish I could find it, though. I'd dig it out with a trowel, I'd burn it out with a hot coal held in my bare fingers. Never mind the absurdity of dealing with genes with such blunt instruments. Her rage at the unfairness of things went beyond reason.

I didn't plan to marry, not for years yet, and even when I did I expected it would only be for a year, long enough to conceive, and then I'd dismiss the husband except for his normal rights with the child. I had no place for bonding with a man in my life. And when I *did* marry it would *not* have been with a weak-kneed semi-vertebrate archivist who allowed himself to be turned into the only servant in a company of lords.

Shedemei had entered this camp determined to make the best of a bad situation, but the more she saw of Zdorab the less she liked him. She might have forgiven him the way he *came* to this company— tricked by Nafai into carrying the Index out of the city, and then bullied into taking an oath to go into the desert with them. A man could be forgiven for behaving in an unmanly fashion during a time of stress and uncertainty and surprise. But when she got here she found that Zdorab had taken a role that was so demeaning she was ashamed to belong to the same species as him. It wasn't that he took upon himself all the tasks that no one else would do—covering the latrines, digging new ones, carrying away Issib's bodily wastes, doing the baking, the washing up. She rather respected someone who was willing to help—she certainly preferred that to the laziness of Meb and Obring, Kokor and Sevet and Dol. No, what made her feel such contempt for Zdorab was his *attitude* toward doing all that work. He didn't *offer* to do it, as if he had a right *not* to offer; he simply acted as if it were his natural *place* to do the worst jobs in the camp, and then performed his work so silently, so invisibly that soon they all took it for granted that the repulsive or unbearably tedious jobs were all Zdorab's.

He's a natural-born servant, thought Shedemei. He was born to be a slave. I never thought there was such a human creature, but there is, and it's Zdorab, and the others have chosen *him* to be my husband!

Why the Oversoul permitted Zdorab to have such easy access to her memory through the Index was beyond Shedemei's comprehension. Unless the Oversoul, too, wanted a servant. Maybe that's what the Oversoul loves best—humans who act like servants. Isn't that why we're all out here, to serve the Oversoul? To be arms and legs for her, so she can make her journey back to Earth? Slaves, all of us . . . except *me*.

At least, that's what Shedemei had been telling herself for all these weeks, until at last she realized that she, too, was beginning to fall into the servant category. It came to her today, as she carried water up from the stream for Zdorab to cook and wash with. She used to do this job with Hushidh and Luet, but now Luet was too weak from all her vomiting—she had lost weight, and that was bad for the child—and Hushidh was nursing her, and so it fell to Shedemei. She kept waiting for Rasa to notice that she was hauling the water all alone, for Rasa to say, "Sevet, Dol, Eiadh, put a yoke on your shoulders and haul water! Do your fair share!" But Rasa saw Shedemei carrying the water every day now, saw her carry the water right past where Sevet and Kokor were gossiping as they pretended to card camel hair and twine it into string, and Aunt Rasa never said a thing.

Have you forgotten who I am! she wanted to shout. Don't you remember that I am the greatest woman of science in Basilica in a generation? In ten generations?

But she knew the answer, and so she did not shout. Aunt Rasa *had* forgotten, because this was a new world, this camp, and what one might have been in Basilica or any other place did not matter. In this camp you were either one of the wives or you were not, and if you were not, you were nothing.

Which is why, today, with her work done, she went looking for Zdorab. Servant or not, he was the only available male, and she was sick of second-class citizenship in this infinitesimal nation. Marriage would symbolize her bowing to the new order, it would be another kind of servitude, and her husband would be a man for whom she had nothing but contempt. But it would be better than *disappearing.*

Of course, when she thought of actually letting him do his business with her body, it made her skin crawl. All she could think of was Luet throwing up all the time—that's the result of letting men treat you like a bank in which to deposit their feeble little sperm.

No, I don't really feel that way, thought Shedemei. I'm just angry. The sharing of genetic material is elegant and beautiful; it's been my life. The grace of it when lizards mate, the male mounting and clinging, his long slender penis embracing the female and searching out the opening, as deft and prehensile as a baboon's tale; the dance of the octopuses, arms meeting tip to tip; the shuddering of salmon as they drop eggs, then sperm, onto the bottom of the stream; it is all beautiful, all part of the ballet of life.

But the females always get to have some choice. The *strong* females, anyway, the *clever* ones. They get to give their ova to the male who will give them the best chance of survival—to the strong male, the dominant male, the aggressive male, the intelligent male—not to some cowering slave. I don't want my children to have slave genes. Better to have no children at all than to spend years watching them grow up acting more and more like Zdorab so that I'm ashamed of the very sight of them.

Which is why she found herself at the door of the Index tent, ready to walk in and propose a sort of semi-marriage to Zdorab. Because she felt such contempt for him, she intended it to be a marriage without sex, without children. And because he was so contemptible, she expected him to agree.

He was sitting on the carpet, his legs crossed, the Index on his lap, his hands together on the ball, his eyes closed. He spent every free moment with the Index—though that wasn't really all that much time, since so few of his moments were free. Often Issib was with him, but in late afternoons Issib took his watch at the garden—the long arm of his chair was quite effective at discouraging baboons from exploring the melons, and had been known to bat birds out of the air. It was Zdorab's time alone with the Index, rarely more than an hour, and the one respect that the company paid to him was to leave him alone then—provided that dinner was already cooking and somebody else didn't want to use the Index, in which case Zdorab was casually shunted aside.

Looking at him there, his eyes closed, she could almost believe that he was communing with the great mind of the Oversoul. But of course he didn't have the brains for that. He was probably just memorizing the main entries in the Index, so he could help Wetchik or Nafai or Luet or Shedemei herself locate some bit of information they wanted. Even with the Index, Zdorab was the pure servant.

He looked up. "Did you want the Index?" he asked mildly.

"No," she said. "I came to talk to you."

Did he shudder? Was that the quick involuntary movement of his shoulders? No, he was *shrugging,* that's what it was.

"I expected that you would, eventually."

"Everyone expects it, which is why I *haven't* come till now."

"All right then," he said. "Why now?"

"Because it's plain that in this company the unmarried people are going to slip further and further into oblivion as time goes on. *You* may be content with that, but I am not."

"I haven't noticed you slipping into oblivion," said Zdorab. "Your voice is listened to in councils."

"Patiently they listen," said Shedemei. "But I have no real influence."

"No one does," said Zdorab. "This is the Oversoul's expedition."

"I didn't think you'd grasp it," said Shedemei. "Try to think of this company as a troop of baboons. You and I are getting thrust farther and farther to the edges of the troop. It's only a matter of time until we are nothing."

"But that only matters if you actually care about being *something*."

Shedemei could hardly believe that he would put it into words that way. "I *know* that you have utterly no ambition, Zdorab, but I don't intend to disappear as a human being. And what I propose is simple enough. We just go through the ceremony with Aunt Rasa, we share a tent, and that's it. No one has to know what goes on between us. I don't want your babies, and I have no particular interest in your company. We simply sleep in the same tent, and we're no longer shunted to the edge of the troop. It's that simple. Agreed?"

"Fine," said Zdorab.

She had expected him to say that, to go along. But there was something else in the way he said it, something very subtle . . .

"You wanted it that way," she said.

He looked at her blankly.

"You wanted it this way all along."

And again, something in his eyes . . .

"And you're afraid."

Suddenly his eyes flashed with anger. "Now you think you're Hushidh, is that it? You think you know how everybody fits with everybody else."

She had never seen him show anger before—not even sullen anger, and certainly not a hot, flashing scorn like the one she was seeing now. It was a side of Zdorab that she hadn't guessed existed. But it didn't make her like him any better. It reminded her, in fact, of the snarling of a whipped dog.

"I really don't care," she said, "whether you wanted to have sex with me or not. I never cared to make myself attractive to men—that's what women do who have nothing *else* to offer the world than a pair of breasts and a uterus."

"I have always valued you for your work with genetics," said Zdorab. "Especially for your study of genetic drift in so-called stable species."

She had no answer. It had never occurred to her that anyone in this group had read, much less understood, any of her scientific publications. They all thought of her as someone who came up with valuable genetic alterations that could be sold in faraway places—that's what her relationship had been with Wetchik and his sons for years.

"Though I couldn't help but regret that you didn't have access to the genetic records in the Index. It would have clinched several of your points, having the exact genetic coding of the subject species as they came off the ships from Earth."

She was stunned. "The Index has information like *that?*"

"I found it a few years ago. The Index didn't want to tell me—I realize now because there are military applications of some of the genetic information in its memory—you can make plagues. But there are ways to get around some of its proscriptions. I found them. I've never been sure how the Oversoul felt about that."

"And you haven't told me till now?"

"You didn't tell me you were continuing your research," said Zdorab. "You did those papers years ago, when you were fresh out of school. It was your first serious project. I assumed you had gone on."

"This is the kind of thing you do with the Index? Genetics?"

Zdorab shook his head. "No."

"What, then? What were you studying just now, when I came in?"

"Probable patterns of continental drift on Earth."

"On *Earth!* The Oversoul has information that specific about Earth?"

"The Oversoul didn't *know* it had that information. I kind of had to coax it out. A lot of things are hidden from the Oversoul itself, you know. But the Index has the key. The Oversoul has been quite excited about some of the things I've found in its memory."

Shedemei was so surprised she had to laugh.

"I suppose it's amusing," said Zdorab, not amused.

"No, I was just . . ."

"Surprised to know that I was worth something besides baking breads and burying fecal matter."

He had struck so close to her previous attitude that it made her angry. "Surprised that *you* knew you were worth more than that."

"You have no idea what I know or think about myself or anything else. And you made no effort to find out, either," said Zdorab. "You came in here like the chief god of all pantheons and deigned to offer me marriage as long as I didn't actually *touch* you and expected me to accept gratefully. Well, I did. And you can go on treating me like I don't exist and it'll be fine with me."

She had never felt so ashamed of herself before in her life. Even as she had hated the way everybody else treated Zdorab as a nonentity, she had treated him that way herself, and in her own mind had given no thought for his feelings, as if they didn't matter. But now, having stabbed him with the contemptuousness of her proposal of marriage, she felt she had wronged him and had to make it right. "I'm sorry," she said.

"I'm not," said Zdorab. "Let's just forget everything about this conversation, get married tonight and then we don't have to talk again, agreed?"

"You really don't like me," said Shedemei.

"As if you have ever cared for one moment whether I or anyone else liked you, as long as we didn't interfere too much with your work."

Shedemei laughed. "You're right."

"It seems that we were both sizing each other up, but one of us did a better job of it than the other."

She nodded, accepting the chastening. "Of course we *will* have to talk again."

"Will we?"

"So you can show me how to get to that information from Earth."

"The genetic stuff?"

"And the continental drift. You forget that I'm carrying seeds to replenish lost species on Earth. I need to know the landforms. And a lot more."

He nodded. "I can show you that. As long as you realize that what I have are forty-million-year-old extrapolations of what *might* happen in another forty million years. It could be off by a lot—a little mistake early on would be hugely magnified by now."

"I *am* a scientist, you know," she said.

"And I'm a librarian," said Zdorab. "I'll be glad to show you how to get to the Earth information. It's sort of a back door—I found a path through the agricultural information, through pig breeding, if you can believe it. It helps to be interested in everything. Here, sit across from me and hold on to the Index. You *are* sensitive to it, I hope."

"Sensitive enough," said Shedemei. "Wetchik and Nafai both took me through sessions, and I've used it to look things up. Mostly I just use my own computer, though, because I thought I already knew everything that was on the Index in my field."

Now she was sitting across from him, and he set the Index between them and they both bowed forward to lean their elbows on their knees and rest their hands on the golden ball. Her hands touched his, but he did not move his hands out of the way, and there was no trembling; just cool, calm hands, as if he didn't even notice she was there.

She immediately caught the voice of the Index, answering Zdorab's inquiries, responding with names of paths and headings, subheads, and catalogs within the memory of the Oversoul. But as the names droned on she lost the thread of them, because of his fingers touching hers. Not that she felt anything for him herself; what bothered her was that he felt nothing at all for *her*. He had known for more than a month that she was going to be his wife, or at least that she was expected to; he had been watching her, certainly he had. And yet there was not even a glimmer of desire. He had accepted her proscription of sexual relations between them without a hint of regret. And he could endure her touch without showing the slightest sign of sexual tension.

Shedemei had never felt more ugly and undesirable than she did right now. It was absurd—until a few minutes ago she had had such contempt for this man that if he *had* expressed any sexual interest she would have been nauseated. But he was not the same man now, he was a much more interesting person, an intelligent person with a mind and a will, and while she didn't exactly feel a great flood of love or even sexual desire for him, she still felt enough new respect that his utter lack of desire for her was painful.

Another wound in the same old place, opening all the fragile scabs and scars, and she bled afresh at the shame of being a woman that no man wanted.

"You're not paying attention," said Zdorab.

"Sorry," she said.

He said nothing in reply. She opened her eyes. He was looking at her.

"Nothing," she said, brushing away the tear that clung to her lower eyelashes. "I didn't mean to distract you. Can we start again?"

But he didn't look back down to the Index. "It isn't that I don't desire you, Shedemei."

What, was her heart naked, that he could see right through her pretenses and see into the source of her pain?

"It's that I don't desire *any* woman."

It took her a moment for the idea to register. Then she laughed. "You're a zhop."

"That's really an old word for the human anus," said Zdorab quietly. "There are those who might be hurt at being called by such a name."

"But no one guessed," she said.

"I have made quite *sure* that no one would guess," said Zdorab, "and I'm putting my life in your hands telling *you.*"

"Oh, it's not as dramatic as that," she said.

"Two of my friends were killed in Dog Town," he said.

Dog Town was where men who didn't have a woman in Basilica had to live, since it was illegal for an unattached male to live or even stay overnight inside the city walls.

"One was set upon by a mob because they heard a rumor he was a zhop, a peedar. They hung him by the feet from a second-story window, cut off his male organs, and then slashed him to death with knives. The other one was tricked by a man who pretended to be . . . one of us. He was arrested, but on the way to prison he had an accident. It was the oddest sort of accident, too. He was trying to escape, and somehow he tripped and in the act of falling, his testicles somehow came off and got jammed down his throat, probably with a broomhandle or the butt of a spear, and he suffocated on them before anybody could come to his aid."

"They do *that?*"

"Oh, I can understand it perfectly. Basilica was a very difficult place for male humans. We have an innate need to dominate, you see, but in Basilica we had to deal with the fact that we had no control except as we had influence with a woman. The men living outside the walls in Dog Town were, by the very fact they didn't live inside, branded as second-raters, men that women didn't want. There was the constant imputation that Dog Town men weren't real men at all, that they didn't have what it took to please a woman. Their very identity as males was in question. And so their fear and hatred of *zhops*"—he said the word with scorching contempt—"reached peaks I've never heard of anywhere else."

"These friends of yours . . . were they your lovers?"

"The one who was arrested—he had been my lover for several weeks, and he wanted to continue, but I wouldn't let him because if we went on any longer people would begin to suspect what we were. To save our lives I refused to see him again. He went straight from me into the trap. So you see, Nafai and Elemak aren't the only ones who have killed a man."

The pain and grief he was showing seemed deeper than anything Shedemei had ever felt. For the first time she realized how sheltered her scholarly life had been. She had never had such a close connection with someone that she would feel their death *this* strongly, so long after. If it *was* long after.

"How long ago?"

"I was twenty. Nine years ago. No, ten. I'm thirty now. I forgot."

"And the other one?"

"A couple of months before I—left the city."

"He was your lover, too?"

"Oh, no—he wasn't like me that way. He had a girl in the city, only she wanted it kept secret so he didn't talk about it—she was in a bad marriage and was marking time till it ended, and so he never spoke about her. That's why the rumor started that he was a zhop. He died without telling them."

"That's—gallant, I suppose."

"It was stupid beyond belief," said Zdorab. "He never believed me when I told him how terrifying it was in Basilica for people like me."

"You told him what you are?"

"I thought of him as a man who could keep a secret. He proved me right. I kind of think—that he died in my place. So that I could be alive when Nafai came to take the Index out of the city."

It was so far beyond anything she had experienced—beyond anything she had imagined. "Why did you keep on living there, then? Why didn't you go to someplace that isn't so—terrible?"

"In the first place, while there are places that aren't so bad, I don't know of any place that I could actually get to that is actually safe for someone like me. And in the second place, the Index was in Basilica. Now that the Index is out of there, I hope the city burns to the ground. I only wish that Moozh had killed every one of the strutting men of Dog Town."

"The Index was that important to you, to make you stay?"

"I learned of its existence when I was a young boy. Just a story, that there was a magic ball that if you held it, you could talk to God and he would have to tell you the answer to any question you asked. I thought, How wonderful. And then I saw a picture of the Index of the Palwashantu, and it looked exactly like the image in my mind of the magic ball."

"But that's not evidence at all," said Shedemei. "That's a childhood dream."

"I know it. I knew it then," said Zdorab. "But without even meaning to, I found myself preparing. For the day when I'd have the magic ball. I found myself trying to learn the questions that it would be worth asking God to answer. And, still without meaning to, I found myself making choices that took me closer and closer to Basilica, to the place where the Palwashantu kept their sacred Index. At the same time, being a studious young man helped me conceal my—defect. My father would say, 'You need to set down the books now and then, go and find some friends. Find a girl! How will you ever marry if you never meet any girls?' When I got to Basilica I used to write to him about my girlfriends, so he felt much better, though he would tell me that the way Basilicans marry, for just a year at a time, was awful and against nature. He really didn't like things that were against nature."

"That must have hurt," said Shedemei.

"Not really," said Zdorab. "It *is* against nature. I'm cut off from that tree of life that Volemak saw, I'm not part of the chain—I'm a genetic dead end. I think I read once, in an article by a genetics student, that it was not unreasonable to suppose that homosexuality might be a mechanism that nature used to weed out defective genes. The organism could detect some otherwise unnoticeable genetic flaw, and this started a mechanism that caused the hypothalamus to remain stunted, causing us to be highly sexual beings but with an inability to fixate on the opposite sex. A sort of self-closing wound in the gene pool. We were, I think the article said, the *culls* of humanity."

Shedemei blushed deeply—a feeling she rarely had and didn't like. "That was student work. I never published it outside the scholarly community. It was speculation."

"I know," he said.

"How did you even find it?"

"When I realized that I was expected to marry you, I read everything you wrote. I was trying to discover what I could and could not tell you."

"And what did you decide?"

"That I'd better keep my secrets to myself. That's why I never spoke to you, and why I was so relieved that you didn't want me."

"And now you *did* tell me."

"Because I could see that it hurt you, the fact that I didn't want you. I hadn't planned on that. You didn't come across as someone who would ever want the love of a contemptible crawling worm like me."

Worse and worse. "Was I so obvious in my attitude?"

"Not at all," he said. "I deliberately cultivated my wormhood. I have worked hard to become the most unnoticeable, despicable, spineless being that anyone in this company will ever know."

And now, thinking of what happened to his two friends, she understood. "Camouflage," she said. "For you to remain single and not be suspected of what you are, you had to be sexless."

"Spineless."

"But Zdorab, we're not in Basilica now."

"We carry Basilica with us. Look at the men here. Look at Obring, for instance, and Meb—doomed by their particular lack of gifts to be at the bottom of any pecking order you can imagine. Both of them aggressive and yet cowardly—they long to be on top, but haven't the gumption to take on the big men and take them down. That's why they're doomed to follow men like Elemak and Volemak and even Nafai, though he's the youngest, because they can't take risks. Imagine the rage built up inside them. And then imagine what they'd do if they learned that I was the monstrous thing, the crime against nature, the unmanly man, the perfect image of what they fear that they are."

"Volemak wouldn't let them touch you."

"Volemak won't live forever," said Zdorab. "And I don't trust my secret to those who won't keep it."

"Are you that sure of me?" said Shedemei.

"I have put my life into your hands," said Zdorab. "But no, I'm not that sure of you. Like it or not, though, we've been forced together. So I've taken a calculated risk. To tell you, so that I have one person here that I don't have to lie to. One person who knows that what I seem to be is only a pretense."

"I'll make them stop treating you so—so unregardingly."

"*No!*" cried Zdorab. "No, you mustn't. Things will be better when we're married, for both of us—you were right about that. But you must let me remain invisible, as much as possible. I know best how to deal with what I am, believe me—you've never even imagined it, you said so yourself, so don't bull your way into my survival strategy and start trying to fix things because you'll end up killing me if you do. Do you understand that? You're brilliant, one of the finest minds of our time, but you know absolutely nothing about this situation, you are hopelessly ignorant, you will destroy anything you touch, so keep your *hands off.*"

He spoke with unbelievable vehemence and power. She had not imagined him capable of talking this way. She loathed it—being put in her place so firmly. But when she thought about it, instead of reacting viscerally, she realized that he was right. That for now, at least, she really *was* ignorant and the best thing she could do was let him continue to handle things however he thought best.

"All right," she said. "I'll say nothing, I'll do nothing."

"Nobody expects you to be *proud* to be married to me," said Zdorab. "In fact, they'll all think of it as a noble sacrifice you're making. So you won't lose any status by being my wife. It'll make you sort of heroic to them."

She laughed bitterly. "Zdorab, that's how I thought of it myself."

"I know," he said. "But that's not how *I* thought of it. I even hoped —imagine, having the right to be alone in the same tent with the keenest scientific mind on the planet Harmony—every night—with nothing to do but talk!"

It was so sweetly flattering and yet, for reasons she couldn't quite grasp yet, it was also vaguely tragic.

"That's a marriage, after a fashion, don't you think? We won't have babies like the others, but we'll have *thoughts.* You can teach me, you can *talk* to me about your work and if I don't understand I can promise you that I'll educate myself through the Index until I do. And maybe I can tell you some of the things I've found."

"I'd love that."

"We can be friends, then," he said. "That'll make ours a better marriage than most of *theirs.* Can you imagine what Obring and Kokor talk about?"

She laughed. "Do you think they actually *do?*"

"And Mebbekew and Dol, both playacting and secretly loathing each other."

"No, I don't think Dol hates Mebbekew, I think she actually *believes* the part she's playing."

"You're probably right. But they're pretty awful, don't you think? And *they're* going to have children!"

"Terrifying."

They laughed, long and loud, till tears ran down both their faces.

The door parted. It was Nafai.

"I clapped," he said, "but you didn't hear me. Then I realized you were laughing and I thought I might come in."

Both of them immediately grew sober. "Of course," said Zdorab.

"We were just discussing our marriage," said Shedemei.

Shedemei could see the relief spread over Nafai's face as if the shadow of a cloud had just passed. "You're going ahead and doing it," he said.

"We were just stubborn enough to want to wait until it was our idea," said Zdorab.

"I believe it," said Nafai.

"In fact," said Zdorab, "we ought to go tell Rasa and Volemak, and besides, you wanted to use the Index."

"I did, but not if you're not done with it," said Nafai.

"It'll still be here," said Shedemei, "when we're ready for it again." And in moments they were outside the tent, heading for—where?

Zdorab took her by the hand and led her to the cookfire. "Dol was supposed to be watching here," he said, "but she usually runs off—she needs her little nap, you know. It doesn't matter—I let Yobar touch the cookpot once, and he must have spread the word about how it feels, because the boons don't come anywhere near here now, even when it smells as good as this."

It *did* smell good.

"How did you learn to cook?"

"My father was a cook," said Zdorab. "It was the family business. He was good enough that he was able to afford to send me to Basilica to study, and I learned a lot of what he knew. I think he'd be proud of what I've been able to do in these piss-poor conditions."

"Except the camel cheese."

"I think I've found an herb that will improve it," said Zdorab. He lifted the lid of the cookpot. "I'm trying it tonight—there's twice as much cheese in this as usual, but I don't think anybody will mind." He lifted the stirring spoon and she saw how cheesily the liquid strung and glopped off of it.

"Mmm," she said. "Can't wait."

He detected the irony in her voice. "Well, it's not as though you don't have ample reason to be suspicious of anything that looks like it might taste like the cheese, but I figure that we've all had years of loving cheese and only a couple of months of hating it, so I should be able to win you all back if I do it right. And we *will* need the cheese—it's too good a source of animal protein for all the nursing mothers we're going to have."

"You've got it all planned out," she said.

"I have plenty of time to myself, to think," he said.

"In a way," she said, "you're really the leader of this group."

"In a way," he said, "you'd best not say that in front of anyone else or they'll be sure you've lost your mind."

"You're the one who decides what we'll eat and when, where we'll void ourselves, what we'll plant in the garden, and you guide us around in the Index—"

"But if I do it right, no one ever notices," he said.

"You take responsibility for us all. Without ever waiting to be told."

"So do all good people," he said. "That's what it *means* to be a good person. And I *am* a good person, Shedya."

"I know that now," she said. "And I should have known it before. I interpreted all you did as weakness—but I should have known that it was wisdom and strength, freely shared with all of us, even the ones who don't deserve it."

And now at last it was time for tears to come to *his* eyes. Just a little shining, but she saw, and knew that he knew that she saw. It occurred to her that their marriage would be far more than the sham she had intended. It could be a real friendship, between the two people who had least expected to find friends and companions on this journey.

He stirred the pottage and then replaced the lid, leaving the spoon hooked over the side.

"I imagine this is the safest place we could come and talk, if we didn't want to be disturbed or overheard," she said. "Because I don't imagine anybody ever comes near the cookfire if they can help it, for fear of being asked to work."

Zdorab chuckled. "I'll always be glad for your company while I'm working here, as long as you understand that cooking is an art, and I *do* concentrate on it sometimes while I do it."

"I hope I can tell you things so stimulating and interesting that you ruin the soup sometimes."

"Do it too often and they'll be pleading with us to get a divorce."

They laughed, and then again their laughter trailed off into silence.

"Why don't I go and tell Aunt Rasa?" said Shedemei. "She'll want to do up a wedding for us tonight, I'm sure. She'll be even more relieved than Nafai was."

"And we want it as public as possible," said Zdorab.

She understood. "We'll make sure everybody sees that we are definitely man and wife." And the unspoken promise: I will never tell anyone that we are *not* man and wife at all.

Shedemei turned to leave, to look for Rasa, but Zdorab's voice detained her. "Shedya," he said.

"Yes?"

"Please call me Zodya."

"Of course," she said, though in fact she had never heard his familiar name. No one used it.

"And another thing," he said.

"Yes?"

"Your student article—you were wrong. About genetic culls."

"I said it was just speculation . . ."

"I mean, I *know* you were wrong because I know what we are. In the ancient science, the Earth science that I've been exploring through the Index: it's not some internal mechanism of the human body. It's not genetic. It's just the level of male hormones in the mother's bloodstream at the time the hypothalamus goes through its active differentiation and growth."

"But that's almost random," said Shedemei. "It wouldn't mean anything, it would just be an accident if the level happened to be low for those couple of days."

"Not really random," said Zdorab. "But an accident all the same. It means nothing, except that we're born crippled."

"Like Issib."

"I think when Issib sees me walking, sees what I can do with my hands, that he would gladly trade places with me," said Zdorab. "But when I see him with Hushidh, and see her pregnant as she is, and see how the others have given him real respect because of that, how they recognize him as being one of *them*, then there are moments—only moments, mind you—when I would gladly trade places with *him*."

Shedemei impulsively squeezed his hand, though she was not one who was apt to make such affectionate gestures. It seemed appropriate, though. A friendly thing to do, and so she did it, and he squeezed back, so it was all right. Then she walked briskly away, looking for Lady Rasa.

And as she went, she thought: Who would have believed that finding out my husband-to-be is a zhop would come as such wonderful news, and that it would make me like him *more*. The world is truly standing on its head these days.

Alone in the Index tent after Shedemei and Zdorab left, Nafai did not hesitate. He took the Index—still warm from their hands—and held it close to him and spoke almost fiercely to the Oversoul. "All this time you've been telling me that Father's dream of the tree didn't come from you, but you never mentioned that you have his whole experience in your memory."

"Of course I do," said the Index. "It would be remiss of me not to record something as important as that."

"And you knew how much I wanted a dream from the Keeper of Earth. You *knew* that!"

"Yes," said the Index.

"Then why didn't you give me my father's dream!"

"Because it was your father's dream," said the Index.

"He told it—it isn't secret anymore! I want to *see* what he *saw!*"

"That's not a good idea."

"I'm tired of your deciding all the time what's a good idea and what isn't. You thought that killing Gaballufix was a *fine* idea."

"And it was."

"For *you*. You've got no blood on *your* hands."

"I have your memory of it. And I didn't do too badly by you out in the desert, when Elemak was plotting to kill you."

"So . . . you saved my life because you wanted my genes in our little gene pool."

"I'm a computer, Nafai. Do you expect me to save your life because I *like* you? My motives are a great deal more dependable than human emotions."

"I don't want any of that from you! I want a dream from the Keeper."

"Exactly. And having me put your father's dream into your mind is *not* the same thing as having a dream from the Keeper. It's merely having a memory report from me."

"I want to see those Earth creatures that the others have seen. The bats and angels."

"Which they *think* are Earth creatures."

"I want to have the taste of the fruit of the tree in my mouth!"

Even as he said it—as his lips silently formed the words, as the cry of anguish formed in his mind—Nafai knew that he was being childish. But he wanted it, wanted so badly to know what his father knew, to have seen what Luet saw, what Hushidh saw, what even General Moozh and Luet's strange mother, Thirsty, saw. He wanted to know, not what they told about it, but what it looked like, felt like, sounded like, smelled like, tasted like. And he wanted it enough that even if he was being childish, he had to have it, he *demanded* it.

And so the Oversoul, regarding it as undesirable to have the male it had earmarked as the eventual leader of the party be in such an anguished and therefore unpredictable state, gave him what he asked for.

It came on him all at once, as he held the Index. The darkness that Father had described, the man who invited him to follow, the endless walking. Only there was something more, something Father hadn't mentioned—a terrible disturbing feeling of wrongness, of unwanted, unthinkable thoughts going on in a powerful undercurrent. This wasn't just a wilderness, it was a mental hell, and he couldn't bear to stay in it.

"Skip past this part," he said to the Index. "Take me past here, get me out of here."

All at once the dream stopped.

"Not out of the *dream*," said Nafai impatiently. "Just skip the dull part."

"The Keeper sent the dull part as much as it sent anything else," said the Index.

"Skip to the end of it where things start happening."

"That's cheating, but I'll do it." Nafai hated it when the Index talked like that. It had learned that humans interpreted resistance followed by compliance as teasing, and therefore it now teased them as a way of simulating natural behavior. Only because Nafai knew that it was only a computer doing the teasing, and not a person, it was merely tedious, not fun. Yet when he complained about it, the Index merely replied that everybody else liked it and Nafai shouldn't be such a killjoy.

The dream came back again, and immediately he was plunged into the darkness, the walking, the back of the man leading him, and that awful mental undercurrent that was so painful and distracting. But then he could hear his Father's voice pleading with the man to tell him something, to lead him out of the place. Only it was not his Father's voice. It was a strange voice that Nafai had never heard before, except that in his mind he kept perceiving it as his *own* voice, only it was Father's thought that this voice was his own, not Nafai's, because his own voice sounded nothing like this and neither did Father's. Until finally Nafai realized that this was how his Father's voice sounded *to his father*. In a dream, of course, Father wouldn't hear the voice everyone else hears. He'd hear the voice he thinks he hears when he's speaking. Only it's not even *that* voice, it's much younger, it's the voice he learned to think of as his own when he formed his identity as a man. Deeper than his real voice, more manly, and younger.

Except Nafai couldn't shake the powerful conviction that, no matter how he analyzed it, this *was* his *own* voice, not Father's at all, though it was also completely wrong for his voice. And then Nafai realized that of course, if the Index was playing back for him his memory of Volemak's experience of the dream, it would be filtered through Volemak's consciousness, and therefore would have all of Volemak's attitudes inextricably tied to it.

That's what that undercurrent was of distracting, meaningless, confusing, frightening thoughts. It was Father's stream of consciousness, constantly evaluating and understanding and interpreting and responding to the dream. Thoughts that Father wouldn't even have been particularly conscious of himself, because they hadn't surfaced yet—including scraps of ideas like This is a dream, and This is from the Oversoul, and I'm really dead, and This is not a dream, and all kinds of contradictory thoughts jumbled up and piled on top of each other. When *Father* was having these thoughts they arose out of his own unconscious mind and his own will sorted them out, and the thoughts responded to his will, terminated a thought as soon as he wanted to move on to another. But in Nafai's mind, with all of this replayed, the thoughts did *not* respond to his own will, and in fact were superimposed on his own stream of consciousness. Therefore he was having twice as many under-the-breath thoughts as he usually had, and half of them did not respond to his will in any way, so it was at once confusing and terrifying, for his mind was out of control.

Father had given up talking to the man and now was crying out to the Oversoul, pleading with him. It was humiliating to hear the fear, the anxiety, the *whining* in Father's voice. He had *said* that he was pleading, but Nafai had never actually heard his father take this self-abasing tone with anyone, and it was like seeing his father going to the toilet or something disgusting like that, he *hated* seeing his father this way. I'm spying on him. I'm seeing him as he sees himself at his worst moments, instead of seeing the man he presents to the world, to his sons. I'm stealing his self from him, and it's wrong, it's a terrible thing for me to do. But then maybe I should know this about my father, how *weak* he is. I can't rely on him, a man who whimpers like this to the Oversoul, begging for help like a baby . . .

And then he thought of how he himself had pleaded with the Index to show him Father's dream and realized that, in their own minds, even the bravest and strongest of men must have moments like these, only no one ever saw them because they never acted on them outside their dreams and nightmares. I only know this about Father because I'm spying on him.

At that moment, just as he was about to ask the Index to stop the dream, it changed, and suddenly he was in the field that Father had described. At once Nafai wanted to find the tree, but of course he could only look where Father looked in the dream, and could only see it when Father saw it.

Father saw now, and it *was* beautiful, and a great relief after all the darkness and bleakness. Only Nafai not only felt his own relief, but also had Father's relief superimposed on his, and therefore it wasn't relief at all, but more tension, and more distraction and disorientation and it didn't help that, instead of walking to the tree in an orderly way, Father sort of just *went* to it. He *thought* of it as walking but he really just got closer suddenly and there he was at the tree.

Nafai felt Father's desire for the fruit, his delight at the smell of it, but because he was faintly nauseated by the movement toward the tree and faintly headachy because of the constant undercurrent of Father's thoughts, the smell did *not* arouse any desire in Nafai. Rather it made him sick. Father reached up and picked a fruit and tasted it. Nafai could feel that Father found it delicious, and for a moment, as the taste came into Nafai's mind, it *was* delicious, powerfully, exquisitely delicious in a way Nafai could hardly have imagined. But almost immediately the experience was subverted by Father's own reaction to it, his own associations with the taste and the smell of it; his reactions were so powerful, Father had been so overwhelmed by the taste that his feelings were out of control, and Nafai could not contain them. It was physically painful. He was terrified. He screamed to the Index to stop the dream.

It stopped, and Nafai let himself fall sideways onto the carpet, gasping and sobbing, trying to get the madness out of his mind.

And in a little while he was all right again, because the madness *was* gone.

"You see the problem I have communicating clearly with humans?" said the voice inside his head. "I have to frame my ideas so clearly and loudly, and even then most of them think that they're hearing nothing but their own thoughts. Only the Index makes it possible for real clarity of communication with most people. Except you and Luet—I can talk to the two of you better than anybody." The voice of the Index was silent for a moment. "I thought you were going to go insane there for a while. It wasn't pretty, what was happening inside your head."

"You warned me."

"Well, I didn't warn you of all *that* because I didn't know it would happen. I've never put one person's dream inside somebody else's head before. I don't think I'll do it again, either, even if somebody gets very upset because I said no."

"I agree with your decision," said Nafai.

"And you were very unkind to judge your father that way. He's a very strong and courageous man."

"I know. If you were listening in, you know that I figured that all out."

"I wasn't sure if you'd remember that. Human memory is very unreliable."

"Leave me alone," said Nafai. "I don't want to talk to you or anybody right now."

"Then let go of the Index. You can always walk away."

Nafai removed his hand from the Index, then rolled over, got to his knees, to his feet. His head reeled. He was dizzy and felt sick.

He staggered outside the tent. Issib and Mebbekew were there. "We're on our way to dinner," said Issib. "Did you have a good session with the Index?"

"I'm not hungry," said Nafai. "I don't feel well."

Mebbekew hooted. It sounded to Nafai very much like the pant-hoots of the baboons. "Don't tell me *Nafai's* going to try to get out of work by claiming to be sick all the time. But I guess it's worked so well for Luet that he figures it's worth a try, right?"

Nafai didn't even bother to answer Meb. He just staggered away, looking for his tent. I've got to sleep, he thought. That's what I need, to sleep.

Only when he got there and lay down on the bed, he realized he couldn't possibly sleep. He was too agitated, too nauseated, his head was swimming and he couldn't think but he also couldn't *stop* thinking.

So I'll go hunting, thought Nafai. I'll go out and find some small helpless animal and I'll kill it and tear its skin off and rip its guts out and I'm sure I'll feel better because that's the kind of man I am. Or maybe when the smell of the guts hits me I'll throw up and *then* I'll feel better.

No one saw him on the way out of camp—if they had seen him, walking so unsteadily and carrying a pulse, they probably would have stopped him. He crossed the stream and went up the hills on the other side. They never hunted in that direction because that was the side where the baboons slept in the cliffs and because if you went too far in that direction you'd get close enough to the villages in the valley called Luzha that you might run into somebody. But Nafai wasn't thinking clearly. He only remembered that once before he had been on the other side of the stream and something wonderful had happened, and right now he very much wanted for something wonderful to happen. Or to die. Whatever.

I should have waited, he said to himself over and over again, when he could think well enough to know what he was thinking. If the Keeper of Earth wanted to send me a dream, it would have sent me a dream. And if it didn't, I should have waited. I'm sorry. I just wanted to know for myself, but I should have waited. I can stand the waiting now, only now you'll never send me a dream, will you, because I cheated, just as the Index said, I cheated, and so I'm not entitled . . . in fact I'm worthless now, I've ruined my own brain by what I insisted the Oversoul do for me, and now I'm going to be sick in the head forever and neither you nor the Oversoul nor Luet nor anybody else will have any use for me and I might as well drop off the edge of a cliff somewhere and die.

It was sundown when he realized that he had no idea of where he was, or how far he had wandered. He only knew that he was sitting on a rock on the crest of a hill—in plain sight, if there were some bandit looking for someone to rob, or a hunter looking for prey. And even though he had his head in his hands and was looking at the ground, he was aware that someone was sitting across from him. Someone who had not yet said anything, but who was watching him intently.

Say something, said Nafai silently. Or kill me and get it over with.

"Oo. Oo-oo," said the stranger.

Nafai looked up then, for he knew the voice. "Yobar," he said.

Yobar wiggled a little and hooted a few more times, in delight, apparently, at having been recognized.

"I don't have anything for you to eat," said Nafai.

"Oo," said Yobar cheerfully. He was probably just grateful for someone to notice him, since he had been ostracized by the troop.

Nafai reached out a hand to him, and Yobar strode boldly forward and laid his forehand in Nafai's.

And in that moment, Yobar was not a baboon at all. Instead, Nafai saw him as a winged animal, with a face at once more fierce and more intelligent than a baboon's. The one wing flexed and stretched, but the other wing did not, for it was the hand that Nafai held in his own. The winged creature who had taken Yobar's place spoke to him, but Nafai couldn't understand his language. The creature—the angel, Nafai knew that's what it was—spoke again, only now Nafai understood, vaguely, that it was warning him of danger.

"What should I do?" asked Nafai.

But the angel looked around and became more agitated and then, seeming to be quite frightened, it let go of his hand and leapt skyward and flew, circling overhead.

Nafai heard a sound of something hard scraping over rock. He looked back down at the rocks around him and saw what had made the noise. A half dozen of a larger, fiercer creature. The rats from the dreams the others had had. They were heavier and stronger-looking than the baboons had been, and Nafai well knew from the stories of other desert travelers that baboons were far stronger than a full-sized man. The teeth were fierce, but the hands—for they were hands, not claws—looked terrible indeed, especially because many of them held stones and seemed prepared to throw them.

Nafai thought of his pulse. How many of them can I kill before they hit me with a stone and knock me down? Two of them? Three? Better to die fighting than to let them take me without any cost at all.

Better? Why would it be better? Bad enough that one should die. What's to be gained by killing more, except that they'd feel more justified in having slain me.

So he set down his pulse on the ground in front of him, and clasped his hands across his knees, and waited.

They waited also. Their arms were still poised to throw. The angel still circled overhead, a silent witness except for occasional high-pitched squeals.

Then, suddenly, Nafai realized he had something in his hand. He opened his hands and saw that he was holding a fruit. He recognized it immediately as one of the fruits of the tree of life. He lifted it to his lips and tasted it, and ah! It was as Father had said, as Nafai had tasted for just a moment before, the most exquisite sensation he could imagine feeling. Only this time there was no distraction, no confusion, no disharmony; he was at peace inside himself, and healed.

Without thinking, he took the fruit from his lips and offered it to the rat directly in front of him.

The rat looked down at his hand, then up at Nafai's face again, then down at the fruit.

Nafai thought of laying the fruit down and letting the rat pick it up himself, but then he realized that no, it would be wrong to let the fruit touch the ground, to let it be picked up like a rotting windfall. It should be taken from a hand. This fruit should always be taken from the tree itself, or from someone's hand.

The rat sniffed, moved forward, sniffed again. And then it took the fruit out of Nafai's hand and took it to its lips and bit down. The fruit squirted, and some of the juice of it struck Nafai in the face, but he hardly noticed, except to lick his lip where it ran. For he couldn't take his eyes off the rat. It was frozen in place, unmoving, the juice of the fruit dribbling from the sides of its mouth. Have I poisoned it? thought Nafai. Have I killed it somehow with this fruit? I didn't mean to.

No, the rat had not been poisoned, merely stunned by it. Now it began making urgent sounds in its throat, and it scurried to its nearest companion, who took the fruit from its mouth with its own teeth. And so that one fruit passed around the circle, each one taking it into its mouth directly from the mouth of the one before, all the way around the circle until it came back to the first one. And that one came forward and offered its mouth to Nafai, the remnant of the fruit still there, still visible.

Nafai's face was not built to a point the way the rats' faces were, and so he had to reach out and take the fruit with his hand. But he put it at once in his own mouth, dreading what it would taste like now, but knowing he must do it. To his relief the flavor of the fruit was unchanged. If anything, it was sweeter now, for having been shared by these others.

He chewed, he swallowed. Only then did they also swallow whatever juice and bits of fruit remained in their mouths.

They came forward and laid at his feet the stones they had been holding to use as weapons. The pile was a pyramid in front of him. Fourteen stones. Then they filed away among the rocks.

At once the angel swooped back down, circled around him, chirping madly, flapping and flapping, until it landed heavily on his shoulders and enfolded him in its wings.

"I hope this means you're happy," said Nafai.

In answer the angel said nothing, but flew away itself.

Then Nafai stood and saw that he was not on the crest of a rocky peak at all, but was in a field, beside a tree, and near him was a river, and beside the river a path with an iron railing. He saw all that his father had seen, including the building on the other side.

And then, when he expected the dream to end—for he knew it was a dream—it changed. He saw himself, standing in the midst of a huge multitude of people and angels and rats, and they were all watching a bright light coming down out of the sky. They had been waiting, he understood. They had all been waiting, and now it was here. The Keeper of Earth.

Nafai wanted to get nearer, to see the face of the Keeper of Earth. But the light was too dazzling. He could see that it had four limbs, just from the shape of it, four limbs and a head, but beyond that the light simply blinded him as if the Keeper were a small star, a sun too bright to look into without burning your eyes.

Finally Nafai had to close his eyes, squint them shut to relieve them from the pain of staring into the sun. When he opened them, though, he knew he would be close enough, he knew he would see the face of the Keeper.

"Oo."

It was Yobar's face he was staring into.

"Oo yourself," whispered Nafai.

"Oo-oo."

"It's almost dark," said Nafai. "But you're pretty hungry, aren't you?"

Yobar sat back on his haunches expectantly.

"Let's see if I can find anything for you."

It wasn't hard, even in the dusky light, because the hares on this side of the valley hadn't grown scarce yet. When full night came, Yobar was still tearing at the corpse, devouring every scrap of it, breaking open the skull with a rock to get at the soft brains. Yobar's hands and face were covered with blood.

"If you have any wit at all," said Nafai, "you'll get home fast with what's left of this meat and all the blood on you so some female will make friends with you and let you play with her baby so you can make friends with *it* and become a full-fledged member of the troop."

It was unlikely that Yobar understood him, but then he didn't have to. He was already trying to hide the body of the hare from Nafai, preparatory to stealing it and running away. Nafai made his life easier by turning a little bit away so that Yobar would seize the opportunity and run. He heard the scampering of Yobar's feet and said silently to him, Buy what you can with this hare's blood, my friend. I've seen the face of the Keeper of Earth, and it is you.

Then, regretting at once the disrespectful thought, Nafai spoke silently to the Keeper of Earth—or to the Oversoul, or to nobody, he didn't know. Thank you for showing me, he said. Thank you for letting me see what Father saw. What all the others saw. Thank you for letting me be one of those who know.

Now, if someone could help me find my way home.

Whether it was the Oversoul helping him or simply his own memory and tracking ability, he found his way home by moonlight. Luet had been worried—so had Mother and Father, and others too. They had put off Shedemei's and Zdorab's wedding, because it would be wrong to do that on a night when Nafai might be in danger. Now that he was back, though, the wedding could go on, and nobody asked him where he had gone or what he had been doing, as if they knew it was something too strange or wonderful or awful to be discussed.

Only later that night, in bed with Luet, did he speak of it. First of feeding Yobar, and then of the dream.

"It sounds like everyone was satisfied tonight," said Luet.

"Even you?" he asked.

"You're home," she said, "and I'm content."

6

Pulses

They stayed in their camp in the Valley of Mebbekew, by the River of Elemak, longer than they intended. First they had to wait for the harvest. Then, despite the anti-vomiting herbs that Shedemei learned about from the Index, Luet was so weakened from pregnancy that Rasa refused to let them begin the journey and risk her life. By the time Luet's morning sickness had ended and she had regained some strength, all three pregnant women—Hushidh, Kokor, and Luet—were large enough in the belly that traveling would have been uncomfortable. Besides, they had been joined in their pregnancy by Sevet, Eiadh, Dol, and Lady Rasa herself. None of them were as sick as Luet had been, but neither were any of them much disposed to mount camels and ride all day and then pitch tents at night and strike them in the morning while subsisting on hard biscuit and jerky and dried melon.

So they ended up staying in their camp for more than a year, till all seven babies were born. Only two of them had sons. Volemak and Rasa named their boy Oykib, after Rasa's father, and Elemak and Eiadh named their firstborn son Protchnu, which meant *endurance*. Eiadh made mention of the fact that only her husband, Elemak, was as manly as Volemak, to put a son in her as Volemak had sired nothing but sons.

By and large the others ignored her boasting and enjoyed their daughters.

Luet and Nafai named their little girl Chveya, because she had sewn them together into one soul. Hushidh's and Issib's daughter was the first birth of the new generation, and they named her simply Dza, because she was the answer to all the questions of their life. Kokor and Obring named their daughter Krasata, a name meaning *beauty* that had been rather in fashion in Basilica. Vas and Sevet named their daughter Vasnaminanya, partly because the name meant *memory*, but also because it was related to Vas's name; they called her Vasnya. And Mebbekew and Dol named their daughter Basilikya, after the city which they both still loved and dreamed of. Everyone knew that Meb meant his daughter's name to be a constant reproach to those who had dragged him from his proper home, so everyone picked up on the nickname Volemak thought of for her, and so called her Syelsika, meaning *country girl*. Of course this annoyed Meb, but he learned to stop protesting since it only caused the others to laugh at him.

Oykib and Protchnu, Chveya and Dza, Krasata, Vasnya, and Syelsika —on a cool morning more than a year after their parents had all come together in the Valley of Mebbekew, the babies were loosely wrapped in cool traveling clothes and laid in hammocks slung across their mothers' shoulders, so the babes could nurse during the day when they grew hungry. The women, except childless Shedemei, did none of the work of striking tents, though as the children grew they would soon be expected to resume their duties. And the men, strong now, tanned and hardened from a year's life and work in the desert, strutted a little before their wives, proud of what babies they had made together, full of their lofty responsibility to provide and care for wives and children.

All but Zdorab, of course, who was as quiet and unprepossessing as ever, with his wife still childless; the two seemed almost to disappear sometimes. They were the only members of the company unconnected to Rasa and Volemak by blood or marriage; they were the only childless ones; they were considerably older than any of the others of their generation except Elemak; no one would have said that they were *not* fully the equals of the rest of the company, but then, no one actually believed that they *were*, either.

As the company gathered to go, Luet, with Chveya asleep in her sling, carried an overripe melon on her shoulder down to where the baboon troop was pursuing its normal business. The baboons seemed agitated and jumpy, which was hardly surprising, considering the tumult up at the human camp. As Luet passed the perimeter of their feeding area, they kept glancing up at her, to see what she was doing. Some of the females approached, to see her baby—she had let them touch Chveya before, though of course she could never let them play with her the way they played with their *own* children; Chveya was far too fragile for their rough fondling.

It was a male, not a female, that Luet was looking for, and as soon as she moved away from the curious females, there he was—Yobar, the one who had been an outcast less than a year ago, and who now was best friends with the oldest daughter of the matriarch of the tribe; he had as much prestige as a male could get in this city of women. Luet brought the melon to where Yobar could see what she had. Then, turning slightly away so he wouldn't be too frightened, she cast it down on a rock and the melon burst open.

As she expected, Yobar jumped back, startled. When he saw that Luet was not afraid, however, he soon came closer to investigate. Now she could show him what she wanted him to see—the secret that they had so carefully kept from all the baboons during their year in this place. She reached down, picked up a fragment of rind with plenty of the meat of the fruit still clinging to it, and ate noisily.

The sound of her eating drew the others, but it was Yobar—as she had expected—who followed her example and began to eat. He made no distinction between fruit and rind, of course, and seemed to enjoy both equally. When he was full, he jumped around, hooting and frolicking, until others—especially young males—began to venture forward to try the fruit.

Luet slowly stepped back, then turned and walked away.

She heard footsteps padding behind her. She glanced back; Yobar was following her. She had not expected this, but then Yobar had always surprised her. He was intelligent and curious indeed, among animals whose intelligence was only a little short of the human mind, and whose curiosity and eagerness to learn were sometimes greater.

"Come if you will, then," said Luet. She led him upstream to the garden, where the baboons had long been forbidden to go. The last of the third crop of melons was still on the vine, some ripe, some not yet. He hesitated at the edge of the garden, for the baboons had long since learned to respect that invisible boundary. She beckoned to him, though, and he carefully crossed the edge into the garden. She took him to a ripe melon. "Eat them when they look like this," she said. "When they *smell* like this." She held the melon out to him, still attached to the vine. He sniffed it, shook it, then thumped it on the ground. With enough thumping, he broke it. Then he took a bite and hooted happily at her.

"I'm not done yet," said Luet. "You have to pay attention through the whole lesson." She held out another melon, this one not ripe, and though she let Yobar sniff it, she wouldn't let him hold it. "No," she said. "Don't eat these. The seeds aren't mature, and if you eat them when they look like this, you won't have a crop next year." She set the unripe melon down behind her, and pointed to the broken ripe melon in pieces around Yobar's feet. "Eat the ripe ones. Shedemei says the seeds will pass right through your digestive system unharmed, and they'll sprout right in your turds and grow quite nicely. You can have melons forever, if you teach the others to eat only the ripe ones. If you teach them to *wait.*"

Yobar looked at her steadily.

"You don't understand any of the words I'm saying," she said. "But that doesn't mean you don't understand the lesson, does it? You're a smart one. You'll figure it out. You'll teach the others before you move on to another troop, won't you? It's the only gift we can leave for you, our rent for using your valley this past year. Please take this from us, and use it well."

He hooted once.

She got up and walked away from him. The riding camels were ready for mounting now; they had been waiting for her. "I was just showing the garden to Yobar," she said. Of course Kokor rolled her eyes at that, but Luet hardly noticed—it was Nafai's smile, and Hushidh's nod, and Volemak's "Well done" that mattered.

On command, the camels lurched to their feet, burdened with tents and supplies, dryboxes and coldboxes full of seeds and embryos, and—above all—with not sixteen but twenty-three human beings now. As Elemak said only last night, the Oversoul had better lead them to their destination before the children get too big to ride with their mothers, or else it had better find them more camels along the way.

The first two days' travel took them northeast, along the same route they had taken from Basilica. It had been a year since they came that way, however, and almost nothing looked familiar—or at least nothing looked more familiar than anything else, since all grey-brown rocks and yellow-grey sand begin to look familiar after the first hour.

Mebbekew rode beside Elemak for a short way, late in the second afternoon. "We passed the place where you sentenced him to death, didn't we?"

Elemak was silent for a moment. Then: "No, we won't pass it at all."

"I thought I saw it."

"You didn't."

They rode in silence for a while more.

"Elemak," said Mebbekew.

"Yes?" He didn't sound as if he was enjoying the conversation.

"Who could stop us if we simply took our share of the tents, and three days' supplies, and headed north to Basilica?"

Sometimes it seemed to Elemak that Mebbekew's shortsightedness bordered on stupidity. "Apparently you've forgotten that we have no money. I can assure you that being poor in Basilica is even worse than being poor out here, because in Basilica the Oversoul won't give a lizard's tit for your survival."

"Oh, and we've been so well taken care of *here!*" said Meb scornfully.

"We were at a well-watered location for more than a year and not *once* did any travelers or bandits or eloping couples or families on holiday ever come near us."

"I know, we might as well have been on another planet. An uninhabited one! I can tell you, when Dolya was too pregnant to move, the baboon females were starting to look good to me."

Never had Mebbekew seemed more useless than now. "I'm not surprised," said Elemak.

Meb glared at him. "I was joking, pizdook."

"I wasn't," said Elemak.

"So you've sold your soul, is that it? You're Daddy's little boy now. Nafai senior."

Mebbekew's resentment of Nafai was only natural—since Nafai had shown him up so many times. But Elemak had long since decided to endure Nafai, at least as long as he stayed in his place, as long as he was *useful.* That's all Elemak really cared about now—whether a person contributed to the survival of the group. Of Elemak's wife and child. And it wouldn't hurt for Mebbekew to recall exactly how much *more* useful Nafai was than Meb himself. "We've lived a year together," said Elemak. "You've eaten meat that Nafai killed during every week of that year, and you still think he's nothing more than Father's favorite?"

"Oh, I know he's more than just that," said Mebbekew. "Everyone knows it. In fact, most of us realize that he's worth more than *you.*"

Mebbekew must have seen something in Elemak's face, then, for he dropped back and stayed in line directly behind Elemak for some time.

Elemak knew that Meb's little insult was meant to enrage him—but Elemak was not going to play along. He understood what Mebbekew wanted: out of his marriage, away from the crying of his baby, and back to the city, with its baths and commodes, its cuisine and its art, and, above all, its endless supply of flatterable and uncomplicated women. And the truth was that if he went back, Mebbekew would probably do as well as ever in Basilica, with or without money; and Dol, too, would certainly find a good living there, being an almost-legendary child actress. For the two of them, Basilica would be a lot better than anything that lay ahead of them in the foreseeable future.

But that issue is closed, thought Elemak. It was closed when the Oversoul made such a fool of me. The message was clear—try to kill Nafai and you'll only be made to bumble and fumble around like a half-wit, unable even to tie a knot. And now it wouldn't be Nafai he'd have to overcome in order to change their destination, it would be Father. No, there was no escape for Elemak. And besides, Basilica had nothing for *him.* Unlike Meb, he wasn't content to hop from bed to bed and live off any woman who'd take him in. He needed to have stature in the city, he needed to know that when he spoke, men listened. Without money, there was little hope of *that.*

Besides, he loved Eiadh and was proud of little Proya, and he loved the desert life in a way that no one else, not even Volemak, could ever understand. And if he went back to Basilica, Eiadh would eventually not renew his marriage contract. He would again be in the unmanly position of having to look for a wife solely in order to maintain himself in the city. That would be unbearable—*this* was how men were meant to live, secure with their women, secure with their children. He had no desire to break up his family *now.* He had stopped dreaming of Basilica, or at least had stopped wishing for it, since the only kind of life worth living there was out of reach to him.

Only Meb and Dolya still had fantasies of returning. And, useless as they both were, it wouldn't hurt the company one bit to let them go.

So as Elemak and his father were choosing the site for that night's camp, he broached the subject. "You know that Meb and Dolya still want to go back to Basilica."

"They have so little imagination, I'm not surprised," said Volemak. "Some people only have one idea in their lives, and so they can hardly bear to let it go."

"You know that they're also nearly worthless to us."

"Not as worthless as Kokor," said Father.

"Yes, well, it's hard to compete with *her*."

"None of them are *completely* worthless," said Father. "They may not do their share of work, but we need their genes. We need their babies in our community."

"Our life would be much easier . . . a lot less conflict and annoyance . . . if—"

"No," said Volemak.

Elemak seethed. How dare Father not even let him finish his sentence.

"It's not by my choice," said Volemak. "I'd let anyone go back who wanted to, if it were up to me. But the Oversoul has chosen this company."

Elemak stopped paying attention almost as soon as Father mentioned the Oversoul. It always meant that the reasonable part of the discussion was over.

When they camped for the night, Elemak determined that during his watch, if Meb and Dolya decided to slip away, he'd make sure he didn't happen to notice them. It would be easy enough to find the way —the desert wasn't all that challenging through here, and they'd have the best chance of the whole journey to return to civilization. Which wasn't that good a chance, admittedly—there would be as great a risk of bandits as ever. Perhaps more, now that Moozh ruled in Basilica and would drive rough and uncivilized men from the city. Maybe the Oversoul would watch out for them and help them get back to Basilica—and maybe not. Whatever happened, Elemak wouldn't block their attempt, if they made one.

But they didn't. Elemak even stood a longer watch than usual, but they never slipped out of their tent, never tried to steal a camel or two. Elemak finally woke Vas for his watch and then went to bed, full of fresh contempt for Meb. If it had been *I* who wanted to leave the group and live somewhere else, I would have taken my wife and baby and *left*. But not Mebbekew. He takes *no* for an answer far too easily.

At midmorning on the third day of travel, they reached the point where, to return to Basilica, they would have traveled north. Elemak recognized the spot; so, of course, did Volemak. But no one else did; no one realized that when they continued eastward instead of turning straight north, they were closing their last hope of restoring something like their old life.

Elemak didn't feel at all sad about it. He wasn't like Mebbekew—his life had centered in the desert all along. He had only returned to Basilica in order to sell his goods and find a wife, though of course he always enjoyed the city and thought of it as home. It's just that the idea of *home* had never meant that much to him—he didn't get homesick or nostalgic or teary-eyed about it. Not till Eiadh gave birth and he held Proya in his arms and heard the boy's firm loud cry and saw his smile. And then home, to him, was the tent where Eiadh and Proya slept. He had no need of Basilica now. He was too strong in himself to hunger for a particular city the way Meb did.

But if this caravan was going to be Elemak's world for the next few years, he was determined to make sure his position in this small polity was as dominant and important as possible. In the valley, where Zdorab's garden brought in half the food and Nafai was as good at hunting as Elemak himself, there was no way for Elemak to fully emerge, secure in his position of leadership. Now, though, on camelback again, even Father deferred to Elemak's judgment on many, many issues, and while the Oversoul chose their general direction, it was Elemak who determined their exact path. He could look back over the company and find Eiadh, her eyes on him whenever she wasn't busy with nursing the baby. The journey was reminding her of how essential he was to the survival of the whole enterprise, and he loved the pride she took in that.

The Oversoul had told Father that if they found a good safe route and had plenty of supplies, sixty days of steady traveling would bring them to their destination. But of course, sixty days of traveling was out of the question. The babies could never endure that long a stretch of heat and dryness and instability. No, they would have to find another secure place and rest again. And perhaps another after that. And in each place, they would probably have to stay long enough to put in a crop and harvest it to feed them on the next leg of their journey. A year. A year in each place, perhaps three years to make a sixty-day journey. Yet through it all, it would be Elemak truly leading them, and by the end of it everyone should be turning to me for leadership, with Father reduced to nothing more than what he ought to be—a wise old counselor. But not the true leader, not anymore.

That will be me, by right. If I decide then that the Oversoul's destination is the place where I want to lead the group, then that's where I'll lead them, and they'll get there safely and in good time. If I decide otherwise, of course, then the Oversoul can go hang.

The Nividimu River wasn't a seasonal river—it rose from natural springs in the rugged Lyudy Mountains, which were high enough to catch snow in the winter. But the flow was never much, and when the river dropped steeply down the Krutohn Valley and reached the low, hot, dry desert, it sank into the sand and disappeared many kilometers before reaching the Scour Sea.

It was because of the Nividimu that the great north-south caravan trail climbed steeply up into the Lyudy Mountains and then followed the river down, almost to the point where it disappeared. It was the most dependable source of drinkable water between Basilica on the north and the Cities of Fire to the south. Perhaps a dozen caravans a year passed along the banks of the Nividimu, and so it was almost to be expected that the Index would instruct them to make camp for a week in the foothills of the Lyudy Mountains while a northbound caravan with a heavy military escort made its way up the valley and then down the twisting road out of the mountains.

The worst thing about the wait was that they couldn't make any fires. The military escort, the Index told them, was nervous and eager to find an enemy. Smoke would be taken as a sign of bandits, and the soldiers wouldn't wait to find out otherwise before slaughtering them all. So they ate the most miserable traveling rations and sat around getting annoyed with each other, waiting for the day that Volemak told them that the Index had decided they could leave.

It was on the second day, as Elemak and Vas were hunting together —for Vas had some talent as a tracker of animals—that they lost the first pulse. Vas probably shouldn't have been carrying one, but he asked for it, and it would have been too humiliating to forbid him to have one. Besides, there was always the chance that he'd surprise a dangerous beast of prey that had tracked the same quarry, and then he'd need the pulse to defend himself.

Vas was not usually clumsy. But as he crabwalked along a narrow ledge over a defile, he stumbled, and as he caught himself the pulse slipped out of his hand. It bounced on a rocky outcropping, and then sailed out into space and on into a canyon. Vas and Elemak never heard it strike bottom. "It could have been me," he kept saying, when he told the story that night.

Elemak didn't have the heart to tell him that it might have been better for everyone if it *had* been him. They only had four pulses, after all, and no way of getting more—eventually they would lose their ability to recharge themselves from sunlight, which was why Elemak was so careful about keeping two of them hidden away in a dark place. With one pulse gone, now one of the hidden ones had to come out and into use for hunting.

"Why were you hunting, anyway?" asked Volemak, who understood what the loss of the pulse might mean in the future. He directed his question at Elemak, which was proper, since it was Elemak's decision to take two pulses out into the desert that day.

Elemak answered as coldly as if he thought Volemak had no right to challenge his decision. "For meat," he said. "The wives can't nurse properly on hard biscuits and jerky."

"But since we can't cook the meat, what did you expect them to do, eat it raw?" asked Volemak.

"I thought I could sear the meat with the pulse," said Elemak. "It would be rare, but . . ."

"It would also be a waste of power that we can ill afford," said Volemak.

"We need the meat," said Elemak.

"Should I have jumped after the pulse?" asked Vas, nastily.

"Nobody wants *that*," said Elemak scornfully. "This isn't about *you* anymore."

Hushidh watched the conversation in silence, as she usually did when there was conflict, seeing how the threads connecting them seemed to change. She knew that the lines she saw between people were not real, that they were simply a visual metaphor that her mind constructed for her—a sort of hallucinatory diagram. But their message about relationships and loyalties and hatreds and loves was real enough, as real as the rocks and sand and scrub around them.

Vas was the anomaly of the group and had been all along. No one hated him, no one resented him. But no one loved him, either. There was no great loyalty binding anyone to him—and none binding him to anybody else, either. Except the strange bond between him and Sevet, and the even stranger one between him and Obring. Sevet had little love or respect for her husband Vas—theirs had been a marriage in name only, for convenience, with no particular bond of loyalty between them, and no great love or friendship, either. But he seemed to feel something very powerful toward her, something that Hushidh did not understand, had never seen before. And his bond with Obring was almost the same, only a bit weaker. Which should not have been the case, since Vas had no reason to be closely tied to Obring. After all, hadn't Obring been the one who was caught in bed with Sevet the night that Kokor surprised them and almost killed her sister? Why should Vas feel a strong connection to Obring? Its strength—which Hushidh recognized by the thickness of the cord she saw connecting them—rivaled the strength of the strongest marriages in the company, like the one between Volemak and Rasa, or what Elemak felt toward Eiadh, or the growing bond between Hushidh herself and her beloved Issib, her devoted and sweet and brilliant and loving Issib, whose voice was the music underlying all her joy . . .

That, she knew, was not what Vas felt toward Sevet or Obring—and toward everyone else he seemed to feel almost nothing. Yet why Sevet and Obring, and no one else? Nothing connected *them* except their one-time adultery . . .

Was *that* the connection? Was it the adultery itself? Was Vas's powerful link with them an obsession with their betrayal of him? But that was absurd. He had known of Sevet's affairs all along; they had an easy marriage that way. And Hushidh would have recognized the connection between them if it had been hate or rage—she had seen plenty of *that* before.

Even now, when Vas should have been connected to everyone in the company by a thread of shame, of desire to make amends, to win approval, there was almost nothing. He didn't care. Indeed, he was almost satisfied.

"We could more easily have afforded the power to cook the meat," said Sevet, "back when we had all four pulses."

It astonished Hushidh that Vas's own wife would bring up Vas's culpability.

But it was no surprise when Kokor followed her sister and pounced even more directly. "You might have watched your step in the first place, Vas," she said.

Vas turned and regarded Kokor with mild disdain. "Perhaps I should have learned about working carefully and efficiently by following *your* example."

Quarrels like this started far too easily and usually went on far too long. It didn't take a raveler like Hushidh to know where this argument would lead, if it was allowed to continue. "Drop it," said Volemak.

"I'm not going to take the blame for our having no cooked meat," said Vas mildly. "We still have three pulses and it's not my fault that we can't light fires."

Elemak put a hand on Vas's shoulder. "It's me that Father holds responsible, and rightly so. It was my misjudgment. There should never have been two pulses on the same hunting trip. When we blame *you* for our lack of meat, you'll know it."

"Yes, we'll start eating *you*," said Obring.

It was funny enough that several people laughed, if only to release the tension; but Vas did not appreciate the joke's having come from Obring. Hushidh saw the odd connection between them flare and thicken, like a black hawser mooring Vas to Obring.

Hushidh watched, hoping that they might quarrel just long enough for her to understand what it was between them, but at that moment Shedemei spoke up. "There's no reason we can't eat the meat raw, if it's from a fresh kill and the animal was healthy," she said. "Searing the outside a little just before eating it would help kill any surface contamination without using much power. We have a good supply of antibiotics if someone *does* get sick, and even when we run out of *those*, we can make fairly adequate ones from available herbs if we need to."

"Raw meat," said Kokor in disgust.

"I don't know if I *can* eat it," said Eiadh.

"You just have to chew it more," said Shedemei. "Or cut it into finer pieces."

"It's the *taste* of it," said Eiadh.

"It's the *idea* of it," said Kokor, shuddering.

"It's only a psychological barrier," said Shedemei, "which you can easily overcome for the good of your babies."

"I don't know why someone without a baby should be telling the *rest* of us what's good for us," snapped Kokor.

Hushidh saw how Kokor's words stung Shedemei. It was one of Hushidh's most serious worries about their company, the way that Shedemei was becoming more and more isolated from the women.

Hushidh talked about it with Luet rather often, and they had been doing their best to deal with it, but it wasn't easy, because much of the barrier was in Shedemei herself—she had persuaded herself that she didn't *want* children, but Hushidh knew from the way Shedemei focused so intently on all the babies in the group that unconsciously she judged her own value by the fact that she had no children. And when some shortsighted, unempathic little birdbrain like Kokor threw Shedemei's childlessness in her face, Hushidh could almost see Shedemei's connections with the rest of the group dropping away.

And the silence after Kokor's remark didn't help. Most of them were silent because that's how one responded to unspeakable social clumsiness—one gave it just a long enough silence to serve as a rebuke to the offensive one, and then one went on as if it had not been said. But Hushidh was sure that was not how *Shedya* interpreted the silence. After all, Shedya was not well versed in high manners, and she was also relentlessly aware of her childlessness, so to her the silence no doubt meant that everyone *agreed* with Kokor, but was too polite to say so. Just one more injury, one more scar on Shedemei's soul.

If it were not for the intense friendship between Shedemei and Zdorab, and the much slighter friendship that Luet and Hushidh had cultivated with Shedya, and Shedya's great love and respect for Rasa, the woman would have no positive connection with the rest of the company at all. It would be nothing but envy and resentment.

It was Luet who finally broke the silence. "If meat is what our babies need, then of course we'll eat it seared, or even raw. But I wonder— are we so close to the edge, nutritionally, that we can't go a *week* without meat?"

Elemak looked at her coldly. "You can treat *your* baby as you want. Ours will always suckle on milk that has been freshened with animal protein within three days."

"Oh, Elemak, do I *have* to eat it?" asked Eiadh.

"Yes," said Elemak.

"It'll be fine," said Nafai. "You'll never notice the difference."

They all turned to look at him. His remark was quite outrageous. "I think I can tell whether meat is raw or cooked, thank you," said Eiadh.

"We're all here because we're more or less susceptible to the Oversoul," said Nafai. "So I just asked if the Oversoul could make the meat taste acceptable to us. Make us *think* that there's nothing wrong with it. And it said that it could do that, if we didn't try to resist it. So if we don't dwell on the fact that we're eating raw meat, the Oversoul can influence us enough that we won't really be aware of the difference."

No one answered for a moment. Hushidh could see that Nafai's almost casual relationship with the Oversoul was quite unnerving to some of them—not least to Volemak himself, who only spoke to the Oversoul in solitude, or with the Index.

"You asked the Oversoul to *season our food?*" asked Issib.

"We know from experience that the Oversoul is good at making people stupid," said Nafai. "You went through it with me, Issya. So why not have the Oversoul make us just a little stupid about the taste of the meat?"

"I don't like the idea of the Oversoul messing with my mind," said Obring.

Meb looked at Obring and grinned. "Don't worry," he said. "I'm sure you can be adequately stupid without help."

The next day, when Nafai brought home a nolyen—a small deerlike creature, barely a half-meter from the shoulder to the ground—they cut it up and seared the meat and then ate it, rather gingerly, until they realized that either raw meat wasn't so bad or the Oversoul had done a good job of making them insensitive to the difference. They'd get by without fire whenever they had to.

But the Oversoul couldn't give them a new pulse to replace the lost one.

They lost two more pulses crossing the Nividimu. It was a stupid, unnecessary loss. The camels were reluctant to make the crossing, even though the ford was wide and shallow, and there was some jostling as they were herded across. Still, if all the loads had been competently and carefully tied in place, none of them would have come loose, none would have spilled their contents into the ice-cold water.

It took a few minutes before Elemak realized that this was the camel that carried two of the pulses; until then he had concentrated on getting the rest of the camels across before trying to retrieve the load. By the time he found the pulses, in a poke, wrapped in cloth, they had been immersed for a quarter of an hour. Pulses were durable, but they had not been meant for use under water. Their seals had been penetrated and the mechanism inside would corrode rapidly. He saved the pulses, of course, in the hope that perhaps they would *not* corrode, though he knew the chance of that was slim.

"Who packed this camel?" Elemak demanded.

No one seemed to recall having packed it.

"That's the problem," said Volemak. "The camel obviously packed itself, and it wasn't good with the knots."

The company laughed nervously. Elemak whirled on his father, prepared to castigate him for making light of a serious situation. When he met Volemak's gaze, however, he paused, for he could see that Volemak was taking things very seriously indeed. So Elemak nodded to his father and then sat down, to show that he was going to let Volemak handle it.

"Whoever loaded this camel knows his responsibility," said Volemak. "And finding out who it is will be very simple—I have only to ask the Index. But there will be no punishment, because there's nothing to be gained by it. If I ever feel a need, I will reveal who it was whose carelessness cost us our security, but in the meantime you are safe in your cowardly refusal to name yourself."

Still no one spoke up.

Volemak said no more, but instead nodded toward Elemak, who got up and held the last pulse in front of him. "This is the pulse we have used *most,*" he said. "Therefore this is the one whose charge is least durable, and yet it's all we have to bring us meat. It *could* last a couple of years—pulses have lasted that long before—but when this one is no longer workable, we have no other."

He walked to Nafai and held out the pulse to him. Nafai took it gingerly.

"You're the hunter," said Elemak. "You're the one who'll make best use of it. Just make sure you take care of it. Our lives and the lives of our children depend on how you fulfil this duty."

Nafai nodded his understanding.

Elemak turned to the others. "If anyone sees that the pulse is in any danger whatever, you must speak or act at once to protect it. But except for such a case, no one but Nafai is to touch the pulse for any reason. We'll no longer use it even to sear the meat—what meat we eat during dangerous passages, we'll eat raw. Now, let's get down this valley before we're discovered here."

By late afternoon they were at the place where caravans either went on south, into the inhabited valleys where the cities of Dovoda and Neeshtchy clung to life between the desert and the sea, or southeastward into the Razoryat Mountains, and then on down into the northern reaches of the Valley of Fires. Volemak led them up into Razoryat. But it occurred to more than one of them that if they went south into Dovoda or Neeshtchy, there would be more pulses they could buy, and decent food, for that matter. And above all, other faces, other voices. Hardly a one of them that didn't wish they could, at the very least, visit there.

But Volemak led them on up into the hills, where they camped that night without a fire, for fear it would be seen by some dweller in the distant cities.

It was slow travel, from then on, for the Index warned Volemak that there were three caravans coming north through the Valley of Fires, two of them from the Cities of Fire and another from the Cities of the Stars, even farther to the south. To most of them those were names out of legend, cities even older and more storied than Basilica. Tales of ancient heroes always seemed to begin, "Once upon a time in the Cities of the Stars," or "Here is how things were in the old days, in the Cities of Fire." They hoped, many of them: Perhaps that's where the Oversoul is taking us, to the great ancient cities of legend.

To avoid the caravans, however, they had to travel away from the road. In the desert that had been easy enough—the road was barely distinguishable from the rest of the desert, and it made little difference what path, precisely, one followed. But here it mattered a great deal, for the terrain was strange, and more difficult and confusing than in any other place in Harmony. They came down out of the mountains and saw at once that it was a greener place, with grass almost everywhere, and vines, and bushes, and even a few trees. It was also rocky and craggy, and the land was strangely stepped, as if someone had pushed together a thousand tables of different sizes and heights, so that every surface was flat, but no two surfaces met at a level. And between the grassy tables were cliffs, some only a meter or so high, but some towering a hundred meters, or five hundred.

And the strangeness grew even greater as they moved down into the Valley of Fires, for there were places where vents in the earth or cracks in a cliff gave off remarkable stenches. Most of them made faces and tried to breathe through their mouths, but Elemak and Volemak took the stinks very seriously indeed, often finding circuitous routes that avoided the vent where the gas was coming from. Only when Zdorab discovered that the Index could provide them with immediate spectroscopic analysis of the gas, at least during daylight, were they able to be sure which gases—and therefore which stinks—were safe to breathe.

Even more frightening—though Elemak assured them that it was much safer—were the smokeholes and the open flames. They would see them from miles away, either thick columns of smoke or bright flames, and they learned to bend their course toward them, especially after Shedemei assured them that they would certainly not explode. When they camped near the open flames, they used them to cook their meat and even bake fresh bread, though only Zdorab, Nafai, and Elemak were willing to do the actual cooking, since it involved running near enough to the flames to leave the meat and the loaves where there was enough heat to cook flesh—which, of course, meant that the heat could cook the cooks if they didn't get out fast enough. They would all help dress the meat that Nafai had killed, put it on griddles, and then cheer madly as Nafai, Zdorab, and Elemak, each in turn, ran toward the fire, set down a griddle of meat, and then ran back to cooler air. Fetching the meat was even harder, of course, since it took longer to pick up the hot griddles than to set down the cool ones, and sometimes when they came back their clothes were smoking.

"It's only our sweat steaming," Nafai insisted, when Luet announced she *preferred* to have her meat raw and keep her husband alive.

But there weren't *that* many fires that were usable, since they were not often located near sources of water, and as often as not they ate cold food.

It was a place of glorious beauty, the Valley of Fires, but there was also something frightening about it, to be confronted at every turn by evidence of the terrible forces that moved inside the planet they lived on—forces strong enough to lift solid rock hundreds of meters straight up in the air.

Glorious, frightening, and also inconvenient, they realized, when they came to a place where the route they had chosen funneled them into a cul-de-sac—a deep, hot lake, surrounded by five-hundred-meter cliffs on both sides. There was no getting across the lake, and no getting around it either. They would have to backtrack several days' journey, Volemak and Elemak decided, and choose another route even farther from the regular caravan roads, and much closer to the sea.

"Couldn't the Oversoul have seen *this?*" asked Mebbekew, rather caustically.

"The Index showed this lake," said Volemak. "That's why we came this way. What the Oversoul could not tell us was that there was no way around it on either side."

"Then the last three days of traveling are *wasted?*" Kokor whined.

"We've seen things that aren't even dreamed of in Basilica," Lady Rasa answered.

"Except in *nightmares,*" said Kokor.

"Some artists have been known to take sights like these and turn them into song," said Rasa. "Which reminds me—we've heard neither you nor Sevet sing this whole year and more, except when you sing to your babies. Nor Eiadh, for that matter—she never had a chance to try her career as my daughters did, but she has the sweetest voice."

Hushidh could have told her to save her breath—there would be no singing until something changed among the women. It was the old quarrel between Sevet and Kokor, of course. Sevet either could not sing anymore or chose not to, all as a result of the damage Kokor did by striking her on the larynx when she caught her in bed with Obring. And as long as Sevet wasn't singing, Kokor dared not sing—she feared Sevet's vengeance if she did. And Eiadh was hopelessly intimidated by the two older girls, who had been quite famous in Basilica, especially Sevet. Kokor had made it clear that if *she* couldn't sing, she didn't want to hear Eiadh's wretched little voice like a mockery of music. Which was unfair—Eiadh *did* have talent, and the very thinness of her voice might have been called bell-like purity if someone besides Kokor had been the critic. But whenever Eiadh did try to sing, Kokor made such a show of grimacing and *enduring* that Eiadh soon lost heart and never tried again. So there would be no songs in their company about the grandeur and majesty of the Valley of Fires.

There was another kind of poetry, though, and another kind of artist, and Hushidh and Luet were the audience as Shedemei rhapsodized about the forces of nature. "Two great landmasses, once a single continent but now divided," she said. "They pressed against each other like your two hands laid side by side on a table. But then they began to rotate in opposite directions, with the center right where your thumbs touch. Now they press toward each other at the fingertips, crushing into each other, even as they pull away from each other at the heels of the hands."

Shedemei was explaining this as she sat on the carpet in Luet's tent, holding both their babies sitting up on her knees, her arms around them, her hands in front of her, demonstrating. The babies seemed fascinated indeed—there was something in the color or intensity of Shedemei's voice that all the babies in the company were drawn to, for Hushidh saw how alert they all became when she spoke. Often Shedemei could quiet a fussy infant when the child's own mother could not—which meant that Kokor and Sevet never let Shedemei near their babies, out of jealousy at being shown up—and Dol was always dropping off her little Syelsika for Shedemei to tend, often leaving her until Dol's own breasts were so sore that she had no choice but to fetch her baby and nurse it.

Only Luet and Hushidh, it seemed, sought out Shedemei's company, and even *they* had to use their babies as an excuse—could you help us with our babies while we bathe? So it was that Shedya sat on the carpet in Luet's tent while the two sisters sponged the dirt of the several days' journey from each other's backs and washed each other's hair.

"The crushing at the fingertips raises the great mountains of the north," said Shedemei. "While the parting at the heels created the Scour Sea, and then the Sea of Smoke. The Valley of Fires is the upwelling at the center. Someday, when the tearing apart is done, Potokgavan will sink into the sea and the Valley of Fires will be an island in an ever-widening ocean. It will be the most glorious and isolated spot on all of Harmony, the place where the planet is most alive and dangerous and beautiful."

Chveya, Luet's daughter, made a gurgling sound in the back of her throat. Like a growl.

"That's right, Veyevniya," said Shedemei, using her own silly name for Chveya. "A place for wild animals like you."

"And what about the thumbs?" asked Hushidh. "What happens there?"

"The thumbs, the fulcrum, the center—that's Basilica," said Shedemei. "The stable heart of the world. There are other continents, but no place on any of them where the water is so hot and cold and deep or the land so old and unchangeable. Basilica is the place where Harmony is most at peace."

"Geologically speaking," said Hushidh.

"Humanity's little disturbances—what are they?" asked Shedemei. "The smallest unit of time that ever matters is the generation, not the minute, not the hour, not the day, not even the year. Those all come and go and are done in a moment. But the generation—that's where the true changes come, when a world is really alive."

"Is humanity dead, then, since we've gone forty million years without evolution?" asked Luet.

"Do you think these children aren't evolution in progress?" asked Shedemei. "Speciation comes at times of genetic stress, when a species —not a mere individual or even a tribe—is in danger of destruction. Then the vast variety of possibilities within the species is winnowed down to those few variations that offer particular advantages to survival. So a species seems to be unchanged for millions of years, only to have change come suddenly when the need arises. The truth is that the changes were present all along—they simply hadn't been isolated and exposed."

"You make it sound like a wonderful plan," said Luet.

"I know—that's how it's always taught among women, isn't it? The Oversoul's plan. The patterns of generation: coupling, conception, gestation, birth, nurturing, maturation, and then coupling again—all the plan of the Oversoul. But *we* know better, don't we? The machine in the sky is merely an expression of humanity's will—part of the reason why we have *not* undergone speciating stress in forty million years. A tool to keep us as widely varied as possible, without ever achieving power enough to destroy ourselves and our world, as we did on Earth. Isn't that what Nafai and Issib learned? Isn't that why we're here? Because this *isn't* a plan of the Oversoul, because the Oversoul is losing the power to keep humanity self-tamed. Yet I can't help but think that it might be a *good* thing to let the Oversoul wither and die. In the generations that came after that, in the terrible stresses that would come, maybe humanity would speciate again and develop something new." She leaned down to little Dza and poofed in her face, which always made Dza laugh. "Maybe *you* are the new thing that humanity is supposed to become," said Shedemei. "Isn't that right, Dazyitnikiya?"

"You *do* love children so," said Luet, with a wistful tone.

"I love *other people's* children," said Shedemei. "I can always give them back, and then have time for my work. For *you*, poor things, it never ends."

But Hushidh was not deceived. Not that Shedemei didn't mean what she said—far from it. Shedya was quite sincere in her decision that it was perfectly all right for her not to have children—that she actually preferred it that way. She meant it, or at least *meant* to mean it.

Hushidh was convinced, however, that the powerful bond between

Shedemei and every baby in the camp was really the infants' unconscious response to Shedemei's irresistible hunger. She wanted babies. She wanted to be part of the vast passage of the generations through the world. And more than that—as Hushidh watched the love between her and Zdorab grow into one of the strongest friendships she had ever seen, Hushidh became more and more certain that Shedemei wanted to bear Zdorab's child, and it made Hushidh yearn more and more for that longing to come true.

She had even asked the Oversoul why it was that Shedemei didn't conceive, but the Oversoul had never answered—and Luet said that when *she* asked, she got the clear answer that what went on between Zdorab and Shedemei was none of her business.

Maybe it's none of our business, thought Hushidh, but that doesn't mean we can't wish that Shedemei had all that she needs to make her happy. Didn't the Oversoul bring everyone into the company because *all* their genes were needful? Was it possible that the Oversoul had erred, and either Zdorab or Shedemei was sterile? Awfully clumsy of her, if that's what happened.

Even now, Shedemei was explaining how Zdorab was the one who had discovered the geological history of the Valley of Fires. "He plays the Index like a musical instrument. He found things in the past that even the Oversoul didn't know that she knew. Things that only the ancients who first settled here understood. They gave the memory to the Oversoul, but then programmed her so that she couldn't find those memories on her own. Zdorab found the back doors, though, the hidden passageways, the strange connections that led into so many, many secrets."

"I know," said Hushidh. "Issib marvels at him sometimes, even though Issya himself isn't bad at getting ideas out of the Index."

"Oh, indeed, I know that," said Shedemei. "Zdorab says all the time that Issib is the real explorer."

"And Issib says that's only because he has more time, being useless at everything else," said Hushidh. "It's as if they both have to find reasons why the other is much better. I think they've become good friends."

"I know it," said Shedemei. "Issib is able to see how fine a man Zdorab really is."

"We all understand that," said Luet.

"Do you?" said Shedemei. "Sometimes it seems to me that everyone thinks of him as a sort of universal servant."

"We think of him as our cook because he's the best at it," said Hushidh. "And our librarian because he's the best at *that.*"

"Ah, but only a few of us care about his archival skills; to most of the people in our company, his culinary skills are the only things they notice about him."

"And his gardening," said Luet.

Shedemei smiled. "You see? But he gets little respect for it."

"From some," said Hushidh. "But others respect him greatly."

"I know Nafai does," said Luet. "And I do."

"And I, and Issib—and Volemak, too, I know that," said Hushidh.

"And isn't that everybody that matters?" asked Luet.

"I tell him that," said Shedemei, "but he persists in playing the servant."

Hushidh could see that, for this moment at least, Shedemei was closer to opening her heart to someone than ever before on this journey. She hardly knew, though, how to encourage her to go on—should she prod with a question, or keep silence so as not to impede her?

She kept silence.

And so did Shedemei.

Until at last Shedemei sniffed loudly and put her nose down near Chveya's diaper. "Has our little kaka factory produced another load?" she asked. "*Now* is the time when my permanent aunthood pays off. Mama Luet, your baby needs you."

They laughed—because of course they knew that Shedemei was as likely to change a baby's diaper as not. This business of giving the baby back to the mother whenever taking care of it was a bother was only a joke.

No, not *only* a joke. It was also a wistful regret. Shedemei's reminder to herself that, like her husband Zdorab, she was not really one of the company of women. She had been on the verge, Hushidh knew it, of telling *something* that mattered . . . and then the moment had passed.

As Luet cleaned her baby, Shedemei watched, and Hushidh watched her watching. Near the end of her bath, Luet was wearing nothing but a light skirt, and the shape of her motherly body—heavy breasts, a belly still loose and full from the birthing not that many months ago—was sweetly framed as she knelt and bent over her baby.

What does Shedemei see when she looks at Luet, whose figure was once as lean and boyish as Shedemei's is still? Does she wish for that transformation?

Apparently, though, Shedemei's own thoughts had taken a different turn. "Luet," she said, "when we were at that lake yesterday, did it remind you of the Lake of Women in Basilica?"

"Oh yes," said Luet.

"You were the waterseer there," said Shedemei. "Didn't you want to float out into the middle of it, and dream?"

Luet hesitated a moment. "There was no boat," she said. "And nothing to make one out of. And the water was too hot to float in it myself."

"Was it?" said Shedemei.

"Yes," said Luet. "Nafai checked for me. He passed through the Lake of Women too, you know."

"But didn't you wish that you could be—for just a little while—the person you were before?"

The longing in Shedemei's voice was so strong that Hushidh immediately understood. "But Luet *is* the same person," said Hushidh. "She's still the waterseer, even if she now spends her days on camelback and her nights in a tent and every hour with a baby fastened to her nipple."

"*Is* she the waterseer, then?" asked Shedemei. "She *was*—but *is* she? Or are we nothing more than what we're doing *now*? Aren't we truly only what the people we live with *think* we are?"

"No," said Hushidh. "Or that would mean that in Basilica I was nothing *but* the raveler, and Luet was nothing *but* the waterseer, and you were nothing *but* a geneticist, and that was never true, either. There's always something above and behind and beneath the role that everyone sees us acting out. *They* may think that we *are* the script we act out, but *we* don't have to believe it."

"Who are we then?" asked Shedemei. "Who am *I*?"

"Always a scientist," said Luet, "because you're still doing science in your mind every hour you're awake."

"And our friend," said Hushidh.

"And the person in our company who understands best how things work," added Luet.

"And Zdorab's wife," said Hushidh. "That's the one that means the most to you, I think."

To their surprise and consternation, Shedemei's only answer was to lay down Dza on the carpet and lightly run from the tent. Hushidh caught only a glimpse of her face, but she was weeping. There was no doubt of that. She was weeping because Hushidh had said that being Zdorab's wife meant more to her than anything. It was what a woman might do if she doubted her husband's love. But how could she doubt? It was obvious that Zdorab's whole life was centered around her. There were no better *friends* in the company than Zodya and Shedya, everyone knew that—unless it was Luet and Hushidh, and they were sisters so it hardly counted.

What could possibly be wrong between Zdorab and Shedemei, that would cause such a strong woman to be so fragile on the subject? A mystery. Hushidh longed to ask the Oversoul, but knew she'd get the same answer as always—silence. Or else the answer Luet already got—mind your own business.

The best thing and the worst thing about turning back and taking another route south was that they could see the sea. In particular, they could see Dorova Bay, an eastern arm of the Scour Sea. And on clear nights—which all the nights were—they could see, on the far side of that bay, the lights of the city of Dorova.

It was not a city like Basilica, they all knew that. It was a scrubby edge-of-the-desert town filled with riffraff and profiteers, failures and thieves, violent and stupid men and women. They told each other that over and over, remembering tales of desert towns and how they weren't worth visiting even if they were the last town in the world.

Except that Dorova was the last town in the world—the last town in *their* world, anyway. The last they would ever see. It was the town they could have visited more than a week ago, when Volemak led them up into the mountains from the Nividimu and they left the last hope of civilization behind—or the last danger of it, for those who had that perspective.

Nafai saw how others looked at those lights, when they gathered at night, fireless, chilly, the bundled infants smacking and suckling away as they drank cold water and gnawed on jerky and hard biscuit and dried melon. How Obring got tears in his eyes—tears! And what was the city to him, anyway, except a place to get his hooy polished. Tears! And Sevet was no better, with her simple, steady gaze, that stony look on her face. She had a baby at her breast, and all she could think of was a city so small and filthy that she wouldn't have stepped into its streets two years ago. If they had offered her twenty times her normal fee to come and sing there, she would have sneered at the offer—and now she couldn't keep her eyes off of it.

But looking was *all* they could do, fortunately. They could see it, but they had no boat to cross the bay, and none of them could swim well enough to cross that many kilometers without a boat. Besides, they weren't at the beach, they were at least a kilometer above it, at the edge of a craggy, rugged incline that couldn't decide whether to be a cliff or a slope. There might be a way to get the camels down, but it wasn't likely, and even if they did, it would be several days' journey back along the beach, *with* the camels—and without them, there would be no water to drink and so they couldn't make it at all. No, nobody was going to be able to slip away from the group and make it to Dorova. The only way there was if the whole group went, and even then they would probably have to go back the way they came, which meant a week and a half at least, and probably one of the caravans from the south to contend with along the way. And it was all meaningless because Father would never go back.

And yet Nafai couldn't stop thinking about how *much* these people wanted that city.

How much *he* wanted it.

Yes, there was the trouble. That's what bothered him. *He* wanted the city, too. Not for any of the things *they* wanted, or at least the things he imagined that they wanted. Nafai had no desire for any wife but Luet; they were a family, and that wouldn't change no matter where they lived, he had decided that long ago. No, what Nafai wanted was a soft bed to lay Chveya in. A school to take her to. A house for Luet and Chveya and whatever children might come after. Neighbors and friends—friends that he might choose for himself, not this accidental collection of people most of whom he just didn't like that much. That's what those lights meant to him—and instead here he was on a grassy meadow that sloped deceptively downward toward the sea, so that if you just squinted a little you couldn't really tell you were a kilometer above sea level, you could pretend for a few moments that it was just a stroll across the meadow, and then a short ride on a boat across the bay, and then you'd be home, the journey would be over, you could bathe and then sleep in a bed and wake up to find breakfast cooking already, and you'd find your wife in your arms beside you, and then you'd hear the faint sound of your baby daughter waking, and you'd

slip out of bed and go get her from her cradle and bring her in to your
wife, who would sleepily draw her breast from inside her nightgown
and put it into the mouth of the baby that now nestled in the crook of
her arm on the bed, and you'd lie back down beside her and listen to
the sucking and smacking of the baby as you also heard the birds
singing outside the window and the noises of morning in the street not
far away, the venders starting to cry out what they had to sell. Eggs.
Berries. Cream. Sweet breads and cakes.

Oversoul, why couldn't you have left us alone? Why couldn't you
have waited another generation? Forty million years, and you couldn't
wait for Luet's and my great-grandchildren to have this great adventure? You couldn't have let Issib and me figure out how to build one of
those marvelous ancient flying machines, so we could go to wherever
you're taking us in just a few hours? Time, that's all we needed, really.
Time to live before we lost our world.

Stop whining, said the Oversoul in Nafai's mind. Or maybe it wasn't
the Oversoul. Maybe it was just Nafai's own sense that he had indulged
himself too much already.

It was morning, just before dawn, at the spring the Index had told
them was named Shazer, though why anyone should have bothered to
name such an obscure place, and why the Oversoul had bothered to
remember, Nafai could not begin to guess. Vas had had the last watch
of the night, and then came and woke Nafai so they could hunt together. Three days since they last had meat, and this was a good campsite so they could take two days to hunt if need be. So Vas would catch
sight of something, or find some fresh animal trace; Nafai would trail
after him and, when the quarry was near, creep silently forward until
the animal came in sight. Then Nafai would take the sacred pulse, aim
so carefully, trying to guess which way the animal would move, and
how far, and how fast, and then he would squeeze the trigger and the
beam of light would burn a hole into the heart of the creature, sear it so
that the wound would never bleed, except for a hot wet smoke that
would stain the sand and rocks it fell on red and black.

Nafai was tired of it. But it was his duty, and so when Vas scratched
softly on the cloth of the tent, near where he knew Nafai's head lay,
Nafai awoke at once—if he had not already been awake, coasting on
the verges of a dream—and got up and dressed without waking Luet or
Chveya and took the pulse out of its box and joined Vas outside in the
chilly darkness.

Vas nodded a greeting to him—they tried to avoid speaking, lest they wake babies unnecessarily—and then turned slowly, finally pointing toward the downhill slope. Not toward the city, but still toward the sea. Downward. Nafai normally thought it was a stupid plan to go downhill on the hunt, since it would mean carrying the game back uphill to get it to camp. But this time he *wanted* to go down. Even though he would never abandon their quest, even though he had no thought of betraying either Father or the Oversoul, nevertheless there was a part of him that longed for the sea, and for what lay across the sea, and so he nodded when Vas pointed toward the seaward slope of the meadow.

When they were well away from the camp, and over the brow of the hill, they stopped and peed, and then began the difficult descent into the tumble of rocks that led downward. All the slope ahead of them lay in shadow, since the dawn was coming up behind them. But Vas was the tracker, and Nafai had long since learned that he was both good at it and very proud of his prowess, so things went better if Nafai didn't try to second-guess him.

It wasn't an easy climb, though the darkness was easing with every moment that passed, for dawn seemed to light the sky from horizon to horizon far more quickly here than it ever had in Basilica. Was it the latitude? The dry desert air? Whatever the cause, he could see, but what he saw was a confusion of cliffs and crags, ledges and outcroppings that would challenge the nimblest of animals. What kind of creature do you hope to find, Vas? What kind of animal could live here?

But these were just Nafai's normal doubts—fearing the worst even as he knew that there was plenty of vegetation here, and there'd be no difficulty finding game. It would just be hard to get it home. Which was another reason why Elemak had always sent a hunter and tracker together, either Nafai and Vas or, back when there was more than one pulse, Elemak as hunter and Obring as tracker. When they were successful, the team would come home with each man carrying half a beast over his shoulders. It happened more often with Nafai and Vas, however, in part because Nafai was the best shot, and in part because Obring could never really keep his mind on tracking well enough to do a good job, so that Elemak ended up having to divide his concentration to do both jobs.

Vas, though, could concentrate very well, seeing things that no one else had noticed. Vas could follow the same prey relentlessly for hours and hours. Like a fighting dog that gripped with its teeth and never let go. It was part of the reason why Nafai succeeded so much more often —because Vas would bring him to the prey. The rest of the success, however, was Nafai's own. Nobody could approach so near to the prey in silence; nobody's aim was as steady and true. They were a good team, and yet in all their lives they had never imagined that they'd be good at hunting. It would never have crossed their minds.

Soon enough, Vas found something—a small mark. Nafai had long since given up trying to see all the things that Vas saw—to him it didn't look like an animal sign, but then it often didn't. Nafai just followed along, keeping his eyes open for predators that might decide that human beings were either a threat or a meal. The animal's trail led farther and farther down the slope, so far that by midmorning Nafai could see a clear and easy route that would lead down to the beach. For reasons he wasn't proud of, he wanted to go down that path and at least put his feet in the water of Dorova Bay. But Vas was not going that way—he was leading them across the face of an increasingly steep and dangerous cliff.

Why would an animal have chosen *this* route? Nafai wondered. What kind of animal is it? But of course he said nothing; it was a point of pride, to maintain perfect silence throughout the hunt.

Just as they reached the most dangerous part of the passage, where they would have to traverse a smooth surface of rock with no ledge at all, only friction to keep them from falling down fifty meters or more, Vas stopped and pointed, indicating that the prey was on the other side of the traverse. That was bad news. It would mean that Nafai would have to make the passage with his pulse out and ready to fire—that, in fact, he would have to aim and fire from that very slope.

But after all this tracking, they couldn't give up and start over just because it was momentarily difficult.

Vas pressed himself against the cliff wall, and Nafai passed behind him, then drew the pulse out of the sling he carried it in and moved ahead onto the difficult traverse.

At that moment the thought came into his head: Don't go on. Vas is planning to kill you.

This is stupid, thought Nafai. It's one thing to be afraid of the traverse—I'm only human. But if Vas wanted to kill me he had only to shrug when I was passing behind him on the ledge just now.

Don't take another step.

And leave the family without meat, because I got a sudden attack of jitters? Not a chance.

Nafai swallowed his fear and moved across the face. He arched his body out a little, so that there would be the greatest possible pressure and therefore the greatest possible friction on the soles of his climbing boots. Even so, he could feel that there was too much give—this was very dangerous indeed, and shooting from this point would be almost impossible.

He reached the point where he could at last see all of the area that had been hidden before, and now he stopped and looked for the animal. He couldn't see it. This sometimes happened—especially because they hunted in silence. Vas would lead him to an animal with good natural camouflage, and when Nafai got within range the animal would see or smell him and freeze, becoming almost completely invisible. Sometimes it took a long time before the animal moved and Nafai could see him. This was going to be one of those waiting games. Nafai hated it that he would have to do his waiting on this traverse, but he was perfectly visible now, and if he moved any closer the animal would bolt and they would have to start over.

He gingerly shifted his hands so that all his weight was on his feet and the hand *without* the pulse, then brought the pulse to where he could easily aim at any point on the face of the mountain before him. Was the animal in those shrubs? Perhaps behind a rock, ready to emerge at any moment?

Holding the same pose in that awkward place was hard. Nafai was strong, and used to holding still for long periods of time—but this posture was one he had never had to hold before. He could feel sweat dripping down his forehead. If it got in his eye it would sting mercilessly, mixed as it was with dust from his face. Yet there was no way he could move to wipe it away without spooking the animal.

An animal I haven't even seen.

Forget the animal. Just get off the face of this rock.

No, I'm stronger than that. I need to get the food for the family—I won't go back and say we'll have no meat today because I was afraid to wait in stillness on a rock.

He could hear Vas moving behind him, traversing the rock. That was stupid—why was Vas doing that?

To kill me.

Why couldn't he shake that idea? No, Vas was coming because he could tell that Nafai hadn't seen the animal yet, and he wanted to point it out. But how would he do *that?* Nafai couldn't turn to look at him, and Vas couldn't pass him to get into his field of view.

Oh, no. Vas was going to *talk* to him.

"It's too dangerous," said Vas. "You're going to slip."

And just as he said it, the friction holding Nafai's right foot in place suddenly gave way. His foot slipped inward and down, and now with the abrupt movement his left foot couldn't hold and he began to slide. It must have been very quick but it felt like forever; he tried to dig in with his hand, with the butt of the pulse, but they both just rubbed along the rock, doing almost nothing even to slow his fall. And then the rock grew steeper and he wasn't sliding, he was falling, falling, and he knew he was going to die.

"Nafai!" screamed Vas. "Nafai!"

Luet was at the stream, washing clothes, when suddenly there came a clear thought into her mind: (He's not dead.)

Not dead? Who's not dead? Why should he be dead?

(Nafai is not dead. He'll come home.)

She knew at once that it was the Oversoul speaking to her. Reassuring her. But she was not reassured. Or rather, she *was* reassured to know that Nafai was all right. But now she had to know, *demanded* to know what had happened.

(He fell.)

How did he fall?

(His foot slipped on the face of the rock.)

Nafai is sure-footed. *Why* did his foot slip? What is it that you're not telling me?

(I was watching Vas very carefully with Sevet and Obring. Watching all the time. He has murder in his heart.)

Did Vas have something to do with Nafai's fall?

(Not until they were traversing the rock did I see the plan in his mind. He had already destroyed the first three pulses. I knew he meant to destroy the last one, but I wasn't concerned because there are alternatives. I never saw it in his mind, not until the last moment, that the simplest way to destroy the last pulse was to lead Nafai to a dangerous place and then push his foot so he would fall.)

You never saw a plan like that in his mind?

(All the way down the mountain he was thinking of a route to the sea. How to get down to the bay so he could walk to Dorova. That's all that was in his mind as he led Nafai after quarry that didn't exist. Vas has remarkable powers of concentration. He thought of nothing but the path to the sea, until the very last moment.)

Didn't you warn Nafai?

(He heard me, but he didn't realize it was my voice he was hearing. He thought it was his own fear, and he fought it down.)

So Vas is a murderer.

(Vas is what he is. He will do anything to get his vengeance on Obring and Sevet for their betrayal of him back in Basilica.)

But he seemed so calm about it.

(He can be cold.)

What now? What now, Oversoul?

(I will watch.)

That's what you've been doing all along, and yet you never gave any of us a glimpse of what you saw. You knew what Vas was planning. Hushidh even saw those powerful bonds between him and Sevet and Obring and you never told her what they *were*.

(This is how I was programmed. To watch. Not to interfere unless and until the danger would damage my purpose. If I stopped every bad person from doing bad things, who would be free? How would humans still be human, then? So I let them plan their plans, and I watch. Often they change their minds, freely, without my interference.)

Couldn't you have made Vas stupid and forgetful long enough to stop this?

(I told you. Vas has a very strong ability to concentrate.)

What now? What now?

(I will watch.)

Have you told Volemak?

(I told *you*.)

Should *I* tell anyone?

(Vas will deny it. Nafai doesn't even realize that he was the victim of a would-be murderer. I told you because I don't trust my own ability now to predict what Vas will do.)

And what can *I* do?

(You're the human. You're the one who's able to think of things that exceed your programming.)

No, I don't believe you. I don't believe that you don't have a plan.

(If I have a plan, it includes you making your own decisions about what to do.)

Hushidh. I have to tell my sister.

(If I have a plan, it includes you making your own decisions.)

Does that mean I *mustn't* consult with Hushidh, because then my decision wouldn't be my own? Or does it mean that consulting with Hushidh is one of the decisions I need to make on my own?

(If I have a plan, it is for you to make your own decisions about your own decisions about your own decisions.)

And then she felt that she was alone again; the Oversoul was not talking to her.

The clothes lay in the grass beside the stream, except for the one gown of Chveya's that she had been washing; that one she still held in the stream, her hands freezing cold now because through all this conversation with the Oversoul she had not moved.

I must talk to Hushidh, and so that's the first decision I will make. I'll talk to Hushidh *and* Issib.

But first I'll finish washing these clothes. That way no one will know anything is wrong. I think that's the right thing to do, to keep anyone from knowing that something's wrong, at least for now.

After all, Nafai is all right. Or at least Nafai is not dead. But Vas *is* a murderer in his heart. And Obring and Sevet are in danger from him. Not to mention Nafai, if Vas even suspects that Nafai knows what Vas tried to do to him. Not to mention *me*, if Vas realizes that I also know.

How could the Oversoul have let things get to such a point? Isn't she responsible for all of this? Doesn't she know that she has brought terrible people along with us on this journey? How could she make us travel and camp for so many months, for a *year* and more, for many years ahead, with a *murderer?*

Because she hoped that he would decide not to murder after all, of course. Because she has to allow humans to be human, even now. Especially now.

But not when it comes to killing my husband. That is going too far, Oversoul. You took too great a chance. If he had died I would never have forgiven you. I would refuse to serve you anymore.

No answer came from the Oversoul. Instead it came from her own heart: An individual's death can come at any time. It isn't the task of the Oversoul to prevent it. The Oversoul's task is to prevent the death of a world.

* * *

Nafai lay stunned in the grass. It was a ledge invisible from above because of the way the cliff bowed out. He had fallen only five or six meters, after sliding down the face of the rock for a while. It was enough to knock the breath out of him; enough that he blacked out. But he was uninjured, except for a sore hip where he landed.

If he had not fetched up on the ledge, he would have plummeted another hundred meters or more and surely died.

I can't believe I lived through this. I should never have tried to kill the animal from that position. It was stupid. I was right to be afraid. I should have listened to my fears and if we lost that animal, fine, because we can always find another beast to follow and kill. What we can't find again is another father for Chveya, another husband for Luet, another hunter who isn't needed for other tasks.

Or another pulse.

He looked around and realized that the pulse wasn't on the ledge. Wasn't anywhere that he could see. He must have let go of it as he fell, and it must have bounced. Where was it?

He crept to the lip of the ledge and looked over. Oh, yes, straight down, except for a few small outcroppings—if the pulse struck them, then it would have bounced and kept on falling. There was nowhere that the pulse could have fetched up and stopped except at the bottom of the cliff. If that's where it was, Nafai couldn't possibly see it from here—it would be lost in the bushes. Or were those treetops?

"Nafai!" It was Vas, calling for him.

"I'm here!" Nafai cried.

"Thank God!" cried Vas. "Are you injured?"

"No," said Nafai. "But I'm on a ledge. I think I can get off to the south. I'm about ten meters below you. Can you move south too? I may need your help. There's nothing below me but a deadly fall, and I don't see any obvious way to get up to where you are."

"Do you have the pulse?" asked Vas.

Of course he had to ask about the pulse. Nafai blushed with shame. "No, I must have dropped it as I fell," he said. "It's got to be at the bottom of the cliff, unless you can see it somewhere up there."

"It's not here—you had it with you as you fell."

"Then it's at the bottom. Move south with me," said Nafai.

He found, though, that it was easier to talk about moving along the face of the cliff than it was to do it. The fall might not have injured him seriously, but the terror of it had done something to him, oh yes—he could barely bring himself to get to his feet, for fear of the edge, for fear of the fall.

I didn't fall because I lost my balance, thought Nafai. I fell because friction simply wasn't strong enough to hold me in that dangerous place. This ledge isn't like that. I can stand securely here.

So he stood, his back to the cliff, breathing deeply, telling himself to move, to sidle south along the ledge, around the corner, because there might be a way to get up. Yet the more he told himself this, the more his eyes focused on the empty space beyond the edge of the cliff, not a meter from his feet. If I lean just a little, I'll fall. If I fell forward now, I'd plunge over the side.

No, he told himself. I can't think that way, or I'll never be good for anything again. I've taken ledges like this a hundred times. They're nothing. They're easy. And it would help if I faced the cliff instead of facing the empty space leading down to the sea.

He turned and stepped carefully along the ledge, pressing himself rather closer to the cliff than he would have in former times. But his confidence increased with every step he took.

When he rounded the bend in the cliff, he saw that the ledge ended —but now it was only two meters from this ledge to the next one up, and from there it was an easy climb back to where he and Vas had come down less than an hour ago. "Vas!" he called. He continued until he stood directly under the place where the ledge above was nearest. He could almost reach far enough onto the ledge to lift himself by his own arms, but there was nothing to hold on to, and the edge was crumbly and unreliable. It would be safer if Vas helped him. "Vas, here I am! I need you!"

But he heard nothing from Vas. And then he remembered the thought that had come into his mind as he was starting the dangerous traverse: Don't go on. Vas is planning to kill you.

Is it possible that that was a warning from the Oversoul?

Absurd.

But Nafai didn't wait for Vas to answer. Instead he reached his arms as far as they could go onto the ledge above, then dug his fingers into the loose grassy soil. It slipped and came away, but by scrabbling constantly, grabbing more and more, he was able to get enough of a purchase that he could get his shoulders above the edge of the cliff, and then it was a relatively easy matter to swing a leg up onto the ledge and pull himself to safety. He rolled onto his back and lay there, panting in relief. He could hardly believe that he had done such a dangerous thing so soon after falling—if he had slipped at any time while clambering up onto this ledge, he would have had a hard time catching himself on the ledge below. He was risking death—but he had done it.

Vas came now. "Ah," he said. "You're already up. Look—this way. Right back to where we were."

"I've got to find the pulse."

"It's bound to be broken and useless," said Vas. "It wasn't built for a fall like that."

"I can't go back and tell them that I don't have the pulse," said Nafai. "That I *lost* it. It's down there, and even if it's in forty pieces, I'll bring those pieces home."

"It's better to tell them you broke it than to tell them you lost it?" asked Vas.

"Yes," said Nafai. "It's better to show them the pieces than have them always wonder whether, if I had only looked, I might have found it. Don't you understand that this is our families' *meat* supply we're talking about?"

"Oh, I understand," said Vas. "And now that you put it that way, of course I see we must search for it. Look, we can come down this way—it's an easy enough path."

"I know," said Nafai. "Right down to the sea."

"Do you think so?" asked Vas.

"Down that way, and jogging to the left—see?"

"Oh, that *would* probably work."

It made Nafai faintly ashamed, that *he* had noticed the route to the sea, while Vas had not even thought of it.

Instead of going down to the sea, however, they scrambled down to the brush where the pulse must have fallen. They didn't have to search long before they found it—split in half, right down the middle. Several small internal components were also scattered here and there in the bushes, and without doubt there were others that they didn't find. There would be no repairing this pulse.

Still, Nafai put the pieces, large and small, into the sling he had made for carrying the pulse, and tied it closed. Then he and Vas began the long climb up the mountain. Nafai suggested that Vas should lead, since he would do a better job of remembering the way, and Vas agreed at once. Nafai didn't give the slightest hint that he didn't dare let Vas walk behind him, where he couldn't see what he was doing.

Oversoul, was that warning from you?

He didn't get any answer from the Oversoul, or at least not a direct answer to his question. What he got instead was the clear thought that he should talk to Luet when he got back to camp. And since that was what he would have done anyway, especially after an experience like this, being so close to death, he assumed that it was his own thought, and the Oversoul had not spoken to him at all.

7

The Bow

The loss of the pulse was such a blow that neither Volemak nor Elemak made any effort to keep the situation calm—not until it was already almost out of control. There lay the pieces of the pulse, spread out on a cloth; nearby were the two water-damaged pulses that Elemak had saved. Zdorab sat by them, the Index in his lap, reading out the numbers of the broken parts. Almost everyone else stood—few were calm enough to sit—waiting, watching, pacing, grumbling as he tried to find out if one whole pulse could be salvaged from the parts.

"It's no use," said Zdorab. "Even if we had all the parts, the Index says that we don't have the tools that would be needed, and no way of making them without spending fifty years achieving the appropriate level of technology."

"What a brilliant plan the Oversoul had," said Elemak. "Keep all of humanity at a low level of technology—so low that even though we can manufacture pulses, we don't understand how they work and can't repair them if they break."

"It wasn't the Oversoul's plan," said Issib.

"Does it matter?" said Mebbekew. "We're going to die out here now."

Dol burst into tears, and for once they sounded real.

"I'm sorry," said Nafai.

"Yes, well, how glad we all are that you're remorseful," said Elemak. "What were you doing in a dangerous place like that anyway? You had the sole surviving pulse, and that's what you do with it?"

"That's where the animal was," said Nafai.

"If your quarry had leapt from the cliff, would you have followed?" asked Volemak.

Nafai was devastated that Father had joined in with Elemak's tongue-lashing. And Elemak himself was far from finished. "Let me put it to you plainly, my dear little brother: If you could have chosen whether you or the pulse would land on the ledge instead of bouncing down to destruction, it would have been more convenient to everybody if you had arranged for it to be the pulse!"

The unfairness of it was almost unbearable. "I'm not the one who lost the first three."

"But when we lost the first three, we still had a pulse left, so it wasn't quite as serious," said Father. "You knew it was the last pulse, and still took such a chance."

"Enough!" said Rasa. "We all agree, including Nafai, that it was a horrible mistake to put the pulse at risk. But now the pulse is gone, it can't be repaired, and here we are in this strange place with no way to kill meat. Perhaps one of you has thought of what we're going to *do* now, besides heaping blame on Nafai's shoulders."

Thank you, Mother, said Nafai silently.

"Isn't it obvious?" said Vas. "The expedition is over."

"No, it isn't obvious," Volemak answered sharply. "The Oversoul's purpose is nothing less than saving Harmony from the same destruction that came to Earth forty million years ago. Are we going to give that up because we lost a weapon?"

"It's not the weapon," said Eiadh. "It's the meat. We need to find meat."

"And it isn't just a matter of having a balanced diet," added Shedemei. "Even if we made camp right here and planted crops immediately—and it's not the season for it, so we couldn't anyway—but even if we did, we'd have no harvest of basic protein crops until long after we suffered from serious malnutrition."

"What do you mean by *serious* malnutrition?" asked Volemak.

"Some deaths by starvation, primarily among the children," said Shedemei.

"That's awful!" wailed Kokor. "You've practically killed my baby!"

Her cry set off a chorus of whining. In the din, Nafai silently spoke to the Oversoul: *Is* there some other way?

(Do you have a suggestion?)

Nafai tried to think of a hunting weapon that could be made from materials at hand. He remembered that the Gorayni soldiers had been armed with spears, with bows and arrows. Would either of those do for hunting, or were they only useful in war?

The thought came into his head: (Anything that will kill a man will probably kill any other animal. To hunt with a spear requires a group of hunters to drive the prey—otherwise it's rare to get close enough for the kill, even with an atlatl to extend your throw.)

Then what about the bow and arrow?

(A good bow has a range four times that of the pulse. But they're very hard to make.)

What about a second-rate bow, with a range only about the *same* as a pulse? Could you teach me how to make one of *those?*

(Yes.)

And do you think I could find prey with it, or does it take too long to learn the skill?

(It takes as long as it takes.)

That was probably as good an answer as he was likely to get from the Oversoul, and it wasn't a bad answer at that. There was a hope, at least.

When Nafai's attention returned to the others, they had apparently goaded Volemak beyond his patience. "Do you think *I* planned all this?" he asked. "Do you think *I* asked the Oversoul to lead us to this hideous place, to have babies in the desert and wander aimlessly through wilderness without enough to eat? Do you think *I* wouldn't rather be in a house? With a bed?"

Nafai could see that Volemak had surprised everyone by joining his own complaints to theirs. But it hardly reassured them—some looked frightened indeed, to have their pillar of strength show a crack. And Elemak's face barely concealed his contempt for Father. It was not Volemak's proudest moment, Nafai could see that—and it was so unnecessary. If he had only asked the Oversoul the questions Nafai had asked, he would have been reassured. There *was* a way.

Vas spoke up again. "I tell you, all of this is completely unnecessary. Nafai and I found a fairly easy way down the mountain. We may not be able to bring the camels, but then, if we're simply walking around the bay to get to Dorova, all we need to carry is a day's provisions and water."

"Abandon the camels?" said Elemak. "The tents?"

"The coldboxes and dryboxes?" asked Shedemei.

"Some of you stay here then," said Mebbekew, "and lead the camels around the long way. Without the women and babies it won't take more than a week, and in the meantime the rest of us will be in the city. Give us a couple of months and we'll be back in Basilica. Or wherever the rest of you decide to go."

There was a murmur of assent.

"No," said Nafai. "This isn't about *us*, this is about Harmony, about the Oversoul."

"Nobody asked if I wanted to volunteer for this noble cause," said Obring, "and I for one am sick of hearing about it."

"The city's right over there," said Sevet. "We could be there so quickly."

"Fools," said Elemak. "Just because you can see the city, just because you can see the beach you'd walk along to reach it, that doesn't mean you could walk it easily. In a single day? Laughable. You've got stronger in the past year, yes, but none of you are in fit condition to walk that far carrying a baby, let alone the liters of water you'd need, and the food. Walking in sand is hard work, and slow, and the more heavily burdened you are the more slowly you go, which means that you have to carry *more* provisions to last you through the longer journey, which means you'll be more heavily burdened and travel even more sluggishly."

"Then we're trapped here till we *die?*" wailed Kokor.

"Oh, shut up," said Sevet.

"We're not trapped here," said Nafai, "and we don't have to abandon the expedition. Before there were ever pulses, human beings were able to kill meat. There are other weapons."

"What, will you strangle them?" asked Mebbekew. "Or use that wire of Gaballufix's, to cut off their heads?"

Nafai steeled himself to resist his own anger at Mebbekew's taunting. "A bow. Arrows. The Oversoul knows how they're made."

"Then let the Oversoul make them," said Obring. "That doesn't mean that any of us know how to *use* them."

"For once Obring is right," said Elemak. "It takes years of training to become a good bowman. Why do you think I brought pulses? Bows are better—they have a longer range, they never run out of power, and they do less damage to the meat. But I don't know how to use one, let alone make one."

"Neither do I," said Nafai. "But the Oversoul can teach me."

"In a month, perhaps," said Elemak. "But we don't have a month."

"In a day," said Nafai. "Give me until sundown tomorrow. If I haven't brought back meat, then I'll agree with Vas and Meb that we have to go to Dorova, at least for a while."

"If we go to Dorova, it's the end of this foolish expedition," said Meb. "I'll never get back on a camel for any reason except to go *home.*" Several agreed with him.

"Give me a day, and I'll agree with you," said Nafai. "We're not running out of provisions yet, and this is a good place to wait. A day."

"A waste of time," said Elemak. "You can't possibly do it."

"Then what harm will it do to let me prove it to you? But I say I *can* do it, with the Oversoul to help me. The knowledge is all there in its memory. And the game is easy to find here."

"I'll track for you," said Vas.

"No!" said Luet. Nafai looked at her, startled—she had said nothing till now. "Nafai will do this alone. He and the Oversoul. That's how it has to be." Then she looked up at him, steadily and intently.

She knows something, thought Nafai. Then he remembered again the thoughts that came to him on the mountain this morning—that Vas had been trying to kill him. That Vas caused his fall. Did the Oversoul speak clearly to her? Were my fears justified? Is that why she'd rather send me out alone?

"So you'll leave in the morning?" asked Volemak.

"No," said Nafai. "Today. I hope to make a bow today, so I can have tomorrow for the hunt. After all, my first few targets may get away."

"This is stupid," said Meb. "What does Nafai think he is, one of the Heroes of Pyiretsiss?"

"I'm not going to let this expedition fail!" shouted Nafai. "That's who I am. And if I won't let a broken pulse stop us, you can bet all the snot in your nose that I won't let *you* get in the way."

Meb looked at him and laughed. "You've got a bet, Nyef, my sweet little brother. All the snot in my nose says you'll fail."

"Done."

"Except we haven't specified what *you* give *me* when you fail."

"It doesn't matter," said Nafai. "I won't fail."

"But if you do . . . then you're my personal servant."

Meb's words were greeted with derision by many around the circle. "Snot against servitude," said Eiadh contemptuously. "Just what I'd expect of *you*, Meb."

"He doesn't have to take the bet," said Meb.

"Set a time limit on it," said Nafai. "Say—a month."

"A year. A year in which you do whatever I command."

"This is sickening," said Volemak. "I forbid it."

"You already agreed to it, Nafai," said Mebbekew. "If you back out of it now, you'll stand before us all as an oathbreaker."

"When I lay the meat down at your feet, Meb, you'll decide then what I am, and it won't be on oathbreaker, that's certain."

And so it was agreed. They'd wait until sundown tomorrow for Nafai to return.

He left them, hurried to the kitchen tent, and gathered what he'd need—biscuit and dried melon and jerky. Then he headed for the spring to refill his flagon. With his knife at his side, he'd need no more.

Luet met him there, as he knelt beside the pool, immersing the flagon to fill it.

"Where's Chveya?" he asked.

"With Shuya," she answered. "I needed to talk to you. Instead we had that . . . meeting."

"And I needed to talk to you, too," he said. "But things got out of hand, and now there's no time."

"I hope there's time for you to take *this*," she said.

In her hand was a spool of twine.

"I hear that bows don't work without a string," she said. "And the Oversoul said that this kind would be best."

"You asked?"

"She seemed to think you were about to rush off without it, and that you'd regret the lack of it by and by."

"I would have, yes." He took it, put it in his pouch. Then he bent to her and kissed her. "You always look out for me."

"When I can," she said. "Nafai, while you were gone, the Oversoul spoke to me. Very clearly."

"Yes?"

"Was Vas near you when you fell?"

"He was."

"Near enough that he could have caused it? By, for instance, pushing your foot?"

Nafai instantly recalled that terrible moment on the face of the rock, when his right foot first slipped. It had slid inward, toward his left foot. If it had just been friction giving way, wouldn't the foot have slid straight down?

"Yes," said Nafai. "The Oversoul tried to warn me, but . . ."

"But you thought it was your own fear and ignored it."

Nafai nodded. She knew how the Oversoul's voice felt—like your own thoughts, like your own fears.

"You men," she said. "Always afraid of being afraid. Don't you know that fear is the most fundamental tool that evolution uses to keep a species alive? Yet you ignore it as if you hoped to die."

"Yes, well, I can't help what testosterone does to me. You'd enjoy being married to me a lot less if I didn't have any."

She smiled. But the smile didn't last long. "Something else the Oversoul told me," said Luet. "Vas is planning . . ."

But at that moment Obring and Kokor sauntered over. "Having second thoughts, little brother?" asked Kokor.

"My thoughts often come in threes and fours," said Nafai. "Not one at a time, like yours."

"I just wanted to wish you well," said Kokor. "I really hope you bring home some scruffy little hare for us to eat. Because if you *don't* then *we'll* have to go to a *city* and eat *cooked* food, and that would be just awful, don't you think?"

"Somehow I think your heart isn't in your kind words," said Nafai.

"If I thought you had a chance of succeeding," said Obring, "I'd break your arm."

"If a man like you could break my arm," said Nafai, "I really *wouldn't* have a chance."

"Please," said Luet. "Don't we have trouble enough?"

"Sweet little peacemaker," said Kokor. "Not much for looks, are you, but maybe you'll grow old gracefully."

Nafai couldn't help it. Kokor's insults were so childish, so much like what passed for cleverness among schoolchildren, that he had to laugh.

Kokor didn't like it. "Laugh all you want," said Kokor. "But I can sing my way back to wealth, and Mother still has a household in Basilica that I can inherit. What does your *father* have for *you*? And what kind of household will your little orphan wife establish for you in Basilica?"

Luet stepped forward and faced Kokor; Nafai noticed for the first time that they were almost the same height, which meant Luet had been growing this past year. She really *is* still a child, he thought.

"Koya," said Luet. "You forget whom you're speaking to. You may think that Nafai is just your younger brother. In the future, though, I hope you'll remember that he is the husband of the waterseer."

Kokor answered with defiance. "And what does that matter *here?*"

"It doesn't matter at all . . . *here*. But if we were to return to Basilica, dear Koya, I wonder how far your career will go if you're known to be the enemy of the waterseer."

Kokor blanched. "You wouldn't."

"No," said Luet, "I wouldn't. I never used my influence that way. And besides—we're not going back to Basilica."

Nafai had never seen Luet act so imperious before. He was enough of a Basilican to feel somewhat overawed at the title of waterseer; it was easy to forget sometimes that the woman he took to bed every night was the same woman whose dreams, whose words, were whispered house to house in Basilica. Once she had come to him at great risk, leaving the city in the middle of the night to wake him and warn him of danger to his father—and on that night she did not show any sign that she was aware of her lofty role in the city. Once she had taken him, when he was being chased by Gaballufix's men, and led him down into the waters of the Lake of Women, where no man was allowed to go and return alive—and even then, as she faced down those who would have killed him, she had not taken this tone, but rather had spoken calmly, quietly.

And then it dawned on Nafai—Luet wasn't putting on this air of haughty majesty because it was any part of *her*. She was acting this way because this is how *Kokor* would have acted, if she had even the tinest shred of power. Luet was speaking to Nafai's half-sister in language that she could understand. And the message was received. Kokor plucked at Obring's sleeve and the two of them left.

"You're very good at that," said Nafai. "I can't wait to hear you use that voice on Chveya, the first time she sasses you."

"I intend to raise Chveya to be the kind of woman with whom that voice would never need to be used."

"I didn't even know you *had* that voice."

Luet smiled. "Neither did I." She kissed him again.

"You were telling me something about Vas."

"Something Hushidh saw but didn't understand; the Oversoul explained it to me. Vas hasn't forgotten that Sevet betrayed him with Obring and brought public humiliation to him."

"No?"

"The Oversoul says he plans to murder them."

Nafai hooted once in derision. "Vas? He was the picture of calm. Mother said that she'd never seen anybody take a bad situation so well."

"He saves up his revenge for later, I guess," said Luet. "We have plenty of evidence now to suggest that Vas isn't quite as calm and cooperative as he seems."

"No," said Nafai, "he's not, is he? Meb and Dol, Obring and Kokor, they whine and moan about wanting to go back to the city. But not Vas. He takes it silently, seems to go along, and then sets out to destroy the pulses so we *have* to go back."

"You've got to admit, it was a clever plan."

"And if he happens to kill me in the process, well, that's the way it goes. It makes me think—if Gaballufix had been as subtle as Vas, he would be king of Basilica by now."

"No, Nafai. He'd be dead."

"Why?"

"Because the Oversoul would have told you to kill him in order to get the Index."

Nafai looked at her, uncomprehending. "*You* throw this up to me?"

She shook her head firmly. "I remind you of it so you don't forget how strong *you* are. You are more ruthless *and* more clever than Vas, when you know you're serving the Oversoul's plan. Now go, Nafai. You have a few hours of daylight left. You *will* succeed."

With the touch of her hand on his cheek still alive in the memory of his skin, with her voice still in his ear, with her trust and honor still hot inside his heart, he did indeed feel like one of the Heroes of Pyiretsiss. Most particularly like Velikodushnu, who ate the living heart of the god Zaveest, so that the people of Pyiretsiss could live in peace instead of constantly conspiring to get the advantage over each other and tear down those who succeeded. The illustration in the version of the tale that Nafai had read showed Velikodushnu with his head jammed into the gaping chest cavity of the god, even as Zaveest flayed the hero's back with his long fingernails. It was one of the most powerful images of his childhood, that picture of a man who ignored his own inextinguishable agony in order to consume the evil that was destroying his people.

That's what a hero was, to Nafai, what a *good man* was, and if he could only think of Gaballufix as Zaveest, then it was good and right to have killed him.

But that idea only helped him for a moment; then, once again, the horror of having murdered Gaballufix as he lay drunk and helpless on the street returned to him. And he realized that perhaps that memory, that guilt, that shame, that horror—perhaps that was his own version of having his back flayed open by Zaveest even as he consumed the heart of the most vicious of the gods.

Never mind. Put it back where it belongs, in memory, not in the forefront of thought. I am the man who killed Gaballufix, yes, but I'm also the man who must make a bow, kill an animal, and bring it home by nightfall tomorrow or the Oversoul will have to begin again.

Obring ducked through the door of Vas's and Sevet's tent. It was the first time he had been with Sevet with any kind of privacy since Kokor caught the two of them bouncing away back in Basilica. Not that it was *really* privacy, with Vas there. But in a way the fact that he sanctioned this meeting meant that, perhaps, the long freeze-out was over.

"Thanks for stopping by," said Vas.

There was enough irony in Vas's tone that Obring realized he must have done something wrong, and Vas was reproving him. Oh—maybe he had taken too long getting here. "You said to come without Kokor, and I can't always just walk away. She always asks where I'm going, you know. And then watches to make sure I go there."

From the curl of Sevet's lip, Obring knew that she was enjoying the idea of him in such bondage to Kokor. Though if anyone should understand his predicament, Sevet should—wasn't she, too, in Vas's relentless custody? Or perhaps not—Vas wasn't vindictive like Kokor. Vas didn't even get angry that night more than a year ago. So maybe Sevet hadn't been suffering the way Obring had.

Looking at Sevet, though, Obring could hardly remember why he had been so eager to have her. Her body had certainly collapsed since the old days. No doubt having a baby had done part of it—the thick abdomen, the too-full breasts—but it was in her face, too, a kind of jowliness, a grimness around the eyes. She was not a beautiful woman. But then, it wasn't really her body that Obring had loved, was it? It was partly her fame, as one of the leading singers in Basilica, and partly—admit it to yourself, Obring, old man—that she was Koya's sister. Even then, Obring had wanted to stick it to his pretty, sexy, contemptuous wife and prove to her that he could get a better woman than her if he wanted to. No doubt, however, he had proven nothing of the kind, for Sevet almost certainly slept with him for similar reasons—if he had *not* been Kokor's husband, Sevet wouldn't have wasted the saliva to spit on him. They were both out to hurt Kokor, and they had succeeded, and they had been paying for it ever since.

Yet now here they were, together at Vas's invitation, and it seemed like things might be improving now, that Obring might actually be *included* in something in this miserable company so dominated by Volemak's and Rasa's children.

"I think it's time we put an end to this whole stupid expedition, don't you?" said Vas.

Obring laughed bitterly. "That's been tried before, and then Nafai pulled his little magic tricks."

"Some of us have only been biding our time," said Vas. "But this is the last chance—the last reasonable one, anyway. Dorova is in plain sight. We don't need Elemak to guide us there. Yesterday I found a route down the mountain. It isn't easy, but we can do it."

"We?"

"You and Sevet and me."

Obring looked over at where their baby, Vasnya, lay sleeping. "Carrying a baby? In the middle of the night?"

"There's a moon and I know the way," said Vas. "And we're not bringing the baby."

"Not bringing the—"

"Don't get stupid on me, Obring—give it a little thought. Our purpose isn't to get away from the group, our purpose is to get the whole group to give up the expedition. We aren't doing this for ourselves, we're doing it for *them*, to save them from themselves—from the Oversoul's absurd plans. We're going to Dorova so they *have* to follow us. We couldn't take babies with us, because they'd slow us down and they might suffer from the journey. So we leave them behind. Then they have to bring Vasnya to me and Sevet, and they have to bring Kokor and Krassya to *you*. Only *they* take the long way round, so the babies are safe."

"That makes . . . a kind of sense," said Obring.

"How kind of you to say so," said Vas.

"So if Nafai comes back without meat, we leave that night?"

"Are you such a fool you believe they'll keep their agreement?" asked Vas. "No, they'll find some other excuse to go on—putting our children at risk, taking us farther and farther from our last hope of a decent life. No, Briya, my friend, we wait for nothing. We force their hand before Nafai and the Oversoul have a chance to pull another trick."

"So . . . when do we leave? After supper?"

"They'd notice it and follow us and stop us immediately," said Vas. "So tonight I'll volunteer for late watch and you volunteer for last watch. A while into my watch, I'll get Sevet up and then scratch the tent for you. Kokor will think you're merely getting up to take your watch and she'll go right back to sleep. There's a good moon tonight— we'll be hours on our way before anybody else wakes up."

Obring nodded. "Sounds good." Then he looked at Sevet. Her expression was as impenetrable as ever. He wanted to get past that mask, just a little, and so he said, "But won't your teats get sore, leaving the baby behind when you're nursing?"

"Hushidh produces enough milk for four babies," said Sevet. "It's what she was born for."

Her words were hardly tender, but at least she had spoken. "Count me in," said Obring.

Then he had a second thought. A doubt about Vas's motive. "But why *me?*"

"Because you're not one of *them,*" he said. "You don't care about the Oversoul, you hate this life, and you're not caught up in some foolish notion of family loyalty. Who else could I get? If Sevet and I did this alone, they might decide to keep our baby and go on. We needed somebody else with us, to split another family, and who was there besides you? The only other unconnected people are Zdorab and Shedemei, who don't have a baby so they do us no good at all, and Hushidh and Luet, and they're thicker with the Oversoul than anybody else. Oh, and Dol, of course, but she's so besotted with Mebbekew, God knows why, and such a lazy coward anyway, that she wouldn't come with us and we wouldn't want her if she would. That leaves *you,*

Obring. And believe me, I'm asking you only because you're a little less repugnant to me than Dolya."

Now *that* was a motive that Obring could believe. "I'm in, then," he said.

Shedemei waited until she saw Zdorab head for Volemak's tent. He would be borrowing the Index, of course—with no cooking allowed these days, he had more free time for study. So she excused herself from the group washing clothes, asking Hushidh to pick up Zdorab's and her laundry from the shrubs when it was dry. When Zdorab came through the door of the tent, the Index carefully tucked under his arm, Shedemei was waiting for him.

"Did you want to be alone?" Zdorab asked.

"I wanted to talk to *you*," said Shedemei.

Zdorab sat down, then set the Index aside so she wouldn't think he was impatient to use it—though of course she knew that he was.

"Dorova is our last chance," said Shedemei. "To return to civilization."

Zdorab nodded—not agreement, only a sign that he understood.

"Zodya, we don't belong here," she said. "We're not part of this. It's a life of endless servitude for you, a life in which all my work is wasted. We've done it for a year—we've served well. The reason for your oath to Nafai was to keep you from giving the alarm in Basilica back when it would have meant soldiers capturing him if you returned to the city. Well, that's hardly likely to happen *now*, don't you think?"

"I don't stay here because of my oath, Shedya."

"I know," she said, and then, despite herself, her tears came.

"Do you think I don't see how you suffer here?" he said. "We thought that having the outward form of marriage would be enough for you, but it isn't. You want to belong, and you can't do that as long as you don't have a child."

It made her furious, to hear him analyze her that way—clearly he had been watching and deciding what her "problem" was, and he was wrong. Or at least he was only half right. "It isn't about *belonging*," she said angrily. "It's about *life*. I'm nobody here—I'm not a scientist, I'm not a mother, I'm not even a good *servant* like you, I can't plumb the depths of the Index because its voice isn't as clear to me—I find myself echoing *your* wisdom when I talk to others because nobody can even *understand* the things *I* know—and when I see the others with their babies I want one of my own, I'm *hungry* for one, not so I can be like *them* but because I want to be part of the net of life, I want to pass my genes on, to see a child grow with a face half-mine. Can't you understand that? I'm not reproductively handicapped like you, I'm cut off from my own biological identity because I'm trapped here in this company and if I don't get out I'll die and I will have made *no difference in the world.*"

Silence was thick in the air in their tent, when she was done with her impassioned speech. What is he thinking? What does he think of me? I've hurt him, I know—I've told him that I hate being married to him, which is not true really, because he is my true friend—who else in all my life have I been able to pour out my heart to, until him?

"I shouldn't have spoken," she said in a whisper. "But I saw the lights of the city, and I thought—we could both return to a world that values us."

"*That* world didn't value me any more than this one," said Zdorab. "And you forget—how can I ever leave the Index?"

Didn't he understand what she was proposing? "Take it," she said. "We can take the Index and hurry around the bay. We have no children to slow us down. They can't catch us. With the Index you will have knowledge to sell as surely as I have—we can buy our way out of Dorova and back to the wide world in the north before they can get this caravan back north to chase us. *They* don't *need* the Index—don't you see how Luet and Nafai and Volemak and Hushidh all talk to the Oversoul without the help of the Index?"

"They don't *really* need it, and so we aren't *really* thieves for taking it," said Zdorab.

"Yes of course we're really thieves," said Shedemei. "But thieves who steal from those who don't need what they're taking can live with their crime a little more easily than thieves who take bread from the mouths of the poor."

"I don't know that it's the magnitude of the crime that decides whether the criminal can live with it," said Zdorab. "I think it's the natural goodness of the person who commits the crime. Murderers often live with their murders more easily than honest men live with a small lie."

"And you're so honest . . ."

"Yes, I am," said Zdorab. "And so are you."

"We're both living a lie every day we spend with this company." It was a terrible thing to say, and yet she was so desperate for change, for *something* to change, that she hurled at him everything that came to mind.

"Are we? Is it a very big lie?" Zdorab seemed not so much hurt as . . . thoughtful. Pondering. "Hushidh mentioned to me the other day that you and I are among the very closest bondings in this caravan. We talk about everything. We have immense respect for each other. We *love* each other—that's what she saw, and I believe her. It *is* true, isn't it?"

"Yes," whispered Shedemei.

"So what is the lie? The lie is that I'm your partner in reproduction. That's all. And if that lie became the truth, and there were a child in your belly, you would be whole, wouldn't you? The lie would no longer tear at your heart, because you would *be* what now you only seem—a wife—and you could become a part of that net of life."

She studied his face, trying to find mockery in it, but there was none. "*Can* you?"

"I don't know. I was never interested enough to try, and even if I had been, I would have had no willing partner. But—if I can find some small satisfactions from my own imagining, by myself, then why couldn't I—give a gift of love to my dearest friend? Not because *I* desire it, but because *she* desires it so much?"

"Out of pity," she said.

"Out of love," he said. "More love than these other men who jump their wives every night out of a desire no deeper than the scratching of an itch, or the voiding of a bladder."

What he was offering—to father a child on her—was something she had never considered as a possibility. Wasn't his condition his destiny?

"Doesn't love show its face," he went on, "when it satisfies the need of the loved one, for that loved one's sake alone? Which of these husbands can claim *that?*"

"But isn't a woman's body—repulsive to you?"

"To some, perhaps. Most of us, though, are simply . . . indifferent. The way ordinary men are toward other men. But I can tell you things to do that can awaken desire; I can perhaps imagine other partners out of my past, if you will forgive me for such . . . disloyalty . . . in the cause of giving you a child."

"But Zdorab. I don't want you to give *me* a child," she said. She was uncertain how to say this, since the idea had only just come to her, but the words came out clearly enough. "I want *us* to have a child."

"Yes," he said. "That's what I mean, too. I'll be a father to our child —I won't have to pretend to do *that.* My condition is not, strictly speaking, hereditary. If we have a son, he'll not necessarily be . . . like me."

"Ah, Zodya," she said, "don't you know that in so many ways I want our sons to be *just* like you?"

"Sons?" he said. "Don't try to net your fish before you reach the sea, my dear Shedya. We don't know if we can do this even once, let alone often enough to conceive a single child. It may be so awful for both of us that we never try again."

"But you *will* try the once?"

"I will try until we succeed, or until you tell me to stop trying." He leaned toward her and kissed her cheek. "The hardest thing for me may well be this: That in my heart, I think of you as my dearest sister. Coupling with you might feel like incest."

"Oh, do try not to feel *that* way," she said. "The only problems we'll have with that are when a child of Luet's falls in love with a child of Hushidh's—double first cousins! You and I are genetically remote."

"And yet so close to each other," he said. "Help me do this for you. If we can do it, it will bring us so much joy. And running away, stealing from our friends, parting from each other, defying the Oversoul—what joy could that ever bring? This is the best way, Shedya. Stay with me."

Nafai found the wood easily enough—the Oversoul did have a fair idea of what kinds of vegetation grew where in this area, and of course knew perfectly well which woods were chosen by the bowmakers of different cities and cultures. What the Oversoul could *not* do was give Nafai any skill with his hands. Not that Nafai was unusually clumsy. It was just that he had never worked with wood, or with knives, really, except for gutting and flaying game. He spoiled two potential bows, and now it was coming on evening and he hadn't even begun to make arrows, the bow was causing him such grief.

You can't acquire in an hour a skill that others take a lifetime to develop.

Was it the Oversoul speaking in his mind, when this thought came? Or was it the voice of despair?

Nafai sat on a flat rock, despondent. He had his third piece of bow-wood across his knees, his knife in hand, freshly whetted and sharp. But he knew little more now about working with wood than he did at the start—all he had was a catalog of ways that knives could slip and ruin wood, or that wood could split in the wrong places or at the wrong angle. He had not been more frustrated since the time when the Oversoul put Father's dream into his mind and it nearly drove him mad.

Thinking back to that time made him shudder. But then, thinking about it, he realized that it might also be a way to . . .

"Oversoul," he whispered. "There are master bowmakers in this world. Right now, this very moment, there is a bowmaker whittling a piece of wood to shape it properly."

(None with tools as primitive as yours,) said the Oversoul in his mind.

"Then find one and fill him with the idea of whittling one with a simple knife. Then put his thoughts, his movements into my mind. Let me have the feeling of it."

(It will drive you mad.)

"Find a bowmaker in your memory, one who *always* worked this way—there must have been one, in forty million years, one who loved the feel of the knife, who could whittle a bow *without thinking.*"

(Ah . . . without thinking . . . pure habit, pure reflex . . .)

"Father was concentrating so hard on everything in his dream—that's why I couldn't bear to have his memories in my mind. But a bowmaker whose hands work without thought. Put those skills in me. Let me know how it feels, so that I also have those reflexes."

(I've never done such a thing. It wasn't what I was designed to do. It might still make you mad.)

"It might also make a bow," said Nafai. "And if I fail at this, the expedition is over."

(I'll try. Give me time. It takes time to find one man, in all the years of human life on Harmony, who worked so mindlessly . . .)

So Nafai waited. A minute, two minutes. And then a strange feeling came over him. A tingling, not in his arms, really, but in the *idea* of his arms that constantly dwelt inside his mind. A need to move the muscles, to work. It's happening, thought Nafai, the muscle memory, the nerve memory, and I must learn how to receive it, how to let this body of mine be guided by someone else's hands and fingers, wrists and arms.

He shifted the knife in his hand until it felt comfortable. And then he began to wipe the knife across the surface of the wood, not even letting the blade bite, just feeling the face of the sapling. And then, at last, he knew—or rather felt—when the wood invited the blade to dip into its surface, to peel away the thin bark. He pulled the knife through the wood like a fish moving through the sea, feeling the resistance of the wood and learning from it, finding the hard places, the weak places, and working around them, easing up where too much pressure would split the wood, biting hard where the wood cried out for discipline from the blade.

The sun was down, the moon just rising when he finished. But the bow was smooth and beautiful.

Green wood, so it won't hold its spring long.

How did I know that? thought Nafai, and then laughed at himself. How had he known any of this?

We can choose the saplings that we need and make greenwood bows from them at first, but also save others, season them, so that the bows we make later will last. There are plenty of stands of wood on our way south that will do for our needs. We won't even have to wait here for bow-wood gathering.

Carefully he looped and knotted one end of the twine Luet had given him, and tightened it around the narrow waist of the string-nock he had cut in one end of the bow. Then he drew the twine along the length of the bow to the other end, looped it around the other string-nock, and tightened it down. Far enough that there would be constant tension on the string, so that when he released an arrow the string would not wobble, but would return to perfect straightness, so the arrow would fly true. It felt right, as if he had done it a thousand times, and he easily and skillfully tied the loop in the twine, cut off the long excess, and then strung it into place.

"If I think about it," he whispered to the Oversoul, "then I can't do it."

(Because it's reflex) came the answer in his mind. (It's deeper than thought.)

"But will I remember it? Can I teach it to others?"

(You'll remember some of it. You'll make mistakes but it will come back to you, because it's now deep in *your* mind, too. You may not be able to explain well what you do, but they can watch you and learn that way.)

The bow was ready. He unstrung it again and then began work on the arrows. The Oversoul had led him to a place where many birds nested—he found no shortage of feathers there. And the short straight arrow shafts came from the tough woody reeds growing around a pool. And the arrowheads from obsidian crumbling out of the side of a hill. He gathered them all, having no idea of how to work with them; yet now the knowledge poured out of his fingers without ever reaching his conscious mind. By dawn he would have his arrows, his bow, perhaps in time enough for him to get a few hours of sleep. After that it would be daylight, and his real test: to track and follow his prey, and kill it, and bring it home.

And if I do, what then? I will be the hero, striding back into camp, triumphant, with the blood of the kill on my hands, on my clothing. I will be the one who brought meat when no one else could have. I will be the one who made it possible for the expedition to go on. I will be Velikodushnu, I will be the savior of my family and my friends, everyone will know that when even my father shrank from the journey I was the one who found a way to continue, so that when we go forth among the stars and human feet again step on the soil of Earth, it will have been *my* triumph, because I made this bow, these arrows, and brought meat home to the wives . . .

Then, in the midst of his imagined triumph, another thought: I will be the one held responsible from then on if anything goes wrong. I will be the one blamed for every misfortune on the journey. It will be *my* expedition, and even Father will look to me for leadership. On that day Father will be irretrievably weakened. Who will lead then? Until now, the answer would have been clear: Elemak. Who could rival him? Who would follow anybody else, except the handful who will do whatever the Oversoul asks? But now, if I return as the hero, I will be in a position to rival Elemak. Not in a position to overwhelm him, though. Only to rival him. Only strong enough to tear the company apart. It would lead to bitterness no matter who won; it might lead to bloodshed. It must not happen now, if the expedition is to succeed.

So I can't return as a hero. I must find a way to bring back the meat we need to live, to feed the babies—and yet still leave Father's leadership unweakened.

As he thought and thought, his fingers and hands continued at their work, expertly finding the straightest reeds and nocking them for the bowstring, slicing them in deft spirals for the feathers, and splitting and lashing the other end to hold the tiny obsidian arrowheads.

* * *

Zdorab lay beside Shedemei, sweating and exhausted. The sheer physical exertion of it had almost defeated him. How could something that brought the two of them so little pleasure be so important to her—and, in its own way, to him? Yet they had accomplished it, despite his body's initial disinterest. He remembered something that an old lover of his had once said—that when it came down to it, human males could mate with any creature that held still long enough and didn't bite very hard. Perhaps so . . .

He had been hoping, though, in the back of his mind, that when he finally mated with a woman there would be some place in his brain, some gland in his body that would awaken and say, Ah, so *this* is how it's done. Then the days of his isolation would be over, and his body would know its proper place in the scheme of nature. But the truth was that nature had no scheme. Only a series of accidents. A species "worked" if enough of its members reproduced faithfully and often enough to keep it going; so what if some insignificant percentage—*my* percentage, Zdorab thought bitterly—ends up being reproductively irrelevant. Nature wasn't a child's birthday party; nature didn't care about including everybody. Zdorab's body would be cycled back through the wheels and gears of life, whether or not his genes happened to reproduce themselves along the way.

And yet. And yet. Even though his body had had no particular joy from Shedemei's (and certainly hers had finally become exhausted from the effort to please *his*), yet there was joy in it on another level. Because the gift had been given. Sheer friction and stimulation of nerves had won in the end, sparking the reflex that deposited a million hopeful half-humans-to-be into the matrix that would keep them alive for the day or two of their race toward their other half, the all-mother, the Infinite Egg. What did *they* care whether Zdorab had lusted after Shedemei or merely acted out of duty while desperately trying to fantasize another lover of a reproductively irrelevant sex? Their life was lived on another plane—and it was on exactly that plane that the great net of life that Shedemei so worshipped was woven together.

I have finally been caught in that net, for reasons that no gene could plan for; I was greased at birth, to slip away from the net forever, but I have been caught anyway, I have *chosen* to be caught, and who is to say that mine is not the better fatherhood, because I acted out of pure love, and not out of some inborn instinct that captured me. Indeed, I

acted *against* my instinct. There's something in that. A hero of copula-
tion, a *real* cocksman, if the others only knew. Anybody can pilot his
boat to shore in a fair wind; I have come to shore by tacking in contrary
winds, by rowing against an ebbing tide.

So let the little suckers make it to the egg. Shedemei said it was a
good time for them to have their competition for survival. Let one of
them, a strong and sturdy one, reach his microscopic goal and pierce
that cell wall and join his helical deoxyribonucleic acid to hers and
make a baby on our very first try, so I don't have to go through all of
this again.

But if I have to, I will. For Shedemei.

He reached out and found her hand and clasped it in his. She did
not awaken, but still her hand closed ever so slightly, gently enclosing
his.

Luet could hardly sleep. She couldn't stop thinking about Nafai, worrying about him. In vain did the Oversoul assure her: He's doing well, all
will be well. It was long after dark, long after Chveya slept from her
last suckling of the night, before Luet drifted off to sleep.

It was no restful sleep, either. She kept dreaming of Nafai sidling
along rocky ledges, creeping up the face of sheer cliffs with sometimes
a bow in one hand, sometimes a pulse, only in her dream the cliff
would grow steeper and steeper until finally it bent backward and
Nafai was clinging like an insect to the underside of the cliff and finally
he would lose his grip and drop away . . .

And she would come half-awake, realize it had been a dream, and
impatiently turn her sweaty pillow and try to sleep again.

Until a dream came that was not of Nafai dying. Instead he was in a
room that shone with silver, with chromium, with platinum, with ice.
In her dream he lay down upon a block of ice and the heat of his body
melted into it, and he sank and sank until he was completely inside the
ice and it closed over him and froze. What is this dream? she thought.
And then she thought, If I know that this is a dream, does that mean
that I'm awake? And if I'm awake, why doesn't the dream stop?

It did not stop. Instead she saw that, instead of being trapped in the
ice, Nafai was sinking all the way through it. Now the shape of his back
and buttocks, his calves and heels, his elbows and fingertips and the
back of his head began to bow downward at the bottom of the ice
block, and she thought—what holds this ice in the middle of the air

like this? Why didn't it also hold Nafai? His body bulged farther and farther downward, and then he dropped through, falling the meter or so to the shining floor. His eyes opened, as if he had been asleep during his passage through the ice. He rolled out from under the block, out of the shadow of it, and as soon as he stood up in the light, she could see that his body was no longer what it had been. Now, where the lights struck him, his skin shone brightly, as if it had been coated with the finest possible layer of the same metal the walls were made of. Like armor. Like a new skin. It sparkled so . . . and then she realized that it was not reflecting light at all, but rather it was giving off its own light. Whatever he was wearing now drew its power from his body, and when he thought of any part of himself, to move a limb, or even just to look at it, it fairly sparked with light.

Look at him, thought Luet. He has become a god, not just a hero. He shines like the Oversoul. His is the body of the Oversoul.

But that's nonsense. The Oversoul is a computer, and needs no body of flesh and bone. Far from it—caught in a human body it would lose its vast memory, its light-fast speed.

Nevertheless, Nafai's body sparkled with light as he moved, and she knew that it was the Oversoul's body he was wearing, though it made no sense to her at all.

In the dream she saw him come to her, and embrace her, and when she was joined to him, she could feel that the sparkling armor that he wore grew to include her, so that she also shone with light. It made her skin feel so alive, as if every nerve had been connected to the molecule-thin metal coating that surrounded her like sweat. And she realized—every point that sparks is where a nerve connects to this layer of light. She pulled away from Nafai, and the new skin stayed with her, even though she had not passed through the ice that gave it to him. It is his skin I'm wearing now, she thought; and yet she also thought: I too am wearing the body of the Oversoul, and am alive now for the first time.

What does this dream mean?

But since she was asking the question in a dream, she got only a dream answer: She saw the dream Nafai and her dreamself make love, with such passion that she forgot it was a dream and lost herself in the ecstasy of it. And when their coupling was done, she saw the belly of her dreamself grow, and then a baby emerged from her groin and slid shining into Nafai's arms, for the babe, too, was coated with the new skin, alive with light. Ah, the child was beautiful, so beautiful.

(Wake up.)

She heard it like a voice, it was so clear and strong.

(Wake up.)

She sat bolt upright, trying to see who had spoken to her, to recognize the voice that lingered in her memory.

(Get up.)

It was not a voice at all. It was the Oversoul. But why was the Oversoul interrupting her dream, when surely the Oversoul had *sent* the dream in the first place?

(Get up, Waterseer, rise up in silence, and walk in the moonlight to the place where Vas plans to kill his wife and his rival. On the ledge that saved Nafai's life you must wait for them.)

But I'm not strong enough to stop him, if murder is in his heart.

(Being there will be enough. But you *must* be there, and you must go now, for he is on watch now, and thinks that he and Sevet are the only ones awake . . . he will soon be scratching on Obring's tent, and then it will be too late, you'll not make it to the mountain unobserved.)

Luet passed through the door of her tent, so sleepy that she still felt as if she were in a dream.

Why must I go down the mountain? she asked, confused. Why not just tell Obring and Sevet what Vas plans for them?

(Because if they believe you, Vas will be destroyed as a member of this company. And if they don't believe you, Vas will be your enemy and you will never be safe again. Trust me. Do this my way, and all will live, all will live.)

Are you sure of this?

(Of course.)

You're no better at telling the future than anybody else. How sure are you?

(The odds of success are, perhaps, sixty percent.)

Oh, wonderful. What about the forty percent chance of failure?

(You are such an intelligent woman, you'll improvise, you'll make it work.)

I wish I had as much faith in you as you seem to have in me.

(The only reason you don't is because you don't know me as well as I know you.)

You can read my thoughts, dear Oversoul, but you can never know me, because there is no part of you that can feel the way I feel, or think the way I think.

(Do you imagine I don't know that, boastful human? Must you taunt me for it? Go down the mountain. Carefully, carefully. The path is visible by moonlight, but treacherous. Obring is awake now; you have made it just in time. Now stay ahead of them, far enough that they can't hear you, far enough that they can't see.)

Elemak had noticed when Sevet and Obring both took extra flagons from the stores. He knew at once what it meant—that there was a plan to make a run for Dorova. At the same time, though, he could not believe that *those* two would ever have come up with a plan together— they never spoke to each other privately, if only because Kokor made sure they had no opportunity. No, there was someone else involved, someone who was better at this sort of deception, so that Elemak hadn't noticed his or her theft of an extra flagon.

And then, just before night, Vas had volunteered for the hated late watch, the second-to-last one before morning. Obring had taken the last watch already. It didn't take a genius to realize that they intended to leave on Vas's watch. Fools. Did they think they could make it down the mountain and across the waterless sand of the beach around the bay on two flagons of fresh water each? Not carrying babies they couldn't.

They aren't going to take their babies.

The thought was so outrageous that Elemak almost didn't believe it. But then he realized that it must be true. His loathing for Obring redoubled. But Vas . . . it was hard to believe that Vas would do such a thing. The man doted on his daughter. He had even named her for himself—would he leave her, heartlessly?

No. No, he has no intention of leaving her. Obring would leave his baby, yes. Obring would leave Kokor, for that matter—he chafed constantly in his marriage. But Vas would not leave his baby. He has another motive now. And it does not include escaping to the city with Sevet and Obring. On the contrary. His plan is to tell us that Sevet and Obring left for the city after he was asleep from his watch, and he followed them down the mountain, hoping to stop them, but instead he found their dead bodies, fallen from a cliff . . .

How do I know all this? wondered Elemak. Why is this all so clear to me? And yet he could not doubt it.

So he gave himself the middle watch, and at the end of it, after he had wakened Vas and returned to his tent, Elemak did not let himself sleep, though he lay still with his eyes closed, breathing in a heavy imitation of sleep, in case Vas came to check on him. But no, Vas did not come. Did not come, and did not go to Obring's tent. The watch dragged on and on, and finally against his will Elemak *did* sleep. Perhaps only for a moment. But he must have slept because he awoke with a start, his heart pounding with alarm. Something . . . some sound. He sat upright in the darkness, listening. Beside him he could hear Edhya's breathing, and Proya's; it was hard to hear anything else beyond that. As quietly as possible he arose, went to the door of his tent, stepped outside. Vas was not on watch, and neither was anyone else.

Quietly, quietly he went to Vas's tent. Gone, and Sevet, too—but baby Vasnaminanya was still there. Elemak's heart filled with rage at the monstrosity of it. Whatever Vas was planning—either to abandon his daughter or kill the child's mother—it was unspeakable.

I will find him, thought Elemak, and when I do he will pay for this. I knew there were fools on this journey, fools and dolts and weaklings, but I never knew there was someone so cruel-hearted. I never knew that Vas was capable of this. I never knew Vas at all, I think. And I never will, because as soon as I find him he'll be dead.

It was so easy, leading them down the mountain. Their trust in him was complete. It was the payoff for his year of pretending not to mind that they had betrayed him. If he had ever shown even a spark of anger, beyond a certain coldness toward Obring, there was no chance the man would have trusted him enough to come along like a hog to the slaughter. But Obring *did* trust him, and Sevet too, in her sullen way.

The path itself had some difficulty—more than once he had to help them through a tricky place. But in the moonlight they often couldn't see how very dangerous a passage it was, and whenever it was hard, he would stay and help them. So carefully taking Sevet's hand and guiding her down a slope, or between two rocks. Whispering: "Do you see the limb you must hold on to, Obring?" And Obring's answer, "Yes," or a nod, I see it, I can handle it, Vas, because I'm a *man.* What a laugh. What a joke on Obring, who is so pathetically proud to be included in this great plan. How I will weep when we come down to carry the bodies back up the mountain. How the others will cry for me as I hold my little daughter in my arms, crooning to her about her lost mother, and how she is an orphan now. An orphan—but one named for her father. And I will raise her so no trace of her traitorous mother remains in her. She will be a woman of honor, who would never betray a good man who would have forgiven her *anything* but to give her body to her own sister's husband, that contemptible, slimy little social climber. You let him empty his little tin cup into you, Sevet, my dear, and so I will have done with you.

"Here's the place where Nafai and I tried to cross over," he whispered to them. "See how we had to traverse that bare rock, shining in the moonlight?"

Obring nodded.

"But the ledge that saved his life is the real path," said Vas. "There's one hard place—a drop of two meters—but then it's a smooth passage along the face of the cliff, and then we reach the easy part, right down to the beach."

They followed him past the place where he had silently watched Nafai's struggle. When it was clear that Nafai was going to make it after all, then he had called out and come to help him. Now he would help them down onto the ledge. Only he would not climb down to join them. Instead he would kick Obring in the head and send him over the side. Sevet would understand then. Sevet would know why he had brought her here. And she would, at long last, beg him for forgiveness. She would plead with him for understanding, she would weep, she would sob for him. And his answer would be to pick up the heaviest stones he could find and throw them down on her, until she had to run along the ledge. He would drive her to the narrow place and still he would throw stones until finally she stumbled or was knocked off balance. She would fall then, and scream, and he would hear the sound and treasure it in his heart forever.

Then, of course, he would climb down the true path to the bottom, and find their broken bodies where the pulse had been. If one of them happened somehow to still be alive, he would have no trouble breaking a neck or two—it wouldn't be surprising to anyone, to find their necks broken in the fall. But he doubted they'd live. It was quite a long fall. The pulse had been completely shattered. That annoying little pizdoon Nafai would have been just as broken up if he hadn't found that invisible ledge to land on. Ah, well, Nafai was only an annoyance—Vas didn't care much whether he lived or died, as long as the pulses were all destroyed so they would have to head back to civilization. And now, before they *did* turn back, was his chance to have his revenge and yet no one would suspect him. "I think they must have heard me following them, because they were going much too fast, especially for nighttime travel. And then I saw they were heading for that ledge. I knew how dangerous it was, I called out to them, but they didn't understand, I guess, that I was warning them away. Or maybe they didn't care. God help me, but I loved her! The mother of my child!" I'll even shed a tear for them, and they'll believe me. What choice will they have? Everyone knows that I long since forgave and forgot their adultery.

I'm not a very demanding man. I don't expect perfection from others. I get along and do my part. But when someone treats me like a worm, as if I didn't exist, as if I didn't *matter,* then I don't forget, no, I never forget, I never forgive, I simply bide my time and then they see: I *do* matter, and despising me was the gravest error of their lives. That's what Sevet will be thinking as the stones strike her and she has no place to flee to except the open air as she falls to her death: If only I had been true to him, I would live to raise my daughter.

"Here," he said. "Here's the place where we have to drop down to that lower ledge."

Sevet was clearly frightened, and Obring put on a mask of bravado that showed his fear as clearly as if he had simply wet himself and whimpered. Which he would do soon enough. "No problem," he said.

"Sevet first," said Vas.

"Why me?" she said.

"Because the two of us can lower you down more safely," said Vas. And mostly because then I can kick Obring in the head as soon as I lower *him,* and you'll already be trapped on the ledge where you can see everything but do nothing.

It was going to work. Sevet squatted at the lip of the ledge, preparing to turn and go over the side. And then there came that other voice, that unexpected, terrible voice.

"The Oversoul forbids you to go down, Sevet."

They all turned, and there she stood, shining in the moonlight, her white gown flapping a little in the wind, which was stronger where she stood.

How did she know? thought Vas. How did she know to come here? I thought the Oversoul would consent to this—simple justice! If the Oversoul had not wanted him to do this, to make Obring and Sevet pay for their crime, then why didn't he stop him before? Why *now*, when he was so close? No, he wouldn't let her stop him at all. It was too late. There would be *three* bodies at the bottom of the cliff, not two. And instead of climbing back up the mountain, he would take three flagons of water and head for Dorova. He would get there and leave again long before any accusations could overtake him. And in Seggidugu or Potokgavan, wherever he ended up, he would deny everything. There *were* no witnesses, and none of these people would have standing anyway. He would lose his daughter—but that would be fit and fair punishment for killing Luet. It would all be even. He would owe no debt of vengeance to the universe, and the universe would owe no debt of vengeance to him. All would be balanced and settled and right.

"You know me, Sevet," said Luet. "I speak to you as the waterseer. If you go down that ledge you'll never see your child again, and there is no greater crime in the eyes of the Oversoul than for a mother to abandon her child."

"As *your* mother did to you and Hushidh?" said Vas. "Spare us your lies about crimes in the eyes of the Oversoul. The Oversoul is a computer set by some distant ancestor to keep his eyes on us, and nothing more—your own husband says so, doesn't he? My wife is not superstitious enough to believe you."

No, no, he shouldn't have said so much. He should have *acted*. He should have taken three steps and shoved the frail-bodied girl off the edge. She couldn't possibly resist him. Then, having seen him do murder, the others would be all the quicker to obey and be on their way— to safety, to the city, they *think*. To argue with her was stupid. He was being stupid.

"The Oversoul chose the three of you to be part of her company," said Luet. "I tell you now that if you go over that edge, you will not live to see daylight, not one of you."

"Prophecy?" said Vas. "I didn't know that was one of your many gifts." Kill her now! he screamed inside, and yet his own body didn't heed him.

"The Oversoul tells me that Nafai has made his bow and arrows, and they fly straight and true. This expedition will continue, and you will continue with it," she said. "If you go back now, your daughters will never know that you once abandoned them. The Oversoul will fulfil her promises to you—that you will inherit a land of plenty, and your children will be a great nation."

"When were any of those promises for *me*," said Obring. "For Volemak's sons, yes, but not for *me*. For me it's nothing but taking orders and getting yelled at because I don't do everything the way King Elemak wants me to."

"Stop whining," said Vas. "Don't you see that she's trying to ensnare us all?"

"The Oversoul sent me here to save your lives," said Luet.

"That's a lie," said Vas. "And you know it's a lie. My life has not been in danger for a single moment."

"I tell you that if you had succeeded in your plan, Vas, your life would not have lasted five more minutes."

"And how would this miracle have happened?" asked Vas.

That was when Elemak's voice came from behind him, and he knew that he had lost everything.

"I would have killed you myself," said Elemak. "With my bare hands."

Vas whirled on him, furious and, for once, unable to contain his rage. Why *should* he contain it? He was as good as dead now, with Elemak here—so why not speak his contempt openly? "Would you!" he cried. "Do you think you're a match for me! You've never been a match for me! I've thwarted you at every turn! And you never guessed, you never *suspected*. You fool, strutting and bragging about how only you know how to lead our caravan—who was it who did what you couldn't do, and turned us back?"

"Turned us back? It wasn't *you* that . . ." But then Elemak paused, and Vas could see understanding come to his eyes. *Now* Elya knew who had destroyed the pulses. "Yes," said Elemak. "Like the coward and sneak you are, you endangered us all, you put *my* wife and *my* son at risk, and we didn't catch you because it never occurred to any of us that anyone in our company could be so slimy and vile as to deliberately—"

"Enough," said Luet. "Say no more, or there'll be accusations that must be dealt with openly, which can still be handled in silence."

Vas understood at once. Luet didn't want Elemak to say outright that Vas had destroyed the pulses, not in front of Obring and Sevet, or there'd have to be a punishment. And she didn't want him punished. She didn't want him killed. Luet was the waterseer; she spoke for the Oversoul; and that meant that the Oversoul wanted him alive.

(That's right.)

The thought was as clear as a voice inside his head.

(I want you alive. I want Luet alive. I want Sevet and Obring alive. Do not force me to choose which of you will die.)

"Come back up the mountain," said Elemak. "All three of you."

"I don't want to go back," said Obring. "There's nothing for me here. The city's where I belong."

"Yes," said Elemak, "in a city your weakness and laziness and cowardice and stupidity can be concealed behind fine clothing and a few jests and people will think you're a man. But don't worry—there's plenty of time for that. When Nafai fails and we return to the city—"

"But *she* says that he's made his bow," said Obring.

Elemak looked over at Luet and seemed to see the confirmation in her eyes. "Making a bow is not the same thing as knowing how to use it," he said. "If he brings home meat, then I'll know the Oversoul is truly with him, and more powerful than I ever thought. But it won't happen, Waterseer. Your husband will do his best, but he'll fail, not because he wasn't good enough but because it can't be done. And when he fails, we'll turn north and return to the city. There's no need for you to have done this."

Vas listened and understood the real message. Whether or not Elemak actually believed Nafai would fail, he was speaking in such a way that Sevet and Obring would think that nothing more had been going on here than an attempted escape to the city. He did not intend to tell them that Vas had been meaning to kill them.

Or perhaps he didn't know. Perhaps Luet didn't know. Perhaps when she spoke of the three of them dying if they went down onto the ledge, she meant that Elemak would kill them to prevent their escape. Perhaps it was all still a secret.

"Go back up the way you came," said Elemak. "Agree to that, and there'll be no punishment. We still have time enough before morning that no one beyond the five of us will need to know what happened."

"Yes," said Obring. "I will, I'm sorry, thank you."

He is so *weak*, thought Vas.

Obring passed Elemak and began to scramble back up the path. Sevet silently followed him.

"Go on ahead, Luet," said Elemak. "You've done good work here tonight. I won't bother asking the waterseer how she knew to be here before them. I'll only say that if you hadn't delayed them, there would have been killing here tonight."

Were the others out of earshot? Vas wondered. Or was Elemak still thinking only of his *own* killing—that he would have caught them and punished them for trying to escape?

Luet passed them by, and followed the others up the mountain. Vas and Elemak were alone.

"What was the plan?" asked Elemak. "To push them as you lowered them down onto the ledge?"

So he knew.

"If you had harmed either one of them, I would have torn you apart."

"Would you?" asked Vas.

Elemak's hand snaked out and took him by the throat, jamming him back against the rock wall behind him. Vas clutched at Elemak's arm, then at his hand, trying to pry the fingers away. He couldn't breathe, and it *hurt*, Elemak wasn't just pretending, wasn't just demonstrating his power, he meant to kill him, and Vas filled with panic. Just as he was about to claw at Elemak's eyes—anything to get him to let go— Elemak's other hand seized Vas's crotch and squeezed. The pain was indescribable, and yet he couldn't scream or even gasp because his throat was closed. He gagged and retched, and some of his stomach bile *did* manage to force its way past the constriction in his throat; he could taste it in his mouth. This is death, he thought.

Elemak gave a final squeeze, both to Vas's throat and to his testicles, as if to prove that he hadn't been using his full strength all along, and then released him.

Vas gasped and whimpered. The pain in his crotch was, if anything, worse, a throbbing ache, and his throat also ached as he sucked in air.

"I didn't do this in front of the others," said Elemak, "because I want you to be useful. I don't want you to be broken or humiliated in front of the others. But I want you to remember this. When you start plotting your next murder, remember that Luet is watching you, and the Over-soul is watching you, and, more to the point, *I'm* watching you. I won't give you a millimeter of slack from now on, Vasya, my friend. If I see any hint that you're planning any more sabotage or any more subtle little murders, I won't wait to see how things turn out, I'll simply come to you in the middle of the night and break your neck. You know I can do it. You know you can't stop me. As long as I live, you will take no vengeance against Sevet or Obring. *Or* me. I won't ask for your oath, because your word is piss from your mouth. I simply expect to be obeyed, because you're a sneaky coward who is terrified of pain, and you will never, never stand against me again because you will remember how you feel right now, at this moment."

Vas heard all this and knew that Elemak was right, he would never stand against him, because he could never bear to feel the fear and pain he had just gone through, was still going through.

But I *will* hate you, Elemak. And someday. Someday. When you're old and feeble and helpless, I will put things back in balance. I'll kill Sevet and Obring and you won't be able to stop me. You won't even know that I did it. And then one day I'll come to you and say, I did it in spite of you. And you'll rage at me and I'll only laugh, because you'll be helpless then and in your helplessness I will make you feel what you made *me* feel, the pain of it, the fear, the *panic* as you can't breathe even enough to scream out your agony—oh, you'll feel it. And as you lie there dying, I'll tell you the rest of my vengeance—that I will kill all your children, too, and your wife, and everything and everyone you love, and you can't stop me. Then you'll die, and only then will I be satisfied, knowing that your death was the most terrible death that can be imagined.

But there's no hurry, Elemak. I will dream of this every night. I will never forget. *You* will forget. Until the day that I make you remember, however many years it is before that day comes.

When Vas was able to walk, Elemak dragged him to his feet and shoved him up the trail leading to the camp.

At dawn, everyone was back in place, and no one but the participants knew of the scene that had played itself out in the moonlight, halfway down the mountain.

The sun was scarcely up when Nafai strode across the meadow toward the camp. Luet was awake—though barely so—nursing Chveya as Zdorab passed around biscuits smeared with sugary preserves for breakfast. She looked up and there he was, coming toward them, the first sunlight catching in his hair. She thought of how he had looked in her strange dream, sparking and sparkling with the light of his invisible metal armor. What did that mean? she wondered. And then she thought, What does it matter what it meant?

"Why are you back!" cried Issib, who was holding Dazya on his lap on his chair while Hushidh was off peeing or whatever.

In answer, Nafai held up the bow in one hand, five arrows in the other.

She leapt to her feet and ran to him, still holding the baby—though Chveya soon lost her grip on Luet's breast and began to protest at all this bouncing when she was trying to eat. The baby was fussing rather loudly, but Luet paid no attention to her as she kissed her husband, clung to him with her free hand.

"You have the bow," she said.

"What is a bow?" he asked. "The Oversoul taught me how to make it —it took no skill of mine. But what *you* accomplished . . ."

"You know, then?"

"The Oversoul showed me in a dream—I woke when it ended and came back at once."

"So you know that we're saying nothing about it."

"Yes," he said. "Except to each other. Except for me to tell you that you are a magnificent woman, the strongest, bravest person that I know."

She loved to hear those words from him, even though she knew they weren't true—that she had not been brave at all, but terrified that Vas would kill her right along with the others. That she had been so relieved when Elemak came that she almost wept. Soon enough she'd tell him all of that. But for now she loved to hear his words of love and honor, and to feel his arm around her as they walked together back to camp.

"I see you have the bow, but no meat," said Issib, when they got nearer.

"So you've given up?" asked Mebbekew, hopefully.

"I have until sundown," said Nafai.

"Then why are you here?" asked Elemak.

Everyone had come out of the tents now, and were gathered, watching.

"I came because having the bow is nothing—the Oversoul could have taught any of us how to do that. What I need now is for Father to tell me where to go to find game."

Volemak was surprised. "And how should I know that, Nyef? I'm not a hunter."

"I have to know where to find game that is so tame that I can creep up on it very close," said Nafai. "And where it's so plentiful that I can find more when I miss my first attempts."

"Take Vas with you, then, to track," said Volemak.

"No," said Elemak quickly. "No, Nafai is right. Neither Vas nor Obring will go with him this morning as trackers."

Luet knew perfectly well why Elemak insisted on *that*—but it still left Volemak nonplussed. "Then let Elemak tell you where to go to find game like that."

"Elemak doesn't know this country any better than I do," said Nafai.

"And I don't know it at all," said Volemak.

"Nevertheless," said Nafai, "I will only hunt where you tell me to. This is too important to leave it up to chance. Everything depends on this, Father. Tell me where to hunt, or I'll have no hope."

Volemak stood in silence, looking at his son. Luet didn't really understand why Nafai was doing this—he had never needed Volemak to tell him where to search for game before. And yet she sensed that it was very important—that for some reason the success of the expedition hinged on its being Volemak who decided where the hunt would take place.

"I will ask the Index," said Volemak.

"Thank you, Father," said Nafai. He followed his father into his tent.

Luet looked around the company as they waited. What do they make of this? Her eyes met Elemak's. He smiled a tight little smile. She smiled back, not understanding what it was *he* thought was going on.

It was Hushidh who clarified it for her. "Your husband is the clever one," she whispered.

Luet turned in surprise—she hadn't noticed Hushidh coming to her.

"When he came back with the bow and arrows, it weakened Volemak. It weakened him yesterday, in fact, when it was Nafai who insisted on trying to continue. All the bonds that held this company together weakened then. I could see it when I got up this morning—fracture. Chaos verging. And something worse, between Vas and Elemak—a terrible hatred that I don't understand. But Nafai has now handed the authority back to his father. He could have snatched it for himself and torn us all apart, but he didn't—he gave it back, and already I can see us settling back into old patterns."

"Sometimes, Shuya, I wish I had *your* gift instead of mine."

"Mine is more comfortable and practical sometimes," said Hushidh. "But you are the waterseer."

Since Chveya was tugging away on Luet's breast, slurping obscenely, as if passionately eager to get all she could before Luet took off running somewhere again, it was hard for Luet to take her noble calling all that seriously. She answered Hushidh with a laugh. Her laugh was heard by those who could not have heard their hushed conversation; many turned to look at her. What could possibly be amusing, they seemed to be wondering, on a morning like this, where our whole future is being decided?

Nafai and Volemak emerged from the tent. Volemak's air of puzzlement was gone. He was firmly in command now; he embraced his son, pointed toward the southeast, and said, "You'll find game there, Nafai. Come back soon enough and I'll allow the meat to be cooked. Let the Dorovyets wonder why there's a new column of smoke coming from across the bay! By the time they can come and investigate, we'll be on our way south again."

Luet knew that many heard those confident words with more despair than hope—but their longing for the city was a weakness in them, nothing to be proud of, not a desire to be indulged. Vas's sabotage might have turned them back, but that would have made all their lives meaningless, at least compared to what they were going to accomplish when Nafai succeeded.

If he succeeded.

Elemak spoke to Nafai then. "Are you a good shot with that thing?" he asked.

"I don't know," said Nafai. "I haven't tried it yet. It was too dark last night. I do know *this*—I can't shoot far. I don't have strong enough muscles in the right places yet, for drawing a bow." He grinned. "I'm going to have to find some animal that's very stupid, very slow, or deaf, blind, and upwind of me."

No one laughed. Instead they all stood and watched him stride away, heading unwaveringly in the exact direction his father had pointed.

From then on it was a tense morning in the camp. Not the tension of quarrels barely contained—they had experienced *that* often enough—but the tension of waiting. For there was nothing to do but care for the babies and wonder whether Nafai would, against all probability, bring back meat with his bow and arrows.

The only exception to the general air of glum nervousness was Shedemei and Zdorab. Not that they were *happy*, really—they were as quiet as ever, going about their business. But Luet could not help but notice that they seemed more—what, *aware* of each other today. They kept *looking* at each other, with some barely contained secret.

It didn't dawn on Luet until late in the morning, when Shedemei was holding naked Chveya while Luet washed the second gown and diaper that her daughter had managed to soil that morning. Shedemei couldn't stop giggling right along with Chveya while they played, and as Luet wondered about Shedemei's unaccustomed lightness of spirit, she realized: Shedemei must be pregnant. At long last, after everyone had concluded that she was sterile, Shedya was going to have a baby.

And, being Luet, she did not hesitate to ask the question outright—after all, they were alone, and no woman kept a secret from the water-seer, if she wanted to know it.

"No," said Shedemei, startled. "I mean—I might be, but how could I know so soon?"

It was only then that it occurred to Luet for the first time: Shedemei had not been pregnant till now because she and Zdorab had never coupled. They must have married for convenience, so they could share a tent. They had been *friends* all this time, and they were so *aware* of each other, Shedemei was so *happy* today because last night they must have made their marriage real for the first time.

"Congratulations anyway," said Luet.

Shedemei blushed and looked down at the baby, tickling her a little.

"And maybe it *will* be soon. Some women conceive immediately. *I* did, I think."

"Don't tell anyone else," said Shedemei.

"Hushidh will know that something has changed," said Luet.

"Her then, but no one else."

"I promise," said Luet.

But there was something in Shedemei's smile then that told her that while she knew *part* of the secret, perhaps, there was more that was yet untold. Never mind, Luet said silently. I'm not one of those who has to know everything. What goes on between you and Zdorab is none of my affair, except as you make it plain to me. But whatever happened, I know this: It has made you happier today. More hopeful than I've seen you in this whole journey.

Or perhaps it is *I* who am more hopeful than ever before, because we weathered such a terrible crisis this morning. And, best of all, because Elemak was on the side of the Oversoul. So what if Vas is a sneak and a murderer in his heart? So what if Obring and Sevet would leave their babies? If Elemak was no longer the enemy of the Over-soul, then all would be well indeed.

Nafai came home before noon. No one saw him coming because no one was looking for him so early. Suddenly he was there at the edge of the tents.

"Zdorab!" he called.

Zdorab emerged from Volemak's tent, where he and Issib had been working with the Index together. "Nafai," he said. "I guess this means you're back."

Nafai held out the skinless carcass of a hare in one hand and an equally naked and bloody yozh in the other. "Neither one's very much by itself, I suppose, but since Father said we could make stew if I got back early enough, I say start up a fire, Zodya! We have fat-riddled animal protein to put in our bellies tonight!"

Not everyone was overjoyed to know that the expedition would go on—but they were all glad of the cooked meat, the spicy stew, and the end of the uncertainty. Volemak was positively jovial as he presided over the meal that night. Luet wondered at that—wouldn't it have been easier for him, now, to let the mantle of authority slip away, to pass it to one of his sons? But no. Heavy as the burden of authority might be, it was far lighter than the unbearable weight of losing it.

She noticed as they sat and ate together that Nafai stank from his exertions of the day. It wasn't exactly an unfamiliar odor—no one could maintain Basilican standards of hygiene here—but it was unpleasant. "You smell," she whispered to him, while the others listened to Mebbekew chanting out a bawdy old poem he had learned in his theatrical days.

"I admit it, I need a bath," said Nafai.

"I'll give you one tonight," said Luet.

"I was hoping you'd say that," he answered. "I see you give them to Veya and I get so jealous."

"You were magnificent today," she said.

"Just a little whittling while the Oversoul pumped knowledge into my head. And then killing animals too stupid to run away."

"Yes, all of that—magnificent. And more. What you did with your father."

"It was the right way to do it," he said. "Nothing more than that. Not like what *you* did. In fact, it's *you* that deserves to be pampered and babied tonight."

"I know it," she said. "But I have to bathe you *first*. It's no fun being babied by someone who smells so bad it makes you choke."

In answer, he embraced her, burying her nose in his armpit. She tickled him to break free.

Rasa, looking across the fire at them, thought: Such children. So young, so playful. I'm so glad that they can still be that way. Someday, when real adult responsibilities settle on them, they'll lose that. It will be replaced by a slower, quieter kind of play. But for now, they can cast away care and remember how good it is to be alive. In the desert or the city, in a house or a tent, that's what happiness means, isn't it?

8

Plenty

The next morning they loaded the camels and moved southeast. No one said anything about it, but everyone understood that they were moving to put some distance between them and Dorova Bay. It was still no easy task finding a way through the Valley of Fires, and several times they had to backtrack, though now Elemak usually rode ahead, often with Vas, in order to scout a path that led somewhere useful. Volemak would tell him in the morning what the Index advised, and Elemak would then mark a trail that led to the easiest ascents and descents from plateau to plateau.

After a few days, they found another spring of drinkable water, which they named Strelay, because they would use their time there to make arrows. Nafai went out first and found examples of all the kinds of tree that the Oversoul knew would make good bows; soon they had gathered several dozen saplings. Some of them they made into bows at once, for practice and for their immediate hunting needs; the rest they would carry with them, allowing them to season into wood that would hold its spring. They also made hundreds of arrows, and practiced shooting at targets, men and women alike, because, as Elemak said, "There may come a time when our lives depend on the archery of our wives."

Those who had been good shots with a pulse were as good with the bow, after some practice, but the real challenge was developing the strength to pull far enough and steadily enough to hit more distant targets. There wasn't a one of them without aching arms and backs and shoulders for the first week; Kokor, Dol, and Rasa gave up early and never tried again. Sevet and Hushidh, however, developed into rather good archers, as long as they used smaller bows than the men.

It was Issib who thought of dyeing the arrow shafts a bright unnatural color so spent arrows would be easier to retrieve.

Then they moved on again, from fountain to fire, practicing archery as they went. They began to be proud of the strength in their arms. The competition in archery among the men became rather fierce; the women noticed but mentioned only among themselves that the men cared about no targets but the ones placed far enough away that Sevet's and Hushidh's smaller bows could not accurately reach them. "Let them have their game," said Hushidh. "It would be too humiliating for any of them to be beaten by a woman."

Without meaning to, they were soon running parallel to the caravan route, and rather close—they were back to raw meat for a while. Then one morning Volemak came out of his tent, holding the Index, and saying, "The Oversoul says we must now head west into the mountains until we come to the sea."

"Let me guess," said Obring. "We won't be able to see a city there."

No one answered him. Nor did anyone else mention their last venture near the Scour Sea.

"Why are we heading west now?" asked Elemak. "We've gone barely half the length of the Valley of Fires—the caravan trail doesn't come to the sea again until it reaches the Sea of Fire, due south of here. All we're doing is going far out of our way to the west."

"There are rivers to the west," said Volemak.

"No there aren't," said Elemak. "If there were, the caravaners through here would have found them and used them. There'd be cities there."

"Nevertheless," said Volemak, "we're going west. The Oversoul says that we'll need to make a long camp again—to plant crops, to harvest them."

"Why?" asked Mebbekew. "We're making good progress. The babies are all thriving well. Why another camp?"

"Because Shedemei is pregnant, of course," said Volemak, "and getting sicker with each passing day."

They all looked at Shedemei in surprise. She blushed—and looked no less surprised than the others. "I only began to suspect it myself this morning," she said. "How can the Oversoul know what I'm only guessing at?"

Volemak shrugged. "He knows what he knows."

"Pretty poor timing, Shedya," said Elemak. "All the other women are holding off on pregnancy because they're nursing, but now we have to wait for you."

For once Zdorab spoke up sharply. "Some things can't be *timed* precisely, Elya, so don't lay blame where there was no volition."

Elemak looked at him steadily. "I never do," he said. But then he dropped the matter and set out to the west, blazing a trail for the caravan.

Their route led up into real mountains—volcanic ones, with some relatively recent lava flows that had not yet been broken into soil. Issib used the Index to come up with information about the area—there were at least fifty active and dormant volcanos in this range of mountains fronting on the Scour Sea. "The last eruption was only last year," he said, "but much farther to the south."

"Which may be the reason the Oversoul is sending us to the sea this far north," said Volemak.

Hard as the climb was, coming down the other side of the mountain range was harder—it was steeper and more heavily overgrown. Indeed, it was almost a jungle high on the slopes of the mountain.

"The winter winds come off the sea," said Issib, "and there are squalls almost every day in summer, too. The mountains catch the clouds, force them up into the colder atmosphere, and bring down whatever moisture is in them. So it's a rain forest here in the mountains. It won't be as wet down by the sea." They were becoming used to Issib being the one who explored the Index; during days of travel, he was the only one with no other duties, and he carried the Index with him, one hand constantly on it, exploring. Zdorab had shown him so many tricks and back doors that he was almost as deft now as the librarian himself. And no one disparaged the value of the information Issib provided, because it was all he *could* provide.

They were in the middle of a tricky passage down a tangled ravine when they felt an earthquake—rather a violent one, which threw two of the camels off their feet and set the others to stamping and turning in confusion.

"Out of the ravine!" cried Issib at once.

"Out? How?" answered Volemak.

"Any way we can!" shouted Issib. "The Index says that this earthquake jarred loose a lake high up in the mountains—anything in the ravine is going to be swept away!"

It was a particularly bad time for an emergency—Elemak and Vas were far ahead, blazing a trail, and Nafai and Obring were hunting higher up in the mountain. But Volemak had been journeying far longer than Elemak, and had resources of his own. He quickly sized up the walls of the ravine and chose a route up through a jumble of rocks into a side canyon that might lead to the top. "I'll lead the way," he said, "because I'm the one who knows best what camels can do. Luet, you bring the women and children along—Meb, you and Zdorab herd the pack animals after us. Supplies first, cold- and dryboxes last. Issib, you stay within earshot of them, and stay in touch with the Index. Tell them when there's no more time. When they have to abandon the rest of the camels and save themselves. They *must* save themselves, as must you, Issya—more important than anything else. Do you understand?"

He was asking everyone, and everyone nodded, wide-eyed, terrified.

"Elemak is in the ravine," said Eiadh. "Someone has to warn him."

"Elya is fit to hear the voice of the Oversoul himself," said Volemak. "The water is coming faster than anyone can ride to catch up with him. Save his baby and his wife, Edhya. Now come *on.*" He turned his camel and began the ascent.

Camels were not made for climbing. Their sedentary pace was maddening. But steadily they climbed. The earth shook again, and again—but the aftershocks were not as violent as the first had been. Volemak and the women made it to the top. Volemak had a fleeting thought of going back down to help, but Luet reminded him that in several places the path was not wide enough for two camels to pass—far from helping, he'd slow down the evacuation.

All the camels were above the floor of the ravine when Issib cried out, "Now! For your lives!" As soon as he saw that Meb and Zdorab both had heard, he turned his own camel and pushed his way in among the pack beasts. However, he could not control his animal forcefully enough to make headway faster than the rest. As Meb overtook him, he reached out and took the reins from Issib's feeble grasp, then began to drag Issib's camel faster and faster. Soon, though, they reached a narrow place where the two camels couldn't pass side by side, especially because of the bulk of Issib's chair. Without hesitation—without even waiting for his camel to kneel to let him dismount—Meb slid off to the ground, let go of his own camel's reins, and dragged on the reins of Issib's mount, hurrying it through the gap.

Moments later, Zdorab came through the same narrow place, then came up beside them. "The Index!" he shouted.

Issib, who couldn't lift it, pointed to the bag on his lap. "It's looped to the pommel!" he shouted.

Zdorab maneuvered his animal close; Meb held Issib's camel steady. Deftly Zdorab reached out, unlooped the bag, and then, brandishing it high like a trophy, rode on ahead.

"Leave me now!" Issib shouted at Meb.

Meb ignored him and continued to drag his camel upward, passing the slower pack animals.

Soon they came to a place where Zdorab, Luet, Hushidh, Shedemei, Sevet, and Eiadh waited on foot. Mebbekew realized that he must be near the top now—Zdorab must have left the Index with Volemak, and Rasa and the other women must be keeping the infants on high ground. "Take Issib!" shouted Meb, handing the reins to Zdorab. Then Meb rushed back down the canyon to the next pack beast. He thrust the reins of the animal in Luet's hands. "Drag him up!" he cried. To each woman in turn he gave the reins of a pack animal. They could hear the water now, a roaring sound; they could feel the rumbling in the earth. "Faster!" he cried.

There were just enough of them to take the reins of all the pack animals. Only Meb's own mount, now last in line, was untended. She was clearly frightened by the noise of the water, by the shaking of the earth, and didn't stay close behind. Meb called to her, "Glupost! Come on! Hurry, Glupost!" But he kept tugging on the reins of the last pack animal, knowing that the coldboxes it carried would be more important, in the long run, than his own mount.

"Let go, Meb!" cried Zdorab. "Here it comes!"

They could see the wall of water from where they were, that's how high it was—higher, in fact, than the top of the ravine, so that they instinctively ran even higher up the slope they were standing on. Those at the top were never in danger of being swept away, though, for the water stayed lower than they were.

However, the water that was snagged into the side canyon they had climbed through shot up into it with such force that it rose higher than the main body of water in the ravine. It slammed into the last two camels and then into Meb, lifting them all off their feet and heaving them the rest of the way up the side canyon. Meb could hear women screaming—was that Dol, howling out Meb's name?—and then he felt the water subsiding almost as fast as it had risen, sucking him downward. For a moment he thought of letting go of the reins and saving himself; then he realized that the pack camel had braced itself and was now more secure on the ground than Meb himself. So he clung to the reins and was not swept away. But as he hung there, pressed against the side of the camel that he had saved, and which was now saving him, he saw his mount Glupost get dragged off her feet and sucked down into the maelstrom in the ravine.

In moments, he felt many hands on him, prying the reins from his fingers, leading him, sopping wet and trembling, up to where the others waited. Volemak embraced him, weeping. "I thought I had lost you, my son, my son."

"What about Elya?" wailed Eiadh. "How could he save himself from that?"

"Not to mention Vas," said Rasa softly.

Several people looked at Sevet, whose face was hard and set.

"Not everyone shows fear the same way," murmured Luet, putting an end to any hard judgments anyone might be inclined to make about the difference between Eiadh's and Sevet's reaction. Luet knew well that Sevet had little reason to care much whether Vas lived or died— though she wondered how much Sevet herself actually knew.

What was most in Luet's heart was the fact that Nafai was also not with them. He and Obring were almost certainly on high ground, and safe. But they would no doubt be deeply worried.

Tell him that we're safe, she said silently to the Oversoul. And tell *me*—is Elemak alive? And Vas?

Alive, came the answer in her mind.

She said so.

The others looked at her, half in relief, half in doubt. "Alive," she said again. "That's all the Oversoul told me. Isn't it enough?"

The water subsided, the level dropping rapidly. Volemak and Zdorab walked down the side canyon together. They found it a tangle of half-

uprooted trees and bushes—not even the boulders were where they
had been.

But the side canyon was nothing compared to the ravine itself. There
was nothing left. A quarter hour ago it had been lush with vegetation—
so lush that it was hard to make way through it, and they had often had
to lead the camels through the stream itself in order to pass some of the
tangles of vegetation. Now the walls of the ravine, from top to bottom,
had not a single plant clinging to them. The soil itself had been scoured
away, so that bare rock was exposed. And on the floor of the ravine,
there were only a few heavy boulders and the sediments left behind by
the water as it dropped.

"Look how the floor of the ravine is bare rock near the edges," said
Volemak. "But deep sediment in the middle, near the water."

It was true: already the stream that remained—larger than the original one—was cutting a channel a meter deep through the thick mud.
The new banks of the stream would collapse here and there, a few
meters of mud slipping down into the water. It would take some time
before the floor of the ravine stabilized.

"It'll be green as ever within six weeks," said Zdorab. "And in five
years you'd never know this happened."

"What do you think?" asked Volemak. "If we stay to the edges, is it
safe to use this as a highway down to the sea?"

"The reason we were using the ravine in the first place was because
Elemak said the top was not passable—it keeps getting cut by deep
canyons or blocked by steep hills."

"So we keep to the edges," said Volemak. "And we hope."

It took a while at the top of the ravine to check the camels' loads and
be sure nothing had come loose during the scramble to safety. "It's
better than we could have hoped, that we lost only the one camel," said
Volemak.

Zdorab led his own mount forward, and held out the reins to Meb.

"No," said Meb.

"Please," said Zdorab. "Every step I take on foot will be my way of
giving honor to my brave friend."

"Take it," whispered Volemak.

Meb took the reins from Zdorab. "Thank you," he said. "But there
were *no* cowards here today."

Zdorab embraced him quickly, then went back to help Shedemei get
the women with babies onto their camels.

It turned out that neither Zdorab nor Meb nor Volemak did much riding the rest of that day. They spent their time on foot, patrolling the length of the caravan, making sure the camels never strayed toward the thick and treacherous mud in the middle of the ravine. They had visions of a camel sinking immediately over its head. The footing was wet, slimy, and treacherous, but by keeping the pace slow, they soon reached the mouth of the ravine, where it emptied into a wide river.

There had obviously been much damage here, too, for the opposite side of the river valley was a mess of mud and boulders, with many trees knocked down and much bare soil and rock exposed. And the rest of the way down the river they could see that both banks had been torn apart. Ironically, though, because the force of the flood had been less intense here than in the ravine, their passage through the debris it left behind would be far harder.

"This way!"

It was Elemak, with Vas behind him. The two of them were on foot, but they could see that their camels were not far behind. They were on higher ground. It would be a steep but not very difficult climb to reach them.

"We have a path here through the high ground!" called Elemak.

In a few minutes they were gathered at the beginning of Elemak's path through the forest. As husbands and wives embraced, Issib noticed that the forest here was considerably less dense than it had been higher up the mountain. "We must be near sea level now," he said.

"The river makes a sharp bend to the west over there," said Vas, one arm around Sevet, his baby held against his shoulder. "And from there you can see the Scour Sea. Between this river and the one to the south it's open grassland, mostly, a few trees here and there. Higher ground, thank the Oversoul. We felt the earthquakes, but when they passed we didn't think anything of them, except to worry that it might have been worse up where you were. Then suddenly Elya insisted we needed to go to the higher ground and look over the area, and just as we got there we heard this roaring noise and the river went crazy. We had images of seeing all the camels floating by, with all of you still riding on top of them."

"Issib was warned through the Index," said Volemak.

"It's a good thing we *weren't* all together," said Issib. "Four more camels, and we would have lost them. As it was, Meb lost his mount—because he was saving pack animals, I might add."

"We can wait for the stories until we're at our camp for the night," said Elemak. "We can reach the place between rivers before nightfall. There's little moon, so we want to have the tents up before dark."

That night they stayed up late around the fire, partly because they were waiting for dinner to cook, partly because they were too keyed-up to sleep, and partly because they kept hoping that Nafai and Obring would find the camp that night. That was when the stories were told. And as Hushidh bade Luet good-night in the tent where she would be sleeping alone with her baby, she said, "I wish you could see as I see, Luet. That flood did what nothing else could have managed—the bonds between us all are so much stronger. And Meb . . . the honor that flows to him now . . ."

"A nice change," said Luet.

"I just hope he doesn't strut too much about it," said Hushidh, "or he'll waste it all."

"Maybe he's growing up," said Luet.

"Or maybe he just needed the right circumstance to discover the best in himself. He didn't hesitate, Issya says. Just dismounted and risked his own life dragging Issib to safety."

"And Zdorab took the Index, and then led us back down . . ."

"I know, I'm not saying Meb was the only one. But you know how it is with Zdorab. That gesture he made, giving his mount to Meb. It was a generous thing to do, and it helped bind the group together—but it also had the effect of erasing the memory of Zdorab's own role in saving us. Our minds were all on Mebbekew."

"Well, maybe that's how Zodya wants it," said Luet.

"But we won't forget," said Hushidh.

"Hardly," said Luet. "Now go to bed. The babies won't care how little sleep we got tonight—they'll be starving on schedule in the morning."

It was only a few hours after dawn when Nafai and Obring returned. They had been far from the flood, of course, but they had also been on the wrong side of it, so that coming home they had to find a place to cross either the ravine itself or the river. They ended up dragging the camels across the river upstream of the ravine, making a long detour around the worst of the destruction, and then crossing the river in shallow marshes and sand bars near the sea—at low tide. "The camels are getting less and less happy about crossing water," said Nafai.

"But we brought back two deers," said Obring happily.

With everyone reunited, Volemak made a little speech establishing this place as their campsite. "The river to the north we will name Oykib, for the firstborn boy of this expedition, and the river to the south is Protchnu, for the firstborn boy of the next generation."

Rasa was outraged. "Why not name them Dza and Chveya, for the first two *children* born on our journey?"

Volemak looked at her steadily without answering.

"Then we had better leave this place before the boys are old enough to know how you have honored them solely because they have penises."

"If we had had only two girls, and two rivers, Father would have named the rivers for *them*," said Issib, trying to make peace.

They knew it wasn't true, of course. For several weeks after they got there, Rasa insisted on calling them the North River and the South River; Volemak was just as adamant in calling them the River Oykib and the River Protchnu. But since it was the men who did more traveling, and therefore crossed the rivers more often, and fished in them, and had to tell each other about places and events up and down the rivers' lengths, it was the names Oykib and Protchnu that stayed. Whether anyone else noticed or not, however, Luet saw that Rasa never used Volemak's names for the rivers, and grew silent and cold whenever others spoke their names.

Only once did Nafai and Luet discuss the matter. Nafai was singularly unsympathetic. "Rasa didn't mind when women decided everything in Basilica, and men weren't even allowed to *look* at the lakes."

"That was a holy place for women. The only place like it in the world."

"What does it matter?" said Nafai. "It's just a couple of names for a couple of rivers. When we leave here, no one else will ever remember what we named them."

"So why not North River and South River?"

"It's only a problem because Mother made it a problem," said Nafai. "Now let's *not* make it a problem between *us.*"

"I just want to know why *you* go along with it!"

Nafai sighed. "Think, for just a moment, what it would mean if I had called them the North and South rivers. What it would have meant to Father. And to the other men. Then it really *would* have been divisive. I don't need anything more to separate me from the others."

Luet chewed on that idea for a while.

"All right," she said. "I can see that."

And then, after she had thought a little more, she said, "But you didn't see anything wrong with naming the rivers after the boys until Mother pointed it out, did you?"

He didn't answer.

"In fact, you really don't see anything wrong with it now, do you?"

"I love you," said Nafai.

"That's not an answer," she said.

"I think it is," he said.

"And what if I never give you a son?" she said.

"Then I will keep making love to you until we have a hundred daughters," said Nafai.

"In your *dreams*," she said nastily.

"In *yours*, you mean," he said.

She made the deliberate decision not to stay angry with him for this, and as they made love she was as willing and passionate as ever. But afterward, when he was asleep, it worried her. What would it mean to them for the men to make their company as male-dominated as Basilica had been female-dominated?

Why must we do this? she wondered. We had a chance to make our society different from the rest of the world. Balanced and fair, even-handed, *right*. And yet even Nafai and Issib seem content to unbalance it. Is the rivalry between men and women such that one must always be in ascendancy at the expense of the other? Is it built into our genes? Must the community always be ruled by one sex or the other?

Maybe so, she thought. Maybe we're like the baboons. When we're stable and civilized, the women decide things, establish the house-holds, the connections between them, create the neighborhoods and the friendships. But when we're nomadic, living lives on the edge of survival, the men rule, and brook no interference from the women. Perhaps that's what civilization *means*—is the dominance of the female over the male. And wherever that lapses, we call the result *uncivilized, barbarian . . . manly.*

They spent a year between the rivers, waiting for Shedemei's baby to be born. It was a son; they named him Padarok—*gift*—and called him Rokya. They might have moved on then, after the first year, but by the time little Rokya was born, three of the other women had conceived—including Rasa and Luet, who were the most fragile during pregnancy.

So they stayed for a second harvest, and a few months more, until all the women but Sevet had completed their pregnancy and borne a child. So there were thirty of them that began the next stage of the journey, and the first generation of children were walking and most of them beginning to talk before they were on their way.

It had been a good two years. Instead of desert farming, they had lush, rain-watered fields on good soil. Their crops were more varied; the hunting was better; and even the camels thrived, giving birth to fifteen new beasts of burden. Making saddles was harder—none of them had ever learned the skill—but they found a way to put two toddlers on each of the four most docile animals, which always traveled in train with the women's camels. When the children first tried out the saddles, some of them were terrified—camels ride so high above the ground—but soon enough they were used to it, and even enjoyed it.

The journey was easy through the savanna along the seacoast; they ate up the kilometers as they never had before, even on the smooth desert west and south of Basilica. In three days they reached a well-watered bay that the men were already familiar with, having hunted and fished there during the past two years. But in the morning, Volemak dismayed them all by telling them that their course now lay, not south as they had all expected, but west.

West! Into the sea!

Volemak pointed at the rocky island that rose out of the sea not two kilometers away. "Beyond it is another island, a huge island. We have as long a journey on that island as we have had since we left the Valley of Mebbekew."

At low tide, Nafai and Elemak tried fording the strait between the mainland and the island. They could do it, with only a short swim in the middle. But the camels balked, and so they ended up building rafts. "I've done it before," said Elemak. "Never for a saltwater crossing, of course, but the water here is placid enough."

So they felled trees and floated the logs in the bay, binding them together with ropes made of the fibers of marsh reeds. It took a week to make the rafts, and two days to take the camels across—one at a time—and then the cargo, and then, last of all, the women and children. They camped on the shore where they had landed, as the men poled the rafts around the island to the southwestern tip, where again they would need the rafts to ferry everyone and everything to the large island. In another week the company had traversed the small island and crossed to the large one; they pushed the rafts into the water and watched them float away.

The northern tip of the large island was mountainous and heavily forested. But gradually the mountains gave way to hills, and then to broad savannas. They could stand at the crest of the low rolling plain and see the Scour Sea to the west and the Sea of Fire to the east, the island was so narrow here. And the farther south they went, the more they understood how the Sea of Fire earned its name. Volcanos rose out of the sea, and in the distance they could see the smoke of a minor eruption from time to time. "This island was part of the mainland until five million years ago," Issib explained to them. "Until then, the Valley of Fires came right down onto this island, south of us—and the fires still continue in the sea that has filled the space between the two parts of the valley."

Growing up in Basilica, most of them had never understood the forces of nature—Basilica was such an unchanging place, with so much pride in its ancienthood. Here, even though the timespans were measured in the millions of years, they could clearly see the enormous power of the planet, and the virtual irrelevancy of the human lives on its surface.

"And yet we're *not* irrelevant," said Issib. "Because we are the ones who see the changes, and know them, and understand that they *are* changes, that once things were different. Everything else in the universe, every living and non-living thing, lives in the infinite now, which never changes, which always is exactly as it is. Only *we* know the passage of time, that one thing causes another and that we are changed by the past and will change the future."

The island widened, and the ground became more rugged. They all recognized it as being the same kind of terrain as the Valley of Fires— the continuation of that valley that Issib had predicted. But it was quieter—they never found a place where gases from inside the earth burned on the surface—and the water was more likely to be pure. It was also drier and drier the farther south they went, though they were rising up into mountain country.

"These mountains have a name," Issib told them, from the Index. "Dalatoi. People lived here before the island split away from the main-land. In fact, the greatest and most ancient of the Cities of Fire was here."

"Skudnooy?" asked Luet, remembering the story of the city of misers who withdrew from the world and supposedly held most of the gold of Harmony in hidden vaults beneath their hidden city.

"No, Raspyatny," said Issib. And they all remembered the stories of the city of stone and moss, where streams flowed through every room in a city the size of a mountain, so high that the upper rooms would freeze, and those who lived there had to burn fires to melt the rivers so that the lower rooms would have water all year.

"Will we see it?" they asked.

"What's left of it," said Issib. "It was abandoned ten million years ago, but it *was* made out of stone. The ancient road we're following led there."

Only then did they realize that they were indeed following an ancient road. There was no trace of pavement, and the road was sometimes cut by ravines or eroded away. But they kept returning to the path of least resistance, and now and then they could see that hills had been cut into to make a place for the road to go, and the occasional valley had been partly filled in with stone which had not yet worn down to nothing. "If there had been more rain here," said Issib, "there'd be nothing left. But the island has moved south so that this land is now in the latitudes of the Great Southern Desert, and so the air is drier and there's less erosion. Some of the works of humankind leave traces, even after all this time."

"Someone must have used this road in the past ten million years," said Elemak.

"No," said Issib. "No human being has set foot on this island since it fully split off from the mainland."

"How can you know that!" Mebbekew scoffed.

"Because the Oversoul has kept humans from coming here. No one even remembers that this island exists. That's how the Oversoul wanted it. To keep things safe and ready . . . for us, I guess."

They saw Raspyatny for a whole day before they reached it. At first it simply looked like an oddly textured mountain, but the closer they got, the more they realized that what they were seeing were windows carved into the stone. It was a high mountain, too, so that the city carved into the face of it must be vast.

They camped northeast of the city, where a small stream flowed. They followed the stream and found that it flowed right out of the city itself. Inside, it made cascades and the walls near it were thick with moss; it was much colder than the desert air outside.

They took turns exploring, in large groups, leaving some in charge of
the children and animals while the others clambered through the rem-
nants of the city. Away from the stream, the city had not been so badly
eroded inside, though nowhere was the interior as well preserved as
the outer wall. They realized why, when they found a few traces of an
aqueduct system that had, just as the legend said, carried water into
every room of the city. What surprised them, though, was the lack of
internal corridors. Rooms simply led into each other. "How did they
have any privacy?" asked Hushidh. "How did they ever have any time
to themselves, if every room was an avenue for people to walk right
through?"

No one had an answer.

"More than two hundred thousand people lived here, in the old
days," said Issib. "Back when this whole area was farther north, and
much better watered—all the land outside was farmed, for kilometers
to the north, and yet their enemies could never attack them successfully because they kept ten years' worth of food inside these walls, and
they never lacked for water. Their enemies could burn their fields and
besiege them, but then they'd starve long before anyone in Raspyatny
ever felt the slightest want. Only nature itself could depopulate this
place."

"Why wasn't all of this destroyed in the earthquakes of the Valley of
Fires?" asked Nafai.

"We haven't seen the eastern slope. The Index says that half the city
was wiped out in two great earthquakes when the rift first opened and
the sea poured through."

"It would have been glorious to see a flood like *that*," said Zdorab.
"From a safe place, of course."

"The whole eastern side of the city collapsed," said Issib. "Now it's
just a mountainside. But this side stayed. Ten million years. You never
know. Of course, the streams are eroding it away from the inside,
making the outside more and more of a hollow shell. Eventually it'll
cave in. Maybe all at once. One part will break, and that'll put too
much stress on what is left, and the whole thing will come down like a
sandcastle on the beach."

"We have seen one of the cities of the heroes," said Luet.

"And the stories were true," said Obring. "Which leads me to wonder whether the city of Skudnooy might be around here somewhere,
too."

"The Index says not," said Issib. "I asked."

"Too bad," said Obring. "All that gold!"

"Oh, right," said Elemak. "And where would you sell it? Or did you think you'd eat it? Or wear it?"

"Oh, I'm not allowed even to *dream* of tremendous wealth, is that it?" said Obring defiantly. "Only practical dreams allowed?"

Elemak shrugged and let the matter drop.

After leaving the vicinity of Raspyatny—and it took them another whole day to pass around the western side of the city, which really seemed to have covered the whole face of the mountain—they made their way through a high pass, which once again seemed to have been made almost uniform in width in order to accommodate a heavily trafficked road. "Once this was the highway between the Cities of Fire and the Cities of the Stars," said Issib. "Now it leads only to desert."

They came out of the pass and a vast, dry savanna spread out below them; they could see that the island narrowed here, with the Sea of Stars to the east and, far to the west, the blue shimmer of the southern reaches of the Scour Sea. As they descended, they lost sight of the western sea; instead, at the urging of the Oversoul, they hugged the eastern shore, because more rain fell there, and they could fish in the sea.

It was a hard passage—dry, so that three times they had to dig wells, and hot, with the tropical sun beating down on them. But this was exactly the sort of terrain that Elemak and Volemak had both learned to deal with from their youth, and they made good time. Ten days after they came down from the pass through the Dalatoi Mountains, the Oversoul had them strike south when the coastline turned southeast, and as they climbed through gently rolling hills, the grass grew thicker, and here and there more trees dotted the landscape. They passed through low and well-weathered mountains, down through a river valley, up over more hills, and then down through the most beautiful land they had ever seen.

Stands of forest were evenly balanced with broad meadows; bees hummed over fields of wildflowers, promising honey easily found. There were streams with clear water, all leading to a wide, meandering river. Shedemei dismounted from her camel and probed into the soil. "It isn't like desert grassland," she said. "Not just roots. There's true topsoil here. We can farm these meadows without destroying them."

For the first time in their journey, Elemak didn't bother riding ahead to confer with Volemak about a campsite. There was no place that they passed through where they could *not* have stopped and spent the night.

"This land could hold the population of Seggidugu and they could all live in wealth," said Elemak. "Don't you think so, Father?"

"And we're the only humans here," he answered. "The Oversoul prepared this place for us. Ten million years, it waited here for us."

"Then we stay here? This is where we were coming?"

"We stay here for now," said Volemak. "For several years at least. The Oversoul isn't ready yet to take us out into the stars, back to Earth. So for now this is our home."

"How *many* years?" asked Elemak.

"Long enough that we should build houses of wood, and let our poor old tents become awnings and curtains," said Volemak. "There'll be no more journeying by land or sea from this place. Only when we rise up into the stars will we leave here. So let us call this place Dostatok, because it has plenty for our needs. The river we will name Rasa, because it is strong and full of life and it will never cease to supply us with all we need."

Rasa nodded her head gently to acknowledge the honor of the naming; as she did, she had the tiniest smile, which Luet, at least, recognized as a sign that Rasa knew her husband was trying to be conciliatory in his naming.

They made their settlement on a low promontory overlooking the mouth of the River Rasa, where it poured into the Southern Ocean—for that was how far south they had come, leaving the Scour Sea and the Sea of Stars behind them. Within a month they all had houses of wood, with thatched roofs, and in this latitude they had a growing season almost all the year, so it hardly mattered when they planted; there were some rains almost every day, and heavy storms swept over quickly, doing no damage.

The animals were so tame they had no fear of man; they soon domesticated the wild goats, which clearly were descended from the same animals that were herded in the hills near Basilica—camel's milk at last became a liquid that only baby camels had to drink, and the term "camel's cheese" became a euphemism for what well-fed babies left in their diapers. In the next six years, more babies were born, until there were thirty-five young ones, ranging in age from nearly eight years to several newborns. They farmed their fields together, and shared equally from the produce; from time to time the men would leave and hunt together, bringing home meat for drying and salting and skins for tanning. Rasa, Issib, and Shedemei undertook the education of the children by starting a school.

Not that their lives were one unrelenting tale of joy and peace. There were quarrels—for an entire year Kokor would not speak to Sevet over some trivial slight; there was another quarrel between Meb and Obring that led to Obring building a house farther from the rest of the group. There were resentments—some felt that others weren't working hard enough; some felt that their kind of work was of greater value than the labor of others. And there was a constant undercurrent of tension between the women, who looked to Rasa for leadership, and the men, who seemed to assume that no decision was final unless Volemak or Elemak had approved it. But they weathered all these crises, all these tensions, finding some balance of leadership between Volemak's loyalty to the purposes of the Oversoul, Rasa's clear-sighted compassion, and Elemak's hardheaded assessments of what they needed to survive. Any unhappiness that they might harbor in their hearts was kept in check, buried under the hard work that marked the rhythms of their lives, and then dissolved in the moments when joy was bountiful and love unstinted.

Life was good enough over the years that there was not a one of them who did not wish, when they thought of it at all, that the Oversoul would forget that they were there, and leave them in peace and happiness in Dostatok.

9

Perimeter

When Chveya was seven years old she had understood perfectly how the world worked. Now she was eight, and there were some questions.

Like all the children of Dostatok, she grew up understanding the pure and simple relationships among families. For instance, Dazya and her younger brothers and sisters belonged to Hushidh and Issib. Krassya and Nokya and their younger brothers and sisters belonged to Kokor and Obring. Vasnya and her brother and sister belonged to Sevet and Vas. And so on, each set of children belonging to a mother and father.

The only oddity in this clear picture of the universe, at least until Chveya was eight, had been Grandfather and Grandmother, Volemak and Rasa, who not only had two children of their own—the brothers Okya and Yaya, who might as well be twins because, as Vasnya had said once, they had but one brain between them—but also were, in some vague way, the parents of all the other parents. She knew this because, in odd moments, she had heard adults call Grandmother not only "Lady Rasa" or "Grandmother" but also "Mother," and she heard her own father and Proya's father Elemak and Skiya's father Mebbekew call Grandfather "Father" more often than not.

In Chveya's mind this meant that Volemak and Rasa were the First

Parents, having given rise to all of humanity. Now, she knew in the forepart of her mind that this was not accurate, for Shedemei had made it plain in school that there were millions of other humans living in faraway places, and clearly Grandfather and Grandmother had not given life to all of *them.* But those places were legendary. They were never seen. The whole world was the safe and beautiful land of Dostatok, and in that place there was no one, or so it seemed, who had not come from the marriage of Volemak and Rasa.

To Chveya, in fact, the world of the adults was remote enough to satisfy any need she had for strangeness; she had no need to wonder about mythical lands like Basilica and Potokgavan and Gorayni and Earth and Harmony, some of which were planets and some of which were cities and some of which were nations, though Chveya had never grasped the rules for which term went with each name. No, Chveya's world was dominated by the continual power struggle between Dazya and Proya for ascendancy among the children.

Dazya was Oldest Child, which conferred on her enormous authority which she cheerfully misused by exploiting the younger children whenever possible, converting it to personal service and "favors" which were received without gratitude. If any of the younger ones failed to obey, she would freeze them out of all games simply by letting it be known that if "that child" were part of a game or contest, she would not participate. Dazya's attitude toward the girls more near her own age was much the same, though it was more subtle—she didn't insist on humiliating personal services, but she *did* expect that when she decided things would be done a certain way, all the other girls would go along, and anyone who resisted was politely ostracized. Since Chveya was Second Child, and only three days younger, she saw no reason to accept a subservient role. The result was that she had a lot of time to herself, for Dazya would brook no equals, and none of the other girls had the spine to stand up to her.

At the same time that Dazya had forged her kingdom among the younger children and the older girls, Proya—Elemak's eldest son, and Second Boy—had made himself prince among princes. He was the only person who could ridicule Dazya and laugh at her rules, and all the older boys would follow him. Dazya would, of course, immediately ostracize the older boys, but this meant nothing to them since the games they wanted to join and the approval they craved were Proya's. The worst humiliation to Dazya was that her own brother Xodhya would join with Proya and use Proya's power as a shield for his own independence from his older sister's rule. Chveya's own younger brother Zhyat, and sometimes even Motya, a year younger than Zhyat and not really one of the older boys, joined with Proya regularly, but she didn't mind at all, for that meant even more humiliation for Dazya.

Of course, at times of struggle Chveya would join with the older girls in alternately sneering at and snubbing the rebel boys, but in her heart Chveya longed to be part of Proya's kingdom. *They* were the ones who played rough and wonderful games involving hunting and death. She would even act the deer if they would only invite her to play, letting them hunt her and shoot at her with their blunt-tipped arrows, if only she could be part of them instead of being miserably trapped in Dazya's demesne. But when she hinted at this desire to her brother Zhyat, he made a great show of gagging and retching and she gave up the idea.

Her greatest envy was reserved for Okya and Yaya, the two sons of Grandmother and Grandfather. Okya was First Boy and Yaya was Fourth Boy. They could easily have dislodged Proya from his position of seniority among the boys, especially because the two brothers did everything together and could have thrashed all the other boys into submission. But they never bothered, only joining in Proya's games when they felt like it, and giving no concern at all to who was in charge. For they fancied themselves to be adults, not children at all. "*We* are of the same generation as your parents," Yaya had once said to her, quite haughtily. Chveya had thereupon pointed out that Yaya was considerably shorter than her and still had a teeny-weeny hooy like a hare, which caused the other children to laugh in spite of their awe for Yaya. Yaya, for his part, only looked at her with withering disdain and walked away. But Chveya noticed that he also stopped peeing in front of the other children.

When Chveya was brutally honest with herself, she had to admit that the reason she was so often completely isolated from the other children was because she simply could not keep her mouth shut. If she saw someone being a bully or unfair or selfish, she said so. Never mind that she also spoke up when somebody was noble or good or kind—praise was quickly forgotten, while offenses were treasured forever. Thus Chveya had no real friends among the other children—they were all too busy making sweet with Dazya or Proya to give real friendship to

Chveya, except Okya and Yaya, of course, who were even more aloof and involved with each other in their supposed adultness.

It was when Chveya turned eight years old and saw how little heed anyone but her own parents paid to her birthday, after the enormous fuss made over Dazya's birthday, that she entirely despaired of ever being a person of significance in the world. Wasn't it bad enough that Dazya lorded it over everybody so outrageously as it was—why did the adults have to make a festival out of Dazya's birthday? Father explained, of course, that the festival wasn't about Dza herself, but rather because her birthday marked the beginning of their whole generation of children—but what did it matter if the adults thought of it that way or not? The fact remained that with this festival they had affirmed Dazya's iron rule over the other children, and in fact had even given her a temporary ascendancy over Proya himself, and Okya and Yaya had sulked through the whole party when they were snubbed and lumped in among the children, which they felt was wrong since they were *not* part of the younger generation. How could the adults so heedlessly and destructively have intervened in the children's hierarchy? It was as if the adults did not think of the children's lives as *real.*

It was then that Chveya reached her profound insight that the adult world and the children's world were probably identical in the way they worked, except that the children were perpetually subservient to the adults. It began in a conversation with her mother as she combed Chveya's hair after her bath. "The younger boys are, the more disgusting they are," Chveya said, thinking of her second brother Motya, who had just discovered how much tumult he could cause by picking his nose and wiping it on his sisters' clothing, a practice which Chveya had no intention of tolerating, whether he did it to her or to little Zuya, who couldn't defend herself.

"That's not necessarily true," said Mother. "They simply find different *ways* of being disgusting when they get older."

Mother said it offhandedly, like a joke, but to Chveya it was a grand illuminating moment. She tried to picture Krassya's father, Obring, for instance, picking his nose and wiping it on Mother, and knew that it could never happen. But perhaps there were other disgusting things, adult things, that Obring might do. I must watch him and find out, thought Chveya.

She didn't question that it was Obring she should watch—she had often seen the way Mother grew impatient when Obring spoke in council meetings. She had no respect for him, and neither did Father, though he hid it better. So if any adult male might exemplify disgusting behavior, it would certainly be Obring.

From now on, Chveya would focus all her attention on the adults around her, watching to see who was the Dazya of the mothers and who was the Proya of the fathers. In the process, she began to understand things that she had never understood before. The world was not as clear and simple a place as she had thought till now.

The most shocking revelation came on the day she discussed marriage with her parents. It had recently dawned on her that eventually the children would all grow up and pair off with each other and have babies and start the whole cycle all over again—this because of some vile remark by Toya about what Proya really wanted to do to Dazya. Toya had meant it to be an obscene horror, but Chveya realized that, far from being a horror, it was probably a prophecy. Wouldn't Proya and Dazya be the perfect pair? Proya would be just like Elemak, and Dazya would probably smile at Proya with complete devotion the way Eiadh did with Elemak. Or would Dazya be like her mother Hushidh, so much stronger than her husband Issib that she even carried him around and bathed him like a baby? Or would Proya and Dazya continue their struggle for supremacy all through their lives, trying to turn their own babies against each other?

That thought led Chveya to wonder which of the boys *she* would marry. Would it be one of the boys of the first year, her own age? That would mean either Proya or Okya, and the thought of either one repelled her. Then what about boys of the second year? Dazya's little brother Xodhya, Proya's little brother Nadya, or the "adult" Yaya— what a proud selection! And the children of the third year were the same age as her revolting brother Motya—how could she *dream* of marrying someone *that* young?

So she broached the subject with her parents as they were eating breakfast on a morning when Father was not going hunting, so they could eat together. "Will I have to marry Xodhya, do you think?" she asked—for she had decided that Xodhya was the least disgusting of all the alternatives.

"Definitely not," said Mother, without a moment's hesitation.

"In fact," said Father, "we would forbid it."

"Well, *who* then? Okya? Yaya?"

"Almost as bad," said Father. "What is this, are you planning to start a family anytime soon?"

"Of course she's thinking about it, Nyef," said Mother. "Girls think about such things at this age."

"Well, then, she might keep in mind that she isn't going to marry a full uncle and *certainly* not a full double first cousin."

These words meant absolutely nothing to Chveya, but they hinted at dark mysteries. What unspeakable thing had Xodhya done to become a "full double first cousin"? So she asked.

"It's not what *he* did," said Mother. "It's just that his mother, Hushidh, is my full sister—we both have the same mother and the same father. And Zaxodh's father, Issib, is your father's full brother— they both have the same mother and father, who happen to be Grandmother and Grandfather. That means that you have *all* your ancestors in common—it's the closest blood relation among all the children, and marriage between you is out of the question."

"If we can possibly avoid it," added Father.

"We can avoid *that* one, anyway," said Mother. "And I feel almost as strongly about Oykib and Yasai, because they are *also* sons of both Rasa and Volemak."

Chveya took all this in with outward calm, but inwardly she was in turmoil. Hushidh and Mother were full sisters, but *not* daughters of Grandmother and Grandfather! And Father and Issib were full brothers, as were Oykib and Yasai, and this fullness of their brotherhood was because they all *were* sons of Grandmother and Grandfather. Yet the very use of the word *full* implied that there were some here who were *not* full brothers, and therefore *not* sons of both Volemak and Rasa. How could that be?

"What's wrong?" asked Father.

"I just . . . who is it that I *can* marry?"

"Isn't it a little early . . ." began Father.

Mother intervened. "The boys who disgust you today will look far more interesting to you as you get older. Take that on faith, my dear Veya, because you won't believe *that* particular prophecy until it comes true. But when that wonderful day comes . . ."

"Dreadful day, you mean," muttered Father.

". . . you can certainly cast your gaze on Padarok, for instance, because he's not related to anybody at all except his baby sister Dabrota and his parents, Zdorab and Shedemei."

That was the first time Chveya realized that Zdorab and Shedemei weren't kin to the others, but *now* she remembered that she had long disliked Padarok because he always referred to Grandmother and Grandfather as Rasa and Volemak, which seemed disrespectful; but it was *not* disrespectful at all, because they really *weren't* his grandmother or grandfather. Did everybody else understand this all along?

"And," added Father, "because there's only one Rokya to service the nubile young girls of Dostatok . . ."

"Nyef!" said Mother sharply.

". . . you'll have no choice but to also—how did you say it, my dear Waterseer?—oh yes, *cast your gaze* upon Protchnu or Nadezhny, because their mother, Eiadh, is no kin of anybody else here, and their father, Elemak, is only my half-brother. Likewise with Umene, whose father, Vas, is not kin of ours, and whose mother, Sevet, is only my half-sister."

Never mind about Proya and Nadya and Umya. "How can Sevet be only half your sister?" Chveya asked. "Is that because you have so many brothers that she can't be a whole sister to you?"

"Oh, this is a nightmare," said Mother. "Did it have to be this morning?"

Father, however, went ahead and explained about how Volemak had been married to two other women in Basilica, who gave birth to Elemak and Mebbekew, and then had married Rasa long enough to have Issib; and then Lady Rasa "didn't renew" the marriage and instead married a man named Gaballufix, who was also Elemak's half-brother because *his* mother had been one of Volemak's earlier wives, and it was with Gaballufix that Lady Rasa had given birth to Sevet and Kokor, and then she didn't renew *him* and returned to marry Volemak permanently and then they had Nafai and, more recently, Okya and Yaya.

"Did you understand that?"

Chveya could only give a stupefied nod. Her entire world had been turned upside down. Not just by the confusion of who was really kin to whom after all, but by the whole idea that the same people didn't have to stay married all their lives—that somebody's mother and father might end up being married to completely different people and have children who thought of only one of them as Mother and the other one as a complete stranger! It was terrifying, and that night she had a terrible dream in which giant rats came into their house and carried off

Father in his sleep, and when Mother woke up she didn't even notice he was gone, she simply brought in little Proya—only full-sized now, because this was a dream—and said, "This is your new father, till the rats take *him.*"

She woke up sobbing.

"What was the dream?" asked Mother, as she comforted her. "Tell me, Veya, why do you cry?"

So she told her.

Mother carried her into Father's and her room and woke Father and made Chveya tell *him* the dream, too. He didn't even seem interested in the most horrible thing, which was Proya coming into their house and taking his place. All he wanted to know about were the giant rats. He made her describe them again and again, even though she couldn't think of anything to say about them except that they were rats and they were very large and they seemed to be chuckling to each other about how clever they were as they carried Father away.

"Still," said Father, "it's the first time in the new generation. And not from the Oversoul, but from the Keeper."

"It might mean nothing," said Mother. "Maybe she heard of one of the other dreams."

But when they asked her whether she had heard stories of giant rats before this dream, Chveya had no idea of what they were talking about. The only rats she had heard about were the ones that were constantly trying to steal food from the barns. Did other people dream of giant rats, too? Adults were so strange—they thought nothing of families being torn apart and children having half-brothers and half-sisters and other monstrosities like that, but a dream of a giant rat, now, *that* was important to them. Father even said, "If you ever dream of giant rats again—or other strange animals—you must tell us at once. It can be very important."

It was only as Luet was covering her up again in bed that Chveya was able to ask about the question that was gnawing at *her.* "Mother, if you ever don't renew Father, who will be our new father then?"

Instantly a look of understanding and compassion came to Mother's face. "Oh, Veya, my dear little seamstress, is *that* what's worrying you? We left laws like that behind when we left Basilica. Marriages are forever here. Till we die. So Father will always be the father in our family, and I will always be the mother, and that's it. You can count on that."

Much reassured, Chveya settled down to sleep. She thought several thoughts as she was drifting off: How awful it must have been, to live in Basilica and never know who would be married to your parents from year to year—you might as well live in a house where the floor might be the ceiling tomorrow. And then: I am the first of the new generation to have a dream of giant rats, and somehow that is very wonderful so I must be very proud of myself and if I'd known that I would have dreamed about giant rats before. And then: Rokya is the boy who is no kin to anybody, and so he's the very best one to marry, and so I shall marry him and *that* will show Dazya who's the best.

Nafai and Luet got little sleep that night. Each had keyed in on a different aspect of Chveya's dream. To Luet, what mattered was that one of the children had finally shown some of the ability that the Oversoul had been selecting for. She knew it was vain of her, but she felt it appropriate that the firstborn of the waterseer should be the first to have a meaningful dream. She could hardly bear to wait until she could first take her daughter into the water of the river to see if she could learn to deliberately fall into the kind of sleep that brought true dreams, the way Luet had schooled herself to do.

To Nafai, on the other hand, what mattered was that after so long a silence, someone had received some kind of message at all. And the message, however vague it was, however tied to childish puzzlements, was nevertheless from the Keeper of Earth, which somehow made it more important than if it had come from the Oversoul.

After all, they had conversation with the Oversoul all the time, through the Index. The Index only allowed them access to the Oversoul's memory, however. It did not let them plumb the Oversoul's plans, to find out through the Index exactly what the Oversoul expected them to do this year or the next. For that they waited, as they had always waited, for the Oversoul to initiate things through dreams or a voice in their own minds. All these years in Dostatok, and the Oversoul had sent no dream, no voice, and the only message the Index had for them, beyond their own research into memory, was: Stay and wait.

But the Keeper of Earth was not tied to any plan or schedule of the Oversoul; it sent its dreams through the lightyears from Earth itself. It was impossible to guess what the Keeper's purpose was—the dreams it sent seemed to get tangled up in the concerns of the person having the dream, just as happened with Chveya's dream of the rats. Yet there were themes that kept recurring—hadn't Hushidh dreamed of rats also as enemies, attacking her family? This seemed to hint that somehow these large rats were going to be a problem to them on Earth—though there were also the dreams that showed the rats and angels of Earth linked with humans as friends and equals. It was so hard to make sense of all of it—but one thing was certain. The dreams from the Keeper of Earth had not stopped coming, and so perhaps something would happen soon, perhaps the next stage of their journey would begin.

For Nafai was growing impatient. Like all the others, he loved the way they lived at Dostatok, yet he could not forget that this was not the object of their journey. There was an unfinished task ahead of them, a journey through space to the planet where humankind originated, the return of humans for the first time after forty million years, and Nafai longed to go. Life in Dostatok was sweet, but it was also far too closed and neat. Things seemed to have *ended* here, and Nafai didn't like the feeling that somehow the future had been tied off, that there would be no more changes other than the predictable changes of growing older.

Oversoul, said Nafai silently, now that the Keeper of Earth has awakened again, will you also awaken? Will you also set us on the next stage of our journey?

Nafai was keenly aware of how different were his and Luet's responses to Chveya's dream. He was at once disdainful and envious of Luet's attitude. Disdainful, for she seemed to have let Dostatok become her whole world—what she cared most about was the children, and how this meant that they might also become visionaries, and most specifically how wonderful it was that their Chveya was the first to dream true dreams. How could this matter compare to the news that the Keeper of Earth was stirring again? And yet he envied her for very connectedness with their present life in Dostatok—he could not help but think that she was far happier than he, because her world *did* center around the children, the family, the community. I live in a larger world, but have little connection with it; she lives in a smaller one, but is able to change it and be changed by it far more than I.

I can't become as she is, nor can she become like me. Individual people have always been more important to her than to me. It's my weakness, that I don't have her awareness of other people's feelings. Perhaps, had I been as observant, as empathic as she, I would not have inadvertently said and done the things that made my older brothers hate me so much, and then our whole path through life might have been different, Elya and I might have been friends all along. Instead, even now when Elemak gives me respect as a hunter and listens to me in council, there is still no closeness between us, and Elemak is wary of me, watching for signs that I seek to displace him. Luet, on the other hand, seems to cause no envy among the other women. As Waterseer, she could just as easily be seen as a rival to Mother's dominance over the women as Elemak is the rival to Father's leadership, and I am the rival to Elemak, but instead there is no sense of competition at all. They are one. Why couldn't Elemak and I have been one, and Elemak and Father?

Perhaps there is something lacking in men, so that we can never join together and make one soul out of many. If so then it is a terrible loss. I look at Luet and see how close she is to the other women, even the ones she doesn't like all that well; I see how close she and the other women are to the children; and then I see how distant I am from the other men, and I feel so lonely.

With those thoughts Nafai finally slept, but only a few hours before dawn, and when he got out of bed he found Luet just as weary from undersleeping, stirring the morning porridge virtually in her sleep. "And there's no school today," Luet said, "so we have all the children and there's no hope of a nap."

"Let them play outside," said Nafai, "except the twins of course, and we can probably leave them with Shuya and then we can sleep."

"Or we could take turns ourselves, instead of imposing on them," said Luet.

"Take turns?" said Nafai. "How dull."

"I want to *sleep*," said Luet. "Why is it that men are never so tired that they stop thinking about *that?*"

"Men who stop thinking about *that*, as you so sweetly call it, are either eunuchs or dead."

"We need to tell your parents about Chveya's dream," said Luet.

"We need to tell *everybody*."

"I don't think so," said Luet. "It would cause too much jealousy."

"Oh, who but you will care about which child was first to have true dreams?" But he knew as he said it that *all* the parents would care, and that she was right about needing to avoid jealousy.

She made a face at him. "*You* are so completely above envy, O noble one, that it makes me envious."

"I'm sorry," he said.

"And besides," she said, "it wouldn't be good for Chveya if a big fuss were made about this. Look what happened to Dza when we made her birthday into a festival—she's really quite a bully with the other children, and it worries Shuya, and that public fuss only made her worse."

"There are times when I see her making the other children run meaningless errands for her that I want to slap her silly," said Nafai.

"But Lady Rasa says—"

"That children must be free to establish their own society, and deal with tyranny in their own way, I know," said Nafai. "But I can't help but wonder if she's right. After all, hers was an educational theory that thrived only in the womb of Basilica. Couldn't we see our own conflicts early on in our journeying as a result of exactly her attitude?"

"No, we couldn't," said Luet. "Particularly because the people who caused the *most* trouble were the ones who spent the *least* time being educated by Lady Rasa. Namely Elemak and Mebbekew, who left her school as soon as they came of age to decide for themselves, and Vas and Obring, who were never students of hers."

"Not so, my dear reductionist, since Zdorab is the best of us and *he* never studied with her, while Kokor and Sevet, her own daughters, are just as bad as the worst of the others."

"You only *prove* my point, since *they* went to Dhelembuvex's school and not your mother's at all. Zdorab is an exception to everything anyway."

At that point the twins, Serp and Spel, toddled into the kitchen, and frank adult conversation was over.

By the time they both got free enough to take a nap, the day's activities had wakened them so thoroughly that they didn't want to sleep. So they headed for Volemak's and Rasa's house to confer about the dream.

On the way they passed a group of older boys competing with their slings. They stopped and watched for a while, mostly to see how their own two older boys, Zhatva and Motiga, were doing. The boys saw them watching, of course, and immediately set out to impress their parents—but it wasn't their prowess with the sling and stones that most interested Luet and Nafai, it was how they were with the other boys. Motiga, of course, was an incessant tease—he was keenly aware of being younger than the other boys and his silly pranks and clowning were his strategy for trying to ingratiate his way into the inner circle.

Zhatva, however, being older, was there by right, and what worried his
parents was how pliant he was—how he seemed to worship Proya, a
strutting cock-of-the-walk who didn't deserve so much of Zhatva's respect.

A typical moment—Xodhya got hit in the arm by Motya's careless
swinging of his loaded sling. His eyes immediately filled with tears,
and Proya taunted him. "You'll never be a man, Xodhya! You'll always
just be coming near!" That was a play on his name, of course, and a
rather clever one—but also cruel, and it did nothing but add to
Xodhya's misery. Then, without any of the boys being particularly
aware of it, Xodhya turned in his misery to Zhyat, who offhandedly
threw his arm around Xodhya's shoulder as he barked at his little
brother Motya, "Be careful with your sling, monkey brains!"

It was a simple, instinctive thing, but Luet and Nafai smiled at each
other when they saw it. Not only did Zhatva offer physical comfort to
Xodhya, without a hint of condescension, but also he drew attention
away from Xodhya's pain and incipient tears and threw the blame
where it rightly belonged, on Motya's carelessness. It was done easily
and gracefully, without giving the slightest challenge to Proya's authority among the boys.

"When will Zhyat see that *he's* the one the other boys turn to when
they're in trouble?" asked Nafai.

"Maybe he fills that role so well because he *doesn't* know that he's
filling it."

"I envy him," said Nafai. "If only I could have done that."

"Oh? And why couldn't you?"

"You know *me,* Luet. I would have been yelling at Protchnu that it
wasn't fair for him to tease Xodhya because it was Motya's fault and if it
had happened to Protchnu he'd be crying too."

"All true, of course."

"All true, but it would have made Protchnu my enemy," said Nafai.
He hardly needed to point out the consequence of *that.* Hadn't Luet
lived through it with him often enough?

"All that matters to me is that our Zhatva has the love of the other
boys, and he deserves it," said Luet.

"If only Motya could learn from him."

"Motya's still a baby," said Luet, "and we don't know what he'll be
except that it'll be something loud and noticeable and underfoot. The
one that I wish could learn from Zhatva is Chveya."

"Yes, well, each child is different," said Nafai. He turned and led Luet away from the stone-slinging and on toward Father and Mother's house. But he well understood Luet's wish: Chveya's loneliness and isolation from the other children was such a worry to them both—she was the only complete misfit among all the older children, and they didn't understand why, because she did nothing to antagonize the others, really. She simply didn't have a place in their childish hierarchies. Or perhaps she had one, but refused to take it. How ironic, thought Nafai—we worry because Zhatva fits in *too* well in a subservient role, and then we worry because Chveya refuses to accept a subservient role. Maybe what we really want is for our children to be the dominant ones! Maybe I'm trying to see my own ambitions fulfilled in them, and that would be wrong, so I should be content with what they are.

Luet must have been thinking along the same lines, because she said, out of the silence between them, "They're both finding their own paths through the thickets of human society, and well enough. All we can really do is observe and comfort and, now and then, give a hint."

Or turn bossy little Queen Dza upside down and shake her until her arrogance falls out. But no, that would only cause a quarrel between families—and the last family that they would ever quarrel with would be Shuya's and Issya's.

Volemak and Rasa listened with interest to their tale of Chveya's dream. "I've wondered, from time to time, when the Oversoul would act again," said Father, "but I'll confess that I haven't been asking, because it's been so good here that I didn't want to do anything to hasten our departure."

"Not that anything we might do *could* hasten our departure," said Mother. "After all, the Oversoul has her own schedule to keep, and it has little to do with us. She never cared whether we spent these years at that first miserable desert valley, or that much better place between the North and South rivers, or here, which is quite possibly the most perfect spot on Harmony. All she cared about was getting us together and ready for when she needs us. For all we know, it's the children she plans to take on the voyage to Earth, and not us at all. And that would suit me well enough, though I'd really prefer it if she took the great-grandchildren, long after we're all dead, so we'll never have to see them go and break our hearts missing the voyagers."

"It's how we all feel sometimes," said Luet.

Nafai held his tongue.

It didn't matter. Father saw right through him. "All but Nafai. He's ready for a change. You're a cripple, Nyef. You can't stand happiness for very long—it's conflict and uncertainty that bring you to life."

"I don't like conflict, Father," protested Nafai.

"You may not *like* it, but you thrive on it," said Volemak. "It's not an insult, son, it's just a fact."

"The question is," said Rasa, "do we *do* anything because of Chveya's dream?"

"No," said Luet hastily. "Not a thing. We just wanted you to know."

"Still," said Father, "what if some of the other children are having dreams from the Keeper but haven't told anybody about them? Perhaps we should alert all the parents to listen to their children's dream tales."

"Put the word out like that," said Rasa, "and you know that Kokor and Dol will start coaching their daughters on what dreams they ought to have, and get nasty with them if they don't come up with good giant rat dreams."

They all laughed, but they knew it was true.

"So we'll do nothing for now," said Father. "Just wait and see. The Oversoul will act when it's time for him to act, and till then we'll work hard when there's work to be done, and in the meantime try to raise perfect children who never quarrel."

"Oh, is that the standard of success?" asked Luet, teasingly. "The ones who never quarrel are the good ones?"

Rasa laughed wryly. "If that's the case, the only good children are the ones who have no spine at all."

"Which means no descendent of yours, my love," said Father.

The visit ended; they returned home and went on with the day's work. But Nafai was not content to wait and see. It troubled him that there had been so few visions, and that now the only one to receive anything from the Keeper was Chveya, and her the loneliest child, and too young to make real sense of her own dream.

Why *was* the Oversoul delaying so long? It had been in quite a hurry to get them out of Basilica nine years ago. They had given up everything they had ever expected their lives to bring them, and plunged into the desert. Yes, things had turned out rather well in the end, but it *wasn't* the end, was it? There were more than a hundred lightyears ahead of them, the part of their journey they had completed so far was nothing, and there was no sign of resuming it.

Answer me!

But there was no answer.

It took another dream to stir Nafai to action. It was Luet this time; Nafai woke from a sound sleep to find her whimpering, moaning, then crying out. He shook her awake, speaking soothingly to her so she would be calmed as she emerged from her dream. "A nightmare," he said. "You're having a nightmare."

"The Oversoul," she said. "She's lost. She's lost."

"Luet, wake up. You're having a dream."

"I *am* awake now," she said. "I'm trying to tell you the dream."

"You dreamed about the Oversoul?"

"I saw myself in the dream. Only young—Chveya's age. The way I used to see myself in dreams."

It occurred to Nafai that it hadn't been all *that* long since Luet *was* Chveya's age. She had been a child when he met and married her, barely in her teens. So when she saw herself as a child, how different could it be from how she saw herself now? "So you saw yourself as a child," said Nafai.

"No—I saw a person who *looked* like me, but I thought, This is the waterseer. And then I thought, No, this is the Oversoul, wearing the face and body of the waterseer. Which is what many women believed about me, you know."

"Yes, I know that," said Nafai.

"And then I knew that I was seeing the Oversoul, only she was wearing my face. And she was searching, desperately. Searching for something, and she kept thinking she had found it, only then she looked in her hands and she didn't have it. And then I realized that what she was chasing, around and around, was a giant rat, and then as she caught it and embraced it, it turned into an angel and flew away. Only she hadn't noticed the transformation and so she thought the rat had slipped away. I think the reason we're waiting here is that the Oversoul is confused about something. Searching for something."

But Nafai's thoughts had hung up on the fact that there were rats and angels in her dream. "This is a dream from the Keeper?" asked Nafai. "But how could the Keeper have known a hundred years ago that the Oversoul would be having trouble *now*?"

"It's only our *guess* that the dreams we've had from the Keeper are traveling at lightspeed," said Luet. "Perhaps the Keeper knows more than we're giving her credit for."

It grated on Nafai's nerves when the women who knew about the Keeper at all simply assumed that it would be a female, as they imagined the Oversoul to be. Somehow it seemed all right with the Oversoul, but faintly arrogant with the Keeper. Perhaps just because Nafai knew the Oversoul was a computer, but had no idea what the Keeper of Earth might be. If it really *was* a god, or something like a god, he resented the thought that it *had* to be female.

"Perhaps the Keeper is watching us and knows us very well, and is trying to wake us up—and through us wake up the Oversoul."

"The Oversoul isn't asleep," said Nafai. "We talk to it all the time through the Index."

"I tell you what I saw in my dream," said Luet.

"Then in the morning let's go and talk to Issib and Zdorab and see what they can get out of the Index about it."

"Now," said Luet. "Let's go now."

"Wake them in the middle of the night? They have children, that would be irresponsible."

"In the middle of the night there won't be interruptions," said Luet. "And it's almost dawn."

It was true; the first light was brightening the sky outside their parchment-glazed window.

Zdorab woke instantly, coming to open the door even before Nafai and Luet reached it. Shedemei appeared in a moment, and after a few whispered words she left to go summon Issib and Hushidh. They gathered then at the house where the Index was kept. Luet told them all her dream, and Zdorab and Issib at once began searching through the Index, trying to find answers.

Luet grew impatient first, as they waited in silence. "I'm useless here for now," she said. "And the children will want me."

"Me too," said Hushidh, and Shedemei reluctantly left with them, each returning to her house. Nafai knew that when it came to searching the Index, he wasn't much use, either—it was Issib and Zdorab who had made exploration of the Oversoul's memory their life's work, and he couldn't compete with them. He knew that the women would resent his tacit assumption that he could stay and Luet needed to leave . . . but he also knew that it was true. The children's routines revolved around Luet, who was always there, while Nafai was so often gone on hunting expeditions that his presence or absence barely made a difference in their lives. Not that they didn't *care* whether he was there or not—they cared a great deal—but it didn't change the normal events of their day.

So Nafai stayed in the Index House as Zodya and Issya asked it questions. He heard their murmuring, and now and then one would ask him a question, but he was truly useless to them.

He reached out his hand across the table and rested the back of his fingers against the Index. "You're looping, aren't you," he said.

"Yes," said the Index. "I realized that as soon as Luet had her dream from the Keeper. Issib and Zdorab are already working to find the loop."

"It must be in your primitive routines," said Nafai, "because you could find it and program your way out of it if it were your own self-programming."

"Yes," said the Index again. "Zdorab assumed that at once, and that's where we're exploring."

"It must be a loop where you think you've found something only you haven't really," said Nafai, remembering the dream.

"Yes," said the Index. It couldn't be sounding impatient, could it? "Issib insisted on that from the start, so we're trying to find something that I can't detect myself. It's very hard to search my memory to find what I haven't detected."

Nafai realized that all his thoughts were doing nothing but following far behind Zdorab and Issib, and so he sighed and took his hand away from the Index, sat back in the chair, and waited. He loathed being a spectator at important events. It's what Elemak has so often said about me, Nafai told himself nastily. I have to make myself the hero of every story I take part in. What was it he said that time? That someday if he didn't stop me I'd find a way to be the protagonist of Elemak's own autobiography. Thus I fancy myself to be vital to the process of discovering what has the Oversoul going in circles, wasting its time, wasting our time . . .

Wasting our time? This is a *waste* of time, to live in peace and plenty with my wife and children? May I waste the rest of my life, then.

Like a hunt, around in circles, the poor Oversoul is tying itself up in knots, covering the same ground without realizing it.

And as he thought this, Nafai envisioned the path he took on his most recent hunt as if he were above the ground, looking down at it like a map, seeing his own path drawn out among the trees, watching as he went in twisting, interlocking circles, but never quite passed the same tree from the same direction so he never guessed it *except* by seeing the map.

That's what the Oversoul needs to do—see its own tracks.

He reached out and touched the Index and said so to the Oversoul.

"Yes," said the Index—still maddeningly unreproachful. "Zdorab already suggested that I look through my recent history to find repetitive behavior. But I don't track my own behavior. Only human behavior. I have no autobiography stored here, except insofar as my actions impinge on humanity. And apparently whatever I'm doing that has me in a loop has no direct effect on humanity—or is so primitive that I'm unaware of it. Either way, I can't retrace my own steps."

Stymied again, Nafai didn't take his hand away. It might be too disturbing to the others, to keep touching the Index and then removing his hand.

Disturbing? No. He simply didn't want the embarrassment of having them know that *again* his would-be contribution was futile.

He was still sleepy. Luet's dream had woken him too early, and sitting here now, with nothing to do, he began to doze. He laid his head down on the table, resting on his other arm; still his fingers touched the Index.

He went back to that image of himself seen from above, a map being traced behind him as he hunted in circles through the woods. Maybe I really do that, he thought, drifting on the edge of sleep. Maybe I really move in circles.

"No you don't," said the Index. "Except when the animal you're tracking moved that way."

I might, said Nafai silently. I might drift around and around in large circles, casting for the tracks of some beast, never realizing that I'm seeing my own tracks. Maybe sometimes I hunt myself. Maybe I find my own tracks and think, what an exceptionally large beast, this will feed us for a week, and then I track myself and track myself and never catch up until one day I come upon my own body, lying there exhausted and starving, *dying* so that in my madness I now imagine myself detached from my body and . . .

I was dozing, he said silently.

"Here's the map of all your journeys," said the Index. "You'll see that you never make circles, except when tracking a beast."

Nafai saw in his mind a clear map of the land all around Dostatok, clear up to the mountains and beyond, showing all his journeys.

I've really covered this territory, haven't I, said Nafai silently.

But even as he said it, he saw it wasn't true. There was an area where none of his hunts had ever taken him. A sort of wedge right up among the mountains, tending toward the desert side of them, where none of his paths went.

Do you have a map of the others' hunting trips? asked Nafai.

Almost at once, a map that he "knew" was Elemak's hunts was superimposed on his own, and then a map of Vas's and Obring's hunts, and the group hunts. They interlocked until they formed a tight net all around Dostatok.

Except for that wedge in the mountains.

What's in that place in the mountains, where none of our paths meet?

"What are you talking about?" asked the Index.

The gap in the maps. The place where no one has been.

"There *is* no gap," said the Index.

Nafai focused on the spot, giving it all its attention. There! he shouted inside his mind.

"You speak to me as if you were pointing, and I can see you giving great attention to something, yet there is no point on the map that you're singling out above any other."

Could there be something here that is hidden even from yourself?

"Nothing on Harmony is hidden from me."

Why did you bring us to Dostatok?

"Because I've prepared this place for you to wait until I'm ready."

Ready for what?

"For you to carry me on the voyage to Earth."

And why should we have come *here* to wait?

"Because this is the nearest place where you could sustain your lives until I'm ready."

The nearest place to what?

"To yourselves. To where you are."

This was getting circular again, Nafai could see. He tried a different tack. When will you be ready for us to carry you to Earth? Nafai asked.

"When I call you forth," said the Index.

Call us forth from where, to where?

"From Dostatok," said the Index.

To where?

"To Earth," said the Index.

To Nafai it was clear—the empty place on the map, which the Index could not see, was also the place where they would gather to leave for Earth—again, a place that the Index could not name.

"I can name any place on Harmony," said the Index. "I can report to you any name that any human has ever given to any spot on this planet."

Then tell me the name of *this* place? asked Nafai, again focusing on the gap in the hunting maps.

"Point to a place and I'll tell you."

On a whim, Nafai mentally drew a circle all around the gap in the paths.

"Vusadka," said the Index.

Vusadka, thought Nafai. An ancient-sounding name. But not dissimilar to the word for a single step just outside a door. He asked the Index: What does Vusadka mean?

"It's the name of this place."

How long has it had this name? asked Nafai.

"It was called this by the people of Raspyatny."

And where did they learn this name?

"It was well known among the Cities of the Stars and the Cities of Fire."

What is the oldest reference to this name?

"What name?" asked the Index.

The Oversoul could not have forgotten already. So he must have run into the block in its memory again. Nafai asked: When is the oldest reference to this name in the Cities of Fire?

"Twenty million years ago," said the Index.

Is there an older reference in the Cities of the Stars?

"Of course—they're much older, too. Thirty-nine million years ago."

Did Vusadka have a meaning in the language they spoke then?

"The languages of Harmony are all related," said the Index.

Again it was being non-responsive. Nafai tried another circling approach that might bring him the information he needed: What is the word in the language of the Cities of the Stars thirty-nine million years ago that most closely resembles Vusadka without *being* Vusadka?

"Vuissashivat'h," answered the Index.

And what did that word mean, to them?

"To disembark."

From what?

"From a boat," said the Index.

But why would this place in the mountains be given a name that is related to a verb meaning to disembark from a boat? Was there once a shoreline that touched here?

"These are very ancient mountains—before the rift that created the Valley of Fires, these mountains were already old."

So there was never a shoreline that touched this land of Vusadka?

"Never," said the Index. "Not since humans disembarked from their starships on the world of Harmony."

Because it used the modern word *disembark* in reference to the original starships, Nafai knew at once that the Oversoul had done its best to confirm what he already had surmised: that Vusadka was the very place where the starships had landed forty million years ago, and therefore the very place where, if there were any possibility of a starship still existing, it would most likely be.

And another thought: *You* are there, aren't you, Oversoul? Where the starships landed, that's where *you* are. All your memories, all your processors, all are centered on this very place.

"What place?" asked the Index.

Nafai stood up, fully awake now. The scraping of his stool across the wooden floor brought the others out of their reveries. "I'm going to find the Oversoul," Nafai said to them.

"Yes," said Issib. "The Oversoul showed us its conversation with you."

"Very deftly done," said Zdorab. "I would never have thought of starting with the map of the hunting trips."

Nafai almost didn't tell them that he hadn't done that deliberately; it felt good to be thought clever. But he realized that if he let them continue to think this about him, it would be a kind of lie. "I was just dozing," said Nafai. "The hunting trip thing was just a mad idea on the edges of a dream. The Oversoul knew that it could not know that it knew, and it recognized that through the map it could communicate with me, that's all. It had to fool itself into telling me."

Issib laughed. "All right, then, Nyef," he said. "We'll agree that you really aren't very bright at all."

"That's right," said Nafai. "All I did was hear it when the Oversoul found an oblique way to call me past barriers in its own mind. Tell the others that I've gone hunting, if anyone asks. But to Luet and your wives, of course, you can tell the truth—I'm off searching for the Oversoul. Both statements are true."

Zdorab nodded wisely. "We've had peace here all these years," he said, "because this was a good land and there was room for us all and plenty to share. No one will be glad to think of uprooting ourselves again. Some will be less glad than others—it's just as well to postpone telling them until we actually know something."

Issib grimaced. "I can imagine a *real* battle over this one. I almost wish we hadn't had so long a time of happiness here. This will divide the community and I can't begin to guess what damage might be done before it's through."

Nafai shook his head. "It doesn't have to be that way," he said. "The Oversoul brought all of us on this journey. The Keeper of Earth is calling to all of us as well."

"All are called," said Zdorab, "but who will come?"

"At this moment," said Nafai, "I will *go*."

"Remember to take a bow and arrows, then," said Issib. "Just in case you find supper for us on the way." He didn't say: So that our story of your having gone hunting will be believed.

It was a good idea in any event, so Nafai stopped by his house to get the bow and arrows.

"And if you hadn't needed those," said Luet, "you wouldn't have stopped by and bid me farewell or explained anything at all, would you?" She sounded quite annoyed.

"Of course I would," said Nafai.

"No," she said. "You probably already asked the other two to let me know where you had gone."

Nafai shrugged. "Either way, I made sure you'd know."

"And yet it was *my* dream, and Chveya's," she said.

"Because *you* had the dreams, *you* own the outcome of it?" he asked, getting just as annoyed as she was.

"No, Nyef," she said, sighing impatiently. "Because I had the dream today, I should have been your partner in this. Your fair and equal partner. Instead you treat me like a child."

"I didn't ask them to tell *Chveya*, did I? So I hardly treated you like a child, I think."

"Can't you just admit you acted like a baboon, Nafai?" asked Luet. "Can't you just say that you treated me as if only men mattered in our community, as if women were nothing, and you're *sorry* you treated me that way?"

"I didn't act like a baboon," said Nafai. "I acted like a human male. When I act like a human male it doesn't make me any less *human*, it just makes me less *female*. Don't you ever tell me again that because I don't act like a woman wants me to act, that makes me an animal."

Nafai was surprised by the anger in his own voice.

"So it comes to this in our own house, too," said Luet softly.

"Only because you brought it to this," said Nafai. "Don't ever call me an animal again."

"Then don't act like one," said Luet. "Being civilized means transcending your own animal nature. Not indulging it, not glorying in it. *That's* how you remind me of a male baboon—because you can't be civilized as long as you treat women like something to be bullied. You can only be civilized when you treat us like friends."

Nafai stood there in the doorway, burning inside with the unfairness of what she was saying. Not because she wasn't speaking the truth, but because she was wrong to apply it to *him* this way. "I *did* treat you as my friend, and as my wife," said Nafai. "I assumed that you loved me enough that we weren't competing to see who *owns* the dreams."

"I wasn't angry because you appropriated the results of my dream," said Luet.

"Oh?"

"I was hurt because you didn't share the results of *your* dream with *me*. I didn't jump up from bed and go tell Hushidh and Shedemei my dream, and then ask them to tell you about it later."

Only when she put it that way did he understand why she was so upset. "Oh," he said. "I'm sorry."

She was still angry, and his apology was too little too late. "Go," said Luet. "Go and find the Oversoul. Go and find the ruins of the ancient starships in the ancient landing place. Go and be the sole hero of our expedition. When I go to sleep tonight, I'll expect to find you starring in my own dreams. I hope you have a tiny role in mind for *me* to play. Perhaps holding your coat."

Almost Nafai let her words hurl him out the door. She had as much as repeated Elemak's insult to him—and she *knew* how much Elemak's words had hurt him because he had confided it to her long ago. It was cruel and unfair of her to say it now. She of all people should have known that it wasn't his desire to be a hero that impelled him now, it was his passion to find out what would happen next, to *make* the next thing happen. She, if she loved him, should have understood. So he almost left right then, letting her bitter words travel with him all the way up into the mountains.

Instead he strode into the children's room. They were still asleep, except for Chveya, who perhaps had been wakened by their low-key but intense quarreling. Nafai kissed each one, Chveya last. "I'm going to find the place where the best dreams come from," he whispered, so as not to wake the other children.

"Save room in all the dreams for me," she whispered back.

He kissed her again and then returned to the kitchen, which was the main room of the house, where Luet was stirring the porridge in the pot by the fire.

"Thank you for finding room for me in your dreams," he said to her. "You're always welcome in mine, too." Then he kissed her, and to his relief she kissed him back. They had resolved nothing except to reaffirm that even when they were angry at each other, they still loved each other. That was enough to send him on his way content instead of brooding.

He would need to have his heart at peace, because it was obvious that the Oversoul was protecting the hidden place without even knowing that it was doing so. At least, so he surmised, for *something* must have turned them all aside whenever they were hunting, keeping them from going to Vusadka, and it was certainly the Oversoul's talent for making people forget ideas it didn't want them to act on. Yet the Oversoul hadn't been able to see that place itself, or even see that it could not see it. This certainly meant that the Oversoul's own deflection routines must have been turned against the Oversoul itself, so it wasn't likely that the Oversoul would be able to turn them off and let Nafai pass. On the contrary—Nafai would have to fight his way through, as he and Issib had fought their way past the Oversoul's barriers back in Basilica so long ago, fighting to think thoughts that the Oversoul had forbidden. Only now it wasn't just ideas that he had to struggle to think of. It was a place where he had to struggle to go. A place that even the Oversoul couldn't see.

"I must overcome you," he whispered to the Oversoul, as he walked across the meadows north of the houses. "I must get past your barriers."

(What barriers?)

This was going to be so hard. It made Nafai tired just to think of it. And there'd be no clever trick to get around it, either. He would just have to bull his way through by brute force of will. If he could. If he was strong enough.

It was dusk, and Nafai was near despair. After a day's travel just to get here, he had spent this whole day doing the same useless things, over and over. He would stand outside the forbidden zone and ask the Oversoul to show him the map of all the paths taken by all the hunters, and easily see which direction he needed to travel in order to reach Vusadka. He would even scratch an arrow or write the direction in the dirt with a stick. And then, after setting boldly forth, he would soon find himself back outside the "hidden" area, a hundred meters from where he had written the direction. If he had written "northeast," he would find himself due west of the writing; if his arrow pointed toward the east, he would find himself south of it. He simply couldn't get past the barrier.

He railed against the Oversoul, but the answers he got showed the Oversoul to be oblivious to what was going on. "I want to go southeast from this spot," he would say. "Help me." And then he would find himself far to the north and the Oversoul would say, in his mind, You didn't listen to me. I told you to go southwest, and you didn't listen.

Now the sun was down and the sky was darkening fast. He hated the idea of returning to Dostatok tomorrow, a complete failure.

(I don't understand what you're trying to do.)

"I'm trying to find you," said Nafai.

(But here I am.)

"I know where you are. But I can't get to you."

(I'm not stopping you.)

It was true, Nafai knew it. The Oversoul might not even be doing this. If the Oversoul could be given the power to block human minds, to turn humans away from actions they were planning, then couldn't the first humans on Harmony have set up another set of defenses to protect this place? Defenses not under the Oversoul's control—indeed, defenses that warded away the Oversoul itself?

Show me all the paths I've taken today, said Nafai silently. Make me see them here on the ground.

He saw them—faint shimmerings, which coalesced into threads on the ground. He saw how they began, time after time, heading straight toward the center of the circle around Vusadka. Then they stopped cold, every one of them, and began again not very far to the north or south, obliquely coasting along the borderline.

That really struck him—how precise the border was. He must be penetrating no more than a meter or so inside it before he was turned away. In fact, he could draw a line on the ground marking the exact border of the Oversoul's vision. And because he could, he did. He used the last half-hour of light to mark the border with a stick, scratching a line or digging a shallow trench several hundred meters.

As he marked the border of his futility, he could hear the hooting of baboons in the near distance, calling sleepily to each other as they headed for their sleeping cliffs. It was only when he was done, when full darkness had descended and the baboons were quiet again, that he realized that while some of their calls had begun outside the border, clearly they all ended up within it.

Of course. The border is impervious to humans, but other animals have not been altered to be susceptible to this kind of fending. So the baboons cross the boundary with impunity.

If only I were a baboon.

He could almost hear Issib say, quietly, "And you're sure that you're not?"

He found a grassy place on highish ground and curled up to sleep. It was a clear night, with little chance of rain, and though it cooled off more here than it did back near Dostatok—he was near the desert, and the air was noticeably drier—he would be comfortable tonight.

Comfortable, but it would still be hard to sleep.

He dreamed, of course, but couldn't be sure if the dream had meaning or was simply the result of his sleeping lightly and so remembering more of the normal dreams of the night. But in one of the dreams, at least, he saw himself with Yobar. In the dream Yobar was leading him through a maze of rock. When they came to a tiny hole in the rocks, Yobar ducked down easily and climbed through. But Nafai stood there looking at the hole, thinking, I'm not small enough to fit through there. Of course, this was not true—Nafai could see it, even in the dream, the hole was not that small. Yet he couldn't seem to think of squatting down and squirming through. He kept looking for a way to get through while standing upright.

Yobar came back through the hole and touched him by the hand. And when he did, Nafai suddenly shrank down and became a baboon.

Then he had no trouble at all getting through the hole. Once he was on the other side, he turned back to human size immediately. And when he turned around to look at the tiny hole, it had changed—it was now as tall as an adult human, and he could pass through standing up.

In the morning, that was the dream that showed the most promise of being worthwhile. He lay, shivering now and then in the predawn breeze, trying to think of some way to use some insight from the dream. Clearly the dream was reflecting his knowledge that the baboons could pass easily through the barrier, while he, a human, could not. Clearly if he turned into a baboon he could cross the barrier too. But that was exactly what he had wished for the night before, and wishing wasn't likely to make anything useful happen.

In the dream, thought Nafai, the hole seemed to be too small for me to get through. But I *could* have got through it easily at any time, because it was really as tall as a man. The barrier was only in my mind —which is true of this barrier as well. The more firmly I try to cross the barrier, the more firmly I'm rejected. Well, maybe it's the *intention* to cross the boundary that pushes me away.

No, that's foolish. The barrier must surely have been designed to fend away even people who were completely unaware of the boundary. Wandering hunters, explorers, settlers, merchants—whoever might inadvertently head toward Vusadka—the barrier would turn them away.

But then, it would take only the mildest of suggestions to turn away someone who had no firm intention of heading toward Vusadka—they wouldn't even notice they were being turned. After all, did any of us ever notice that we were avoiding that area on all our hunting trips during all these years in Dostatok? So those original paths didn't define a sharp, clear border the way that I'm defining it *now*. And our paths didn't turn all that sharply . . . we just lost track of our prey, or for some other reason turned gradually away. So the *force* the barrier uses must increase with my firm intention to cross it. And if I somehow were able just to *wander* through here, the barrier's strength might be much weaker.

Yet how can I casually and accidentally wander where I know full well that I *must* go?

With that thought, his plan came to him full-blown; yet he also hardly dared to think it clearly, lest it trigger the barrier and fail before he tried it. Instead, he began to focus on a whole new intention. He must hunt now, and bring prey to feed the children. He himself was certainly hungry, and if he was hungry then the young ones must be famished. Only the young ones he thought of feeding were the young baboons. He remembered the baboons of the Valley of Mebbekew and felt himself responsible for bringing them meat—as Yobar had scavenged food, to please the females and strengthen the young.

So he set out in any direction that morning, not particularly orienting himself toward Vusadka, and searched until he found the pellets of a hare. Then he stalked his prey until, within the hour, he was able to put an arrow through it.

It wasn't dead, of course—arrows rarely killed immediately, and he usually finished the animal off with his knife. But this time he left it alive, terrified and whimpering; he drew the arrow from its haunch and carried it by the ears. The sounds it made were exactly what he needed —the baboons would be much more interested in a living but injured animal. He had to find the baboons.

It wasn't hard—baboons fear few animals, and defend themselves from *those* by being alert and giving good warning to each other. So they made no effort to be quiet. Nafai found them foraging in a long valley that stretched from west to east, with a stream flowing down the middle. They looked up when they saw him. There was no panic—he was still a safe distance away—and they looked at the hare with great curiosity.

Nafai moved closer. Now they became alert—the males stood on their foreknuckles and complained a little about his approach. And Nafai felt a great reluctance to come nearer to them.

But I *must* come nearer, to give them meat.

So he took a few more steps toward them, holding the hare out in front of him. He wasn't sure how they'd take this offering, of course. They might take it as proof that he was a killer, or perhaps as a suggestion that he already *had* his prey and so they were safe. But some of them had to be thinking of the hare as meat that they could eat. Baboons weren't the world's best hunters, but they loved meat, and this bleating hare had to look like a good meal to them.

He approached slowly, feeling more reluctance with every step. Yet he also saw that more and more of them—especially the juvenile males —were looking from him to the hare. He helped them think more of the meat by averting his own gaze whenever they looked at him—he knew it would only challenge and frighten them if he made eye contact.

They backed away from him, but not far. As he had expected, their natural tendency was to retreat toward their sleeping cliffs. He followed them. He kept thinking. This is not a good idea. They don't need this meat. But he shouted down the thoughts, trying to focus on one thing: These mothers need the protein, their babies need to have it from their milk. I've got to get this meat to them.

You can't, this is stupid, you should drop the hare and then retreat.

But if I do, then the hare will go to the strongest males and not to the females at all. Somehow I've got to get this nearer to *them*, so it can benefit the young ones. That's my *job*, as the hunter for this tribe, to bring them food. I've got to feed them. I can't let anything stop me from reaching them.

How long did it take him? It was so hard to keep his mind on what he was doing. Several times he felt as though he had just wakened, though he knew he had not been asleep, and then he shook himself and pushed on, relentlessly heading toward the females, who increasingly arrayed themselves toward the sleeping cliffs.

I have to get behind them, closer to the sleeping cliffs than they are, he thought. I've got to get on the side where the females are.

He began to sidle northward, but he never let his attention waver from the females. And, around noon, he finally found himself where he wanted to be—between the baboons and their sleeping cliffs. The hare had finally fallen silent—but the baboons wouldn't be bothered by the fact that it had already died, since it was alive when it arrived, and besides, they weren't all *that* fussy, if the meat was warm. So Nafai tossed the hare toward them, aiming for the center of the group of females.

Pandemonium broke out, but things went about as Nafai had planned. Some of the juvenile males made a play for the hare, but the older males stood their ground against Nafai himself, for he seemed, at least momentarily, to be a threat. Thus the hare was back among the females, who easily brushed away the juveniles. The hare hadn't been dead after all—it squealed again as the dominant females tore into it, devouring whatever they could get their teeth into. The fact that baboons didn't bother with killing their prey before eating it had bothered Nafai when he first lived in close proximity to baboons back in the desert, but he was used to it now, and was delighted that his plan had worked and the females had got to the meat first.

As the males began to realize that they were missing out on the treat, they grew more and more agitated, and at last Nafai began to back away, closer and closer to the sleeping cliffs; when he was finally far enough away, the males charged into the group, scattering females and pummeling each other in their struggle for scraps of hare. Some of them did indeed come away with big pieces, but Nafai knew that the females had got more than their usual share of the meat. That made him feel good.

Now, though, it would be best for him to get as far from the baboons as possible. A *long* way away, up this valley. In fact, it wouldn't hurt if he found more prey up here, to bring back to them.

Gradually, though, as he headed farther and farther away from the baboons, he realized that his reluctance was getting easier and easier to fight off. Daringly, he let himself remember his real purpose in coming here. At once his reluctance to proceed returned—it became almost a panic inside him—but he did not lose control of himself. As he had hoped, the barrier was strongest at the borderline. He could overcome *this* level of interference—it was more like what he had felt back in Basilica, when he and Issib were first trying to push past the Oversoul's barriers and think about forbidden things.

Or maybe I'm feeling easier about it because the barrier has *already* pushed me away toward the border—maybe without realizing it I've been defeated.

"Am I outside or inside?" he whispered to the Oversoul.

No answer came at all.

He felt a thrill of fear. The Oversoul couldn't see this area itself—what if, when he crossed the border, he simply *disappeared* from the Oversoul's sight?

Then it occurred to him that this could be precisely why the force of the resistance might be weaker now. Maybe, without the Oversoul realizing it, this barrier had combined its own strength with the Oversoul's power—at the border. But in here, where the Oversoul itself could not penetrate, the barrier had only its own aversive power to draw on, and that's why it was defeatable.

It made sense to Nafai, and so he continued to head eastward, toward the center of Vusadka.

Or had he been heading north? For suddenly, as he crested a hill, he saw a completely barren landscape before him. Not fifty yards away, it was as if someone had built an invisible wall. On one side was the verdance of the land of Dostatok, and on the other side was stark desert—the driest, most lifeless desert Nafai had ever seen. Not a bird, not a lizard, not a weed, *nothing* with life in it was beyond the line.

It was too artificial. It had to be a sign of another kind of barrier, another borderline, one that excluded all living things. Perhaps it was a barrier that *killed* anything that crossed it. Was Nafai expected to cross this?

"Is there a gateway somewhere?" he asked the Oversoul.

No answer came.

Carefully he approached the barrier. When he was near enough, he reached out a hand toward it.

Invisible it might be, but it was tangible—he could press his hand against it, and feel it sliding under his hand, as if it were faintly slimy and constantly in motion. In a way, though, the very tangibility of it was reassuring—if it kept living things out by blocking their passage, then perhaps it didn't have any mechanism for killing them.

Can I cross? If humans *can't* cross this boundary, then why bother to have the mental barrier so far back? True, it might be simply a way of preventing humans from seeing this clear borderline and making a famous legend out of it, attracting undue attention to this place. But it was just as possible, as far as Nafai knew, that the barrier of aversion was designed to keep humans away because a determined human being *could* cross this physical barrier. One barrier for humans, farther out; and another barrier for animals. It made sense.

Of course, there was no guarantee that just because something made sense to Nafai it would therefore have any relation to reality. For a moment he even thought of returning to Dostatok and telling them what he had discovered so far, so they could explore the Index and find out if there was some clever way to cross the barrier.

As far as Nafai knew, however, the very thought of returning to Dostatok might be a sign of the barrier working within his mind, trying to get him to find excuses to go away. And maybe the barrier had some kind of intelligence and was able to learn, in which case it might never be fooled again by his device of concentrating on his urgent need to feed the baboons rather than his *real* purpose of getting past the barrier. No, alone as he was, it was up to him to make a decision.

It will kill you.

What was that, the Oversoul talking in his mind? Or the barrier? Or just his own fear? Whatever the source, he knew that the fear was not irrational. Beyond that barrier nothing was alive—there must be a reason for that. Why should he imagine that he would be the exception, the one living thing that could cross? After all, when the barrier was built in the first place there must have been plants on both sides of the barrier, and even if it were impassable, life should have continued on both sides. Perhaps forty million years of evolution would have made the flora and fauna of the two sides quite different from each other, but life should have flourished, shouldn't it? Mere isolation couldn't kill off all life with such brutal thoroughness.

It will kill you.

Maybe it will, thought Nafai defiantly. Maybe I'll die. But the Oversoul brought us here for a purpose—to get us to Earth. Even though the Oversoul couldn't think directly of Vusadka, or at least could not speak of it to humans, nevertheless Vusadka had to be the reason the Oversoul had brought them *here*, so close to it. So, one way or another, we have to get past this barrier.

Only *we* are not here. Only *I* am here. And it's quite possible that no one will ever be here again, if I don't succeed this time. If I fail, then that's fine, we'll try *then* to seek another way in. And if I succeed in crossing the barrier and then find that something beyond it kills me before I can get back, well, the others will at least know, from the fact that I never return, that they have to be more careful about getting into this place.

Never return.

He thought of his children—quiet, brilliant Chveya; Zhatva, wise and compassionate; mischievous Motiga; bright-spirited Izuchaya; and the little twins, Serp and Spel. Can I leave them fatherless?

I can if I must. I can because they'll have Luet as their mother, and Shuya and Issya to help her, and Father and Mother too. I can leave them if I must because that would be better than returning to them, having failed to fulfil the purpose of our lives for no reason better than fear of my own death.

He pressed against the barrier. It seemed not to give at all under his hand. The harder he pressed, the more it seemed to slide around under his hand. Yet with all that illusion of sliding, his hand did not actually slip to the right or the left, up or down. In fact, the friction seemed almost perfect—while pressing inward he *couldn't* slide his hand across the surface, even though it felt like the surface was madly sliding in every direction under his hand.

He stepped back, picked up a rock, and lobbed it at the barrier. It hit the invisible wall, stuck for a moment, and then gradually slid downward.

This thing isn't a wall at all, realized Nafai, not if it can grab the stone and then let it slide down. Could it even *sense* what the thing is that struck it, and respond differently for stones than for, say, birds?

Nafai picked up a clod of turf. He saw with satisfaction that there were several grubs and an earthworm in it. He heaved it at the barrier.

Again it stuck for a moment and then began to slide downward. But not at the same rate. The dirt went first, cleanly separated from the roots. Then all the vegetable matter slid down, leaving only the grubs and the earthworm on the face of the barrier. At last they, too, slid down.

This barrier is able to sort out what strikes it, thought Nafai. It is able to tell the difference between living and dead, between animal and vegetable. Why not between human and nonhuman?

Nafai looked down at his own clothing. What would the barrier make of *that?* He had no idea how the barrier sensed the nature of the things that struck it. Perhaps it could tell before he touched it that he was human. But there was also the chance that the clothing would disguise him a little. Of course, he had no idea whether that would be good or bad.

Again he picked up a rock, but this time he didn't lob it, he threw it as hard as he could. Again it stuck on the barrier.

No, this time it stuck *in* the barrier. Nafai could see by pressing his hands to the barrier on either side of the stone, as it slid downward, that the stone had actually embedded itself in the barrier.

Nafai took his sling from his belt, laid a stone in the pocket, swung it vigorously, and hurled it at the barrier.

It stuck, and for a moment Nafai thought that it was going to behave like the other items.

Instead, the rock clung for a moment and then dropped down *inside* the barrier.

It had crossed! It had had enough momentum and it had passed through. The barrier had slowed it so much that it *almost* didn't make it, but it had kept just enough momentum to make it through. The only trouble was that Nafai had no idea how to hurl himself at the barrier with anything like the force that the stone had had. Even if he could, the force of striking it might kill him.

Maybe the barrier has different rules for humans. Maybe, if I try hard enough, it will *let* me through.

Oh, yes, of *course* it will, Nafai, you fool. The whole barrier system was set up to exclude humans, so of *course* it will let you pass through.

Nafai leaned back against the barrier to think. To his surprise, after a couple of moments the barrier began to slide him down toward the ground. Or rather, it slid his *clothing* toward the ground, taking him with it. It had done nothing of the kind to his hands. When he touched the wall with bare skin, it had let him stay in place and did not move him at all.

With difficulty he pulled himself away from the invisible wall. It *clung* to his clothing as it had held the rocks, the dirt, the grass, the grubs and the worm. There *are* different rules for humans, he realized. This wall *does* know the difference between me and my clothing.

Impulsively he stripped off his tunic, baring his arms. Then he swung his arm as fast as he could, hurling his fist into the barrier. It stung like hitting a brick wall—but it passed through.

It passed through! His fist was on the other side of the barrier, just like the stone that had passed. And where his arm stuck through the barrier he couldn't feel anything unusual at all. He could unflex his fist on the other side and wiggle his fingers, and though the air was perhaps a bit cooler there, there was no pain, no distortion, no obvious problem at all.

Can I follow my hand through the wall?

He pushed forward, and was able to slowly push his arm in right to the shoulder. But when his chest reached the barrier, he was blocked; when he twisted for a better angle, his head also came up against the barrier and stopped.

What if I'm stuck here forever—half in and half out?

In alarm he pulled away, and his arm came out easily enough. He could feel some resistance, but nothing painful, and nothing pressed against his skin to hold him. In a few moments he was free.

He touched the arm and hand that had been on the other side and couldn't find anything wrong with them. Whatever kept life from thriving on the other side hadn't killed him *yet*—if it was a poison, it wasn't immediate, and it certainly wasn't the barrier itself.

He reviewed the rules he had learned for crossing the wall. It had to be bare skin. He had to strike it with some force. And if he wanted his whole body through, he'd have to strike the barrier with his whole body at once.

He stripped off his clothing, folding it neatly and laying it on top of his bow and arrows. Then he piled some rocks on top of them so they wouldn't blow away. Silently he hoped that he would indeed need these clothes again.

For a moment he contemplated leaping face first against the wall, but didn't like the idea—striking it with his fist had felt like hitting a wall, after all, and he didn't relish doing that with his face *or* his groin. Not that it would feel wonderful to do it backfirst either, but it was the lesser of two evils.

He walked a ways along the edge of the barrier until he came to a place where there was a fairly steep hill. He walked to the top and then, after a few deep breaths and a whispered farewell to his family, he ran headlong down the hill. Within moments his running was completely out of control, except that when he neared the wall he planted a foot and flung his body in a wild spin designed to lay him flat against the barrier.

Flat was not what he achieved at all. Instead his buttocks passed through first, and then, as he slowed, his thighs and his body up to the shoulders. His arms and head remained outside the barrier, even as his feet fell through and struck the stony ground on the other side. His heels hurt, but he hardly cared about that, because here he stood, his body inside, his arms and head outside.

I've got to get back outside, he thought, and try it again.

Too late. In the last moments before he stopped moving at all, his shoulders had passed inside. He was stuck again as he had been before, unable to bring his body along to follow his arms. The key difference this time was that his head was outside the barrier, and his chin and ears seemed to be reluctant to follow him inside. Worse, he couldn't even bring his arms all the way inside, because he needed the full weight of his body to pull them through, and with his chin hung up on the barrier he couldn't do it.

This has got to be the stupidest way anyone ever found to die, thought Nafai.

Remember your geometry, he told himself. Remember *anatomy*. My chin may be at too sharp an angle from my neck for me to pull it through, but at the top of my head there's a smooth, continuous curve. If I can just jut my chin forward and pull my head back . . . assuming that I don't rip my ears off in the process . . . but those can flex, can't they?

Slowly, laboriously, he tilted his head back and felt himself pulling through. I can do it, he thought. And then my arms will be easy enough.

His head came through all at once, at the end, his face fully inside the barrier. Only his arms continued to protrude through to the outside.

He meant to pull his arms through at once, after resting for just a moment, but as he rested, panting from the exertion, he realized that his need to breathe only increased, and was growing desperate. He was suffocating somehow, even as he drew great draughts of strange-smelling air into his lungs.

Strange-smelling air, dry and cool, and he wasn't getting any oxygen. Even as the panic of suffocation rose within him, his rational mind realized what he should have known all along: The reason that nothing lived behind the barrier was that there was no oxygen in here. It was a place designed to eliminate all decay—and most decay, the rapidest of it, was linked to the presence of oxygen, or oxygen and hydrogen joined to form water. There could be no life, and therefore not even microbes to eat away at surfaces; no water to condense or freeze or flow; no oxidation of metals. And if the atmosphere also failed to support anaerobic life-forms, there'd be little within the barrier to cause decay except sunlight, cosmic radiation, and atomic decay. The barrier had been set up to preserve everything within it, so it could last for forty million years.

This sudden comprehension of the purpose of the barrier was no comfort. For his rational mind was not particularly in control right now. No sooner had he realized that he could not breathe than his hands, still sticking through the barrier, began clutching for air, trying to pull him back through the barrier. But he was in exactly the same situation he had been in before, on the outside, when only an arm was through the wall. He could push his arms deeper into the barrier, but when his face and chest reached the wall, he could go no farther. His hands could touch the breathable air on the other side, but that was all.

Made savage by fear, he beat his head against the barrier, but there simply wasn't leverage—even with panic driving his muscles—to get force enough to push his face through to the breathable air. He really was going to die. Yet he still struck his head against the barrier, again, again, harder.

Perhaps with the last blow he stunned himself; perhaps he was simply weakening from lack of oxygen, or merely losing his balance. Whatever happened, he fell backward, the resistance of the barrier slowing his fall as his arms slipped inside through the invisible wall.

This is fine, thought Nafai. If I can just get to where the slope goes the other way, I can run down toward the barrier and get through again, only this time face first. Even as he thought of this cheerful plan, he knew it wouldn't work. He had spent too long already trying to get through the barrier right here—he had used up too much oxygen inside his own body, and there was no way he had enough left to climb another hill and make another downward run before he blacked out.

His hands came free and he fell backward onto the stony ground.

He must have struck very hard, for to him it sounded like the loudest, longest thunderclap he had ever heard. And then wind tore across his body, picking him up, rolling him, twisting him.

As he gasped in the wind, he could feel that somehow, miraculously, his breathing was *working* again. He was getting oxygen. He was also getting bruised as the wind tossed him here and there. On the stones. On the grass.

On the grass.

The wind had died down to a gusty breeze—he opened his eyes. He had been flung every which way, perhaps fifty yards. It took him a while to orient himself. But, lying on grass, he knew he was outside the barrier. Was the wind another defense mechanism, then, hurling intruders through the wall? Certainly his body was scraped and bruised enough to bear that interpretation. He could still see a few dust devils whirling in the distance, far within the dead land.

He got up and walked to the barrier. He reached out for it, but it wasn't there. The barrier was gone.

That was the cause of the wind. Atmospheres that had not mixed in forty million years had suddenly combined again, and the pressure must not have been equal on both sides of the barrier. It was like a balloon popping, and he had been tossed about like a scrap of the balloon's skin.

Why had the barrier disappeared?

Because a human passed through it completely. Because if the barrier had not come down, you would have died.

To Nafai it seemed like the voice of the Oversoul inside his head.
(Yes, I'm here, you know me.)

"I destroyed the barrier?"

(No, I did. As soon as you passed all the way through, the perimeter
systems informed me that a human being had penetrated. All at once I
became aware of parts of myself that had been hidden from me for
forty million years. I could see all the barriers, knew at once all their
history and understood their purpose and how to control them. If you
had been some exceptionally determined intruder who didn't belong
here, I would have told the perimeter systems to let you die; they
would have immediately been hidden from me again. That has happened twice before, in all these years. But you were the very one I
meant to bring here, and so the purpose of the barrier was finished. I
ordered its collapse, bringing oxygen to you and, therefore, to the rest
of this place.)

"I appreciate that decision," said Nafai.

(It means that decay has reentered this place. Not that it has been
wholly excluded. The barrier excluded most harmful radiation, but not
all. There *has* been damage. Nothing here was meant to last *this* long.
But now that I can find myself instead of running into the perimeter
system blocks, maybe I can figure out why I was looping.

(Or Issib and Zdorab can figure it out—they're at the Index even
now, and the moment you passed through the perimeter, the blocks
went down for them, too. I've shown them everything you did, and
they're now searching through the new areas of memory opened to all
of us.)

"Then I made it," said Nafai. "I did it. I'm done."

(Don't be a fool. You got through the barrier. The work is only just
beginning. Come to me, Nafai.)

"To *you?*"

(To where I *am.* I have found myself at last, though I had never been
able to think of searching for myself until now. Come to me—beyond
those hills.)

Nafai searched for his clothes and found them scattered—winds that
could blow his body around had easily snatched his clothing out from
under the stones. What he needed most were shoes, of course, to make
the trek across the stony ground. But he wanted the other clothes, too
—eventually he'd have to come home.

(I have clothing waiting for you there. Come to me.)

"Yes, well, I'm coming," said Nafai. "But let me get my shoes on whether you think I need them or not." He also pulled on his breeches, and pulled his tunic over his head as he walked. And the bow —he searched a moment for his bow, and didn't give up until he found a piece of it and realized that it had broken in the wind. He was lucky that none of his bones had done likewise.

At last he headed out in the direction that the Oversoul showed him inside his mind. It took perhaps a half hour of walking—and he wasn't quick, either, his body was so bruised and sore. Finally, though, he crested the last hill and looked down into a perfect bowl-shaped depression in the earth, perhaps two kilometers across. In the center of it, six immense towers rose up out of the ground.

The recognition in his mind was instantaneous: the starships.

He knew the information came from the Oversoul, along with many facts about them. What he was seeing was really protective shells over the tops of the ships, and even then, only about a quarter of each ship rose above the ground. The rest was underground, protected and thoroughly linked into the systems of Vusadka. He knew without having to think about it that the rest of Vusadka was also underground, a vast city of electronics, almost all of it devoted to maintaining the Oversoul itself. All that was visible of the Oversoul were the bowl-shaped devices that pointed at the sky, communicating with the satellites that were its eyes and ears, its hands and fingers in the world.

(For all these years, I have forgotten how to see myself, have forgotten where I was and what I looked like. I remember only enough to set certain tasks in motion, and to bring you near here to Dostatok. When the tasks failed, when I began looping, I was helpless to help myself because I couldn't find where to search for the cause. Now Zdorab and Issib and I have seen the place. There has been damage to my memory —forty million years of atomic decay and cosmic radiation has scarred me. The redundancy of my systems has compensated for most of it, but not for damage within primitive systems that I couldn't even examine because they were hidden from me. I have lost the ability to control my robots. They were not meant to last this long, even in a place without oxygen. My robots were reporting to me that they had completed all safety checks on the systems inside the barrier, but when I tried to open the perimeter the system refused because the safety checks had not been completed. So I initiated the safety checks again, and the robots again reported that all was complete, and on and on. And I couldn't discover the loop because all of this was at the level of reflex to me—like the beating of your heart is to you. No, even less obvious. More like the production of hormones by the glands inside your body.)

"What would have happened if you could have broken out of the loop?" asked Nafai.

(If I could have found myself, I would have recognized the problem and brought you here at once.)

"You mean you could have shut down the barrier?"

(I wouldn't have needed to. Shutting it down was within your power all along. That's what the Index was for.)

"The Index!"

(If you had brought the Index with you, you would have met no resistance at any point. No mental aversion, and when you touched the Index to the physical barrier it would have gradually dissolved itself— avoiding the winds, which were not helpful, since they stirred dust into the air.)

"But you never told us the Index could do that."

(I didn't know it myself. I *couldn't* know it. All I knew was that whoever was coming to the starships would have to have the Index. Then, when the safety checks were completed, the perimeter system would have opened everything up to me and I would have understood what was needed and could have told you what you needed to do.)

"So my nearly suffocating myself to death and then getting bruised up in the windstorm wasn't a stupid waste of perfectly good panic."

(Forcing your way in here was the only way I would ever have broken out of my loop. I have read the memory of the perimeter system and I am delighted at the way you used the baboons to draw you through.)

"Didn't you show me that in my dream? That I needed to follow a baboon through the barrier?"

(Dream? Oh, I remember now, you dreamed. No, that wasn't from me.)

"From the Keeper, then?"

(Why must you look for an outside source? Don't you think your own unconscious mind is capable of giving you a true dream now and then? Aren't you willing to admit to yourself that perhaps it was your own mind that solved this problem?)

Nafai couldn't keep himself from laughing in delight. "I did it, then!"

(You did it. But you aren't done. *Come* to me, Nafai. I have work for you to do, and tools for you to do it with.)

Nafai strode down the hill into the valley of Vusadka. The place of disembarkation. The place where human feet had first touched the soil of Harmony, and where those first settlers had placed the computer that would protect their children from self-destruction for so many years that to them it must have seemed the protection would be forever.

But it would not be forever. It was dying already. And now Nafai was walking among the towers of the starships, the first human being to tread in their footsteps since they built this place. Whatever the Oversoul meant for him to do now, he would do it, and when it was done, human beings would return again to Earth.

10

Shipmaster

Volemak and Rasa called the community together the moment Zdorab and Issib finished reporting what they had learned from the Index. It had been a long time since a meeting had been called without Elemak knowing in advance what it was about. It worried him. At some level it *frightened* him, but since he could not live with the idea of fear, he interpreted it as anger. He was *angry* that a meeting was called without his knowledge, without Father having sought his advice in advance. It suggested to him that the meeting was Rasa's, somehow—that the women were making some play for power and had deliberately cut him out of the process. Someday the old hag will push too hard, thought Elemak, and *then* she'll find out what power and strength really are—and that she doesn't have any.

This was the filter of interpretation through which Elemak received the morning's news. Chveya and Luet had dreamed . . . ah, yes, the *women* trying to assert their spiritual leadership, the waterseer and her no-doubt-well-coached daughter angling for the old dominance Luet had back in Basilica. And then Nafai, Issib, and Zdorab had searched the Index for information, and Nafai—of course, it had to be Luet's *husband*, the Oversoul's favorite boy—had found a secret place that none of them had visited in all their hunts. Such nonsense! Elemak had covered every kilometer of the surrounding country in his hunts and explorations—there *was* no hidden place.

So Nafai had taken off on a hunt for a non-existent place, and only this morning had figured out a way past all the barriers. Once a human being made it inside, the barrier came down, and now Nafai was walking among the ancient starships, while in the meantime Issib and Zdorab were able to find things through the Index that no one had guessed at before. "This is the landing place," Father explained. "We are living now at the site of the First City, the oldest human settlement on Harmony. Older than the Cities of the Stars. Older than Basilica."

"There was no city here when we came," said Obring.

"But this *place*," said Father. "We have brought the human race full circle. And even now, Nafai is walking where the ancient fathers and mothers of us all first set their feet upon the soil of Harmony."

Romantic bushwa, thought Elemak. Nafai could be napping in the noonday sun right now for all anybody here knows. The Index was just a way for the weaklings of their company to assert control over the strong ones.

"You know what this means, of course," said Father.

"It means," said Elemak, "that because of what people who have nothing better to do have supposedly learned from a metal ball, our lives are going to be disrupted *again*."

Father looked at him in surprise. "Disrupted?" he asked. "What do you think we came here *for*, except to prepare for a journey to Earth? The Oversoul itself was caught up in a feedback loop, that's all, and Nyef finally broke through and set it free. The disruption is *over* now, Elya."

"Don't pretend that you don't know what I mean," said Elemak. "We have plenty here. A good life. In many ways a better life than we would have had in Basilica, hard as that is for Obring to believe. We have families now—wives and children—and our lives are good. We work hard, but we're happy, and there's room for our children and our children's children here for a thousand years and more. We have no enemies, we have no dangers beyond the normal mishaps of being alive. And you're telling me that *this* is the disruption, while wasting our time trying to get into *space* is our normal course? Please, don't insult our intelligence."

Elemak could sense easily enough who was with him in this. As he painted the true picture of what this all would mean, he could see Meb and Vas and Obring nodding grimly, and their wives would go along easily enough. Furthermore, he could see that he had put some doubt in the minds of some of the others. Zdorab and Shedemei especially had thoughtful expressions, and even Luet had glanced around at her children when Elemak spoke of how good their lives were, how they faced no danger, how they could have a good future here in Dostatok.

"I don't know what Nafai found, or if he found anything at all," Elemak went on. "I honestly don't care. Nyef is a good hunter and a bright fellow, but he's hardly suited to lead us into some hideous danger using forty-million-year-old starships. My family and I are not going to let my little brother make us waste our time in the foolish pursuit of an impossible project. Nyef's murder of Gaballufix forced us all to leave Basilica as fugitives—but I've forgiven him for that. I certainly *won't* forgive him if he disrupts our lives again."

Elemak kept his expression calm, but inwardly it was all he could do to keep from smiling as he watched Luet's feeble attempt to absolve her husband of guilt for Gaballufix's murder. Her words didn't matter —Elemak knew he had done the job thoroughly with the first blow. Nafai was discredited even before he returned. It was his fault we left the city; we forgive him for that; but nothing he says is going to change the way we live here. Elemak had provided the reasonable justification for total resistance to this latest maneuver by the women and their little male puppet. The proof of his success was the fact that neither Father nor Mother—nor anyone else, except Luet—was mounting any kind of defense, and *she* had been sidetracked onto the issue of why Nafai killed Gaballufix. The idea of starships and hidden lands was dead.

Until Oykib walked out into the middle of the meeting area. "Shame on you all," he said. "Shame on you!"

They fell silent, except Rasa. "Okya, dear, this is an adult conversation."

"Shame on *you*, too. Have you all forgotten that we came here because of the Oversoul? Have you all forgotten that the reason we have such a perfect place to live is that the Oversoul prepared it for us? Have you forgotten that the only reason there weren't already ten cities here was because the Oversoul kept other people away—except us? You, Elemak, could *you* have found this place? Would *you* have known to lead the family across the water and down the island to here?"

"What do you know of this, little boy?" said Elemak scornfully, trying to wrench control back from this *child*.

"No, you wouldn't," said Oykib. "None of you knew *anything* and none of us would *have* anything if the Oversoul hadn't chosen us all and brought us here. I wasn't even born when a lot of this happened, and I was a baby through most of the rest, so why do *I* remember, when you older ones—my older and wiser brothers and sisters, my *parents*—seem to have forgotten?"

His high piping voice grated on Elemak's nerves. What was going on here? He knew how to neutralize all the adults—he hadn't counted on having to deal with Father's and Rasa's new spawn as well. "Sit down, child," said Elemak. "You're out of your depth."

"We're *all* out of our depth," said Luet. "But only Oykib seems to have remembered how to swim."

"No doubt you coached him on what to say," said Elemak.

"Oh, yes, exactly," said Luet. "As if any of us knew in advance what *you* would say. Though we should have. I thought these matters were all settled long ago, but we should have known that you would never cease to be ambitious."

"Me!" shouted Elemak, leaping to his feet. "*I'm* not the one who staged this phony visit to an invisible city, which we know about only because of supposed reports from a metal ball that only *you* can interpret!"

"If you would lay your hand on the Index," said Father, "the Index would gladly speak to you."

"There's nothing I want to hear from a computer," said Elemak. "I tell you again, I will not put my family's lives and happiness at risk because of supposed instructions from an invisible computer that these *women* persist in worshipping as a god!"

Father rose to his feet. "I see that you are disposed to doubt," he said. "Perhaps it was a mistake to share the good news with everyone. Perhaps we should have waited until Nafai came back, and we could all go to the place he found, and see what he has seen. But I thought that there should be no secrets among us, and so I insisted that we tell the story now, so no one could say later that they were not informed."

"A little late to try the honesty approach, isn't it, Father?" asked Mebbekew. "You said yourself that when Nafai left day before yesterday, he was searching for this hidden place and he *thought* it was probably where the first humans disembarked from their starships. Yet you didn't think of telling us all *then*, did you?"

Father glanced at Rasa, and Elemak felt completely confirmed in his suspicions. The old man was dancing to the old lady's tune. She had insisted it be kept secret before, and had probably counseled him against telling now, knowing her.

Nevertheless, it was time for Elemak's next move—he had to seize the high ground, now that Oykib had undercut his previous position. "Let's not be unfair," said Elemak. "We've only heard *about* Nafai. We don't have to decide anything or *do* anything yet. Let's wait until he gets home, and see how we feel then." Elemak turned to Oykib, who still stood in the middle of the group. "As for you, I'm proud that my next-to-last brother has such fire in him. You're going to be a real man, Oykib, and when you grow old enough to understand the issues instead of blindly following what others tell you, your voice will be well listened to in council, I can assure you."

Oykib's face reddened—with embarrassment, not anger. He was young enough to have heard only the clear praise and completely missed the subtle insult. Thus I wipe *you* out, too, Okya, dear brother, without your even realizing it.

"I say this meeting is over," said Elemak. "We'll meet again when Nafai comes back, except, of course, for the little conspiratorial meetings in the Index House where all this was cooked up in the first place. I have no doubt that *those* meetings will continue unabated." And with those words he put a sinister meaning into any kind of conversation that Rasa's party entered into, thus deeply weakening *them.*

These poor people—they thought they were so clever, until they actually came up against somebody who understood how power worked. And because it was Elemak who dismissed the meeting, and in effect announced the next one, he had gone a long way toward stripping Father of his leadership in Dostatok. The only test now was whether the meeting actually broke up with Elemak's departure. If he walked away, but the meeting went on substantially intact, then Elemak would have a much tougher time establishing leadership—in fact, he would have lost ground today.

But he needn't have worried. Meb arose almost at once and, with Dol and their children in tow, followed him away from the meeting; Vas and Obring and their wives also got up, and then Zdorab and Shedemei. The meeting was over—and it was over because Elemak had said it was over.

Round one for me, thought Elemak, and I'll be surprised if that isn't the whole match. Poor Nafai. Whatever you're doing out in the woods, you're going to come home and find all your plots and plans in disarray. Did you think you could really face me down from a distance and *win?*

There was no writing anywhere, no signs, no instructions.

(No one needs instructions here. I am with you always in this place, showing you what you need to know.)

"And they were content with this?" asked Nafai. "All of them?" His voice was so loud in the silence of this place, as he scuffed along the dustless catwalks and corridors, making his way downward, downward into the earth.

(They knew me. They had made me, had programmed me. They knew what I could do. They thought of me as—their library, their all-purpose instruction manual, their second memory. In those days I knew only what they had taught me. Now I have forty million years of experience with human beings, and have reached my own conclusions. In those days I was much more dependent on *them*—I reflected back to them their own picture of the world.)

"And their picture—was it wrong?"

(They did not understand how much of their behavior was animal, not intellectual. They thought that they had overcome the beast in them, and that with my help all their descendants would drive out the beast in a few generations—or a few hundred, anyway. Their vision was long, but no human being can have *that* long a vision. Eventually the numbers, the dimensions of time, become meaningless.)

"But they built well," said Nafai.

(Well but not perfectly. I have suffered forty million years of cosmic and nuclear radiation that has torn apart much of my memory. I have vast redundancy, and so in my data storage there has been no meaningful loss. Even in my programming, I have monitored all changes and corrected them. What I could not monitor was the area hidden from myself. So when the programs there decayed, I could not know it and could not compensate for it. I couldn't copy those areas and restore them when any one copy decayed.)

"So they didn't plan well at all," said Nafai, "since those programs were at your very core."

(You mustn't judge them harshly. It never occurred to them that it would take even a million years for their children's children to learn peace and be worthy to enter this place and learn all about advanced technologies. How could they guess that century after century, millennium after millennium, the humans of Harmony would never learn peace, would never cease trying to rule over one another by force or deception? I was never meant to keep this place closed off for even a million years, let alone forty million. So they built well indeed—the flaws and failures in my secret core were not fatal, were they? After all, you're here, aren't you?)

Nafai remembered his terror when he had had no air to breathe, and wasn't sure that they hadn't cut it all a little fine.

"Where are *you*?" asked Nafai.

(All around you.)

Nafai looked, and saw nothing in particular.

(The sensors there, in the ceiling—those are how I see you right now, and hear you, besides my ways of seeing through your eyes, and hearing your words before you say them. Behind all these walls are bank after bank of static memory—all of that is my self. The machinery pumping air through these underground passages—they are also me.)

"Then why did you need me at all?" asked Nafai.

(You are the one who broke me out of my loop and opened up my vision to include my own heart, and you ask me that?)

"Why do you need me *now*?"

(I also need you—all of you—because the Keeper has sent you dreams. The Keeper wants you, and so I will bring you.)

"Why do you need *me*?" he asked, clarifying the question even further.

(Because my robots were all controlled by a place in my memory that has become completely untrustworthy. I have shut them down because they were reporting falsely to me. No one ship of these six has a fully uncorrupted memory. I need you to collect and test the memory in every part of the ships and bring good memory together until we have one perfect ship. I can't do this myself—I have no hands.)

"So I'm here to replace broken machines."

(And I need you to pilot the starship.)

"Don't tell me you can't do that yourself."

(Your ancestors did not let their starships pass completely under the control of computers like me, Nafai. There must be a starmaster on every ship, to give command. I will carry out those commands, but the ship will be yours. *I* will be yours.)

"Not me," said Nafai. "Father should do this."

(Volemak didn't come here. Volemak didn't open this place.)

"He would have, if he'd known."

(He knew what you knew. But you acted. These things are not accidental, Nafai. It isn't coincidence that you are here and no one else is. If Volemak had found this place and forced his way in, risking his own life for the sake of coming here, then he would wear the cloak. Or Elemak, or Zdorab—whoever came would have that responsibility. It was you. It is yours.)

Almost Nafai said, I don't want it. But that would be a lie. He wanted it with his whole heart. To be the one chosen by the Oversoul to pilot the starship, even though he knew nothing about piloting anything—that would be wonderful. More glory and accomplishment than he ever dreamed of in his childhood. "I'll do it then," said Nafai, "as long as you show me how it's done."

(You can't do it without tools. I can give you some of them, and teach you how to make the rest. And you can't do it without help.)

"Help?"

(There will be thousands of memory plates to move from one ship to another. You will grow old and die if you try to do it all yourself. Your whole village will need to work together, if we are to have a reliable starship that contains all of the memory that I will need to bring to the Keeper of Earth.)

At once Nafai tried to imagine Elemak doing any job under his direction, and he laughed aloud. "If that's so, then you'd better put someone else in charge. They won't follow me."

(They will.)

"Then you don't understand human nature very well after all," said Nafai. "The only reason we've had peace among us these past few years is that I've stayed pretty much in my place, as far as Elya is concerned. If I suddenly come back and tell them that I'm the starmaster and they have to help me put together a starship . . ."

(Trust me.)

"Yeah, right. I always have, haven't I?"

(Open the door.)

Nafai opened the door and stepped into a dimly lighted room. The door closed behind him, shutting off much of what light there had been. Blinking, Nafai soon grew accustomed to the dimmer light and saw that in the middle of the room, hanging in the air with no obvious means of support, was a block of—what, ice?

(Much of it is water.)

Nafai approached it, reached out, touched it. His finger went in easily.

(As I said. Water.)

"How does it hold this shape, then?" asked Nafai. "How does it float in the air?"

(Why should I explain, when in a few moments the memory will be yours just for the thinking of it?)

"What do you mean?"

(Pass through the water and you will emerge wearing the cloak of the starmaster. When that is in place, linked to you, then all my memories will be yours, as if they had been yours all along.)

"A human mind could never hold such information," said Nafai. "Your memory includes forty million years of history."

(You will see.)

"Having Father's memory of his vision in my mind almost drove me mad," said Nafai. "Won't that happen this time, having yours?"

(I will be with you as I have never been with you before.)

"Will I still be *myself?*"

(You will be more yourself than ever before.)

"Do I have a choice?"

(Yes. You can choose to refuse this. Then I will bring another, and she *will* pass through the water, and then *she* will be starmaster.)

"She? Luet?"

(Does it matter? Once you have chosen not to be starmaster, what right do you have to concern yourself with the person I then choose to take your place?)

Nafai stood there, looking at the miraculous block of water resting in the air, and thought: This is less dangerous than passing through the barrier, and I did *that*. He also thought: Could I bear to follow the starmaster, knowing for the rest of my life that I *could* have been starmaster, and refused? And then: I have trusted the Oversoul so far. I have killed for it; I have nearly died for it. Will I now refuse to take the leadership of this voyage?

"How do I do it?" asked Nafai.

(Don't you know? Don't you remember when Luet told you of her vision?)

Only now, with the Oversoul's reminder, did Nafai remember what Luet had said, of seeing him sink down into a block of ice and emerge from the bottom, glowing and sparkling with light. He had thought it had some metaphorical meaning. But here was the block of ice.

"I sink down from the top," said Nafai. "How do I get above this?"

Almost at once, a meter-wide platter skimmed across the floor toward him. Nafai understood that he was to stand on it. But when he did, nothing happened.

(Your clothing will interfere.)

So he removed his clothing for the second time that day. Doing so reminded him of all the scratches and bruises he had suffered from the buffeting of the wind. Naked, he stepped again on the disk. Almost at once it rose straight up into the air and carried him above the block.

(Step off onto the water. It will support you like a floor.)

Having just put his finger easily into the side of the block, Nafai had his doubts, but he did as he was told—he stepped onto the surface of the block. It was smooth, but not slippery; like the surface of the barrier, it seemed to be moving in every direction at once under his feet.

(Lie down on your back.)

Nafai lay down. Almost at once the surface under him changed, and he began to sink down into the water. Soon it would cover his face, he realized. He wouldn't be able to breathe. The memory of his recent suffocation was still fresh inside him—he began to struggle.

(Peace. Sleep. You'll not lack for air, or anything else. Sleep. Peace.)

And he slept as he sank down into the water.

Elemak was surprised to find that it was Shedemei at the door. All things were possible, of course—she might actually be coming here to join him. But he doubted it—it was far more likely that she was here to try to negotiate some settlement on Rasa's behalf. In which case she wasn't a bad choice as an emissary. He had nothing against her, and she had no awkward family connections. Besides, hadn't she and Zdorab stood up at the end of the meeting, accepting Elemak's authority to dismiss it? It was worth hearing what she had to say.

So he ushered her in and let her sit down at the table, along with Meb, Obring, and Vas. Then, when she was seated, Elemak sat across from her and waited. Let *her* speak first, and thus let him know what to expect from her.

"Everyone advised me against coming to you," she said. "But I think they underestimate you, Elemak."

"They have before," said Elemak.

Meb chuckled. That annoyed Elemak—he wasn't sure whether Meb was laughing at *them* for having underestimated Elemak, or laughing at Elemak for making such a claim. One was *never* sure, with Meb, whom he was mocking. Only that he was mocking *somebody*.

"There are some important things that you seem not to understand," said Shedemei. "And I think you need to know *everything* in order to make wise decisions."

Ah. So she was here to teach him about "reality." Well, it was worth listening, if only so he could better plan how to undercut her position at the next meeting. He nodded for her to continue.

"This isn't a conspiracy to take authority away from you."

Right, thought Elemak. You start out by denying it, and you've as good as confirmed to me that that's *exactly* what's going on.

"Most of us know that you're the natural leader of this group, and with some exceptions, we're content with it."

Oh, yes. "Some" exceptions indeed.

"And the exceptions are more among *your* followers than you imagine. Here at this table there is more hatred and jealousy of you than has ever been found among those who gather in the Index House."

"Enough of that," said Elemak. "If you came here to try to sow distrust among those of us who are trying to protect our families from the meddlers, then you can leave now."

Shedemei shrugged. "I've said it, you've heard it, I care little what you do with the information. But here's the fact: The only person you're fighting right now is the Oversoul."

Meb hooted once. Shedemei ignored him.

"The Oversoul has at last got access to the starships. It's going to take a massive effort by all of us to cannibalize five of the ships to make one ship ready to fly. But it's going to be done, whether you approve or not. The Oversoul is hardly going to let you block her now, when she's come so far."

Elemak heard with amusement the way Shedemei persisted in referring to the inanimate computer as if it were a woman.

"When Nafai returns, he's going to be wearing the starmaster's cloak. It's a device that links him almost perfectly to the memory of the Oversoul. He's going to know far more about you than you know about yourself, do you understand me? And there are other powers that come along with the cloak—a focus of energy, for one thing, that makes the pulse look like a toy."

"Is this a threat?" asked Elemak.

"I'm telling you the simple truth. The Oversoul chose Nafai because he has the intelligence to pilot the ship, the loyalty to serve the Oversoul's cause well, and the strength of will that broke down a supposedly impenetrable barrier and allowed the expedition to continue. *Not* because Nafai was conspiring against you. If you had ever shown a scrap of loyalty to the Oversoul's cause, she might have chosen *you.*"

"Do you think pathetic flattery like this will move me?"

"I'm not flattering you," said Shedemei. "I already said—we know you're the born leader of this company. But you've chosen *not* to be the leader of the Oversoul's expedition. That was your *own* choice, freely made. So when it comes down to it, when you realize that you have lost the leadership of this group forever, you can blame no one but yourself."

He felt anger growing within him.

"Nor would you have been the second choice," said Shedemei. "There was some doubt that Nafai would accept the cloak—for the very reason that he knew you would reject his leadership. At that point the Oversoul made her second choice. She asked *me* whether I would accept the burden of leadership. She explained to me more about what the cloak does and how it works than she even explained to Nafai, though by now he undoubtedly knows all. I accepted the offer. If it hadn't been Nafai, it would have been me. Not you, Elemak. You did not miss this great office narrowly. You were never in the running, because you rejected the Oversoul from the start."

"Perhaps you had better leave now," said Elemak softly.

"But this doesn't mean that you can't have a valued, important role in the community," she went on, seeming not to hear him, seeming not to notice that he boiled with rage. "Don't force the issue, don't force Nafai to humiliate you in front of the others. Instead work with him, and he will gladly let you take as much of the leadership as the Oversoul will let him surrender to you. I don't think you've ever realized how Nafai worships you. How he has always wished he could be like you. How he has longed for your love and respect more than that of any other person."

"Get out of my house," said Elemak.

"Very well," said Shedemei. "I see that you are a person who refuses to revise his view of the world. You can only bear to live in a world where all the bad things that happen to you are someone else's fault, where everyone must have conspired against you to deprive you of what is your due." She rose and walked to the door. "Unfortunately, that world happens not to be the *real* world. And so you four will sit here and conspire to take over the rule of Dostatok, and it will come to nothing, and you will be humiliated, and it will have been nobody's fault but your own. Yet even then, Elemak, you have our deep respect and honor for your considerable abilities. Good night."

She closed the door behind her.

Elemak could hardly control himself. He longed to leap after her, hit her again and again, beat the unbearable condescension out of her. But that would be a show of weakness; to maintain control of these others, he had to make it clear that he was unaffected by such nonsense. So he smiled wanly at them. "You see how they want to make us stupid by making us angry," said Elemak.

"Don't tell me you're *not* angry," said Meb.

"Of course I am," said Elemak. "But I refuse to let my anger make me stupid. And she also gave us some valuable information. Apparently Nafai's going to be coming back with some kind of magic cloak or something. Maybe it's nothing more than an illusion, like those masks that Gaballufix dredged up to have his soldiers wear back in Basilica, so they all looked alike. Or maybe there's some real power in it. But far from making us back down, that will simply force us to act all the more quickly and cleanly—and permanently."

"Meaning?" asked Vas.

"Meaning that we will *not* permit *anyone* to leave here and go join Nafai, wherever he is. We will make him come to us. And when he does, unless he immediately backs down and accepts our decisions, we'll eliminate his ability to make further problems."

"Meaning?" insisted Vas.

"Meaning kill him, you dolt," said Obring. "How stupid do you have to be?"

"I knew he meant that," said Vas quietly. "I just wanted to hear him say it with his own mouth, so that he can't claim later that he never meant any such thing."

"Oh, I see," said Elemak. "You're worried about responsibility." Elemak couldn't help but compare Vas with Nafai—for all his other faults, Nyef had never shrunk from his responsibility for the death of

Gaballufix. "Well, the responsibility is mine. Mine alone, if you insist on it. But that also means that after we've won, the authority is mine."

"I'm with you," said Meb. "To the hilt. Does that mean that when it's done, I share authority with you?"

"Yes, it does," said Elemak. If you even know what authority is, you poor simpering baboon. "It's as simple as that. But if you haven't got the heart to put in the knife along with us, that doesn't mean you're our enemy. Only keep silence about our plan, join with us in preventing others from joining Nafai, and stay out of the way when we kill him—if it comes to that."

"I'll agree to that," said Obring.

Vas also nodded.

"Then it's done."

Nafai awoke on the floor of the room. Above him hung the block of water. He didn't feel any different.

That is, until he started trying to think of things. Like when he tried to feel, from the inside, whether anything was different about his own body. All of a sudden a great gush of information flowed into his mind. He was conscious for a moment of all his bodily functions, and had a detailed status report on all of them. The output of his glands; his heartrate; the amount of fecal matter built up in his rectum; the current deficiency of fuel for his body's cells, and how his fat cells were being accessed to make up the shortfall. Also, the rate of healing of all his bruises and scrapes had been accelerated, and he felt much better.

Is this what the Oversoul has always known about me?

At once the answer came, and now it truly was a clear voice—even clearer than when the Oversoul spoke through the Index. (I never knew this much about you before. The cloak has connected with every nerve in your body, and reports on your condition continuously. It also samples your blood in various places and interprets and acts to enhance your condition many times a second.)

Cloak?

At once an image flashed into his mind. He could see himself from the outside, as the Oversoul no doubt saw him through its sensors. He could see his body as he rolled out from under the block and rose to his feet. His skin sparkled with light. He realized that most of the light in the room came from him. He saw himself run his hands over his own skin, trying to feel the cloak. But he felt nothing at all that was different from his normal skin.

He wondered if he would always shine like this—if his house would always light up like this whenever he was inside.

The thought had no sooner come to him than the Oversoul's voice responded. (The cloak responds to your will. If you wish it to go dark, it will. If you wish it to build up a powerful electrical charge, it will—and you can point your finger and send an arc of energy in whatever direction you choose. Nothing can harm you while you wear this, and you can be deeply dangerous to others—yet if you have no wish to harm someone, the cloak will be passive. Your children can sleep in the dark, and you can hold your wife as you always have. Indeed, the more physical contact you have with others, the more your cloak will extend to include them, and even respond, in a small way, to your will.)

So Luet will also wear this cloak?

(Through you, yes. It will protect her; it will give her better access to my memory. But why do you ask me these things? Instead of thinking of questions, why not simply cast your mind back and try to remember, as if you had always known about the cloak. The memories will come to your mind easily and clearly, then. You'll know all there is to know.)

Nafai tried it, and suddenly he had no more questions about the cloak. He understood what it meant to be shipmaster. He even understood exactly what the Oversoul needed him to do to prepare a starship for departure.

"We don't have enough lifetimes among us, including our children, to do all of this," said Nafai.

(I told you that I'd give you the tools to work with. Some aspects of the robots are unsalvageable now, but other parts can be used. The machines themselves are perfectly workable—it's only my program to control them that is defective. Parts of it can be reactivated, and then you and the others can set the robots to doing the meaningless tasks under your direction. You'll see.)

And now Nafai "remembered" exactly what the Oversoul had determined was possible. It would take some serious work for several hours to get the robots working, but he could do it—he remembered how. "I'll get started at once," he said. "Is there anything to eat here?"

No sooner had he asked than he remembered that of course there was no food here. It made him impatient to think of having to leave this place and go hunt for food. "Can't you bring the others here? Have them bring food, and . . . I don't see why we should have to take a day's journey every time someone comes here. We can rebuild our village here—there's plenty of water in the hills to the south, and plenty of lumber. We can spend a week doing that and save ourselves many days of travel each year until the ships are done."

(I'll pass the word. Or you can tell them yourself.)

"Tell them myself?" And then he remembered: Since the Oversoul's memory was now "his" memory, he could speak to the others through the Index. So he did.

"You're not going," said Elemak.

Zdorab and Volemak stood before him in bafflement. "What do you mean?" said Volemak. "Nafai needs food, and we need to mark out the new village. I assumed you'd want to come along."

"And I say you're not going. Nobody's going. We're not moving the village, and nobody is moving from here to go join Nafai. His attempt at seizing power here has failed. Give it up, Father. When Nyef gets hungry enough, he'll come home."

"I'm your father, Elya, not your child. You can decide not to go yourself, but you have no authority to stop me."

Elemak tapped his finger on the table.

"Unless you're threatening to use violence against your father," said Volemak.

"I have told you the law of this place," said Elemak. "Nobody leaves this town without my permission. And you don't have my permission."

"And if I disobey your presumptuous, illegal command?" said Volemak.

"Then you're no longer part of Dostatok," said Elemak. "If you're caught skulking around here, you'll be treated as a thief."

"Do you think the others will consent to this?" asked Volemak. "If you raise a hand against me, you'll earn only the disgust of the others."

"I'll earn their obedience," said Elemak. "I advise you . . . don't force the issue. No one takes food to Nafai. He comes home, and the charade about starships ends."

Volemak stood in silence, Zdorab beside him. Their faces were inscrutable.

"All right," said Volemak.

Elemak was surprised—could Father be giving in so easily?

"Nafai says he'll come home now. He has the first robots recommissioned and working. He'll be home in an hour."

"In an hour!" said Meb, who was standing nearby. "Well there it is. This Vusadka place was supposed to be a whole day's journey away."

"Nafai only just got the paritkas working. If they function well enough, we won't have to move the village."

"What's a paritka?" asked Meb.

Don't ask, you fool, Elemak said silently. It just plays into Father's hands.

"A flying wagon," said Volemak.

"And I suppose you're talking to Nafai right now?"

"When we don't have the Index with us," said Volemak, "his voice is as hard to distinguish from our normal thoughts as the Oversoul's voice normally is. But he's talking to us, yes. You could hear him yourself, if you only listened."

Elemak couldn't help laughing. "Oh, yes, I'm sure that I'm going to sit here and listen for the voice of my faraway brother, talking in my mind."

"Why not?" asked Zdorab. "He already sees everything that the Oversoul sees. Including what's going on in your mind. For instance, he knows that you and Meb plan to kill him as soon as he gets back here."

Elemak leapt to his feet. "That's a lie!" Out of the corner of his eye, he could see Meb getting a panicked look on his face. Just keep your mouth shut, Meb. Can't you recognize a wild guess when you hear one? Just don't do anything to *confirm* their guess. "Now get back to your house, Father. You too, Zdorab. The only way Nafai will be in any danger is if he attacks *us* or tries to mutiny."

"This isn't the desert now," said Volemak. "And you're not in command."

"On the contrary," said Elemak. "Desert law still applies, and I am the leader of this expedition. I have been all along. I only deferred to you, old man, out of courtesy."

"Let's go," said Zdorab, drawing Volemak out of Elemak's house.

"And deprive Elemak of the chance of showing exactly how malicious he really is?"

"Not malicious, Father," said Elemak. "Just fed up. It's you and Nyef, Rasa and Luet and your group who started this. Nobody asked you to start this stupid business about traveling out among the stars.

Everything was going fine—you're the ones who decided to change all the rules. Well, the rules *have* changed, and for once they don't favor you. Now take your medicine like a man."

"I grieve for you," said Volemak. Then Zdorab had him out the door and they were gone.

"They knew," said Mebbekew. "They knew what we were planning."

"Oh, shut up," said Elemak. "They *guessed,* and you nearly blurted out a confirmation of their guess."

"I didn't," said Meb. "I didn't say a thing."

"Get your bow and arrow. You're a good enough shot for *this.* "

"You mean we aren't going to wait and talk to him first?"

"I think Nafai will talk more reasonably if he has an arrow in him, don't you?"

Meb left the house. Elemak rose to his feet and reached for his bow over the fireplace.

"Don't do it."

He turned and saw Eiadh standing in the doorway to the bedroom, holding the baby on her hip.

"Did I hear you correctly, Edhya?" asked Elemak. "Are you telling me what to do?"

"You tried to kill him once before," said Eiadh. "The Oversoul won't let you. Don't you realize that? And this time you might get hurt."

"I appreciate your concern for me, Edhya, but I know what I'm doing."

"I know what you're doing, too," said Eiadh. "I've watched you with Nafai for all these years, and I thought, at last, Elya has learned to give Nafai his proper respect. Elya's stopped being jealous of his little brother. But now I see that you were just biding your time."

Elemak would have slapped her face for that, except that the baby's head was in the way, and he would never harm his own child. "You've said enough," he warned.

"I'd beg you to stop because you love me," said Eiadh, "but I know that would never work. So I'm begging you to stop for your children's sake."

"For their sake? It's for *their* sake that I'm doing this. I don't want their lives disrupted for the sake of Rasa's conspiracies to get control of Dostatok and turn this into a village of women like Basilica."

"For their sake," said Eiadh again. "Don't make them see their father humiliated in front of everyone. Or worse."

"I can see how much you love me," said Elemak. "Apparently your bets are on the other side."

"Don't shame them by letting them see that you're a murderer in your heart."

"Do you think I don't understand this?" said Elemak. "You've had a yen for Nafai ever since Basilica. I thought you'd outgrown it, but I was wrong."

"Fool," said Eiadh. "I admired his strength. I admired yours, too. But *his* strength has never wavered, and he's never used it to bully other people. The way you treated your father was shameful. Your sons were in the other room, listening to how you talked to your father. Don't you know that someday, when you're old and frail, you may hear that same kind of disrespect from *them?* Go ahead, hit me. I'll set down the baby. Let your sons see how strong you are, that you can beat up a woman for no greater crime than telling you the truth."

Meb burst through the door. He had his bow and arrows. "Well?" he said. "Are you coming or not?"

"I'm coming," said Elemak. He turned to Eiadh. "I'll never forgive you for that."

She smirked at him. "In an hour you'll be asking for *my* forgiveness."

Nafai knew as he approached exactly what to expect. He had the memories of the Oversoul. He had heard the conversations between Elemak and his fellow plotters. He had listened as he ordered everyone to keep the children in their houses. He had felt the fear in everyone's hearts. He knew the damage Elemak was doing to his own family. He knew the fear and rage that filled his heart.

"Can't you make him forget this?" asked Nafai.

(No. That wasn't one of the powers I was given. Besides, he's very strong. My influence over him is oblique at best.)

"If he had chosen to follow you, he would have been better for your purposes than I am, wouldn't he?"

(Yes.) It might as well speak plainly, since it could keep no secrets from Nafai now.

"So I'm second choice," said Nafai.

(First choice. Because Elemak doesn't have it in him to recognize a purpose higher than his own ambition. He's far more crippled than Issib.)

Nafai sped south, the paritka skimming over the ground, automatically finding a smooth route at a pace Nafai found unimaginable. He cared nothing for the miracle of this machine. It was all he could do to keep from weeping. For now, as he focused on the people of Dostatok instead of the labors of restoring a starship, he "remembered" things that he had never guessed. The struggles and sacrifices Zdorab and Shedemei had made for each other. The cold hatred Vas felt for Obring and Sevet, and, ever since Shazer, for Elemak. Sevet's bitter self-loathing. Luet's and Hushidh's pain as their husbands treated them more and more like Elemak's idea of what wives should be, and less and less like the friends they were supposed to be.

Issib, who depends on Hushidh for everything in his life, how shameful for him to regard his wife as something less than a partner in all his work! And how *more* shameful for me, when my wife is the greatest of women, at least as wise as I am, that I have made her feel as she felt when I left her.

For he had seen all their hearts from the inside, and that is a vision that leaves no room for hate. Yes, he knew that Vas was a murderer in his heart—but he also "remembered" the agony that Vas went through when Sevet and Obring brought such shame on him. Never mind that Nafai himself had never thought that humiliation was an excuse for murder. He knew how the world looked from Vas's point of view, and it was impossible to hate him after that. He would *stop* him from getting his revenge, of course. But even as he did, he would understand.

Just as he understood Elemak. Understood how Nafai himself looked through Elemak's eyes. If only I'd known, thought Nafai. If only I'd seen the things I did that made him hate me.

(Don't be a fool. He hated your intelligence. He hated how you *loved* being intelligent. He hated your willing obedience to your father and mother. He hated even your hero-worship of Elemak himself. He hated you for being yourself, because you were so similar to him, and yet so different. The only way you could have kept him from hating you would have been to die young.)

Nafai understood this, but it changed nothing. Knowing all that he knew did not change the fact that he longed for things to be different. Oh, how he longed to have Elemak look at him and say, "Well done, Brother. I'm proud of you." More than those words from Father, Nafai needed to hear them from Elemak. And he never would. The best he would get from Elemak today was his sullen compliance. The worst would be Elya's dead body.

"I don't want to kill him," whispered Nafai, over and over.

(If you don't want to, then you won't.)

And then, again and again, Nafai's thoughts came back to Luet. Ah, Luet, why did it take this cloak to make me understand what I was doing to you? You tried to tell me. Lovingly at first, and in anger lately, but the message was the same: You're hurting me. You're losing my trust. Please don't do it. And yet I didn't hear. I was so caught up in being the best of the hunters, in living the man's life among men, that I forgot that before I was really a man, you took my hand and led me down to the Lake of Women; you not only saved my life, you also gave me my place with the Oversoul. All that I am, all that I have, my self, my children, I received it all at your hands, Luet, and then rewarded you shamefully.

(You're nearly there. Get control of yourself.)

Nafai pulled himself together. He could feel how the cloak worked within him, healing the skin around his eyes from the reddening that had come with his tears. Instantly his face gave no sign of having been in tears.

Is this how it will be? My face a mask, because I have this cloak?

(Only if you want it to be.)

Nafai "remembered" where Elemak and Mebbekew had gone, to lay an ambush for him. Vas and Obring were back in the village, making sure everyone stayed indoors. Elya and Meb were waiting, bows in hand, to kill Nafai as he approached.

Nafai's first thought had been to simply go around them, where they couldn't see him. Then he thought of flying past them so quickly they couldn't shoot. But neither course would be useful. They had to commit themselves. They had to put the arrows in him, unprovoked. "Let them strike me," said Nafai. "Help Meb with his aim—he'll never do it without your help—calming him, helping him concentrate. Let both arrows hit me."

(The cloak doesn't stop pain.)

"But it will heal me, once I pull the arrows out, right?"

(Well enough. But don't expect miracles.)

"All of this is a miracle," said Nafai. "Help Elemak miss my heart, if you're worried."

Elemak missed his heart, but not by much. Nafai slowed the paritka enough that they could get a clear aim. He could see, only an instant after the Oversoul itself saw, how the paritka frightened them both; how Meb almost lost his nerve, almost threw down his bow and ran. But Elemak never wavered, and his murmured command held Meb at his post, and then they aimed and fired.

Nafai felt the arrows enter his body, Elemak's buried deep in his chest, Meb's arrow through his neck. The latter arrow was more painful, the former more dangerous. The pain of both was exquisite. Nafai almost lost consciousness.

(Wake up. You've got too much to do to nap now.)

It hurts it hurts, Nafai cried out silently.

(It was *your* plan, not mine.)

But it was the right plan, so Nafai didn't pull the arrows out until the paritka brought him into the center of the village. As he had expected, Vas and Obring were terrified when they saw the paritka fly in and hover over the grass of the meetingplace, Nafai slumped in the seat, an arrow protruding from his chest, another stuck clear through his throat.

Luet, called Nafai silently. Come out and pull the arrows from me. Let everyone see how I was ambushed. That I carried no weapon. You must do your part.

He could see as if through Luet's own eyes; the kind of closeness that had almost driven him mad, back when he received his father's vision so long ago, was now much more easily borne, for the cloak protected him from the most distracting aspects of the Oversoul's recorded memories. He saw clearly what her eyes saw, but only hints of her feelings, and almost none of that stream of consciousness that had maddened him before.

He saw how her heart leapt within her at the sight of him, and how she was stricken by the sight of the arrows in him. How she loves me! he thought. Will she ever know how I love *her*?

She cried out. "Come out, all of you, and see!"

Almost at once Elemak's voice came from the distance. "Stay in your houses!"

"Everybody!" cried Luet. "See how they tried to murder my husband!"

They were pouring out of the houses, adults and children alike. Many of them screamed and cried at the sight of Nafai, the arrows in him.

"Look—he didn't have even a bow with him," she said. "They shot at him with no provocation!"

"It's a lie!" cried Elemak, striding into the village. "I thought they'd try something like this! Nafai put the arrows in himself, to make it look like an attack."

Now Zdorab and Volemak were there with her, and they were the ones who reached up and pulled the arrows from him. The one in his neck had to be broken and pulled out from the arrowhead side. Elemak's arrow tore his chest badly coming out. He felt the blood rush out of both wounds, and speech was still impossible for him, but Nafai also could feel the cloak working within him, healing him, keeping the wounds from killing him.

"I refuse to let you blame us for this," said Elemak. "Nafai's an expert at playing the victim."

But Nafai could see that no one was buying Elemak's lies, except perhaps Kokor and Dol, who were never terribly bright and were easily deceived.

"No one believes you," said Father. "Nafai himself knew that you were planning this."

"Oh, really?" asked Elemak. "Well, if he's so wise now, why did he stroll right into this supposed ambush?"

Nafai put the answer in his father's mind.

"Because he wanted everyone to see your arrows in him," said Father. "He wanted everyone to see clearly who and what you are, so there's never any doubt about it."

"Most of us saw it all along," said Rasa. "We hardly needed Nafai to bear such wounds."

"It doesn't matter," said Luet. "Nafai wears the cloak of the Oversoul. He's the starmaster now. The cloak is healing him. There's nothing Elemak and Mebbekew can do to harm him now."

Am I ready yet? Nafai asked. The pain had subsided considerably. (Almost.)

Elemak was keenly aware that no one was with him now, except Meb, who had no choice. Even Vas and Obring were averting their gaze from him—there'd be no support from *them*. But then, he had never expected any. "Whatever we did," said Elemak, "we did for the sake of our children, our wives—and *your* wives and children, too. Do you really want to leave here? Is there a one of you who wants to leave this place?"

"None of us *want* to go," said Luet. "But we all knew that this was the plan from the beginning—to take us to Earth. That was never a secret. No one lied to you."

And then—the crowning insult—Eiadh added her voice to Luet's. "I don't want to leave Dostatok," she said. "But I would rather wander in the desert forever than have a decent man killed to keep us here."

She spoke with fire, and Elemak felt it burn within him. My own wife, and she damns me with her accusations.

"Ah, you're all so brave *now!*" he cried. "But yesterday you agreed with me. Did any of you really think that our peace and happiness here would be preserved without bloodshed? You've all known it from the beginning—as long as Nafai was free to stir things up, there'd be mutiny and dissension among us. The only hope we have of peace is what I tried to do more than eight years ago."

(Now.)

He rose to his feet. To his surprise, he was unsteady, lightheaded. At once he "remembered" why—the cloak took energy from his own body when it had to, and the process of healing him so quickly was sucking strength from him faster than the cloak could replenish itself from the sunlight. However, he also knew that this temporary weakness would not stop him from doing all that he needed to do.

"Elemak," he said. "I've wept all the way here. It fills me with anguish, what you've tried to do. If only you'd bend enough to accept the Oversoul's plan—I would have followed you gladly if you had only done that. But all along, it's been you, your ambition to rule, that has torn us apart. If you hadn't plotted with them, *led* them, do you think these weak ones would ever have resisted the Oversoul? Elemak, don't you see that you've brought *yourself* to the edge of death? The Oversoul is acting for the good of all humanity, and it will *not* be stopped. Do you have to die before you'll believe that?"

"All I know is that whenever the Oversoul gets mentioned, it's you or your whiny wife or your mother the queen who's angling for control."

"None of us has sought to rule over you or anybody else," said Nafai. "Just because you live every waking moment with dreams of controlling other people doesn't mean that the rest of us do. Do you think that it's my *ambition* that created this paritka I'm standing on? Do you think it's Mother's *plotting* that holds it off the ground? Do you think it was

Luet's—what did you call it, *whining?*—that brought me here, a day's journey in an hour?"

"It's an ancient machine, that's all," said Elemak. "An ancient machine, just like the Oversoul. Are we going to take our orders from *machines?*"

He looked around for support, but the blood on Nafai's throat and tunic was too fresh; no one met his gaze except Mebbekew.

"We're moving the village to the north, near Vusadka," said Nafai. "And all of us, including the older children, will work with the Oversoul's machines to restore one starship. And when it's ready, then *all* of us will enter the starship and rise up into space. It will take us a hundred years to reach Earth, but to most of us it will seem like a single night, because they'll sleep through the whole voyage, while to the rest of us it will seem like a few months. And when the voyage ends, we will come out of the ship and stand on the soil of Earth, the first humans to do so in forty million years. Are you telling me that you mean to deprive us all of *that* adventure?"

Elemak was silent; so was Mebbekew. But Nafai knew what was passing through their minds. A grim resolve to back down now, but at the first opportunity knock him unconscious, slit his throat, and throw his body in the sea.

It would not do. They had to be convinced of the futility of resistance. They had to stop their plotting and concentrate their efforts on making the ship spaceworthy.

"Don't you see that you can't kill me, even though at this very moment, Elemak, you're imagining slitting my throat and throwing my body into the sea?"

Elemak's rage and fear redoubled within him. Nafai could feel it, striking at him in waves.

"Don't you see that already the Oversoul is healing the wounds in my throat, in my chest?"

"If they were real wounds at all!" cried Meb. Poor Meb, who still thought that Elemak's original lie might be revived.

In answer, Nafai plunged his finger into the wound in his own throat. Because the scar tissue was already forming, his finger had to tear its way in—but no one could miss the fact that Nafai's finger was into the wound nearly to the third knuckle. A couple of people gagged; the rest gasped or moaned or cried out in sympathetic pain. And, in truth, the pain *was* considerable—worse as he pulled his finger out than when he plunged it in. I must learn to avoid theatrical gestures like that, thought Nafai.

He held up his bloody finger. "I forgive you for this, Elemak," said Nafai. "I forgive you, Mebbekew. If I have your solemn oath to help me and the Oversoul as we build a good ship."

It was too much for Elemak. The humiliation was far worse now than it had been in the desert eight years before. It could not be contained. There was nothing in his heart but murderous rage. He cared not at all now what others thought—he knew he had already lost their good opinion anyway. He knew he had lost his wife and his children—what was left? The only thing that could heal any part of the agony he felt inside was to kill Nafai, to drag him to the sea and plunge him in until he stopped kicking and struggling. Then let the others do what they wanted—Elemak would be content, as long as Nafai was dead.

Elemak took a step toward Nafai. Then another.

"Stop him," said Luet. But no one got in his way. No one dared—the look on Elemak's face was too terrible.

Mebbekew smiled and fell in step beside Elemak.

"Don't touch me," said Nafai. "The power of the Oversoul is in me like fire. I'm weak right now, from the wounds you gave me—I may not have the strength to control the power I have. If you touch me, I think you'll die."

He spoke with such simplicity that his words had the plain force of truth. He could feel something crumble inside Elemak. Not that the rage had died; what broke in him was that part of him that could not bear to be afraid. And when that barrier was gone, all the rage turned back into what it had really been all along: fear. Fear that he would lose his place to his younger brother. Fear that people would look at him and see weakness instead of strength. Fear that people wouldn't love him. Above all, fear that he really had no control over anything or anybody in the world. And now, all those fears that he had long hidden from himself were turned loose within him—and they had all, all of them, come true. He had lost his place. He looked weak to everyone, even his children. No one here could love him now. And he had no control at all, not even enough control to kill this boy who had supplanted him.

With Elemak no longer moving forward, Meb, too, stopped—always the opportunist, he seemed to have no will of his own. But Nafai well knew that Meb was less broken in spirit than Elemak. He would go on plotting and sneaking, and with Elemak out of the picture, there would be nothing to restrain him.

It was clear to Nafai, therefore, that he had not yet won. He had to demonstrate clearly, unforgettably, to Meb and Elemak and to all the others, that this was not just a struggle between brothers, that in fact it was the Oversoul who had overcome Elemak and Meb, not Nafai at all. And in the back of his mind, Nafai clung to this hope: that if Elya and Meb could come to understand that it was the Oversoul who broke them today, they might eventually forgive Nafai himself, and be his true brothers again.

Enough power to shock them, said Nafai silently. Not to kill.

(As you intend, the cloak will act.)

Nafai held out his hand. He could see the sparking himself, but it was far more imposing when he saw through the eyes of others. By accessing the Oversoul he could see dozens of views of himself at once, his face a-dazzle with dancing light, growing brighter and brighter. And his hand, alive with light as if a thousand fireflies had swarmed around it. He pointed his finger at Elemak, and an arc of fire like lightning leapt from his fingertip, striking Elemak in the head.

Elya's body spasmed brutally and he was flung to the ground.

Have I killed him? cried Nafai in silent anguish.

(Just shocked him. Have a little trust in me, will you?)

Sure enough, Elemak was moving now, writhing and jerking on the ground. So Nafai extended his hand toward Meb.

"No!" cried Mebbekew. Having seen what happened to Elemak, he wanted no part of it. But Nafai could see that in his heart, he was still plotting and scheming. "I promise, I'll do whatever you want! I never wanted to help Elemak anyway, he just kept pushing me and pushing me."

"Meb, you're such a fool. Do you think I don't know that it was Elemak who stopped you from murdering me in the desert, when I stopped you from killing a baboon?"

Meb's face became a mask of guilty fear. For the first time in his life, Mebbekew had come face to face with one of his own secrets, one that he thought no one could know; there'd be no escaping from the consequences now. "I have children!" cried Mebbekew. "Don't kill me!"

The arc of lightning again crackled through the air, connecting with Meb's head and knocking him to the ground.

Nafai was exhausted. He could barely stand. Luet, help me, he said silently, urgently.

He felt her hands on his arm, holding him up. She must have climbed into the paritka beside him.

Ah, Luet, this is how it should always be. I can never stand without you beside me. If you're not part of this I can't do it at all.

In answer, all he could feel from her was her love for him, her vast relief that the danger was over, her pride at the strength he had shown.

How can you be so forgiving? he asked her silently.

I love you was the only message for him that he could find in her heart.

Nafai decided that the paritka should settle to the ground, and so it did. Luet helped him step from it, and with their children swarming around him, she led him back to the house. Over the next few minutes, all the others came to the house to see if they could help. But all he needed was to sleep. "Look after the others," he whispered. "I'm worried that the damage might be permanent."

When he awoke, it was near dusk. Zdorab was in their kitchen, cooking; Issib, Hushidh, Shedemei, and Luet were gathered around his bed. They weren't looking at him . . . they were talking among themselves. He listened.

They spoke of how sorry they felt for Eiadh and Dol, and for their children. Especially Proya, who lived for the pride he felt in his father, Elemak. "He looked as if he had just seen his father die," said Luet.

"He did," said Hushidh. "At least, it was the death of the father that he knew."

"The damage from this day will be a long time healing," said Shedemei.

"Was it damage?" said Luet. "Or the beginning of the process of healing wounds that we had only ignored for the past eight years?"

Hushidh clucked her tongue. "Nafai would be the first to tell you that what happened today wasn't healing, it was war. The Oversoul got her way today—the starship will be outfitted, and Elemak and Mebbekew will work as hard as anyone, when they recover from this. But the damage was permanent. Elemak and Mebbekew will always see Nafai as their enemy. And anyone who serves Nafai."

"Nobody serves Nafai," said Luet. "We only serve the Oversoul, as Nafai himself does."

"Yes," Shedemei agreed quickly. "We all understand that, Luet. This wasn't Nafai's battle, it was the Oversoul's. It might have been any of us with the cloak."

Nafai noticed that, however close she might come to the edge, *this* time Shedemei wasn't telling that she was the one who would have had the cloak if Nafai had refused it. She would keep that now as private knowledge, between her and Zdorab. Elemak and Mebbekew, Vas and Obring—they weren't likely to tell anybody, if they had even understood what she told them last night. She would always know that she was the Oversoul's next choice for the leadership of the colony—that was enough for her, she was content.

"He's awake," said Luet.

"How do you know?" asked Issib.

"His breathing changed."

"I'm awake," said Nafai.

"How are you?" asked Luet.

"Still tired. But better. In fact, *good.* In fact, not even tired." He propped himself up onto one elbow, and at once felt a little light-headed. "On second thought, *definitely* still tired." He lay back down.

The others laughed.

"How are Elya and Meb?"

"Sleeping it off, same as you," said Shedemei.

"And who has *your* children?" Nafai asked them.

"Mother," said Issib.

"Lady Rasa," said Shedemei. "Zdorab decided you'd want *real* food when you woke up, so he came over and cooked."

"Nonsense," said Luet. "He just knew how worried I'd be and didn't want me to have to worry about cooking. You haven't asked about *our* children."

"Actually, I don't have to ask about anybody's children," he said. "I know where they are."

There was nothing they could say to that. Soon they brought food in to him, and they all ate together, gathered around the bed. Nafai explained to them what kind of work would be required at the starship, and they began to think through the division of labor. They didn't talk long, though, because Nafai was clearly exhausted—in body, if not in mind. Soon they were gone, even Luet; but Luet returned soon with the children, who came in and embraced their father. Chveya especially clung to him. "Papa," she said, "I heard your voice in my heart."

"Yes," he said. "But that's really the voice of the Oversoul."

"It was your voice, when you thought you were dying," she said. "You were standing on a hill, about to run down and throw yourself through an invisible wall. And you shouted to me, Veya, I love you."

"Yes," he said. "That was *my* voice, after all."

"I love you too, Papa," she said.

He slept again.

And woke in the middle of the night, hearing a breeze from the sea as it played through the thatch of the roof. He felt strong again, strong enough to rise up into the wind and fly.